PIERCE EGAN'S

PILGRIMS OF THE THAMES

IN SEARCH OF THE NATIONAL

ILLUSTRATED BY PIERCE EGAN THE YOUNGER

SOURCE of the THAMES

MOUTH of the THAMES

FIRST BRIDGE over the THAMES

LAST BRIDGE of the THAMES

THE

PILGRIMS OF THE THAMES,

IN SEARCH OF THE

NATIONAL!

BY

PIERCE EGAN,

AUTHOR OF "LIFE IN LONDON," "DUBLIN," "LIVERPOOL;" "LIFE OF
AN ACTOR;" "SHOW-FOLKS;" ETC.

THE ILLUSTRATIONS,

DESIGNED, ETCHED, AND DRAWN ON WOOD, BY

PIERCE EGAN, THE YOUNGER.

DEDICATED TO HER MOST GRACIOUS MAJESTY, QUEEN VICTORIA.

LONDON:

W. STRANGE, 21, PATERNOSTER ROW;
AND ALL BOOKSELLERS.

1838.

"STAR PRESS"
20, Cross-Street, Hatton-Garden,
JAMES TURNER.

Dedication.

TO HER MOST EXCELLENT MAJESTY,

QUEEN VICTORIA.

MOST GRACIOUS SOVEREIGN,

If a life of deep experience has enabled me in
THE PILGRIMS OF THE THAMES, IN SEARCH OF
THE NATIONAL, to depict scenes, which, at the time they
amuse, may instruct the Public; I may perhaps be pardoned,
for most humbly and respectfully, thus inscribing my efforts to
your Majesty; who has ever the welfare of your people at
heart.

That LITERATURE, THE FINE ARTS, SCIENCES, &c., may
bloom healthily, and brightly, under your Majesty's protection,
—who, while you foster the more elevated Rose, will not neglect
the humble Violet;—that your Majesty may long, very long,
reign over a brave and free people, the Mistress of their HEARTS,
as you are of a Kingdom, which is MISTRESS OF THE WORLD;
and that in promoting the Peoples' you may secure your own
happiness, is the sincere wish of,

YOUR MAJESTY'S
Very humble, and
Most devoted Servant,
PIERCE EGAN.

London, January 1st. 1838.

CONTENTS.

CHAPTER IX.

A few preparatory words on authorship—shewing that it is more advantageous to have Nature for a guide than trust to the imagination; and giving the preference to mix with society in general, than cogitating in the closet, if characters and real life are to be truly depicted. Be it so:—Where shall we go? above, or below bridge?—The question at issue—difficult to decide; both attractive to the echo. An invitation to TURF's cottage puts an end to the argument. MAKEMONEY's recollections of former days respecting the Banks of the Thames—Dress and manner of the people—an immense change for the better. Millbank; to wit—An extraordinary character of the olden times—a thief and a honest man in the same person; completely illustrating Pope's maxim, that "the proper study of mankind is man." Curious definition of champagne, versus ale, by one of the Pilgrims—a matter of taste. Outlines of a Race-course—a study, perhaps worthy of contemplating by persons who seek after pleasure. Flats and Sharps—Fools and Deep Ones—Peers and Tradesmen—all in motion. Thimbles applied to a very different purpose from their original intention. The magical garter, and the gilded pill; or, how to twist an argument. A head without brains; or, a sketch of a thoughtless fellow—a tale for inexperienced young men. The long wished-for anecdotes related by TURF—The Match-Girl; or a woman with the fine bust. A peep in the mirror—wretchedness and beggary personified. The transformation What can't gold do!

CHAPTER X.

The Pilgrims turn Pic-nic-ians!—Why should not a Pic-nic be a medium for a Pilgrimage? Who's to be there? Characters of all sorts; great and small, learned and unlearned, "extremes meet." The preliminaries for starting adjusted, a slight mistake! Diamond for Diana, and prospect of no dinner; possible probability of the provisions presence, and passionate propensity, "pro" pungency, in a pretty petticoat. A steamer in hot weather, a broiler, and no sinecure! Makemoney overcome; Sprightly not flourishing; nor Flourish sprightly! The females in a stew for fear of being fried. The punster punless; and the pedant pensive! The children in mischief, and Mrs. Brindle in agony! The landing, hurra! here's the provender. The dinner! accidents and offences, "Keep your hands from picking and stealing!" The Stroll—Fortune telling in Richmond Park—Makemoney cajoled by a flattering black-eyed gipsey girl. "Ah old gentleman, we've caught you, have we? Ha! ha! ha! What did she say—eh?—"Such stuff as dreams are made of." Let's have tea—agreed. Oh, dear—dear—I thought so, my dress is spoiled! Never mind, "children will be children." Now for home, "domus amica, domus optima!"—"Rise gentle moon." A Hero and Leander in humble life. Boat song—the lover to his mistress; fatal termination! "The course of true love never did run smooth!" Well, here we are—our "journey's happy ended,"—Good night. "Bonus Nocte!"

CHAPTER XI:

MAKEMONEY's invitation to Charles Turf, Esq., to dine with him in London—accepted by the latter. Continuation of the interesting adventures of the Match-Girl; strange, but true. Love-letters, or rather bargains of a Smithfield character—Vice reduced to a trade, and beauty a marketable commodity; but face painting not amongst the faults of the Match-Girl. The dangers of fascination—FLOURISH's opinion and dislike of very beautiful women—some truth connected with his remarks. A female without a heart—yet not devoid of susceptibility—a touch of the pathetic—the afflicted father, fond mother, and inconsiderate son—grey hairs still respected. Greatness of the Match-Girl. Introduction of young RENTROLL, a country gentlemen—a neck-or-nothing sort of personage—all to-day, and let to-morrow provide for itself—A masquerade visit; or, how to pay off old debts. Dangerous to be safe. Prowess of the Match-Girl—the sprig of quality reduced beneath the rank of a commoner—revenge sweet. No security in disguise, or I am not what I seem

PLATES TO FACE.

The Frontispiece to face the Title.

PILGRIMS OF THE THAMES

IN SEARCH OF THE

NATILONAL!

———◆———

CHAPTER I.

THOUGHTS ON THE ORIGINALITY OF THE SUBJECT—AND TRUTH AND FACTS THE LEADING FEATURES OF THE ARGUMENT.

IF ROMANCE is the *forte* of an author, whenever he makes up his mind to sit down to write a book, he may, if circumstances require it, exclaim, with the late Lord Byron, " I want a HERO.? "

However, fortunately for us, we are not left in that predicament ; we have not to " lean upon our elbows," lost, as it were, in *cogitation ;* neither have we any thing to do with *Romance* in any shape whatever. No! our castles are not of the " Otranto" build ; nor do we deal in matters like the " Mysteries of Udolpho," it not being our intention to speak in—*parables !*

Corridors and subterraneous passages, likewise, are not necessary to illustrate our characters, as it will be seen they do not depend upon stage effect—abrupt entrances ! awful exits ! trapdoors ! or blue fire ; and ghosts and grinning spectres are much too frightful to be introduced for the *amusement* of our readers ! Therefore, nothing of the phantasmagoria kind will be attempted ; reality being the decided object in view ; and our heroes and heroines are to be met with every day in the public walks of life ! sometimes on board of steamers ; at others *inside,* or on the *tops* of stage-coaches ; and not unfrequently to be seen on the *outsides* of horses. They are flesh and blood to the very touch ; and words are not put into their mouths like puppets ! but they *speak* for themselves, either " good, bad, or indifferent !'

Invention is, therefore, entirely out of the question ; and far be it from us to *make* characters—that is to say, like parts written for actors, according to the rank and situation they hold on the boards of a theatre—an " *Uncle Foozle,*" to wit, for Mr. Farren ;

or a ready-cut and dried sailor for Mr. T. P. Cooke! Our aim is totally different, and takes a higher ground;—the " dramatis personæ " that we are about to represent, being composed of persons who caught the eyes of the Pilgrims under peculiar circumstances ; or crossed their paths during their pilgrimage on the BANKS OF THE THAMES !

As a matter of course, it will appear that some of our aspiring personages are decorated in the fashionable apparel of a Stultz or a Nugee, for the best of all reasons—because fashion is their very soul, and *dress* their only idol ! while the other part of them are, from dire necessity, compelled to wear a garment, purchased perhaps either at *Rag Fair* or *Monmouth-street*—no matter where, so that it answers the purpose of wearing apparel.

Yet *taste*, with a certain class of society, is considered of the utmost importance—for instance, in the trifling article of snuff, without the peculiar scent given to it by the addition of the *Tonquin Bean*, would be pronounced by the connoisseur of the ' Canisters !' shocking ! wretched, and abominable stuff ! while, on the contrary, downright " Irish Blackguard " would be hailed as a delicious treat to the *proboscis* of other individuals, and asserted, with equal firmness, that none but gentlemen make use of the above article—therefore, " Who's to decide when doctors disagree ?' However, we take our heroes as we find them, and chance it—whether running against my Lord Duke, with his glittering star, backed by his high birth, parentage, and education ; or coming in rude contact with " Sweep, soot ho ! " with only his bag and brush to carry him through the world ! From such a variety of persons passing in review, some of NATURE's unmeaning compositions will shew themselves—who, to supply their defects, endeavour to set themselves off to the best advantage, by exhibiting a dashing exterior, to obtain *importance* in the eyes of society ; and if PERRING's fashionable light hats cover many *lighter* heads—it is no matter about *brains*—if the effect of attraction is obtained by the wearers of them !

Our heroines, too, will be found real women, positively females from top to toe—it not being our wish, if we had the power, like Glendower, to call " spirits from the vasty deep ! " nor to enlist Venus, Juno, Psyche, and all the other captivating goddesses, from the splendid court of Jupiter's beauties, under our banners, to dazzle the eyes and bewilder the senses of our patrons ! No ! we are anxious to exclude any thing in the shape of temptation ; therefore, nothing like a *Venus di Medicis* will be prominent amongst them :—

> Ladies, like variegated tulips,
> 'Tis to their changes half their charms we owe ;
> Fine by defect, and delicately weak ;
> Their happy spots the nice admirer take.

Although among our pages may be found ladies with pretty faces—

good figures—genteel gait—interesting address—and handsomely dished up in gros-de-Naples silk-dresses—diamond ear-drops—fingers covered with rings—hair, in glossy ringlets—united with every thing that *art* can render effective to ornament their persons—and give attraction to their appearance. Such females as you may cast your eyes upon at the Italian Opera—the Theatres—Epsom and Ascot Races—Kensington Gardens—Regent Street, &c. from my Lady Duchess down to the humble maid of all work—*Fairies*, and other imaginary creatures, are exclusively left to the writers of *romance* !

ORIGINALITY and decided features being our peculiar aim ; although it is asserted by the *Quidnuncs*—a set of persons who wish to be thought wiser and better informed than other folks, " that there is nothing new under the Sun !" But as a set-off against the above old, and *stale* adage, we agree with the dramatist :—

> Severe their task, who in this critic age,
> With fresh materials furnish out the stage !
> Not that our fathers drain'd the comic store,
> Fresh characters spring up as heretofore ;
> NATURE with *Novelty* does still abound ;
> On every side fresh follies may be found.

However, it will be admitted the *Age* varies—the *Times* alter—and that *Fashion* is continually changing all the modes of life ;—so much so, that, in the course of a few fleeting years, society assumes a different *aspect* altogether ; yet however, it is not altogether improbable that we may jostle against some *soi-disant* English Don Juans—Chevaliers Faublas'—Don Quixottes, &c., but rather more likely that we may meet with beings similar to Tom Jones, Peregrine Pickle, and Paul Clifford ! Should such characters appear, pen and ink drawings shall not be wanting to illustrate their achievements, and if we can but hold the mirror up to Nature, and shoot folly as it flies—we shall then feel gratified that we have accomplished our task ; therefore, in order to deserve success, we set sail boldly, under the old proverb, a faint heart ne'er won a fair lady !

CHAPTER II.

An Outline—or, rather a Pen and Ink Sketch of PETER MAKE-MONEY—*a thorough-bred Cockney—his obscure origin in early life—great rise—immense luck—and experience in society. A retired wealthy citizen, who had filled the Offices of Sheriff, Alderman, and Lord Mayor. His observations on Men and Manners—Opinions worth knowing.*

A wit's a feather, and a chief a rod,
An honest man's the noblest work of God.

PETER MAKEMONEY was, at one period of his career, a man of considerable importance in the City of London, but whose first onset in life was rather in an humble capacity : however, from his rigid attention to business, and industry, he was soon enabled to shake off his obscurity—and, like several other persons connected with mercantile affairs in this immense Metropolis, he rose step by step, until he arrived at the important situation of an Alderman. He looked back with astonishment at his rapid success in life, being scarcely the possessor of a shilling at one time ; when he retired from business with an immense fortune. He had served the office of Sheriff with great activity and credit to himself ; and also filled the Civic Chair to the general satisfaction of the public.

Makemoney was a strait-forward character in every point of view—and a highly impartial magistrate. He was a friend to the poor—the distressed in circumstances—and the unfortunate, generally, in him found a friend. Yet he was a terror to the wicked and profligate ; but, nevertheless, he always tempered justice with mercy ; and if he thought there appeared any thing like sorrow or reformation about the criminal, when brought before him, he did every thing in his power to give the culprit a chance to effect so desirable an object. He endeavoured to " see his way" clearly upon every subject ; and any thing like the slightest bias of an improper feeling, never appeared in his conduct or his decisions. He did his duty fearlessly upon all occasions ; and, although a very plain man in his habits and mode of life, yet he was most anxious to preserve the dignity of his situation as the Lord Mayor of the greatest city in the world : and by his liberality he considerably increased, rather than diminished the smallest particle of the splendour which attached to the office.* He was

---

* It should seem that Makemoney, in order to preserve the dignity of the character attached to the person of the Lord Mayor, adopted the following mode to

firm in his manners, dignified in his conduct, and nothing like parade or ostentation was observed by his most intimate friends. He felt proud that he had been thought worthy by his fellow citizens to fill so important an office; but nevertheless he had no political ambition to gratify, and Peter Makemoney preserved his independence to the end of the chapter.

In his magisterial capacity he was accessible upon all occasions; and although many of the interruptions he received came under the denomination of " *troublesome,*" he never shewed impatience to any of his applicants, and they always left his presence well pleased with his affability and condescension: indeed, Peter was anxious to obtain the good opinion of every body. He completed his Mayoralty with immense popularity: and also with great joy to himself, that he was enabled once more to retire into private life. He disliked the pomp and shew; although he admitted it was necessary to the importance of the Chief Magistrate: and Makemoney often declared he felt himself a hundred times happier in his own humble residence, than when receiving all the honors and attentions in the splendid Mansion allotted to the Lord Mayor.

However, it could be scarcely said of him, that he was indebted to any thing like education for his rise in life; or what is generally termed education—although he had had a great deal to do with *Books*—his occupation being more to *sell* them, to make an addition to his purse, than *reading* works for the improvement of his mind: but, it is quite certain, that he owed much to *observation:* and treasured up the following lines of POPE as most excellent advice:

> 'Tis strange the MISER should his cares employ,
> To gain those riches he can ne'er enjoy!
> It is less strange the PRODIGAL should waste
> His wealth, to purchase, what he ne'er can taste!
> Something there is more needful than *expense,*
> And something precious e'en to *Taste*—'tis SENSE!
> Good sense which only is the gift of Heav'n,
> And, though no *Science,* fairly worth the Seven!

Calculation was also an immense assistance to him in his daily pursuits;—but *Economy*—invaluable *Economy*—all powerful *Economy,* that often times gives, not only independence to the mind—but frequently fortune to the adopter of it—was the inti-

---

answer two purposes:—From early habits, when the fatigue of business was over for the day, he always indulged in the habit of smoking his pipe over a glass of grog; but for the Lord Mayor to be seen with a pipe in his mouth before his *decorated* servants at the Mansion House, he thought might produce some remarks and sneers not very palatable to his feelings. He, therefore, retired for an hour or two, every evening, to his old chimney corner at his private residence (as the humble Peter Makemoney) to enjoy his whiffs in comfort; and then returned, like a " giant refreshed," to sustain the duties imposed upon him, as chief magistrate of the City of London.—" *Domus amica—domus optima.*"

mate and steady friend of Peter Makemoney. It is true those excellent notions, united with industry, and persevering conduct, had been of immense assistance to him in his progress through life ; they had not only rendered him a good and confidential servant, but had taught him the necessity of putting by money every year towards producing an easy sort of independence against old age.

But he had been promoted, step by step, from one situation to another in the establishment, till his *word* had become almost *law*. His never-tiring conduct to increase the interest of the concern, was made so evident by his superior knowledge with every circumstance connected with it ; nay more, transactions of every description went through his hands—and he was the *go-between* on all occasions. It might be truly said, that *his* decision was final—that his master had become little more than a " Looker-on " as it were—and troubled himself scarcely about any thing else, but his expenditure and profits.

Peter Makemoney, it should seem, had only flattered himself that, from his long services and attention, he might one day or another, whenever his employer thought fit to retire from business, or death took him out of the concern, realize a small share in it ; that is to say, such a share as might be given to him for his peculiar knowledge of conducting such an immense establishment, provided it got into the hands of new proprietors.

But it had never entered his thoughts, great as his ambition might have been to have arrived in the trade as a person of importance—that he should become the whole and sole possessor of his master's large property. Yet so it turned out in the sequel. His master had not a relative in the world that he was aware of —neither *chick* nor *child ;* and did not follow the example of the rich and fortunate foundling boy—who, after he had amassed together upwards of 100,000*l.* by his exertions in trade—advertized in the public newspapers a handsome sum, if any person could give him an accurate knowledge whether his father or mother were living ; or indeed, any of his relations, that he might share his fortune with them—so much did he feel himself *alone* in this great metropolis :—

" Ah, my Pylades, what's this world without a friend ?"

On the contrary, Makemoney's employer felt perfectly satisfied, that he had found a sincere friend ; a good servant ; and a person who had been through life attached to his interests. That was enough. He could not find a better, or more deserving man to leave his property to, than PETER. In consequence of this decision his master made his will in the most private manner ; and, barring his confidential solicitors, to whom he left handsome legacies for their trouble, the disposition he had made respecting his great wealth remained a profound secret : but Death, who spares no man, at length overtook him ; and

Peter Makemoney, to his utter astonishment, by such an unexpected slice of luck—became a man of immense property.

Thus at one *stride*—if he did not realize the appellation of a *great* man—his good fortune resounded from the East India House to St. Paul's Church Yard, that he had become one of the most wealthy persons in the City of London. This *shower of gold* as it might be termed, did not overwhelm his feelings ; and rather strange to state, it did not alter the man " *a jot.*" In his intercourse with society—his good sense taught him not to be too much *elevated* with sudden prosperity.

It is true Peter had been fond of money, being perfectly aware the comforts it brought to the possessors of it ; but, nevertheless, nothing like the term of miser attached to his character—and he was quite capable of granting an *accommodation* or doing a good action, without being paid for it. He also kept a good table ; yet he was no *gourmand.* Although it has been the prevailing *satire* on the Court of Aldermen from time immemorial of their *greedy* attachment to good living,* almost to gluttony, yet it was well-known that Makemoney had adopted in his own person the sensible and healthful adage of " eating to live ; and not living to eat." He was a temperate man altogether, though he did not regulate his meals by any particular *system ;* neither did he refrain from taking a glass or two of generous wine when in the company of his friends ; or at other times when such refreshment was deemed necessary.

Peter was a thorough cockney, to the utmost extent of the phrase—except knocking about the *v*'s and the *w*'s. The sound of Bow bells, to his ears was delightful music ; and the sight of " *Old Best,*" (as he termed St. Paul's Cathedral,) the delight of his eyes ; in fact, he had seen nothing else but *Lon 'on,* and he

---

* A well known facetious Baronet, connected for several years with the Corporation of London, distinguished for his jolly looking face, and his *penchant* for the good things of this life—in the character of an Epicure—if not a *Gourmand !* was very fond of turtle soup, regardless of the expence. He one morning called at a tavern contiguous to Guildhall, after transacting some business—and asked for a basin of turtle soup ! It was little more than a thimble-full in the eye of the Baronet—and he put it out of sight, instanter. ' How much ?' said he to the waiter. ' Thirteen and sixpence,' was the reply. Clapping his hands upon his stomach he thus argufied the topic. ' Thirteen shillings and sixpence a small basin !—soon gone !—rather expensive, to be sure ; and scarcely a taste ! But as I am not indebted to any body—I do not see any just cause why I should die indebted to my own flesh and blood—and cheat my stomach. No ! that will never do.—Starvation is not my creed ! Here, waiter, another basinful ; and bring something like a basin this time—you made a mistake last time—and brought the soup in a *tea-cup !*' Description falls short to portray the delighted voracious eyes of the Baronet ; but like Sir John Falstaff over a cup of sack, he smacked his lips and devoured the contents of it with peculiar *gout.* Then pulling out his purse—' Here, waiter, is one pound eight for you. Twenty eight shillings might have been laid out much worse ! There is nothing *immoral* in a basin of turtle soup—the Society for the Suppression of Vice do not take cognizance of such things—therefore there is no offence in it.' He then left the tavern to enjoy his dinner. Facts are stubborn things.

thought there was no place like London ; and, excepting High-gate and Hampstead (the cockney's round), the *Metropolis* was the only place that he called his home.

According to the " Sayings and Doings" of a celebrated author, though we cannot call accurately to our memory whether he had ever made use of the adage of a devoted Londoner in favor of the place of his nativity,—" that he would sooner be *hanged* in LON-DON, than *die* a natural death in the country !" But, neverthe-less, Peter insisted there was an excuse for this sort of partiality, and that it came under the denomination of an " amiable weak-ness !"

Be that as it may, Makemoney has often been heard to answer, when the question has been put to him about his remaining so much at home ? " In the first place," said he, " I could not spare the time—the quantity of business I always had to transact would not permit it ; and, secondly, it would not do for me, a man of my years, to risque my neck on the high hills of SWITZ-ERLAND, look like a fool in ITALY, and be absolutely lost, as it were, on the banks of the Rhine ; or, in other words, be found in the ludicrous situation of what is termed ' *a cockney adrift* !'

" No, no—I am quite content to explore the resources of my own country, now the tide has turned, and my fortunes permit me to do it—nay, more, the advantages which present themselves contiguous to my native city, which I have often heard urged, that for interest to the mind, attraction to the lovers of prospects, and situations, cannot be excelled, either to the merchant, the artist, or the historian—therefore, I am determined that my PILGRIMAGE shall not extend beyond the Banks of the Thames !"

Peter Makemoney was now quite at his ease : he had come into the possession of more cash, by the above-mentioned bequest, than he could ever spend in a rational sort of way—even if his life were prolonged to a greater extent than falls to the lot of man. A splendid fortune was at his command, besides a good round sum which he had acquired by honest industry, in the capacity of a servant.

Business, as a matter of course, had had its day with him—he, therefore, relinquished it, and only kept his Alderman's gown as a sort of amusement ; or, rather to occupy in some measure his leisure time. He despised any thing like ostentation ; and self-importance he was equally disgusted with ; but his home and fire-side were great objects to his mind : he was also fond of a game at whist or cribbage : in fact, there was a sort of *Hoyle* about his play and judgment, but he severely exclaimed against any thing that partook of *gaming*, in the slightest degree.

He was an excellent companion—a social fellow—and he had no objection to a pipe and a glass in their proper place, and par-ticularly fond of a good song. He was in raptures, even at the recollection of the late Charles Incledon's Black-eyed Susan, and Tom Moody :—" the Italian Opera House might be fine, as to music ; but the best of them" said he, " were a hundred miles behind our English ballad-singer."

Makemoney always thought the Theatre not only a rational, but a place of information, united with amusement ; and that a good play improved society in their feelings towards each other. It was delightful to see and hear the animated applause which came from all parts of the house when the character of a villain met with punishment for his crimes.

He was also a stickler for what might *now* be termed the old school of acting, and considered the late John Kemble classical to the echo : Mrs. Siddons, the greatest creature of them all ; and entertained an opinion, that a century might occur before such another actress appeared on the boards of any theatre. Little Kean, too, a none-such—all fire and intellect ; quite in earnest with every character he represented ; and thought it was a great loss to the drama that he had made his exit from the stage so prematurely in life ! The comedy of Elliston he pronounced delightful—nay more, perfection !

" Talk of *making* love," observed Peter, in extasy, " there was not an actress on the stage, during his day, ever engaged with him in comedy, so earnest were his professions of attachment to her, that I have heard it asserted, she actually fancied him her lover in reality !

" But, alas !" said he, " they have had their day and gone ! I may be wrong—but no matter—yet I have often regretted that a sort of *immortality* could not be spread over actors of such splendid talents, which might enable us 'old ones' to communicate their beauties for the amusement, if not for the instruction of the rising generation."

Peter was a kind master, and frank and free to all those persons about him. He was a great enemy to all *pretenders ;* and he never assumed a knowledge that did not belong to his character. The only thing that Makemoney ever *boasted* of, was, that he considered himself one of the *luckiest* fellows in existence. He had had nothing else but good luck throughout his life—every thing was prosperous that he undertook—and he did not consider himself *unlucky* because he had remained a bachelor ; and when asked the reason he had never changed his situation, he laughingly replied, that his time had been always too much occupied for him to devote any of it to love ; yet, nevertheless, he professed great admiration for the sex,—" but," said he, " I am now too old to make a fool of myself—and I have made up my mind that I will not become the laughing-stock of my friends, by entering into any indiscreet, or foolish marriage."

c

CHAPTER III.

The advantages attached to property ; or, win gold and wear it ! MAKEMONEY'S spontaneous notions of a Pilgrimage on the BANKS OF THE THAMES—" Home, sweet Home," against any other Air in the history of music ; contrasted with Switzerland, Italy, the Rhine, &c. The Pilgrims —MAKEMONEY, FRANK FLOURISH, and JAMES SPRIGHTLY (otherwise " Young Neverfret !") in search of the NATIONAL.

> Three Pilgrims, blithe and jolly,
> Sworn foes to melancholy,
> Went out strange things to see !

PETER'S liberal advice to his Nephew, full of pith, and nothing else but orthodox. An outline of " Young Neverfret," scarcely out of his leading strings ; and a Sketch of FLOURISH ; quite a character ! MAKEMONEY'S admonition to his brother Pilgrims, previous to their starting—' a stitch in time saves nine'—FLOURISH'S opinion against duelling—a safe card—prevention better than cure—A few words in praise of Greenwich Hospital, truly NATIONAL !

PETER MAKEMONEY was a jolly Momus-looking sort of fellow, about five feet four inches in height—a kind of low comedy sort of person—a facetious, smiling countenance, and decently dressed old man—who might have played a fatherly part, without reprehension, as to *look*, in one of Beaumont and Fletcher's comedies —yet not one of the flinty-hearted sort of personages generally found in those dramas, but more applicable to the fine feelings of an " *Old Dornton*," in the Road to Ruin.

His apparel was of the very first quality, as to *goodness*—the best cloth always selected ; and no grumbling as to the price of the suit of clothes—a first-rate workman employed to make them, and who well knew the outline of the human figure ; but, nevertheless, it had been said, that, let Makemoney be dressed after any style of fashion, new or old, he never lost sight of the man in trade. All the united taste of the tailors in London could not have changed his appearance : there was a certain sort of rotundity about his person which defied the term " gentility ;" although it had never been disputed that it did not come under the denomination of " *respectable*." But he never quarrelled with his looks :—

> O, that this too, too solid flesh would melt,
> Thaw, and resolve itself into a dew.

DRESS was not at all Makemoney's hobby; and, for the accommodation of himself, he would not have had a looking-glass throughout his dwelling, so little did he value the decorative powers to set off a man: yet he was not an enemy to *dress*, and decided cleanliness and an air of respectability were the leading features seen in his establishment. True, there was nothing of the Adonis character about him; but he was a weighty man in his person as well as his purse, and more inclined to grow fat since he had retired from business: he, therefore, felt determined, for the few years Providence might lengthen his existence, to be comfortable and happy, and to spend his time, either *in* or *out* of doors, in the most pleasant manner that he or any of his friends could suggest. He also felt emphatically the adage, " That the right end of life is to live and be jolly!" " To be sure it is," said Peter, " and when you have plenty of money in your pocket, good health, and a disposition to be happy in yourself, there cannot be much reason to call yourself to account how you have spent your time!"

Makemoney started to be pleased—his mind was made up for pleasure—and to walk or ride, were questions of no importance for his consideration. *Time* was of no object to him—a week, a month, or a quarter of a year—so that the period was occupied happily, and the journey answered the intended purpose: neither did he make any tiresome preparations for his travels.

An umbrella was his principal attendant, and a box of first-rate cigars his most pleasant companion, to fill up those hours dedicated to recreation and comfort. Like the inimitable STERNE, his luggage was extremely light—cleanliness was his object—but *dress*—studied dress—that is to say, an attention to fashionable apparel, was quite out of his calculation: two or three shirts put into his carpet-bag, accompanied by a Guide to the River, and a small note-book, to " *book*," as he termed it, any little touches of eccentric characters that might cross his path during his pilgrimage on the BANKS of the THAMES, which might refresh his memory when he returned home, were all he took with him; any thing more, he said, would be superfluous.

One night, during the enjoyment of his pipe, Makemoney observed to his nephew, that he had made up his mind to have a little jaunt—" some persons," said he, " might be inclined to call it a *Tour*—but, at all events, it could not come under the denomination of travels—FOREIGN PARTS being entirely out of the question: however, one point I have settled, and that is, my boy Jem, you shall be my companion.

" But I do not intend to sally forth, like the renowned *Don Quixotte*, to attack windmills; neither should I wish you, in your capacity as my squire, to display all the singularity and whim of a *Sancho Panza*—because neither of us, possessing the fun and wit of a CERVANTES, should circumstances come in our way worthy of recital, we could not communicate them with the fire, spirit, and talents of that justly celebrated author. Therefore, we do not set forth to *make a book*. But you now know my outline, and you will act accordingly. Wolves and tygers we shall not meet with in the shape of beasts, whatever we may do in the characters of men; neither shall we have any thing like Mount Vesuvius to frighten us, or to retard our pursuit. No, no—our tour will be quite a safe and pleasant thing! We always shall be in sight of land, although we shall not complain of the want of water: for instance, if the wind blows too strong or cold for us on one day, or the rain comes down in torrents on the next, we can return home on the same night, if our inclinations prompt us so to do; and having said so much, I will now name the place —OLD FATHER THAMES."

" Delightful!" replied his nephew. "How often have I listened with the most inexpressible pleasure to hear your old friend, Mr. Folio (the compiler), deliver himself in nearly the following words, in praise of his own country :—' Switzerland,' said he, ' I am ready to admit, may be quoted for its romantic hills, again and again; ITALY, for its beautiful, serene sky, repeatedly with delight; the RHINE, also, for its splendid scenery, with all the enthusiasm connected with poetic feelings; and NAPLES for its carnivals, gondolas, music, &c., while pleasure holds her seat in the memory. In truth, there are few, if any countries, but what possess some eminent situations, regarding prospects and interesting circumstances, to recommend them to the notice of the traveller; nay, more, positively to extort from him the highest panegyric on their extent and grandeur: but, in turn, may it not be urged, that we have in our own country subjects of the most fascinating description to call our attention, and also worthy of our enquiry; for instance, the BANKS of the THAMES—equal, in point of excellence and greatness, to any known spot in the world, leaving its rich prospects and variegated scenery entirely out of the question. True—if the BANKS of the THAMES do not possess fabulous LEGENDS, to give them a peculiar sort of interest with the lovers of romance; nevertheless, their emphatic situation and decided character, in the eyes of Europe, add an importance to them that no other possess in the scale of nations at the present moment—whether viewed in point of naval architecture, extensive and unrivalled commerce, ships from all countries,—also crowded with steam and pleasure-boats—the whole forming such a magnificent picture, which stamps the English nation the pride and envy of the world without competition."

" Aye, my friend Folio was a great enthusiast in favour of his country, I must allow," replied Makemoney,—" but, nevertheless, I will second every word that he has asserted to be the truth—the BANKS OF THE THAMES are unequalled! and only think of the beauties he has described with so much effect attached to their situation; besides the advantages of their being so contiguous to London. Yes, yes,—be it remembered when you lose sight of Dover ; or climbing the hills in foreign parts ; besides, being in a country, perhaps, where you do not know a single sentence to make yourself intelligible—laughed at for your ignorance—and reduced to the misery of standing an hour or two dripping wet—being frozen as cold as a statue—and not able to comfort yourself with a change of clothes—or a good fire-side to forget your troubles.

" Then, my dear boy, when home, dear native home, is within our grasp—almost, as you may say, to keep St. Paul's in your eye as a land-mark—and that fine, substantial structure,—yet a fig for its architecture, or its regularity of design—whether it belongs to the Doric, Ionic, Gothic, Corinthian, or Composite, it matters not to me, (without any offence I hope to Sir John Soane,) but when, I repeat, I can behold my hobby—and a prime *hobby* it is—the Bank of England—I apprehend no danger from *my* jaunt, or tour. Such being the case, my dear Jem, we can start at an hour's notice, unincumbered with any thing like the formality of luggage—our minds free and spirits good—and our pockets full, to enjoy the various scenes which present themselves to our observation, when we commence our Pilgrimage."

It may, perhaps, be necessary to introduce to the notice of the reader, before we proceed any further, Mr. James Sprightly, but amongst his companions designated as young " *Neverfret !*" or rather, if things, or men, could always be called by their proper names—*Spendmoney* would have been the most correct title, for the beloved nephew of the old Alderman.

JEM, (for such his uncle familiarly called him,) was about twenty-three years of age, and in *look*, what the fair sex might have termed rather handsome ; to be *well dressed* at all times, was a peculiar feature with his notions of taste ; studiously *polite,* under the idea that civility is always amiable, and costs nothing. *Gentlemanly* in his behavour, which not only renders a man pleasing and acceptable to all his friends and acquaintances, but a good passport to society in general ; he was likewise viewed as a young man of *spirit*, which conveys that nothing mean, low, or contemptible ought to be connected with the composition of such a being ; but polished with those delightful requisites—feeling, generosity, and honour. All these qualifications, we must aver, he possessed in a greater or less degree.

Sprightly was a great favourite with his uncle ; nay, propriety would not quarrel with the appellation in calling PETER MAKE-MONEY *his* father. JEM was the only son of an affectionate sister, a widow, who had been left in rather narrow circumstances, and previous to her death, her brother Peter had made a solemn promise to her, that he should not want for the care of a father in his progress to manhood ; and he kept his promise with the strictest sense of honour : nay, more, the uncle had evinced that degree of attention towards him—shewed so much real interest and anxiety for his future welfare—that very few fathers could boast of displaying such laudable conduct with truth and sincerity, which young Jem had experienced under the rearing of his uncle MAKEMONEY.

He had been well taught; his education not superlative, but liberal; to which might be added, that his uncle had left no stone unturned to put him on his guard; and likewise to convey to his ear some invaluable instructions respecting the ways of the world.

" I am anxious," said he to his nephew, " to point out to the ' young adventurer ' upon his entrance into life, the immense advantages resulting from experience, and the conversation and advice from persons in years, who have trod the thorny paths of the world; that is, to look before he leaps, and deliberate before he resolves; and also to make the best use of his wealth, if the smiles of Fortune have placed him on an eminence above other persons—and to be humane, charitable, and considerate towards his fellow creatures; likewise, I feel interested that he should avoid meanness and servility of disposition; but above all, not to think too much of himself—something after the manner that I am myself—ALONE; but to admit the *possibility* that there are other persons in existence as well-informed as himself; perhaps, somewhat wiser, and better read in the intricate ways of the world. Also, that the ' young adventurer ' should, upon all occasions, be JUST before he is *generous ;* and to endeavour by fair and honourable means to increase his property. To resist CANT in all its specious shapes—to reject HUMBUG—expose DECEIT—despise fulsome and uncalled-for FLATTERY—and to be GENTLEMANLY in every point of view. ' KNOWLEDGE is power ;' as such it is described by one of our greatest law-givers—my Lord BACON—and that immense power is only to be obtained by a clear, cool, and dispassionate view of society. *Outside* appearances must ever go for little in the account of human nature with men of sense. The world is still deceived by ornament, it is too true, but nevertheless, my wishes are, that the *mind* of the ' young adventurer ' should act as a JURY, to hear both sides of the question, and not to condemn *unheard ;* but to look after the *substance,* and to avoid being imposed upon by the *shadow !*"

In return, JEM proved that he was tractable, kind, and attentive to his uncle during his boyhood, and received those instructions with the right sort of impression on his mind ;—namely, that they were intended for his good, and future respectability in life. In truth, the conduct displayed on every occasion by his uncle, might be called *orthodox,* that is to infer, he had endeavoured, to the utmost extent of his power, to " train up a child in the way he should go, that when he is old, he will not depart therefrom."

JAMES SPRIGHTLY, as the term goes, was viewed as a good young man, and highly respected by every family to whom he had had the honour of an introduction. He was not a " harem-scarem " sort of fellow who would dash at every thing, regardless of the consequences ; nor too *precise* and *demure,* to make objections where none existed.   He was acquainted with several young men like himself, and with them he had visited several places in London openly, and well worthy of his study and observation ; and perhaps, others on the *sly,* that had much better remain unknown ; but, neverthless, it should seem, that James Sprightly, the darling nephew of his uncle, had come out of the " dregs of iniquity " none the worse ; nay, better, much better, for the visit.   Yet, however, the experiment might be considered dangerous.

> Vice is a monster of so frightful mien,
> As to be *hated,* needs but to be seen ;
> Yet seen too oft, familiar with her face,
> We first endure, then pity, then embrace.

The contrast which he had witnessed between bad and good society had so disgusted him, that, to use his own words,—" One pill was more than a dose."   He had been out of his " leading-strings " for a year or two, that is to say, he had become a MAN according to law—at the precise period of twenty-one years of age ; but as to " *years of discretion* "—an undefined sort of term, and for which no Act of Parliament has yet been passed, to settle that most important point in the lives of both the male and female sex, we are compelled to leave that " knotty point," or rather postpone it,—to be settled by the conduct of Mr. James Sprightly himself, at some future period of his existence.

Though not so well read in the ways of the world as his uncle, yet he had paid some attention to men and manners ; and he had been far from an idle observer in his walks through society.   He also well knew the value of *circumspection* and *obedience.*   He was, likewise, a tolerably good actor—his *entrances* and *exits* were made to a nicety ; and he had *measured* the ways and feelings of his uncle with all the accuracy of a superior tailor, who prides himself of never having *mis*-fitted any of his customers in the whole course of his business.

Thus far they had gone on well together ;—his uncle's word was law, and the nephew had acted up to it, to the very spirit and letter.   Old Makemoney was too liberal in disposition to be harsh, or to curb his nephew's feelings ; in fact, he had not witnessed any line of conduct that had called forth from him any thing like remarks of severity.   " Young men will be young men," said he, " and I do not expect to find old heads upon young shoulders—neither do I wish to see it ! Any thing out of its place I dislike.   I am more inclined to be of Sir Oliver's opinion in the School for Scandal, in speaking of Charles Surface, ' For my part, I hate to see prudence clinging to the green suckers of youth ; tis like ivy round a sapling, and spoils the growth of the tree.'

" For myself," observed Uncle Makemoney, " when I was

twenty years of age, my notions were rather confined and stupid, but I could not perceive it then ; and not so liberal as I have since wished them to have been.   At thirty, my experience had then taught me to view a variety of circumstances respecting Men and Manners in a totally different light ;   at forty, and every succeeding year, I was inclined to laugh at my own ignorance—to draw comparisons—ask myself a few questions—and endeavour to become and act like a useful and rational member of society.

" My situation in business, and my character getting abroad as a rich man, as a matter of course introduced me to numerous characters in every point of view :—the high born Peer—the Member of Parliament—the Spendthrift—the Deep One—the poor, but honest deserving character—the specious, hypocritical man ; and the downright swindler, &c. ; and to say that I have not been imposed upon, tricked, swindled, and almost cheated, with my eyes open, by artifices that I could not suspect, and plans so well laid, that I was not able to detect, until too late to remedy the evil—therefore, I do not expect too much from young men ; and if they will only listen to their elders in experience, half the difficulties are overcome : at the same time I will not proclaim myself a wiser man than society are inclined to give me credit for—but admitting, at times, I was severely pinched by such delusions, yet ultimately they proved of good effect to my understanding, and, like a ' burnt child that dreads the fire,' I was never deceived a *second time*, however speciously the artifice might have been dressed up, on the same sort of attack."

Such was the description which Peter Makemoney gave of himself, not only for the future guidance of his nephew, but when seated with several young men, who were anxious to become acquainted with the mode he had adopted to raise himself in the estimation of society—a *desideratum*, that all young persons of enterprise and knowledge would feel desirous to hear, or, in other words, to take a leaf out of the book of Mr. Peter Makemoney.

" Do not *gamble*," said his uncle, " nor get drunk—for they are both the forerunners of every other crime ; the drunkard is a *beast-besotted*, and does not know, at times, what follies he commits ;—the Gamester is reckless, without a heart—and plans the destruction of others with as much coolness and ice-like feelings, as the most *routine* transaction in the world—therefore, avoid both these crimes, and my hopes and wishes will be confirmed, that you will be able to make your way through life in the most pleasant manner !"

" Excellent—capital ! my dear uncle," answered Jem, " I never heard you make a speech in the whole course of my life, half so intelligible ! Good advice—Banks of the Thames—Trips by Steam Boats—Greenwich, Vauxhall, Richmond, Windsor, &c. all by turns !—Variety is charming ! That's the time of day ! Never fret ! Be alive ! A fig for expense !—I am delighted beyond measure !"

" Well, then, we will be off without delay ; and I have invited *Frank Flourish* to make a third," said his uncle ; " we cannot be dull in his company !"

" I do not like to differ with you, sir, upon any subject—but perhaps that invitation had been better let alone," replied Jem, " he is such a mixture——"

" True ; but nevertheless, he is the very fellow for us," said his uncle, " you will find him better than any Map, Guide, or Itinerary, however correct they may be ; and excepting his foolish nonsense, and strange peculiarities, there are many worse acquaintances than *Frank Flourish* to be met with in this world. He will never be at a loss if a house or a knocker is at hand—he accosted twenty persons in our journey to High-gate, with all the familiarity of old acquaintances."

" I am satisfied, sir ;—your word is law to me. If he can please you, I have not the slightest objection of his being of the party. My fears were only on account that some of his follies might get us into a *row ;* or some unpleasant dilemma;" answer-ed the nephew.

" We will risque that ; surely two of us can manage him ; however, we will lecture Flourish a little on the subject, pre-vious to our starting ;" said Makemoney, " and I think we can make him tractable."

The other Pilgrim, Frank Flourish, Esq., invited to make the Tour with them on the BANKS OF THE THAMES, was, in the present state of society, termed a *Character ;* at least, he had endeavoured to make himself *somebody* in the eyes of the circles he visited. Frank pretended to *know* everything, but the real fact was—in the scale of talent—this good opinion, which he had formed of himself, was very much questioned ; but, never-theless, he had mixed a great deal with the different classes of society ; and abating the above sort of *conceit,* he shewed him-self at times, as a man of some *nous.*

But he was *uneven*—often upon stilts—and frequently, what he had vehemently urged on the previous day, he would as strenu-ously deny on the next. But then he was *rich*—very rich, and upon that account, it was said he was *endured ;* indeed, it is too often seen, that riches, nine times out of ten, obtain a preference in society. Some of his acquaintances urged that he put on this *strangeness* of disposition ; others, that he was not half such a fool as he made himself ; indeed, various opinions had been ex-pressed respecting his capability.

Yet he was a good-natured man, and not easily to be put out of countenance. The *assurance* he possessed was enough to defy brass itself. He was useful in this respect, to those per-sons who might be in want of a leader ; or rather, a *pioneer,* to clear the way for them. He would go any where !—Ask all manner of questions !—and introduce himself to the greatest stranger on the earth, without a *blush,* in the most familiar manner. Frequently, he proved himself, to a certain extent, a complete *Marplot ;* and had seemed to have modelled himself after the celebrated Paul Pry ! This latter hero of bronze and impertinence, he acknowledged for his prototype ; observing, at the same time, there was something very imposing and forgiving about the words—"I beg pardon ! I hope I don't intrude." And Frank thought it utterly impossible that any person could be so cruel as to find fault with him for acting up to the—*polite !*

However, his personal appearance did much for him; although he did ot possess the elegant figure, nor the fine face of a Canning ; neither the beau ideal of a handsome man, like the late Sir Thomas Lawrence ; nevertheless, there was a certain something about FLOURISH, which intimated to the spectator, that he was above the rank of a plebeian in society ; and might be termed, without any offence to the phrase—"*gentlemanly !*"

Indeed, all the old and young women pronounced him a " fine man !" His taste for dress was also excellent ; although, if a jury of tailors were summoned to decide on that most important feature at the West End of the town, we have no doubt but Beau Brummel and the Baronet Sir Lumley Skeffington, in their zenith, would have had a decided majority in their favour, as to the " cut, good taste, and prime fit " of their clothes.

But in his *meridian,* " the CITY," it is said, that FRANK FLOURISH had it nearly all his own way ; indeed, there was something of the *band-box* always about his appearance out of doors—a new made pin could not have looked better. " The CITY ! Psha !" observed one of the West End to Flourish, " do not talk of the City, when fashion is the topic ; or else, you will rapidly get below freezing point in an instant, and be laughed at as a complete Goth, or Vandal ! If you must make comparisons, and introduce ' *the City !*' talk about its ' good,' and not ' fashionable men ;' and then your argument will be admitted sterling, and have a *backer* in the ' good ' Rothschild !"

FLOURISH was about five-feet, ten inches in height ; and although he was a remarkably well made man, we do not intend to urge that he might have been selected as a model in " the *Life !*" at the Royal Academy. At all events, his appearance was prepossessing : his address was easy and confident, and he entered a room amidst the most scrutinizing looks of the company, with as much ease as an old actor walks over the boards of a theatre---in truth, he was that sort of personage which the female sex give the preference to, and admire as a " well-bred man !"

But if Flourish had any *forte* belonging to him, it was to find fault with almost every thing, indeed he wished to appear rather fastidious : this was the weakest part of his behaviour---he thought it gave him the character in the eyes of his friends and the world, as a man of superior judgment. He found *fault* with his Papa and Mamma, as he said, for not having given him greater abilities---" they ought to have done so---I have found fault with myself ; and as I possess that liberality of disposition, surely I have a right to object to the behaviour of other persons---more especially, as I only do it in a ' *critical*' way, to expose *ignorance*, and shew *wisdom.*" Such was the outline of the third Pilgrim, who was on the eve of starting on a Pilgrimage to improve the minds of his Majesty's liege subjects ; or, that travellers see strange things !

" Psha !" said Makemoney, " do not profane the word ' critical !' also leave ignorance and wisdom out of the question, and attend to me. Take my advice before you start : I wish you to be more careful in your remarks to strangers---and do not presume too much upon your riches---and then we shall stand not only a good chance of keeping out of mischief, but return home in whole skins."

It had been whispered about by some of Flourish's acquaintance, that for his impertinence he had been in danger several times of being kicked---horsewhipped---and other degrading circumstances---but, as no proof had appeared, and it was only hearsay evidence, such reports went for nothing in the estimation of Uncle Makemoney, or his nephew.

" Danger ! a whole skin ! never mind, my dear Sir," answered Flourish, with a self-approving smile on his countenance, " you will not meet with the shadow of danger in my company ; I have made up my mind never to fight a *duel ;* although I have not registered an oath in Heaven on the subject ; no, no, let fools fight duels---wise men know better. If ignorant people will take offence, when no offence is meant---it only shews a want of judgment---and then, I say, if they are obstinate, there is the *law* for them. I am for the LAW---there is time to cool upon any question at issue---and you can punish your opponent, if not convince him, by deputy. Besides, Sir John Falstaff's opinion has quite decided me upon such matters ; when he asserts, that ' honour cannot restore a leg---and discretion is the better part of valour !' The law of the land is also against duelling ! and have I not another good authority in Old Hudibras---although the words may have been disputed as the text of the author, yet I will take them for granted, and not question their import :

> The cock that fights and runs away,
> May live to fight another day !
> But he that is in battle slain,
> Will never rise to fight again.

Therefore, rest assured, my dear Makemoney, that I detest the sight of a bullet ; and the smell of gunpowder, of all others, is the most obnoxious to my olfactory nerves—nay, quite shocking ! —and I will not waste another word about it. But I never can become a *murderer*, to take away a man's life, because he differs in opinion with me, is most certain. Call me coward, puppy, *shubberoon*, or what you may, I will never deviate from the plan I have adopted—I will endeavour to keep the line, as you seem so very particular—but we must have a little fun, quiz, and all that sort of thing, though we are Pilgrims in disguise. You used not to be so tenacious, sir; you would not make Puritans of us, I am sure."

"Never fret, but keep your temper, my dear uncle," said his nephew; therefore, let us be alive—get ready—pack up—be off—sail down the Thames—look out—be merry and wise—Time is on the wing—a few hours will change the scene! No chest of drawers wanting, Frank—no toilette—Nature unadorned—carpet-bag will do—clean face—a cigar or two in the box—put on a sailor's jacket, if you like—no nonsense—be at the scratch to a second—remember, to-morrow! Breakfast at eight—afloat by ten—a whiff or two before we part to-night—grog stiff—to bed soon—be stirring with the lark, my good fellow! then all will be right—and that is what I call the time of day—doing the trick, when travellers are on the move. But never fret." The above sentences were all given with the rapidity of a *Goldfinch*, describing the races at Newmarket.

"I shall be in time," replied Flourish, "but I should like to hear the outline of our first day's trip, before we start."

"Why, my dear Frank," replied Makemoney, "the first shrine that we shall pay our devoirs to will be Greenwich Hospital; the very sound of which fills my heart with love of country. Well may foreigners observe, that our Hospitals are palaces—the compliment is a just one, but not a jot more than it deserves. You will see nothing like Greenwich Hospital I believe upon the *Rhine,* or any where else, except close to Old Father Thames: but, much as I may admire it as a splendid piece of architecture, its *manly* contents I love one hundred times better; and if you will allow me to repeat some original lines from a manuscript in my possession, I think you will have a correct description of it :—

> See that beautiful edifice—
> NATIONAL to the very echo!—Where
> Lion-hearts and lamb-like feelings are laid up
> In ordinary? 'Tis Humanity's figure
> Head! The receptacle of true courage and
> Honor! The pride of Englishmen, and the boast
> Of Great Britain! Where timber-toes shew love of
> Country! And the loss of an arm displays more
> Importance in the eye of the public than
> The exterior of a Peerage. Here may
> Be seen Jack Junk, of the Thunder Man-of-War,
> Relating his battles to Bill Mainstay over
> A glass of grog—and the latter exclaiming,
> 'Aye, my ould tar, come the three quarters of the
> World in arms, England never did, and never
> Shall lie at the proud foot of a conqueror.
> Give us your flipper, shipmate, and while there is
> A plank left in the vessel, we'll stick to her,
> And cry,—Old England, for ever! Huzza! huzza! huzza!

"Is not that NATIONAL?" exclaimed Makemoney; "but in such matters I must confess myself an enthusiast."

"Something very like it," replied Flourish, "and strictly in unison with my feelings—the brave defenders of their country merit every return that can be granted for their services."

"Then, for the Park and its amusements; also a peep at the Fair, and all the *et cetera* that attends upon a day's adventures. Nothing shall come amiss to us; and, as jolly Pilgrims, we will mix with the holyday folks like one of the party. I love to see the girls merry, and the boys happy---who appear like birds out of a cage; and thinking, as it were, every minute an hour from boxing-day to Easter-Monday until the lively period arrives! I was once young myself, and I cannot forget the days of my boyhood."

"Glorious feelings, sir," observed Jem, "but never fret!— Young! you are young! you will always be young, if you can but think so; you are as young as ever! Only get on—push along---sport a toe---quick step--please and be pleased, and leave old age to those who can't help themselves. Let us be off like shots---hit the mark---shoot flying---bring down your birds ---and that's the time of day!

"Besides," answered his uncle, "I love to see the old pensioners enjoying themselves: the sight of those veterans, the remnant of their country's greatness, gives my mind a secret pleasure that I cannot communicate. It also puts me in mind of old times. Well, after all, there is nothing like the old times---least wise, the old ones think so, and that is all the same to us. Then to-morrow morning, my boys, we'll start by one of the steamers ---enjoy the breezes from Old Father Thames---land at the Hospital stairs---mix with the gay and lively throng---and then make ourselves as merry and comfortable as the best amongst them! Now, you have my outline on the subject."

"An outline, sir," replied Flourish, in extacy, "it is a *finished* picture! I am in raptures---I shan't sleep a wink for thinking upon it; the mere anticipation of the pleasure and fun that we shall meet with, delights me beyond measure."

"My dear, good uncle," said Jem, "may you live a thousand years!---may you never die!---so look out, Flourish---the Tower ---steam-boats---holyday folks---pretty lasses---prime boys--- bands of music---dancing---singing---mirth and good humour, and all that sort of thing, to make our existence a treat! Sleep, did you say, Flourish!---I want no sleep---I am wide awake for a start---delays are dangerous!"

"Not quite so fast, young man," observed Makemoney, "all in good time; therefore, we'll take a glass of grog together before we separate." They were all on the *qui vive*---full of anticipation. Several funny and amusing anecdotes were told over the glass; and Makemoney, who was on his mettle, every now and then burst forth singing, "O! the days when I were young!" Cigar after cigar was disposed of in quick time---the supper o'er---all's well---merry and wise---and "good night!"

CHAPTER IV.

*The pleasures of anticipation—the Pilgrims preparing to
start—Who's for Greenwich? Holiday Folks! Smiling
faces; Children six feet high; Pleasure the order of the
day! The Tower recognized as an old land-mark, and
the Custom House praised for its magnificence.—Lots of
Characters on board of the Steamer! Off she goes—The
eloquent dealer in Literature—(quid pro quo)—the
luxury of a Newspaper—Introduction of TIM BRONZE,
without being introduced; a living Vampire and Victim
hunter—Description of the necessary CUTS in Society—
Secrets worth knowing to a Young Man on his entrance
into life! The soi-disant Duchess and her two daughters
—Generals in petticoats enlisting recruits! PICTURESQUE
DOLEFUL, a tally undertaker, one of the woeful disciples
of LAVATER; but a useful personage to ensure a decent
finish to the last exit! SCAPEGRACE, a dark and terrific
portrait of human nature; or, a man may smile and be a
villain. OLD FATHER THAMES in all his glory—MAKE-
MONEY in extacy—a bit of the NATIONAL! A sound reply to an Alarmist of the Olden Times!*

THE pleasures of anticipation had fastened so strongly upon
all their feelings, that the Pilgrims, on retiring to rest, had
rather *dozed*, than slept during the night; and who, in consequence, left their beds at a much earlier hour than usual,—
the time appearing to hang heavily upon their hands, until the
signal was given for starting—so eager were they to commence
their Pilgrimage.

The mind of Makemoney now being as free as air, the cares of
business completely at an end---and nothing to claim his attention, but pleasure and happiness---he was almost as much a *boy*,
regarding the object in view, as his junior companions; he was
equally as good in health, and young in spirits---indeed,
his constitution was so unimpaired by irregularlty of conduct---
that if he did come under the denomination of rather a " *middle-aged* " looking gentleman, he was in possession of more
agility and strength than most of the young men of his acquaintance; and he might quote from *Adam*, in " As You Like It,"
with the utmost propriety and truth.

> Tho' I look old, yet I am strong and lusty,
> For in my youth I never did apply
> Hot and rebellious liquors in my blood:

P Egan Sunf delt

CONCERTING the PILGRIMAGE

Nor did I with unbashful forehead woo
The means of weakness and debility;
Therefore my age is as a lusty winter—
Frosty, but kindly: let me go wi h you,
I'll do the service of a younger man
In all your business and necessities.

The Pilgrims met together at breakfast in high spirits. "Now, my boys,---brother Pilgrims," said Makemoney, "the time is arrived, and the game is in view, as the anxious sportsman says, when the hunter's horn invites him to the chase; therefore, let us understand each other---to be free, jovial, and all that sort of thing; but at the same time, let our conduct be such, that we may not have to reflect upon it with regret!"

"Reflect! regret! perish such phrases," replied Flourish in a high tone of extacy, "and substitute in their stead, pleasure! I am sure we shall have to remember our Pilgrimage with extacy---it will form a delightful epoch in our lives. We shall enjoy the picturesque---get more acquainted with the *National* ---obtain a better insight into character---and meet with lots of adventures. We do not mean to go hand over head; but to enjoy every circumstance that crosses our path, with interest and good humour.

"Never fret, my dear uncle," observed Jem, "we are the proper sort of folks to do what is right to each other; I am quite aware what you mean---that is, to stear clear of what is vulgarly termed, '*larking*;' but do not let us mar our trip with any thing like cold, icy sort of feelings---rigid propriety--- caution---fear---to be as demure as an old nurse at a christening, and to be afraid to look and act for ourselves. No, let us enter into the scene with all the spirit it deserves :---

We are the boys,
That fear no noise—
Where thundering cannons rattle.

"Well, let it be so," replied Makemoney, full of jollity--- "I merely threw out a hint; and I shall not *sermonize*, as you call it, any more on the subject."

The clock had struck eleven, when the Pilgrims sallied forth for the scene of action; but they were full early at the Wharf, acting upon the excellent maxims of Makemoney, always to have a quarter of an hour to spare, rather than be five minutes too late---by which means they had some time to make a few remarks, and look about them, before the last bell gave warning that the steamer was ready to start.

"This bustling scene is delightfully interesting to me," said Makemoney, as the holyday folks, young and old, were pushing along towards the steamer; "pleasure seems to sit upon every brow, and shews the necessity and great advantages derived from *relaxation*---not only upon the minds and habits of the persons employed in business, but in a political point of view.

Relaxation, properly directed, tends towards the preservation of good order and obedience to the laws---produces contentment, and adds stamina and security to the Government. I like to see the middling classes of society enjoy themselves without restraint; and if some of them do appear for a short time as wild as birds out of a cage, they, nevertheless, in general, return to their duty with pleasure and alacrity. I shall always support those good old customs. See the apprentice boy, more happy than the prince---in fact, the higher walks of life cannot possess such real feelings of enjoyment---the journeyman, equally alive to a day's pleasure, and independent in mind and conduct as the first peer in the realm---and the shopkeeper, relaxing from the fatigues of business, quits his counter with all the importance and feeling of a man in the first station in the country. The votary of pleasure, too, in order to occupy a few leisure hours to pick up something new, may be seen, *incog.*, viewing the habits and manners of the middling and lower classes of society;---the caricaturist, who is on the alert to sketch new characters after nature; and the pretty lasses, full of love and anticipation to enjoy a day's pleasure with their sweethearts. The name of Greenwich---its hill, and unrivalled park, which nothing can excel---is the great focus of attraction."

"That's the time of day, uncle," replied Jem, "they are not only excellent remarks, but full of liberality, and permit me to second them: it is also a convincing proof to me the advantages to the mind of mixing with the different grades of society."

Flourish had scarcely put his foot on board, before he observed, "Aye, there is my old acquaintance, the Tower, but not altered a brick in appearance since I was a youngster. The Tower is always a sort of land-mark to me on my exit or entrance into London; but that is a splendid building, I must confess," looking through his eye-glass at the Custom-House; "but a friend of mine, a very accurate creature to a dot, tells me it is not half so big, nor any thing like such an elegant ssructure as the Customs on the banks of the Liffey! That is strange, too, I think------"

" Don't think about it, Frank," replied Makemoney, rather sharply, " Make no more foolish remarks! What is the use of large premises, elegant, perhaps in point of architecture; but as to importance in the eyes of the merchant, mere empty shew, if there is no business to support them. But------"

Here the argument was cut short, owing to the bustle of the scene, and also by the volubility of a man in the character of a newsman, with a handfull of morning newspapers, who thus addressed Makemoney: " Don't you want a newspaper, Sir! I can suit every body! I am like the Public Ledger, open to all parties, and influenced by none; and I am decidedly in favour of the Liberty of the Press. Here is the cream of all the talent in the Metropolis for you---the advantages of information---and the

The STEAM PACKET

power of knowledge. News from the four quarters of the world:
---Let me say to you, Ladies and Gentlemen, that reading a
newspaper early in the morning, is like unto a gun charged in
the hands of a sportsman, who is prepared to make a hit, and
bring down his bird: which, on the other hand, may be compared to the reader, who goes forth and scatters the contents of
his knowledge for the benefit of numerous companies. The mind
must be fed as well as the body; therefore, to those persons
that require literary food, I present myself as their caterer.
All persons, you know, sir, must live in this world; and they
must work, too, according to that New Poor Law Act! But
no matter—it is of no use to grumble, I suppose; yet I hope
there is room for us all. So, my worthy masters, here they are,
pick and choose,—from the *Great Giant* down to the *Tap-tub!*
all piping hot from the machines—containing important debates in
both Houses of Parliament—foreign news—crim. con. intelligence, theatricals, police, murder, rapes, &c. Do buy one, sir—
you cannot lay out your money better! A newspaper is one of
the most amusing things in the world—positively a luxury under any circumstance; but on board of a steamer, you are at the
end of your journey before you can say Jack Robinson."

"The *Giant* and the Tap-tub!" echoed Makemoney, smiling
—" they are curious designations, arn't they, Mr. Newsman?"

"They are nick-names, I admit, sir," replied the newsman;
" but there are *giants* as well as *pigmies* in literature. It is a
sort of cant which runs through society; but, nevertheless,
such designations sometimes apply with more effect, and give a
better character to a man or a book, than words of a more com-
monplace description. But for my own reading, sir, I am for
quality instead of quantity; but taste is every thing; and some
writers have the power of communicating in a few lines what
others cannot effect in three columns: therefore, sir, I am for
brevity."

"You are a critic," said Makemoney.

"Not in the slightest degree, sir," observed the vender of
newspapers. "I run here—I go there—I pick up what I can—
I hear sensible men argufy the topic on most subjects of the
day, and I lose nothing. I have no pretensions to be a critic,
but I am an observer—a plain matter-of-fact man—nothing
more—and only read as I run—and I am always on the trot;
therefore, I have no time to digest any of the articles: indeed,
I may say, I swallow them by wholesale, and retail them to my
customers afterwards."

"You are an amusing fellow, at all events," replied Makemoney, " and if any man can sell a newspaper, I should think
you are the person to procure customers."

"You flatter me, sir," said the newsman, "but what little I
know is owing, in a great measure, to the rapid strides of the
march of intellect; a kind of railway-road of communication to

E

our pericraniums. Our *eyes* are clearer than heretofore, our *ears* are 100 per cent. of more advantage to us, and listen with more interest; and our minds, sir, are divested of prejudice—we are more liberal in our decisions—such are the advantages and blessings of a free press! What shall I do for you?—here is the Giant, sir, or——"

" The Giant, as you call it, "replied Makemoney, " is a great creature, I must admit, for talent and early information; but since I have been man and boy for the last forty years, it has made as many *leaps*, backwards and forwards, as *Harlequin*, and quite as many *changes*, and become as party-coloured as his jacket—it blows hot and cold with the same mouth—and *vacillating*, to answer particular purposes, to the end of the chapter —it can turn, turn, and turn again, and yet be a newspaper! No—I must have a more stable commodity for my money, Mr. Newsman."

" All right, I dare say, sir; as I perceive you look before you leap," answered the seller of newspapers; " and very proper, I make no doubt. But, nevertheless, I like to tell my customers what they are going to get for their money. I have, sir, a character to lose :—My name is Jack, the publisher, but more familiarly known and called ' the walking index; or steam boat companion;' but I am scarcely allowed to get forty winks during the night, and a peep-o'-day boy into the bargain. However, I do not wish to appear here, sir, like a counsellor without his brief—therefore, I skims over the contents of each newspaper before I brings them out of the office; by which means, as the actors say, I am up in the part; and I then know what I have in store for my worthy patrons—the Whigs, the Tories, Conservatives, the Radicals, Independents, &c. I have no doubt, sir, but amongst your acquaintances, you are a very great quidnunc—I hope without offence; but as that is neither here nor there, only let me recommend to your notice the *Tap-tub;* I beg your honor's pardon, I should have said the *Morning Advertiser*. But it is a nick-name given to that paper by the vulgar part of society; because it is supported by the publicans of the Metropolis. It is, however, an excellent paper—greatly improved; and for my individual reading, I like it the best of any; it has numerous paragraphs, and a tiny bit of every thing that is going on in London, and you are not deluged with Parliamentary news. Besides, it ought to have the support of every body."

" Why so?" asked Makemoney, " does it display greater talent than any other newspaper?—Are the articles better written?"

" Not that I am aware of, sir," replied Jack, the publisher; " but I will leave the talents of the writers to speak for themselves. However, I am always anxious to promote its sale, for the best of all reasons. Out of the profits of the Morning Advertiser, a school has been established for many years, for the sons and daughters of indigent or deceased publicans, and upwards of a hundred and fifty boys and girls are entirely supported—besides the best education that can be procured for them."

"This is a recommendation for the Morning Advertiser, I must confess," said Makemoney.

"It is a magnificent building in Kennington Lane; and it would do your heart good, sir, to behold it—it is worthy the name of a palace," observed the newsman. "Besides this splendid work of charity, several alms-houses have been erected in the Kent Road, for the reception of the aged, infirm, and distressed publicans and their widows—with a most liberal allowance for their comfort and support. Therefore, sir, to the utmost of my abilities, I will promote the interest of a newspaper which has for its *stimulus*—the protection of youth from beggary, if not crime; and ultimately sends them forth into the world as good, and enlightened members of society. Too much cannot be said for such a meritorious institution—and which leaves all *party*-matters at an immeasurable distance."

"Bravo!" exclaimed Makemoney, "you are a philanthropist—give me the Morning Advertiser, and there is half-a-crown for yourself. Good feelings at all times ought to be encouraged, and I will never take a glass of wine at an inn, or a public-house, but I will recommend to their notice a newspaper so laudably established, and which exhibits so much humanity towards the orphan and distressed child. But you ought to have been a member of parliament, instead of a newsman; for I am sure, from the manner you have told your story, you would cut a much better figure than many M. P's. I could mention. Ha! ha! You are eloquence personified."

"Thank you, sir, for the compliment," replied the newsman, "I wish you a pleasant trip—a fine day—and plenty of fun." He then touched his hat, and scampered off to another part of the vessel, to sell the remainder of his papers.

Makemoney immediately retired to the most unfrequented part of the steamer, to read, or rather devour the contents of the newspaper—"Without which," he said, "he always appeared at fault, and in want of something the whole of the day." Our uncle perfectly coincided with the *chattering* newsman, that a well-conducted newspaper was one of the greatest luxuries to the mind in the whole field of literature: the variety of topics for argument it produced, *immense;* and the transitions from grave to gay, were pleasant in the extreme. No man, he urged, wanted company when he had a newspaper with him. The stocks, and list of bankrupts, were his first objects of perusal, as a man of business—then the *new* publications, just like an old coachman likes to hear the smack of the whip, he had an eye to what was going on in the trade—and lastly, the *et cetera*, until the whole of the columns were disposed of; in fact, he was a complete literary glutton in this respect.

During the time Makemoney was making a *meal* of the Morning Advertiser, the two other Pilgrims, Frank and Jem, were on the alert, viewing the crowd and entrance of the passengers on beard of the ——steamer, tumbling in, as the old saying has it, thick and three-fold.—"Here are lots of characters," cocking up his eye-glass, said Flourish, on the titter;' "and I must have a touch at some of them during our short voyage to Greenwich. I have got a page or two open for them in my pretty little note book, for the amusement of my friends at some future period. Hallo! I must not be quite so fast! The coast is not so clear as I could wish. I perceive an old enemy of mine on board, and if I do not 'sheer off,' a broadside will be the result."

"Surely, you do not mean to assert that you are afraid of a bailiff," said Jem, "or a dun?"

"A bailiff, or a dun? Psha! They are trifles, and may be settled with, on knowing the amount of their demand?" replied Flourish; "but the enemy I mean, if he does not upon the present occasion assume the shape of a *water pirate*, he is well known as a *land shark*, and bites at every thing within his reach."

"I cannot understand you," answered Jem; "you are speaking in parables."

"Well, then, I will soon enlighten your understanding," replied Flourish; "you see that tall shabby-genteel looking man, who has got the Captain of the vessel in tow, and who appears to be laughing heartily at his remarks; his name is TIMOTHY BRONZE, but familiarly called *Tim*, and I, unfortunately, know him. He is a complete sturdy beggar: I never knew any thing like him: he will not be *shook* off at any price. I have tried to CUT him in all directions, but in vain: He is well known in the fashionable circles by the title of 'CUT-and-*Come*-again!' and I verily believe if you could *cut Tim* in half—one part or the other would attack you—perhaps both!

"No doubt but you have heard of a celebrated broken-down man of fortune, who was so reduced in a pecuniary point of view—as to assume the character of 'Jeremy Diddler' off the stage; and who made it his boast that he had *borrowed* in *single* shillings from his friends and acquaintances (otherwise victims), to the tune of FIVE HUNDRED POUNDS!"

"I think I have heard my uncle"—said Jem—"speak of such a character as you have just described."

"Be that as it may," replied Flourish, "I am sure BRONZE is a greater warrior in point of levying contributions on his friends! He first requests the loan of a few pounds—until he comes down to *coppers*—he is worse than a horse-leech—he will bleed you to death; and if you do not relieve his wants—he will abuse you in a sort of pathetic style, and so work upon your feelings that it is almost impossible to resist his *importunities*. But Bronze has lost every thing like the feelings of modesty—and, to get rid of his company, you must purchase his *absence*.

" He is a troublesome customer," answered Jem, " at all events ; but are you acquainted with his origin ?"

" He commenced life with a decent property ; and his parents were gentlefolks ;—but, from a wrong *bias*, he not only disposed of his patrimony in a few years, but he got twice the amount in debt with his tradesmen ; and, for a long time, ' *John Doe* and *Richard Roe*' were continually in pursuit of him. The King's Bench—Fleet—Horsemonger Lane—and Whitecross Street Prisons, in succession, were his lodgings after he had lost house and land ; but, nevertheless, when shut out from his extensive range of society, and confined to a small space within the gates of a prison—even amongst the wretchedly distressed, needy, and starving debtors he found out VICTIMS ; nay more, he had the art, and possessed the soft tones of persuasion in so great a degree, that, *steeled* as the minds of the persons who sold articles of provision in the prison might be against credit, from the numerous tricks that had been practised on their credulity—yet Bronze with the utmost *sang froid* got into their debt—by which he acquired a second title—" THE VICTIM HUNTER !"

" He must be a clever fellow," said Jem, " thus to impose upon people ; Indeed, a person with such talents—it is almost impossible to be on your guard against."

" His stories are not only well told, but well timed ;" answered Flourish, " and his anecdotes pointed and rich ; and his knowledge of life and character, superlative. He makes himself a feature in every company : and appears to be perfectly at home, if seated by the side of a *sweep*, and not at a loss when in the company of a senator ! It has been said of Bronze, that he had the art of persuasion so much at his command, as almost to seduce a bird from a tree. In company with him you forget his rogueries—although he tells them about his friends A. and B.—but so pleasantly, that he must be a stoic indeed who does not join in the laugh. Excepting debts, Bronze never did any thing to affect his personal liberty ; and it must be low-water mark indeed with him amongst the " *Sufferers*" if he appears in public badly dressed."

" Then that is the case with him now," said Jem, " for all the *nap* appears to have been brushed off both his hat and coat !"

" I have no doubt but he has *victimized* so many Sufferers, that he has not a *chance* left amongst them : his *memory*, excepting what he owes, is of the most tenacious description : indeed, several of his victims have offered to make a bet, that if it suited his purpose, and an object was to be gained by it—that he would retail Sir Richard Phillips' MILLION OF FACTS, without a halt !

" He likewise makes it a point with himself to *read* every BOOK that is likely to give him the lead in conversation ; it is impossible to *compete* with him—he is a cold, calculating fellow, and I would almost swear, that his last thoughts at night, and the first in the morning were—to get the whip-hand of everybody! I have been *punished* severely for my credulity!"

"To a weak mind," said Jem, "this Bronze must be a dangerous acquaintance; and, according to your statement, he swindles you first, and then laughs at you afterwards."

"A sensible man, aye, and one of experience, he *deceives* with the utmost dexterity," answered Flourish: "over his cup of coffee he literally devours the contents of the Penny Magazine, Chambers' Journal, &c. His manners are prepossessing, and he is polite to the echo. The slightest acquaintance he attacks first under the name of a *loan;* and to those persons that he has '*done brown*,' as the term goes, he begs them to place it to the benevolent and humane account, under the name of '*a gift.*' Besides, you are aware, sir, that 'Charity covereth a multitude of sins.'"

"You cannot hide yourself," said Jem—"let him come. I do not mind a shilling or two, just to have a specimen of his talents—how he carries on the war! I perceive he has recognized your person, as he is approaching towards us."

"You will regret it," answered Flourish; "he wants a new *victim,* and you will suit his purpose."

BRONZE now addressed Flourish, in his pathetic style, by saying, "Hard up, you see, sir! (*pointing to his clothes*) Dress bad!—tailors shy!—the world cruel!—old friends have bad memories!—every thing is turned upside down—friendship, attachment, and respect, positively kicked out of doors!—generosity only known by name!—hearts have changed their sides, and feeling—did I use such an obsolete term?—I beg pardon—nothing else but *sentiment* remains for the unfortunate!"

"'Pon my honor, Mr. Bronze," said Flourish, "if this statement be true, "the world is turned upside down, indeed."

"But what are my troubles to any other person!" answered Bronze, with a deep-fetched sigh. "There was a time, Mr. Flourish, when I was in my prosperity! Ah, that's gone by! but now I have that within (*placing his hand on his heart*) which passeth show! (*Then whispering to Flourish, but audible enough for young Sprightly to hear*) I have not broken my fast to-day; and the steward has brushed by me so often with such delicious-looking plates of ham and beef, new-laid eggs, &c., which have made me so faint and ill, and also rendered me desperate, that I have been almost tempted to throw myself overboard! But *suicide!* You know *suicide* is quite out of my taste, more especially a watery grave! No, no—I must not disgrace the character of my ancestors, but go down to the family vault in a regular "*hic jacet*" manner. But if I am wretched myself, to see my friend, Frank Flourish, Esq., look so well, is an unspeakable pleasure and happiness."

Notwithstanding the character given of Bronze by Flourish

to Jem, for insinuation and plausibility, and the caution also not to be led away by his artifices, yet the latter was so *touched* by his pathetic mode of delivery, his piteous-looking face, and his mournful gestures, that almost unconsciously he slipped half-a-crown into the hand of Bronze. The countenance of the latter instantly changed to a smile ;—he made Jem a most profound bow, observing, " I perceive, sir, you are a perfect gentleman ; and that generosity and good feelings are not altogether banished from society. Accept, likewise, sir, my best thanks, nay, gratitude ; and I am now enabled to defy the taunts of the steward, with his passings and re-passings of plates of ham, &c."—bowing himself out of sight.

" Ha! ha! ha!—you really, Jem," said Flourish, " must excuse my laughing so heartily at your expence—I was certain such would be the fact. He has duped by his representations of misery much more experienced persons than you can profess to be. Bronze is an excellent actor : he is master of the passions, and can *laugh* or *cry*, just as the scene may require his exertions. For this time, I must say that you have only paid for your learning : but, depend upon it, he will make more attacks upon your feelings ; therefore, I once more advise you to be on your guard."

" Never fret!" replied Jem, " I did it with the best intentions. His tale was so well told, that I confess I was off my guard ; but, nevertheless, I will not make any promises, as it appears to me that a man like Bronze, who has studied the weakness of human nature, may almost, with his capabilities, *talk* you over to any thing he may advance : however, I will keep a good look out, should he ' try it on ' with me in future; that is as much as I can promise."

" Once more, my friend," answered Flourish, " let me give you the benefit of my experience. Bronze has told you that the world is turned upside down—I deny this position *in toto*—the world is not changed in the slightest degree—the dress and fashion of the exterior of mankind may have undergone some revolution—but the mind—the feelings—and the general conduct of society—respecting particular occurrences will always remain the same. PROPERTY will ever claim respect and attention ; the idea of *gain* is paramount with most men—but broken down men of fashion—ruined gamesters—spendthrifts, and thoughtless fellows,—an acquaintance with whom can produce little else but loss of time as well as money—must expect to meet with rebuffs—and the once-welcome door is shut against them, as a natural, if not a sensible consequence—and they are only recognized to be *neglected !*"

" Such advice," replied Jem, " must be invaluable at all times —therefore, proceed, and I shall listen to you with the most profound attention."

" The world is not changed." said Flourish ; " things go on

as usual ;—*St. Paul's* stands on the same bit of ground ; and Regent Street has not altered its course a jot! It is the *Man* that is changed! Bronze is metamorphosed into the sturdy beggar—the once-dashing swell on the town has now spent all his money—and the out-door *Pauper* only remains.   Squandering and economy are features—like *borrowing* and lending—must always be the same.   He is compelled to live upon his own resources—therefore, *invention* is all the capital he has to work upon—and new schemes must be resorted to daily to carry on the war of contributions : *borrowing* is now become so familiar to him—that he will not be refused—and he almost insists upon the *loan* with the authority of a *demand ;* without you have resolutely made up your mind to ' *cut him off*' on the instant ; for if you *parley* with him only a *second*, it is *ten* to *one* but he carries his point.   His manners and conversation are so interesting, that the cash is almost insensibly extracted from your pocket ! But you must positively learn the SWORD EXERCISE, which I will teach you without the use of a sword—the CUTS of which will prove far more severe than any blade of *steel*, made by the first cutler in the Kingdom—then give ear to a short history of the *different* CUTS—that whenever you are assailed by any person like Bronze you may *cut* him in the following style, as circumstances may require.   If you can, in the first instance, produce a CUT—severe enough to prevent the intruder ' *Come-ing again !*' That I should pronounce the CUT *glorious !*"

" The *shy* CUT ! or, I am off !—*(Pointing.)*— ' That's the way to the Refuge for the Destitute !' as if you were showing some person the way to that institution.

" The *won't see* CUT ! or, I have no notion of always looking at one object !   This cut ought to be got by rote, and always at the fingers' end of a young rich man, entering into life— according to the good old proverb, ' None are so blind as them that won't see !'   This will prevent a great deal of trouble.

" The *half-nod* CUT ! that is to say, when you are *compelled*, positively compelled, just to give a *wink ;* in case you cannot *bolt* without it.

" The *'pon my honor* CUT ! 'Pon my soul, Charles, you are so much altered that I really did not know you !   I am in great haste !—You must excuse me !—Good bye, I wish you well !' But remember that you do not stop to hear a word of reply ;— but *cut*, and be off like a shot.

" The *apology* CUT ! that is, whenever you are charged with knowing any person that you are ashamed of. ' Why, I can't say I ever saw the fellow before !—True !—I have met him in tolerable company—at that period, it was very well ; he then had a carriage—fine house, and all that sort of thing, which characterised the gentleman ; but now the case is altered. They do say, that ——— but, no matter,—he is become quite a wretch !   It is impossible to stand it !   Bob is worse than a blood-sucker! You must not be thought to know such folks! I am quite right! Poverty is a d—d bad acquaintance, even in Sunday clothes, and the sooner it is CUT the better."

"Ha! ha! ha! upon my word," said Jem, "there is something so impressive and judicious in your advice, that I must endeavour to adopt it."

"Adopt it!" cried Flourish; "if you do not *adopt* it, you will soon become a nice *victim* for the deep Bronze and his associates! I must now inform you of the IAGO CUT (that is, behind the back—vulgarly termed *back-biting*), and the cruelest *cut* of them all: but then you know, as Shakspeare says, 'we must be cruel, only to be kind!' I act upon it, morning, noon, and night; indeed, I would not set up my opinion in opposition to such unanswerable authority. I am now giving the *Iago* CUT to Bronze. But, hold—I see him returning to us."

Bronze appeared in great agitation, and seemed rather to hesitate a short time—something like an actor making himself up for a part—the more to betray a sort of unhappiness of mind, to give effect to the deceit he was about to practise on Sprightly: his face, in unison with his actions, was a picture of sorrow. He thus addressed his victim :—"I really am ashamed; nay, I beg ten thousand pardons, sir—but necessity—cruel necessity—has no law. Therefore, to be brief, I cannot pay my fare. In my hurry to be in time, I left my purse on my dressing-table—I am mortified beyond description at my carelessness and stupidity. It is devilish annoying, an't it, sir? If it is not inconvenient to you to lend me half a crown, it would be new life to me at the present moment. I will return it, 'pon my honor—*honor* with me is a sacred virtue! and when I get back to town, consider the loan in your pocket. If the amount of the fare was a pound or two," assuming an air of importance, "I would tell the captain of the steamer to call upon me; but it is such a *trifle*, it would make one look so perfectly ridiculous, that I am sure, sir, you are too much of a man of respectability—although I am a stranger to you, but well known to your friend, Squire Flourish—to let me be left in *pledge*, and become the derision of the passengers for so small a sum. I have the *feelings* of a gentleman, rest assured, and this painful moment touches me to the quick—if I—— but my silence must speak the rest."

"Well, sir," replied Sprightly, "I cannot resist the appeal, and I shall trust to your honor. Here is the half-crown."

"Spare my remarks, sir," answered Bronze, putting up his handkerchief to his eyes; "I am overwhelmed with gratitude —my heart is too big—God bless you, noble young man!—I cannot utter one word more!" He then hopped off, with the agility of a dancing-master, to the further end of the vessel in an instant, laughing in his sleeve at his success in thus victimising the friend of Flourish a second time."

"Bravo!" exclaimed Flourish, smiling, "I must give Bronze

F

credit for his *inventive* talents—at the same time, I detest his rogueries.   But he has not done with you yet awhile—you are too good a subject for him : he will make another attempt, and he will almost stand *kicking* before you can shake him off.   I will give you an instance.   Bronze has served me much worse, as to attacks upon my purse : but at length I detected his real character—I then became decided, and gave him the *Cut*, FINALE! as I thought, but to no purpose.   The last resource I had left was to put myself into a great rage, in order to get rid of him—when I urged that I was sorry to see that he had lost sight of the character of a man and a gentleman ; that he had also become a downright sturdy beggar ; nay, more, a mean, contemptible wretch—an accomplished swindler—and I wanted words to express my hatred of his conduct—and if he would give me a *penny*, I would give him five pounds, if ever he provoked me to speak to him again during my life."

" Such heart-breaking words, which were enough to excite a stone almost to enter into a combat for defence of character, had not the slightest effect upon *his* feelings : neither did they alter his countenance at all ; and he replied, with the utmost *sang froid*, ' You are angry now, Squire Flourish—out of temper with the unfortunate, distressed, miserably afflicted Bronze. Something, I am sure, has *ruffled* your disposition, but, nevertheless, you shall not excite me to quarrel with my best friend ! No, no, I know better ; and when we meet again, you will be more yourself, and have banished the circumstance from your mind.'   And you saw that he came up to me with the most perfect assurance, as if nothing had happened between us ; therefore, let us cut all discourse about the most *incorrigible* Diddler in the world.   Only beware of the third attack."

" With all my heart," said Sprightly.   " I am ready to take another view ; and a more pleasing part of the picture already presents itself. Here are some dashing females in sight, and who appear to me to be out of place, but worthy of our attention."

" To be sure they are," replied Flourish, " and this already is one of the advantages resulting from our pilgrimage—a sort of preface to the view of mankind which we have pictured to ourselves : indeed, we might have lingered at home by our firesides, until we had literally been devoured up by *ennui*, and lost sight of every thing like taste and spirit.   *Still*-life will not do for my book ; I am for the reality of the thing.   I love to meet with speaking eyes—ruby lips—pearly teeth—palpitating bosoms—rosy cheeks—animated countenances—fine figures—elegant address—sensible minds—and nothing else but lively interesting companions, exactly after the manner of the poet—

' Heaven in her eye—
In all her gestures dignity and love.' "

" Is not this ebullition of yours, Flourish, rather of too romantic a description ?" said Sprightly ; "a fancy sketch—too rho-domontade—"

" Not a bit, my dear boy—woman is a complete romance alto-gether. I have studied the sex—I am well read in all their lit-tle tricks and fancies, calculated to make conquests and enslave the unwary ; in fact, I am armed at all points when a woman is the theme. Therefore," observed Flourish, " look to me, and you will be out of harm's way."

" If that is the fact," replied Sprightly, " then your judgment and advice must be invaluable ; but, according to my reading on the subject, I have always understood that women have not only proved the greatest conquerors, and better generals than the men, but some of our wisest creatures have been outwitted by them."

" Yes, in the antique school—a century or two, or more, such things have occurred, I believe ; but in modern times, that feature is completely altered—*experience* has made fools wise ; and men are not tricked as heretofore. The sex, in general, in the hands of a skilful man, are almost reduced to mere playthings. True, they may enjoy their hours of coquetry—revel in flirtation—and have a host of *danglers* in their train ; but women now are short-lived as to any thing like sovereign power."

" I hope, I may find it so," said Sprightly, " but I confess I am more inclined to be a sceptic, than otherwise. However, you have now an opportunity of giving me a taste of your quality. The ladies are before you, and I claim your opinion."

" You shall have it," replied Flourish, putting up his glass : " fat, fair, and forty, at all events ; verging, perhaps, toward *sixty ;* but imposing as to outside appearance, and duchess like ; though not of peerage-quality, I dare be sworn ; however, I am not exactly decided on the latter point.—Duchesses and persons of high rank, seldom honor plebeians with their presence—ex-cepting in election matters."

" You have overshot the mark, I am sure, as to age," observed Sprightly, " her corpulency rather tends to put more years on her *looks*, than she really possesses. I would say thirty ; and under forty, I would wager a dozen of wine. But in other respects, I have my doubts. Yet, I would ask, why not a duchess have a little *freak* on the sly, as well as my lord duke *incog.* to take a peep at human nature in her holiday clothes ? It is a sort of *masquerading*, only without concealing the face."

" I may have been, perhaps, a little too fast concerning her *antiquity ;* but then she is dished-up so much after what is termed—*lamb*-fashion, that a better judge than myself might be deceived. Her colour is excellent, if it is real : and her *face*, rather inclines to the term of *handsome ;* however, at all events, it is well got up, if my tell-tale glass does not deceive me ; to be sure there is something more like the *Hottentot Venus* about her person, than the *Venus di Medici ;* but that circumstance, I am inclined to admit, is more her misfortune, than to be viewed as a failing : yet, what *art* could do for her, has been done ; and after all, I must say, she is a 'tight article,' in spite of her bulky appearance.

"Fashion, extreme fashion, has been studied from her head to her feet ; and style predominates, whether becoming or not. Her fingers covered with rings, and her gloves taken off every now and then, to show their value to the eyes of her astonished spectators ; which, to my taste, appertains too much towards the 'vulgar.' But, nevertheless, she appears to nod with something like grace ; and there is also something about her smiles, air, and carriage, that denotes she has mixed with good society ! in short, I am determined to '*make her out.*' Greenwich, at holiday time, is very questionable ; surely, she cannot be destined for the Park ? I would say, most likely for Gravesend, Margate, Dover, or, perhaps, the opposite coast,—her intended route to Paris ; and sheer necessity may have compelled her to take her passage on board this steamer, on account of saving time. No matter, I will find her out. Let Frank Flourish alone, for his display of talents, when *discovery* is the point at issue."

"Go it, my dear Frank," said Jem, "I perceive you are upon *stilts* already ; but take care that your Pegasus don't throw you off ; and, Phæton like, you get consumed in the attempt. But proceed—I'll not interrupt you."

"I may be wrong," replied Frank ; "perhaps, I am elevating their rank in society too much ; for, after all their dashing appearance, they may be for the Park. Women are funny articles ; according to Pope :—

Men, some to business, some to pleasure take,
But ev'ry woman is at heart a RAKE.

And enjoy under the rose the game of '*kissing in the ring.*' I'll talk to them upon the subject by and bye ; and, perhaps, I may ultimately come in for a chaste salute or two, from the introduction, that is to say, from the manner in which I put myself forward in accosting them. I will first play '*the amiable*' with the old duchess, acting up to the old adage, 'that more flies are caught with honey than vinegar ;' and no sugar candy shall be sweeter than the compliments I will bestow upon her. For her daughters, time shall speak of my success."

"Don't make too sure the young females are her daughters," said Sprightly ; "she does not, in my opinion, look old enough to be pronounced their mamma."

"No matter, I shall be able to give you a complete history of them in due time. Birth—parentage—education— their connections—and movements in life—if they prove worth powder and shot. I am the boy," replied Flourish, "to worm out secrets, and ascertain pedigree. Voyages of discovery are delightful to me.   But stop, I'll be hanged if I do not perceive among the crowd on board—*Picturesque Doleful*, the *finisher*. —Ha! ha!"

" Who, in the name of fortune, is he ?   I never heard of such a designation in my whole life," observed Sprightly.

" To be intelligible on the subject," replied Flourish, " he is well known as the *tally*-undertaker, at the East end of the town.   Doleful undertakes, for a trifling sum per week, to give a decent funeral to the members of his club ; and he has established several of them about town."

" I never heard of such a thing before," said Sprightly.

" Live and learn, my boy ! Ha ! ha ! perhaps you would have no objection to become a member ?" remarked Flourish ; " As the saying goes, we are all born, but not buried ; and there is no ascertaining the events of this life ! But yet, you may perceive there is a consolation in most things—if we can but appreciate it. I maintain, the idea is grateful to our feelings—that the last token of respect which can be paid to our remains will be done by such means, and that without any obligation to your friends ; and effectually prevent the horrid necessity which sometimes occurs in society, to bury a man by subscription.   I think I see him trying to put a smile on his solemn face ! Well, it is holiday time, and that accounts for it.—Ha ! ha !"

" A smile, did you say, Flourish ? I should rather call it a horribly ghastly *grin ;*" replied Sprightly : " the living skeleton was a corpulent man, by comparison to Doleful ! I should think a sudden gust of wind would shiver him into a thousand pieces : he seems to hang together by a mere thread ! a piece of geometry ! and whenever he is called to the tomb of the Capulets, it is very likely that a mutiny will arise amongst the worms over his body —instead of flesh, versus bones ! Doleful certainly would do for the incantation scene of Der Freizchutz."

" I'll bet a wager he has had one hundred extra cards printed to distribute amongst the visitors at Greenwich, in case any accidents should occur," said Flourish ; " such as breaking their necks by violently running down the hill, and other little casualties which occur at Fair time !

" Doleful is a prime fellow for a good look out for Coroners' Inquests, nay, it is said, that he pays one or two reporters —' *Penny-a-liners,*' as the dons of the press denote them— poor fellows—who are glad to catch hold of any thing in the shape of information, to make the pot boil ! Be it so—any thing is better than idleness.

" However, I must tell you the following anecdote, which was in general circulation some years ago, and generally accredited as a fact :—A parcel of young fellows, much more fond of mischief than propriety, were determined to have a ' *lark*' with *Picturesque* Doleful, in order to put his courage to the test with the dead ! He having frequently boasted that he could enter a church yard at the most dreary hour of the night—take a comfortable nap in a solemn vault—or, be locked up in the most lonesome part of a cathedral for a week together without feeling the slightest fear! Doleful asserted that he looked upon the dead with as much quiet of mind as if they were persons in a sound sleep!

" The young men had made up their minds to cast lots who should be the person to *act* the part of a *dead* man—but one of them, a daring sort of person, that nothing could daunt, or divert him from his purpose—

> When church-yards yawn,
> And Hell itself breathes forth contagion to the world,

resolutely offered himself to carry the above scheme into execution.   He was to *sham* dead! His companions were then to go rather late in the evening to the house of Doleful for a shell!— but previous to which some of the party were to get him out of doors, and to detain him at a public house, that no interruption should occur to frustrate their plan!

" Two or three of them then went and told a pitiful story; that one of their friends had met with an accident, and was killed on the spot, and they required a *shell* to put the body into it, and they would bring the body as soon as possible to the house of the undertaker. They procured the shell without the slightest trouble, and the *supposed* dead man was conveyed to the domus of the Picturesque, with all the solemnity of a real transaction : and placed in a room set apart for such purposes.

" The party who had taken Doleful under their especial care, plied him constantly with plenty of ale, and dram after dram, until the Tally Undertaker was completely intoxicated, when they saw him home! Upon his arrival, he was informed by his man, who was put up to the secret, and well paid to be silent— that an accident had happened, and the body was in a shell.   It was a capital job,—the friends of the dead man were rich ; and he must ' *stand* something to drink,' on account of their giving him the preference as an undertaker !

" ' I'll stand any thing,' said Doleful, as groggy as a sailor three sheets in the wind—reeling from one end of his shop to the other, and continually hiccoughing—a convincing proof that the *Picturesque* was ' how come you so?' ' But I shan't look at the corpse to-night—I have other fish to fry !' and with a ghastly smile upon his countenance, which he intended for a joke, observed—' the corpse can't *bolt* to-night, you know ; and I shall find it in the morning where I left it !' and staggered off to bed, where he soon fell asleep, snoring as loud as a humming top. After he had been in bed about an hour, the supposed dead man, who had been enjoying himself over some brandy-and-water with his companions, in the room close to Doleful's apartment, put a shroud over his frame, whitened his face to have the appear-

IN SEARCH OF THE NATIONAL.

ance of a *ghost*, and, with a dark lanthorn, he immediately went to the bedside of the undertaker ; but previous to which he had placed one of his hands in a jug of cold water, to give it the icy, clammy feel of death !

" Doleful was so sound asleep that he only started a little on the ' cold hand ' being rubbed over his face ; but on the repetition of it, when the light of the lanthorn opened upon him, and shewed the ghost-like figure of the supposed dead man, the agony of mind displayed by Picturesque was frightful. His eyes rolled, and his tongue almost forsook its office, and in faultering accents he could scarcely exclaim—' Where am I ?—O, Lord, forgive me my sins !—What do you want with me ?—I never did harm to any body in my life !—O spare me ! '

" ' I want to get out,' said the supposed dead man, in a sepulchral tone. ' Wretch ! do you want to bury me alive ? What business had you to confine me in a *shell*, and steal me from my peaceful abode ? But I'll serve you out for such conduct. Did you mean to make a *Guy* of me, and sell me to the Hospital coves as a *stiff'un !* So prepare yourself for an exit, Old Doleful ! '—catching hold of his shirt, at the same time giving him three precious slaps on his head ; and, in a hollow voice, said, ' Picturesque, farewell for the present. I'll call for you to-morrow night at twelve. So be ready ! No shuffling nor excuses will do for me.'

" The companions of the supposed dead man having got their *cue*, rushed into the room, and, with loud shouts of horrid laughter, yells, groans, &c., danced about the room, nearly depriving Old Doleful of his senses. The *dead*-alive man then put some blue fire into his lanthorn to make a blaze, when, with a most uproarious noise, they vanished—the place immediately became dark, and all was as silent as death.

" The undertaker was too much alarmed to stir, but covered himself all over with the clothes, in dreadful anxiety lest the ghost should pay him another visit—suffering under violent perspirations—until, overcome with fatigue of mind and fright, he fell asleep.

" Not getting up at his usual time, his man knocked at his room door, calling it was getting late. ' Come in, Bill,' said Doleful ; ' I have had the devil and his imps visiting me to-night, and *walloped* me like boxers ! '

" ' Nonsense, master ! you have been dreaming !' said Bill ; ' your head has been wool-gathering—you are out of your mind ! If you run on with such stuff, I must get a straight-waistcoat for you.'

" ' Out of my mind !' said Doleful ; ' I never was more correct in my life. But run and see if the corpse is safe that I left in the *shell* last night.'

" ' You certainly are wandering, master—you are as mad as a March-hare,' replied Bill ; ' you left no corpse last night—you certainly have taken leave of your senses. But, to satisfy your mind, I'll go and see.' His man returned immediately, laughing—'If you left a corpse there last night, master, the corpse has *bolted*, for there is not the ghost of any dead man in the next room, or any thing like it. Rouse yourself, master—it must have been a dream.'

" 'A dream, indeed! you are a stupid fool, Bill,' answered Picturesque—'the old devil and his frightful imps promised to call for me to-morrow night at twelve o'clock!'

" ' They never shall have you, master,' said Bill ; ' but if they have the courage to come, we'll give them a warm reception, and no mistake! I'll not leave you till after that hour. They shall not touch your old jacket! So think no more about it. Don't humbug yourself about a foolish dream—get up—your breakfast has been waiting for you upwards of an hour—and I'll go and fetch a drap of *jacky* to raise your spirits.'

" His friends, in general, persuaded him that it could be nothing else but a dream," said Flourish ; " but Doleful always stuck hard and fast to it that it was a reality! But the undertaker has always been considered a half-witted fellow—a mere simpleton—easily imposed upon, and persuaded to any thing—and I have no doubt but we shall have some joke with him before the day is at an end.

" But hold, if my eyes do not deceive me, I see the notorious *Jack Scapegrace,* entering the steamer. Yes, it is him, dressed out as fine as a peacock. New clothes from top to toe! I should like to know who *suffers!* He is on some *secret* expedition—a *woman*, perhaps ; but I would rather say after the *pelf*! Fun, or mere pleasure, I am sure, is out of the question ; but on recollection, I think we had better avoid him. He has recognized us, and I do not like his *looks*, they mean mischief. Since his last examination before your uncle, he has not openly dared to insult me ; but nevertheless, his behaviour has been any thing but gentlemanly, because I would not notice him."

" Do not pervert the name of gentleman," replied Sprightly, " if you value the truth. It is true I am speaking at random ; but if I dare hazard an opinion, I should assert he had more pretensions to the character of a swindler, or a thief, than any thing else. Therefore, I should say, avoid such a man, if you value your respectability or your person; and although he got over the last charge brought against him cleverly, still I have very great doubts on the subject. But at all events, my advice is, to be on the *civil* list with him—and keep your tongue within your teeth. A contemptuous look will almost irritate him to kick up a row ; and he carries too many guns for you, Flourish, —a word and a blow is the way he settles *his* accounts. He has got a fist like an anvil for hardness of quality ; and not at all particular, when it suits him, to use it very roughly. Although he appears to be *alone*—depend upon it, he has several asso-

ciates lurking about the steamer, should any thing offer to require their assistance. He is, to sum up his character, nothing
better than a *well-dressed* ruffian."

" You are not far from the mark," answered Flourish, " and,
as our friend Catalogue has it, we will pass him over as a very
bad lot. His mode of life is truly mysterious, and how he lives
is a matter of doubt; yet, he will, if possible, introduce himself
to the notice of good society. He never appears to be in want
of cash; is cool, cautious, and calculating; and appears to have
a motive for every thing he does."

" He is more of a bravo, or bully, I think, than absolutely a
man of courage; although *fear* does not appear to belong to
him. However, in my opinion, he is a dangerous fellow—either
in the character of a friend or a foe! He is slow in resentment;
but nevertheless, he treasures up his anger for a time when it
will best suit his purpose; and I am sure since we have *cut* his
acquaintance, it rankles in his mind, and he flatters himself that
he will be able to revenge himself, sooner or later, for such sort
of contempt. 'He can smile, and smile again, and yet be a
villain;' but once more, my dear Frank," said Sprightly, " avoid
him. This is all owing to making an acquaintance in the
first instance with Scapegrace, without an introduction. For my
own part, I shall avoid such an error in future."

" True, my boy," answered Flourish, " sensibly urged, and a
good hint into the bargain; or, rather a guide for us during our
Pilgrimage. All is not gold that glitters—men are not always
what they seem—and the women are——"

" Stop, stop, my dear Frank, a word or two about the fair
sex," said Sprightly; " the *Duchess*, as you have designated
her, I have my doubts respecting her person and appearance
altogether; and what little I know about society in general,
teaches me that her eye speaks volumes—it is a penetrating one
—there is a sharpness and fire attached to it, that you do not
meet with in the heads of modest, unassuming females—her
look is too wanton and knowing for my taste—although she may
attempt to conceal it; therefore, take care you do not meet with
your match, if not decidedly your mistress. She appears to me a
kind of Argus in society—she sees everything, I should say, at a
glance—is up to every move on the board—and has forgotten
more, much more, than you and I have ever seen or heard in our
intercourse with life, or can positively remember."

" Not quite so fast!—You are calculating without your host,
Sprightly," observed Flourish, " you make up your mind too
hastily—the female in question is a perfect stranger to both you
and me, and you are running down the *Duchess*, as I call her,
with a vengeance, and also calumniating her character without
any rhyme or reason. People are not to be taken by their *looks*
—for, of all other criterions, that is the most dangerous; but
you are inexperienced in such matters, and that accounts for it."

" I may be wrong in my conjectures; but it is only a private opinion between ourselves, and which goes for nothing as to a matter of decision; but nevertheless, I confess, I do not like her appearance;—her face is a sort of index to my feelings as to her notions—and I should rather say, that the Duchess comes, (as a matter of course,) from the *West*, and not the East end of the town. Indeed, I will bet a wager—'May Fair and its neighbourhood, against Wapping and the Docks!' that *speculation* is her forte on this trip—she is on the look out—and if the day turns out pleasantly and beaus are to be picked up—entangled, and ultimately made victims—why then her scheme is answered. If not, the expence is so trifling, that a failure on her part—once in a way, can be put up with, without any complaints—Ha! ha!"

" You may laugh at your own ideas upon the subject," said Flourish, rather touched with the remarks of his friend, " but you may depend upon it, before the day has expired, the laugh will be in my favour; and you will acknowledge that you have taken a wrong view of the matter at issue."

" Be that as it may, I have only to urge, brother Pilgrim, if you are not above taking advice," observed Jem, " to have a care, and be not too profuse in your *devotions* to the ABBESS; and also on your guard respecting *vows* to the Nuns! Do not be too clever!—neither entertain an opinion that you know too much to be outwitted; and, likewise, be not more confident than you ought to be in yourself. Quiz! quiz! by all means, if you like to ' shew' your talent, wit, and knowledge of the world; and ' go it' as much as you think proper. But, remember, if a *row* should occur, I am not one of the party. True, I would not stand by and see you wantonly ill-treated; but do not let it appear against you as the author of any disturbance. I see my uncle coming towards us. Only one word more:—Remember! Pray keep the line."

" Well, brother Pilgrims," said Makemoney, putting the newspaper into his pocket, " the last bell has rung, and we shall soon be off." The band struck up God save the King, when the ——— left St. Catherine's Dock. " Is this not a prospect worth a Jew's eye? Talk of foreign parts, indeed; Is there such another sight like it to be seen any where?—and if I possessed the oratorical talents of some of our great folks in Parliament, I would describe it in glowing colours:—

> This ancient City,
> How wanton sits she, amidst Nature's smiles!
> Nor from her highest turret has to view,
> But golden landscapes and luxuriant scenes—
> A waste of wealth, the store-house of the world.
> Here fruitful vales, far stretching, fly the sight—
> There sails, unnumber'd, whiten all the stream,
> Float on the waves, and break against the shore!

Does not Old Father Thames look delightfully to-day, surrounded by such a numerous offspring—old and young, all in pursuit of pleasure and happiness? And I will insist upon it, my dear nephew, that the THAMES—Old Father Thames—and his next-door neighbour, the Ocean, combine every thing that must please and attract the coldest spectator; but to a cockney, a man born in London, if you like the expression better, unutterable delight and satisfaction.

"Only take a peep down the River—view the different ships from all parts of the world—the steamers, as it were, flying along the water,—the wherries full—barges all in motion—commerce in all its bearings, or myriads of persons all on the *qui vive*, either for pleasure, trade, or enterprise. See the anxious merchant waiting for the arrival of his vessels from a far distant clime, laden with goods, &c. to replenish his empty warehouses, and also view the sailor's joyful return to his native shore, after an absence of several years ;—does not the sight of the Thames bring forth recollections and feelings to his mind, that neither painting nor pen can depict :—

> And as the much-lov'd shore we near,
> With transport we behold the roof,
> Where dwelt a friend, a partner dear,
> Of faith and love a matchless proof.

Therefore, brother Pilgrims, excuse my partiality, prejudice, weakness—call it what you will—the BANKS OF THE THAMES for me. I am satisfied with my own country."

" Mr. Makemoney," observed a gentleman very near to him; " I have been listening to the description you have been giving of the Thames, to your nephew, with the greatest delight; and I am very glad to find that you still continue the same true-born Englishman, and are not to be laughed out of those good old notions, ' that there is nothing like home!' Here is another friend of your's on board—Mr. Fearful. Shall I tell him you are here, as I know he will be glad to see you?"

" Most certainly, Mr. Briton," replied Mr. Makemoney; and, during his slight absence, he said to his nephew and Flourish, " I will have a bit of fun with Charles Fearful, Esq. one of the best-tempered creatures in the world; but for the last forty years of his life he has been the most terrible *alarmist* I ever knew. At every change of government, if contrary to his way of thinking, or any little disturbances, he contemplated nothing else but destruction to all our public establishments, and a total annihilation of property; and almost prepared himself to lay down and die!"

At this juncture a tall, thin, classical looking gentleman made his appearance; a Sir Peter Teazle sort of personage; and when the congratulations were over at meeting with each other, after an absence of several years, Makemoney, with a smile on his countenance, thus addressed him—" Well, Mr. Fearful, all the fine old establishments, I am happy to say, still remain entire.   The political whirlwinds that you so much dreaded when last I had the pleasure of seeing you, have done not the slightest damage whatever.

" St. Paul's Cathedral stands as firm as ever; Westminster Abbey has not moved a jot: the House of Commons is as strong as a rock—and the House of Lords still remains a *fixture.*   The Tower of London continues as formidable as heretofore :—Windsor Castle stands in the same place—but improved in every point of view—not a tree missing in its fine splendid Forest—the KING, ' God bless him,' still remains in health, with undisputed prerogative ; and long may he continue to reign over a brave and free people.

" Not a shadow of a picture defaced in the National Gallery, and the British Museum increased beyond all degrees of comparison for the benefit of the student and reader. All the good old edifices—the antique, rich spires—hundreds of places of worship remain also in *statu quo ;* the national representation has been improved, and we are getting on, as an improving race of intelligent beings altogether. Therefore, I hope, my dear friend, all your fears have long ceased to exist—all apprehensions for the worst are at an end, and you may now lay down in quietness, and your repose secure."

" True, Mr. Makemoney, " I cannot refute several of your assertions ; but, nevertheless, we live in strange if not in troublesome times—*alteration* seems the watchword.   You must excuse me, my old friends, if I still have my doubts."

" I have done, Mr. Fearful, as I perceive you are perfectly incurable !   But, rest assured, difference of opinion will never alter our *friendship.*"

CHAPTER V.

*The Steamer afloat—FLOURISH at fault—" the amiable" want-
ing—afraid to attack the Duchess—DOLEFUL and Coroners'
Inquests; or, the World's End! a hoax—A few words
more respecting SCAPEGRACE, but not quite ripe for exposure. MAKEMONEY delighted—his description of the variety seen in a Trip by Steam—Cocknies adrift—Fresh-
water Sailors; versus, the Rough Sons of the Ocean—De-
barking from the Steamer—Greenwich Park—Kissing in
the Ring—National habits ought to be preserved; a legal
opinion on the subject. An invitation to dinner; a rhetorical display, vulgarly termed the gift of the gab! WIL-
HELMINA and SERAPHINA, a pair of female Portraits—
live and learn, stay at home, and know nothing—What a
world we live in!—The self-sufficient FLOURISH completely outwitted.*

DURING the previous harangue, or rather piece of satire from
Makemoney to the *Alarmist,* Flourish had been strolling up and
down the deck of the steamer, *ogling* the old Duchess and her
two daughters, but he could not exactly make up his mind in
what manner he should address her; and not the slightest circumstance had occurred on which he could make any point of
conversation. No opening being left to him but to make a direct attack, he felt quite at a loss, hesitated, and could not assume courage enough to enact " *the amiable !*" although he had
brushed up his hair two or three times—placed his shirt-collar in
the best point of view—put his diamond pin in a prominent situation—looked at himself, again and again—still he appeared
waiting for something like a *cue* to commence the siege.

Whether his ardour might have been damped by the *definition*
given of the Duchess by his brother Pilgrim, James Sprightly,
did not appear, but his unblushing impudence, which had, upon
all other occasions, prompted him forwards, it should now seem
had totally deserted him, in case he might meet with a *Tartar*
in disguise. Yet, nevertheless, he was determined not to be
idle: and, on passing Doleful, he appeared more at his ease, and
ventured, with a sort of insolent freedom, to ask him " if he was
not going to Greenwich to attend a Coroner's Inquest ?"

Doleful, harmless in the extreme. screwed up his melancholy
phiz, not quite a yard and a half in length, and almost as hollow

as a lanthorn, with a great deal of civility, observed, 'No, sir, I never heard of any such thing!'"

"I am quite surprised at that," answered Flourish, with a face of clay, and without moving a muscle, while young Sprightly was ready to burst his sides with laughter; "you are a *finisher*, I believe (Doleful stared at him with the most piteous aspect) —I mean, an undertaker; that is, you put people out of sight very 'cheap.' Yes, yes, I am right—I well remember you *finished* off in good style Churchwarden *Swallow-Mutton*, who was choked with a bone at a vestry-supper; and so extremely low were your charges, that had I not have known you to have been a man of strict integrity in all your dealings, I should have thought you had not come honestly by your materials."

"Have you got a card about you?" Doleful put his hand in his pocket, and gave Flourish one. (Jem, on witnessing this circumstance, was so overcome with risibility, that he was compelled to run to another part of the steamer, in order not to spoil the joke)—"That's right; I will recommend you to a job directly. Now, if you go to the 'World's End'—that is, I mean the sign of it, at Greenwich—there is a Coroner's Inquest sitting, and the foreman of the jury, a friend of mine, *John Hookham Snivey, Esq.*, will make it all right for you to bury him. A poor simple chap had laid a wager that he would climb up to the steeple of Greenwich Church, but, unfortunately for himself, he made only one false step, which caused his exit before he expected, and he never told any person *how* the accident happened."

"How very shocking!" replied Doleful; and, pulling out his pocket-book, noted down the 'World's End,' and 'Hookham Snivey, Esq.' with all the gravity attending a real circumstance, and quite pleased with the job he had in view, not being bound down to any precise terms of *contract*, exclaiming, at the same time, to himself, "I shall leave the Park and the *casualties* to themselves to-day—'a bird in the hand is worth two in the bush at any time.'"

Flourish, strutting off like a crow in a gutter, in a sort of audible whisper to his brother Pilgrim Jem, said, "I have finished off *Old Doleful* in good twig;" but before he could congratulate himself on the success of his joke, "*Finished off!*" muttered a voice, "I should like to finish you off a little bit, for imposing on a simple tradesman!" Flourish, with his face half turned round, recognized the well-known countenance of the daring Scapegrace! but he wisely took no notice of it.

"Aye, you may look; its me," said Scapegrace, in a low voice, but a murderous tone of accent, "I owe you *one* upon an old account—and perhaps I may chance to *wing* you, some day, when you least expect it! It won't do now, I perceive; but the time will come—and then—if you get off as well as the *Old Shroud Maker* has done—think yourself lucky! Now that's what I mean—and no mistake!"

This sort of side-wind murmur, and coming when least expected from the dangerous and determined Scapegrace, almost produced an attack of the *ague* on the frame of Flourish; at another time, it might completely have *paralysed* his efforts: but the latter was too well supported on board of the steamer to experience any rough treatment—so he ' pocketed the affront,' as the safest mode to get rid of it—by putting it off with a smile!

Makemoney, whose time had been occupied with several other objects, on returning to his friends, felt rather surprised at the sight of Scapegrace close to the elbow of Flourish, and, to all appearance, his lip quivering with rage, and his face looking more like a disappointed demon than a Christian, and ejaculating ' *Revenge!*' Makemoney, with great eagerness, said—" Has that fellow, Scapegrace, been saying any thing unpleasant to your feelings in the shape of a threat! I know he is perfectly capable of such an action: and I am sure we do not stand at all well in his estimation; and, if he had a convenient opportunity, I think he would not mind to do any of us an injury. He bears the character of a vindictive fellow—therefore, keep out of his clutches—give him no cause for reproach—but more anon, when I am at leisure!"

Flourish thought it the most prudent method to put a stop to any more argument on the subject, by observing—" I did not hear him say any thing, although, in passing by me, he appeared in anger, as if some person had irritated him. However, I heed him not!" yet thinking to himself, at the same time, that it might be as well for him, if he remained quiet during the short voyage to Greenwich.

" He may be a desperate character, and in an assassin-like manner, be inclined to take a cowardly advantage of us in private; provided he could conceal himself, and without the fear of detection! But let him, if he dare, come to an open contest," said Sprightly, in a high-spirited tone of challenge—" and although I hate and despise anything like boasting, I care not for the threats of fifty Scapegraces! Therefore, at present, let us not bestow another thought upon him. Do not let such a fellow as that, whom no one knows any thing about, *mar*, in the slightest degree, our pursuits or pleasure. A good general, I am told, is always prepared for his enemy—therefore, only keep a good look out; and I am certain it is out of his power, or malice, to do either of us any harm. A fig for his threats, Flourish, if he did make any! Yet I have some faint recollection of the subject of his anger towards us! But another time!"

Here the discourse was finished, and Scapegrace was forgotten, by the band playing the animating gallopade from the opera of *Gustavus*—the company gaily promenading up and down the deck, and several of them from the movement of their feet quite anxious to commence the ' *Gallope!*' But no leader, or master

of the ceremonies, presented themselves to give the eclat necessary to the dance ; and Flourish still tardy about making up his
mind to challenge the fair daughters of the 'old Duchess,' to
join the party on the 'light fantastic toe.' the tune was permitted
to finish, and the deck resumed its former appearance.

Old Makemoney then addressed his nephew, in a quiet,
colloquial manner, "Travelling in a steamer, more especially on
the Thames, where scarcely any thing like danger is apprehended is, in my humble opinion, of the most delightful description ;
for instance—refreshments can be had at any time, in case the
breezes should operate on the appetite, and hunger require sustenance : an elegant cabin for retirement—books for those who
have a taste for reading ; and where, frequently, several ladies
may be seen quite wrapped up in excitement at the tale of the
last new novel.

"The lovers of prospects and other objects are equally amused
on the deck—and a taste for naval architecture may also be gratified. The great variety of company you meet with connected with
all ranks in the scale of society—the different remarks you likewise
hear on all passing subjects upon politics, theatres, police, &c.
are highly worthy of the attention of any author who is fond of
exercising his pen on the subject of men and manners. The delight of popping on an old acquaintance by accident. Viewing
others cogitating over a cigar—a few scientific persons engaged
at chess. Here and there a few parties may be seen at drafts,
dominoes, cribbage, &c., while some of the juvenile company
are enjoying themselves skipping about the deck, or in the shape
of a dance.

"You may also behold lots of young cockneys, of both sexes,
puzzling the man at the helm, it being their first trip by steam,
with all sorts of questions, as to ' What's that ere place ?' or
' this ere castle ?' Travelling by steam also gives the steady
merchant a little respite from business—and his mind perhaps, at
ease, is at work on the calculating system from the beginning to
the end of his journey, and when he hears the man sing out—
' Gravesend ! Herne Bay ! Margate ! or Dover !' He feels
astonished, as well as pleased, that he has accomplished his
place of destination in such a very short time.

" You may also see the ' man of pleasure,' full of gallantry,
making himself agreeable to the ladies by his polite attention
and conduct to their little wants, and with his spy-glass, he is
the very essence of communication, pointing out the situations
and names of all the places as they pass along ; obtaining the
character of ' what a nice man—a perfect gentleman,' with the
whole sex on board. Sometime hearing the remarks—' Really,
my dear mamma, it is more than delightful to meet with such
intelligent persons.'

" Well, for my part, I must give a preference to steam before
any other sort of conveyance—the weather cannot affect your

person—you are enabled to retreat from the attacks of the wind and rain ; besides, you are not subjected to trifling quarrels about ' putting up,' or ' leaving the glasses down !' as in a stage coach: no dust to annoy your feelings, or spoil your clothes ;—you experience the pleasure of walking up and down the deck—not only enjoying the requisite towards health and exercise ; but you have the gratification to know, at the same time, that you are rapidly proceeding with your journey, and that your progress is not retarded by stopping at the doors of inns on the road to change horses, or coachmen !

" Many other circumstances might be pointed out in favour of steam navigation, if it were necessary to show its great convenience and immense utility—it also conveys a picture of real life —abounding with characters of every description ; only witness the veteran tar, nearly three sheets in the wind, a passenger by the steam-boat to join his ship, laughing at the remarks of *fresh-water* sailors, and the fears expressed by the ladies of the approaching danger, talking of the boisterous winds, and the roughness of the sea !—' Rough ! my darlings—Ha ! ha ! there an't a thimble-full of wind stirring, and on the rough *sea*, as you call it, why there's not a *ripple* to be seen. My eyes, if you had been along with me and my shipmate Jack Dreadnought, who sits beside me, in the Bay of Biscay, then you might have said OLD BOREAS had opened his doors, and went to work with a new pair of bellows—that Daddy Neptune had been kicking up a row in his berth below, and set the foaming billows in rapid motion, making all the craft, big and little, dance mountains high without any music. But never mind, my hearties, every one to his calling—(*singing.*)—

But sailors were born for all weathers—
Great guns let it blow high—blow low!
Our duty keeps us to our tether,
And where the gale drives we must go!

Here, steward, bring us a glass of stiff grog—none of your six upon four stuff—that I may drink to all ' *sound hearts and true bottoms !*' The *tout ensemble*, to me, is of the most inviting description ; and if you, my worthy brother Pilgrims, enter into the same sort of spirit on the subject, I feel assured that all our trips connected with the Banks of the Thames will not only prove gratifying to our feelings, but instructive to our minds.'

Greenwich Hospital was now in sight, and boats from the shore putting off for the steamer. The Pilgrims immediately were ready to get on land ; the Duchess and her companions were equally on the alert : and Doleful appeared so anxious to be off, that he had nearly jumped over the waterman's wherry into the water, so eager was the undertaker to reach the land.

Scapegrace, also, as it were, slunk out of the steamer. Flourish, it should seem, had now screwed his courage to the sticking place, thinking his only chance might be now or never—im--

H

mediately went up to the Duchess, and begged he might have the honour of seeing her safe in the boat, and also to the shore: Makemoney and his nephew making for the land in another wherry, viewing with merriment the operations of Flourish.

"Really, sir, your offer is very kind," replied the Duchess, with a sort of agreeable simper on her countenance; "but I cannot think of being so troublesome to a perfect stranger: yet, nevertheless, permit me to return you thanks for your gentlemanly conduct to unprotected females."

Flourish, flattered up to the eyes by this reply, swallowed the bait with all the greediness of a perch; and positively insisted on performing "the amiable" to ladies who were so much in want of a male friend. The row was but short to the shore; but during the little period which occured, the Duchess was determined to make the most of it—a *conquest* being in view. She, therefore, appeared the very mirror of attraction—her smiles, affability, condescension, and politeness, were truly conspicuous. The young ladies, who had also had their cue—*giggled* a little, shewed a kind of simplicity, and affected a sort of coyness, that, whenever Flourish put any questions to them, as if shy, they turned their heads from his face. Makemoney and Jem, at this juncture, bowed in recognition to Flourish, which the latter returned by a nod.

"You are nodding to your friends, I presume. I am sorry we should have been the cause of your *separation*. I beg pardon," said the Duchess, "the corpulent gentleman is perhaps your——"

"O la, ma!" observed one of the young ladies, in an audible whisper, yet quite loud enough for any person to hear, "is he not very much like our butcher? It is him, I am sure; and I thought so when I first saw the fat man on board of the boat."

"Hush! hush! my dear Seraphina," replied the Duchess, as if in great confusion; "you should not have interrupted the gentleman in his reply: besides, it is extremely rude to make any remarks on the dress of any person. But you will be kind enough to excuse them, sir, as this is the first time they have ever been suffered to *gaze* or to mix with the world; at least, upon such an occasion. You are very foolish children; and I hope no more caution from me will be found necessary."— This was urged with so much propriety, that a *Saint* might have been imposed upon, much more the self-important Flourish.

"Well, and I think Seraphina is right, after all," observed the other young lady, with a toss of the head, "for I know him by the cut of his coat! Butchers always wear such coats."

"Wilhelmina, my child," answered the Duchess, to all appearance quite angry; "worse and worse—O fie!—if you cannot say any thing more to the purpose, I must impose *silence* upon you for the rest of the day. I am shocked!"

" Like their butcher! Cut of his coat, &c. These folks of
the upper circles have a precious deal of assurance belonging
to them," thought Flourish ; and, indeed, he was so much taken
by surprise, that he had nearly forgot to reply to the Duchess.
However, not appearing to notice those impertinent remarks,
and recollecting himself, he said, " O yes, yes. He is a man of
great respectability in the City : also in the possession of immense property, and a truly worthy creature. But no matter:
You will allow me, as we are very near the shore, to see you
safe to the place of your destination, or to your friends at Greenwich."

" Why, really, sir, I am almost ashamed to inform you," turning her head, replied the Duchess, " as I have no doubt but you
will think me a very foolish woman ; but, at the same time, I
know your kindness will excuse the fond mother. My girls are
just arrived from school, and, in a good-natured, thoughtless
moment, I promised them—not thinking of what I was about—
that they should visit Greenwich Hospital and the Park ; and
the cunning jades have taken me by surprise. Indeed, I
was not at all aware it is what is called the holyday time,
until I was on board the steam-boat. But they are both mad-
caps—rich ; and they know it—large fortunes in their own
hands ; that is to say, when they come of age ; and they will
hardly, on that account, submit to any thing in the shape of control. It is true, sir, we are here incog., and not dressed well
enough to meet with any of our friends and acquaintances, who
are of the very first consequence in the upper circles of society.
Indeed, not for the [' Indies of gold,' would I be seen by any
persons from the West End ; although being here could not be
construed into any thing more than a mere harmless frolic.
Thank my stars, I am rich enough to be above any thing like
malice. Yet, you know, sir, that we cannot be too much upon
our guard—people will talk, and too often make mountains of
molehills ! But you, I am confident, sir, are not only a gentleman by birth and good-breeding ; and when we are in the company of a person of that superior description, we are quite certain to experience nothing else but gentlemanly treatment."

Flourish made a most profound bow for the compliment which
had been just paid to him, and replied, " I hope so, my dear
madam, and any thing in my power you may command, sans ceremonie. Therefore, I will accompany you to the Park, if you
have no objection."

" Objection, sir ; oh no, indeed !' answered the Duchess, with
a most agreeable smile ; " on the contrary, for myself, I shall be
proud in the extreme of your company ; and I will answer for
my mad-caps of girls, that they will be delighted by the attentions of a gentleman of your excellent taste and accomplishments."

The boats had by this time deposited their contents on the

shore.   Scapegrace often looked behind him, with a sort of fierceness about his aspect, that seemed to say, ' I will be with you at some future period, when you least expect it—I am for revenge !'—but he was not perceived by any of the Pilgrims. Doleful had no sooner landed than off he started, running at the top of his speed for the " *World's End*," or rather the sign of it, with his hand upon his ruler, with an intent to measure the dead man for his coffin ; so strongly did the idea possess him that he was to get the job from the foreman of the Coroner's Inquest.   Flourish was convulsed with laughter, although in company with the Duchess and her daughters—so much did he pride himself with the success of his joke upon poor Doleful.

Makemoney and his nephew now came up to Flourish, during the time the Duchess and the girls had walked forwards a few steps, while the former discharged the boatmen.   " Won't you join us ? " said Frank.   " You will not regret it, take my word. She's a lady of importance, I have no doubt, from the West end of the town—of rank—and rich : her daughters have got splendid fortunes—they are out upon a little frolic, but decidedly *incog*. If you neglect this opportunity you will miss a treat.   I have found that she is positively a diviuity ! affable in her manners, fascinating in her conversation, and neither proud nor ostentatious—taking things as she finds them, and anxious to have a peep at the middling and lower classes of society, with all that *gaite de cœur* connected with a woman of quality !   She has recognized you and Jem as my two friends ; therefore, three and three will make excellent *couples* for a stroll in the Park—so join us, my dear fellows, without the slightest reserve.   Remember what the old song says—

We're Pilgrims, blithe and jolly,
Sworn foes to melancholy,
And come out some fun to see !

So do not repent of the offer I have made, when it is too late. Come and join us !

" For myself," answered the uncle, " I must decline.   I am too old, and not fit company for such dashing females.   I should feel out of my element—a plain matter-of-fact man like myself would only be troublesome ; but, nevertheless, I will not deprive my nephew, if he feels any desire, to pass the evening with you.   I am no churl, but I must decline your pleasant offer.   However, I will meet you in the evening, depend upon it.   In the mean time, I shall make myself comfortable and happy—there are plenty of subjects to keep one alive here, which present themselves.   You must excuse me, Frank."

" I will not leave you, uncle," said Jem.   " No, no—I'll stick to the good old oak, and NATIONAL into the bargain," patting, in a friendly manner, his uncle on the back ; " I shall be safe under its branches, and out of harm's way.   No decoy ducks for

GREENWICH PARK

me. I repeat, all is not gold that glitters! I am young in life —*knowing* a little, but not *knowing* enough; and I will not give a chance away. I shall want words—be shy—bashful—at fault—look foolish—and be *quizzed* to death! No, it won't suit me. You, Frank, shall be the hero of the tale—the merit of this adventure shall belong entirely to yourself! But, as a friend, I say do not make any mistakes. Don't put your foot in it! The *knowing ones* are done sometimes. My uncle and I will meet you at Richardson's Show, in the Fair, from half-past eight till nine—we shall be punctual.

" You are quite wrong, I am sure, in your conjectures—your apprehensions groundless; nay, your suspicions are unjust," replied Flourish; " I tell you again they are ladies—every thing about them bespeak it. Do you think I am so easily imposed upon? Well, you shall have your opinion, and if they trick me I will forgive them. I was not born yesterday. But I will not press you. No, no—Liberty Hall is my motto: I am pledged to them for a stroll in the Park, and I cannot look so ridiculous as to break my word. I will be punctual to you at Richardson's, when I shall be able to report progress. So adieu, my worthy brother Pilgrims, for the present, and for only a short period." Flourish immediately joined the Duchess and her girls, and they were soon out of sight.

Makemoney and his nephew took another direction, and both parties were anxious to get to the Park. The streets were thronged with people—the coaches from London arriving every quarter of an hour overloaded with passengers—shatter-o'-dans —taxed carts—flys—covered vehicles—vans, waggons, &c., breaking down almost with the weight of their luggage; every person so anxious to arrive early at Greenwich: the public-houses crowded to excess—the cook-shops literally besieged, and their contents devoured like an attack from cormorants. The whole forming a lively but glorious scene of bustle and confusion; vividly portraying the pleasure and delight the holydays are hailed with by the people in general.

" If I am not mistaken," said Makemoney, " Flourish with all his boasted knowledge of life, will have to pay dearly for this frolic;—there is something about them that does not please me; —they are *knowing ladies*, to a certainty, and there is also a sort of impudent leer about their eyes, that do not belong to modest females. No, no, modest women are different creatures altogether. But they have found out Frank's weak point—they have flattered him—and he is foolish enough to believe that he is deserving of such compliments. No matter, he is a rich single man; and, therefore, if he will sin with his eyes open, let him be punished for it. It has been said, that *experience* makes fools wise!—Be it so."

" True, dear uncle," answered Jem, " he in general finds fault with every thing; and almost with every body; therefore

I am the more surprised at this sudden alteration in his feelings: but for *himself*—he thinks he is the standard of perfection; and he imposes upon you in such an insinuating sort of style that you can scarcely withstand his remarks. For instance, ' My dear boy, Jem,' said he; 'I admit that you are a clever, high-spirited, well-informed young man, and in reality you do possess a much greater knowledge of the world then could be expected for so young a man. But would you, Jem,—and let us argue the question fairly,—place your experience in competion with mine?' Therefore, let Flourish take his chance—it is most certain we have all our weak moments—and perhaps we ought to think ourselves lucky, if during our pilgrimage connected with the Thames, we escape *free!* After all, he may not be *serious.*"

" Liberal, boy, liberal!" exclaimed the uncle, " I like that sort of generous allowance which you have made for the infirmities of human nature; it ought to obtain praise—nay, more, it ought to be recommended, as a point well worthy of consideration, to all our friends and acquaintances through the different walks of society. Mankind might not then be inclined to prove such harsh judges, as they too often do, upon *outside* appearances, giving undue weight to them, instead of relying only upon *facts.*"

" Every body seems happy here, uncle," said Jem, " from the highest to the lowest person; and mirth and good humour appear to predominate in every party. I am quite delighted with the scene, although it does partake, in a great measure, of *rudeness.*"

·' True, Jem: but surely you would not expect *etiquette* at Greenwich Fair," replied Makemoney: " in my humble opinion, in promoting the happiness of the lower classes of society, you increase the strength of the nation. I must confess, I am fond of old customs—I have a great veneration for those sort of land-marks—they hand circumstances down from father to son—and they keep alive features not only in private parties, but connected with the rise and fall of nations; which, otherwise, might be totally forgotten, or sunk into oblivion.

" I love to keep birth-days—and like the return of the holy-days at Christmas, Easter, Whitsuntide, &c., it tends to break the business-like chain of confinement—and employment, and work of every description, is returned to with a pleasing zest, that cannot be felt without the benefit of *relaxation.*

" I am quite aware it may be strongly urged against the revival of such places as Fairs, Races, &c.; that they are the means of bringing crowds together, and that riots sometimes occur; it is likewise a harbour for designing folks to assemble together, to entrap the unwary; there is little doubt but there is a great deal of truth in these remarks—but notwithstanding, I am of the late Sergeant Best's legal opinion, now Lord Wynford—' that we ought to take care to preserve our national habits, manners, and customs. From the union of these,' the learned Sergeant boasted, ' has arisen our national spirit—our love of independence, of justice, and of our country.—THE TRUE AND ONLY SOURCES OF ALL OUR GREATNESS AND ALL OUR HAPPINESS. Wakes and their amusements are amongst the customs, and are the fruits of our liberty. He who would destroy them, would make a change in our manners and habits, the extent of which we cannot see ; and for the consequence of which, no good man would chuse to answer.' "

"Excellent !" replied Jem, " and as I feel rather dry, and require a little refreshment before we proceed on our Pilgrimage in Greenwich ;—if you have no objection we will walk into a tavern, or one of the booths, and drink the health of the late Sergeant Best, for those noble sentiments ;—which, I am sure, cannot be too often repeated—and which all lovers of their country must cherish and admire ;—they are so truly English !"

" With all my heart and soul !" said Makemoney, glowing with animation, " and in a bumper !"

We will now leave them to the enjoyment of their repast, and take a peep at the movements of the Duchess and her daughters."

" It is well, perhaps," thought Flourish, on leaving his brother Pilgrims, " that I did not say any thing to them about the butcher, the cut of his coat, &c., calculated to excite angry feelings against the ladies ; however, it appears I am all right in their estimation, and old Makemoney a good *foil* to me."

" Your friends, then, will not join us ?" said the duchess.

" It is, I assure you, madam, a matter of regret to them," replied Flourish, " but a previous engagement prevents them from the enjoyment of your delightful company."

" You are a flatterer, I perceive, sir," answered the Duchess, with one of her most fascinating smiles; " but I am sorry for their absence, as we might then have been so agreeably paired off. Give me leave to say, sir, you are a bold man to encounter three females ! I am afraid you will have to regret your temerity, or rather, like Macheath observes :—

> How happy could I be with either,
> Where t'other dear charmer away !

Ha ! ha ! ha ! You must excuse me, sir, but perhaps, I am making a little too free at so short an acquaintance : indeed, it has always been my fault to be too communicative ; however, I hate your distant, cold, proud, reserved sort of folks. No, I belong to a different sort of world—my feelings are of another cast : If I like a person, or feel pleased with their manners, I cannot help making free with them, that is to say—rank them amongst my friends. Yet, sir, you may think me too candid in this respect ?"

" You overwhelm me, madam, with delight," answered Flourish; " it is this sort of frankness which belongs to persons of superior intecourse with society; and which the advantages of education give them over other individuals, who are confined to a different sphere; therefore, madam, I hope you will be more *candid*, as you term it, and let me be benefitted by your remarks and conversation. I will close here, lest any further observations of mine might be deemed *flattery*, which I assure you, is far, very far removed from my intention; therefore, may I hope that you will proceed without the slightest reserve !"

" Your politeness, sir, emboldens me to enter into that freedom of conversation," said the Duchess, assuming an air of gravity; " which otherwise I most certainly should have hesitated in doing; for, after all, females, however well educated they may have been, and positively *drilled* into every thing connected with genteel life are very inferior to the well-bred gentleman and elegant scholar! Ha! ha! No, no—there is no sort of comparison—but the man of gallantry who seems outwardly to pay the most devout attention to a female, like the actor who has to deliver a speech *aside*, has often been heard to denominate the ladies—" *mere playthings of an hour !*"

" You wrong yourself, my dear madam," said Flourish; " and I am afraid the last sentence was rather too *satirical !*"

" This is not fair, my dear ma !" said Miss Seraphina; " You engross the whole of the gentleman's conversation to yourself."

" A few words more, my dear girl," replied the Duchess, " and then you can say what you please. But I was merely going to account for our being here, to inform the gentleman that you were tired out with your frequent visits to the Italian Opera; the Zoological has become a perfect bore; the Coliseum was very well in its way; lounging at the Bazaars had ceased to become attractive, and that you were determined to enjoy a little RURAL FELICITY by way of a change in your amusements. That you were more anxious to tread on a carpet of green, and enjoy the sweet fragrance of the air, than waltzing on chalked floors, and being oppressed with the heat proceeding from the effects of gas light, or wax candles."

" Charming ! mamma, you have described our feelings to a nicety," said Wilhelmina; " too much of one thing is good for nothing—and at the West end, you know, it is one continued *routine* from morning to night. It is enough to make one yawn only to think of it."

" True, my dear Willy," observed Seraphina; " Only look at those persons having a little delightful rural exercise from that high hill—I long to be with them. Do you think it would be *indecorous*, mamma, if we were just to have a little scamper down the hill ? I am sure it would do us good, and improve our health. We shall only be taken for well-dressed rustics—perhaps country milliners—but no matter for once——"

" Yes, mamma, you must consent ! " echoed Miss Wilhelmina ; " it will be only viewed as a little bit of *rusticity*."

" Why, my dears," replied the Duchess, " you seem quite *wild*, and more like birds who have had the doors of their cages left open by accident, than young ladies whose education and pursuits should have taught you better manners. But you are so persevering, that you will not be denied. However, if I thought your uncle, the Admiral, would not pounce upon you—and that is not at all unlikely, as he might have some duty to perform at the Hospital—perhaps I might, for once, indulge your whims. But he's a fine old soul, and, jolly tar-like, he might only join in the laugh. But pray take care you do not run down the hill too fast, as it is not very lady-like you know, girls, for females to be seen tripping up their heels."

" You will perhaps, sir, have the goodness just to join us for a run or two," said Miss Seraphina ; " it will have such a strange appearance for us to run down the Hill without the protection of a gentleman. I am sure you will not refuse a challenge from a lady."

" Certainly not, my dear young ladies," replied Flourish, quite gallant ; " if your mamma will remain by herself for a few moments, only to laugh at our folly."

" You have my free consent," replied the Duchess ; " therefore, on my account, lose no time."

Miss Seraphina and her sister commenced the race with all the rude ardour of romps, and nothing like the appearance of *delicate* females. Flourish, in truth, was so pulled about by each arm that he was panting for breath ; and, after a run or two, he was compelled to decline the contest. Though the latter did not perceive it, yet it should seem that the young ladies were more anxious to *display* their well-turned ancles, covered with rich silk stockings, elegantly clocked, than to *conceal* them from the eyes of the public, and were quite indifferent as to bashfulness. After the race had terminated, they all three joined in the laugh at the weakness of Flourish's constitution. During the space of time that Flourish was recovering his exhausted breath, he perceived old Doleful running as fast as he could towards him— who, upon reaching him, observed,—" I beg your pardon, sir ; I cannot find the ' *World's End !* ' and I am afraid I shall lose the job."

Flourish could scarcely look at Doleful, from the effects of risibility, at the great simplicity displayed by the tally undertaker. " Egad," said Flourish, " I beg your pardon—I have made a mistake—how could I be so stupid !—I mean ' *the Man struggling to get through the World!* '—but there is such a similarity between them, that any person might have committed an error quite unintentionally. However, you shall be correct now, as I will write it down for you ; but if you do not make haste you will be too late."

I

Away ran Doleful, but in his haste he tripped up against a stone, and down he measured his whole length on the ground ; which Flourish perceiving, proposed to the ladies to have a stroll to some other part of the Park. On turning round, just to have a last look at Doleful, he perceived the thread-paper sort of figure of the undertaker on his legs, *hopping* as fast as he could for ' *the Man struggling to get through the World !* ' Flourish was now totally unable to proceed until he had enjoyed an immoderate fit of laughter at the successful *hoax*, a second time which he had played off on old Doleful : but on taking out his pocket-book, to write the direction for the undertaker, he accidentally let fall one of his cards, unperceived by himself, but which was carefully picked up by one of the young ladies, who, after looking at the name, immediately concealed it in her *reticule.*

" Did I not see that grim spectre-looking sort of man on board the steamer ? " asked the Duchess. " What a horrid fright for a human being ! "

" Yes, madam," replied Flourish ; " he is a *cheap* undertaker by profession—always looking out for a job. Therefore, to have a little bit of fun, I found him a *subject,* and he is gone to look after the said imaginary being to bury him. Will you allow me—ha ! ha !—to recommend him to the notice of your Ladyship ? "

" For mercy's sake, sir, don't frighten me to death ! He is more terrible-looking than any of the horrid skeletons in the German Opera. But it was cruel of you," said the Duchess ; " O fie ! " Yet, nevertheless, in spite of their sympathy, they all joined most heartily in the laugh at the *finisher's* expence.

On recovering from their laugh, they had not proceeded far from the above spot before Flourish perceived a large ring, composed of young men and girls, enjoying themselves at a rural game, which is very conspicuous at holyday time in Greenwich Park, called " KISSING IN THE RING ! " It is truly simple in its nature, and does not require the least instruction to become perfect : for instance, the female selects one of the males whom she appears to prefer to any other person present, when she touches him on the back, and then runs away from him as fast as she can, until the man she has touched overtakes her. The female is then taken into the ring, when she is saluted by her admirer, and also by the clerk of the ring. She is then left as a pledge until she is relieved by some other aspiring lover from the ring. Therefore, those ladies who are fond of *kissing,* here may be gratified to the utmost extent of their wishes.

Flourish now thought he had an opportunity to have a bit of fun with the young ladies, when he thus addressed them :— " Now, young ladies, it is my turn to challenge ; what do you say to a game at *Kiss in the Ring?* It is a game I am very fond of. Therefore, my dear Miss Seraphina, let me beg the favour of a slight touch from you, that I may have the inexpressible felicity of a chaste salute from those vermillion lips. Afterwards, another touch from my dear Miss Wilhelmina; and then I shall be doubly blessed. Nothing can be more simple, I assure you. Suppose we commence the game——"

" You astonish me, Mr. Flourish, at the boldness of your request," said Miss Seraphina, with a sort of disdainful air, " I hate kissing!—'tis a vulgar practice, as well as an immodest one. But if I did consent to kiss, I should say, with Juliana, in the Honeymoon, ' I only *kiss* where I love."

" Bravo!" answered Flourish, " I admire your spirit, not to say your good taste; but you know it is only RURAL FELICITY! We do not expect it in drawing-rooms; but it is all fair at fair-time! Come, come, do not be so cold. I once more challenge you to the ring. You have given me a good specimen that you are nimble on the foot, and there is a probability I might not catch you."

" Stop, stop, Mr. Flourish, not quite so fast," replied Miss Wilhelmina; " I say much more than my sister—it is a most filthy practice—so much *slabbering* about it, to let every rude beast salute your lips, be what his breath may. It is quite shocking—so think no more about it. Come, let us be walking, and seek for subjects more interesting than an unmeaning kiss!"

Flourish felt quite surprised, nay, abashed at this unexpected check—and was rather confounded at the freedom with which they used his name! How could they have acquired it? thought he. He was almost at a stand-still for a reply; but, however, he determined to rally them slightly on their coyness, and to try if he could not reduce their pride a little. " Every one to his taste," said Flourish: " but I should like to have one harmless run;—there really are some very nice girls in the ring, that a duke might not be ashamed to salute—some of the choicest gifts of Nature!"

" You are only joking, Mr. Flourish," said the Duchess, " I am sure; and you are determined to be facetious! A gentleman of Mr. Flourish's pretensions in society would not like to be discovered making himself an equal amongst such a herd of common-place sort of folks. Therefore, if you have no objection, we will move forwards to a spot more congenial to all our taste and feelings—True, as you say, sir, it is Fair time—but, in some cases, we ought never to lose sight of our dignity."

" Perhaps you may be right, madam," answered Flourish; " you have called me by the name of Flourish—are you certain that is my proper designation?"

" We are quite certain of that circumstance," replied the Duchess—" You are better known to us than you expect—or you might have been assured, that we should not have trusted ourselves in any other company but that of a gentleman. we are also aware that you are a rich man—highly connected—and that, like ourselves, you have descended a few steps from your proper station in society, to have a day's fun at Greenwich!" The conversation received a short pause for a few minutes, but in passing a very large moveable tavern, Miss Seraphina observed to her sister, " Something smells very nice, indeed! I declare it has made me quite hungry! I wonder now whether the articles of food at these places are good! If I thought they were, I would not mind, for my part, just having a sandwich, by way of a lunch, and also to stay one's appetite, as it will be so very late before we get home to dinner. Nobody will know us! and if they should, why every body must take refreshment, you know."

" I declare, too, that I am almost dying for something! We came out in such a hurry, that I had scarcely any breakfast: I have no objection," observed Wilhelmina; " but ma is so very particular—she never will put her notions of quality on the shelf, if it were only for a few minutes! What delightful looking ham! the beef, too, appears delicious—and the pickles looked really inviting to a degree. Only look, ma, what a stylish booth!"

This dialogue being overheard by a man at the door, whom some persons might designate as a *Touter*, he immediately commenced the following harangue:—" I beg pardon, young lady, the term is obsolete! Our ancestors, the good old folks that are dead and gone, kept *Booths*, I admit—but this building, my fair damsel, is called a TAVERN: only look at the elegance of it, and you will allow that the expression was wrong; but most of us, at times, young lady, are apt to make mistakes—and none of us are infallible.

" This Tavern was designed by our very first architects—Sir John Soane, and the great Nash—I do not know which, but I should rather say they both had a hand in it; indeed, so much was its architecture admired at Ascot Races, that the late King George IV., in raptures with the composition of it, ordered it immediately to be served up to him like a joint of meat; but, as that could not be done, this great King of Taste was content to view it through one of Dollond's five hundred guinea telescopes, when he not only pronounced it ' Prodigious!' but ' a Palace in miniature!' "

" How very astonishing!" cried the Duchess; " I would not have believed the story, if I had not have heard it from this man's lips!"

" Therefore," said the man, resuming his discourse; " you cannot do better than to walk in—seat yourselves down comfortably—and call for what you please. Lots of quality dine here every day, at this particular season of the year. You will find every thing here in apple-pye order; and we are complimented on our good taste by the most magnificent people in society. But where's the wonder? We employ Monsieur Ude, the celebrated cook,—there never was such a cook born before; nor there never will be such a cook born again!—who makes all our pastry during this splendid CARNIVAL.

"We spare no expense!—Profit we do not care about!—Our only aim being to give satisfaction!—We are every-day sort of tavern keepers! We are *here*—THERE—and at every place, where the quality show themselves—we are strongly connected with the PEERAGE; therefore, permit me to say, ladies and gentlemen, that character—yes, character—aye, I repeat it—character with us, is the leading feature of this most splendid Arabian-night sort of establishment. There is nothing like it in the world!

"Our wines are rich, mellow, and old! and we can challenge the East or West India Docks—and as the sporting gentlemen say at Epsom, we can give any tavern-keeper under the globe —TWELVE, and beat him. Our Bees-wings are worth a Jew's-eye—and we have got a patent from the king and queen of the bees, on that particular point of excellence.

"The Champagne that we have in our cases, I want words to describe its beauty, independent of its high flavour! Talk of pink—its nothing else but pink. Our Sherry never was bought —it could not be bought—it is part of a present which came from the King of Spain; but that is neither *here*, nor *there*,— only a few bottles of it are left—therefore, I think this hint is worth its weight in gold—and the lovers of fine wines would pay a premium, if they knew where they could purchase it.

"Our table-cloths are as white as snow—knives as sharp as razors—plate of all descriptions, but no *plated* articles whatever. Remember it is the CROWN, and the *Crown* does nothing by halves—and our *Anchor* teaches us to HOPE that you will be more than satisfied with our superior refreshments."

"What an extraordinary fellow," said the Duchess, "he must certainly be some broken-down counsellor; why Lord Brougham, nor Sir Robert Peel neither, could have spoken more to the purpose. I declare it was quite an oratorical flourish! The invitation is excellent, and I feel half subdued already. If I thought we could *slide* into this tavern, as it were, without being recognized by any of our friends, I have half a mind to consent."

"You will not be seen by any person, ma!" answered Miss Seraphina, "there are times when I think pride should relax a little; and if you agree with the old proverb that ' necessity has no law,' where can be the objection? Hunger, I have heard it said, will break through stone walls; I am sure prejudices are much more easily overcome. I am so hungry, that I shall do any thing presently, regardless of propriety."

"Pray, ma! do *unbend?* You will be ill. I am sure you must be faint," echoed Wilhelmina; "well, I shall judge for myself, and enter this tavern *sans ceremonie!*"

" Well, well, you really are such coaxing, persuading, teazing sort of girls, that I suppose I shall have no peace if I do not comply with your request. But mind, girls, if your rich and particular aristocratic old uncle, the General, a P. and Q. sort of character, should hear of it, mind you must take all the blame! But I certainly should not like to see you dying with hunger."

" Now really, my dear madam," observed Flourish, " I think you are too particular, you ought not to stand upon such niceties. You are only here for ten minutes, to partake of a lunch, and gone the next ; I assure you, I have seen persons of the first respectability in life take refreshments at this tavern."

" There, mamma! you hear what Mr. Flourish has to say upon the subject," said Wilhelmina, " and now I will not take any refusal."

" Then say no more, my dear girls," replied the Duchess, " we will go in : but lose no time, give your orders for what you should like best, without Mr. Flourish will have the kindness to tell the people what is necessary to place on the table for gentlefolks."

The waiters were not in the least dull, after such an understanding between the parties, and catching hold of the last sentence, they were satisfied that some good customers were before them. The table was soon spread out with every delicacy the tavern afforded, in great profusion, and no time was lost by the Duchess and her daughters to commence operations.

" *Sans ceremonie !*" said Miss Seraphina, " let us make ourselves all at home."

No rough dairy maid, hungry groom, or shepherd's boy, ever displayed better appetites ; or, more tact in disposing of ham, fowls, beef, &c., than the Duchess and her daughters did : they appeared more like cormorants, who had been kept without food for several days—cut and come again—laughing and joking with each other on the subject : although, but a few minutes before, they had displayed the *squeamishness* of the most fastidious persons in the world.

" I declare," said Miss Wilhelmina, with the bone of a fowl in her fingers,—" I never relished any thing half so well in my life—this trip by water has given me quite an appetite."

" It is quite delightful !" observed Seraphina, " if you call this RURAL FELICITY—I shall never be tired of it ; but I suppose it is the novelty of the thing—I really am ashamed of myself."

They did not trouble Mr. Flourish to give orders, but boldly called for every thing they wanted. Flourish was so struck with astonishment, that he could scarcely taste a bit himself, ruminating what strange sort of folks the people of quality were.

When the Duchess, with the utmost sang froid, said to the waiters, " I think I heard you praising your *Pink* Champagne ; you had better bring a couple of bottles !" Flourish looked unutterable things, but said nothing. "Girls," observed the Duchess, with a sort of satirical smile upon her face, "this is one of our gala days! and I think, as it is growing late, we may as well make a dinner of it instead of a lunch; and I shall allow you both to take a glass of Champagne; Mr. Flourish, I am sure, will join us."

Mr. Flourish nodded consent, and said "Certainly!" but his articulation was very faint—and his former spirits seemed on the vane. He looked dull. The Champagne soon disappeared; in truth, so did every thing else.

"I always take a glass of Madeira, my dear mamma, after my dinner, you know; therefore," said Seraphina, "you have no objection that my sister and I should have one each to-day."

"By all means, my dear," replied the Duchess, "but let me recommend, after cold fowl, ham, &c., a little *Eau d' vie* as a preventive to spasms! Therefore, waiter, bring some brandy with the Madeira."

"The fruit looks delightful," said Wilhelmina; "therefore, you may bring the dessert as soon as you like, waiter."

The waiter, as quick as lightning, brought order after order made by the ladies. "Here is the Madeira, madam; and I have also brought for your taste some of the finest red Port in the world, and Sherry to match with it, to save you trouble."

"You have done perfectly right," answered the Duchess; "I see you are a clever man; and at my next rout I shall want such a clever assistant-waiter like yourself; but you must let me have your card before I go, that I may send to you."

The Duchess rallied Flourish on his lowness of spirits, which he denied, and evidently assumed to be cheerful; when the former drank to the girls, and the young ladies returned the compliment to their mamma. They were all in high mirth and good humour, and called upon Flourish to give them some toasts. He began to find himself getting a little *queer*, but his guests did not appear any the worse for the portion of the Champagne which they had drank; but, nevertheless, the girls were inclined to "break out" several times, had it not have been for the "stern frown" which the Duchess put on, as a cue for them to be quiet: however, to prevent any mistakes, the Duchess apologized to Flourish, and observed it was growing rather late, and they must think of getting back to London; she was also sorry, nay, afraid, that they had kept him so long from his friends."

Flourish begged of the Duchess not to mention it: he had never before been in such delightful company—*time* positively flew—and regretted they must part, but "not for ever!"

"By no means," replied the Duchess; "that would be grievous indeed."

"Part for ever!" echoed the girls; "perish the thought! Mamma, have you not given Mr. Flourish our card?"

" Here it is, Mr. Flourish," with a smile displaying at the same time a magnificent card case, said the Duchess ; " The Honorable Mrs. ———, Grosvenor-square : where we shall be most happy to see you at any time you can make it convenient ; or, at our villa, as my Seraph. will have it—the girl is so romantic in her ideas ; but I designate it no more than a mere cot—a plain, simple-looking cottage,—but fitted up truly in character, after the style of his late Majesty George the Fourth's private retreat in Windsor Great Park.   Therefore, sir, you can take your choice—at the cottage we rusticate ; or, I should rather say, *unbend.*"

The bill was now presented to our hero—but, on looking at the bottom of it, the *figure* altered his countenance a little ; however, he made no remark—his gallantry forbade it.

The Duchess, who was far from a novice, and who could read the face of Flourish, apologized for the omission of her purse, as she felt anxious to take a share in the expences ; but Flourish would not listen to any such thing. No, no—the ladies never paid in his company.

" You are a perfect gentleman, I am sure, sir, and I know you will excuse me, as I am without my purse," observed the Duchess, " I shall require the loan of five pounds from you to pay for a glass coach to carry us to our town house. It quite slipped my memory to have ordered the carriage ! I hope I am not making too free."

" No more free than welcome, madam ; I am happy it is in my power to serve you."   The preliminaries being thus settled for return to London, Flourish escorted the ladies to the best house in the town, and put the Duchess and her daughters into a post chaise. " Adieu, sir ;" " Farewell, ladies ;" were often repeated between them, but no *chaste* salutes ! The post-chaise was soon out of sight—and Flourish left to reflect at the termination of his adventure with some little *astonishment* !

CHAPTER VI.

FLOURISH asking himself a few questions ! Perplexed with doubts ! Satire a bitter weapon ; and men, in general, afraid of being laughed at. A hint or two respecting the dangers of blind confidence ; or persons having too good an opinion of their own sagacity. Travellers see strange things, and are rather too apt to praise other countries in preference to their own : nevertheless, Greenwich Fair and the Park contrasted with the Carnival at Naples. The Dance—not the Tarantula ; but equally as exciting to the feelings—nothing else but gay moments—touch and take—please your taste—running kisses—dangerous to be safe—" O the days when I were young"—quality and quantity—both in the field :—

Poor Pauline ! you know what I mean,
There's more to be fear'd from a fall on the grass,
Than a race on the frozen river !

MAKEMONEY's love of country again displayed. SPRIGHTLY over head and ears in love ! The ARTISTS at work—DRAWing the Flats—and the Pilgrims let into the secret !

LOURISH, for a few seconds, stood like a man in a *trance* ; the transition he had experienced was great in the extreme—from gay to grave in an instant—the Duchess and the two prattlers, Seraphine and Wilhelmina, out of sight like a shot,

K

galloping towards London—leaving Flourish a complete picture of loneliness. He seemed lost to every thing around him—but at length, starting from his reverie, he mentally exclaimed—

> Can such things be,
> And overcome us like a summer's cloud,
> Without our special wonder?

Or, to use a vulgar phrase, but quite in point, that a fool and his money were soon parted: indeed, he appeared astonished at his own conduct—*wheedled,* as it were, out of a truly expensive, nay, extravagant dinner—positively a *Clarendon* touch—united with the loan of five pounds! And all this politeness—liberality—condescension, and generosity, to perfect strangers! What a change in circumstances, in the course of a fleeting hour or two! How are we beguiled—entrapped—decoyed—induced—but no matter—such are the adventures of real life.

Flourish, it should seem, was carried away by an *impulse* he had never felt before. It had hitherto been his boast that he always " looked before he leaped !" but, in the present instance, he was hurried on so precipitately, that he had not an opportunity of making good his retreat. His gallantry was put to the test—and although few men had a greater regard for the cash than Flourish, yet he startled at the idea of being thought a shabby fellow! He could not make up his mind to say NO! The fascinating Duchess, who was well read in the ways of men, with her interesting daughters, were too much for him; and yes, yes, and yes, were the replies to all their questions.

The greater portion of the errors that mankind too often *split* upon, arise from the flattering unction with which they please their minds, namely, the superior intuitive knowledge and experience which they *think* they possess, generally, over their fellow creatures; and it is from this sort of confidence, rather say blindness, that they are tricked, imposed upon, nay, laughed at, for exhibiting such weakness of disposition. In the first place, take the legal Wrangler at the top of his bent for talents, experience, acuteness, and wisdom; and, at times, the " glorious uncertainty of the law" throws him over the bridge, and all his *profundity* goes for nothing.

You may also travel through the various *grades* of society, step by step, and a thick volume would not be half large enough to shew *how* men—who think themselves *knowing,* well informed, up to every thing, armed at all points, and who not only flatter themselves, but who often assert, with a self-approving smile, that if A. or B. can impose upon their understanding, they will forgive them—are cheated with the utmost ease and simplicity.

The inveterate gambler, who lives by his wits—always calculating, whether *foul* or fair, to reduce his winnings to a certainty; goes to sleep with some new scheme in his head, and his first thoughts, on rising in the morning, are to put his well-laid plans into execution, and success must be the result. Yet, when he resorts to the table at night, with his mind made up of unmeasured good fortune—confident to the echo—it has often been seen that he has become one of the greatest flats and victims, in consequence of his opponent having found out what is termed "a new *pull*," and of which he is as ignorant as the veriest *novice*.

But one more instance will suffice :—A celebrated juggler, the Sieur ———, highly distinguished for what is termed the art of Legerdemain, or Hocus Pocus, exhibited some years ago at Bartholomew Fair with immense success. His tricks with the cards were astonishing; his fame resounded from one end of the Fair to the other; and the general assertions were that he dealt with, or had a patent from the "Old One!" for his *diablerie!* In addition to his fame, as one of the Emperors of Conjurors, he filled his pockets with cash; and retired, at the conclusion of the Fair, highly gratified with his exertions and good fortune. However, a well-known gambler, at that period, laid a *plant* for him; he declared that the Sieur was a first-rate conjuror, but that he had no more knowledge of games than a mere child. This challenge had the desired effect: the Sieur felt irritated at the threat thus to reduce his importance; yet, nevertheless, appeared to treat it with contempt—feeling confidently that no man could more adroitly shift a card, *palm* a deuce or tray, than he could. The Sieur immediately offered to play at any game from a guinea to £100. The parties met; but, in the course of the night, the conjuror was not only laughed at, but *tricked* out of every farthing that he possessed in the world: at the same time, the Sieur well knew that he had been *cheated*, but he could not detect the *pull* of his opponent. These are only the common, nay *routine*, circumstances which occur every day in life with MEN; but when a woman is the feature —lovely woman—whose mere *looks* can conquer—whose eyes speak volumes—whose tongue enchants—whose manners fascinate—and whose figure enraptures—and for whom a ten years siege was fought—some little allowance will be made for the *self-important* Flourish—who had made up his mind in the *closet* not to be subdued and overcome—who had also erected himself into the hero in *still* life; but in the public walks of society proved, that, with all his boasted insight into human nature, he was in reality nothing more than a mere *novice*.

Flourish, on recollecting himself, and recovering in some degree from his stupor, the appointment with his brother Pilgrims immediately flashed across his mind, and prepared himself to meet them at Richardson's Theatre in the Fair.

On his way towards this latter scene of confusion, he was wrapt up in *thought*, cogitating on his singular adventure with the Duchess. On reflection, he was astonished, delighted, yet confounded, at such a mixture of behaviour—from pride and haughtiness, at times, down to the extreme of vulgarity. It was above his comprehension—he could not " make them out !" He felt puzzled ; but still he entertained an opinion they were not *common* sort of people ; and that, from their freedom of conversation on general topics, they had or did move in good circles of society. And then *their* card—a high-sounding designation. However, he would not decide on the conduct of the Duchess and her daughters, until he had had another interview with them : his judgment, he presumed, might then be more satisfactory, if not correct. Until that period arrived, he was determined to be as close as a pill-box, and " *mum,*" in a great measure, to any questions from Makemoney and his nephew, respecting their general behaviour, his expences, and their place of abode.

During the time which occupied Flourish with the ladies, Makemoney and Jem had not been idle spectators of the numerous attractions which Greenwich presents to the visitors during the holydays. Heroes are to be discovered in abundance, and heroines out of number ; and we very much doubt whether the " Carnival of Naples," highly as it has been spoken of by travellers, could compete with the varieties of fun, frolic, humour, spree, adventures, and anecdotes, which are to be met with, during a day's pleasure in the renowned Greenwich Park !

Distant objects are frequently highly coloured by travellers to give them importance ; and we have heard mole-hills magnified into huge mountains ! Here no gondolas are required to heighten the delightful scene upon the Thames ; nor poignards found necessary to revenge an insult—but wherries, filled with well-dressed females and smart young men, all in eager anticipation to partake and enjoy the amusements at this peculiar season of the year.

It is a fine field for observation ; and, to any thing like an active mind, amusement is to be found from " peep o'day" until the sun goes down. The middling and lower classes of society are here seen to perfection without the aid of a microscope, and the ENGLISH CHARACTER, in all its glowing colours, from youth to extreme old age.

We are not aware that the watermen on the Thames have any peculiar songs or airs connected with their occupations, while the boatmen of other rivers abroad are said to be highly distinguished for musical sounds by travellers ; nothing to compete with Tasso and Ariosto : but here and there, in a row up to Vauxhall or 'down to Greenwich, a few *touching* notes may be heard to escape the lips of those watermen who have a taste for music—what many persons call " *snatches*"—but truly national ! and of both a comic and serious description :—

> " There was a waterman, one Jack Street,
> Who used to ply along the Thames river ;
> He had serv'd aboard his Majesty's fleet,
> Pull away ! yo-e-yo !

He ply'd with sculls, a scull-cap wore,
And it was noticed how he swore:
  Right foddi, viddi, voddi, pull away!
  Right foddi, viddi, voddi, pull away! .

" *The Life of Poor Jack*," " *My Poll and my Partner Joe*,"
and

" Did you not hear of a jolly young waterman,
Who at Blackfriars Bridge used for to ply," &c.

Not only the words, but the music also, from the pen of the
late Charles Dibdin, Esq., which tend to enliven the feelings to a
recollection of the brave deeds of our warlike countrymen; and .
equally as harmonious to the ear, if there are persons who can be
inclined to think that *excellence* may be produced in England,
without the passport of FOREIGN aid to be added to it. When
the above songs were first produced, they had such an effect upon
the feelings of the young men, all over the country, that thousands were induced to enter as volunteers in the navy. However,
we have one little point in our favor, connected with a British
composer,* which rather makes Englishmen feel that they have
something *National* belonging to them, even in music :—

When the wind blows,
Then the mill goes!

equal to any thing heard on the rivers, or canals abroad, where
delightful harmony is the subject in question.

Makemoney and Sprightly in their rambles through the park,
did not come in contact with Flourish and the ladies, being too
much occupied with their own pursuits. The nephew wished
his uncle to have a turn at ' *Kiss in the Ring!*' " You will
only have to run for it.—Ha! ha! ha! and if it is not worth
fetching—it is not worth having !"

But the *Old Gentleman*, as he termed himself, thought it
would be rather out of character. " I may," said he, " look and
long, or look back to the days of my youth. No, no, it is too
late in the day for me to play at ' kiss in the ring,' but when you
are tired of the sport, you will find me in the enjoyment of my
pipe at yonder tavern."

" Be it so," replied Jem, " I have to thank you for your accommodation; indeed, I must gratefully acknowledge you are at all
times anxious to afford me amusement. I will soon join
you; as I shall require some refreshment after this pleasant exercise."

Sprightly joined the merry party with all the lively spirit and
wildness of a young colt—he was all animation—his eyes were

---

* When Bishop was on the Continent, he met with the late Von Weber at a
party; but the latter splendid musician could not recollect the name of the
former eminent English composer. However, in order to shew that the excellence
of Bishop's composition had a holdfast upon his mind—he ran to a piano-forte in
the room, and began playing the air alluded to in the Miller and his Men. A
more truly gratifying compliment could not have been paid to any man of talent.

full of fire—he had the look of a gentleman—and very superior altogether to the young men who had congregated together upon this occasion. He was not long before he received a slight touch upon the back from one of the most lovely young females in the group, as a pleasing indication to him, that he was to have the pleasure of kissing her—if he caught the prize.

Sprightly answered the *touch* with the speed of a greyhound, and he very soon made a capture of his fascinating challenger; but he did not stand upon the punctilios of the game—and kissed o'er and o'er again, with the most ardent raptures which beauty inspires, without the least opposition, nay, it should seem they were more agreeable than otherwise. Upon entering the ring with his fair captive, he again imprinted a dozen or more kisses on her lips—which called forth the remarks of a young man rather in an angry tone, who had observed his attentions :—

"I think, sir," said he, "you are making rather too free with the lips of that lady. *One* kiss, according to the rules of the game, ought to have satisfied you."

"I beg pardon, young man," replied Sprightly, "there are no *rules* laid down for *kissing*, that I ever heard of. One hundred kisses would not have satisfied me, had it been left to my choice. Indeed, I should never be satisfied with kissing such a lovely pair of vermilion lips. But you are not the clerk of the ring! Then by what right have you to call me to account for kissing the lady ?"

"By the best of all rights——her husband !"

"Most undoubtedly," said Sprightly, "that alters the case; but if you will let your young and lovely wife, play at kiss in the ring, why, all I can say is, you must take the consequences! A wife of mine, if she was as ugly as *ugliness* itself, should not play at kiss in the ring, either with or without my leave—but for a *divinity* like yours——"

This handsome compliment—elegant flourish—or piece of well-timed flattery—call it what you will—not only appeared to please, but raised the spirits of the young lady, who observed —"La, my dear Charles, what a piece of fuss you are making about a harmless kiss. The gentleman is not to blame in the slightest degree. He has not acted rudely towards me; but on the contrary, polite and genteel more than otherwise. We both complied with the rules of the game. Nothing else! I touched him—he followed me—and after all, it is nothing more than a 'chaste salute!' And considered all *fair*—at fair time. Therefore, do not be jealous, my love, about such trifles!"

"Trifles !" muttered her husband, "I beg you will quit the ring immediately, Fanny. Such trifles may lead to——"

"I shall not quit the ring, sir, without you give up the game too! Such remarks are uncalled for; and let me warn you, Charles, not to be jealous without a cause. I am sure I saw you kiss a female eight or ten times; nay, you seemed as if you could

P. Egan Sun delt

KISS in the RING.

have devoured her lips! In truth, you acted more like a lover than a married man! You compel me to forget myself."

"My sweet young lady," said Sprightly, "let me beg pardon, I have been the innocent cause of this little unpleasantness between you: depend upon it, sir, I will not offend again. I will not kiss your pretty wife any more."

"There is no offence in it at all, sir," replied the lady, "you are not to blame; therefore no apology is necessary. If my husband did not think it wrong in the first instance, why did he ask me to join the sport? You need not——"

"No more, Fanny," said her husband, sharply. "I wish you a good·day, sir," and putting his wife under his arm, he walked off at a smart pace to another part of the Park.

Sprightly appeared quite pleased that the above little *fracas* had terminated so quietly; and turning on his heel, began to sing to himself the last part of the well-known beautiful glee on this subject:—

> May his soul rest in heaven!
> He deserv'd it, I'm sure—
> Who was first the inventor of kissing!

Sprightly soon joined his uncle, and upon his relating the above adventure to him; Makemoney observed—"Aye, my boy, you see the danger attached to kissing other men's wives—whether by accident or design; therefore, avoid it in future! Private property, you know, ought always to be respected; landmarks claim attention at all times; and there are boundaries to all things! A young married female may be compared to a *tinder-box*—a *spark* is likely to make it burst into a *blaze;* and *fire* often proves our master! Then do not become a *Lucifer*—Ha! ha! ha!"

Sprightly made no reply; but he had scarcely seated himself, when the music, and lots of fine girls engaged in the dance, in another part of the tavern appropriated for the votaries of Terpsichore, attracted his attention.

"You must excuse me, uncle," said he, "I should like to have only one dance, and when your pipe is out, give me a call, and I will attend your summons immediately; or, perhaps, if it was not deemed so vulgar, (as the *cant* is, that they do these things better in France,) you might have been inclined to have had a step or two, upon the old English system,—' hail fellow, well met.' "

"My dancing days, I am rather afraid, my boy, are nearly, if not quite over," replied Makemoney; " if I even felt disposed to join the gay throng. The hilarity of the scene is delightful; and the dancing altogether considerably better than I expected to witness at a fair; indeed, some of the females would not disgrace a Ball Room; therefore, I must insist upon it, *that they cannot do these things better in France!* They might have done so when STERNE made the assertion, some sixty or seventy years ago, but since that period the English people have made such rapid improvements in every subject connected with ease, elegance, and the Fine Arts, that it becomes a question with me whether we are a jot behind them in such parties as are to be seen tripping it away on the light fantastic toe in holiday time! They have their *manner* of doing things, and we have our *mode*. But the *cry* is against us, I must admit, with a *travelled* few, who wish to have something *foreign* for breakfast—*foreign* for dinner—*foreign* for tea—and *foreign* for supper, in order to assume an importance, which they do not possess—to call it judgment would be a perversion of the phrase."

" Bravo, my uncle, I am delighted with your love of country—your anxiety to do it justice," said Sprightly; " and no one will deny but that you are an Englishman from the crown of your head to the sole of your foot."

" The fact is, they can do nothing better in France than we can in England," observed Makemoney; " I may be laughed at, I am aware, for this display of *nationality*—but let us *scan* our amusements only:—the French never had such a singer as the late Charles Incledon; and again, it would puzzle them to find such a vocalist as Mr. Braham. We'll leave the wooden walls and those fellows that wear the blue shirts out of the question! Ha! ha! ha!

" And if Sterne could pop his head out of his tomb at the present moment, he would proudly acknowledge the great improvement and change of circumstances which have taken place for the better, since he penned his Sentimental Journey!

" Their Opera dancers (my judgment may be treated with contempt) may have a *feather* in weight the advantage of us; but, nevertheless, Oscar Byrne perfectly satisfied them on their own boards in Paris, that he well knew the use of his feet as a dancer of the first quality! Ducrow, in the Circle at Franconi's, extorted from them the exclamations of Bravo! and *Superbe!* and T. P. Cooke, in the *beautiful* monster, as they termed his personification of that imaginary being, obtained their applause as a touch of the *magnificent!* As a climax—our Vestris, who relies on her HEAD instead of her *heels;* I have great doubts whether it is possible that Madame can be rivalled in any shape or degree; but to be excelled is entirely out of the question! Yet I am ready to pay every respect and deference to the French nation as a great people—masters of the art of war as soldiers—and well skilled in all the sciences, literature, &c. But that they do things better in France, perish the thought! For myself, I never did, nor I never will harbour such an idea.

" Be on your guard respecting ' the *Sisterhood;* '—they appear to have mustered very strongly upon this occasion; but, to be sure, holiday time is their harvest;—however, they are dangerous articles at all times to young men, when flushed with the juice of the grape, and the fascinating dance!"

" Never fear, sir," replied Sprightly; " your advice is well meant—but those sort of ' characters ' never claim my attention; —the term may be harsh, I admit—but I loathe and detest the name of a *prostitute*—they cease to be women in my estimation. A female who can forget what is due to her sex, I—"

" Not so fast, my boy," observed Makemoney; " Virtue I admire; I have the highest veneration for Chastity in a female; and propriety of conduct is above all other considerations. I never can become the apologist for vice in any shape—but it is the CAUSE—and I feel more inclined, five times out of six, to pity than harshly condemn unfortunate creatures, without knowing the CAUSE of their deviating from the paths of rectitude, and rushing headlong, as it were, into destruction. I repeat, be on your guard ——"

" I am no *Joseph*, uncle!" said Sprightly, " neither do I boast of more propriety of conduct than other young men; ' *gay* women,' to my feelings, are a perfect annoyance! Therefore, I am prepared against rude or vulgar attacks that may be made upon me; or, any artful stratagem laid to attract my attention."

" I shall be glad to find it so, my boy—Ha! ha! ha! I have often found that ' great talkers' do the least," said Makemoney; " yet your notions are formed on the right basis."

" In any mixed company, but more especially an assemblage of persons at a *hop* at Greenwich Fair! *Etiquette* is entirely lost sight of—and *character* not an object of enquiry! Duels are not likely to take place on account of the introduction of improper persons; although a row—a disfigured nose—and a black eye, might be the result of a visit to them, by being rather too attentive to the partner of another man." However, Sprightly had made up his mind not to be drawn aside by the *glances* of the gay creatures; but he did not give his word and honour that he would be as cold as *ice* to females of another description, who might be inclined to sport a toe in the all-inviting dance.

One, two, nay three, dances did not satisfy the high-spirited Sprightly; but, nevertheless, when the signal was given to depart, he kept his word, although with a sort of reluctance.

" I think I never saw so sweet a girl before in the whole course of my life—a perfect rose in full bloom, and smelt as sweet—it is true, upon my honor, uncle. I was over head and ears in love in a minute, and I was rude enough to gaze on her till she was out of countenance; nay, more, I was so fascinated that I attempted to praise her, and would have taken hold of her hand, but she repulsed me; and her suitor, I suppose, coming up to ask what was the matter, she blushingly answered, ' *Nothing!*' Otherwise, I might have got into another row, and likely to have been punished for my insolence. However, luckily, you called me at the instant, or else perhaps I might have lost sight of the

bounds of discretion.   But you know, uncle, what *Filch* sings
in the Beggar's Opera :—

> ' 'Tis woman that seduces all mankind,
>   By her we first were taught the wheedling arts :
> Her very eyes can cheat ; when most she is kind,
>   She tricks us of our money —with our hearts ! '

But, thank my stars, I have escaped.   I would not come in *contact* again with her eyes for a trifle !   I am afraid my resolution
would not be good for much !   I never saw such *eyes* before—I
was positively rivetted to the spot !   I shall never forget her
glances—they electrified my very *heart*, and I feel it there
now———"

"Electrified! a fiddle-de-dee !" replied his uncle, laughing ;
"why you are quite in the heroics !   I am afraid, from your
conversation, the glass or two of wine you have drank has raised
your spirits above fever-proof—your pulse must be high indeed.
Venus ! Juno ! Cleopatra ! all eclipsed in a dancing-booth at
Greenwich Fair !   Psha !   You had better try the effects of a
glass of soda-water to restore you to a state of convalescence,
that we may go and keep our appointment with Flourish."

"True," said Jem ; "I should not like Flourish to have the
laugh against me, as I well recollect his admonitions at a former
period.   'Tis weakness of mind,' said he, ' and badness of taste.
Horrible ! horrible ! my dear Jem, don't think of it.   In matters
of love you must be as cold as ice—feeling must be always banished in such cases, and remain at freezing point—and then hesitate before you make up your mind on matters connected with
love.   They only are *lunatics* who are violently in love—'tis a
species of madness, make the best of it.'   Therefore, I should
not like to encounter any of his *sneers* upon the subject."

It was now drawing near the hour of appointment to meet
Flourish at Richardson's, and they had only a few minutes to
spare to keep accurately their time : in consequence of which
they hurried forwards to the gate to quit the Park, and were
soon enveloped, before they were aware of it, in a dense crowd
of persons, all directed towards the same object ; but they appeared not to move an inch towards gaining the public road.
The screams of the women, rows, and noise, were quite annoying to all the ears of the persons engaged in this pushing sort
of contest.

"Don't push so," said, to all appearance, a very genteel young
man ; "it is all useless."

"Why," answered another person, "its this fat fellow here,
big enough for three people," alluding to Makemoney ; "some
brewer's servant in disguise, who has borrowed his master's
clothes on the sly, to cut a bounce in the Park for a day ; but
it won't do for us—such porpoises should stay at home, and not
annoy other people with their ponderous bulk !"

"You are a rascally impertinent fellow," said Makemoney, almost gasping for breath; "and if I had you in my ward I would commit you for your insolence."

"O Lord!" said a woman, "I shall be killed!—for God's sake, let me out: I shall be squeezed as flat as a pancake."

"Squeezed! I believe you," said an elegantly dressed young fellow; "it is this giant of a chap that does all the mischief. He is a second Daniel Lambert! D—n me, but he'd squeeze St. Paul's into a nutshell—he is a walking flatting mill. What a fine assistance he'd be to Macadamise the roads—he would do the work of fifty men! I will recommend him to the Commissioners."

"Aye do, my dear fellow," observed a man in the garb of a quaker, "recommend him to any body, so that we may get rid of him; if the beast remains any longer with us we shall all be reduced to a jelly—I have lost several pounds weight already. He has no more feeling than a horse, and rides over people as if they were nothing more than stones."

"Beast!" echoed Makemoney, "is it come to this, that a gentleman is to be abused in such a manner, and have no means of redress? Only let me get out of this mob, and I'll have one or two of you blackguards before the magistrates to answer for such infamous conduct."

"Ha! ha! ha!" resounded from one end of the crowd to the other. "Will no person have the kindness to remove the elephant? but never mind, his keepers will soon be after him. I wonder the men at the gate did not refuse such an overgrown animal admittance."

Makemoney became violently incensed at these remarks beyond all endurance: he was hemmed in on all sides; and, just as he was about making a desperate effort to shew his anger, he received a tremendous blow on his hat, which drove it down over his eyes, and hindered him from seeing; and he could not get up his hands to remove the obstruction. His nephew was equally in as bad a situation, and covered with perspiration, from the intense heat of the crowd, when he cried out, "Thieves! thieves! Police!"

"Here's another troublesome fellow," observed a decent old man; "but I suppose it is to answer his purpose—picking pockets."

"Picking pockets!" exclaimed Sprightly, in a violent rage. "How dare you, scoundrel, to charge me with such a crime! If I was near you, for your villanous assertion, I would annihilate you! Do I look like a thief?"

"What do I care for your looks," answered a ruffianly sort of fellow; "but if *looks* are taken into account—then I say, at all events, that you do look more like a thief than a horse! You need not give yourself any airs! Do you suppose any person here cares a farthing for your upstart consequence?"

The whole of the crowd were covered with dust, and no remedy at hand, until the officers of justice routed the phalanx; when Makemoney and his nephew, quite exhausted, made their way into the street. Upon getting into the air, they both sat down, puffing and blowing like broken-winded horses; and Makemoney was a few minutes before he could recover his breath.

"I hope you have not lost any thing, sir," observed one of the policemen, " as you appeared to me to have been surrounded by some suspicious characters."

"Egad," replied Makemoney, " I never thought of that: in fact, I was more afraid of suffocation than any thing else—I could not draw my breath—and the insolence I received from several rascals, that I never thought any thing about my property. However, I will now look after it." On feeling his fob-pocket, a cold sweat came over his face in an instant, when he replied, with astonishment, " It's gone!"

" Gone!—What's gone, uncle?"

" My gold watch and seals! Oh, the rascals! Was there ever such a set of deep villains in the world," said Makemoney; " I had no idea of it."

" You had better search, and see if your money is all right," answered the officer.

" Do not frighten me to death," said Makemoney. " Indeed, I am almost afraid to look into my pockets." On searching them—" That is gone too, purse and all. Well, I am surprised, I must admit; as it appeared to me that I was surrounded by nothing else but genteel company—gentlemen eager to get through the gate. Thieves never entered my head. However, it will be a lesson to me, and I shall know better how to act another time."

" Yes," replied the officer, " some of the SWELL MOB were at work, I have no doubt; and it is by their elegant appearance they are enabled the better to carry on their depredations. They would deceive a conjuror—they are up to so many tricks and fancies."

After the agitation of the moment had subsided a little, Makemoney said to his nephew, " Jem, I hope you have not lost anything! They had not to complain of your bulk annoying them. Let us hear."

" I will see, sir; but my paying attention to you, I have not thought about the matter; but no doubt I am safe enough. I should say, it was impossible to rob me! I have been in numerous crowds upon various occasions, but I never lost a farthing in the whole course of my life!"

" Don't make too sure," answered Makemoney; " neither young nor old escape the swell mob, I suppose?" to the policeman.

" Why," replied the officer, " they are not particular in that respect—all is fish that comes to net : they never let a chance go by them."

On searching his pockets, the nephew, in a violent rage, exclaimed, " By G-d, I have lost my pocket-book, notes, memorandums, &c., and all my loose cash. I thought, now I recollect it, I felt a sort of *tugging* at my pockets ; but I did not suspect I was being robbed."

" There has been no *tugging*, sir," said the policeman ; " you may perceive your coat has been cut with a sharp instrument. You could not have felt it."

" Then I am not the only victim !" answered Makemoney, half inclined to smile and be jocose about his loss ; " we now are poor Pilgrims, indeed ! without money, it is true, but not without a home. Therefore, it might have been worse ; and the best thing we can do is to put a good face upon the matter, and try to forget the circumstance as soon as possible."

" You, sir, are a rich man," replied Jem, " and the loss, I am aware, is a more aggravating sort of thing than the actual value you have been robbed of ; but to me it is of a more serious nature, being entirely dependant on your bounty. It is, notwithstanding, truly mortifying to be served out in such a manner, without the slightest chance of recovering the property lost, because the thief or thieves are unknown to either of us.

" Never mind, Jem," said Makemoney, " you shall be none the worse for it." On searching his pockets once more—" Come, come," said he, " the rogues have not been quite so treacherous as I expected—they have not taken all I had. I find I have got a couple of sovereigns safe in my waistcoat ; and we shall see Flourish soon, and I know he has always plenty of money about him ; therefore, we cannot be at a loss to carry on the Pilgrimage. So let us imitate JOB—be patient under our sufferings—put up with our losses, and like *stoics*—shew a merry face—that Flourish may not have the laugh against us, and meet him with all the fun and good humour attached to our character, as if nothing had happened."

" There is nothing like philosophy in this life, sir," answered Jem, " I am convinced ; and *silence* also is the best friend a man can have on his side, if he knows how to turn it to his advantage : therefore, I once more urge silence, sir, when you see Flourish."

" Your advice is good," replied his uncle, " and respecting our loss, I shall be as close as a pill box !"

CHAPTER VII.

The SHOW FOLKS! Talents outside of the Theatre; or, HOW to " pull 'em in!" An original Comic Song, embellished with patois, but quite in character; and a word or two respecting the chances and profession of an Actor. Recollections of the late MUSTER RICHARDSON, entitled to RECORD, according to the INTRINSIC value set upon mankind by a great public writer. The miseries attached to Strollers sixty years ago. The dangers of a double-bedded apartment! The serious effects from too much learning—the light headed PIG to wit—a caution to Students. A glance at the CHOICE SPIRITS of the olden times—Players, Poets, Painters, Authors, &c.

Praising what is lost
Makes the remembrance more dear!

The late EDMUND KEAN and the Show Folks—his flattering reception at the Court of George the Third—Talent will make its way. A wet scene; or, too much of water hadst thou, OXBERRY! The flight of Ducks! a singular adventure. How to avoid an Act of Parliament: a Play Bill for Dummies! Liberal Traits of the late Mrs. JORDAN—more anon. Comparisons (not odious) between the illustrious JOHN KEMBLE, of classical notoriety, and the matter-of-fact Showman. Hear, and decide! A few sentences by way of EPITAPH—a trifling remembrance to the memory of the late Muster Richardson :—

Praises on tombs are trifles vainly spent.

MAKEMONEY and Sprightly now made towards the fair with all the haste in their power; and after encountering a good deal of bustle and pushing against the holyday people in the streets, who all appeared to be in a great hurry, they arrived amongst the show folks :—

Behold the Fair!
Crowded to excess with smiling, joyous
Faces! And a glorious scene of noise,
Bustle, and confusion, from one end
Of it to the other! With ev'ry thing
To attract the eye, please the fancy, and
Amuse the mind! A complete picture of
A free people—rude independence to
The echo! Pushing and jostling along
With that prevailing spirit of freedom
Inherent in the breasts of Englishmen:
JACK with his JILL, and in thought of value
Equal to the richest man in the Fair!

Rank entirely out of the question!
Such are the feelings of Britons.   Hear the
Rival Clowns challenging each other for
A battle of brains! The loud laugh! Huzzas
Of the crowd at the quaint sayings—funny
Faces—and salt-box tricks of the old
Mountebanks.   Valk up! Valk up! The Players
Are here, by the King's permission, to
Amuse his kind, loving subjects, at this
Particular season of the year, and
No mistake! Come, my worthy Masters and
Mistresses, lose no time, if you wish to
See and hear the unknown conjuror
From the other side of the world, who
Can make every hair of your head as
Thick as a broomstick, by the touch of his
Magic wand—if you don't obey his call!
Hallo! Hallo! Here's the *larned*
Pig, who can tell more with his feet than all
The *Nobs* put together at the high-bred
Universities with their heads! Only
Come and see! Look out! Look out! Wonders will
Never cease! There never wos such times as
These are! Open your eyes, and pick your ears—
This is the booth that contains the only
Man Salamander in the world, who can
Whop the Fire King into shivers! He is
Employed by the Steam Navigation
For the next five hundred years—because his
Breath is hotter than any fiery
Furnace! He can propel six steam vessels
At once, by the movement of his tongue!
Come up here! Come up here! And see the horse
That can beat the celebrated TAGLIONI
For stepping out—and give that prime piece of
Furniture any thing she asks.   All the
Zoologicals are mad to get him : But
They won't! ' *Go-it-along* ' isn't to be had!
Here, my little boys and girls, come and take ·
A peep, and see what you can see ! You can't
Lay out a halfpenny better to improve
Your mind, and become acquainted with rich
Historical facts against you ' come out'
In life! Look and behold, on the left side
Of the picture, the weeping willow which
O'erhangs the tomb of the great Napoleon
At St. Helena! and then turn your eyes
To the right, and view the splendid
Monument in St. George's Chapel, Windsor,
Erected to the late Princess Charlotte,
Shewing you " to this complexion you
Must come at last!" Never mind such epitaphs—
Have a swing? Exercise is the thing for
Health—so, lose no time, but up you go! What
A pity it is, this Carnival lasts
Only for *three days!* A severe blow to
The FUNNIMENTS of LONDON—so full of
Whim, frolic, uproar, noise, row, mirth, and good
Humour! Well calculated to disperse
The ' *Blue* Devils,' and please mankind—at the
End of which it becomes like the baseless

Fabric of a vision—touch and go—
Until Time flies to give *another* Fair
A local habitation !

They had scarcely ascended the platform at Richardson's Theatre, when Flourish appeared close at their heels. "Well, my boy," said Makemoney, "I am glad to see you again, and may now assert, that we PILGRIMS are once more complete. I hope, Flourish, yon have had a pleasant afternoon of it—the company of the ladies truly felicitous—and that you have also parted with them pleasant and happy ? Protestations of love ! —friendship without interest ; and all that sort of thing, which hangs upon the lips of a man of fashion and gallantry, when bidding adieu, or taking farewell of ladies."

"Why, sir, that is not exactly the real state of the case," said Flourish, "I hope I shall never lose sight of true gallantry, or that kind of attention and politeness, which are at all times due to ladies. But you are quite aware that I should not have left your excellent company, and also that of your nephew, but I have the poet's excuse for it :—

When a lady's in the case,
All other things must give place !

Therefore, on the score of politeness, I strolled about the park with them for an hour or more ; when I took a most respectful leave of the Duchess and her two daughters ; but with no renewal of another meeting—no protestations of love—nor any thing else, that could induce them to suppose, that I was anxious to meet again ! No, no—I am not to be caught with *shadows*—fine clothes and outside show are " *trifles* light as air" with me, although, I must admit, their society was delightful ; and upon all the different topics of the day, they were truly eloquent—literature, music, the fine arts, fashion, &c. But Frank Flourish, however the term may be reproachful—is a more *calculating* sort of fellow ! ' He looks before he leaps !' "

"Bravo, Frank," observed Jem, "bad taste on your part was impossible ! and weakness of mind entirely out of the question ! Cold as ice !—Freezing point !—Love is madness !—Lunatics only are in love !—Ha ! ha ! I know, (winking his eye to his uncle,) you was the lad not to be had. Frank Flourish is too well read in the ways of the world, to be picked up as a flat !"

" Enough of this," replied Flourish, half nettled at the echo of his former advice. " Let us know how you have passed your time in my absence. I have no doubt but it was very *methodical ?*"

" *Methodical*, indeed! and let me tell you, Frank, there was nothing like *method* about it !" said Jem. " On the contrary, it was all gaiety, and the spur of the moment. ' *Kissing in the Ring,*' was one of the delightful movements on the turf ; but nevertheless, I could not persuade my uncle to enter into the pleasures of the game.

GREENWICH FAIR

P. Egan Jun.ᵈᵉˡ

" Then *dancing*, with the merriest group of young men and women I ever witnessed—no master of the ceremonies to control one's choice, and *etiquette* not known. A glass or two of wine, to exhilarate our spirits, laughing at all sorts of merriment which crossed our path—I own we were not dull a minute—all jollity and happiness, while my uncle took his grog, and cogitated pleasantly over his pipe.

" But I should have liked to have had your opinion of one of the loveliest females I ever saw in the course of my travels—that is to say, to my fancy! A perfect divinity!—an angel!—in truth, she was of so superior a *caste*, that I want words to describe her attractive appearance; and I do insist, the *Haidee* of Lord Byron did not surpass her in beauty; but I have lost sight of her for ever:—

> Round her she made an atmosphere of life,
> The very air seem'd lighter from her eyes,
> They were so soft and beautiful, and rife
> With all we can imagine of the skies,
> And pure as Psyche ere she grew a wife,
> Too pure even for the purest human ties;
> Her overpowering presence made you feel,
> It would not be IDOLATRY to KNEEL!"

" Stop, stop, my dear Jem, you must have been drinking—this is too *inflated*, for any thing like a rational being who walks abroad with his eyes wide open," observed Flourish; " there is no time to be lost—I must prescribe for you—therefore, *bleeding* without delay, is the first step that must be taken—salts, ice cream, cold baths, nay, every thing that is cold, must be administered—you are in a high fever—you will become dangerous, and must have a keeper, or else a strait-waistcoat, if something is not done to turn the course of your thoughts.

" I am positively alarmed for your *safety!*—Your brains must be in an uproar, and if a change does not take place, every hair on your head must come off! You, Jem Sprightly, the once decent, well-behaved, solid, discreet, envied, and to be *copied* young man! Impossible!—you are bewitched!"

" Hold, hold, I say, hold, Flourish!" urged Makemoney, " or else I shall think that you have been making too free with the bottle, if I may judge from your discourse; therefore, let us lose no more time on such nonsense—downright stuff! But listen to what I have got to propose to you both; the last ten minutes has been positively trifled away—so let us display something like common sense."

" Excuse me, sir," answered Frank, " I scorn to give you the slightest offence; but, I believe, you never had time to become acquainted with the '*tender passion!*' and that accounts for your remarks upon it; but, nevertheless, I am always ready to acquiesce in any thing you may propose—as I feel rather anxious to finish the day in a style worthy of jolly PILGRIMS!"

This conversation was interrupted by a man, dressed for the

M

purpose, on the platform of Richardson's Show, haranguing the
mob outside, and throwing bills amongst them :—" Look this
way—look here—and behold the classical ground of the Fair—
and leave the shows of the wild beasts for the enjoyment of the
Chaw-bacons! the Yokels! the Clod-hoppers! the Johnny
Raws! and the Know-nothings! 'Tis here we have a splendid
treat for the men of sense—we are patronised by the House of
Peers, for our elegance of appearance and style ; and supported
by the Members of Parliament, for our good diction and elocu-
tion! Only ask them! when they will report progress, and tell
you, by their Speaker, that half an hour spent under our roof is
worth more than six months' ease, lolling on a sofa, and devoured by *ennui!* We are not the growth of a day! I beg you
will take into your consideration, in the first instance, we
are the descendants of the great Roscius, almost as long ago
when Adam was a little boy: in addition to which, let me refresh your memories, that we are likewise related to the great
Shakspeare, who lived in the reign of Queen Elizabeth, and who
was hand and glove with our immortal bard : also with
the Congreves—the Otways—the Cibbers—Ben Jonson—Beaumont and Fletcher—down to more modern times ; when the
illustrious Brinsley Sheridan flourished with his brilliant pen, for
the amusement of society—succeeded by the inimitable Sheridan
Knowles, of the present day. We rise with the lark, and
every minute of our time is devoted to study, in order to please
and gratify the public. Then, I say,—Walk-up, walk up,
walk-up, ladies and gentlemen !—The players—the players are
here, and no mistake ; we are not mountebanks ! No, nor fellows
with cups and balls, to cheat your eyes and pick your pockets.
Ours is the legitimate drama !—tragedy, comedy, opera, melo-
drame, farce, song, dance, &c.

" It is our *forte* to interest the mind—please the fancy—raise
the spirits—and drive ' DULL CARE ' to his hiding place : therefore, we can enact ' Othello,' for those persons who prefer Tragedy ; and ' John Bull,' for the Comedy folks ; ' Love in a
Village,' for the Opera customers ; the ' Tower of Nesle,' for
excitement and melo-dramatic minds ; ' High Life below Stairs,'
for the lovers of Farce ; the ' Twopenny Postman,' for the admirers of comic singing ; *Pantomime,* for the young folks—the
juvenile part of the audience, who like to witness the capers
and agility of Harlequin, the graceful attitudes of Columbine,
and the fun and humour produced by the grimaces of the Pantaloon and Clown ; and for the TAGLIONI's—the followers of
Terpsichore—we can give them *sixteen,* and then dance all the
breath out of their bodies afterwards!

" I should like to know what we can't do ! ' Why, we can
draw,' as Shakspeare says, ' spirits from the vasty deep!' I
call your attention only to *look* at the company—view them as
they pass up and down the parade ; and, independant of their

manly forms and exquisite shapes, you will perceive talent strongly developed in all their countenances—persons of immense abilities—men of superior mind—and females of intellect and character—none of your slip-slop sort of the sex, who can only make *tea* and *coffee ;* but females that might challenge the collection of beauties at Windsor Castle—not for that distinguished trait alone : no—I say no—as we are all aware that beauty is but skin-deep !

" But do not take my word. Come in to the Theatre, and see them perform, and then you will be able to judge for yourselves. Our manager is an *old stager* in the service of the public, and he has got at his fingers' ends a due knowledge of taste, so as to be able to please all palates. We can either extort the sympathetic tear, or produce roars of laughter ; and, as a test of the excellence of the company, the applause which has been bestowed upon their exertions has repeatedly shook the walls of the Theatre ; but we don't mind trifles—we live upon applause —it is our delight and support—nay, more, it is meat, drink, washing, and lodging, to us, who are patronized by the public.

" I state thus much only to point out to you, ladies and gentlemen, what ' *great creatures* ' belong to our stage ! and bear in mind our liberality, that we charge you nothing for *looking* at them as they pass in review, on the good old principle, of ' taste before you buy ! '

" Drury Lane Theatre, I admit, is a much larger place of amusement, but we are *multum in parvo ;* that is to say, my worthy masters and mistresses, who do not understand University learning, means, ' much in little.' Here you can see and hear without the aid of magnifying glasses : ours is the true school for performers—deny it who dare. The greatest actor on the English stage was brought out by *Muster* Richardson—think of that, ladies and gentlemen—and also remember there is only ONE *Muster* Richardson in the dramatic line ; therefore, what is due to *Muster* Richardson, render unto Muster Richardson.

" Our wardrobe is superior, in point of real value, to any of the Theatres ; and our scenery will bear the strictest scrutiny for excellence ; the greatest painters of the day having been engaged to give it beauty and effect. And if the specimen which I have given to you, in rearing one of the greatest actors on the stage, is not enough to convince you of our superiority of talent, I will open all the doors and let you in *gratis*—which means, nothing !

" Then do not lose your valuable time ; let me impress upon you not to be too late, if you wish to procure good seats, and to have your minds enlightened. So I repeat—' Walk up ! walk up, ladies and gentlemen : the players—the players are here ! Allow me, sir (to Makemoney) the honor of presenting you with a bill of the performances, in which you will find chapter and verse for all that I have asserted—besides the prices of admission, the names and characters of the performers, &c. &c. ; and I flatter myself we shall have your generous patronage :—

A CHANGE OF PERFORMANCE EACH DAY.

RICHARDSON'S THEATRE.

This day will be presented a New Grand Melo-Drama, with New Scenery, Dresses, Properties, &c., entitled The

MURDERER'S BRIDE;

OR, THE HOUR OF TRIAL.

Appius Claudius (a Decemvir) Mr. COOPER.
Lucius Julious (Nephew of Appius, in love with Virginia), Mr. SMITH.
Siccius Dentatus (Father of Virginia), Mr. GROVE.
Publius (a Roman Officer), Mr. LEWIS.
Officers, Guards, Banner Bearers, &c. &c.
Virginia   (Betrothed to Julious)   -   Mrs. SMITH.
Spectre of the Murdered Lucretia, Miss WALTON.

In the course of the Piece,
A Variety of Splendid Scenery by the First Artists.
The Piece concludes with the

DISCOVERY OF THE REAL ASSASSIN, AND THE DEATH OF APPIUS CLAUDIUS.

The Entertainments to conclude with a new Comic Harlequinade, with new Scenery, Tricks, Dresses, and Decorations, called

HARLEQUIN FAUSTUS !

OR, THE DEVIL WILL HAVE HIS OWN.

Luciferno, Mr. THOMAS.
Dæmon Amonzor, afterwards Pantaloon, Mr. WILKINSON.
Dæmon Ziokos, after Clown, Mr. HAYWARD.
Violoncello Player, Mr. Hartem.   Baker, Mr. Thompson.
Landlord, Mr. Wilkins. Fisherman, Mr. Rae.
Doctor Faustus - (afterwards Harlequin) - Mr. SALTER.
Adelada (afterwards Columbine), Miss WILMOT.
Attendant Dæmons, Sprites, Fairies, Ballad Singers, Flower Girls, &c. &c. &c.

The Pantomime will finish with

A SPLENDID PANORAMA,

Painted by the first Artists.

Boxes, 2s. Pit, 1s. Gallery, 6d. [Romney, Printer, Lambeth.

" Who can refuse to witness the performance of the above veteran's company of comedians," said Makemoney, " after such an eloquent appeal to the lovers of theatrical amusement ?—so let us go in and take our seats."

" Do you think there is any truth in what that fellow has asserted about a late distinguished actor ? " observed Flourish ; " or is it what they term *gag*, done with the intent to humbug the people at the Fair. He has certainly got the gift of speech. I do not think any of T. P. Cooke's ' *yarns*,' as they are called, were ever better spun out. I never heard a fellow lay it on so thick—he would almost make you believe the moon was made of green cheese ; yet he seemed to please the crowd, who not only laughed heartily at his remarks, but loudly applauded his exertion."

" Although the speech seems to be spontaneous, and a sort of extempore oration," replied Makemoney, " yet he is well *studied* in it ; and he repeats it perhaps fifty times a day without deviating a single word. It is a complete piece of *mechanism ;* but then the great art of *delivering* it *is,* to give it the appearance of reality emanating from the ebullition of the moment. The man was certainly correct about that great actor once being a member of Richardson's Company. Although such speeches are generally full of romance, yet they are not destitute of humour and talent, and I never thought my time lost in listening to them."

" Well, then," said Sprightly, " let us go in and have a taste of their quality ; we can easily leave the Theatre if we disapprove of the performances. Besides, I am very partial to a comic song."

Makemoney, Flourish, and Jem, were liberal with their applause, and were highly delighted with the following comic chant, called " The Strolling Ballad-Singer turned Manager."

> My history should you like to know,
> I'll tell it off like criss-cross row—
> A *chanter* once ! it was my fate,
> But now I'm like a man of state,
>   For I've got a snug theatre !
> Of various booths I'm now *Lessee,*
> The *blunt* is down—I've paid the fee—
> Oh ! I tipt it to them all in *screens,*
> Or else I couldn't get the scenes,—
>   O to make a pretty feature :
>   So now, Mr. Chant,
>   Is become quite gallant—
> And known as a " Great Creature," &c.

[SPOKEN.] Enter Mr. Multum-in-parvo ! so he is called by my first author—meaning, to do every thing in no time at all. I believe it is from the *Greek*—but we will not stand upon trifles ! He has got COMEDY on one side of his face, and TRAGEDY on the other ; and MELLOW-DRAM in his stomach ! His *stomach* is prodigious ! You are fond of a dram, an't you *Multum ?* [MULTUM. Yes, most noble Don, it gives *spirits* to my *hacting !*] He has got *Uproar* in his belly ; no, no, *Comic Opera*, I mean, and *Pantomime* in his legs. He is engaged to *laugh,* or *cry* according to my orders. He can *laugh* for a fortnight, without being out of breath! and *cry* for a month without shedding a tear. The whole mob of Rosciusses put together—male and female, are not a *patch* against my Multum. The great theatres have offered more cash for him than would fill the Bank of England to get him from me; but Multum is engaged to me during his whole natural life, and a day after it; but all their tricks won't do at any price—he is above *Price*—and he shan't go at no price! When the weather is dull, and customers wanting at my theatre, why, I make him laugh the whole of the day, and when the sun shines, then he cries by way of contrast, to shew the spectators his talents; which makes the people outside laugh, and makes me laugh because we pull them in.

So now you see, Mr. Chant,
Is become quite gallant,
And known as " a Great Creature !"

Yes, Authors now pay me great court,
The newspapers do *me* report!
Such lots of actors—a *precious bore*,
And *musicians* by the score!
Bow-ing at *my* theatre!
With Harlequins and Pantaloons,
And mobs of girls " come, buy my brooms!"
Tight rope dancers—and *all* " The Graces !"
The public jostling for *good* places!
O 'tis such a pretty feature!
So now you see, &c.

[Spoken]. *Good* Places! To be sure I can! No Prime Minister in the world has got so many Places as I have to bestow upon you. Only come in—I will give you all *good places*, and change them every half hour, if you like it so best. I'll do every thing to make the *wisit* pleasant! Besides, you will have the advantage of listening to the unheard of capabilities of Mr. Multum. He can *parley woo* to the people at Calais, while he holds a conversation with the country folks at Dover! His lungs are superior to an *India Rubber* Manufactory for *stretching*; he has offered to bet a week's salary that he gives orders to any of his Majesty's ships in the most distant part of the globe, at the same moment he is taking his instructions from the Lords of the Admiralty. His terms are now under the consideration of the Board of Red Cloth. He can *talk* all the Barristers to a *stand still*, or else he would be of no use.

So now you see, Mr. Chant,
Is become quite gallant,
And known as " a Great Creature !"

" Could you have killed time in a better or more pleasing manner for half an hour," said Makemoney, after leaving the Theatre. " I know there are many persons who treat with the most sovereign contempt such performances: however, I am not one of that number. Richardson, as a showman, has been before the public for forty years, and with great success."

" Killed time, my dear sir," replied his nephew; " I think you are in error, when you call it killing time! I did not expect to see a Kean or a Macready; but, nevertheless, abating a little too much *rant*, I was not so blind to merit but I could perceive talents, abilities, and an anxiety to please; and if we may judge as a criterion from the applause which were bestowed on their exertions, I should say the audience were gratified. I hate any thing in the shape of *hyper-criticism*."

" Indeed, *fastidious* as I am termed, and generally considered to find too much fault with every thing," answered Flourish, " I

must confess, the scenery, &c., and viewed as a whole performance, was far better than I could have anticipated; and, in
truth, I had not the slightest idea that the thing was half so
complete as it is. But it must be extremely fatiguing for the
actors to perform so many times a day—thirteen or fourteen, at
the least, I have been told—I cannot think how they stand it."

" I am glad to find that you have still a spark of liberality
left in your composition. The life of a travelling showman," said
Makemoney, " must have been full of adventures, and I feel assured, if it could be related, would afford a fund of amusement."

Since the above circumstances occurred, Muster Richardson
has ceased to exist; and the author trusts that the anecdotes,
incidents, &c., connected with the career of the above eccentric
showman, will not be viewed in the shape of a digression; but,
on the contrary, quite connected with the object of the PILGRIMS
of the THAMES in SEARCH of the NATIONAL!

Scarcely had the celebrated GEORGE COLMAN, whose " Broad
Grins " so often set the table in a roar, been summoned to
" that bourne from whence no traveller returns; " and the inimitable JACK BANNISTER, who, for upwards of half a century,
had sent thousands of his Majesty's loving subjects laughing
heartily to their beds, made his final exit from the *stage* of
life—when *Muster* John Richardson also received a notice to
quit—thus followed in rapid succession three men, in the
short space of a few days, who had done the Theatrical World
" some service, and they know it."

> Death! great proprietor of all! 'tis thine
> To tread out empire, and to quench the stars:
> The sun himself by thy permission shines;
> And one day thou shalt pluck him from his sphere.

Mr. D'Israeli, a celebrated writer, and a great observer of
the lives and actions of men, thus sets *his* value upon mankind:
—" We have before us," said he, " a list of nearly three hundred
persons who had attained a great age, in no instance less than
one hundred, men and women in all parts of the united kingdom, during the term of years beginning with 1807 and ending
in 1823, both included, and we cannot discover throughout the
whole catalogue a SINGLE NAME that had linked itself with
an *expression* or a DEED worthy to be remembered for *an*
HOUR!!!"

Such a *reflection* as the above cannot be levelled against the
character of the late *Muster* Richardson, whose whole life was
quite a history of " Sayings and Doings " to the end of the chapter; in truth, *his* life was full of bustle, incident, and situation;
and when public amusements were the theme of discourse,
scarcely a little boy or girl in the Metropolis, or elsewhere, but
remembered the name of RICHARDSON, the Showman! with
pleasure; and perhaps, now, with regret!

During the late Deptford Fair (Monday, May 30, 1836), the

writer of this article called on *Muster* Richardson, his usual custom, if he happened to be in the vicinity of any of the Fairs, to see if any thing like *Novelty* occurred : when the showman complained severely about the reduction of prices ; and he observed, with a *sneer*, that when a Patent Theatre admitted persons at a tizzy per head, the poor mummer could not be found fault with for opening his doors to the public for *browns*. Richardson had never before taken less than *sixpence* each during his career. "But nevertheless, Muster," said he, "so help me ——, it is too bad ; my expences are just the same ; and, do what I will, I cannot keep pace with my opponents. Only look at Lee's company of performers—and they are clever folks too—within one or two booths of mine, who amuse their visitors for one penny ' a *nob* ;' and who are carrying all before them. Theatricals are going fast to the dogs ; and it is high time I should have done with them."

Amidst other conversation with myself and Mr. Johnston, his money-taker, he said, "I think, *Muster* Pierce Egan, I have lived long enough to tell the world *how* I have bustled my way through it ; you have known me for many years—are up to a thing or two with your pen—and, with my assistance, you could inform the public *summut* about my Travels, Life, and History, that might amuse them (little anticipating at that period he was so near his end)—I wish to appear grateful for the patronage I have received ; and, although I am nothing more than a humble showman, I have been respected and well treated by all classes of society, in every part of the kingdom ; and wherever I have pitched my tent *once*, I have been repeatedly sent for to come again."

"Your request shall be complied with," I replied ; "and, as far as an allowance can be made for the infirmities of human nature, it shall be written after the sterling adage of *Shakspeare* —' nothing to extenuate, or set down aught in malice !' "

He then briefly related several anecdotes (whilst he was handling the coppers for admission) at which he laughed very heartily, and said, "When you have a leisure hour or two, call on me at Woodland Cottage, and I will tell you every movement of my life." We then parted. In about four months afterwards the call was made at Woodland Cottage, according to agreement, when Muster Richardson opened his *Budget*, and related the principal features of his career. But, on the writer calling again on Muster Richardson, merely to inform him that he had committed all the anecdotes to paper, on the door being opened, he was informed that Muster Richardson had departed this life at seven o'clock *that* morning : but, through the kindness of Mr. Johnston, every particular has been obtained which occurred since, and the writer of the RECOLLECTIONS *of the late* MUSTER RICHARDSON has the satisfaction to be enabled to pledge himself for their AUTHENTICITY !

THE LATE MUSTER RICHARDSON,

THE ECCENTRIC SHOWMAN.

To use his own words, which were a "round unvarnished tale," his first recollection of himself was that of a poor little urchin, the very climax of poverty, in the workhouse of Great Marlow, in Buckinghamshire, the place of his birth. After filling several menial situations in the above town, he started for the metropolis, in order to better his fortune, and gained employment, where he remained for some time, in the cow-house of Mr. Rhodes, at Islington, at one shilling per day. Soon after which period he had acquired some taste for theatricals; and in the year 1782 he first engaged in the theatrical line; or, to use the cant of the stage, "smelt the lamp," and joined Mrs. Penley, who was then performing in a club-room, at the Paviour's Arms, in Shadwell, near Wapping. The pieces were *Chrononhoton-thologos* and *Midas* (the taste of the town at that time), and required several actors; but Mrs. Penley *contrived* to get it up with two men and two women. The receipts generally were from four to five shillings per night. Starvation was almost the order of the day; and, after going from town to town in the country with little better success, he left the stage for a short period, and commenced, in a small way, as a broker in London. His shop turned out lucky, and by industry he accumulated money enough to take the Harlequin in 1796, near the stage-door of Drury Lane Theatre. The Harlequin was frequented by theatrical people—old Mr. Greenwood, the scene-painter, Mr. Banks, old Mr. Russell, the facetious Tony Le Brun, &c.—but getting tired of keeping a public-house, he left the Harlequin, and made up his mind to attend the fairs. He engaged a company to go with him; and young Tom Greenwood and Mr. Banks painted his first set of scenes.

In the above year, *Muster* Richardson first made his appearance in the character of a showman at Bartholomew Fair, where he had to contend with the old favourites of the public. Old Jobson, the great puppet-showman, in one yard; Jonas and Penley (the families of which have both distinguished themselves in the history of the stage), in the George-yard; the celebrated Mrs. Baker, at the Greyhound, in a room up one pair of stairs; O'Brien, the Irish giant, at the King's Head; Sieur Rea, the great conjuror; and also in a one pair of stairs, Richardson and his company exhibited: his platform was built out of the one pair of stairs window, forming an arch over the ginger-bread stalls, with a long pair of steps leading down into the fair. *Twenty-one times* in the day were the performers called upon to act. Richardson's band was selected out of the streets, which consisted of three blind Scotchmen, but noted as clarionet players. The pieces were not very good, and each audience did not fail to abuse the actors as they left the house. Poor old Mrs. Monk generally got upon the stairs to cool herself; and, as the spectators had to pass her on going out, she was generally saluted with many "*damns!*" and "You old b——, you have taken us in!" Mrs. Monk was a good-natured creature, and her only reply was, "What can you expect at a fair?" Upon the whole, the performances passed off tolerably quiet.

Bartholomew Fair then was more distinguished for slack-wire performances, tight-rope, tumblers, dancing-dogs, Punch and Judy, &c., and *meagre* in the extreme, compared with the present day.

Muster Richardson now made the regular tour to most of the large fairs in the kingdom—at Edmonton he appeared with Tom Jefferies, a clown from Astley's, who, in his line, had no competitor; and was allowed by the best judges of *fools* to be without a rival. He had a *lingo* of his own, and his tricks and conversation were so irresistibly comic, that he had the character of "pulling them in" better than any other character.

Shortly after the above period, Mrs. *Carey*, and her two sons, Edmund and Henry, were engaged by Richardson. Edmund (since the celebrated Kean) made his first appearance in *Tom Thumb*, and his mother acted the Queen Dollalolla. At Windsor Fair Edmund again performed *Tom Thumb*; when, to the great astonishment of Muster Richardson, he received a note from the Castle, *commanding* Master Carey to recite several passages from different plays before his Majesty, King George the Third, at the Palace. Richardson was highly gratified at the receipt of the above note, but he was equally perplexed how to comply with the commands of the King. The letter came late on Saturday night; and, as the wardrobe of Master Carey was rather scanty, it was necessary to add to it before he could appear in the presence of royalty. The purse of Richardson was nearly empty; and, to increase his dilemma, all the shops belonging to the Jews were shut, and the only chance left was their being open on the Sunday morning. Among the Jews, Muster Richardson purchased a smart little jacket and trousers, and body linen, and the Manager tied the collar of his shirt through the button-holes with a piece of black ribbon; and, when dressed in his new apparel, Master Carey appeared a smart little fellow.

The King was much pleased with the performance of Edmund, and so were his nobles. Two hours were occupied in his recitations; and he was pronounced an astonishing boy, and a lad of great promise; but the present he received for his performance was rather small, being only two guineas; though, upon the whole, it turned out fortunate for the family. The principal conversation in Windsor for a few days at that time was about the talents displayed by Master Carey before the King; his mother, therefore, took advantage of this circumstance, and immediately engaged the market hall for three nights for recitations for *Edmund*. This was an excellent speculation; the Hall overflowed with company every night. Mrs. Carey joined Richardson on the following Monday at Ewell

Fair; and all the family, owing to their great success, came so nicely dressed, that the Manager scarcely knew them. Mrs. Carey and her children did not quit his standard during the summer.

"In addition to my company," says Richardson, "the next year Mr. Saville Faucit, now Manager of the Margate Theatre, and Mr. Grosette, joined us at Stepney Fair. The latter was a lazy, dirty fellow; and I was compelled to discharge him on account of the want of clean linen. But he played me a trick for it. In the course of the same week, Grosette came and told me he had got a change of dress, and expressed a wish that I should re-engage him. I did so, in consequence of his appearance being improved, and his linen quite clean; but in a few days I found out that Mr. Grosette had made free with my little wardrobe, and dressed himself in one of my shirts, stockings, and neckerchief. He remained with me two or three seasons; after which he distinguished himself as a performer of considerable merit both in the Norwich and Bath companies.

"We left Stepney for Cambridge, and opened our booth at Stourbridge fair; at which place I lost all my money, and experienced great distress. Owing to my refusal to pay taxes upon the ground, I was taken into custody, and should have been committed with my company, had it not have been for the interference of old Mr. Brunton. This veteran of the stage had also a company at Stourbridge fair at the same time. I found out that the magistrates could not commit me, without also sending to prison Mr. Brunton and his actors. The University law is not to suffer any theatre to be opened within a specified number of miles of Cambridge; therefore, the University was liable to lose a part of their privileges by suffering us to perform. Our audiences were so trifling in number, that I was completely ruined; and old Mr. Brunton, witnessing our distress, generously made me a present of five guineas; which feeling disposition I shall always remember with the highest sense of gratitude. At this unfortunate fair to me, all my horses, excepting three, were drowned by the flood; and having no more money than Mr. Brunton's present of five guineas, it was soon exhausted among so many persons. *How* to get to London was the question. At last, I made up my mind to leave two of my waggons in pledge at a public-house yard, and with my three horses proceed with my company to town in the caravan. But to raise the money for the purpose was the difficulty. The landlord of the public-house entertained so bad an opinion of players, that instead of advancing a shilling upon the waggons left in his possession, he demanded a certain sum to be paid per week, for their standing in his yard. I therefore agreed with my clown, Tom Jefferies, who could sing a good low-comedy song, Mr. Brown, a musician, and myself, to *busk* our way up to London. Jefferies was to sing, and Brown and myself to go round with the hat. The plan being settled, we started off without any money in our pockets; but previous to which we bundled the rest of the company, consisting of women and children, into the caravan. We minstrels generally kept two miles before the caravan, and laid siege to every public-house upon the road. Our success was much better than we expected. Tom Jefferies hit upon a song, called ' *Tidi didi tol lol lol, kiss and ti-ti-lara,*' which had a great run at Astley's riding-school. To add to the effect of the above song, Jefferies squinted, which caused much fun and laughter amongst the country folks, and I was not behind hand with my hat in collecting subscriptions. As fast as we got the money we purchased tea, sugar, and other necessaries, and supplied the persons in the caravan; we lived together very well, but we reserved sufficient cash to buy corn for the horses, &c. On my arrival in London, I found a friend, who advanced me a sufficient sum of money to redeem my waggons left with the publican; but, nevertheless, I was still unfortunate. The man that I sent for the waggons, turned out a rascal: he decamped with my cash, taking the horses and harness with him, and from that period to the present hour, I have never heard any thing concerning his flight. I applied again to my friend for assistance—he really was a friend in need, and advanced me money enough to get my waggons once more into my own possession.

" After a short period I again got my company together, and with hired horses, I went to Waltham Abbey. I took a small theatre in that town, the rent of which I paid---fifteen shillings per week. It was all the money too much. My company I considered very strong, consisting of Mr. Vaughan, Mr. Thwaites, Master *Edmund*, his mother, and the whole of the family, Mr. Saville Faucit, Mr. Grosette, Mr. and Mrs. Jefferies, Mr. Reed, Mrs. Wells, and several other performers, who have since been engaged at several of the principal theatres in the kingdom. Notwithstanding we acted the most popular pieces, the night produced only *nine shillings and sixpence.* Starvation stared us in the face, and our situation was so truly pitiable, that the magistrates of the town, out of compassion to our misfortunes, ' *bespoke a night!*' The feeling conduct of the justices of the peace, put us all in high spirits; and every bench and every corner was measured to ascertain what the house would hold, which, upon a fair calculation, we found would produce seven pounds. Under the expectation of receiving this seven pounds, every chandler's, butcher's, and baker's shop was tried, with a promise of payment on Monday night. A rehearsal was called on Sunday morning; but those actors who were so fortunate as to have obtained a dinner upon credit, forgot their parts, in the anticipation of realizing a hearty meal, an *unusual thing* in the company. Mr. Vaughan, who played my first line of business, was obliged to go to London on some pressing occasion, started at five o'clock on the Sunday morning, with a solemn promise to be back in time for the rehearsal the next day ; but he had scarcely departed, when the landlord of the public-house where he lodged, came during the rehearsal and enquired for him. He was told that Vaughan had gone to London. ' Yes,' replied he, ' and he has stolen twelve pair of my ducks.' Thinking of the magistrates bespeak, and the seven pounds, it operated on my feelings like a *lock*-jaw for the instant, and I could not give the man any answer. However, on recovering my speech, I asked the landlord *how* any single man could take away twelve pair of ducks? But he was irritated, and would not hear a word I had to urge in the defence of Vaughan. I, at last, prevailed upon the landlord to keep silent until the next morning, as Vaughan had promised to return without fail by twelve o'clock. On the departure of the landlord, I went to the company, who were at rehearsal, and made them acquainted with the charge of the publican, at the same time, begging one of them to study the part, as I made sure Vaughan had got the ducks. On Monday morning, about eleven o'clock, while the company were at rehearsal, Vaughan, to my surprise, made his appearance. I was very glad to see him. He said he should have been down at Waltham Abbey much sooner, but that he had dined out with a friend, and had a beautiful dinner. I, of course, asked him what were the dishes? His reply was ' Ducks and green peas !' ' Then, by Heaven !' I exclaimed, ' you had the man's twelve pair of ducks.' Vaughan inquired what I meant ; but during the time the story was being told to him, the landlord of the public-house entered, and, calling me on one side, said he hoped that I had not told the young man about the ducks. He was sorry for what he had said, as it since appeared the ducks had gone down with the mill-stream to a farm some two miles off, when Mr. Vaughan left for London, and had likewise returned about the same time as his lodger. Upon the whole the story of the ducks was a fortunate thing for Vaughan, as the landlord of the public-house, to prevent an action for defamation, fed and lodged Vaughan, free of expence, during the remainder of his stay in the town. The magistrates ' *bespeak*,' produced an excellent house ; we divided the receipts, and paid all the money we could amongst the tradesmen who had given us credit.

 "On quitting Waltham Abbey we made our route to be in time for the opening of the Paddington Canal, and erected our booth. By the time of the company's landing we opened, and had an excellent night, the receipts of which put me upon my legs, and I retired for the winter. During the vacation I looked out for new performers, and visited the private theatres. Amongst them MINTON'S, in Queen Anne Street east, claimed my attention. The play was Richard the Third, the part of the

Duke of Gloucester, by Mr. Oxberry. I knew his uncle, and himself, previous to that period ; therefore, I had an immediate interview with Oxberry without any hesitation. The latter performer wished to travel, and I engaged him for the ensuing summer. Oxberry joined my company at Easter, and remained with me for two seasons. At that time a young woman of the name of *Bass*, belonged to us, and in our journey to Ascot races, we stopped to bait our horses at the Swan, Staines Bridge. We were immediately recognized by the watermen, who good naturedly lent the company their boats to take a small excursion on the Thames. *Nine* of the actors got into one of the boats, and amongst them *Billy* Oxberry; in the middle of the river it upset, and the whole of them had a sousing, nay, went to the bottom ! The whole town hearing of the circumstance, rushed to afford them assistance, and with very great difficulty the nine performers were rescued from a watery grave. But Billy Oxberry had the narrowest escape of any of them, owing to Miss Bass rising at the same time with Billy. In going down a second time, Miss Bass caught hold of Oxberry's coat, which had nearly drowned them both ; but by the perseverance and struggling of Oxberry, and prompt assistance being afforded him, they were both preserved to laugh at the incident. The most ludicrous part of this unlucky circumstance was, that not one of them had a change of clothes: they therefore all scrambled into the caravan, took off their wet apparel, and hung them out of the caravan to dry. Oxberry was the most unfortunate of the party : his breeches were made of buckskin, and fitted so tight to his limbs, that it was with the utmost difficulty they could be got off ; and the leather taking a long time to dry, Billy was compelled to walk about Ascot race-course with a full pair of Turkish trowsers.

"About this time, I engaged Mr. Abraham Slader, and Mr. Rose, both of whom, in a few years afterwards, became men of celebrity at Astley's and the Surrey theatres. The former was distinguished for his singing the beautiful ballad of ' Sweet Kitty of the Clyde !' Also, a Mrs. Fitzgerald, who, on leaving my company in the course of a few years, was the *manageress* of the York Circuit ; likewise, Miss Fanny Welding, belonging to Astleys, but afterwards, as Mrs. Pearce, of Covent Garden Theatre. In the course of the year I went to Twickenham Fair ; and Messrs. Copeland and Russell's company were then performing at the Theatre, Richmond. I made up my mind to have *one* private night after the fair was over, and I announced the public performance of *Douglas*, and the *Miller of Mansfield*, Young Norval, by Mr. Saville Faucit. Directly our bills had been circulated in the morning, it was a usual thing on my part, on the day after the fair, to give all the company a treat at Twickenham Ait, with as many eel pies as they could eat, and as much ale as they could drink. We were all very comfortable and merry, and the performers did not want any persuasion to play their different characters with spirit. But in the midst of our happiness, to my astonishment, I received a note from the managers of the Richmond Theatre, with information that it was a benefit that night, at their house, and if I attempted to perform, they would apply to a magistrate, and have myself, and the whole of the company taken into custody. I laughed at this threat; and being quite warm with ale, I returned an answer, with my compliments, that if I was taken up, it should be by the authority of a magistrate, and not by *two vagrants*—like myself.

" Mrs. JORDAN, at that time, lived on Twickenham Common. I went immediately to that justly celebrated actress, and put the letter of the Richmond managers into her hand. Mrs. Jordan said, she could scarcely think they would have been guilty of such an act of meanness; but she knew it was their handwriting. Mrs. Jordan desired me to return to my company, and perform without any fear of their threats: that she would endeavour to make me up a party, or at least, if she could not come herself she would send her children. This most excellent actress and worthy woman kept her word. The next morning the above managers did me another favor, by engaging *Saville Faucit ;* but the latter actor would not consent to quit my service immediately, according to their wishes, but remained in my company till the season closed.

" My next tour was to St. Alban's Fair, where I met with very great encouragement ; and, year after year, my gratitude compels me to think that I have met with some cheerful patronage from the inhabitants and corporation of St. Alban's."

To shew the vicissitudes of the stage, Muster Richardson often observed that superior talents ultimately will be recognised by the public. At Easter, in 1806, at Battersea Fair, the magistrates gave him permission to perform whole pieces for two nights afterwards. He was short of hands, when Edmund Kean applied for an engagement ; and the first night he acted Young Norval ; and on the second Motley, in the Castle Spectre ; and for which the Manager paid him a crown per night ; which sum, however trifling, he thankfully received : " and I am happy to say that his splendid talents have, since that period, not only saved one of the Theatres Royal from ruin, but he has received one hundred pounds per night for his exertions. This was the last time Edmund played for me ; though the rest of his family remained some months afterwards in my company."

A fellow once called on Muster Richardson at Woodland Cottage, during one of his vacations ; who was ragged as a colt, and as dirty as a sweep. On being asked what he wanted, he answered, he was out of an engagement !

" *Engagement !* " echoed Richardson, surveying him from top to toe.

" Yes, I want an engagement. You need not stare so—I am a man of talent ; though perhaps I don't look such ! But you, Governor, are too good a judge to take a man by his *looks !* "

" If I did," said Richardson, " you would not get one. But what can you do ? "

" Do ! any thing—every thing. I can stand upon my head—deliver a message—sing a comic song—dance a hornpipe—*slang* the mob. I can light the lamps—put them out—take care of the wardrobe—act as call-boy ; in short, I am for general *utility ;* and, upon a *pinch,* I can take the money."

" The latter qualification is out of the question ; therefore, we'll *bar* that—*pinching* won't do for me—it is no go in my establishment. I play the first fiddle on that ere suit, muster, myself : no, no, I don't want to make a rogue of you. But where did you come from ? "

" Come from !" answered the fellow ; " all over the kingdom ! I have been *starring* it ! "

" What !—Ha ! ha ! ha !—*starring* it."

" Don't laugh, master. Its true, so help me Bob. I have been starring with a Pig ! whom I taught his letters, and other subjects ; but I bothered his upper works so much that he became *light*-headed."

" Light-headed ! Ha ! ha ! ha ! A pig *light*-headed ! "

" Yes ! He took his *larning* so fast that it turned his brains, and the pig became as mad as a March-hare."

" You astonish me. I have seen and heard a good deal," observed Muster Richardson ; " but this is a new caper—to make a *hanimal* light in his upper story ! Well—go on."

" Astonished, I believe ye ! I could scarcely believe my own eyes ; but, nevertheless, it was true. I took the pig to one of our first *insane* doctors ; but as my *larned* friend, the *Pig,* could not explain the nature of his complaint, the mad physiciner said he could do nothing for him—that it was a new case altogether ; but he would consult the College of Physicians on the subject—at the same time, handing out his morley for the fee."

" Ha ! ha ! ha ! An't you coming it a little too strong ? " said Richardson ; " but no matter—how did you proceed then?"

" Proceed ! I could not proceed at all—my splendid grunter made his exit—and that *floored* me ! For some time I was *insane* myself—all the *blunt* vanished—my toggery all spouted—and I am now anxious for a new start—another *move* on the board ! And as I have not to learn, Muster Richardson, but you have got your head *screwed* on the right way, I have got something more under my hat than you think for. Therefore, you will find me not a bad card—tractable, and worthy of your patronage."

" Well, come in, muster," said the wily showman ; " but first try the effect of soap and water, and look like a man ; and then I'll see if I can find some new rigging from my wardrobe to put you once more upon your pins." This man afterwards proved a valuable acquisition to Muster Richardson, who observed, when speaking of the "*pig starrer!*" that he was a prime make-shift cove, and never grumbled to try to do what he was set about; and that men are not to be taken by their *looks!*

In the zenith of Kean's fame, when his name resounded from one part of the kingdom to the other, as one of the greatest actors ever seen in this country, it is due to his character to state that he called to see his old manager several times in Bartholomew Fair; offering his hand to him with that strong sense and good feeling which elevates the *prosperous* man still higher in the estimation of his friends, and shewing that his recollection of old times and former circumstances had not escaped his memory. Also, when Mr. Kean was the Manager of the Richmond Theatre, he felt it no degradation to write a letter to *Muster* Richardson, requiring, for a short time, the loan of some of his wardrobe!

Muster Richardson arriving from the country one night, several years since, in a hurry, slept in a double-bedded room at one of the coffee-houses under the Piazza in Covent Garden. Early in the morning, before day-light, the person who slept in the bed next to the showman, and whom he had not seen, got up, and took with him the sheets off the bed, and some other portable articles, unperceived. During the time Richardson was at breakfast in the coffee-room, the chamber-maid informed her master of the robbery which had been committed in the house. The latter, without hesitation, challenged Richardson with the theft; and also threatened to send to Bow-street for an officer. In vain Muster Richardson protested against the charge, and declared his innocence, accompanied with an oath; and, at the same time, observed, that if he was taken to the public-office it might ruin his character. "*I am RICHARDSON, the Showman!*" said he.

"Then," said the master, full of anger, "the fellow that's bolted with my sheets is a pal of yours; and if you do not immediately consent to pay for the loss of my property, at all events, you shall undergo an examination at Bow-street."

Richardson thought it much better to pay the sum demanded than to let the subject get wind before the public: but scarcely had three weeks elapsed, when the person who had taken the sheets returned to the tavern and restored the property. It appeared that he was a gentleman, but labouring under very great distress at the moment, had pawned the sheets to raise him a small sum of money; but since that period fortune had turned in his favor, and he was more than anxious to repair his error. He immediately sent for *Muster* Richardson, begged his pardon, returned him the sum of money he had paid, and did every thing in his power to make the *amende honorable.*

"This circumstance will be a warning to me," said the showman to one of his intimate friends: "so help me ——, I'll never sleep in a double-bedded room again as long as I live, when such gallows willins are suffered to prowl about and rob the public, and then plead distress as the occasion; and innocent people are liable to be transported for their tricks. I have no notion of it." The above adventure, perhaps, might be some reason why he preferred sleeping in his caravan ever afterwards.

At Portsdown Fair, some years ago, the next show to Richardson's was kept by a Welshman and his wife, who did every thing in their power to annoy him : in fact, they were jealous of his success and reputation,—overflowing shows crowning his exertions. Muster Richardson, however, by way of a bit of fun, had some goats dressed up, and had them led up and down his platform by the clowns, singing the old well-known stanza—

> Taffy was a Welshman,
>   Taffy was a thief ;
> But Taffy's poor show
>   Won't bring him any beef !

The Welshman did not complain of the appearance of the goats, but did not altogether relish the satire levelled against him ; during the night he had a dummy figure stuffed, dressed exactly like Muster Richardson, and hung it up, with a rope round the neck, early the next morning. This circumstance excited a great deal of merriment throughout the Fair ; and when Richardson appeared on the front of his show, the Welshman pointed to the figure hanging, and asked him if he knew who the culprit was ?

"Know him ! do I know myself?" was the reply; "it is intended for Richardson, the showman, who can beat all his opponents with the greatest ease and certainty, by his performances being so excellent ; and whose actors are so superior, that he can fill his show three times over to any other *Mummer's* once, and *you* know it.—Ha ! ha ! ha !—Its a capital likeness, I think, and I give you credit for your invention. I have only one favour to beg of you, Muster Taffy, as it is likely to do me good, I hope you will let it remain during the fair—it will prove an excellent sign for my friends to find me out!" The Welshman finding it had not the desired effect—to put Richardson out of temper, and make him angry, immediately took down the figure.

The *Paraders*, as they are called, persons who are hired to 'strut and fret their hour' on the platform, in order to attract the attention of the public, were the best looking females he could procure ; and as a matter of business—few men better knew the value of effect on the populace by exhibiting pretty faces, genteel figures, and women who walked proudly, than the late Muster Richardson. He did not boast of any great knowledge with the plays of Shakespeare : but one line, he said, suited *his* purpose :—

" Beauty provoketh thieves much sooner than gold !"

Some suspicious characters were found concealed one night under his booth at Greenwich Fair, whom he supposed had intended to have robbed him of his cash when he went to sleep, but nothing being found upon them but a phosphorus box, the magistrate told Muster Richardson that he could see nothing to detain them according to law !

" But I do," said he, " I have no doubt the gallows willins meant to *blow* me up and my show with their *prosperous* box when they *cotched* me winking ! But I was too leary for their tricks ! The ould showman has'nt lived for nothing—he has always got one eye open when he does go to sleep—they are such a set of rogues in this ere world !"

In the same light as the late *erudite* John Kemble was to the patent theatres, respecting their improvement and advancement towards perfection, may be viewed the exertions of the late *Muster* Richardson towards the SHOW FOLKS ! The difference, in point of intellect, between those great characters was immense —the *illustrious* John, for *sifting*, as it were, the words of Shakespeare, to obtain an accurate phraseology, to render the exits and entrances of actors classical, and to produce the original costume to various historical and other pieces—claimed the well earned tribute of unqualified praise.

On the other hand, the late *Muster* Richardson, without the advantages of a patent right, and a splendid domus to give effect to his exertions, or the assistance of great writers ; not possessing the talents to pore over dusty black-lettered volumes atth e British Museum, and other libraries for information, nevertheless, wrought great changes, effected visible improvements, and elevated the *Show Folks* into importance.

The booths erected for performances at Bartholomew, and other fairs, between forty and fifty years since, when Muster Richardson first showed himself, were of the most wretched description, and mere *stables*, when compared with the moveable theatres of the present day. Muster Richardson, who was a shrewd, cunning, clear-sighted man, saw the deficiency of comfort which was experienced by the visitors, and he spared neither pains, expense, or exertions, until he improved it, and produced a building well worthy of the reception of the public. In consequence of which he became attractive—a great feature with the visitors of fairs ; and the good performances, better actors, intelligent pieces, exalted scenes, comfortable seats, rendered him not only a formidable opponent, but he soon distanced all his competitors, and obtained for himself the appellation of the GREAT SHOWMAN, all over the kingdom.

When the late George Colman's drama of Blue Beard was first produced, it positively took London by storm ; at the ensuing Bartholomew Fair, Muster Richardson, as far as the size of his theatre would permit, exhibited Blue Beard in such a splendid style as to astonish the public : nothing could excel the value and magnificence of his dresses, and, although he could not engage the inimitable *Parisot*, to display her attitudes—shew the illuminated garden with such brilliancy as his predecessor on a more extended scale—or, give the terrific effect to the *blue chamber*, as realized at Drury Lane, yet he achieved much more than was expected, and his theatre was literally besieged with succeeding audiences, crowning his efforts with the loudest shouts of approbation : nay, more, it was a matter of great regret expressed by John Bull, when the fair closed, which deprived the multitude of enjoying the above splendid spectacle at *six-pence* per head.

John Kemble *lived* on the stage and in his closet, and books and dramatic lore were his idols ; he was classical, and nothing else but classical, to the very tip of his little finger ; and *refine-ment* was his decided model of good taste. Muster John Richard-son, (no relation, we believe, to the author of Sir Charles Grandison,) *existed* all his leisure time in his caravan, peeping out at the corner of a little window at the tricks and fancies of mankind, taking measure, at the same time, of John Bull and his family, with all their peculiarities and propensities, noting them down in the tablet of his memory, to turn them to good account when it suited his purpose, often smiling at the thought that—

"Man's a man, for a' and a' that !"

It has been an expressed opinion, nay, quite a mistaken notion, respecting the degradation of actors appearing at a fair—a sort of *squeamishness*, that people in general do not exactly understand. The public, or what is termed the public, must still be the same in point of decision and applause. Surely it will not be urged that because persons are better dressed, and live in a more splen-did house, that they have superior, or more intellectual heads than their neighbours ; the audience in the *boxes* can but dis-play judgment, the visitors in the *pit* shew their opinion, and the *gods*, as they are termed, or, in other words, the *gallery* folks, will have a *say* in the matter, cry encore, and obtain it, in spite of all the rank, birth, and property in the nation.

Then the actor, who having endured the rude noisy interrup-tion of a mob, as it were, and without the advantages of a well-regulated theatre, extorts applause from the audience, proves that he possesses talents, and only wants ' the *opening*,' to pro-cure him fame and fortune, and ultimately, a passport to excel-lence ; confirming the pleasing idea of the poet :—

Full many a flower is born to blush unseen,
And waste its sweetness on the desert air.

Woodward, the splendid comedian of olden times, if ever rivalled, was never excelled ; and who never felt any thing like reduction of consequence, by his performance at Southwark and Bartholomew Fairs ; the inimitable Shuter, one of the greatest mimics of his time ; and Macklin—

The Jew,
That Shakespeare drew.

also exhibited at Bristol, and other fairs; Belzoni, afterwards the great traveller, was at one period of his career, a show-man; and the late Mrs. Mountain's delightful abilities as a vocalist, were not valued a jot the less because she had exhibit-ed for several years over the kingdom at fairs.

Muster Richardson's theatre was open to all parties, and influenced by none: he loved talent—he invited it to *his* boards —and he promoted it—facts are stubborn things, and he had to boast that his humble booth had been the stepping-stone to fame and riches to several of his early actors, amongst whom might be named the two Southbys, clowns; Mr. Thwaites and Mr. Vaughan, who distinguished themselves in America; Saville Faucit, Mr. Grosette, Mr. and Mrs. Jefferies, Mr. Reed, Mrs. Wells, Mr. Oxberry, Mrs. Pearce, Abraham Slader, Mrs. Rose, Mrs. Fitzgerald, and Walbourn and Saunders, the celebrated Dusty Bob and Black Sal; with numerous other actors, that at present we cannot call to our memory.

Muster Richardson often declared that the burletta of *Tom and Jerry*, at Bartholomew Fair, brought him the greatest houses, and most money, he had ever received during his career as show-man. The piece was concocted by Bob Keeley, rehearsed at Stepney Fair, and for which the comedian received five pounds for his trouble. The showman gave a dinner upon the occasion, at which the author of Life in London, in company with (those celebrated characters—Dusty Bob and Black Sal,) Bill Wal-bourn and Saunders, dined off a prime baked shoulder of mutton and potatoes in his caravan, metamorphosed into a tidy parlour; and who enjoyed their meal with as much *gout*, as if they had been seated in the most splendid domus in the world; a drop of *jacky* gave spirit to the affair, which was concluded over some red port that would not have disgraced the table of a king. Muster Richardson took pride to himself for the expensive and elegant dresses which he provided for the three heroes—Tom, Jerry, and Logic; and in point of fact, they were never better dressed at any theatre either in town or country. On quitting the caravan, he filled a glass of wine, and said, here Muster * * * * * * * * * * here's your good health, and when your benefit takes place, I will take ten pounds worth of tickets, and so ought every other manager in the kingdom!

"I have lost a great many actors during my showman-ship," observed Richardson; "poor devils! they works werry hard after all for a bit of wittals; yet I pays them as well as I can for their sarvices, and I always likes to *cognize* (recognize) merit. But when you consider that they are exposed to heats and colds—and all sorts of weather in the open air—perform so often, werry often, in one day, added to a little drinking—it makes out the old saying, that the life of an actor is short, but a merry one! During the *Feer* time they scarcely are allowed time to sleep!

" I have been the means of setting several werry clever fellows a-going in this ere world! When they first came to me for engagements they were mere *cripples*—quite timid—and did not know wot they could do—but they all wanted to begin at the top of the tree, and to *hact* Emperors and Kings! But I tould them of their mistakes. I don't care how *bould* you speaks to the audiences, because I knows they likes *bould* orators; and it always puts me on the fret when I hears the *spectres* (spectators) call out—Speak up!

" Besides, I cured a great many young men who were at first shy, and ashamed to parade up and down the front of my theatre! But I used to say to them, You must *persewere*, and never mind being picked out by an ould acquaintance in the crowd—look at them full in the face, as if they were perfect strangers to you, by which means you will be able to get lots of *sing fryd* (sang froid), and become werry good hactors! I know werry vell wot it is to be timid myself—and that *bouldness* is not to be obtained without a good deal of practice; *non-chance* (nonchalance) requires some time to be mastered! There was that ere Bill Walbourn—I always saw the day-light in him; he was restless to become *sumbody*—he had got a nob on his shoulders, and a pair of heels to his feet!

" Besides, what advantages the young hactors have on my platform—room for the exercise of their limbs—and an hactor without action is like a horse that wants whipping, as he never can get over the ground with ease to himself, or pleasure to the audience. And several of the female women, who have turned out werry good performers; though, at a more advanced part of their lives, they have been rather too proud to acknowledge their first school—yet they never forgot my *lessons!*"

His criticisms, in general, were of the most ludicrous description. In speaking of Mr. Cartlitch, he said, " he was a *bould* speaker, and not afraid of his lungs, as he could be *heer'd* all over the *Feer;* and his *tickilation* (articulation) was so werry fine! But for my ghosts!—ha! ha! ha!—they were the most *spirited* performers in my company."

Had the late *Muster* Richardson been able to have kept a common-place book, and noted down the strange fellows that crossed his path for the last forty or fifty years, the droll incidents he had met with, and the singular circumstances connected with his life, an unsophisticated work, written according to the dictates of NATURE, might have been presented to the public, with great advantages to society, and also been viewed as an invaluable piece of biography. Muster Richardson lived in a world, almost his own, amongst the SHOW FOLKS! but, nevertheless, if he could not use his pen with the facility of a short-hand writer, he did not stand all day with his eyes open, and see *nothing !* On the contrary, he was rather a keen observer of human nature—full of anecdote—and could depict, after his own style, the abilities of various persons, the *shifts* resorted to by characters upon the town, with excellent common sense.

To use his own words, when speaking of Bartholomew Fair for the last fifty years, and of the bucks and bloods, as they were then designated, who frequented the above "*raree show*," to have a peep at what was going on, perhaps may afford some little amusement to the "*moderns*" of the present day.

"Bartholomew Fair, in the olden times," observed Muster Richardson, "was hailed once a year as the rallying point for all the 'CHOICE SPIRITS' in the Metropolis to meet—desirous to please, be pleased, and to give a taste of their various qualities —in the long room of the stable-yard at the French Horn, every evening during the Fair. This meeting was a select affair altogether, being composed of jovial fellows far above the common routine of society ; and rather a difficult matter to gain access to it, if not introduced by a friend, who had the privilege of doing so. The evening was entirely devoted to harmony ; catches and glees were the leading features, with some excellent songs, &c.

The great "pan of the dairy," upon this occasion, or the chairman for the time being, was DICK JOHANNOT—full of life and spirit, as a high-mettled racer—a steeple-chace sort of creature —a bottle of sparkling Champagne uncorked—nothing came amiss to Dick, the well-known celebrated comic singer and actor at old Astley's Amphitheatre. Johannot was a most distinguished favorite with the public ; and, although the senior Astley was a pound, shillings, and pence sort of man, yet Johannot received a splendid salary, and a couple of benefits in the year. He kept his horses and curricle, lived in good style, and was the life of his party. Dick possessed not only a voice of uncommon strength, but the tone of it was truly harmonious: he sang with the greatest ease to himself, and was considered one of the best comic singers of his time. There is nothing like so rich a burletta singer at the present period.

Johannot had a Joe Munden sort of face—he could do any thing he liked with it—twist it in all manner of shapes, but never distort it out of humour: he could roll his eyes of fire with such irresistible effect, that it was impossible not to smile, but more likely to burst out into a roar of laughter.

Dick was truly the cock of the walk upon his own ground : he had the good sense to keep it, to know *exactly* his value, and not to get out of his depth. He was tempted several times with great offers by the managers of both the Theatres Royal, to make an appearance in any character he might select for the occasion. "No, no," was the reply; "I am at the top of the tree here; I have it all my own way, and no rival to annoy my feelings ; therefore, I will let well alone.

" The Theatre Royal has a high-sounding name, and is rather flattering, I must admit; but it will never do for Dick Johannot to become little A at a *big* house. A failure would make a bankrupt of me in the Court of Fun—I should go down below *par*; and, what might be worse, never be able to *rise* again. Besides, I feel convinced there is a *peculiar* atmosphere for actors to breathe; and, what might be considered *great* at the Amphitheatre, might be thought *nothing* of at a Theatre Royal; therefore, I will not chance it." Johannot was the father of the present Mrs. W. Vining, and his great comic song—the CRIES OF LONDON :—

> Like a lark in the morn, with early song,
>   Comes the sweep, with his sweep, soot, oh !
> Next the cherry-cheek'd damsel she trips it along,
>   Any milk, pretty maids, below !
> Any dust ! any dust ! goes the tinkling bell,
>   While sharp in each corner they look ;
> Next the Jew, with his bag—Any clothes to sell ;
>   Any hare-skins, or rabbit-skins, cook !
>   Let none despise
>   The merry, merry cries
>   Of famous London Town !

The facetious TONY LE BRUN, when the fatigues of the Fair were over, used to drop in and exhibit his comic mug to the satisfaction of all parties. Tony, at one period of his life, was one of the inmates at Wargrave, the seat of the spendthrift, larking Lord Barrymore, when private theatricals were the rage of his Lordship. Le Brun was also one of the founders of the *Humbug* Club, established by his Lordship.

Tony only lived for the moment—*To-morrow* never gave him a thought. He was a complete peep-o'-day boy ; and to go to *roost*, as he termed it, before the cock began to crow, was a reflection upon the man, that he was " told out," and had not another word to say for himself. " Time was made for slaves." He was a man of splendid talents; but, as to his application of them, perhaps the less that is said the better.

The anecdote of his shirt has outlived his memory. Tony was never overburdened with a wardrobe, and his stock of linen was scanty in the extreme. He sent his only shirt to the washerwoman—an article that had seen the best of its days for several months ; but the woman was afraid, if she attempted to *rub* it, Tony would be *shirtless*, as there was great damage of it going into pieces; and returned it to him by one of her little children. " Tell your mother," said Tony, erecting himself in a pompous attitude, " she is a lazy beast !—that she has no invention !—without brains ! She might have pinned it against the wall, and thrown soap-suds at it ! "

It was also amongst these wits that SUETT, the celebrated *Dicky Gossip*, used to *unbend* for an hour or two at the English Carnival, and enter into the fun of the thing with more than ordinary spirits ; where he told his tales, cracked his jokes, and sang his comic songs. His slender figure was Comedy itself— he appeared like a man hung upon wires. His singular expression—"Oh dear! Oh la! la! Oh!" and his whimsical laugh, always created intense mirth. His character as an actor is entirely lost to the stage ; there was a *peculiarity* attached to it which cannot be recognized in any of the comedians of the present day. As the chairman of a convivial meeting he had few equals—he never would let " Dull Care " have a seat in his presence. He was an inveterate punster ; and, according to one of his biographers, he died with a *pun* in his mouth. He said to the late Robert Palmer—" Bobby, my boy, the *watchmen* are coming—I hear the *rattles!* " The following impromptu was written by the late Tom Greenwood :—

WIT AND WHEY.

DICK SUETT had dined at Bill Spencer's one day—
Got his *drops* rather soon, and went staggering away ;
But still feeling thirsty, as was often his lot—
His brain all on fire, his copper quite hot—
Reel'd into a pastry-cook's, so his friends say,
There sat himself down, and call'd for some whey :
In an instant 'twas served, but Dick, fond of a *joke*,
Determin'd a laugh at Puff's cost to provoke,
Said, " Halloo, my friend," after taking a drop,
" Where am I? "—" Why, sir, you are *inside of my shop* ; "
" I'm inside your shop! Mr. Pastrycook, hey?
'Tis a lie," replied Dick, " for I'm *over the whey.*"

Amongst this coterie of choice spirits—none took a higher lead, or appeared to greater advantage, than the late PERCY ROBERTS ; he was an artist by profession, and a most excellent engraver. Percy was also a mimic of the first quality, and for several years he was of the most erratic disposition ; he prefered what, at that period, was termed *vagabondizing*, in different parts of the country, in company with the well-known Paddy Rourke, and the late George Nussey : although his talents were of a superior description, and he could have lived with the most comparative ease, like a gentleman. Fortune once or twice bestowed her gifts upon him—to the tune of several thousand of pounds ; but this sunshine was not of long duration—light come, light go, he never appeared to fret, was always gay and happy, and his excuse for getting rid of his money was, that the saving banks were not in vogue then, that he might have secured his cash.

Percy Roberts in person, was viewed as the double of the late George the Fourth, and at the head of the table, his appearance and ' small talk,' were of the most imposing description. He was generally surrounded by young men of property, and who always promptly obeyed his calls towards the expences of the night, when he officiated as chairman. He had a pleasant manner of doing things, and magnifying mole hills into mountains.

'The Gods, my dear boys, always drank nectar,' said he, 'and we are the sons of Anacreon! So, my jolly dogs, lets be happy while we may! Full bowls!—flowing bowls!—The Gods never did any thing by halves!—Waiters, attend and have a plentiful supply of bottles of wine ready: and do you mind, if you do not bring it from the *supernaculum* bin, you will be sent back with it, and get no remuneration. Then singing :—

> O bring me wine! Bring me wine!
> 'Tis a comfort to the mind, &c.

No man was more *awake* to the movements of life, than Percy Roberts; he was affable, polite, interesting, and his manners were sure to make an impression on strangers. He had a good address, but never *profound* upon any subject; he *floated* on the surface, yet he was extremely imposing, and always took the lead in companies where he was present.—His song was always ready when called upon; and he made it a point never to make any excuse. This sort of *readiness* to oblige, made him a favourite in all the convivial societies he visited. Roberts' *mock bravura* was the delight of all companies; and he never sang it without the loudest *encore*. The story of it ran thus :—The wife of a French musical composer had left the baby in the cradle for Monsieur to take care of while she went out to purchase some trifling errand. The child cries—the composer is compelled to leave his score, to take the child out of the cradle, who happens to be disordered in its bowels. The composer, in a rage, not knowing what to do with the baby, exclaims—

> "Must I tear my score?"

Amongst the numerous qualifications which Percy Roberts possessed, he performed the part of clown, for the benefit of Delpini, at the Haymarket Theatre, with considerable applause.

To add to the above list of gay mortals, who were determined to make it appear that the right end of life was to live and be jolly, was the eccentric BILL SWORDS, a low comedian of considerable repute, both on and off the stage—a *gallimaufry* personage—a great man at the free and easy clubs in the Metropolis, and who had always got a benefit on the stocks, at some public house or the other; 'Just,' as he said, 'by way of keeping the devil out of his pockets; and also, to produce him one of those musical sounds which gave him pleasure—the *singing* of his tea-kettle. Swords was a great tea-drinker, but not without the embellishments of French cream—lots of brandy in it. He was a conspicuous feature amongst the choice spirits, for his comic songs, and his droll stories. It was astonishing the interest he used to excite in company by his manner of relating them—they were told with such an air of truth—names were mentioned—dates refered too—and circumstances developed—*facts* he insisted upon, to give them effect—that his auditory could never persuade themselves it was all *romance*. To show how the fashions have altered since that period—respecting the head dress of men, the following song, sung by Swords, was in great repute :

The youth comes up to town to learn all modern foppery,
For London town, no better place, to teach those from the country ;
He soon finds out what is wanting, and like him not sees one in ten,
But rolls into a barber's shop to get a swinging *tail*, and then—
This is the way to be a rolly kiddy O !
The girls will all admire you,
And swear you are the tippy, O !

The versatility of talent displayed at this meeting was truly delightful, the chairman only called on those persons who were capable of amusing the company, and *failures* never occurred, although a great variety of faces presented themselves every evening during the fair. Davy Everard, said to be a natural son of the Roscius—David Garrick, Esq., if in London at the time, always put in an appearance. He felt very proud of his origin, and he took care to let every person know who was his father ; but his *dear* mamma was never heard of. In his benefit bill, he always signed himself a pupil of that great man. It is true, that Garrick noticed him in the early part of his life ; but the habits of Everard were so attached to dissipation, that he ultimately lost his patron. Nevertheless, he was a man of first-rate abilities ; as an English dancer, at that period, he was considered above par, and a student under the celebrated Slingsby. Everard was a fascinating companion—a most excellent *mimic*—and his tales and recitations almost spell-bound his listeners. Day-light, to Everard, was of little use—breaking up a company, or being called a *starter*, were phrases that never applied to his conduct. He never thought of *retiring* until he was either turned out of the house by the landlord, or fell off his chair from the want of repose. The bacchanalian song described Everard to a T.

What have we with day to do?
Sons of care, 'twas made for you.

" If there was one man more than another," observed *Muster* Richardson, " intituled to the phrase of ' choice spirit ' in the true meaning of the word to its fullest extent, it was the late TOM GREENWOOD, the distinguished scene painter of Drury Lane Theatre, and of whom Lord Byron thus noticed in his poem of ' English Bards and Scotch Reviewers:—

Where genius ne'er confines
Her flights, to garnish *Greenwood's* gay designs.

" He never misssed paying me a visit at Bartholomew Fair ; and his presence always afforded me infinite pleasure. Greenwood always appeared delighted with the eccentricity and humour of the scene. Tom was very fond of ' seeing life,' and in accordance with his profession, as a scene painter, he entertained an opinion, that he could never see too much of the peculiarities of human nature. The exertions of Greenwood were directed to please mankind and make them happy.

" He was a most inoffensive creature in disposition, there was nothing presuming about his person, but affable and accessible at all times! He despised the rude insolent blackguard, the impertinent coxcomb, and the overbearing egotist.

" Greenwood could not live without the pleasure of mixing with society ; and when the fatigues of the day were over at the theatre, it was his general custom to mix with authors, poets, painters, actors, &c., who had obtained some eminence in the world, or acquired a name for their abilities.

" In every thing that Greenwood undertook to perform, he was clever and happy ; his prologues and epilogues were excellent, nothing dull or prosing about them.   His peculiar mode of ' returning thanks,' when his health has been drunk, was of the neatest description, and full of point.

" Through his exertions the principal pantomimes were produced at Sadler's Wells, in the best days of one of the best clowns that ever illustrated the boards of any theatre—Joey Grimaldi.

" Nothing could exceed the brilliancy of the scenes painted by Greenwood, in the burletta of Tom and Jerry, got up at the above place of amusement, under the management of the late Mr. Egerton.

" He published a small volume of poetry, intituled. ' Rhyming Reminiscences,' which was well received by the public : and his burletta of the ' Death of Life in London,' performed for upwards of fifty nights with the most flattering success.

" Greenwood was one of the most intimate friends of the late Jack Emery, and Billy Blanchard, distinguished for their convivial talents at the Hygean Society, held at the King's Arms, Holborn.

" Tom was a great enemy to *rows* of any kind, knocking down watchmen was entirely unconnected with his pursuits, keeping out of watchhouses, and appearing before magistrates his decided aim.

" Greenwood was one of the readiest men ever seen in uniting the efforts of his pen with the execution of his pencil. He was an invaluable man to any theatre. The loss of such a person must be generally felt by society : full of talents in his own person, he was a great admirer of them in others ; nothing like envy ever rankled in his bosom, well-knowing the immense difficulty to obtain an eminence in London ; he was liberal in the extreme to rising merit, and whenever he had an opportunity of bestowing his patronage, the tyro always met with a helping hand from the late Tom Greenwood.

" It would be totally impossible," said Muster Richardson, " to pass over a theatrical gent. of the name of Dighton, once the ' great card ' at Sadler's Wells ; indeed, it might be said he was the principal *prop* of that place of amusement. Dighton and Sadler's Wells were almost synonymous ; so great a feature was he at one period of his career. He was distinguished for his performance of Irish characters and comic songs. Dighton was viewed as a good set-off against Johannot at Astley's; and the contrast between them proved of great service to the opposite houses. He was a great favorite with the public, and deservedly so; and when he left the stage the chasm that occurred was never filled up. In addition to his capabilities as an actor, he was the most distinguished caricaturist of his day, and had a style of his own. St. James' and Hyde Parks affording him rich subjects for his pencil, his *likenesses* were so extremely accurate that no one could mistake who they were meant for. His shop-window, in which they were exhibited at Charing Cross, was so crowded with spectators outside, that numerous passengers were compelled to resort to the road to pursue their course. Dighton was a choice spirit, to the very echo!

The meeting previously alluded to was not distinguished wholly for the resort of actors and singers; but persons of literary character were to be seen amongst them. An author, known at that time by the title of *Anthony Pasquin*, celebrated for his poem of the Children of Thespis, and the Lives of Lord Barrymore, and Edwin, the great comic actor: he was also connected with the leading newspapers at that period. Pasquin (otherwise Williams) was a man of considerable abilities, who could handle the out-door subjects better than most men of his time; although he had to compete with the celebrated Major Topham, of the Post, and Sir Henry Bate Dudley, of the Herald. Pasquin was a leading theatrical critic, and very much looked up to by the actors of that period. But, it is urged, there is such an affinity between " choice spirits," that they will find each other out, and assemble together; no matter whether it is in a cellar, a garret, a fair, or a tavern. Talent loves talent— and that accounts for it.

" But," said Muster Richardson, " I have lived to see all those ' choice spirits ' called to their Mother Earth (with a sigh, something like a foreboding that he might soon follow them), and this sort of thing is all gone by now-a-days; and I am sure ' I shall never look upon their *like* again.' There was nothing like a *calculating* fellow amongst them who had any idea of making a purse for another day; yet they were all clever in furnishing expedients, upon the shortest notice, to ' *raise the wind!*' But those ' choice spirits,' as they are termed, never do, nor can they last as long as other men, because the rapidity of their enjoyments consume them: they are faster than race-horses—they are always on the *gallop* through life! But, with all their *nous,* they did not give themselves half a *chance.* Sleep they never count upon, and only succumb to it when nature cannot hold out any longer; and then—they drop off their *perch.*"

" I look back with astonishment," said the showman, " at the time when I first commenced to *amuse* the public (*swindling*, I am aware, some persons call it), in my humble way, respecting the improvement of the theatres, scenery, dresses, &c. ; but, to be candid, I cannot say as much for the *improvement* of the actors. I may be called partial, and my judgment questioned, but I have seen more real talent exhibited at *Feers* than I ever saw at any of the licensed Theatres."

Old Ducrow, father of the present lessee of Astley's Amphitheatre, was a great opponent for several years at the fairs ; and also old Saunders ; but Richardson, if he was deficient in *personal* talents with either of the above active, clever men, had always some little *dodge*, he said, to keep pace with them in producing novelties for the public.

Muster Richardson was extremely liberal to actors who visited his show during the fair, (and several performers belonging to the Theatres Royal, out of curiosity, used to go and see what the performances were *like*,) but he was fond of the profession in general : and on '*passing* them' he would observe to his doorkeeper, "It is all right, Jem, pass that ere gentleman, he is a professional hactor, and belongs to one of the Theatres Royal. We are werry glad to see them: I loves talent.—He is one of us !"

During the career of Muster Richardson, he had, in several Country Fairs, to contend against magisterial authority, who would not listen, he used to assert, either to rhyme or reason. Frequently, after the Fair was over, he wished to have a private night or two to *act* plays ; but the Magistrates either refused their consent, or he was threatened with informations if he *act*ed contrary to their wishes ; the penalty of which, according to the Act of Parliament, is 50*l.* He, therefore, in one town, issued the following singular bill, which he called his *dummy* explanation of the grievances he laboured under :—

The " *MANAGER in Distress*," and under circumstances of *Restraint*, is compelled to put forth a

QUIET

C L A I M   T O   N O V E L T Y,

By commencing with

A PIECE—a new PIECE—and nothing else but an ORIGINAL PIECE, written, or rather PENN-ed, by a well-known

ERRATIC WRITER,

Who has nothing for *his* CHARACTERS to *say*—Speech-making also out of the question—yet, nevertheless, they will address

The audience without WORDS !

A TOUCH-AND-GO thing altogether—twenty minutes in length —not by Shrewsbury, but by the nearest clock in the Town.

The Piece is *legitimate*—the *line* has been kept—and the *denœuement* also in strict accordance with the Patents of the Great Houses (with such *nicety* of taste, that those precious documents have not been robbed of a single particle of *dust*), in which will be depicted, in *silent* sorrow, all the luxury of woe, to the echo that applauds again : but, as a matter of course, GRIEF cannot, must not, ought not to be *encored*—yet with the liberty to enjoy, but not to *repeat* it—set down as the

TONGUE-TIED ACTORS!
OR, THE
DUMMIES

Struggling to make themselves intelligible to JOHN BULL !

" We must speak by the card, or equivocation will undo us ! "
IMMORTAL BILLY.

But tell it not to LIBERTY !—Hear it not, REFORM! Disciples of the PRESS bear it in mind as one of the *imposing* Spectacles of 1832. Weep, Authors, weep !—your occupation's gone ! ! Drop a tear, ACTORS—a legitimate *drop ! ! !* The tear that bedews sweet Sensibility's shrine ! Enough !—too much ! but *exit* ACTING—the Farce is over, and

CHAOS COMES AGAIN ! ! ! !

Behold MELPOMENE devoid of utterance—THALIA quite speechless—and the MANAGER not having one *word* to say for himself !

Can such things be?
And overcome us, like a summer's cloud, without our special wonder !

The noisy, talkative, uproarious Country DAGGERWOOD reduced to a dummy in every town—

" True, 'tis pity ; and pity 'tis, 'tis true ! "

The matronly Lady DAGGERWOOD, with all the numerous little DAGGERS, drawn forth upon this touching occasion, without RE-dress !

ASSISTED BY

A mob of non-legitimates, and a variety of other DUMMIES, whose *features* will *talk*, if their TONGUES are unable to perform their usual office ; and, by way of

LIGHT AND SHADE TO THE PIECE,

A *Caper*, in GRIEF, will take place, with *steps* of the most doleful description ; in which the *heels* of the Performers must SPEAK for them to the audience.

And as sort of a make-weight,

A CUDGELLING MATCH will be introduced (names not being required to illustrate this peculiar rencontre,) between a legitimate *Gog* and a *TINY OPPONENT* in the Minor K.

Q

To which will be added,

A serious LA-MENT, of the most penetrating description, to prevent the Comedy of the " ROAD TO RUIN " being changed to a most *distressing* tragedy.

> I do remember me, when a MINOR became a MAJOR—
> And when that MAJOR descended to a Minor!
> " Over the water to Charley."——" But LAW is LAW ! "

The wind-up will be the appearance of

A GREAT CHARACTER !

ONE OF THE
MOST ILLUSTRIOUS SORT!—EN PASSANT.

In order to render the denouement complete and decisive, and the effect interesting and APPROPRIATE.

———

N. B. The trouble of *listening* to the above Piece will be dispensed with, but to *see* it is a matter of considerable importance to the Theatrical World.

———

☞ Further Particulars in the Bills of the Day.

———

Richardson's mode of discourse and language, owing to the want of education, was rather peculiar, and he had a host of imitators amongst the actors : for instance—" How do you do, Mr. Richardson ? "—his answer was, " Pretty well, thank you—my every thing—as God's my judge, Muster."

He was a shrewd, calculating man, and well knew how to ' measure ' the public. He employed the first-rate scene-painters, Messrs. Grieve, and the late Tom Greenwood ; his dresses were equal, if not superior in costliness, to the Theatres Royal. Facts are stubborn things.—The front of his booth alone cost several hundred pounds.

A few years since, he felt inclined to give up his theatrical concern ; and employed the celebrated George Robins, the auctioneer, to dispose of it ; but with all the tact and knowledge of the world possessed by this distinguished hero of catalogues, no bidder appeared, and it was bought in.

Muster Richardson had an idea, at one period of his life, of bringing out a new piece according to his own experience on the subject, under the title of ' The Fudge Family !' " For," said he, to the person whom he wished to write it from his observations, " no man has had so much to do with the FUDGES in theatrical life, as I have ; I can give a werry good account of them, they are a werry large family." However, nothing more was done towards the production of the piece, than the following bill :—

THE FUDGE FAMILY;

OR,

ACTORS ON THE ROAD TO FAME!

TRAVELLERS see strange Things!!!

Being an Original, Laughable, Whimsical, Poetical, Numerical, Musical, Mathematical, Farcical, Didatical, Lyrical, Comical, Rhapsodical, Theatrical, Provincical, Mimical, Parodical, Operatical, Analytical, Row-ical, Olympical, (not Piratical,) and not in the least

TRAGICAL!

PERFORMANCE.

SHOWING—"That one man in his time plays many parts!" Also, that "Life's a jest!" To die! to sleep! to die all, to die nobly! That's your sort! or, in other words, to make a *good* EXIT! The FUDGE FAMILY will, in consequence, put their shoulders to the wheel, to make a long pull, a strong pull, and a pull altogether, in order to represent a

COLLECTION OF INTERESTING SCENES FROM NATURE,

MIXED UP WITH A TINY BIT OF ART!

By a well-known FANCY writer,

ACT-ing up to the liveliest feelings of his IMAGINATION, to put into a tangible shape, something after the manner of an OPERA, BURLETTA, MELO-DRAMA, EXTRAVA-GANZA, BROAD-FARCE, or rather an OLLA-PODRIDA, including a variety of harmonious SNATCHES from the most approved AIRS in the PLAY World, to hold as it were the Mirror, pointing out the advantages of DRESS and ADDRESS, illuminated by those powerful auxilliaries—

The entrance of FUN—the attendance of MIRTH—the Company of LAUGHTER—the force of RIDICULE—the touching qualities of PATHOS, to illustrate, captivate, and elicit applause at any rate—and the power of EMPHASIS, to bring down the Three Rounders—but above all to display an animated

KNOWLEDGE OF LIFE AND CHARACTER!

PORTRAYING

The iusurmountable difficulties attendant on the Lives of Actors in general, throughout a variety of EXITS and ENTRANCES, —INS and OUTS—UPS and DOWNS, and *changes of the scene* to the end of the chapter—

THAT ENDS OUR strange, eventful HISTORY!

The FUDGE FAMILY has been written with the laudable attempt to please all parties; at the same time, the mind's eye has been on the look-out to avoid giving offence to any body; and in order not to o'erstep the modesty of nature!

The representation of the Fudge Family is intended for this Night only,

A SORT OF DRESS REHEARSAL;

Without a generous, enthusiastic, enlightened, liberal, discerning, high-minded, and laughter-loving PUBLIC, should most spiritedly enter into the TOUCH and GO Sketch of

"HE WOULD BE A PLAYER!"

and add their mighty, and all powerful stamp to it of a taking quality, so as to RUN the piece off its Legs, without making

A CRIPPLE OF IT!

" 'Tis a Consummation most devoutly to be wished!"—Hem!— SHAKESPEARE.

After getting over his difficulties he began to realize money very fast, and for several years past he put by large sums of money. He had no family, was rather an abstemious person in his mode of living, industrious to the echo, and very plain in his manners and dress. But his heart lay in the right place; he was not only alive to a tale of distress, but ready to relieve the object of it. He was a charitable, feeling man, to all intents and purposes; and numbers have been assisted in the hour of need by his liberality, who, we hope, will cherish his memory with respect. At St. Alban's, when a terrible fire took place, and a subscription was set on foot for the uninsured, he subscribed his hundred pounds, styling himself,—"the Showman!"

Property, in general, is so much exaggerated, that a variety of reports had got into circulation, stating Muster Richardson had died worth between thirty and forty thousand pounds; but the true statement is—that his property altogether did not reach ten thousand pounds, and his theatrical concern, dresses, &c., did not fetch, when sold by auction, one thousand pounds. But when it is taken into consideration, that he was the architect of his own fortune—a poor workhouse boy—struggling through immense difficulties—in a most arduous and precarious line of life, and after rendering great assistance to several other persons—it must be viewed in the show department, as a large sum of money! Very few of our greatest actors have died worth so much property; nay, half that sum.

The sudden demise of the great showman was rather unexpected. He had scarcely closed his season for the year at Bartholomew Fair—seen all his waggons safely stowed away—his dresses carefully covered up in the wardrobe—his music collected together and put on the shelf—his company of strollers dismissed to their homes—and prepared himself to enjoy the comforts of Woodland Cottage, (his residence for upwards of thirty-three years,—a neat building, excellently well furnished, and contains some good old paintings.) until the return of Easter Monday should again call him forth to meet his numerous patrons at Greenwich, when the " Grim King of Terrors," the most terrific *spectre* he had ever had to deal with, made his appearance—

" So come along, no more we'll part,
He said, and touched him with his dart."

A few minutes before he died (at seven o'clock on the morning of Monday the 14th,) he observed to his female attendant and friend, Mrs. Johnson, " that his mind was quite comfortable—he was prepared to die—that he had disposed of his property entirely to his satisfaction, and he was quite resigned."

Mr. Cross, of the Surrey Zoological Gardens, he appointed one of his executors; and, according to his wishes, he was buried at Great Marlow, in Buckinghamshire. His remains were conveyed from London in a hearse and four, accompanied by two mourning coaches; his friends being extremely anxious to pay every respect to his memory. A great number of the inhabitants of Marlow went out to meet the funeral procession upwards of a mile from the town; and his body was carried to and from the church by several of the most respectable inhabitants of Great Marlow. Mr. Johnson rendered every attention to the funeral and grave of his worthy predecessor! who was upwards of seventy years of age. At all events the late Muster Richardson was a great feature with the public; and take him for " all in all," you may travel a long distance before you find a better man.

The theatrical concern of the late Muster Richardson has been purchased by Messrs. Johnson and Nelson Lee; the former was in his service for several years; and he felt so much satisfaction at his integrity, that he remembered him in his will to the amount of five hundred pounds, free of legacy duty: (but all his bequests were left free of duty,) and the latter, a person of considerable abilities as an actor, and manager of Sadler's Wells. They will, by their united efforts and experience start well; and produce an improved state of things in the show department. Their wardrobe is entirely new; with a new stage front, painted by Mr. Marshall of Covent Garden Theatre; they are determined to spare neither expense nor exertions to merit the support of the public.

———

In a sequestered spot,
In Great Marlow Church Yard,
after a long career,
Of bustle, incidents, and humour,
Lie the remains of the late

MUSTER RICHARDSON!

The celebrated SHOWMAN!

He was

The HERO of his own TALE,

and

One of the principal

FUNNIMENTS

IN ENGLAND,

For the last Fifty Years:

It was his

RULING PASSION

To make Mankind laugh and forget their cares!

———

" I knew him well, Horatio! "

And, to do him justice, he was the

FAIR-est of the FAIR!

He raised himself from the most wretched obscurity in Life to a NOTORIETY in the eyes of the World that few Men could hope to obtain!

HE WAS THE GREAT OUT-DOOR FEATURE OF AMUSEMENT!

and the name of

RICHARDSON

appeared like a charm at all the Fairs!

He lived by SHOW-ing up the Public!

He had a great predilection for SOUND, and the GONG did great wonders for him—by it he made a great Noise in the Country!

ALL THE WORLD WAS HIS STAGE!

And the canopy of Heaven his dome!

Entrances and *Exits* were his delight!

PANTOMIMES, DANCES, and MELO-DRAMAS, were his forte!

Harlequin, Columbine, and Clown, his " Great Creatures!"

And " Walk up! walk up! walk up!
" The PLAYERS are here! "

were words of the greatest importance

IN HIS BOOK!

But the grim King of Terrors pounced upon him, with the
cue, to say that

THE SHOW WAS OVER,

And that MUSTER RICHARDSON

must

DROP THE CURTAIN!

He bowed content, having reached the summit of Man's Life—
Three Score and Ten Years—
and his

LAST ACT

was,

Previous to his grand EXIT,

that

HE DIED IN GOOD HUMOUR

with

ALL MANKIND!

At Woodland Cottage, Monday, Nov. 14, 1836.

———

PEACE TO HIS MANES!

CHAPTER VIII.

CHARLES TURF, Esq.: a character upon the town—up to every thing—with a LINGO of his own—yet a man of observation, and a most excellent companion. A glance at the Sporting Booth—all sorts of folks—Nature unadorned—Niceties not required—Jack as good as his Master—Independence of feeling to the echo—Looks dangerous, and speech worse—the old adage desirable, " To hear much and speak little." A Song for those that like it—a curiosity in Literature—a scrap for D'ISRAELI. The handsome female with a fine bust—Beauty powerful in all companies. The maker of a Book ; but no READER. A fig for Literature—Authors distanced as to chance, 7 to 4. A figure in rhetoric. The Free and Easy Concert—every body welcome—WEBER not known, and BISHOP not thought of. Babel—to wit, " All round my Cap !" " Tommerhoo !" Silence ! Silence ! Silence ! What a Row ! For shame—when a FEMALE WOMAN shews her ivories ! What low remarks ! Vulgar fellows ! Keep your jaw to yourself ! or else—What? Why ! You'll meet with a stop-jaw ! Indeed ! How liberal ! Enough ! Too much. Who's for Lunnun ? The Costard-monger and his Prad—Every man to his calling. Any port in a storm. The dangers of TICKLING ; or, keep your hands to yourself, Ould Chap ! A glance at low life —Rum Customers. St. Paul's in sight—and the PILGRIMS once more at home.

" WE cannot quit the Fair while there is any thing worthy of our sight and observation," observed Makemoney to his brother Pilgrims ; " besides, novelty and a change of scene render our pilgrimage more interesting."

" Any where you please," replied Flourish: " we look up to you, sir, as our leader, Mentor, guide, &c. ; therefore, make no apology for any place that you take us to visit—I am not at all inclined to be particular. No—I am for research."

" Let us see all we can, uncle," said Sprightly ; " we came out for that purpose. I am anxious to become acquainted with life, in all its various grades."

" You will perceive by the sign (*pointing to a painting of two men in the attitude of self-defence*), that this booth is connected with the Sporting World ; I do not think our day's pleasure would be complete without we visit it, just to see what is going on, and I am almost certain we shall meet with an old friend of mine, CHARLES TURF, Esq. You will be very much pleased with him," said Makemoney to his nephew; " his dialogue is quite his own—that is to say, it is the peculiar *phraseology* made use of by that class of society to which he belongs. He is one of the most independent, lively fellows in the kingdom—full of *point* in his remarks, but here and there interspersed with a few *slang* terms ; yet, nevertheless, he is a man of general knowledge. It is an honor to know him ; and I do not think he has the shadow of a bad trait in his whole composition."

" I hope you will meet with him," said his nephew, " as he will not only keep us alive, but put us up to a thing or two."

" Respecting the properties of a horse," replied Makemoney, " he is eloquent in the extreme, and is well known at Tattersall's. His opinion has great weight ; indeed, his soul and body appear to be quite wrapt up in matters of this kind : he is considered a thorough-bred sportsman. Here he is, sure enough, over his cigar, and he sees us——"

" What, my old friend, Jack Makemoney, I am glad to see you—give us hold of your *flipper*," said Turf ; " done all your dirty work, I hear—that's your sort !—all right for you, my young 'un *(giving a nod to his nephew)*. Now you have *cut* trade, I see, you have time to *unbend* a little ; and above vulgar prejudices, too ! That's the time of day, my flower ! But I certainly did not expect to have seen you at the sporting-booth —I thought you used to be a little *particular* about being seen in such places."

" True, when I was in business I always held it incompatible with my character ; but now having retired," answered Makemoney, " I do not care who sees me any where. To tell you the truth, Mr. Turf, curiosity induced us to enter ; and also for the decided purpose of meeting with you."

" That's right, ould chap," replied Turf ; " the longer we live, you know, the more we ought to learn—and your *curiosity* will be highly gratified ; for there are a number of jolly dogs here, and I will not say there are not some rum customers amongst them, who are not particular as to nicety of lingo ; but if you give no offence, you need not fear being affronted. Pleasant Jem, the cove here, is wide awake to his own interest, and *civility* is his motto. He will not stand any nonsense : he looks well after his customers. Only produce the *tip*, and *Dusty Bob* is as good to him as my Lord Duke—the *cash* is the test of *goodness* with Jem—he don't understand *chalk* ; indeed, he has not got a bit of it in the book—PONTIC won't do here."

" There appears a great many people here : are they all sporting folks, sir ? " asked Flourish.

" That is more than I can answer for," replied Turf, rather sharply : " through my life—you'll excuse me, sir— I have always made my own *game ;* and I let other people play their cards as they like : that is to say, in plain English, I never trouble my head with other people's affairs—it is too *Paul-Pryish* for me."

"That's a little one in for you—therefore, be on your guard," whispered Sprightly to Flourish.

"Do not think me harsh, sir," said Turf; "I see you are a stranger, and I am sure my advice will not be thrown away upon you. *Novices* are likely to get into danger sometimes, from sheer ignorance, when they least expect it ; although, at the same time, they have no intention of giving offence. I am well known here, on the turf, and at most of the sporting places in the kingdom ; and though I publicly say, ' Damn your remarks,' I do not owe a *mag* in the world ; therefore, I do not care for anybody—but that does not apply to you as a stranger ; yet, understand me : there are persons here who do not like to be *looked* at—the stare, or dead-set at them is unwelcome to their feelings —they are apt to think you have an unpleasant motive in doing so towards them. It is a strange world we live in, and you ought to have the eyes of Argus to look about you, to steer clear from difficulties."

"I am quite certain," answered Makemoney, "that my friend Frank will be grateful for your advice ; and I hope you will pardon my curiosity, for both Jem and myself are as much in fault as he has been ; but there is a certain *curiosity* attached to these sort of places, that a person cannot exactly suppress—which must plead our excuse ; but under the *generalship* of Charles Turf, we shall not commit any more errors, although the old proverb does not stand good here," he concluded laughingly,— "'that a cat may look at a king !'"

"May be not, uncle," answered Jem, "but when we are at Rome, we should do as Rome does! Therefore, we will leave it entirely to Mr. Turf, to point out to us, or say what he thinks proper, for our information ; and I am sure we shall not have to complain of his *silence.*"

"The tall, genteel looking young man, you see in conversation with pleasant Jem," said Turf, "is the person, called the Phenomenon, in the sporting world—a chip of the old block, and never defeated in the P. R. He has won several battles ; by the side of him is the ' Pet of the Fancy,' equally conspicuous as a pugilist ; but as that sort of amusement appears to have had its day with the public, and is now nearly laid on the shelf, we shall not say any more on that subject.

"But look to your right,—that little natty fellow, as nice and clean as if he had just come out of a band-box, is *Bob Driver,* the well-known jockey! That's the boy for the winning post! He can manage a horse with as much ease as I do a spinning top! He knows when to make play, and push for the race, with the best of them on the turf—on the Derby, and Oak days, and the St. Leger, at Doncaster, he is a great man! Half a nod from Bob, nay, the slightest wink, to a betting man, is a point gained, and his head is *screwed* on the right way.

"Talk of the *Penny Magazine,* and the *Guide to Knowledge,* they are mere waste paper, when compared with Bob's upper works. It is true, that he cannot *write* a volume, but he can *make* not only as interesting, but perhaps, a more valuable BOOK, than any author that you have got in your catalogue.

"He has not been idle—he has made a purse for himself—and his name is good for a high figure at the *Blunt* Magazine, and no questions asked. Bob always proved himself a good calculator, and never let the opportunity, however dazzling it might appear in his favour, put it to the chance of depriving him of his last sovereign—desperate hazards would not do for Bob—a palace or a workhouse! by which good conduct, he has been able to provide against the wind, rain, quarter-day, tax-gatherers, &c., and all those other disagreeables in life. Besides, Bob always '*comes to scale,*' like a trump. He pays all his bets off hand; and he is nothing else 'but a right one,' and what I call, an ornament to the sporting circles."

The discourse was interrupted here, by loud calls of silence! silence! for a song, and give us the Highwayman of the Olden Times, Bill.

"The song, or rather the parody, you are about to hear," said Turf, "is respecting a noted highwayman, who composed it while he was under sentence of death, and sent it, accompanied with an introductory letter,* to the female he cohabited with,

---

* " My dearest Peg,

" Keep this *chant* (a) as a *rummy-nooseness* of your *infortunate* Bob! and do not 'nap (b) your bib' for wot can't be helped! as some folks you know are born to be *twisted* (c) and others drowned! I think as how it is much better than any last dying speech, birth, parentage, and all that ere sort of caper—but, as to *confession,* why that you are aware, my Peg, is all my eye and Betty Martin. I always did keep secrets; and as to become a *nose*—no, no—I shan't *split* now!

" But you know the *traps* (d) first *nippered* (e) me; the *beaks* (f) then *lumbered* (g) poor Bob; the *big wigs* (h) knocked him down, which rendered your fancy man of no use to you, Peggy, or any body else; and the *nubbing chit* (i) will finish the innings by changing *infortunate* Bob into a *stiff* (k) un! But let me be 'put to bed' (l) decently, for you know, Peg, I never was a shabby or a mean fellow in my life; and, therefore, I should like the *tie-up* of poor Bob to be nothing else but good. I am sure some of my old *pals* will watch in turns, throughout the *darky* (m), to prevent the body-snatchers from selling me for an *ottamy* (n).

" See this done, and I am quite resigned to my fate. When you receive this *scrive* (o) the hand that wrote it will be stiff and motionless—my once bold heart as cold as ice—my courage gone—and my unbounded love for the 'loveliest of *mots*' (p), which touches me more than all the rest, silenced for ever. And I, who never flinched from a trap when he tried to deprive me of my liberty, or boldly called out, regardless of the danger, to a coach and four, 'Stop and deliver!' will be numbered with the dead.

" Therefore, keep your weather-eye up, and look out for squalls when your Bob is off the hooks! Give the kid a kiss, and tell him that the ould chap died game. You'll find some *steeven* (q) in my reader, if you can't gammon the draper out of any crape to hoist signals of distress. My *ogles* (r) are like a river; and

the night before his execution. The hero of the song, was one of the most daring fellows that ever existed, a second *Jerry Abershaw*,* and who set powder, ball, and rope at defiance ; and who was a complete terror to the police officers.

I, who never shed a tear before in my life—have them now streaming down my cheeks. Farewell! I am off—I can say no more—my chaffer sticks to my mouth. From your doating, but

"IN-fortunate, daring BOB."

(*Notes upon the Note.*)—*a.* letter ; *b.* To shed tears ; *c.* hanged ; *d.* officer ; *e.* hand-cuffed ; *f.* justices ; *g.* sent to prison ; *h.* judges ; *i.* Jack Ketch ; *k.* a corpse ; *l.* buried ; *m.* the night ; *n.* skeleton ; *o.* letter ; *p.* cyprians ; *q.* money ; *r.* eyes.

* The annals of the country do not record a more hardened wretch than Abershaw, who was executed at Kennington, about forty years since, for the murder of Price, a police-officer. Being visited the day before his execution by his father in the New Gaol, he said to the afflicted old man, "Father, what signifies your troubling yourself about me, I am only going to H—, to have a game at All Fours with some of my old companions." On the way to execution, near Newington Church, he kicked off his shoes, and threw his hat away. When the halter had been put about his neck, after a horrid imprecation, he said to Little, a fellow-sufferer, "Mind your d—d long legs don't dangle against mine, for I intend to make an easy journey of it." He not only refused to join in prayer with the clergyman who attended on the occasion, but insulted him with the most gross language, and even attempted to kick at him. On account of the desperate temper of this offender, his legs were bound with a cord before leaving the prison. Upon the cap being drawn over his face, he said to the excutioner, "Well, good bye to you. old boy—I wish you better luck than I have had!" and then, by an effort of his strength, sprung out of the cart, when the cord confining his legs snapped. As he rode in the cart, he appeared entirely unconcerned—had a sprig of myrtle in his mouth, his bosom was thrown open, and he kept up an incessant conversation with the persons who rode near the vehicle he was in, frequently laughing and nodding to others of his acquaintance whom he perceived in the crowd, which was immense. The prisons in the Metropolis, at the period alluded to, were not subject to the improved and severe state of discipline which is now observed in the whole of them: they were then all noise and uproar, instead of the "*silent*" system ; and a prisoner could live as much at his ease, and enjoy his comforts, as when outside of the jail, provided he had but the money to pay for them. Lockit's ideas in the Beggar's Opera was the mode acted upon— "Fetters at any price!" In consequence of which, Abershaw passed his time in the most agreeable manner during his confinement ; and, like Macheath, he was visited by his favorite mistresses—drank his wine, and became the hero of the tale. He was a man of gallantry—had received an excellent education, and he also held a superior situation in the navy. Neither was he destitute of talent: he used to relate his numerous robberies on the road, dished up in the style of romances or lively anecdotes ; and laugh heartily at the fright and consternation he had frequently put upon the inoffensive passengers, when he bade them "stand and deliver!" He was quite a feature in the prison ; and nothing scarcely was heard, from one end of it to the other, but the extraordinary feats and adventures of *Jerry Abershaw*. His undaunted resolution and courage never forsook him ; and, under any circumstances, the slightest particle of *fear* was never to be discovered in his composition. He was a terror to the officers ; and two years elapsed before he was taken after he shot Price. He always carried pistols about him, and laid them on the table during meals, that he might be prepared against any sudden attack. However, he was betrayed by a favorite mistress into the hands of the officers of justice : she secured his pistols unperceived by him, then gave the signal, when they rushed upon him, and safely secured him, before he was able to make any resistance. Upon the entrance of the officers

" The parody is considered a fine specimen of the cant language, which may vary a little from the olden times, when Ben Jonson used to quote it ; but there is something so emphatic and peculiar about the *slang*, that in more modern times, two of our greatest poets have called it to their aid—MOORE, in his 'Tom Crib's Memorial to Congress,' and the late LORD BYRON, in his ' Don Juan,' have indulged in such phrases. Likewise the refined author of the ' Last Days of Pompeii,' has not thought it beneath his pen to fill the mouth of his hero—Paul Clifford, with the words most in use with thieves ; and the writer of Rookwood, it should seem, thought that several of his characters, without flash songs, might have appeared dull and spiritless ; from no other motives, I suppose, than to claim attention. I have often been surprised," continued Turf, " to witness the great applause such sort of songs have met with amongst the lower orders ; but there is no accounting for taste."

Silence—silence !—Order—order, &c., when the following song was sung, with all the peculiarities which belongs to such a composition :—

THE SLAP-UP HOUNSLOW HIGHWAYMAN.

Air—" *The fine Old English Gentleman.*"

I'll tip you a prime flash chaunt, made by a good ' *old scout*,' (1)
Of a slap-up Hounslow highwayman, whom all have heard about ;
Who kept the ' *blunted* (2) travelling coves ' all on a sharp look out ;
And the ' Prigs' (3), who tried to ' *quod*' (4) him, Lor he put 'em to the rout !
          Like a slap-up Hounslow Highwayman,
            One of the Olden Time !

His *crib* (5) so snug, was hung around with *wipes* (6), and *pops* (7), and *crows* (8);
With *bess* (9) and *glims* (10), some prime *jemmys* (11) and *slugs* (12) for any foes ;
All round his *squeeze* (13) a *bird's-eye wipe* (14), *cord kickseys* (15), and *high-lows* (16) ;
Oh, he *lush'd* (17) his *flash of lightning* (18), and scorned to be a *nose* (19).
            Like a, &c.

In heat or cold, he was as bold, and sung out ' *Stand*,' to all ;
And though but one score two his years, he'd *crack* (20) the first swell's hall ;
No *high pad* (21) e'er stood so game when *flash'd* at by *pops* and *ball* ;
And tho' he *prigg'd* (22) from all the great, he'd give *blunt* to the small !
            Like a, &c.

But time, tho' prime, is fast in flight, and ' *the twelve* (23) *coves* ' *blackd his try* (24),
The *beak* (25) and *topping chit* (26) proclaimed the *high pad*—he must die !
His *crab shells* (27) he kick'd off like a trump, nor *cockles* (28) once did cry ;
And *snivling pals* stood round the *chit*, to see him *twisted high* (29).
            Like a, &c.

You SWELL MOB this is better far than all your vain parade,
Of *cly faking* (30) at the *spells* (31), or at the Masquerade !

---

he looked for his pistols, but they were gone ; when he said, in an indignant tone, " This treachery, Poll, is the work of your hands, but I'll be revenged." He never saw her afterwards ; in fact, she was afraid to encounter his resentment. Abershaw was afterwards hung in chains on Putney Heath, near to which the memorable duel took place, on a *Sunday*, between the late Right Hon. William Pitt and George Tierney, Esq.

And really much more pleasant*er*—besides you're better paid—
Then leave *smashing* (32) and *pinching* (33) off, and take up the old trade
    Of a slap-up Hounslow Highwayman,
     One of the Olden Time.*

The applause and cheers at the conclusion of the song continued for a minute, and every exertion was made to procure an encore; so highly was it relished by the majority of the visitors in the booth.

"You rarely meet with, now-a-days, slang songs," observed Turf, "except at fairs, and in booths of this description; or at free and easy clubs; but when I was a much younger man, they were very prevalent in companies. However, we are getting more refined in our ideas every day, and every thing that is deemed low and vulgar, is sinking fast into the shade!"

"We are highly indebted to you, sir,' replied Jem, "for the animating and pleasing description you have given us of the jockey, and also the highwayman's parody; but, I hope, you will not take it amiss, if I ask, if you are acquainted with that splendidly fine looking female, who is sitting at the bottom of the table, at the further end of the booth, in company with a gentleman, equally well dressed?"

"Come, come, Jem," answered Makemoney, "I had quite enough; indeed, something too much of the last lady you were in such raptures about! Quite in the heroics! Why you appear to be a general lover!"

"No, no, dear uncle," said Jem, "quite a different character, I should hope. But to admire one of the greatest beauties in the creation, I trust, will never be reckoned a *fault!*"

"I don't know that," urged Flourish, "a *look*, sometimes, proves very dangerous; it too often leads into further enquiries, and you get into a labyrinth, before you know where you are. Handsome women are always dangerous articles to behold; therefore, as I have told you before, turn your eyes on objects less captivating."

"Well observed," replied Turf, "there is great danger about the look of a fine woman. The person, the young one alludes to, is quite a picture! She is a character; and her life quite a history—it is worth hearing, Master Makemoney: her memoirs would make a capital book, and without a bit of *romance* re

---

* For the benefit of country gentlemen of *mo·lern* times, the following glossa,y is added :—

1. Watchman; 2. Monied men; 3. Thief-takers; 4. Jail; 5. House; 6. Handkerchiefs; 7. Pistols; 8. Crow-bar; 9 and 10. Small bar and lantern; 11. A bar for drawing back bolts; 12. Shots; 13. Neck; 14. Spotted neckerchief; 15. Knee breeches; 16. Shoes; 17. Drank; 18. Glass of gin: 19. In former; 20. Housebreaking; 21. Highwayman; 22. Stole; 23 Jury; 24. Sentenced him to death; 25. Judge; 26. Gallows; 27. Shoes—a common practice in former times, the criminal observing "he would not die like a horse, with his shoes on;" 28. Rattles in the throat; 29 Hung; 30. Picking pockets; 31. Theatres; 32. Passing of bad money; 33. Petty larceny thefts.

quired to embellish it. What a bust!—Five to one against the whole race of East and West-enders! And as to her *peepers*, they are like flashes of lightning—there is no standing against them, and they may well be termed the '*windows of the soul*.' She has made sad work amongst the lads!—She is the——— No, never mind! This is not the time, nor place for it; but more anon,—when we meet again, perhaps."

"This is what I call dashing the cup from the lips of a man parched with drought!" observed Makemoney. "Just as we had made up our minds to obtain secrets worth knowing, respecting the '*handsome female with the fine bust!*' the description coldly ends, with—'She is the—no, never mind!' This is too bad, Mr. Turf, it reminds me of the breaking off of stories in the magazines, when your feelings are raised to the highest pitch of excitement—and you are compelled to wait a month at least, before you have any chance of learning the result—and perhaps, then you are again disappointed!"

"Ha! ha! ha! my dear Jack," replied Turf, "your style, I admit, has not displayed much of the heroics; and you were the last person from whom I should have expected a rebuke; but it seems then, that you are not insensible to the charms of a fine female with a handsome bust. Young or old, I see are just the same, when women are the theme of the argument! However, as you seem to be all in a blaze about this elegant piece of furniture for the household of a gentleman, when next we meet, you shall know her whole history, and then, you will say, it was worth waiting two months to hear."

"This is worse and worse, nay, adding fuel to the fire; and most certainly raising our expectations twice as high; but patience, patience, my dear Makemoney, you are aware is a great virtue, and therefore, we must, in this instance, acquiesce to its dictates! But out of this heterogenous mixture of persons," said Flourish, "who all appear characters to me—is there not one more worthy of description? There is a singularly looking personage lighting his cigar."

"I must not touch upon him! he is suspicious of every body who merely takes a glance at his person—he is eying us already —by comparison, he is a barrel of gunpowder, and the slightest *spark* of anger, would make him blow up the whole place in a minute. Therefore, MUM, is a matter not only of prudence, but safety.

"But there are a number of harmless *fanciers* of every description. Some of whom, their time is entirely occupied with the breed of superior dogs, and who can talk of nothing else; others of them, their sole fancy and delight is in the rearing of pigeons, and making matches as to the distance they will fly to a certainty. Cock-fighters are likewise on the *qui vive* here; and in short, every thing connected with the sporting world forms the subject of debate and enquiry, at 'pleasant Jem's' booth.

" But not the least number are the FANCIERS of the FAIR-SEX ; perhaps, the term, if not so sporting, is better in effect, to say, 'admirers of females !' and from the show here to night, you may see, Master Makemoney, that BEAUTY is not confined to the courts of kings and princes, we have some ' GOOD GOODS ' to look at. Some very pretty wild flowers, and if collected together, would make a very handsome nosegay.

" It is true their *toggery* would not compete with the silks, satins, diamonds, and *paint*, displayed by the ladies in the upper circles of society ; but for a fine bit of rude, unsophisticated nature—well-grown, without the trickery of art, and no d—d nonsense—this is the time of day, my pippins. When one can with truth, sing :—

> " If FORTUNE, fickle jade, should e'er wish to *scourge* my name,
> And what she generously gave, would wish to have again :
> O that I'll freely grant, and without the least remorse,
> Only give me what God can grant—health, my wife,. and horse !"

" You are a happy fellow, Charles Turf !" said Makemoney, " full of spirits—let the world wag as it will, I always see you the same. I should like to have a leaf out of your book."

" Well, ould chap," said Turf to Makemoney, " I must bid you a good night. You see, my *prad* is at the door, and on the *fret ;* therefore, off's the word ; but you must come and see me ; my cottage is at Hampton, on the Banks of the Thames, and do not let it be long before I see you, where you will find me happier than a king, I'll bet a hundred ! I will make you comfortable, depend upon it, and you shall experience what the late Charles Incledon used to *chant* so finely—' May we ne'er want a friend, nor a bottle to give him !' But before we part, let me give you a word of advice (whispering into his ear). Keep a good look out after the Young One—he is high bred—and they often prove skittish—won't answer the whip—run out of the course—and kick over the traces : also take care of the collectors—the artists—there are suspicious persons abroad, who might make a mistake, and put their hands into your pockets instead of their own !"

" What ! a second time in one day ?" replied Makemoney ; " that would be too much of a good thing—they have had their *dues* from us already—but *mum* !" pointing to Flourish ; " our wrongs, in this respect, we intend to keep to ourselves, and then we shall not be *sneered* at—for fools !"

" Ha ! ha ! ha ! excuse my laughing !" said Turf ; " as a rich man, you will not mind your loss, however mortifying it may be to your feelings ; but there is a consolation in all things, you can now walk about without any apprehensions of losing any thing. Good night, gents. I shall be happy to see you at my crib." He then mounted his gig and drove off.

" He is really a choice spirit," observed Jem, " there is something so hearty about his manners, that it is a pleasure to be in company. He appears to me a down-right sincere man, anxious to please his friends, at the same time fond of an adherence to the truth !"

" Charles Turf is no flatterer," said Makemoney ; " yet he is not one of those cold, hesitating characters, in bestowing praise, where the person, or talents displayed before him, have required approbation: I have always found him to be a strait-forward man—the same sort of person to morrow, as you find him to-day—he does not meet an old friend with a new face ; he is, therefore, a man whose word is to be relied upon, and rather liberal, than otherwise, in his remarks ; but when called upon to give his judgment, he has the firmness upon all occasions to decide with all the coolness of an equity judge.

" He has no ambition to be thought a better man than he really merits ; and, I must say, take him for ' all in all,' he is one of those upright, cheerful sort of men, not to be met with every day in the walks of society. Therefore, Nephew, there is no harm in your cultivating an acquaintance with him. I am sure we shall be received by him with a most hearty welcome !"

" We must go, uncle, to Mr. Turf's *crib*, as he calls it," replied Jem, " or else we shall not hear any more about the ' *handsome woman with the fine bust !*' and you know we are all very much interested in her memoirs ! I am particularly fond of biography ; more especially, when the biographer is living, and you can depend upon his testimony, being well assured that he does not resort to *invention*, instead of stating plain facts."

" I think," urged Flourish, " we ought to enlist him under our banners as a pilgrim. He would not only be a pleasing addition to our party, but also a great assistance. He is likewise well acquainted with the movements of the world."

" We will now think of starting towards home," said Makemoney, " take a peep here and there as we go along into the different taverns, and, I have been told, we shall hear some good songs, which I am very fond of—it will also give us another feature connected with Greenwich Fair, and point out to us—*that one half of the world* does not know how the other half lives !"

" An excellent proposition," replied Jem, " and I have no doubt, but that we shall meet with plenty of merriment and fun."

The Pilgrims had not proceeded far from the fair, on their road towards London, when they were attracted by the voices of some persons singing, or rather attempting, a glee. " This is the place," said Makemoney, quite full of spirit, " let us go up stairs and see what it looks like. It is all free and easy—every body welcome, and no questions asked."

On entering they found the room was filled with company of the most heterogenous mixture of persons, consisting of 'prentice

s

boys, shop girls, journeymen mechanics, watermen, clerks, shop-men, milliners, straw bonnet makers, &c. &c. A glorious scene of confusion—the room clouded with smoke—people calling out for liquor, and knocking the pots against the tables to claim attention from the waiters ! Several persons who were anxious to hear singing, were bawling out " Silence! silence ! Order !" indeed, it was more like the confusion of *Babel* than anything like a rational company, who had congregated together to amuse one another. The waiters were seen fighting their way through a dense crowd of persons, who standing up, were not inclined to move an inch, and also spilling the porter and ale over the dresses of the females.

Songs without tunes—words without music—rhyme out of question, and not very particular as to the *exact* sense of the author. Sentiment being bawled out on one side of the room, and comic songs on the other—at the upper end of it a blind fidler *teasing* the cat-gut, in order to pick up a few half-pence ; nevertheless, the company all appeared to be happy and merry, and not at all inconvenienced by the confusion of the room. After several attempts were made to procure attention, something like silence was obtained, by the repeated cries of " Attention—Silence for a lady !" A very nicely dressed female, after making a few hems, and apologies to her friends, on account of her bad voice, sang the following parody :—

> All round my cap I vears a green villow,
>   All round my cap for a twelvemonth and a day,
> If any one should ax the reason vy I vears it,
>   Tell them that my false lover is far, far avay.
>
> 'Twas a going of my rounds in the streets I first did meet him,
>   Oh ! I thought he vos a Cupid just come down from the sky—

Very little more was heard of this song, from the noise and buzz around her, but more especially from the rough and hoarse voice of a costard-monger, roaring " What use is that 'ere chant, JEM, you give 'em one that will set 'em all in a blaze, you know what I means—TOMMARROO !" when he began :—

> Ben was a hackney coachman rare,
>   " Jarvy, jarvy !" " Here am I, your honour !"
> O crikey ! how he used to swear—
>   Tommarroo !
> Oh, how he swore whilst he did drive,
> Number three hundred and sixty five !
>   Rum tum tiddle iddle, I gee wo !
>   Rum tum, tiddle iddle, I gee wo !
>
> Now Benny was a knowing cove,
>   Rumti tumti, dum dumdi, diddle um,
> But swore and flogged so whilst he drove—
>   Tommarroo !

The room now resounded with the hoarse voices of a set of fellows trying to have a '*lark*,'—the female who had sung part of

A FREE and EASY GREENWICH FAIR TIME.

the song, was in tears, and her partizans were determined to resent the insult she had received ; but all the explanation they could get was ' *Tommarroo !—Tommarroo !*' like the yells of an Indian war-whoop, bawled into their ears. This produced a skirmish—a row—nay, almost a general fight, when Makemoney, and his brother Pilgrims, who felt it *dangerous* to be *safe*, made for the stairs, and by a quick exit got into the street.

" We made a lucky escape," said Makemoney, " the blows were as thick as hail near my person ; however, I did not receive any of them,"

" Yes, a miss is as good as a mile !" said Jem, " I was very near getting a jaw-breaker from one of those blackguards, who appeared bessotted with liquor !"

" I hope, I shall not have a black eye," remarked Flourish, " but for the instant my head appeared as if it had been knocked off my shoulders, the blow was so extremely violent."

They had scarcely got into the street when they experienced the rain slightly coming down : a fellow belonging to a covered cart thus addressed them :—" Don't your honours want a con-weyance to London ?—If you do, I can tell you, at this late hour, mine is the only wehicle left ; and as I wish to make up my number—only a *bob* a piece ; but you must as how decide di-rectly, as the *chovies* are coming down in rum style, and then you see I shall charge twice as much. Therefore, a stitch in time saves nine, my masters. My *prad* is nothing else but a safe and good 'un ; he vill do his vork, and never refuses ; but he has given me a bit of a *nint*, that he is tired and vishes to get his *night cap* on. I can understand him, and for once in the vay, I should like to oblige Old Jack, that is the reason, or else, I should charge not a *farden* less than *half-a-bull*. So tumble up, my masters, and make yourselves happy, you will mix with a jolly company. I vishes to be off ! To-morrow is a new day, and the *blunt* being rather shy—I must come out to look for it. Poor Jack, and his master, can't go without grub. I does not take any riff-raff, or else my cart might have been full fifty times over. No, no, I am rather a particularish sort of chap in my customers ! So we'll be on the toddle——"

" Any port in a storm," said Flourish, " but will you start directly ?"

" In a pig's whisper," replied the driver, " only make the visit pleasant to the female folks. I have just got my number now with you three swells."

It was a covered cart—a dark night—and Makemoney and his brother Pilgrims did not observe the class of persons they were about to mix with—more women and girls than men ; and the former, it should seem, were not of the most honest or chaste description : but the rain coming down in torrents, they were glad to obtain any thing like a shelter at that late hour of the night. However, they had not proceeded far, when one of the girls, a low-life hussey, said to Makemoney, in a slang tone of voice, " I wish you would keep your hands to yourself, ould fellow—you are making rather more free than welcome."

" What do you mean by that assertion, you impudent minx ? " replied Makemoney, in a rage ; " I have not moved a finger or thumb since I have been in the cart ; but, if I am not mistaken, I felt your hands about my pockets."

" Get out, you nasty old warment ; if you say I wanted to pick your pockets, you'll say any thing. I dare to say you havn't got a *tanner* (sixpence) to bless yourself with, now you have tipped for the *tumbler* (cart). I am not going to be bounced out of my senses, and have my character injured, by such an ould cove. You had much better have been in your bed, if you have got such a bit of household furniture, than taking liberties with young girls."

" Come, I say, ould chap, behave decentish, or else I must valk you out of my wehicle in quick time," said the carman ; " these female vomen here, who are under my protection, though poor, are the right sort of folks wot won't stand any nonsense. But, I say, Nance Grizzle, you must excuse the ould cheese-monger !—he seems a little *fresh*-ish—the vorse for lush—and ould men sometimes are a little foolish, and more *hamorous* than wot becomes them."

Sprightly, in an angry tone, observed to the driver,—" What do you mean by calling the gentleman a cheesemonger ? "

" He is a cheesemonger," replied the costardmonger, " and a rich one too ! I knows him werry well—his name is Butterfirkin, of Puddle Dock !—Lord bless you, I've bought many a slice of cheese of him in my time ! He's out on a bit of a lark ; but he shouldn't pull the girls about—ould men sometimes will be *rummy !* "

" I'd have you be on your guard, Mr. Carman," said Flourish ; " the gentleman you call a cheesemonger is a Magistrate of the City of London ; and if you don't mind your behaviour, you will stand a very good chance of being committed to jail for your insolence. We got up into your cart to avoid the rain, and we will not be insulted either by man or woman ; therefore, I would advise you to let civility be your motto."

This remark from Flourish rather altered the conduct of the driver, who said to himself, " I must draw it mild ; and I shall give Nance a bit of a hint." Then appearing rather angry,— " Come, Nance Grizzle, it won't do as how for you to play your tricks in my wehicle, and injure my bread. You wanted to *frisk* the ould chap—the gemman I mean—I begs his pardon— so the boot is on the other leg ; and if you tries it on any more out you bundle, and no mistake. Every body is safe under my roof ; so gemmen swells you need not be afraid."

" Vy, you blink-eyed buffer—you Jem Sneak," answered the girl ; ' you can turn any *vay* with the vind. But I don't care a pinch of snuff (snapping her fingers at him) for you, or any one half like you. My money is as good as the King's, and I will tell you, Mr. Sneak, a bit of my mind;—if every body had their own I don't know where you'd be,—so put that into your pipe and smoke it. You think you'll be able to *gammon* the swells out of a little more *tip;* but I'll spoil you, my fine *feller*, that's wot I vill—it shall be no go after all. I likes people to be upright and down strait—no half-and-half coves for Nance Grizzle!"

"Now don't you be too *imperent*, Nance," said Jem Sneak; "that tongue of yours is rather too big for your mouth, and will be your downfall in life. I doesn't vant to quarrel with you, but you are too fast—you might be mistaken, you know. He is a gentleman, and I'm sure he would not take any liberties—he is the father of twelve children—a regular church-going man. I tells you, Nance Grizzle, you was mistaken; so drop it, and make it all right, and I'll stand a drap of summut at the next house, as I must give old Jack some heavy whet."

"What, does your horse drink porter?" asked Flourish.

"Drink porter! I believe you, when he can get it," replied Sneak. "Only you hand Jack over a tankard, and you'll soon see how soon he will take the *lining* out of it."

"This is out of the frying-pan into the fire," said Makemoney, in a whisper to Flourish; "but no matter—it is a sketch of real life amongst a certain class of society, and it only adds another event to our day's pilgrimage. We have only to keep our tempers down, and all will yet go pleasant;—but I never heard that I had twelve children before."

"That circumstance," replied Flourish, "is best known to yourself; "and, as you are not before the churchwardens and overseers of the parish to defend the charge, let it rest for the present."

"I knows as how I am a tiny bit of a passionate nature," replied Nance Grizzle; "and as you say the *Swell* meant no harm, and it was a mistake altogether, I will drop it; and I doesn't mind, for once in a vay, just to make all things agreeable—I vill be a *ke-varten* of Peppermint to mix with the *Jacky*. I likes to do the thing wot is handsome! Nance has been in tow with the swells before to-night."

Peace was at length restored, and all was fun and laughter; with bits of songs from one and the other of the assemblage in the cart, until the vehicle discharged its contents at London Bridge: the PILGRIMS then called a coach, and St. Paul's had just struck four when the knocker's rattling peal announced their return at the *domus* of old Makemoney. Flourish kept his *secret* respecting the Duchess and her daughters within his own bosom, as he wished to have a little *private* pilgrimage to himself the first convenient opportunity; and Makemoney and his Nephew let not a sentence drop from them respecting their being robbed at the gate—to prevent lots of jokes from their friends, instead of pity.

"Come," said Makemoney, "we'll have a glass of grog together before we go to bed; and take a slight review of our day's pilgrimage."

"With all my heart," replied Flourish, "as I may laugh now, I hope, without offence; but I was sadly afraid we should have had rather a serious row, on your account, with Nance Grizzle. It was too bad of you, Makemoney, to tickle the girl in the dark."

"Why, I must confess," answered Sprightly, "I did not like the appearance of things at one time; and it might have been unpleasant, particularly to my uncle, to have made our appearance before the Greenwich Magistrates as *disorderlies*. A row and a fight almost appeared inevitable."

"Well, Flourish, you have a right to your joke if you think proper," said Makemoney, "but I am now satisfied she was nothing else but a female pickpocket; and, for fear of detection, she began to cry out first. I pledge my honor I never touched the hem of her garment. However, we will drink success to our next pilgrimage."

"Never mind, uncle," answered Sprightly, "all's well that ends well; and perhaps we may have the laugh next time against Flourish."

"Be that as it may," observed Makemoney, "our pilgrimage has strongly reminded me of the words of Sterne:—' 'Tis thou, Liberty—thrice sweet and gracious goddess—whom all in public, or in private, worship—whose taste is grateful, and ever will be so till NATURE herself can change. No tint of words can spot thy snowy mantle, nor chemic power turn thy sceptre into iron. With thee to smile upon him, as he eats his crust, the swain is more happy than his monarch, from whose courts thou art exiled!' I believe so, if I may judge from what I have seen to-day," urged Makemoney; "and if the pleasure and enjoyment of real liberty are to be witnessed, I assert, without the fear of contradiction, that it is on the BANKS OF THE THAMES. How say you both?

"Agreed!" said Flourish.

"Agreed!" echoed Sprightly.

BON REPOS!

CHAPTER IX.

A few preparatory words on Authorship—shewing that it is more advantageous to have NATURE *for a guide than trust to the imagination ; and giving the preference to mix with society in general, than cogitating in the closet, if characters and real life are to be truly depicted. Be it so :— where shall we go ? above or below bridge—The question at issue—Difficult to decide ; both situations attractive to the echo. An invitation to* TURF'S *cottage puts an end to the argument.* MAKEMONEY'S *recollections of former days respecting the Banks of the Thames—Dress and manner of the people—an immense change for the better. Mill- bank ; to wit—An extraordinary character of the olden times—a thief and a honest man in the same person ; com- pletely illustrating Pope's maxim, that " the proper study of mankind is man." Curious definition of Champagne, versus Ale, by one of the Pilgrims—a matter of taste. Outlines of a Race Course—a study, perhaps worthy of contemplating by persons who seek after pleasure. Flats and Sharps—Fools and Deep Ones—Peers and Tradesmen —all in motion.* THIMBLES *applied to a very different purpose from their original intention. The Magical Garter, and the Gilded Pill ; or, how to twist an Argu- ment. A head without brains ; or, a sketch of a thoughtless fellow—a tale for inexperienced young men. The long wished-for anecdotes related by* TURF—*The Match-Girl ; or, the Woman with the fine Bust. A peep in the mirror —wretchedness and beggary personified—The transform- ation—What can't gold do !*

IT is said that after " a storm comes a calm ; that pleasure is frequently accompanied with pain ; and the fatigues of a journey take some little time before the traveller is enabled to set out again in pursuit of fresh objects.' Granted: and although our PILGRIMS were not called upon to perform *penance,* or com- pelled to put *peas* into their shoes, by way of punishment for their misdeeds in life, like the Pilgrims of olden times, yet, it should seem, they required some indulgence to recruit their strength, in order again to start forward, like " giants refreshed," in search of adventures connected with " flood and field."

Authors, in general—such as the writers of romance, tales of love, or novels of domestic life—sit themselves comfortably down in their closets, with a good fire before them—a library full of books, to give them a *helping* hand if at a loss for a subject ; or perhaps some intelligent friend or acquaintance may give an accidental call, and render assistance to the author, should he be perplexed towards elucidating some knotty point, or clearing up doubts and fears : but we, on the contrary, have nothing " *cut* " and " *dried* " for our pages, and until our three Pilgrims again sally forth, under the canopy of heaven, to endure the rude blast, the pitiless, pelting showers, or perhaps be almost choked and smothered with dust, if they depart from their previous mode of peregrination—that is to say, if they do not embark on board of steamers, and prefer putting into harness their *Bucephalus*, and get over the ground in a cab or stage-coach—our labours are positively at a stand still !

This, as a matter of course, must operate as a drawback to our proceedings, and likewise create delays ; but then the advantages of FACTS are immediately seen, and the loss of time made up by the originality of circumstances presented to the view of the reader.

STILL LIFE is quite a different thing altogether. An author may possess a fine and bold imagination, with a lively, vigorous conception, like the sculptor, who, in his mind's eye, sees the beautiful figure and drapery in the rough, huge block of stone ; and he may also conjure up spirits, " red, black, and grey," to answer his purpose, in order to produce a highly spirited interesting work. Be it so : but then he is likely to " o'erstep the modesty of nature." He may, likewise, to give greater effect to his ebullitions of fancy, *strain* the point, outrage probability, and be in danger of exhibiting the *ridiculous !*

But, on the contrary, when the author only takes NATURE for his guide, he treads on sure ground—he cannot err. His prospects are delightful—his FACTS are strong and conspicuous, as to speak for themselves : his mind is also free—his subjects are not *distorted ;* and the opportunity also presents itself, " nothing to extenuate, or set down aught in malice." CONSIDERATION is, therefore, out of the question : he is not lost in thought, and waiting, as it were, for his ideas to flow *spontaneously*.

No! he has to keep his observations alive—real life for his pen—men and women on the *pave*—with all their light and shade of character, dress, manners, and conversation, from the late ponderous *Daniel Lambert* down to the " Living Skeleton."

For instance—let the artist make a sketch from fancy, and as a picture it may be viewed as a pleasing, pretty, nay, an exquisite performance, and bear the strictest investigation as a work of art. But when the draftsman takes out his pencil on the top of a mountain, and is about to depict the splendid scene before him, he then *grapples* with reality !—he has the *substance* and not the *shadow* to pourtray :—his MIND becomes enlarged : the vast expanse almost creates giant-like ideas : his feelings are all alive to the inviting prospect—the peculiar situation of a tree—

the peeping out, as it were, of some venerable ruin—an old church upon a hill—a slight dash of water with a ship in the distance, and surrounded by lofty hills—places all these subjects in so conspicuous a form for his pencil, that the finest imagination in the world must be as snow before the sun, when put in competition with the BEAUTIES OF NATURE!

Just so, the AUTHOR who has *his* facts to work upon, which enables him not only to write with spirit, but for a time his *inventive* faculties are set at rest, the good or bad man is within his view, he hears the one *talk*, and he sees the other *act;* and marks down both their conduct; and perhaps, he may be surrounded with characters of every description, either eminent in society for their superior talents, or *notorious* for their improper and suspicious demeanour: his tale is then likely to become interesting, in a greater or less degree; *singularity* may attach to his descriptions, but probability is not in danger of being lost sight of—because he has data for his argument, and the author appears rather more in the character of an historian than any thing else, noting down with clearness and perspicuity the time and place where such circumstances have occurred; and can relate his tale with all the glowing animation of truth.

Not so the writer of romance. The reader is taken through long corridors—down trap doors—he sees the shade of some hero in armour, with his vizor up—he finds himself in a lonely vault—overwhelmed with strange noises, and petrified with fear—alarmed by the sound of some dreadful bell—is surrounded by ghosts, hobgoblins, grinning spectres, and the whole et cetera of the phantasmagoric fraternity, like the incantation scene in Der Freischutz, which too often fill weak minds with nervous terror, and employs much time, without adding to the stock of knowledge; while a work which has facts, and every day circumstances for its basis, increase by example our stock of common sense, and adds to our knowledge of the world. Such must be ever acknowledged the great advantages resulting from the works of nature—the society of mankind over the *imagination* of the highest, comprehensive, and most splendid descriptions.

SHAKESPEARE has put into the mouth of Iago the following words: "I'm nothing, if not critical!"—the words likewise apply with as much force to *character* in a review of human nature! Authors and artists must fail in their representations of men and manners—if they are not critically correct as to outline, and almost *verbatim* in their detail, if they feel anxious to give effect to the various personages which come under their observation.

HOGARTH, in some of the most disgusting scenes which occur in life, by the fidelity of his pencil, has rendered them of the most interesting description to mankind; not only as a mark of abhorrence to be avoided, but also as a useful lesson to the young and thoughtless; and SMOLLETT, in his admirable

T

sketches of different persons, in his various novels, would never have been able to produce that strong effect upon the mind of his readers, if he had *minced* the matter; and instead of portraying the reality of the thing, might otherwise have rendered it *mawkish*, and totally unlike what it should be.

True, some persons may be inclined to quarrel with the *broad* humour displayed by that inimitable novelist, whose every page abounds with real facts of truth and human nature; which may be looked for in vain amidst the voluminous writers of the present day.

However, we are most anxious to state, that *obscenity* ought to be avoided in all instances—it may be done without—it ought to be done without—and authors are highly culpable who resort to offensive terms of expression—

" Immodest words admit of no defence !"

But, nevertheless, effective humour, and perfectly in unison with the character which is represented, ought never to be *marred*, or reduced in strength, by anything like far-fetched squeamishness, or an attempt to be *cautious* over much. There are persons to be met with daily amongst the mass of mankind, who have no value for *etiquette*—who study no rules—have no choice of words—no check upon their conversation, or demeanour—that their sort of dialogue may be found fault with by the well-bred and intellectual part of society, is not to be doubted; but surely, the author who is called upon to communicate with his pen, in an artist-like manner, sentences that he has nothing to do with *personally*, may retort, in the phraseology of the Queen to Hamlet—" Those words are not mine !"

In the upper House of Parliament, dignity of expression—gentlemanly demeanour—and the greatest urbanity prevails throughout the arguments—establishing a high character for its elevated situation in the eyes of the public.

In the House of Commons quite a different *character* is to be witnessed—energy of declamation—violent harangues—and fine examples of public spirit. Choice of words are not the desideratum in this splendid assembly of the wit and talents of the country.

A mob has also its character—and the laughable, rude, yet witty sayings, which so often occur in crowds, are worthy of record ! Just so, a fair, where all ranks of people congregate together, to meet with amusement in a variety of shapes, sustains *a character* totally different from any other public meeting.

Character is our decided object—an adherence to truth and nature our constant aim—and let us ask of what value is our description, if we do not relate faithfully the dialogue and manners of all classes ?

During the period which occurred previous to the Pilgrims being prepared to start a second time, Flourish had made up his mind more than once, to have gone privately into the neighbourhood where the card represented the Duchess to have dwelt, to have ascertained the reality of her situation in life—indeed, he was quite feverish on the subject; but some circumstance or another interfered to thwart his inclination, and he was compelled to postpone his journey until a more favourable opportunity presented itself.

Makemoney and Sprightly were equally close on the circumstance of their being robbed in the Park. Thus matters stood on the eve of their departure.

" I should like," observed Flourish, " if it meets with your approbation, to have a turn up the river this time ; but, perhaps, I had better put it to the vote ; and then whatever may occur during the Pilgrimage—fault cannot be found with each other."

" Very fairly proposed," replied Makemoney, " I am for a trip up the river."

· " And so am I," responded Sprightly, " therefore the proposition has been received, as it ought to be—unanimously. It matters not to me whether I go *up*, or *down* the river—the banks of the Thames have so many delightful attractions, that I have no particular choice, being determined to make myself quite at home upon any spot; and all happiness, whether I travel by a stage, an omnibus, or any other vehicle, so that we alight on the banks of the Thames !"

" Your declaration pleases me, nephew," answered Makemoney; " at Turf's cottage, a day or two may be passed in the most agreeable manner ; in the first place, his conversation, anecdotes, and knowledge of life, must afford us a fund of amusement; independant of strolls on the banks of the Thames connected with his residence. I'll not even hint at the female with the fine bust, as any excitement, or cause of attraction."

" You are quite right, Makemoney," replied Flourish, " that subject might be a dangerous one, and likely to do mischief; I would not answer for the consequences when Sprightly becomes wholly acquainted with her memoirs.—Ha! ha! ha!"

" I will make no rash promises," answered Sprightly ; " I am but a man, and very young in the field ; therefore, I will let time and circumstances speak for themselves. I am not *invulnerable !* But rest assured, my friends, I do not second the proposition of a turn up the river on that account ; yet, to tell the truth, I most certainly should like to spend a few hours in the company of Charles Turf, Esq. Besides, he is a sporting character ; and it is the time of year for the Hampton Races, held upon the inviting downs of Moulsey Hurst. The races are not only well-attended by the public in general, but by persons of the highest rank and fashion ; and characters of the greatest notoriety in the kingdom are seen *unbending* at them !"

" True," replied Makemoney, " the spot of ground you have mentioned is delightfully connected with the subject of a most interesting nature—Garrick's Villa!—The Palace at Hampton

Court!—Pope's residence at Twickenham!—independent of other attractions!"

"But, my dear sir," observed Flourish, in great extacy, " why leave out that unparalleled spot for romantic scenery in the world—Richmond Hill? Also, Bushy Park, once the retreat of the late Mrs. Jordan, whose presence gave it an additional importance and weight in society? Then I again propose up the river—it will be a new feature for us, and the contrast will be attractive in the extreme."

The arrival of the following letter, put an end to the argument respecting *above* or *below* bridge :—

Turf Cottage, Banks of the Thames.

"MY DEAR MAKEMONEY,

" There is a kind of charm in the very sound of your name, which must always prove an attraction to those persons who are inclined to write to you. And if I felt inclined to pun on it, I should say the invitation I am about to give you, is to a place, where you are very likely to *lose* money! But as you have no *touch* about you of a sporting character, there is little danger to be apprehended on that point.

" However, there is no time to lose, if you wish to enjoy a day or two's pleasure at Hampton Races—the Course is delightfully situated, and the company in general of the best sort in society.

" Lots of amusement, I have no doubt, will be afforded to you, my dear Friend, more especially, as I have heard you state, you never saw a race in your life. Therefore, as you are quite a novice in those matters altogether, you may put yourself under my care without the least hesitation ; at all events, I will not lead you into any thing like danger ; but point out to you those places, and those characters which will be well worthy of your observation.

" Tell your young friends, Flourish, and Sprightly, it is not a 100 to 1, that they do not meet with the handsome female, they were so much in raptures with at Greenwich, as the lady in question is very fond of sporting her fine figure at races in general.

" I will be in waiting with a carriage for you at Kew Bridge—till then,
          " My dear Friend,
                    " I remain your's truly,
"P. MAKEMONEY, ESQ."   " CHARLES TURF."

" This invitation, I believe," said Makemoney, "will meet with the approbation of all parties ; and we have nothing to do but prepare ourselves for another trip by steam."

The Pilgrims were once more afloat, on the *qui vive* in search of fresh adventures, and ready for any circumstance, or object, which might attract their attention. The steamer was nothing like so crowded as when the holiday folks were all anxiety for Greenwich ; but, nevertheless, there was no lack of passengers, who were rather of a more genteel description than those who had honoured the Greenwich steamer with their presence. The band started them with a favourite air—the weather was all that could be wished—and the Thames was inviting in the extreme.

Flourish made a hasty tour of the deck, paid a visit to the saloon, and also took a peep into the second cabin, to ascertain if any of the *characters* were by chance on board, that called forth his attention on the last Pilgrimage.

On his quick return to Sprightly, he observed, " *Bronze* is not here at all events ; therefore, his absence is a treat. The *Picturesque* Doleful most likely is dancing attendance at the elbow of some coroner, waiting for an accidental job—no annoyance from Scapegrace—and the fascinating Duchess and her two agreeable daughters are not to be found. Therefore, we must put up, as the sportsmen have it—fresh game ; or, birds of another feather !"

" I am glad of it," replied Sprightly, " very glad—variety is charming : but should no objects in the shape of characters, or persons of an interesting, or *outre* description claim our notice, why then we must look out for all the improvements on both sides of the river : until something more lively presents itself to our view."

" With all my heart," answered Makemoney, " we must occupy our minds with something ; St. Paul's cannot call forth any new remarks ; and Blackfriars Bridge has nothing to recommend one word in its favour ; but I cannot pass the Temple Gardens, without observing how many pleasant hours I have spent in them of an evening, after the fatigues of business were over. This liberality of the Benchers, in allowing the public the free use of them for several months in the year, does them great credit. The Temple Gardens also bring to my recollection a young friend of mine, when I was quite a youth, who afterwards made his way in life, by his splendid talents, and superior mind —Counsellor Browbeatem ! He was called to the bar very early in his career ; and ultimately, arrived at the judgment seat. He was the best counsellor to cross-examine any witness, that I ever heard in my life ; indeed, he was so much dreaded by some persons, who feared to encounter his searching remarks, that a Major in the Army observed, that he would almost sooner face a whole fire of artillery, than come under his lash in a court of ustice ; if it suited Counsellor Browbeatem's purpose, he would ' hunt-up ' a witness, as he termed it, and make that witness recollect the whole circumstances of his life—good, bad, or indifferent, if it were essential to the Counsellor's obtaining a verdict,

" Browbeatem always contended for victory, either to clear a prisoner of the accusations brought against him, or on the contrary, to prove his guilt, according to his brief. He was severity itself ; and quite in earnest with every cause that he undertook, either for the plaintiff, or defendant. He has often told me, in private, that he has saved many a rogue from the gallows, who ought to have expiated his offences upon it. ' But they were my clients,' said he, ' and I was paid to do the best for them that I could.' He used to boast, over his cups, that he stood so well with eleven of the judges, that he always claimed the greatest attention from them; but the frown of the twelfth, notwithstanding the Counsellor's *bronze*, and readiness of reply, used, at times, almost to unnerve him.

"Counsellor Browbeatem, I must confess, never appeared to me, half so much 'at home,' as he did at the Old Bailey; although he could make a good speech, on any subject, in the other courts.

"He was termed the '*blowing up*' Counsellor, amongst the vulgar part of society, and in the early part of his life, he had visited all the haunts and night houses of the thieves, in order to make himself a complete master of the cant languages, and slang terms, thet he might have been called a second *Grose*. By which means he obtained a clearer insight as to their transactions and feelings, and he often *astonished* some of the most experienced thieves when he put the questions to them in their own *peculiar* way. He frequently remarked to me, that it had enabled him to be *up* to their movements, and *down* to their tricks! The Counsellor always reprobated the adage—'give a dog an ill name and hang him!' In several cases in which he had been engaged, where the previous bad character of a man was enough to convict him, he was indefatigable to remove that almost overwhelming prejudice, and to prove the innocence of his client. In one or two memorable instances, he succeeded in saving the lives of men, who otherwise might have been found guilty—almost from bad characters alone.

"He was of a most facetious disposition; and in those cases where he could exercise his vein for humour, he has kept the court in roars of laughter, that even the judge, in spite of himself, has lost sight of the gravity of his situation on the bench. He was also a kind and liberal man; and, to his honour be it remembered, in many cases where charity has been required and pointed out to him, he has received his brief without a single shilling. He was indefatigable in his profession—his very soul was in it; and business flocked in upon him in so great a degree, that for many years of his life he was always in his study by six o'clock in the morning: yet, strange to assert, but strictly true, Counsellor Browbeatem's advice to me was, never "*to go to* LAW!"

"And excellent advice too," replied Flourish; "for the glorious *uncertainty* of it frightens all sensible men."

Makemoney, although not a practical man out of doors as to the tricks and ways of the world, from his steady attention to business, nevertheless had been a great reader: he also possessed a tenacious memory, and was an excellent companion to fill up a vacant hour. He was never at a loss for anecdotes, and felt a pleasure in communicating whatever knowledge he had acquired for the benefit of his acquaintances and friends.

"On both sides of the Thames, I perceive," said Makemoney, "great improvements are taking place; and you scarcely advance a yard or two but some new building presents itself to your view. Such is the enterprise and spirit of all classes of society connected with trade and commerce in the Metropolis, since I was a boy; that I am lost in admiration when I reflect upon the subject."

"I never," said Flourish, "pass Waterloo Bridge without praising this unequalled structure; and I think I might assert, without the fear of contradiction, there is not such another bridge to be found in the world."

"I do not think there can be two opinions about Waterloo Bridge," replied Makemoney; "and it is a splendid ornament to this part of the Thames."

On passing through the Bridge,—"Captain," asked Flourish, "what is the name of that handsome building on the other side of the river, near the shot manufactory, and which appears to me to have been recently erected?"

"It is called the New Lion Ale Brewery, the property of Messrs. James and Charles Goding; and a magnificent piece of workmanship it is," replied the Captain: "it may be equalled perhaps, but in my opinion, as a brewery, it cannot be excelled in the Metropolis. It is a treat to go over it. And if, gentlemen, you are fond of a glass of good ALE, fine and sparkling like champagne, the above is the place to purchase it." The Captain, who was a jolly fellow, by way of illustration to his recommendation, began to sing a few lines of the well-known ballad—

> Can any king be half so great—
>   So kind, so good, as I?
> I give the hungry food to eat,
>   And liquor to the dry.
> My labour's hard, but still 'tis sweet,
>   And easy to endure ;
> For while I toil to thrash the wheat,
>   I comfort rich and poor.
> And I merrily sing, as I swing round my flail,
> My reward, when work's over, is a jug of brown ale.

" Champagne is exhilarating, I admit," said Makemoney, " and generally considered a *bon bouche* by all wine bibbers ; but a glass of real good ALE is far more valuable, as to quality, when the human frame is the object of consideration. Champagne makes a Frenchman of you for a few minutes—light, airy, but not lasting—a sort of flash in the pan. But a cup full of humming stingo puts a man's courage on the alert—he is ready for any thing—and his companions soon perceive he has all the animation of a real John Bull about him—English to the back bone ! "

" Bravo, uncle ; still NATIONAL ! " replied Sprightly. " I heard, Captain, the opening of the Brewery was celebrated with great demonstrations of joy."

" There were rare doings, indeed, sir," answered the Captain ; " I partook of Messrs. Godings' hospitality. Two thousand bottles of wine were disposed of without any difficulty : ten barrels of ale were soon drank, not only as a matter of good taste, but out of respect to the donors of the feast : several bushels of hot potatoes, roasted in the stoke hole, were received as a treat : sixteen hundred weight of meat cooked, including the barons of beef, which netted forty-three stone. Over each of the barons a ' beef-eater ' and his page, in the uniform of the Yeoman Guards, were assigned to answer the claims of those who might be disposed to participate in such rich and substantial fare."

" It must have been a very gratifying sight to the visitors," observed Sprightly.

" Every person appeared happy," said the Captain, " and upwards of fifteen hundred visitors dined off old English fare ; including beef, boiled and roasted, veal, hams, tongues, pigeon-pies, with all the *et ceteras* to render such a collation truly inviting. One thousand pounds, I am sure, could not have paid the expenses."

" So many licensed victuallers assembled together must have produced rather a funny appearance," said Flourish, " for they are generally fond of the good things of this life, and can handle a knife and fork better than most other men, owing to their excellent practice ; and also know the taste of a glass of good wine ! Ha ! ha ! ha ! "

"True, sir," replied the Captain, "they were not *niggards* at the tables, nor with the wine; and many of them were 'right merrie' before they departed. It was one of the most joyous scenes I ever experienced: all was mirth and good humour to the end of the chapter. I do not know any building that was ever half so well *christened* as Messrs. Goding's Lion Ale Brewery: it was a rich picture of English hospitality."

"I am sure of it," said Makemoney: "the British merchant never does any thing by halves—his enterprise, liberality, and extension of commerce, go hand-in-hand together; and search the world all over there are nothing, in my humble opinion, like the merchants of old England to be met with."

"But, in order to render the opening of the above splendid Brewery more important in the eyes of the public," answered the Captain, "Messrs. Goding gave a prize-wherry, of the value of forty pounds, called the '*Lady Jane*,' out of compliment to Lady Jane Goding (the wife of one of the brothers). This boat-race not only excited considerable interest, but afforded a vast deal of amusement to the numerous spectators."

"Such spirited conduct deserves success," replied Makemoney; "and when we get to Richmond, we will all drink prosperity, in the Lion Ale, to the brewery."

"Most certainly," echoed Sprightly and Flourish.

Makemoney was quite in a descriptive mood, and thus observed to his brother Pilgrims, in passing Milbank,—"I have known this place for upwards of forty years, and, from the best information I have received on the subject, at the period I allude to, it was the favorite resort of a class of persons, nick-named '*Kiddies!*'—low-life sort of folks—both the young men and their girls. Their dress was also *peculiar* to themselves. The men wore their hair in close curls on the side of their heads, done upon leaden rollers; hats turned or looped up on the sides; and to their breeches eight, and sometimes ten, small buttons were seen at their knees, with a profusion of strings, after the famed 'Sixteen-string Jack;' long quartered shoes, with very large buckles.

"The language of those kiddies was low and illiterate—they never mixed with any other society but flash company, thieves, &c., and were altogether different from the present race of young men.

"Milbank, on the Sunday and Monday afternoons, was crowded with this description of persons—idlers, apprentice-boys, journeymen, &c. It was a difficult matter to obtain a seat in the evening at any of the public-houses on the Bank. There was a numerous attendance of 'cutter-lads,' so designated because they subscribed towards pleasure-boats, to row with four, six, or eight persons—and their cockswain was dressed in a red jacket with gold lace and white petticoat trousers. The above

U

cutter lads made quite a parade of their exertions up and down the River.

"It was one continued scene of rude low-life and gaiety, which lasted for several years; and the *ridiculous* and absurd idea of being thought a 'deep one,' and a '*knowing* character,' was the only great object in view with all these sort of people. The rooms at night were turned into Free and Easy clubs—full of noise and confusion, and obscured in smoke—and scarcely any thing heard but the lowest of flash songs. The following short specimen will not only shew the *taste* of that period, but amply suffice :—

> Behold the City youth, to the garden he does run,
> Where he toddles by the Judies, and thinks it is rum fun :
> Oh, he toddles by their sides, and stands the *Sam* for gin,
> Naps a kiss for his treat, and he bundles home by ten.
>> Ri tal la, ral la !

> Now by more frequent going the bolder he does get,
> And in some *flash panny* he ventures for to sit ;
> Where he learns to patter flash, and to chant a rolling song,
> And to come his 'eyes and limbs,' as the kiddy rolls along.
>> Ri tal la, ral la !

"But, I am happy to say, the scene has long since been changed altogether, and improvement is now the order of the day in every point of view. Nothing of this kind is now to be witnessed on Milbank, and the race of kiddies—thanks to the march of intellect—have become extinct. Men's minds have undergone a complete revolution ; and every thing low, blackguard, and illiterate, is not only viewed as disgusting to the feelings of sensible persons, but shunned in all directions."

"For this picture of men and manners, uncle," said Sprightly, "permit me to thank you kindly : it has proved a very interesting subject to me."

"The only thing disagreeable, decidedly disagreeable to me, on the banks of the Thames, is the *look* of the Penitentiary ; it always produces in me the most unpleasant sensations," observed Flourish ; "its very look is appalling."

"It also reminds me of an extraordinary character who lived very near it for some years," said Makemoney, "who was hanged for forgery : and it was well known, at the same time, that he could neither read nor write."

"Not read, nor write," asked Flourish, "Is it possible !—How could he commit a forgery, I should like to know?"

"He was tried on two counts—one for forgery, and the other for uttering the notes, knowing them to be forged," replied Makemoney ; "you rarely meet with so extraordinary a person, and well might Shakespeare assert—

> "What a piece of work is man !"

"Did he follow any trade or calling?" asked Flourish, "I

should like to hear a little of his history; any thing out of the common routine of the lives of men, either in high or low life, always interests me more than I can express! You will, perhaps, oblige us with a few of his peculiar traits, we cannot know too much of the actions of mankind!"

"I will, as far as my recollection serves me, and likewise, what I have heard of him," replied Makemoney. "*Slender Billy* was the designation he was known by, and was recognized, as well in the neighbourhood of Westminster, as the old Abbey itself!

"He kept a menagerie for beasts of every description, in the Willow Walk, Tothill Fields, and was patronized by some of the first people in the kingdom, who were fond of baiting the bull, the bear, the badger, &c., and also by the collegians, who left the study of Homer, and the elements of Euclid, for the more intimate knowledge of the game bull and the fierce badgers. In fact, numerous M. P.'s were often seen participating in the rude humours of the pit, regardless of the heterogenous mixture of the company; and also, several members of the peerage, did not appear to feel any sort of degradation to patronize the efforts of Slender Billy in his breed of dogs, and other animals calculated to afford amusement."

"There must have been considerable talent attached to him, although in a peculiar way," said Sprightly.

"Yes, and strength of mind, too," answered Makemoney; "only listen to the result.

"Slender Billy was quite a hero in his own way; and a man of considerable importance amongst the thieves. In the cant language, he was viewed as the *safest* fence in the kingdom;— *i. e.* a receiver of stolen goods. His integrity was considered as firm as a rock; and any thing like treachery to his pals was never thought of. Billy was well known to the officers of justice in the above character; and the magistrates in the neighbourhood, were perfectly aware that such a man dwelt within one hundred miles of their office. But the Lacedemonians did not acknowledge *thieving* as a crime, provided the thief was not caught in the fact. This was the creed of Slender Billy!"

"Indeed," said Flourish, "you do astonish me. But how did he escape punishment, when himself and dwelling were so very notorious?"

"For forty years he pursued this career; but during that period he had been in custody several times, *merely* on suspicion, and his plans were so well laid, that he always escaped detection.—Ha! ha! ha! I cannot help laughing, whenever I think of it.—His dwelling house was particularly well situated for concealment, and he adopted the following mode, to render it more secure from the attacks of strangers. He garrisoned it with bull dogs, so as almost to render it impregnable without the use of fire arms, and when any intruders paid him a visit, that he did not like the appearance of, and he generally kept a good look out, Billy never leaving any thing to chance, he let his best friends loose, as he termed his dogs ; this gave him time, if he had any concealed property on the premises, to remove it. Officers, and other persons, were in danger of their lives, if they attempted to contend with the fury and courage of his thorough-bred English bull dogs.

" Billy often used to laugh heartily at this circumstance when relating it to any of his acquaintances—' I never pay any taxes myself,' said he ; ' but I give my dogs the hint, and they inform-ed the parish officers that if they had any desire to get home in a whole skin, to return the house, in their books, as an empty one.'"

" It may be well said," replied Sprightly, " that one half of the world does not know *how* the other half lives !"

" True," answered Makemoney, " but the most extraordinary part of his life is to be developed. He was a housebreaker in his own person ; and a most accomplished workman, to com-plete the object in view without detection. In all his trans-actions with the thieves, he was considered one of the finest specimens of an *honourable* and an *honest* man, that ever existed. He was a straight-forward fellow upon all occasions, and when-ever he gave his word and honour to his companions, it was valued by them equal to the most severe, and binding oath, taken by any pious man. Slender Billy was frequently called upon to divide stolen property amongst thieves ; and in his cha-racter of an *arbitrator*, Lord Eldon could not have been nicer, or more *conscientious* in his decisions to do justice, even to the splitting of a hair.

" To his offspring, (and he had two remarkably fine daughters, who were much admired for their persons,) he was *tenderness* tself ; and felt an overwhelming anxiety to give them excellent educations, to make up for that deficiency in himself, which he often bitterly lamented the want of, to his friends.

" The courage of Slender Billy was of the highest order ; fear was out of the question ; and he possessed a heart that would have done honour to a better cause. Horses and dogs he bought and sold, in rather an extensive manner. However, singular to state, but true, that in bargaining for the purchase of each, on refusal to his terms, he has often in a jocular manner informed the owners, that he must have them for *nothing*, and which promise he repeatedly carried into execution "

" I never heard of such an extraordinary character," observed Flourish ; " I have read the whole of the Newgate Calendar ; but this Slender Billy, as you call him, for his talents distances the whole of them put together."

" In his occupation as a *nacker*, (to kill horses when worn out with age, or owing to accidents,) it was his boast that he had stolen many a poor old horse, rather out of charity to his carcase, than for the value of his flesh. Slender was always viewed as a humane man."

" What a strange mixture of good and bad qualities in the same person," observed Sprightly.

" Yes," said Makemoney, " he was viewed by his associates as one of the *staunchest* men alive ; and whatever affair he was engaged in, Billy proved himself as firm as a rock ; and nothing could tempt him to act the part of a dishonourable fellow.

" For a certain sum of money, he entered into an agreement with a French General, of the name of Austin, who was on his parole in England, with several other French prisoners, to convey them safely and secretly out of this country to France, for which he was treacherously impeached by one of his companions, and sentenced to two years imprisonment."

" Then," urged Flourish, " the adage does not always stand good, ' that there is honour amongst thieves !'"

" The above imprisonment ultimately proved his downfall and death," replied Makemoney ; " the rascally conduct and ingratitude of the Frenchman towards Slender Billy, preyed severely, at times, upon his feelings, during his confinement. He had risqued the safety of his person, added to the expenses of a boat, and the assistance of other persons, to render the escape of the Frenchman more certain, and upon the General's landing on his own soil, notwithstanding his oath and promises to Billy, he was ungratefully cheated out of his reward. He was so enraged at being thus tricked by the rascally Mounseers, as he termed them, that he swore, he would much sooner have forgiven the robbery of the whole of his property in one night, and have been left entirely destitute, than any man should have forfeited to him his *word* and *honour,* in a cause, in which Slender Billy had been engaged."

" I would have had such an ungrateful scoundrel, as that French General, thrown into the sea," observed Flourish ; " and however he might have called out for assistance to save his life, none should have been rendered to him, as an example to other traitors !"

" Severe, but just," replied Makemoney, " and nothing can be considered too harsh for the crime of ingratitude, more especially when liberty and life is in danger from it.

" Slender Billy, during his imprisonment, being still anxious to turn the penny to account, acting upon the old adage—' Get money, honestly, if you can ; but get money,'—and flattering himself that none of his *pals* would betray him, he *dabbled* a little in forged notes ; but he found, to his cost, that he was mistaken in the integrity of his associates, and he was regularly sold. A *plant,* as they call it, (a scoundrel, under the mask of friendship,) was put upon him, and in spite of his knowledge and caution, proved his destruction."

" Honesty is the best policy, after all, in this life," said

Sprightly, " and then a man may lay his head upon his pillow and sleep soundly, without any thing like fear or apprehension disturbing his rest."

" A more cold-blooded plan was never laid for the ruin of a man, than in the following instance," observed Makemoney. " The notes were scarcely purchased, under the mask of friendship for Billy, by one of his associates, when the rascal gave immediate notice to the keepers of Newgate, who were in waiting outside of the door, for the result. They rushed in, and seized violently hold of his person ; but his courage and resolution did not desert him in the hour of distress ! Slender was a very strong man, and determined not to be entrapped while a chance remained to extricate himself from danger, or while he had any strength left ; he wrestled successively with his keepers, and threw them from him with the utmost ease, and shoving his hand, which contained the *marked* notes, brought in by his treacherous associate, into the fire, and holding it there till they were all burnt, exclaimed—' Now its all right, you may search and be d—d !' "

" With such high courage and cool determination," said Flourish, " what essential services might such a man have rendered his country."

" But Billy was wrong in his conjecture," observed Makemoney ; " unfortunately for him, some forged notes were concealed in his bedstead, which he had forgotten, and which, added to corroborating circumstances, proved his overthrow. The Bank of England had been making great exertions to find out the source from whence the forged notes were obtained ; and it is an incontrovertible fact, that Slender Billy could not read, although he was indicted for *forgery!* He had plenty of good notes about him when he was searched by the officers ; and the way he distinguished a large note from the ' one pound ' was, from the length of the words, ' one hundred,' &c."

" Such a person justly deserved punishment for his misdeeds,' answered Flourish, " but he ought not to have lost his life from deceit and treachery."

" He appeared very firm throughout his trial," said Makemoney ; " but, on being turned into his cell, after his condemnation, his feelings were overcome, and he burst into tears. He said, if he had not have been able to have cried, he thought his heart would have burst. But his fortitude returned, and he soon resumed his wonted cheerfulness. He divided his property in the most equitable manner between his family ; and he prepared himself for his awful *exit* with so much firmness as to astonish all his friends. However, singular to state, in opposition to some part of his behaviour, he was a man of strict punctuality and integrity in all his dealings, as to the common transactions of business, and had saved a large sum of money."

" If he could not read nor write," said Flourish, " he must

have had a good head, and have been an excellent calculator, according to his own notion of things."

" The following decision he made, when offered his life, if he would inform against the persons who furnished him with the forged notes, is a convincing proof of his correct notions of honor," observed Makemoney. " Nothing could tempt him from his purpose; urging, that he preferred *death* to dishonor. He had also, he said, solemnly pledged himself, in common with the rest of .his associates, never to *impeach* the concern under any trouble, and that he was now too honourable to forfeit his word."

" There is something about the character of such a man, in spite of his failings, that must excite our pity," said Sprightly. " Had he have received the advantages of education, I have no doubt in my mind but a better fate might have awaited him."

" Upon his being pressed very closely by his intimate friends to save his life," replied Makemoney, " he replied, that if he did *inform* against his pals, he must hang several others, and render their families miserable. Therefore, what happiness could he derive, if he gained his liberty? His life would always be in danger. A pardon, it is said, was offered to him the night before, and also upon the morning of his execution; but he resisted all importunities on the subject—saying, that he must ever afterwards have *crawled* upon the earth in secresy, and never shewn himself in daylight. He, therefore, resigned himself to his fate, and expiated his offences on the scaffold without a sigh, or a desire to live. His exploits would fill a volume."

" And would make a very interesting one, I have no doubt," said Flourish.

" It was the opinion of Slender Billy," resumed Makemoney, " that six hours' rest was quite enough for any man, and that the remaining part of the twenty-four ought to be actively employed *honestly;* but if that could not be done, a man ought not to stand in his own light as to the acquirement of property.

" It was said of Slender Billy, that when St. Paul's Cathedral was robbed of its massy plate, he *received* it without any qualms of conscience; and he also kept a private still, being a great enemy to Excise and Parish Officers. He frequently laughingly observed to his acquaintances, that tailors were of no use of him. He had no choice of *colours;* neither was he particular as to superfine or any other cloth: nay, more, he was never measured for any articles of wearing apparel. He was asked how he managed these circumstances. ' Why,' said he, ' to tell you the truth, ' I always *prigged* * all the dress that ever covered my body.'

---

* No person was better known in his day, in the neighbourhood of Westminster, than the late Slender Billy, and recognized in the following characters: —A safe *fence* (receiver of stolen goods); an expert *cracksman* (a house-breaker); a *peter-man* (cutting the luggage off from coaches); a *nacker* (a killer of horses);

" And now," said Makemoney, " I think a finer illustration of Pope's maxim was never made out than in the case of Slender Billy, that the

" Proper study of mankind is man ! "

The wind was blowing rather fresh, and nearly capsized Flourish's hat, when he observed to the Captain of the steamer, —" I believe you call this part of the river ' *Chelsea Reach ;* ' otherwise, the ' Cocknies' Sea.' "

" Yes, sir," replied the Captain ; " people that don't know any better may laugh at the term of ' Cocknies' Sea ;" but I have seen several accidents occur here entirely owing to the violence of the wind ; and small sailing and other boats have been upset in the Reach : indeed, in several parts of the River Thames I have experienced more severe gales than I have in coming from Scotland."

" We have been so much interested, my dear uncle, with your entertaining anecdotes," said Sprightly, " that we have passed several interesting objects, that otherwise might have engaged our attention ; but as Hampton Races, and a visit to Turf's cottage, being set apart for this trip, other days must be devoted for those places we have passed over."

Richmond was now at hand, and the Pilgrims were on the look out for Charles Turf, whom, as they neared the shore, they

---

a *gin-spinner* (a private still) ; the keeper of a dog-pit, &c., in a *business*-like manner ; yet, nevertheless, in the general acceptation of the phrase, when met with out of either of his *callings*—as a lively, jolly, spirited fellow ! He had no notion of doing things by halves, as he termed it ; and he always liked to treat his friends in a handsome manner when he gave them an invitation to his house. At one of his christenings—for he was fond of birthdays, and keeping up the good old customs of hospitality—he invited a very numerous party, as he said, " to give the *kid* a name." Nothing could exceed the splendour of the repast. The tables groaned under the weight of the good things of this life, which were furnished in the utmost profusion. The *dessert* vied with the first nobleman's banquet in the kingdom for variety and richness of fruit. The wines were of the very best quality, including champagne and other expensive sorts ; and the spirits could not be surpassed for their excellence. In fact, an emperor, or the greatest epicure, could not have found fault with a single article of refreshment that was provided for the guests. The company—rather a most heterogenous mixture of thieves and honest persons—stared and looked at each other with surprize, and were calculating what a vast expense he must have been at in furnishing such an out of the way splendid entertainment. But he soon removed all doubts upon the subject ; and, being rather merry, he filled himself a large rummer full of sparkling champagne, singing a line or two of the well-known flash song,—

" For supper Billy stood,
To treat his curious cronies,' &c.

drinking the whole of their healths ; observing, at the same time, " The more you eat and drink, my friends, the more I shall be pleased, for then I shall think that you like the supper. The *flats* say the *blunt* can do any thing ; but in this case the *blunt* was not required at all, and I have not put myself to the slightest expense—for every thing you see in this room, either *on* or off the table, I have *stolen.* So I again say, make yourselves all happy and comfortable, for it is impossible that either you or I can quarrel about the *price* of it."

espied looking towards them. "Here am I," said he, " you see I know the value of time : and always make it a point to be five minutes *before,* than after, in any engagement I make. However, I am very glad to see you, my jolly Pilgrims—the weather is fine—the day is delightful—the road appears to be crowded with company—and, I have no doubt, I shall be able to furnish you with plenty of amusement of one sort or another. So jump up, my friends, and we shall soon be on the race-course, which you will find a complete scene of excitement from one end of it to the other !

" The spot on which you now stand," observed Turf, " has been distinguished for several great sporting events—besides racing, coursing, &c., most of the principal prize battles have been contested on Moulsey Hurst. However, that sort of amusement has had its day; and it is not my intention to offer any argument either for or against its continuance; but I merely make the remark, that I have seen some of the greatest legislators that ever adorned this, or any other country, sitting down on this beautiful turf, viewing the contests I have alluded to with all the breathless anxiety and suspence that ever attended the most important debates in both Houses of Parliament, and the greatest personage in the kingdom included as one of the anxious spectators."

" Indeed," said Makemoney, " I was not aware of that circumstance ; but nevertheless, in a free country like ours, I do not think the illustrious person at the very head of affairs, can be too much acquainted with the manners and sports of the people over whom he has to preside !"

" Exactly so," replied Turf ; " spoken like a real patriot, and a true politician. From having obtained a thorough knowledge of the people—mixing with them—participating in their habits —and hearing their opinions on the laws and government, in propria persona, he is, by such intercourse, enabled to guard against flatterers—to form a correct judgment in his own mind —and is not likely to be beaten down by powerful sophisticate eloquence on the one side of the question, or give way to browbeating oratory on the other ; provided he had only emancipated from his closet, and left the leading-strings of courtiers and sycophants. And if ever any sovereign, in the history of kings and emperors, had a thorough knowledge of the feelings of his people, it is our present King, God bless him !"

" If all the crowned heads in the world," said Flourish, " had the same opportunity of becoming acquainted—*personally,* with the manners, customs, and sports of the people, over whom they preside, government would be better administered—the cause and effects of liberty would be more generally understood on both sides of the question—and a much greater portion of happiness enjoyed by all ranks of society !"

" I think I heard you say, Makemoney, that you never was

upon a race-course in your life, during the time the races were contested," remarked Turf; " then I will promise you a treat— although I have been upon almost every course in the kingdom, yet, strange to say, it always appears like a new feature to me, from the variety of subjects that continually attract the notice, independant of the sport which occurs between the horses! But to a common observer, a person not interested as a betting man, a race-course is a fine picture of real life; and affords a fine source of amusement.   There is a great mixture of company, no doubt, and you are sure to run against the good, bad, and indifferent part of society.   But if you are careful, and do not mix in the confusion and crowd, you will have very little to complain of, I assure you—therefore, I say, be on your guard !"

" We are very much obliged to you," replied Flourish; " but we are nothing else but careful fellows, and always look before we leap !"

" I am glad to hear it," said Turf ; " but I see some of my friends in the betting stand, that I have some wagers with, during which time, you Pilgrims can take a stroll over the course, and spend a short period in the most pleasant manner you can with the different subjects which present themselves to your notice. Therefore, till I return to you, you will excuse my absence ; but you never can be dull upon a race-course."

The first thing that attracted the notice of the Pilgrims upon the departure of Turf, was a man with a small table, and a crowd of persons listening to his harangue.   He had three thimbles upon the table. and was endeavouring to shew his capabilities by placing peas under them, and continually shifting them, so that no person could name the *particular* thimble under which one of the peas was to be found.   The strange and impudent remarks of the fellow, produced roars of laughter.

" With this small thimble, and this little pea," said he, " it is impossible that any thing like deception can take place; *cheating* is entirely out of the question.   Therefore, I will bet pounds, crowns, pewter, or copper, a five, or ten pound note, or any other sum, large or small, that no lady or gentleman present, can tell under which thimble the pea is to be found !   Can you tell, sir ?" addressing himself to Flourish.

" I don't think the pea is under either of them," replied Flourish, " I saw you throw it away, and here it is, upon the ground."

" You don't know a *pea* from a turnip, I'm sure," said the fellow, " you had better borrow a pair of spectacles the next time you come to the races, for you must be blind !   You can't see at all, and I'll bet you five pounds the pea is under that thimble," (pointing to one of the three).   These rude remarks produced bursts of laughter from the crowd, at the expense of Flourish, who was getting a little angry.

" You may be as saucy as you please, Mr. Thimbleman, to my

friend, but I likewise saw you throw the pea away!" said Sprightly, quite in a passion, " you can't impose upon us so easy as you imagine." Another loud laugh from the crowd, and the persons connected with the gang.

" You are a *moon-raker*, I'm sure," replied the fellow with the thimbles. " You are a nice man to find a mare's nest! You can see what never took place ! I'll bet you five, or ten pounds, that the pea is under the middle thimble ; but stop, I'm wrong, you never had five pence in your pocket in your life time—you are only some journeyman barker to a clothes shop—and you have borrowed a suit of clothes from your master, to cut a bounce for the day at the races—I'm up to you ! But such fellows are of no use to any body—poor fellow, I pity you."

" He's no moon-raker, fellow," said Makemony, quite irritable, " nor a barker to a clothesman, but a young gentleman of property ; therefore, be more choice of your words in future. You know, very well, you threw the pea away!"

" Don't put yourself in a passion, my old cripple, with one leg in the grave !" answered the thimble man, accompanied with a tremendous laugh from the crowd.

" I'll give any man the price of a pint of ale, if he will take this poor insane creature to the lunatic asylum, which is close at hand, and the governor of the charity will reward him well for his trouble ; poor old creature, he is as mad as a March hare !" Roars of laughter followed these remarks.

Flourish, Sprightly, and Makemoney, being entirely off their guard, with this sort of cant—vulgarly called chaff-cutting, were nearly ready to knock the saucy fellow down.

" Well now, you three pretended swells," said the thimble man, "if you were all put into a bag, and well shook together, nine pennor'th of coppers would not be found amongst you.—Nothing else but outside show !"

" You are a lying scoundrel," replied Makemoney, " we have got our pockets full of money !"

" I should like to see it," answered the thimble man. " I'll bet you five pounds the pea is under the outside thimble, and no mistake !"

Flourish, in a whisper to Makemoney, observed—" he said it was under the middle thimble before, he must be wrong, I'm sure !"

When a decently dressed looking man, a confederate in disguise, observed to them, in a kind of whisper, " I would bet him five pounds for his impudence, and make him pay for it.— I saw him throw the pea away myself—you can't lose, it is impossible—bet him !" This advice, or rather stratagem, had the desired effect, and the jolly Pilgrims were completely duped.

" Done for five pounds," cried Makemoney, putting down the note, quite in ecstacy that he should punish the fellow for his impudence.

"A fool and his money are soon parted," (taking up the outside thimble, under which the pea was discovered,) said the thimble man. The roar of laughter was terrific, and several of the fellows cried out—"He certainly is mad, take him off to the lunatic asylum." The astonishment of the Pilgrims is not to be described—the mob now began to hustle Makemoney, who seeing his danger, made the best of his way to another part of the course, followed by Flourish and Sprightly.

After the Pilgrims had recovered from their surprise, and having a hearty laugh at the way they had been decoyed to lose their money, Makemoney observed, rather gravely, "Live and learn!"

"Truly," replied Flourish, "and you are quite aware, my friend, that learning has always proved an expensive article; therefore, as it is a *new reading* to you, don't complain. Turf will have the laugh against us, when we tell him of this adventure."

They had not moved many yards before they observed another *touter*, a fellow haranguing the crowd outside the door of one of the gambling booths, inviting the spectators to walk in and make their fortunes!

"This is the lucky booth," said he, "fortunes are made with the utmost ease, and without the least anxiety! But, remember, nothing venture, nothing win; therefore, walk in, and please yourselves. It is called the game of *Une, Deux, Cinque!* Fifty can play as well as one—and it is not necessary to exchange a single word upon the subject.

"Some persons may wish to *insinuate* it is gambling; but rest assured, ladies and gentlemen, there never was a greater error broached in society; it is positively nothing more than an elegant *amusement*, at which the very first quality in the kingdom are delighted with.

"Only take a peep at the interior, and you will find it fashion itself! The table is magnificent, and the ball, which rolls so interestingly round it, is beautiful, and reminds you of the colours of the rainbow! Therefore, you have only to fix on the *right* colour, and 'good luck' you will find at your elbow! Nothing can be more simple!—You have not to ask yourself a question on the subject! A child can play as well as the antique hero! There is no *shuffling* and *cutting* at this amusement; and trumps are not required to win at this game!

"Some obstinate people will call it a game! But what's in a name?—Nothing! Then, I say, ladies and gentlemen, walk in, out of the heat of the sun and dust. Wine is at your service; and if you *hit* upon the right colour, you are sure to make a HIT!

"We are the most honourable folks to deal with in the world! You can taste before you buy! That is to infer, you can walk in, and see how the amusement is going on, and then amuse yourselves as you think proper. Free will is our motto! We have no *decoy* ducks, but if you will not put money into your pockets, and lay the foundation of a fortune, that is not my fault."

" This man appears more refined in his discourse, than the vulgar thimble fellow, I admit," said Makemoney, " but his invitation may not be a jot the less deceptive ! He does not want for the art of persuasion to induce people to enter the booth ; and he seems to possess that sort of imposing ability, which would make some people almost believe that the moon is made of green cheese !"

" Never mind what he says on the subject," replied Flourish ; " I will try *my* luck—I can leave off when I like.—Besides, I have had a touch at this sport before ! Therefore, I will be your leader in the *amusement,* as the fellow called it at the door. I think, I know as much as any of them about *Une, Deux, Cinque ;* I will show you both how to win money enough to pay all our expences."

" If that is the case," said Sprightly, " there is not much danger to be apprehended in looking at your play, Flourish. Go in, and my uncle and I will follow you."

Flourish pulled out his purse with a smile on his face, and a look of consequence—whispering to Makemoney, on taking out five pound, " I shall soon turn them into twenty-five sovereigns —so here goes !"

" I hope you will," said Makemoney, " to make up for the thimble-rig !"

" Hush !" answered Sprightly, " let that affair be consigned to oblivion."

Flourish's *first* sovereign soon vanished on blue—the second shared the same fate—the third was missing quickly—the fourth gone in a twinkling—and the *fifth,* off like a shot ! Flourish felt his own insignificance ; and Makemoney and Sprightly could not refrain from a fit of laughter.

" It is nothing, sir, when you are used to it," remarked the man at the table, with a smothered grin. " If you had selected the *right* colour, the event must have come off differently. Will you make your game, sir ?"

" Not any more to-day," answered Flourish, " it is not one of my lucky ones." The Pilgrims immediately left the booth, in search of other adventures.

" We may as well see all the tricks and fancies offered to us, now we are on the spot," said Sprightly, " it will prevent loss of time when we go to another race-course : besides we shall not be *had* a second time."

A shabbily dressed looking fellow was next observed by the Pilgrims, flourishing about a *garter* (a piece of list,) in his hand, talking to a small group of persons—" Behold this garter," said he, " and simple as it may look, the king, our gracious sovereign, never had any thing like such a garter in his possession, although he has given so many garters to the brave knights about his person.

"I call it the '*Magical Garter*,' because it is more difficult to unravel than the celebrated clue you have heard talked of by your great grandfathers and grandmothers, which secretly led to Fair Rosamond's bower.

"It was given to me by a great necromancer, who had more eyes in his head than Argus, and more fingers on his hands than the spots in a peacock's tail. There never was so great a creature in the world, before nor since; he out-heroded Herod, by his astonishing feats and performances! And good luck to his memory say I, for he gratuitously bequeathed to me a taste of his quality!

"Then, thus it is, ladies and gentlemen—from a *bob* to a crown—from a sovereign to ten—fifty to a hundred—nay, for any thing you like—a bushel of gold to a sackful of the precious coin! Do not start with surprise, when I tell you I have a waggon-load close by of the glittering ore, just to convince the public of the value set upon me by the Bank Directors; and that I do not stand still for the ready rhino to back myself—that no lady or gentleman on the Race-course are in possession of the secret to fix the garter in this table with a large pin, which I will put into their hands for that particular purpose!

"My trumpeter is now over the Course, offering this challenge to all the world!

"Come (addressing Makemoney), you are fat enough, ould chap, to be an astronomer, if you like it. You consult the stars, at times, I have no doubt—a dealer in the occult sciences; and perhaps a Bartholomew Fair conjuror in disguise! Therefore, I will lay a sum, equal to all the coin in your pockets and the clothes upon your back, that, with all your knowledge of the '*abracadabara*,' you cannot fix this garter with the pin to the table!" A very loud laugh from the crowd, and shouts of applause, followed this speech.

Makemoney could not resist joining in the laugh, although against himself, but replied, rather in an angry tone of voice, "I am no conjuror, nor a wise man; but I am not fool enough to be entangled in your garter."

"Well, don't be out of temper—you are old enough to know better—but you are only in leading strings yet," said the chap with the garter; "if you are a flat you can't help your looks! Perhaps your two friends are clever, and they don't know it. Let them have a try—I am open to all their cunning for a trifle. Come, young swells, you don't prick either *in* or OUT of the garter, for a sovereign. There is a fine chance for you, if you have any thing like *pluck* about you."

This last challenge put Sprightly on his mettle, and in an instant he replied, "Done, for a sovereign—I prick *out* of the garter!" The money was put down; when the garter man observed,—"I like your courage; you are sure to win—if you don't lose! Ha! ha! ha! Now, see what a flat you look like!

Why, you are *in* the garter! Now, I'll lay you another sovereign, if you try again, you are OUT of the garter!" The shouts and loud laughter from the crowd made such a noise that the Pilgrims were glad to make their escape as soon as possible.

In the course of a few minutes they perceived the cheerful countenance of Turf making towards them. "Well, my worthy Pilgrims, I hope you have been highly amused during my short absence."

"Very much amused, indeed," replied Makemoney; "I have been picked up, as you term it, for a customer at the thimble rig, and I am a five-pound note the worse for it."

"Ditto, at Une, Deux, Cinque," said Flourish; "but I was at fault respecting the right colour—I took *blue* instead of red, or else it would not have happened."

"And I," observed Sprightly, "have been punished a little, for endeavouring to become acquainted with the mysterious folds of the garter."

"Ha! ha! ha! Then you cannot laugh at one another, as you have all been *nibbled* a tiny bit," said Turf; "but, my dear Pilgrims, there is nothing like EXPERIENCE in this life: theoretical knowledge goes for very little in the scale of society: I have paid for it—and so must you. After all, perhaps you have laid out your money well. Listen to me. At the *Thimble-rig*, you have not a shadow of chance to win, be you as clear-sighted as possible, without they give you a sprat to catch a herring! Therefore, have nothing more to do with thimbles.

"With the *Garter*, it is precisely the same thing: the man who holds it can either put you *in* the folds or out of them at pleasure: then let this information satisfy you; and leave the tricks of the garter for other customers at a Race-course, and consider one pill a dose.

"At the game of *Une, Deux, Cinque!* you *can* win; and, in my time, I have seen several banks broken belonging to the different tables on a Race-course; or at gambling-houses, when a run of ill-luck has been against them. But *novices* must expect to have a little the worst of it when they first 'come out.' Ha! ha! ha!"

At this juncture, a dirty-looking little man, with a cadaverous face, worn out from the effects of riot, dissipation, and debauchery—scarcely a shoe to his foot, a worn-out hat, and a coat that had done its duty for several years past—hastily pushed by Turf—moving his hat to the latter—and said, " I hope you are well, sir."

" I wonder at the fellow's impudence to address me in public," observed Turf, with great indignation; " a detestable fellow like that———

Providence slubbered it in haste.
'Tis one of her unmeaning compositions,

> She manufactures when she makes a gross.
> She'll form a million such—and all alike—
> Then send them forth, ashamed of her own work,
> And set no mark upon them. Get thee gone!

" In that wretched epitome of a man ; or, rather the wreck of a human being ; you behold a distressing picture and awful example of thoughtlessness and extravagance ; it is frightful to reflect upon it! He was possessed, at different times in his life, of property to the amount of upwards of eighty thousand pounds. His father, a foreigner, was a merchant at the east-end of the town, a dealer in diamonds, a very cunning, sharp, deep sort of man, with no other object in view but to realize money. In fact, money was his idol. His son was born in England, and it might in truth be said, without a mind. What little education he obtained, was like swindling, for his father would never pay any of his schoolmasters without they obtained payment in a court of justice! This might be considered a drawback to improvement, but he never shewed any signs of intellect, and imbibed the greatest portion of his father's worst qualities ! But he never had any idea of the ' main chance,' although from the moment he could lisp, he never saw any thing before his eyes but the most parsimonious conduct in his parent—a complete miser ; who would never part with a shilling without the law compelled him to do so; the great feature in his son's life was *reduction*—instead of increasing his property. Well might it be said of father and son—

Sure such a pair were never seen !

" From quite a youth he appeared to have a *taste* for depravity of the worst kind; and his associates, both male and female, were composed of the lowest grade in society. Nevertheless, he was flattered, caressed, and made the hero of the tale in such companies, because he could administer to their wants, and furnish money to pay the nightly expences of each debauch. The only ambition he was said ever to possess, was to appear something like a well-dressed gentleman; but if he had had a well-furnished hall, and a score or two of tailors every morning at his command, they never could have accomplished the task! His clothes were, at that period, of the first quality, but he never rose higher in the estimation of his own immediate friends, than a tolerably attired *groom* to a man of property.

" He ultimately, by the advice of some of his *cronies*, took to gambling ; and accordingly visited some of the first-rate houses at the west-end, and having lots of money in his possession, he played for heavy stakes. He was quite a novice—impudent and proud—and as headstrong as a horse, he dashed at every thing that presented itself to his view. He would not listen to any thing like advice ; and he has been known to bet the odds— seven to four upon himself, when it has been *two* to one

against him : yet, strange to say, such *extraordinary luck* *
attended him, that he has broken two and three substantial
banks of an evening. But *his* day was for a very short time.
He was found to be by his associates what is termed nothing
else but a rank flat ! He was *floored* upon every suit—he possessed no judgment whatever, and several schemes were laid to
victimize him with the greatest success. From bad to worse,
he ultimately lost sight of every thing like *principle,* and would
join in any robbery to cheat the unwary : his *moral* character
was detestable in the extreme, and much worse than all his
other transactions put together. In the zenith of his riches, he
married a poor girl, according to his account of it, from attachment ; but, from his connection with the most abandoned females, he very soon got rid of her, and allowed a gentleman
ten guineas a week to keep his once dearly-beloved wife, as he
urged, out of " harm's way," which the attorney of this depraved man regularly paid to him.

" But ruin overtook this ' apology' for a human being ; and
from such extravagant conduct and excesses he was reduced to
want and almost beggary ! He then turned *Informer* against

---

* " *Luck*" does wonders frequently at a gaming table, as well as in other pursuits in life ; and it is surprising what *novices* have achieved, although quite ignorant as to any scientific knowledge of the game they have been playing—the
mere effects of *chance.* The following facts may be relied upon :—the brother of
an Admiral, who had a great *penchant* for play—seldom missing a night at the
table of a well-known house—lost a heavy sum of money one night, it is
said, not being quite himself, having indulged a little too much over the bottle,
before he appeared at the table ; in consequence of which he lost every shilling
he had in his pockets, but still was very anxious to play ! He therefore asked the
proprietor of the house to lend him some money to proceed with the game ! " At
any other period, and on any other pursuit " replied mine host, " any sum of
money should be readily at your service, sir ; but in the present instance it is
contrary to the rules of our house to lend money to play against ourselves. Should
you want any trifling sum to pay for a coach home, you have, sir, only to mention
it." " No !" he indignantly replied, " I can walk home ;" rather chagrined at
the refusal of a loan. However, he had scarcely got a few yards from the house
in question, when putting his hand accidentally into one of the outside pockets of
his coat, to his great surprise he found a ten pound note, which he supposed he
must have put in by mistake during the anxiety of play. He immediately returned
to the table, and in the course of the night not only recovered the sum of money
he had lost, but actually went home one thousand five hundred pounds the win-
ner !

Another instance might be quoted as to a *lucky* and an *unlucky* night in the
same person. The son of one of the most celebrated members of the bar, (who
was distinguished not only for the propriety of his general life, but his indefatigable attention to his profession) " but no more like his father than I to Hercu-
les !" won some thousands rapidly in succession at two or three houses in the
early part of the evening ; and congratulating himself on his great success, he
called at a Club House on his road home, where he met with a couple of the most
scientific players at whist, cribbage, and other similar games ; he was persuaded to
play, and he not only lost every shilling that he had about him, but was compelled
to give his I. O. U. for several thousands. Such are the effects and circumstances
connected with gambling. Many other instances, well-known facts in the " play
world," might be introduced, if necessary. There are a few *cool* gamblers, it is
said, that are not to be moved by any circumstances whatever.

2

some of the houses in which he had lost his money—but his character was so bad that his oath had no weight in a Court of Justice, and he was foiled! I understand he now lives like a sturdy beggar on the contributions of shillings and half-crowns from his former associates, whom he *duns* every time he meets them. However, he is despised and shunned, as he ought to be, by every person who values the appellation of—a MAN!

"However we may be taught to feel for the misfortunes of our fellow-creatures," replied Makemoney, "there cannot be the slightest regret expressed for the sufferings or deprivations of such a character as you have just represented to us. Such kind of feelings as he possessed I am totally unacquainted with, and I hope I ever shall be. I did not think it possible that men could degrade themselves so horribly in the eyes of society."

"I do not wonder that you are astonished that the principles of men can be so debased; but you have lately 'come out in life,' and have been more engaged with *books* than men," said Turf; "yet when you mix more with out-door society, who get a livelihood in the best manner they can, either honestly or otherwise, your astonishment will wear off in a great degree."

"Persons in retired situations must be totally ignorant of such fellows," observed Flourish, "and cannot for an instant entertain an opinion that such are the every-day transactions of life."

"I have known broken-down gamblers," replied Turf, "who have lost every shilling they possessed in the world, estates, land, &c., and who could not work, and 'to beg or dig' were ashamed, and who had no means to obtain subsistence, except in a vile capacity, have turned rapidly round, and lost sight of all the principles of honor; and also have become the most inveterate black legs and sharpers ever met with in the walks of life. It is a well-known fact, that in one year in the metropolis so great did the gambling mania prevail in the higher classes, that four young men, who came into princely fortunes, lost every thing they possessed in the world; amounting, it is urged, to nearly two millions of money. And if such men *can* outlive their misfortunes, is it surprising they can undertake to do any thing?"

"You positively alarm me," answered Sprightly, "to think that men can be such idiots—nay, rogues to themselves—and not only embitter every future moment of their existence, but also that of their relatives and friends."

The attention of the Pilgrims was now directed to a ragged fellow, with a printed list of the race-horses, soliciting them to become purchasers. "Come, gentlemen sportsmen," said he, "who's for a bit of the terrible high-bred cattle that are to start for the gold cups, plates, &c., at Hampton Races? Take notice, worthy sporting gentlemen, I offer you none of the low-life tricks of the *garter*, thimbles, or throwing a ball round a table, to deceive your eyes and pick your pockets! No, no—I have a higher game to play at.

"Here you have the real sport for your money—the real thing, and nothing but the real thing. You will witness the talents of the jockies, whose superiority in riding those fine creatures is a treat—all pictures of beautiful horses! You hear the bell ring —see the jockies mount—the race-horses start—and admire their beauty, bone, and action. You also hear the conversation of the betting characters—the immense interest they feel on the horses going off—the hopes, the fears exhibited—the loud shouts of approbation from the crowd when they see the jockies make play, when they are getting near the winning post—and the joy and pleasure expressed when the favourite wins the race.

"Therefore, lay out a tizzy, a deuce, or any sum you like, to encourage poor PUBLISHING JACK,—who toddles from one end of the kingdom to the other, to give a correct list of those terrible, terrible high-bred cattle, for the amusement and information of the Sporting World!"

"I never heard fellows, in the course of my life," said Makemoney, "tell their tales half so well as I have heard to-day upon the race-course; they positively seem to have made it their study to find out the *weakness* of mankind. Ha! ha! ha! They will, if you believe them, persuade you to any thing. Here is the rankest gambling that ever was seen, termed Une, Deux, Cinque, *twisted* into a pleasant amusement; the *folds* of a garter only wants *genius* to unravel it; and the *thimbles* are too small to cheat or deceive any person whatever. I never heard any thing like it; and indeed it may be truly said, cockney as I am, that I have lived in London all my life, and a much greater simpleton in reality than the clodhoppers, as they are called."

"True, uncle," replied Sprightly, "you could not have expected to witness such tricks and fancies in the counting-house of a bookseller's shop. If so, our pilgrimage in search of adventures must have proved nothing else but 'stale, flat, and unprofitable.'"

"Every man to his trade," observed Flourish; "call it *art*, if you please, for every thing out of doors appears to me to be reduced to a complete science. You are *robbed*, according to a system laid down for the purpose; *cheated*, likewise, after the rules of art; and however knowing or experienced a man may consider himself, in the excitement of the moment, he generally gets duped, and becomes—a VICTIM! Plausibility is a very insidious mode of attacking the senses."

"It is the *novelty* of the attack which beats you," answered Turf; "but, after all, you have not had much reason to complain—you have been punished but very little for your *credulity*. However, if you please, worthy Pilgrims, we will take a view of the horses who are about to start, and if you are fond of the sight of high-bred animals, I flatter myself you will be much gratified."

" Any where you like," said Makemoney; " we cannot do wrong, in my opinion, when under your especial care, my friend Turf; at least, I flatter myself we are as safe as when under our own roof."

" Such confidence, on your part," replied Turf, " would be rather *blind* than otherwise. It is true, I might be able to point out to you several improper places that you ought to avoid visiting; but there are moments upon a race-course, when, experienced as I am in the ways of the world, I have found it, as the term goes, ' dangerous to be safe.' Rest assured, I am never too confident.

" However, pleasure is now the order of our movements, so let us push forwards to the starting-post."

Makemoney, in his progress to the appointed place was delighted with the general view of the Course, which was not deficient in point of fashion, elegance, or female beauty. He enjoyed the promenade greatly, and observed to Turf, " You may laugh at me as much as you please, but I am certainly proud of my country, and the NATIONALITY of it—the feature throughout is independence to the echo! The inmates of the splendid barouche and four, embellished with a coronet to give it importance in the eyes of the vulgar, put up with the most convenient place the coachman can find upon the Course; while the proprietor of the *donkey* and pair of hampers, with articles for sale—thinks and *acts* upon it, that he is entitled to the same privilege in this free country; and it is this view of the thing which proves so grateful to my feelings, and makes me proud that I am an ENGLISHMAN!"

" If I had the power of bestowing the honor of knighthood to any man of my acquaintance," said Turf, " it should be upon you, Makemoney, as a real specimen of the *true* John Bull. Ha! ha! ha!"

At this instant a dashingly dressed sort of man, but more like a *Frenchman* in every point of view, than a native of England, hurried by Turf, giving him a familiar nod. " I cannot help smiling," observed the latter, at the *contrast* which has just passed me. He is an Englishman from top to toe, connected with birth, parentage, and education; but on the contrary his delight is always to express himself in favour of other countries; and to run down in the severest style the bad taste of his own. I believe it is admitted that he has travelled a little —and he is well known at the West end of the town by the cognomenation of Captain *Grand ;* or Jack the boaster!!! He is quite a character—and for a *romance*, I think I may say, he is matchless! I do not mean to urge that he *lies* with the intention of doing mischief to the persons he talks about—but merely to give himself an air of importance in the eyes of society to be looked upon as a man of consequence. He knows, or pretends to know, every body who has attained any thing like eminence with the public! Dukes and Lords he mentions as his friends with the greatest familiarity; and authors, poets, painters, actresses, and actors, he will become acquainted with, if impudence can assist him. He does not wait for any introduction; but contrives by some means or another, as it were, to throw himself in their way, and then gives an account of himself—apologising for the liberty he has taken with them! But the *address* of Captain *Grand,* I must confess, is rather prepossessing than otherwise; and he is tolerably well informed on most of the topics of the day. He possesses a trifling independence, which enables him to dress well at all times—added to economical habits—he manages to keep up the appearance of a gentleman. He is to be seen at all the public places of amusement —but he contrives never to pay at any of them—except when dire necessity compels him to shew the cash—indeed, he is well known at all of the theatres in the metropolis—as the ' *very orderly* gentleman !' The Captain is likewise ready at all times to accept of invitations to dinners; and to *act* the ' amiable' upon every occasion when he has not to put his hand into his own pockets : he adopts the well-known adage to the spirit and letter of it—that " fools make feasts, and wise men eat them !" He is a most excellent card player—which is a kind of adventitious income for him—and for his knowledge and coolness at whist and cribbage, he is equal, if not superior to most other persons in private companies, however competent they might be, from possessing a thorough knowledge of the above games. But to do justice to Captain Grand, I never heard him called as a *cheat,* yet I do not remember ever to have heard that he lost a game upon any occasion: by which *luck,* as he called it, he was never short of ready money. In company he always renders himself a feature—a kind of pocket chronologist to his friends— by which knowledge he has established for himself the character of a *reference.*

" Yet notwithstanding his accuracy in the above points, whenever any opportunity offers that he can get upon *stilts* he becomes a perfect *Munchausen,* by the most outrageous improbabilities which he puts forth; and should his veracity be doubted, he declares, upon his honor, that he has too much regard for the truth, to deviate from it, in the slightest particular.

" He is an immense favorite with young persons who have not seen much of the world. *Grand* is a most excellent judge of his company; he soon finds out their weak points—and if he can *victimise* in a genteel manner, he never hesitates; but then he has the *art* of doing it with so much grace and pleasantry, that he appears rather to be conferring a favour than accepting of one.

" However, he has more than once been roughly handled for boasting of having received favours from ladies—of whom he has been detected in not having the slightest knowledge: and, in his own opinion, he fancies himself the most decisive ' *Lady-killer*' in the kingdom. Therefore, my worthy Pilgrims, should he ever cross your path, you will know how to treat him—if not prove a complete match for ' Jack the boaster !' "

" We never can repay you, Sir, for such practical advice," replied Sprightly; " illustrated by facts, and demonstrated in so clear and pleasing a manner. For my part, I could listen to such narratives for ever !"

" We have no time to lose," answered Turf; " let us go and look at the racers ! Those terrible high-bred cattle, as the man with the lists designates them: they are my delight; I am not ashamed to acknowledge it, and those gentlemen who patronize the breed of race horses, in my humble opinion ought not to be classed under the title of—*Gamesters !* It is a sport which ought to be encouraged ; and breeding such fine cattle is an honor to the country !"

" Much as I am against gambling," said Makemoney, " I admire, and would encourage the breed of race horses."

" Notwithstanding there are great prejudices entertained against the sporting world," replied Turf, " it cannot be denied that it offers great encouragement towards promoting the breed of horses, dogs, &c. and many noblemen and gentlemen, attached to British sports, prove the means of giving employment to thousands of persons, who otherwise might remain idle, and become burthensome to their parishes ! I am ready to admit that the attractions of races are alluring to the high-spirited, the thoughtless, and unwary persons, to speculate their money ; that ruin—precipitate ruin, is often the serious consequences, before any such result is anticipated."

" Your candour is admirable," observed Flourish ; " but if men will run headlong beyond their means, and plunge into difficulties without any *why* or wherefore, such inconsiderate characters must take the consequences upon themselves, and ought to be punished for their temerity."

" Ambition is also a great feature in the sporting world, like other movements in life," urged Turf ; " some gentlemen wish to possess the best stud in the kingdom—a crack pack of hounds, and superior animals of every description ; and no doubt great sums of money have been expended in this manner. It also cannot be denied that many characters are to be met with who obtain a livelihood on the *chance* of the thing ; but, nevertheless, it does not follow that all sporting gentlemen are GAMBLERS: indeed, the contrary is the fact. There are numbers of breeders, and names might be mentioned, who never risk a shilling on any event in a *gambling* point of view."

Turf had scarcely finished the above remarks, when Sprightly, quite in ecstacy, roared out to Flourish, "There she is!"

" Who? the Duchess!" asked Flourish.

" No, no! talk of snow before the sun," replied Sprightly, " but the female with the fine bust, who excited so much attention amongst us at the sporting-booth at Greenwich; and she is giving a very familiar nod to you, Mr. Turf, accompanied with a pleasing smile."

" Indeed," said Turf, " then I must return it," and kissed his hand to her; " I perceive it is Charlotte——"

" Charlotte! who?" asked Makemoney. "Has that most lovely woman no other designation but plain Charlotte?"

" No other at present; in fact, she has undergone so many appellations," replied Turf, " that I am quite at fault as to her real name, and that is the truth of the matter. I have, my dear uneasy Pilgrims—ha! ha! ha!—no anxiety to conceal it from you."

" Then I suppose she has been married several times," observed Flourish.

" That circumstance does not follow," said Turf; " the lady in question is fond of variety, and does not continue in the same mind long together. Charlotte has been one of the pretty playthings of fortune, and her run of good luck has been almost unequalled. She is prodigal, changeable, and extravagant, to the echo! Charlotte is a most dangerous acquaintance; and if you never know any more about her but plain Charlotte, that will be quite enough, I assure you."

" Old as I am," replied Makemoney, " I must confess her looks are cent. per cent. in her favor."

" Say no more at present—the horses are about to start," observed Turf, singing a few lines of the much-admired ballad of Charles Dibdin, Esq.—

> See the Course throng'd with gazers, the sports are begun—
> What confusion, but hear! I'll bet you, sir. Done! done!
> Ten thousand strange rumours resound far and near,
> Lords, hawkers, and jockeys, assail the tir'd ear:
> While, with neck like a rainbow, erecting his crest,
> Pamper'd, prancing, and pleas'd, his head touching his breast,
> Scarcely snuffing the air, he's so proud and elate,
> The *High-mettled* RACER first starts for the plate!

Look out, my worthy Pilgrims—now they are off. What a delightful sight to a lover of race-horses—a handkerchief might cover the whole of them. How charmingly Juno moves her legs—she's a picture of a horse;—there is nothing half like her on the Course for beauty, blood, bone, and action. My eyes, how finely they get over the ground. The mare wins the cup for a thousand! *Done!* Once more if you like it! *Done!* I'll do it again, sir! You do, to the end of the chapter. Juno's not the favorite. I don't care for that—she's my favorite; and that's quite enough for me to *lay* upon her. Bar *Spindle*,

Shanks, and Harlequin, and I'll take Juno against the field! There's racing for you—did you ever see such whipping and slashing? Beautiful jockeyship!—Neck and neck! What good ones! It must be a dead heat! No, no—nothing like it! Huzza! Juno's got the lead!—She keeps it!—What a plunge! —Go along, my lovely Juno!—She passes the winning cup!— That's the time of day! Huzza! huzza! huzza!"

After the *excitement* had in some degree abated, in which the Pilgrims appeared delighted beyond measure, and expressed the pleasure they had felt in witnessing the race, to Turf; "I should prove a very bad one to make a bet upon such hasty terminations; great knowledge must be required respecting the speed and various qualities of the different horses engaged in the contest," observed Makemoney.

"You are perfectly right, sir," replied Turf; "judgment, tact, nerve, and courage, are required to *win* upon several occasions. Let me ask you, gentlemen Pilgrims, can there be a finer sight than to view a race well contested? You have an opportunity of beholding the beauty of the animals, their high state of breeding, fine action, and the spirit with which the horses enter into the scene, and who appear to possess as much anxiety to pass their competitors as the *interested* and clever jockies upon their backs. The view from one end of the course to the other, is one of the finest pictures of *anxiety*, impressed upon the countenances of all present, that can be witnessed, respecting the results of the race—eagerly looking out for the winning horse. It is sharp work, while it lasts, both for the men and cattle; and in the short space of a few fleeting minutes, thousands of pounds change masters!"

"It is this view of horse racing that alarms me," said Makemoney, "and reduces the pleasure of the thing to my economic ideas; yet, I am noniggard, and to be merry and wise, is my motto."

"But it is only the indiscreet, desperate, and foolish men, who *risque* their ALL upon a race; such things have occurred I regret to say," replied Turf; "yet they seldom happen; and when men, who possess the slightest common sense, cannot commit any thing like such mad-brained errors—faults, I ought to have called them. Too true, we have seen the pistol and razor put a violent end to the career of such thoughtless characters; yet, it is equally well-known that speculations of a widely different nature, have produced on the minds of some men similar horrid results! However, I should not wish to appear too harsh on the subject; yet, such men can only be classed with madmen and cowards."

"You have properly classed such characters under the denomination of madmen and fools!" said Makemoney, "to be reduced from a state of affluence to beggary, owing to the stride of a horse!"

" But mark the difference, my dear Peter, your career and rise in life has been of so reversed a character, I speak it without offence ! You, my friend Makemoney, have been taught from experience, the value of a single *farthing*, half-pence, shillings, and pounds ! You have placed the various coins upon the top of each other until they multiplied into a large sum ; and thus, step by step, ultimately produced a fortune !

" But, on the contrary, the gentleman you heard offer to bet six hundred to four hundred pounds, was never taught *practically* the value of money. He has never been called upon, under any circumstances whatever, to earn a single shilling towards his subsistence, or to furnish himself with clothes, pay his rent, &c. He was born a gentleman, a fortune ready 'cut and dried to his hands, and solely indebted to his ancestors for every farthing that he possessed in the world ; and according to the vulgar proverb—' He was born with a silver spoon in his mouth !' Therefore, whatever sums, large or small, he offers to bet, does not *alarm* his feelings in the slightest degree ; he only thinks of *winning*, and relies upon his income to bring him through upon every event ! Such are the different habits of mankind ; and while you, Peter, very properly, look upon the immense risque of losing six hundred pounds, well knowing the great difficulty of realizing such a sum of money by your exertions in trade, the sporting gentleman views it as a mere *bagatelle*—even when called upon to pay his losings."

" I must admit," replied Makemoney, " you have placed the matter, in doubt to me, in a more clear light ; and it certainly does account for the vast sums of money that are lost upon race horses, and other species of gambling, with so much *indifference* of feeling. However, such sort of conduct, after all, remains to me a perfect enigma."

" Ha ! ha ! ha ! you do not understand the matter," said Turf, " it might turn out, the gentleman alluded to, who offered six hundred to four hundred pounds, did not risque that particular sum as a dead loss, supposing the event to come off against him, he having laid the above sum merely to *suit* his book. And much, my dear friend, as you have been acquainted with books in general, the *book* in question is an ODD volume that you have no touch of. Although, to those persons who are familiar with such transactions, it is as clear that two and two make four ; and perfectly, according to the system of Cocker."

" Neither do I wish to be instructed in *such* a book ; for rest assured, ignorance in such matters is perfect bliss ! Where hundreds of pounds are disposed of, as a matter of course ; and handfulls of bank notes paid over to each other, with as much indifference as the most trifling milk-score," observed Makemoney. " No, I again repeat, that ignorance is bliss ; and I should set myself down as the greatest fool in existence, if I so far forgot myself as to risque my property in such a manner ; I

really think I should not be able to sleep for a month afterwards
—if one thousand pounds of mine depended upon the *stride* of
a horse.

"It is true, that I have read of a certain dashing courtezan,*
to shew one of her admirers the contempt she set upon the
value of money; a naval officer of high rank, made her a present of a hundred pound note, after a very short acquaintance
with her person. She called the waiter, and ordered two thin
slices of bread and butter, when she placed the one hundred
pound note between them, aud to the surprise of the officer,
swallowed them with a cup of tea; observing at the same time,
with a sneer—'Thus should all *misers* be treated, who put no
value upon the charms of the female sex!'"

"'I have no doubt but you speak the truth," replied Turf,
"according to your feelings; but as many men have many minds,
and as *betting*, in any shape, is a mere matter of taste, we
will drop the subject, and look out for something more in unison
with your ideas. But laying of wagers is the very life and soul
of some men; and if they are not personally *interested* in the
money transactions on a race, or upon any other contest, they
view it with the most perfect indifference. The minds of some
men must be continually excited, as well as the body, to bring
them into action; and there are to be found, in all sorts of
society, individuals, who can talk of nothing else but sporting
events. Others again, on the opera, musical parties, &c. The
drama, and the play-house is the very idol of some folks! The
conversation and love of books, by others, often prove a great
annoyance to some companies; therefore, my friend Makemoney,
it is highly necessary, as the world is constituted, that we should
not think alike."

"Excellent advice," replied Flourish, "and we humble
Pilgrims, as to the ways of the world, are little better than non-
entities, in your presence; we must look up to you, sir, as our
oracle, finger-post, Mentor, guide, indeed, every thing, in our
present situation; and as we are out upon a tour of observation,
men and manners being our decided objects in view, we are
highly indebted to your observations!"

"I hope I am not too troublesome, nor inquisitive," said
Sprightly to Turf; "by asking if you at all know that gentleman on the box of the splendid barouche, on the other side of
the Course; there is something about his appearance, that be-
speaks him a public character, if not, a man who paid more than
ordinary attention to his toilette? It might be said of him, that
he had just stepped out of a band-box; there is so much *nicety*
about his person!"

"Ha! ha! ha! You might have been farther off the bull's
eye; but I only know him, from report," replied Turf, "as

being one of the *fools* of fortune! He is an *outside* man—all show, and designated in the fashionable world—' The man without a head!" He came *out* with a princely fortune—a large sack full of gold ; but as it is said that charity covers a multitude of sins, it might as well be observed, that riches are an excuse for the committal of a great many foibles! At all events, he has not been a *selfish* character! and scorned to keep so large a stock of money to himself, but distributed it in all manner of shapes, for the good of the community ; yet he comes under the denomination of a *fool*, for his liberality ; for a time, he was a good *victim* ; but necessity ultimately gave him another kind of insight into the views of mankind, when he was compelled to adopt a military phrase—to *halt!*

" During his career, he paid attention to the daughter of a person of very high rank in the country, and offered her his hand and fortune ; but she rejected the proposal with the utmost disdain, observing to her parent, who rather urged the match as an advantageous one—' If I marry the man who has proposed for me, I must worship his riches, his person only will be for me to look upon ; for he has not got a head upon his shoulders !' This remark was more *severe* than just—the lady was haughty, proud, and aristocratic ; and would not ally herself to any person—but one who boasted of a long line of ancestry. However, he possesses the manners of a gentleman—polite, good-natured, and affable ; and although he might never be selected to fill the situation of one of our judges, he is not without *Robin|Roughhead's* qualification to make his way through the world, who observed —' If he had not got it in his head, he had it in his pockets !' and that is a general passport in all countries !"

The races were now over, and the company fast quitting the Course ; when Turf observed, " We will now make the best of our way to my cottage."

The Pilgrims most cheerfully acquiesced with Turf's proposition ; but, previous to their quitting the race-ground, Sprightly and his uncle kept a sharp look out to have another peep at the female with the fine bust ; and Flourish was equally on the alert to ascertain if the Duchess and her two daughters were present. Nothing like either of the ladies were to be seen, and the pursuit was given up for the charms of a good dinner. The Pilgrims were wafted across the Thames in the ferry-boat, and the cottage of Turf soon presented itself to their notice.

The exterior of this had but little to attract the attention of the spectator, except neatness ; indeed, any thing like a style of architecture was entirely out of the question : yet it was a comfortable, convenient looking erection—wind and weather proof—and well known as the seat of friendship and hospitality.

But the interior of it was a perfect treat to the visitor— every thing to be seen was consistently in keeping with the name of a cottage ; and this view of the thing was the highest ambition of Charles Turf. It was, according to his own character of the building, erected under the idea of being a contented happy spot for himself, and to prove in reality of the same description to all his acquaintances and friends.

The dinner he gave to the Pilgrims did not display any thing like extravagance nor ostentation ; but, nevertheless, the good things of this life were found in abundance upon the table.

After the removal of the cloth, and the wine began freely to circulate amongst them, Makemoney called upon Turf to give them a toast ; when the latter filled up a bumper, and said,— " *A contented mind, a hundred to one, against any other consideration in life.*"

" Bravo ! " exclaimed Flourish; " you appear to me one of the happiest mortals I ever met with in society, and I should be highly gratified, as you sporting gentlemen say, to take a leaf out of your book, by way of instruction."

" And so should I," echoed Sprightly ; " practice against theory for my money."

" And, *ancient* as I am," said Makemoney, " it has always been my decided opinion that a man is never too old to learn ; therefore, my worthy friend Turf, just give us an outline of your notions of life."

" With all my heart," replied Turf, " if it will afford you Pilgrims the slightest gratification whatever. I have my dog and my gun, whenever I feel inclined for a turn amongst the feathered tribe: I have also three or four horses, which answer all the purposes I require ; and my cabriolet—I prefer to any sort of carriage ; for pride and ostentation do not belong to my notions of life.

" My house is my castle ; but, nevertheless, I retire to rest without using a single bolt—I ought to have said the COTTAGE of CONTENT—my peaceful retreat and abode—where Charles Turf may always be found *happier* than a King, because all his wants are gratified, and every desire is within his reach—I envy no one.

" I am, at times, an angler ; although not so decided a fisherman as Izaak Walton. My greyhounds, I flatter myself, are equal to any ever seen in the kingdom ; and a day's coursing not only affords me great pleasure, but tends to invigorate my constitution.

" My fortune is not great, but, nevertheless, it is ample ; and I am perfectly satisfied with my income, which not only makes me truly happy and comfortable, but it enables me to make persons understand that I can feel and assist the wants of others. I am as free in mind as the air I breathe ! I am subject to no control ; and I go here, there, and every where I please. I have nothing to complain of—*trifles* I never suffer to annoy me for an instant ; and I trust I possess enough common sense not to create imaginary evils !

"Although I do not pretend, nor neither am I a politician, yet I am not insensible to the welfare of my country. I am extremely fond of perusing the contents of a newspaper, just to see how matters are going on in the world, and also to prevent appearing ignorant as to the movements of society. My library is not extensive; neither am I what you call a great reader; but I should feel I was wrong if the works of Byron, Scott, Moore, Campbell, Bulwer, and other men of note, were not to be found in it. I cannot be viewed as a literary man; therefore, on this subject I am afraid I shall appear at fault.

"My garden, in its turn, claims my attention;—flowers afford me great pleasure, and the beauties of nature are ever grateful to my feelings.

"It is true, I am without a wife, but a greater admirer of matrimony does not exist; and the only difficulty which presents itself to me on that subject is—a proper choice! However, I have no doubt the time will arrive, and I don't care how soon, that the Cottage of Content will have a mistress to take her place at my table—for man was not born for himself!

"Yet, under all the circumstances of the case, I do not repine, but make myself *happy* every where. The *country* I prefer, as to selection for a residence; but in LONDON I feel contented, and never grumble if I am detained a day or two longer at any time than I intended.

"It is my maxim not to be too *systematic* in my movements through life; then I cannot be made miserable, nor put out of my way. Regularity of conduct is a desirable thing at all times; but to be too *precise,* in my humble opinion, often proves disagreeable to the man who adopts such line of conduct, as well as troublesome to his friends; therefore, all hours I make agreeable to my feelings. And, if I felt inclined to act upon it, I should, whenever it suited my inclination, 'lie down with the lamb, and rise with the lark.'

"I am ready to admit that several years elapsed, and not without a great deal of trouble, before I obtained the *mastery* over myself. Perfection is not to be obtained, I am well aware; but it is the duty of every individual, if he can, to preserve an equanimity of temper, if possible, under all circumstances of life. And that is the direct road to happiness."

"Excellent advice, indeed," said Makemoney, "and such as I did not anticipate from the lively man of the world, Charles Turf—more like a philosopher; and such maxims, if practically adopled, must prove invaluable. Therefore, I hope, brother Pilgrims, you have treasured up every word delivered to us by the host of the Cottage of Content."

"I have not lost a sentence," replied Sprightly; "nay, more, I shall endeavour to act up to the letter and spirit of it, upon all occasions."

"I am delighted with the opinions of my friend Turf," said

Flourish; "so much so, that I hope I shall never be found wanting to put them into practice."

"And, with deference to our worthy host," observed Makemoney, "I do not think a better opportunity could occur for the recital of the memoirs of Charlotte. A promise to that effect has been made."

"And it shall be kept," replied Turf; "I will endeavour to remember her adventures, and also to relate them with truth and fidelity. Yet, I am almost afraid that you will be inclined to think there is more an air of *romance* attached to her character than reality: but, nevertheless, I pledge myself for the truth of them. However, before I proceed, let me have distinctly all your opinions as to her *looks*, and that, had you have seen her each alone, without my exciting your attention towards her history, you might not have thought it 'stale, flat, and unprofitable.'"

"Nothing, sir, rest assured, without flattery," said Flourish, " can be unprofitable from your remarks; but I think that gravity, united with experience, and the hey-day of blood being over, my much-respected friend Makemoney should be the first to his opinion. At all events, we shall obtain solidity of judgment."

"That is my opinion also," answered Sprightly.

"Ha! ha! ha! and mine too," urged Turf. "He has had, in the way of business, plenty to do with fine women, and great beauties in the *print* line, upon whom he might gaze, gaze, and gaze again, without any thing like unpleasant excitement. We shall now perceive what reality may have upon the feelings of Makemoney, when he looks upon the dashing beautiful heroine, displaying all her charms of attraction upon a race course!"

"Then I am to be laughed at in spite of myself," replied Peter; "to be quizzed outright, as a piece of ice—exhibited as cold as snow—and showed up as insensible to the charms of beauty, and a fine woman, as the slippered pantaloon—sans eyes, sans taste, sans every thing! But I think, with deference to my friend Turf, that he has began at the wrong end of the story—*my* opinion ought not to have the weight of a feather in the scale, where loveliness is the theme of discourse. But Flourish, a professed adept in matters of gallantry, ought not merely to give an opinion, *dry* as a lawyer in consultation over a brief of birthright; but like an *enthusiast* on matters of love, which he professes to be, by a rhetorical flourish embracing the analysis of beauty so finely depicted by Hogarth; and not to have placed the weight upon the shoulders of a man in the downhill of life!"

"My dear Makemoney," replied Turf, "you have read a great number of books, I am aware; and published the memoirs of several extraordinary characters, both male and female! But the story, I am about to relate to you and your brother Pilgrims, is decidedly a collection of facts, and which came immediately under my own observation. I am also intimately acquainted with the whole of the parties connected with it : and if I am not able to embellish it with fine metaphors, and apposite quotations, like some of our celebrated writers and novelists—I am sure you will take the will for the deed, and if I make any slip or deficiency of language, or the introduction of a *cant* phrase or two, now and then, I feel satisfied you will excuse it."

" Excuse, Charles Turf," replied Makemoney, " you surely are joking with us! Tell the story in any manner you please ; and I am sure we shall all be delighted with the memoirs, when they are connected with REAL LIFE ; and also, that we are certain that the relater of them is telling the truth !

" Then, as no opinions are to be had from you, jolly Pilgrims, respecting this ' rare work of nature,' I have only to say, beware of the handsome female with the fine bust," urged Turf. " Be on your guard, in case she should ever cross your path. She has positively ruined three, if not four men, and turned the heads of several others ; besides *victimizing* more thoughtless fellows than I can bring to memory. Indeed, well might Shakespeare exclaim, ' Frailty, thy name is woman !' I again repeat, beware—her smiles are a kind of enchantment—her nod bewitching—her eyes—enough ! "

" I have often been astonished how men can be such fools, led like children by strings, and become the dupes of women, who have nothing else to recommend them than a beautiful face," said Flourish ; " men may be liberal ; nay, more than generous to a pretty woman ; but to suffer themselves to be reduced to beggary and want, are not deserving of any thing like pity."

" Do not be too fast," replied Turf ; " you are young, and perhaps inexperienced ; but, in the course of my life, I have known some of the *deepest* men, who have been in every other transaction of their lives positively misers ; yet, when women have been the source of attraction, and men, who have been fast descending into the vale of years——"

" Stop, stop, my dear Turf ; have the kindness to leave old men out of the question," observed Makemoney, " or you will frighten me out of my wits. Ha! ha! ha! Old men in love, I know, are the greatest fools in existence. But proceed."

" All men, either young or old, in my opinion, are all fools in a greater or less degree, in matters of love. But to my narrative; and, as it is not the very witching time of night," replied Turf, " there is no necessity for you jolly Pilgrims to be alarmed."

" Not in the least," said Sprightly ; " but, on the contrary, we are quite on the *qui vive* to hear your story."

" Well, then, without further preface," answered Turf, " here begins :—This splendid piece of work—one of the freaks of nature—Miss Charlotte Par———no matter, the name is not essential to the fact—was first discovered in the streets of London as a match-girl, near St. Paul's Cathedral.   Neither is her birth, parentage, or education, necessary at all to make out my tale!—Miss Par—— being herself, *alone*.   Her appearance was extremely ragged, with habiliments scarcely enough to cover her person ; without stockings or shoes—her face almost as black as a sweep, and her legs and feet were covered with mud and dirt.

"Her voice, however, was truly musical—nay, harmony itself —and her *cry* of matches, or rather a sort of *chant*, was highly attractive, as she walked through the streets with her basket under her arm :—

> Come, buy my good matches—come, buy 'em of me —
> They are the best matches you ever did see !
> I cry my good matches at fam'd Charing Cross,
> Where sits a black man upon a black horse.
>
> I cry my good matches all thro' the street.
> Where many good people I often do meet !

The match-girl was born in misery, and reared in beggary ; and the few halfpence she collected in the character of a 'female timber-merchant,' as her companions in poverty designated her, were barely sufficient to procure for her half a bellyful of food : in fact, almost starvation stared her in the face.   She had no friends nor relatives to apply to for help or succour.   Her father she had no knowledge of, and her mother died when she was quite a baby ; yet the friendless match-girl was never heard to grumble at her fate, and went out into the streets, either wet or dry, to seek her scanty pittance early every morning.

"At length, in one of her daily peregrinations near the Bank of England, her beautiful face and fine person suddenly attracted the attention of a middle-aged wealthy banker (whose intrigues and amours would fill a volume)—with, ' Will you please to buy any matches, sir ?   Do, sir, buy a ha'porth of a poor girl ! ' The amorous banker was almost rivetted to the spot with surprise—he was quite struck with the match-girl, although under such disparaging circumstances ; but when she pressed her suit, he appeared confused, and hesitated for a reply.   'No, no, I do not want any matches.'   But appearing to recollect himself, he said, in almost a whisper to her ear, ' If you will go of an errand for me, and perform it punctually, I will give you half a crown.'

" The poverty-stricken match-girl, overjoyed at the idea of receiving half-a-crown—so large a piece of his Majesty's coin she had never had in her possession before to call her own—replied, with an agreeable smile, ' You may depend upon me, sir.'

" 'Follow me,' said he; ' but do not say a word !'   He then retired down an obscure alley to avoid the *stare* of the persons in the streets ; and also to prevent being recognized by any of his friends or acquaintances near the Bank ; a well-dressed man

THE MATCH

THE
LOTTERY
OF
LIFE

being seen talking to a poor match-girl, might have excited some suspicions not consistent with his character. He pulled out his pocket book, and with a blacklead pencil wrote a few lines on a slip of paper—directed to Mrs. ——, folded up in the shape of a letter.

" Upon his putting the note into her hand, he enquired if she could read writing? 'No, sir,' said she, 'I am no scholard! I om only a poor ignorant girl, without father, or mother, and I have not a friend in the world !'

" 'So much the better,' replied the banker ; ' never mind, I will send you to a good place ; and if you do but mind what the lady bids you to do, you will not repent of it. I have given you a recommendation to her: therefore, my girl, you have only to obey her orders—and here is the half-crown for you !' "

" ' Thanky, kind gentleman ! God bless you, sir, for noticing a poor girl !' answered the dealer in matches.

" ' I want no thanks,' observed the banker ; ' but make all the haste you can with the note ; and I will call in the evening, to see whether the lady, my friend, approves of you for her servant. You will find her a very nice sort of woman, only obey her commands.'

" ' That I will,' replied the girl.

" The banker then departed, and was out of sight in an instant.

" The wretched match-girl almost cried with joy, to think that she had met with such a charitable, kind-hearted gentleman, and started off with almost a run to be in time with the note. On her arrival at the house where it was directed, not one hundred miles from the Obelisk, in St. George's Fields, and knocking at the door—she was rudely assailed with a gruff voice, not very pleasing, or harmonious to her ear—' Go along you dirty bunter, how dare you disturb people when they are at breakfast, to leave it to answer such beasts as you are ? Go along, I tell you—we want none of your blackguard matches ! —Go along, or else——'

" ' Don't be angry, ma'am,' replied the girl, ' I have got a letter for the lady of the house.'

" ' Got what ?—Oh ! a letter—aye, that alters the case.— Where did you bring it from ?—Give it me.'

" ' I don't know, ma'am, I'm sure,' replied the match-girl. ' A gentleman sent me with it !'

" The letter was taken in to the mistress of the house, while the wretched girl stood trembling at the door, waiting the result.

" But to the poor girl's surprise, the mistress came running to the door, with a smiling face, and said—' Come in, my child : I am glad to see you. Such a recommendation makes you heartily welcome to me. I will make you happy and comfortable. So come in, come in, my dear.'

" After this kind salutation from the mistress of the house—

the servant immediately altered her tone, and endeavoured to keep pace, if not outstrip her employer in kindness—'La! my girl, I am werry sorry I kept you so long at the door in the cold, and spoke so roughly to you. But we are assailed by so many wretches continually, that I am tired of giving answers to them; if I had have known you had been so well recommended to my mistress—I would not, for the vorld, have behaved so queer to you! But you must excuse it—and now I knows as how you belongs to *sumbody*, I'll make it up to you in civility, that's wot I will.'

"The contents of the note ran thus:—

"My Dear Mrs. Feelnot,
                    "Obey my orders instantly! Spare no expence respecting the bearer of this note: she suits my taste! I found her by accident in the streets, not half-an-hour since—I never saw her before—but no matter. Make a bonfire of her wretched garments, and attire her in every thing new, in that sort of dress which accords with my fancy. *New*, I say, from head to foot! *Ablution* will be highly necessary; for she appears, to me, to have been sadly neglected; and it is my intentions to better her prospects in society. I will be with you about nine o'clock this evening, when, I have no doubt, the *transformation* will be effective; and the hitherto wretched, beggarly match-girl, have something like the appearance of a well dressed female! Do not tell her, at present, my name, or situation in life.—In great haste,
                    "Your's, &c.,
                         "HENRY IMPULSE."

"P S. You will also provide a nice little supper; and let the Champagne be of the finest quality. You know I am particular in the wines I drink.

"'What is your name, my dear girl?' asked the mistress of the house; 'that is, your Christian name will be quite sufficient at present; and, although we are quite strangers to each other, we shall soon be on more intimate terms, I'll warrant ye—so make yourself cheerful and happy in every respect. It was a *lucky* moment for you when you met with *my* friend, and whom you may now call *your* friend.'

"'CHARLOTTE PAR——,' replied the girl.

"'Quite enough! quite enough!' answered Mrs. Feelnot; 'but the sooner you get rid of those dirty, wretched, filthy, stinking, disagreeable, nay, disgusting rags, the better. They are odious in my eyes. I hate the sight of *decent* poverty, much more the extreme extent of it. But those days are over with you now, my dear girl; if you but mind what I say to you, and follow the instructions I will give you for your future conduct in life, you may become a rich and bright woman yet.'

"The poor match-girl, although tolerably well versed in matters of low life, and who had so often endured the rude elements in the streets with scarcely a rag to cover her person, often wet through to the skin, and who had no place to dry her clothes, except during the time they were upon her back, as she strolled through the courts and alleys; meeting with little else but rebuffs from one passenger to another, when she solicited any person to buy her matches—was all amazement at this *magical*-like turn in her affairs, and the kind reception she had met with from Mrs. Feelnot. She had not the slightest idea of the *real* cause of it—that she was to become the victim of lust and depravity ; and her youth and beauty it were that had attracted the rich banker. The prospect likewise of *gain*—base, sordid lucre—in the mind of the mistress of this house of iniquity, was the sole cause of her soothing, insinuating manner, to prepare the way for the downfall and ruin of one of her own sex !

" ' Come, my dear Charlotte,' said she, ' we must see if we cannot, by the aid of a little scented soap and warm water, make that pretty-looking face of yours in the dirt even more handsome, when it is rendered nice and clean ! And remember, my dear girl, that cleanliness and attention to your person should be one of the very first considerations to a female on her outset in the world.'

" ' Most certainly, ma'am,' replied Charlotte, ' I shall mind what you say, and endeavour to improve myself under your directions.'

" ' Well said, my girl,' replied Mrs. Feelnot, ' I am not afraid but you will soon become an apt scholar—I like your readiness. Now I look at you, Charlotte, your hair is terribly out of order ; but I will soon have it rectified by my hair-dresser, who is a clever fellow—nay, one of the first chaps in the metropolis, for having the *art* to set off a pretty face to the greatest advantage.

" ' Here, Betty, run immediately to Jem Nicecut, and tell him I shall want him, in the course of an hour or two, to put a young lady's head in order, and to be particular to his time.' Betty was off like a shot ; a nod or a wink was quite sufficient : she was a complete adept in all the arts and manœuvres of her mistress, in the way of infamy, added to a knowledge of the worst part of society, particularly where unfortunate females were the objects in view.

" On Betty's return from the hero of the curling irons, her mistress told her ' to make up a good fire, for I am determined those horrid rags belonging to this neglected, dear girl, shall be consumed to ashes in a few minutes, and no traces whatever of them remain, either to annoy the feelings of Miss Charlotte, or to appear odious in my sight. Is the warm water quite ready, as we are in want of it immediately ?'

" The bath, ma'am, only waits for the use of Miss Charlotte,' replied the wary servant ; ' and you will find every thing quite ready and convenient for your purpose.'

" ' Come, my dear girl,' said Mrs. Feelnot, ' we have no time to lose ; and you will soon find yourself quite another person.'

" The poor match-girl was like a person in a trance ; she could scarcely believe her own ears, or give credence to her eyes. Such kindness, great attention, and preparation, in the course of two or three fleeting hours ! Her naked feet, from pacing through the cold wet streets, now enjoying the warmth and luxury of a splendid Turkey carpet—magnificent mirrors—rich curtains—sofas—with every thing to correspond respecting the household furniture! Sinbad the Sailor, in the Valley of Diamonds, could not have been more surprised than the poor match-girl at such a rapid change in her circumstances!

" 'Now, my dear Charlotte,' said Mrs. Feelnot, placing her person before a very large looking-glass, where she could see herself from head to foot, with a most agreeable smile upon her countenance, 'Take a peep for the last time at the poor, wandering, neglected, poverty-stricken MATCH-GIRL, who has endured the buffets and scorn of the world. Look again at yourself, and bear well in your mind what you NOW are in the eyes of society! It is worth your consideration.

" ' But in the course of the day you shall have another peep at your altered appearance, when you will behold in the same mirror the handsome, beautiful Charlotte! the elegant dressed lady! the envy of the women, and the admiration of the men. So now, my girl, we will proceed to the toilette, and practically experience the wonders it can perform !'

" To portray the feelings of the Match Girl,—or to describe the surprize she underwent from the artful mode of proceeding adopted by Mrs. Feelnot, would be quite impossible. A wretched, beggarly, outcast Match Girl in the early part of the day supplicating the passenger to buy a halfpenny worth of matches to procure her a bit of bread; and before the evening—in the course of a few fleeting hours—to be viewed partaking of an excellent supper—surrounded by all the luxuries of life—complimented on her beauty and shape by a man of taste—drinking champagne and other costly wines before the night expired—was quite enough, nay, far more than enough, to turn more experienced heads than that of a poor match girl—without a friend in the world! But such strange events occur daily in the Metropolis—behind the *curtain* of real life!

" Charlotte underwent the ablutions of the warm bath; and the scientific Nice-cut, the hair-dresser, practised his art with all the talents in his power, to give her head and face an appearance it had never possessed before. Her ragged clothes had been committed to the flames; her legs decorated with rich silk stockings, and her feet fitted with the handsomest kid shoes that could be purchased.

" An elegant silk dress altered to her shape, in the most prompt manner and fashionable style, to give her person and bust the appearance of one of the finest forms that could be imagined.

" In short, all that ART could bestow upon the person, was resorted to by the experienced Mrs. Feelnot; to which was added an elegant, massy gold chain placed round her neck; and some splendid gold rings put on her fingers, to give her hands

THE MATCH GIRL.

an attractive look. Nearly the whole of the day had been consumed in trying on and altering clothes under the direction of a first-rate dress-maker, to render the metamorphose complete, in every point of view.

"Indeed, so immense a change had been effected in such a short period, that much as Mrs. Feelnot had accomplished in former instances, she felt proud, and congratulated herself on the celerity and good taste she had displayed in thus transforming a rude, uncultivated, *dirty,* ragged match-girl, into the appearance of a fine lady, and a person for beauty of character that no one could look upon her without admiration.

"Every thing being settled to the satisfaction of Mrs. Feelnot, and the *transformation* realized, she felt determined to see what effect the *mirror* once more would have upon the senses of the poor girl!

"'Now, my dear Charlotte—Miss Charlotte, I should have said—you shall take a peep in the mirror, and give me your opinion on yourself. You will find the *change* very great in your person; but do not be alarmed—as it is an appearance you will ever afterwards assume in life; nay, much better, when you have done growing, and you become more set as to your figure.'

"The match-girl made no reply, but, on viewing herself in the glass, she appeared to be lost in astonishment, and nearly fainted; her sensations of surprise and joy were so overwhelming that she did not recover herself for some minutes. 'Surely I am bewitched.' Then bursting out into a fit of laughter, afterwards the tears running down her cheeks—'I cannot be Charlotte!'—when Mrs. Feelnot caught hold of her arm, and said, in an exulting manner, 'You are Miss Charlotte! But where's the poor, ragged match-girl, now, my dear? Gone for ever! It is only Miss Charlotte remains with me in her stead. Come, we will quit this apartment for the present, for fear you might be inclined to fall in love with yourself, and become *vain.*'

"'I don't know, ma'am,' replied Charlotte, 'how I shall ever make you amends for the trouble you have had with me. I am but a poor ignorant girl, yet I am willing to learn.'

"'Well, then, only mind what I say, and do as I bid you; and then you will, my dear Charlotte, be sure to make your way in life. I only want you to be *tractable!* But, I am sorry to say, I have done a great deal for several girls in my life-time, but they have nearly all of them proved very ungrateful to me for it. However, I have a better opinion of you, Miss Charlotte —there is something like honesty about your pretty face, that I flatter myself my confidence is not likely to be misplaced.'

"From this sort of insinuating dialogue, and particular attention paid to her by Mrs. Feelnot, with the addition of 'My dear Charlotte!' added to almost every sentence that she addressed to her, it cannot be a matter of surprise that the poor match-girl ultimately became an easy prey to the arts of such an experienced woman in the ways of infamy, who was too well acquainted with the weak side of the sex not to turn it to her own advantage. *Flattery* was one of her grand attacks to her victims in general ; but, in the present instance, Charlotte was beauty herself : she possessed it in a very eminent degree ; and if her *intellect* had kept pace with it, the connoisseurs of fine intelligent women might have travelled a long distance before they had met with such a person as the match-girl."

" Allow me to interrupt your narrative for only a single moment," said Makemoney ; " but I *must* give vent to my feelings of indignation. I would have such a woman as Mrs. Feelnot burnt ! if I had the power of putting such a sentence into practice. Is it not infamous to think that any woman, for the sake of a few filthy pounds, would undertake to destroy the innocence, corrupt the mind, and render a young female odious in the eyes of society for the remainder of her life. Such wretches ought not to be called women—females they cannot be : they are nothing else but monsters in human shape."

" It is impossible to differ in opinion respecting such an infamous character," observed Flourish, " but let me beg of you not to delay the narrative ; therefore, pray, Mr. Turf, proceed."

" ' Come, my dear Charlotte,' said the mistress of the house, ' we will now drink a health in sparkling champagne to *your* friend and mine ; for it is to him that you are indebted for all the fine clothes which you now have upon your back. You will find him a very generous man. He is very rich ; and, as to money, he has got a cart-load of it.'

" ' *Sham*, wot d'ye call it,' asked Charlotte ; ' I never heard of it before. I don't know not what you mean, ma'am.'

" ' Why,' replied the mistress, ' I dare say you do not ; but it is wine of the richest quality, and only drank by people of the first consequence in life. But whatever I tell you, Charlotte, endeavour to keep it in your memory, and become as sensible as you can. Gentlemen do not like *ignarant* women for their companions.'

" ' I shall do my best to please you, ma'am,' answered Charlotte, who scarcely knew whether she stood upon her head or her heels ; in fact, she was almost light-headed : the change of clothes and scene she had undergone in the last few hours were too much for her senses.

" The clock had scarcely struck nine when the wealthy banker appeared, true to his appointment. Impatient to behold the metamorphose wrought in the match-girl, his first question to the mistress of the house was,—if she had received a note he had sent to her by a poor girl that morning ?'

" ' Yes, sir,' she replied, ' and all your directions have been complied with to the utmost extent ; and, if you will go into the drawing-room, you will be able to judge for yourself.'

" He immediately repaired to the room, when he saw the

match-girl sitting upon a sofa ; but he was so dazzled with her appearance, that he hastily shut the door, thinking he had made some mistake, and certainly gone into a wrong room, He returned to Mrs. Feelnot for an explanation ; when she assured him, the female he saw was no other person but the once-ragged match-girl he had sent to her that morning.'

" Impossible ! ' he cried. ' True, I know your tact and industry to perform strange things ; but you certainly are now trying to impose upon me to the best advantage. If not, where are the ragged clothes she had upon her back this morning when I first saw her ? Convince me, by some means or another. Here are no traces left of the poor girl I sent to you.'

' The rags—they were nothing better than rags upon her, which I immediately committed to the fire. But, you may rely upon it, no trick has been put upon you, sir,' urged the mistress of the house, who soon satisfied him of his error.

" The match-girl, who had attracted his attention in her ragged habiliments—beauty in tatters ! But now, when he saw beauty decked out in all the splendour of fashionable array— diamond-like eyes, rendered more sparkling and brilliant by the aid of embellishment and art !—when he saw cheeks, divested of dirt, changed to the ruddy glow of health, with the colour of the rose—a Grecian nose, of the handsomest form—teeth that no dentist could, with all his skill, have *rendered* whiter—and a form, altogether, that might have challenged competition with the finest woman in the kingdom—he could not believe his own eyes, that so beautiful a creature had been obscured under such a bundle of rags !

" Without loss of time, he hired a splendid establishment for her in the country, a few miles from London ; where they lived together, as man and wife, for some time before any doubts were thrown upon the matter.

" It is true, he selected her from the streets, for the worst purposes ; but he became so strongly attached to her afterwards, that he was determined at all events, to make her his companion for life. He was a rich, bold, and determined man, who did not care a pin for the opinions of the world. He, therefore, had her taught to ride by one of the first equestrians of the day ; and also to dance, by one of the most able professors at the Italian opera. She was likewise instructed to read and speak by a celebrated elocutionist. French, as a matter of course ; in short, he spared no expence to employ masters* of every description, to improve her person and mind, to which he

---

* If the scholar should prove an *apt* one, it is astonishing what may be acquired by perseverance and tuition : it is a well-authenticated fact, that the late Countess of Exeter, who was the daughter of an obscure country farmer, in the course of twelve months became a most accomplished woman. The Countess not only reflected great credit on the good taste of the Earl in selecting a female of superior mind for his wife, but also on her exalted situation in life !

added his own indefatigable exertions ; and it is but justice to aver, that if Charlotte did not excel in all the lessons she received from her various tutors, she, nevertheless, imbibed a sufficient portion of them, to render herself a sensible and agreeable partner to her most liberal protector. She, most undoubtedly, would have preferred the character of *wife,* if she could have prevailed upon her admirer to have given her that title to eminence in society ; besides securing to herself something like property in case of the death of the wealthy banker ! Yet, Charlotte was ' his *darling,*' as he pronounced her ; and besides calling her his ' TOT !'   But matrimony was out of the question: however, they lived together, for several years, in the most perfect harmony, under the designation of the old man and his beautiful mistress.   Her conduct was not demure, nor hypocritical, but bold, lively, and interesting ; in truth, there was nothing like pretence about her behaviour, and the banker never evinced the least signs of jealousy.

" If Charlotte did not show great love towards her protector, she was not deficient in gratitude ; and it had never escaped her memory that the banker had been the cause of removing her from the depths of misery and deprivation, to the comforts of a splendid living, and, likewise, giving her an education, which she otherwise would never have obtained under any other circumstances ; therefore, she did not quarrel with her situation in life—being the mistress of the rich banker, Mr. Impulse. She had received many gross insults, and offers, on account of her beauty, from men of rank, during her connection with Impulse ; but she kept them to herself, to prevent a duel on her account —so much regard had she for the life of her protector.

" The banker belonged to that class of persons in society, who come under the denomination of ' not marrying men !' Therefore, any thing like *restraint* upon his inclination was torture to him ; and hitherto he had been one of the most inconstant mortals to the sex in general ; and they had been to him nothing more than the mere ' playthings of an hour.'   But the match-girl in her *dirty* attire, had not only attracted the banker at first sight, in a most extraordinary degree, and after he had had her instructed according to his wishes—nay, moulded her to his way of life and manners, no husband in the world could have paid her more attention than he did, or been more fond of a wife. Yet *marriage* was entirely out of the question.

" The banker was liberal, even to profusion, in supplying her with money ; and his fascinating Charlotte could not be habited too splendidly for his taste ; and no lady in the land dressed better, or wore clothes of a more costly description, than the late match-girl. In this particular point of view, it might be said, that she possessed an *intuitive* knowledge ; and never let any opportunity pass, that offered itself respecting the newest fashions, without applying it to herself, and with increased advantage to her personal appearance. But the *dazzling* scene had had its day ; and her anticipated future bright pros- pects were clouded for a short period by an unexpected event— the death of the wealthy banker, owing to an apoplectic fit. Her grief was not an outrageous display of sorrow, but, never- theless, it was sincere ; and it was felt by her in *private* se- verely, although not recognized in that manner by the public.

" Her immediate loss was immense—the supplies were at an end ; and the relations of the rich banker would have deprived her of every thing she possessed in the world, and, if they could, have again turned her into the streets, to have sought her live- lihood ; but they were defeated. By the sudden demise of her protector, she had not been remembered in his will, although he had promised her to that effect, and no doubt had intended to have kept his promise. But, fortunately for Charlotte, the house she lived in he had purchased for her, in her own name of CHARLOTTE PARTRIDGE. Likewise the plate, which bore her initials—the jewels—household furniture ; in short, every thing belonged to her upon the premises ; and, therefore, decidedly her own property, in spite of all the lawyers in the world to remove a single pin from the threshold.

" Therefore, her situation in life was far removed from dis- tress ; and, in addition to which, she had contrived to lay by a tolerably round sum of money, from the numerous liberal pre- sents Mr. Impulse had made to her during her residence with him. Public report had circulated in her favour that she had been left a splendid fortune by her late protector, and she had too much good sense to contradict it ; but rather strength- ened such floating information, by the secresy and mystery she always displayed on the subject.

" This had the desired effect. A beautiful young woman—a splendid fortune—and a fine establishment—cannot excite the least surprise to assert, brought suitors by the score—full of love, flattery, professions of friendship, and ready to lay down their lives to promote her happiness. But, from the lessons she had received, during the life-time of her ardent admirer, to beware of the tricks and impositions of the world, together with her own experience, and the recollections of her early days, when she had to walk the streets to sell matches before she could get her breakfast, rendered her not quite so easy a conquest as a number of *knowing* men in the town had previously antici- pated, and who were totally ignorant of Charlotte's history.

" She still continued to live in good style, after the decease of Mr. Impulse, but far from a state of extravagance ; and in the ' *widow's weeds*,' it was thought by her greatest admirers, that she even looked more beautiful than heretofore Char- lotte, at this period of her life, was by no means insensible of her *attractions ;* nay, more, and determined to make the most

2 c

of them : therefore, it is strictly my intention to adhere to the advice of the poets :—

> Poets heap virtues, painters, gems at will,
> And shew their zeal, and hide their want of skill:
> 'Tis well—but artists, who can paint or write,
> To draw the naked is your true delight !

" During her residence with the banker, not the slightest whisper was ever heard against her character; and it is the truth that she conducted herself with all the propriety of an *attached* wife ; so much did she feel the force of gratitude. But since that period—since she has mixed with the gay world, without any person to check any sort of impulse which might have appeared to have a wrong basis, her notions of propriety, virtue, and consistency, have taken quite a different direction ; perhaps, more owing to her acquaintance with fashionable rakes, libertines, rich presuming fools, thoughtless and extravagant fellows ; added to the notions of getting money, through the bad advice of Mrs. Feelnot ; whose *first* instructions to Charlotte were, to place no value upon mankind, without *interested* motives—completely illustrating the never-to-be-forgotten proverb, that ' Evil communications corrupt good manners.'

" It is not my wish to ' extenuate, or set down aught in malice,' respecting this beautiful creature ; but it should seem, from her after conduct in life, that Charlotte was one of that class of women who preferred being the mistress of some man of title, or very rich hero, than to become the retired female in domestic life ; and, in spite of all the intreaties and advice she had received from her various tutors, she never could exactly *rub* off the impressions of her early *low* origin, which accounts for her being fond of fairs. Charlotte was quite in ecstacy on a Race-course—delighted beyond expression at the Opera, Theatres, or any other situation where bustle, gaiety, and fashionable movements were to be witnessed ; yet it was her most anxious wish, at all times, that she should obtain the character of a *genteel* woman !

" She had an immense deal of *tact* in her conduct—knew well the meaning of *finesse ;* and, to entangle her lovers, she was a perfect mistress in the art of pleasing. Charlotte sings well, I must admit, but she dances much better. However, I should say, that she has no touch of real *affection* in her composition ; but, nevertheless, she has the address—a fascinating manner—to make all her admirers entertain a strong feeling towards her, that she is quite a creature of attachment, and she only exists in the presence of her lovers ! ' Thus bad begins, but worse remains behind !' "

The servant, at this period, announced to the Pilgrims that the post-chaise ordered to convey them to London had been waiting for some time. Makemoney observed—" There is a time for all things ; and, I regret to say, we must bid you fare-well. But you have furnished us with so much amusement, united with good advice—pointed out various characters on the Course—and, lastly, the interesting memoir of the MATCH GIRL —that I am deficient in words to thank you, my friend Turf. I never spent so happy a day in the whole course of my life : but I shall not rest satisfied until I hear the *conclusion*—another chapter, respecting Charlotte Partridge. Ha! ha! ha!"

"I could set up the whole of the night without winking," said Flourish, "to become acquainted with the whole of her history."

" And I for a month," answered Sprightly; " I am certain her adventures are of no common description. Match-girls, transformed into women of fortune, are not every day circum-stances."

"Depend upon it," replied Turf, "I will comply with all your wishes the next time we meet over a glass of wine."

The hands were shaken together in friendship all round ;— "Good night!" was the last sentence, when the post-boy was ordered to get over the ground as fast as possible; and in quick time the Pilgrims arrived safe, in whole skins, once more in the City of London.

CHAPTER X.

The Pilgrims turn Pic-nic-ians !—Why should not a Pic-nic be a medium for a Pilgrimage? Who's to be there? Characters of all sorts ; great and small ; learned and un-learned—" extremes meet." The preliminaries for start-ing adjusted—a slight mistake ! DIAMOND for DIANA, and prospect of no dinner ; possible probability of the provisions presence, and passionate propensity, " pro" pungency, in a pretty petticoat. A Steamer in hot weather —a broiler, and no sinecure ! Makemoney overcome ; Sprightly not flourishing ; nor Flourish sprightly ! The females in a stew for fear of being fried. The punster punless ; and the pedant pensive ! The children in mischief, and Mrs. Brindle in agony ! The landing—hurra ! here's the provender. THE DINNER—accidents and offences—" Keep your hands from picking and steal-ing !" THE STROLL—Fortune telling in Richmond Park —Makemoney cajoled by a flattering black-eyed gipsey girl. Ah ! old gentleman, we've caught you, have we? Ha ! ha ! ha ! What did she say—eh ?—" Such stuff as dreams are made of." Let's have tea—agreed. Oh ! dear —dear—I thought so, my dress is spoiled ! Never mind, " children will be children." Now for home, "domus amica, domus aptima!"—" Rise gentle moon." A Hero and Leander in humble life. Boat song—the lover to his mistress : fatal termination ! " The course of true love never did run smooth !" Well, here we are—our " jour-ney's happy ended,"—Good Night. " Bonus Nocte !"

" A FEW days since," said Flourish to Makemoney and Spright-ly, " I accepted an invitation to accompany a Pic Nic to Rich-mond ; and as we have not yet made a Pilgrimage to that renowned spot, I anticipated your assent to attend us, and begged your admittance into the circle ; a request which was readily granted."

" You are very good," answered Makemoney ; " I shall feel much pleasure in accompanying you ; there are many associa-tions connected with Richmond, which must interest us ; and I do not see why a Pic Nic should not be an agreeable vehicle for our Pilgrimage."

" Who's to be there ?" asked Sprightly.

" The invitation was tendered me by the daughters of Old

Brindle, the stationer," replied Flourish; " and of several persons mentioned to me by them, there were but two or three with whom I am acquainted."

" Name! name!" said Sprightly.

" Oh, certainly!" laughed Flourish; " the two Miss Brindles, with their ma, of course; Miss Azure, Miss Young, who by the bye is *rather ancient*, and two or more ladies whose names I know not, terminate the female list; the gentlemen consist of Old Brindle; Pundit, the pedant; Tom Buoyant, the inveterate punster; our worthy selves, and a few others: you will find the party composed of opposites, but as ' extremes meet,' I have little doubt but the whole affair will turn out extremely pleasant."

" When is this trip to take place?" enquired Makemoney; " and by what means are we to reach the place of destination?"

" To-morrow, and by the Diana steamer;" was the reply.

" Are we each to carry our quantum of provision in the true style of Pic Nic?" questioned Sprightly, " or is there to be a caterer who will provide for all?"

" Why," returned Flourish, " to prevent the recurrence of a circumstance which occurred to a recent Pic Nic party, where every one brought lamb, and no one brought bread, Mrs. Brindle has taken upon herself the task of furnishing provender; and I imagine from the manner in which the old lady communicated her intention to me, we have nothing to fear on that point."

Although Flourish knew not the names of all the persons composing the party, we feel it our duty to make the reader acquainted with them; leaving it to the occurrences of the day for an improvement of the acquaintance. First came Mrs. Brindle, a good-natured fat old soul, who, in endeavouring to oblige every body, *almost* failed to please any body; and who had, among many other little peculiarities of character, a considerable degree of nervousness; which was ever worrying and flurrying her. Her extreme good-nature had induced her to have two mischievous little scoundrels, who were the schoolfellows of her dull-headed glutton of a son, to spend a month's vacation with him; and thinking the poor dear boys would be so delighted, and receive *so* much benefit from this little excursion, she brought them with her, to the annoyance of every one else, and to the misery of herself; her horrid nervousness keeping her in a state of perpetual anxiety, for fear of some accident occurring to them.

The Miss Brindles were thoughtless, giddy girls; fond of giggling, possessing very little sense, and much frivolity; differing extremely from Miss Azure, who aimed at being admired for her intellect, as much as for her beauty; who wrote poetry in the album of every person she knew possessing one; was never without a book of some awfully learned character upon her person; professed herself a great reader, and prided herself upon the knowledge of languages, *of* which she talked, but *in* which she never conversed ; but occasionally interlarded her speeches with a few common-place idiomatical expressions culled from ' exercise books.' She was accompanied by her mamma, who served as an excellent foil to her; for Mrs. Azure's younger days had been humbler days ; left an orphan in infancy, and in the workhouse, she had not to boast of either tender nurture, or mental culture ; her budding youth having reached riper years, the overseers, with parental solicitude for her future welfare, placed her in the eligible situation of scullion in a public house, where her young ideas were taught

" the scouring of pots,"

of culinary utensils, and how to tend the wants and wishes of the ' unwashed artificers' who honoured the tap-room with their presence ; it was here she imbibed their manners and language ; and as ' the cask retains the flavour of the first liquor which impregnated it,' so Mrs. Azure still retained the speech of her juvenile days ; although the constant rub in later times against a higher grade of society, had removed a portion of the rust which had incrusted her manners. Her buxom beauty and sprightliness attracted the attention of Mr. Azure, who was then light porter in a druggist's warehouse; and as he ' found favour in her sight,' she acceded to an offer of marriage which he made her, became ' bone of his bone, and flesh of his flesh,' and bid adieu to ' heavy wet' and ' glistering the pewter' (as she termed polishing the pots,) for ever ; for, by a series of circumstances which *were* not uncommon in the city, he became master of the concern in which he had entered as light porter.

Mr. and Mrs. Azure, aware of the deficiencies in their own education, had been extravagant in that which they had bestowed upon their daughter ; an exemplification of which, as Theodore Hook says, ' the reader may yet live to see.'

Miss Young, who had ' gazed upon the world' a trifle more than fifty years, was a lady who laboured with infinite industry to be *mis*taken for a Miss who had outlived but twenty summers, but unfortunately for her talents thus *mis*placed, people were rarely so *mis*taken. She stated herself to be a lineal descendant of the renowned Dr. *Young ;* all her day talk was of his ' Night Thoughts ;' and she was for ever quoting from the theological works of various divines, from Jeremy Taylor to Hartwell Horne.

Mrs. Bodger and her daughter concluded the ladies ; Mrs. Bodger was an early friend and associate of Mrs. Azure, and had passed through life under similar circumstances ; she had been a servant of all work, and was now the widow of a *retired* tallow merchant. Like Mrs. Azure, she still spoke the ' language of her youth ;' and the ' ope hof henjoying a leetle fresh hair' had induced her ' to go a gipseyin ;' her daughter was tinctured with a little of the blue of her bosom friend, Miss Azure; but her chief study was satire; she levelled her shafts at every one, and every thing; whether well, or ill-timed was a matter of no moment to her; she forgot that

> Satire should like a polish'd razor keen,
> Wound with a touch that's scarcely felt or seen;

and as there was little, or no real wit, in her pungent remarks, she but too often made herself appear very rude, and very ridiculous.

The gentlemen need but little description; Mr. Brindle was an enthusiast in the *viewing* of nature; he never went a long, or short journey; a sea, or land voyage; took a trip out of town, or ascended the top of his house without his telescope: numberless were the accidents this propensity had entailed upon him; but vain were their effects in curing him; he still, upon every occasion, walked with his telescope to his eye, shifting the focus as he neared, or retired from any object, and as he usually carried a pocket one when he perambulated the streets, as he said, 'To see the time by the farthest church clock,' he frequently descended open cellars, areas, coal gratings, &c. &c., without any previous intention, more speedily than was ever agreeable; and measured his length upon the ground, against his desire, most constantly, and in a manner he thought remarkable.

Mr. Azure was fond of monosyllables and gin; the former he *always* indulged in, the latter, at nights, and in both the latter cases he thought it indispensable.

Mr. Pundit was a pedant, who deemed the ancients the only authors a man should read; his language was precise, and his manners bore a resemblance to his language; yet, on all occasions like the present, he wished to be present; he felt it 'a relief,' he observed, 'to unbend when his mind had been prolapsed in the profluent study of abstruse, and obscure authors.'

Tom Buoyant was a confirmed punster, which is saying everything for him; he was attended by his two friends, Raleigh Walter,, a desperate smoker, and Sam Smerke, or, as he was nick-named, Smiling Smerke, because he was always on the broad grin.

Last, and least, were the two schoolfellows of Master Brindle, who bore the family name of Budd—Bob and Joe Budd, and precious 'buds' they were, only happy when in mischief, and decidedly opposite in every point of character to Master Swallow Brindle, who loved nothing so well as eating; and must have been the very boy who wrote from school to his mother, the most expressive letter ever penned—

" Dear Mother,

" Puddin."

These sweet youths completed the party.

July is known to be rather a warm month, from a slight hint

conveyed in the Almanack—*ecce signum*—'dog days;' and if ever England experienced a day unusually 'hot,' it was that on which our Pilgrims accompanied the *Pic-nic-ians* to Richmond; not a breath of air was stirring, the sky over head was a faint blue, which gradually faded into a pale fewn colour, as it approached the horizon, not a cloud broke—

> " Light shade for the leaves when laid
> In their noon day dreams,'

Terrible were its effects on Mrs. Brindle—poor old soul, it had been almost an Herculean task to her to get the eatables ready in time, but she succeeded—got them packed and sent on board the steamer the night previous to starting, taking upon herself the task of making and cooking all the tarts, pastry, and everything in that way ; she had given herself a good hard day's work over a large kitchen fire, which, in July, is no joke, and is in itself enough to knock up even a person accustomed to it ; but Mrs. Brindle had not only to attend to the puffs and tarts, but also to the young gentlemen, who had forced their way in, and nothing could induce the dears to quit the kitchen while the sweets were about ; ever and anon they were ' seeking what they might devour,' and having outraged every indulgence granted them, had been, ultimately, forcibly expelled ; as might be expected, the contention with the ' youthful hopefuls,' the heat of the weather, the fire, and the anxiety of the well-turning out of her cookery, had completely knocked her up, and instead of keeping her promise to be at the party, she ought to have kept her bed ; but, good natured creature, she imagined that the party would receive a great damper by her absence, and therefore, roused herself in the best manner she was able. The party assembled at her house by nine o'clock, and after two or three little stoppages, caused by ' forgetfulness,' got on board the Diana, at ten minutes to ten, which was the appointed hour for starting. As Mrs. Brindle had prided herself upon the correctness with which all the joints and their concomitants—all the pastry, the dessert, the wines, and liquors—had been packed ; and, as her man servant had saib, safely delivered on board the steamer, she thought to make assurance doubly sure by *seeing* that they were on board : she, therefore, enquired respecting them of the captain, who referred her to the steward, who knew nothing about them ; consequently, they could not be on board ; for if they had been they would have been consigned to his care. Mrs. Brindle grew alarmed ;—luckily, she had brought the man-servant who had taken them the night previous to wait upon them : she immediately sought him out : she found him.

" Jim," she cried.

" Ma'am."

" You took those hampers I sent you with last night safe to the steam-office ?"

" Yes."

" Did you put them, as I told you to do, on board ? "

" No."

" No ! why not ? "

" Too late."

" Why, you never took them home again."

" No, ma'am, I left them at the office."

" Oh ! " (A groan of relief.)

" There's the young man I left 'em with," said Jim, pointing to a person who was talking with the captain.

" That's lucky," said Mrs. B. " Jim, follow me."

Jim obeyed.

" My servant left some packages last night with you to go by this steamer to Richmond," said Mrs. B. to the young man. Judge of Mrs. B.'s horror upon hearing the reply. " He left some packages last night with me, but not for this steamer."

" Not for this steamer ! " reiterated Mrs. B. " For which then ? " she falteringly enquired.

" For the Diamond, ma'am," politely returned the clerk.

" Jim ! "

" Ma'am."

" What did I tell you ?—pray, what name did I tell you ? "

" I forgot the name, ma'am—and that young man said the ' Dimond'—and it sounded like it—so I thought it was all right."

" Jim, you are a downright fool."

Jim mentally disagreed with her.

" We can have them taken out of the Diamond, and put on board this vessel ? " asked Mrs. B. of the clerk.

" Oh no, ma'am," replied the clerk, " the Diamond went to Gravesend at six o'clock this morning."

Mrs. B. felt as if she could sink into the earth   " What ? " she faintly asked.

The clerk repeated the disagreeable intelligence. Mrs. B. mechanically turned to Jim, who looked particularly foolish ;— her indignation was excited at the sight of him.   " Jim," she cried, " you stupid, dull-headed fool; here's a predicament you have placed us in ; here's a t—t—t—t——what shall we do ? "

" I beg your pardon, ma'am," said the clerk; " I presume your packages contain provision for a pic-nic party."

" They do—they do," responded Mrs. B.

" I expect the Diamond will return by eleven o'clock, and your packages can be forwarded to you by a waterman's boat, and I dare say will reach you by the time you will want them."

" You are very, very good," exclaimed Mrs. B., who felt as if the whole world had been taken off her chest. " Jim, you shall stay behind, and when the Diamond returns, get our things from her, and bring them in a boat after us up to Richmond Bridge."

"Very well, ma'am," replied Jim, who was as pleased as his mistress that it was no worse.

"You will have the goodness to see them forwarded," said Mrs. B. to the clerk.

"I will, ma'am," he replied, and bowed low, as he received half-a-crown from her.

The relation of this occurrence excited some merriment among the party.

"Well," exclaimed Makemoney, "although our dinner has gone in the opposite direction to our destination, it is still probable that we shall meet."

"It is *meet* we should," said Buoyant.

"Ha! ha! ha!" roared Smerke.

"What a wretched attempt, Buoyant," sneered Miss Bodger: "really your puns are, like yourself, frightfully hideous, and particularly *pointless*"

"Ha! ha! ha!" grinned Smerke.

"You are *sharp*, however, Miss," replied Buoyant.

"We shall be in a precious mess if he don't come," observed Mrs. Azure.

"Oh, he'll come," said Mrs. Brindle, consolingly.

"If he didn't he should go," cried Mrs. Bodger. "I tell you what, Mrs. Brindle, its all gammon about forgetting the name. I'd lay my life he got drunk; and, if I was you, I'd give him the sack."

"What sack?" asked Mrs. Brindle, innocently.

"Ha! ha! ha!" shouted Smerke.

"Mother!" uttered Miss Bodger, silencingly.

"Mrs.B.—puff—means—puff—discharge—puff—him—puff," —exclaimed Raleigh Walter, as distinctly as his cigar would let him.

"Nay," exclaimed Miss Azure, with affected kindness, "do not be so harsh; mistakes will occur, you know, in the best regulated families, '*comme dit l'autre;*' besides, it is useless to make a grievance of a circumstance which the occurrence obviates the prevention—'*Il faut souffrir patiemmement ce qui est inevitable.*' And, let me observe," she concluded, simperingly, '*Il n'est pas tout-a-fait clair que le mal arrivera.*'"

"No—nor the dinner either," rejoined Flourish.

"The non-existence of mnemonics in domestics causes a frequency of errors," said Pundit.

"Very true, sir," broke in Miss Young, who did not properly understand Pundit's meaning, but was dying to say something about her ancestor; "very true, sir!—

> ' Error in *acts* or judgment is the source
> Of endless sighs ! '

as writes my illustrious antecedent, the great Dr. Young, in the ninth night of the Complaint——"

She would have continued, but her voice was drowned by the vociferation of the captain to the sailors to cast off, and the engineer to clap on. The passengers became sensible of the motion of the vessel, and the dum-dum-dum-dum of the paddle-wheels was predominant.

"Now we are off," exclaimed Sprightly, "and two hours hence I anticipate that my feet will kiss the green bosom of Richmond Hill."

"How poetical!" cried Miss Azure.

'He did press on the green moss——'

Here she was interrupted by a violent screaming and an outrageous scuffling: all eyes were turned on the spot from whence the noise proceeded, and beheld the steward bringing the Master Budds, grasped by the collars of their coats, in his right hand, and Master Swallow, held by the arm, in his left. It is needless to say that a strong opposition was kept up by the youthful party; which developed itself in sundry kickings, strugglings, bitings, &c., and, on the part of Master Swallow Brindle, by a most lusty roaring, as he run, unwillingly, at the pace of ten miles an hour.

"Who do these younkers belong to?" exclaimed the steward—(an old seaman, who had been a boatswain of a man-of-war; was pensioned off for wounds received in his Majesty's service, and, to his pension, added the emolument of a steward's berth in a steamer)—"Who do these younkers belong to?" again roared the steward.

Poor Mrs. Brindle hesitatingly advanced; she dreaded to hear the steward's explanation of this scene; a glance at the boys was quite enough to satisfy her that the intelligence would be far from pleasing. "I believe the children—that is—I brought the children with—that is—what *is* the matter?" she enquired a little more boldly.

"Why, lookee, ma'am," answered the steward; "if these youngsters be you'rn you ought to seize 'em up, and gi' 'em a round dozen, and I'll tell you why—avast there!" he shouted to the boys, who were making desperate struggles to free themselves, accompanied by yells of—"Mrs. Brindle—ma—mum—Mrs. Brindle—oh—oh—oh!—let us go."

"Let them go," said Mrs. Brindle, entreatingly; "and pray do let me know what they have done?"

"Oh, sart'n'y, marm," replied the old man, and he let the boys loose; but attempted to recapture an orange, and sundry lumps of sugar from Master Swallow, who, upon losing them, extended his arms and hands, performed a very speedy dance, and screamed more lustily than before; as silence could only be restored by a restoration of the orange and sugar, this was done, and peace obtained.

"Now," said Mrs. Brindle, "if you please, tell me the meaning of all this."

"If that powder monkey was mine," exclaimed the steward, indignantly, "instead of an orange, I'd giv' him the bight of a topsail sheet over his starn ; but that's neither here nor there ; you see, ma'am, I was on duty in the chief cabin, and somebody sung out for an allowance o' brandy—I turned into my berth to fetch it, when—buntlines and cluelines—I saw the youngsters as busy as topmen shaking out reefs when a fair breeze is springing up ; and what do you think they were after ?"

"Don't know," answered Mrs. Brindle, with a consciousness that something *very* unpleasant was coming.

"Why, there was one had turned up a pot of green paint ; and was painting over the bulk heads till all was blue."

"Fudge !" said Mr. Azure.

"The other was mixing rum, brandy, gin, wine, stout, and water, in a two gallon can, and the third, that youngster sucking the orange, had stretched along the eating haliards, and was raking the fruit locker fore and aft—I boarded 'em in the smoke —and brought 'em up all standing—I made 'em prisoners, and lugged 'em up to be owned, and as they're yours, you must pay all damage."

"How much is it ?" asked Mrs. Brindle, who understood very little more than the last sentence ; but that was quite enough to know. The steward began to enumerate, but as his list run rather long, Mrs. Brindle cut it short by asking if half-a-sovereign would cover the damage ; the seaman replied in the affirmative, and the payment of the money settled the affair.

A lecture on good behaviour followed from Mrs. Brindle to the boys ; to which, as it appealed to their sense, they were completely insensible ; and fully developed their sense of it, by starting off, upon its conclusion, to see what further mischief they could employ themselves in. Mrs. Brindle having herself a misgiving of the efficacy of her lecture, followed them in their peregrinations, just to keep an eye on them, a task by no means delightful.

The intentions of children are usually evanescent ; they were peculiarly so in the Master Budds ; as soon as they formed a desire, they attempted its gratification, the slightest impediment to its attainment gave rise to a fresh design, which, in its turn, was succeeded by another, until they accomplished something, not always agreeable in its effects ; whenever any thing like eatables were the *fruits* of the 'Budd's' campaign, Master Swallow made one of the party, and the prospect of obtaining an apple, ever induced him to follow the *pair*.

The possibility of her dear boy's getting into danger, entailed a stronger necessity upon Mrs. B. to bring up their rear ; and as their operations were of a most desultory nature, without fear, or care for the result, they kept the poor old lady in a perpetual fever and continued jog-trot ; her appearance was truly piteous ; the sun, when endeavouring to show his face through a fog of particularly *cutable* consistency, never looked redder than did the countenance of poor Mrs. B.: her hair, which she had taken such pains to paper, and press, the night before, and that very morning had spent half an hour in combing and pinning, to make all sure, was now hanging in straggling disorder over her forehead and cheeks, her white dress, which had been 'got up' so nicely, so *whitely*, and stiffly, was now flaccid, dingy, and hung upon her like a bathing gown on a nymph performing her saline ablutions; in truth, the sultriness, or, as Mrs. Bodger termed it—the *sweltriness* of the weather, and the heat of the steamer combined, had 'induced a copious exudation,' to use Mr. Pundit's words, and produced the effect we have described.

"Poor Mrs. Brindle has enough to do, to keep those boys from mischief;" said Makemoney, who had been much amused with witnessing their freaks, and Mrs. B's. nervous agitation.

"Yes," replied Sprightly, "and I cannot conceive what motive Mrs. Brindle could have, in bringing those young gentlemen, whose 'little pleasantries' seem to have such unfavourable results."

"No," cried Mrs. Bodger, "I'd a seen the brats at Jericho first, afore I'd a brought 'em; they'll fag her to death; here I'm all a muck a' sweat standing still, and what must she be? why, sweating like a bull to be sure!"

Flourish looked at Sprightly on the termination of this speech, and they both laughed—inwardly, it is true; but Miss Bodger, who had noticed the glance and smile, felt stung, and determined, if possible, to be revenged for it.

"My mother is peculiar in her choice of words," she remarked to Flourish; "but old people have singular ways, you know; your pa, I believe, was so *eccentric* in his language and manners, that he was not admitted in decent society, because in all circles he preferred retaining his early speech and habits—was it not so?"

Sprightly and Makemoney both laughed immoderately, and Flourish, with something like asperity, replied—"You are slightly mistaken, my dear. My father was the younger son of Sir Ralph Flourish, a baronet, and lineal descendant of the Earl Gaspar de Flourish, who came over with William the Conqueror; my father was educated at Eton, and afterwards at Christchurch, Oxford; upon quitting college, he took a fancy to commerce, and in addition to a handsome income, realized a large fortune, of which I am the unworthy possessor," and he made Miss Bodger a low bow.

"I was misinformed," replied Miss Bodger, and slightly coloured; but she was not to be prevented from having another try to repay that smile at her mother's expense; so turning to Sprightly, she said, "Perhaps, I mean you, I am forgetful of names," and she tried to look archly.

Sprightly, who saw the 'cloven foot,' smilingly referred her to his uncle—"who," he said, "knew his father better than himself."

"Yes, young lady," exclaimed Makemoney, "I knew him well for many years, and suffer me to observe, that you are equally mistaken with regard to Sprightly ; but first let me say that it is not the choice of *words,* that we should——"

A crash—a scream—and a tremendous outcry, interrupted the speech of Makemoney ; on seeking the cause, it appeared that Master Swallow had, like a cat with a mouse, been playing with an orange before he devoured it ; his actions had been carefully watched by a dog, of which Flourish was the owner, and a miscalculation in the point of descent of the fruit by Master Brindle, who had been tossing it in the air, caused the orange to fall upon the deck ; immediately the dog perceived the prostrate luxury, he made a bound to obtain it, the success of which was counteracted by Master Swallow's seizing fast hold of his tail ; and as the dog made strenuous efforts to capture it, he compelled Master S. to go through the evolutions of a slide ; at the same moment Mr. Brindle had just directed his glass to Vauxhall Bridge, and was stepping back to bring the glass to a right focus, when the dog bolted through his legs, but as Master S. still kept firmly hold, and being rather too large to pass freely the same opening, Mr. Brindle was propelled at an unusual speed, until Master Swallow found it impracticable to hold any longer, in consequence of the dog's suddenly turning short and impressing his teeth on the young gentleman's digits ; thus sharply admonished, he quitted the tail, and the result of the sudden cessation of the propelling power was, that Mr. Brindle and his son were forcibly deposited in the centre of a party who were playing at cribbage for bottles of stout ; this was the cause of the crash—for bottles and glasses, like many banks—were broken. The scream came from Mrs. Brindle, who had witnessed the catastrophe, and whose fears had magnified the accident into certain destruction of one or both parties, from which horrid conviction she was relieved, by seeing Mr. Brindle arise and politely beg a thousand pardons of the circle into which he had gained admittance unknown and thus abruptly, for unintentionally slightly disturbing their game ; and Master Swallow finding himself minus an orange, and gainer of a bite—

' Crowed like chanticleer,"

giving powerful indications that if he had lost his fruit, he still retained his lungs. Mrs. Brindle upon ascertaining that her dear child had actually been bitten by the dog, grew fearfully alarmed ; frightful visions of hydrophobia assailed her—bitten by a dog in dog days—horror ! she saw him (mentally of course) turn with terror and disgust from water—foam at the mouth——biting—writhing—dying raving mad ; and globules of perspiration cold as ice, chased each other down her broad forehead and fat cheeks ; cutting and cauterizing next presented themselves to her frantic imagination ; cutting out the part affected, and then applying a red-hot iron to the wound—agony ! " My child !—my boy !—my Swallow !" she exclaimed hysterically.

" Oh—oh !—Ha—a—a—a—oh !" screamed her Swallow. " Ha—a—a ! I will have my or—or—orange." A rapid movement with his feet ensued. " Gi—gi—give it to me—oh—oh—oh !" and the yell faded into a faint sniff—a quivering catching of the breath, as Flourish put into his hands the orange, which his dog had laid at his feet ; the recovery of his lost treasure quieted the boy, and with that happy indifference to ' clean and sweet ' which characterizes children (excepting in one instance, where we saw a child refuse a piece of barley sugar which a *black* man had been sucking, and in a fit of *child-like* good nature, took from his mouth, and offered), Master Swallow immediately commenced devouring the *spheroid*, which the dog had well moistened with his saliva. Mrs. Brindle was, however, not so easily satisfied ; she strictly scrutinized the bitten hand, but not finding an incision from the animal's incisors, concluded that cutting would not be required, and ejecting load No. 3 from her chest, admonished her offspring to keep himself quiet for the remainder of the day : she was roused from her lecture by hearing Mr. Pundit exclaim——

" The calidity of the Apollic luminary, has compelled a liquefaction of the colophony, with which the place, against which I have leaned, has been covered, and, I fear, a quantum has attached itself viscously to my coat."

This speech was addressed to Mrs. Bodger, who replied—" I don't know what you mean by collor-funny, but if you mean your coat, why its all over green paint, for you've been leaning agin the board which young Joe Budd has been a painten hon."

Mr. Pundit was a man who felt ill if a speck of dirt got upon his clothes ; he therefore heard that his coat, a light plum, almost a lavender colour, was ornamented across the shoulders with a bright emerald green, with a satisfaction by no means evident.

" The exestuation," said he angrily, " of exiguous juveniles, ever produces mischief, and I feel surprised that Mrs. B. who knows that they are not morigerous, by the frequency of their requiring objurgation, should, maugre this knowledge and the possibility of producing unpleasantnesses, have brought them with her, to the dissatisfaction of every one present, and to her own discomforture." So saying, he indignantly joined the party at the head of the vessel, who were expatiating upon the beauty of the scenery they were passing.

Mrs. Brindle was almost affected to tears by this reflection upon her ; and Mrs. Bodger soothed her by saying—" Hif you hadn't a brought 'em this wouldn't a happened—but what's done can't be hundone, so never mind, don't bother yourself about what he said—I didn't hunderstand him—it was all igh Dutch to me. Where's the kids ?"

"Kids!" reiterated Mrs. Brindle, interrogatively.

"Yes, the young 'uns!" said Mrs. Bodger.

"Oh, the children! oh, the young Budds are asleep with the heat, and Swallow seems fast following," replied Mrs. Brindle.

"Well, that's lucky—ere, come hup to the hother hend, where the hothers hare," cried Mrs. Bodger; and arm in arm they sought the head of the vessel.

"There's—puff—the—puff—Red-house—puff," said Walter.

"A famous place for shooting pigeons," remarked Make-money.

"Yes," replied Buoyant, "and gulls are to be seen there as well."

"Ha! ha! ha!" laughed Smerke.

"Infamous!" said Miss Bodger; "of course then *you* are to be seen there."

"Ha! ha! ha!" yelled Smerke.

"The loud laugh shows the vacant mind!"

uttered Miss Azure, listlessly.

Smerke was silent.

"Now," cried Buoyant, "we reach Chelsea Reach; 'tis said when we reach this Reach, it makes us cockneys retch."

"Ha! ha! ha!" roared Smerke.

"Fudge!" exclaimed Mr. Azure.

"It is very open to the wind here," said Makemoney.

"Yes, uncle," answered Sprightly, "do you remember coming to a sailing match, and being very nearly run down by one of the vessels?"

"I do," responded Makemoney, "and a narrow escape we had; it was all through the stupidity of our waterman, who ran foul of a wherry which he nearly upset, and a sailing boat was just upon us—"

"Which luffed up, and prevented your being run down, I suppose," punned Buoyant.

"Exactly," returned Makemoney.

Battersea, Putney, and Hammersmith bridges, were respectively passed, and commented on, and the mansions, villas, and churches, decking the river's bank, excited critical remarks; Miss Azure was labouring, with great perseverance, to bring all her quotations—English, French, and Italian, into play; while Miss Young never lost an opportunity to drag in some lines from Young, whether *apropos* or not; and if Young could not furnish her with lines to the purpose, she drew upon some theological author whom she had read, and a retentive memory enabled her to produce portions when occasion required; Miss Bodger found opportunities to indulge in her pungent remarks; and Tom Buoyant punned most vigorously; Smerke roared more than ever; Raleigh Walter was emptying his cigar with all speed, and Mr. Azure his gin-bottle; Mrs. Azure and Mrs. Bodger were being drawn out by Flourish, to whom they were

CHELSEA, REACH.

recounting, to the great amusement of Makemoney and Sprightly, a " slap-up gipsey party" which they had enjoyed together some twenty years previous ; while Mr. Pundit was sighing over his painted garment ; and Mr. Brindle, still gazing through his telescope, kept treading on the toes of every one near him, and was continually knocking his shins against the windlass, bits, &c.; exciting the nervous irritability of Mrs. Brindle, which developed itself in the frequent utterance of the interjections, " Ha—ho—oh !" as her husband encountered each of the little accidents just mentioned ; but

> " A change came o'er the spirit of their dream."

The sun, which was increasing in altitude, was also increasing in heat ; the steam likewise dispensed a considerable portion of its warmth on all within its influence, and assisted materially in making the atmosphere insufferably hot. Every one laboured under its effects ; and, notwithstanding the endeavours of the ladies, by means of veils, &c., to

> " Shade their beauty from the sun,"

their efforts were of no *avail*, as Tom Buoyant remarked ; for their foreheads, noses, cheeks, and chins, were suffused, not with a faint blush, but a flush of scarlet ; an accession not very desirable, as being a colour burnt in was not likely easily to be ef-*faced*. The gentlemen loosened their neckcloths, their coats, and waistcoats : vainly did they turn to the four cardinal points in the faint hope of catching a breeze ; but no—not a breath was to be obtained ; and Makemoney, after veering about several times, gave vent to his oppression in a most energetic " Phew !"

" *Qu'il fait chaud,*" said Miss Azure.

" Who? what? kill for shew? What do you mean ?" asked her mother.

" Your daughter alluded to the calidity of the atmosphere," replied Pundit ; " and, veraciously speaking, the Apollic luminary is excessively calorific, and I am in an oppressive state of sudation."

" Thank'ee, sir," was responded by Mrs. A., who remained as wise as before.

Mr. Pundit sighed, and thought of his coat : he tried to see its reflection on the water, but his efforts were without success.

" Silence reigned triumphant." It was very evident that the sudorific powers of the sun were resistless ; and though several efforts were made to keep a conversation afloat, it dwindled into monosyllables, and eventually into silence. Buoyant left off punning, Raleigh Walter smoking, Smerke grinning, Mr. Azure drinking gin, and Mr. Brindle put down his telescope ; Miss Azure ceased French-ising, Miss Bodger pungency ; Miss Young began to dream of her illustrious antecedent ; Mesdames Bodger and Azure forgot ' hold times ' in somnolency ; the Miss Brindles were just beginning to grow serious, and Mrs. Brindle went to look after the boys ; our Pilgrims, who felt the oppressive sultriness no less than the other portion of the party, maugre their great love of the picturesque, sought refuge in the cabin ;—and thus they reached Richmond.

The exclamations of " Richmond! Richmond!" from the steward, and the bustle attendant upon the arrival, awakened the sleepers and dozers ; and as the note of the Swiss horn gathers the shepherd's flock together, so the voice of the steward collected our scattered party into one group. The heat was still intense ; but the slight repose, and the novelty of the arrival, counteracted partially the lassitude which the weather occasioned, and seemed to put a fresh spirit into the Pic-nic-ians ; every one blessed with a peculiar characteristic indulged in it as freely as heretofore. Tom Buoyant commenced :

" I esteem a steamer, although it has been a frier," said he, " because the day is a broiler."

" Ha! ha! ha!" roared Smerke.

" Stuff!" cried Azure.

" Catachrestical!" exclaimed Pundit, superciliously.

" Ha!—puff—devilish—puff—good," puffed Walter.

" *Entre-deux,*" lisped Miss Azure.

" He! he! he!" giggled the Miss Brindles ; " he is so amusing—the wretch!"

" Oh, dreadfully so," sneered Miss Bodger, " particularly to shallow minds."

" I see," said Flourish, a little ungallantly, for he had not forgotten the attack upon his father ; " I see you derive much amusement from him."

" Thank you," she answered ; " but I believe you exceed me in that little particular."

" Where's Mrs. Brindle?" interrupted Mrs. Azure ; " oh, here she comes with those precious boys. Why, what's the matter now?" she inquired of Mrs. B., who looked much distressed, while her boy was crying mightily.

" Matter!" replied Mrs. B.; " look here;" and she turned her back to Mrs. A.; " look here—what d'ye think of that?"

Mrs. Azure directed her eyes to her dress, and there saw sundry large dabs of green paint ; on which, with much labour and ingenuity, had been stuck several pieces of red paper, of smaller dimensions than the spots of paint; while, in various parts, pieces of the dress, in the shapes of diamonds, stars, suns, and moons, had been carefully subtracted with a sharp instrument— possibly a pair of scissors.

" There," continued Mrs. B.; " what do you think of that?"

" Ha! ha! ha!" yelled Smerke, convulsively.

" Mr. Smerke—sir—I am surprised—its no laughing matter, I can assure you," said Mrs. B. in a dignified tone, while the tears stood in her eyes ; " no, sir—if you——"

At this moment Mrs. Bodger's attention was attracted by Mrs. Brindle's tone of voice, and immediately after by her dress.

"Hallo!" she cried, " why, my ighs!—ha! ha! ha!—Where have you been?—Ha! ha! ha!—Oh, you know ; aint you bedizined worser nor a May sweep queen—well, I never——"

" *Marchand qui perd ne peut rire*," exclaimed Miss Azure, whose attention, with that of the rest of the party, had been excited by Mrs. Bodger's exclamation. " What is the matter, *ma chere madame?* " she asked of Mrs. Brindle.

" Why, my dear," replied Mrs. B. afflictedly, " upon finding every one was going off to sleep, I thought I would go and see how and where the boys were, for, you know, they are so lively that they will do any thing, and I thought they might have tumbled into the boiler——"

" Of course," interrupted Buoyant, " that put you in a stew."

" Ha! ha! ha!" laughed Smerke.

" Detestable effort!—pray be silent, Buoyant, and do not expose your extreme insufficiency," remarked Miss Bodger.

" Ha! ha! ha!" accompanied Smerke.

" You are almost as bad as Smerke," she concluded.

Smerke ceased.

Mrs. Brindle proceeded : " I therefore hurried to the cabin, and found two on the sofa, and one on a table, fast asleep ; well, I thought I would not disturb them, and I sat down to take a little rest, and fell a dreaming ; I thought Swallow was tumbling off the vessel into the water ; I rushed forward to save him, and awoke, to find Master Joseph Budd cutting and hacking my dress with a pair of scissors, while Swallow was sticking bits of paper on places which Bob was painting with a green brush ; my anger got the better of my tenderness, and I certainly struck them rather severely ; but don't you think they deserved it? " she inquired of all.

All exclaimed,—" Yes, oh yes! naughty boys," &c. &c.

" You are not, madam," said Pundit, pensively, " the only person who has suffered from their dispensation of that mineral and oleaginous composition ; you will perceive I am likewise a sufferer ; "—and he turned his back to the company.

" Ha! ha! ha!" shouted Smerke.

" Sir," said Pundit, " your cachinnation is offensive."

" Now, gentlemen, if you please," said the captain.

" Boat, sir! Boat! Boat! Here you are, sir! This way, marm! " was uttered successively by several boatmen.

As the party consisted of twenty persons, that is, seventeen adults and the three children, it was necessary to have three boats, and as it was likely to be a lucrative af-*fair* for the watermen, a scuffle ensued between them who should get the party—much shouting and much screaming ensued ; the three boys were seized forcibly by one man and placed in his boat, Mrs. B. followed quickly after them. As she was getting down the steps into the boat, Mr. Pundit was about following, when a scuffle between two watermen ensued just at his elbow; the sudden *lurch* of one of them caused him to dash against Pundit's shoulder, who was on the edge of the stairs; this act gave his descent a frightful impetus, and as there was nothing but Mrs. Brindle's back to stop his speed, his two hands came in contact with it, and caused her instantaneous entrance into the boat; it is needless to say he accompanied her with an impetuous celerity, and that they both discovered themselves in the bottom of the boat, rolling over each other: the violence with which this occurrence took place very nearly caused the turning over of the boat, and drew from the boatmen a horrid exclamation; the two Budds were sent sprawling over one of the seats, and Master Swallow over the side, to the intense agony of his mother, who rising, caught a glimpse of his boots disappearing; she bounded forward, upsetting Pundit, who was also rising, and thrust her hands and arms to her shoulders into the water in time to seize him and drag him into the boat; the suddenness with which she did this, nearly upset the boat a second time, and it required all the skill of the watermen to prevent it. She put Swallow, wet as he was, plump into the lap of Pundit, who had that moment seated himself, holding the sides of the seat most firmly, to prevent having a bathe unwillingly. Pundit had nankeen trousers on, and of course, was soaked to the skin instantly; scarcely any thing worse could have occurred to him: he was thinking thus, when Mrs. Brindle, overcome by the excitement, threw her wet arms around his neck and fainted away; here a new bustle was created, and Mr. Brindle, upon seeing the whole of the affair, which hardly occupied a minute, in his hurry to go to his wife's assistance, let the telescope slip through his fingers. Unfortunately he made a grasp at it, and succeeded only in striking it with the tips of his fingers, and instead of falling, as it would have done, upon the deck, it flew over the side, and the waters closed over it for ever; this, to him, was a greater misfortune than his wife's accident, and it was not till the reiterated offers of salts, scents, and aromatic vinegar, from the ladies, induced him to turn from franticly gazing upon the place where his telescope disappeared, to his wife in a swoon in the boat, he gave one ' longing lingering look behind,' and prepared to attempt the recovery of his wife, being fully convinced of the impossibility of recovering his telescope; or, it is probable, the latter might have called forth his efforts first; however, his assistance was not required, for Mrs. B. came to, and after gazing wildly round her for a moment, gave utterance to a short hysteric scream, and cried—" My child!—my boy!—where's my boy?"

" Your offspring, madam," said Pundit, grimly, " I imbibe gratification in observing, is preserved."

This speech was partially drowned by Master Swallow, who had given birth to a most violent yelling, with a piano accompaniment by the two Budds, who were both hurt by the fall; Mrs. B. upon hearing the well-known tone, caught him to her breast, hugged and wept over him, for be he what he might to other people, he was *her* only child, and she doated on him.

The other boats were now filled, and the party reached the shore, where the only incident of note occurring, was the sudden desire of Mr. Azure to be thought nimble; he made a jump from the boat to the shore, but miscalculating his distance, arrived up to his knees in the water, two feet nearer the boat than he intended.

"Ha! ha! ha!" shrieked Smerke.

"Fool," roared Azure, and darting a look of awful malignity at him, thrust both hands into his coat pockets and stalked up to the town.

The party followed, and proceeded some distance, before Mrs. Brindle could conceive how her son's and her own garments were to be dried; a pastry-cook's shop caught the eye of her son, and the probability of the proprietor allowing them to dry themselves struck her. She went, accompanied by the three boys, into the 'Original shop for Maids of Honour,' and easily obtained the required favour.

The remainder of the party proceeded to the Hill; we have before stated that it was a cloudless day, and, consequently, the view was exquisite.

"Well," exclaimed Makemoney, "this is, indeed, beautiful; we are well repaid for our fatigue: who will assert, after seeing this view, that Richmond Hill does not equal any spot in the world for a prospect?"

"There is something very chaste and varied," observed Sprightly.

"Chaste!" reiterated Makemoney; "why, France with her beautiful vines—Italy, with her blue skies and broad lakes—the Rhine, with its woody heights, or Switzerland, with its mountain scenery, owns nothing more beautifully diversified, more simple, or more characteristic."

"It is delightful," cried Miss Azure, who saw an opportunity to quote. "It is—

'A most living landscape, and the wave
Of woods, and cornfields, and the abodes of men,
Scattered at intervals, and wreathing smoke
Arising from such rustic roofs—'

lends a charm which makes it heaven to gaze on."

Miss Young who, for the preceding two hours, had been unable to introduce her 'illustrious antecedent,' was very unwilling to let this opening pass without making the most of it, so, scarcely waiting the termination of Miss Azure's remark, she burst forth with extraordinary velocity—"True, my dear; very true, it is, indeed, most exquisite; it makes me say, in the words of my truly great predecessor, Complaint, Night 4,—

" O most adorable ! most unador'd !
Where shall that praise begin, which ne'er should end ?
Where'er I turn, what claim on all applause.'

and, as Bishop Heber says,

" From the soft vernal sky, to the soft grassy gronnd,
There is beauty above me, beneath, and around."

and, I repeat with Dyer—

" How close and small the hedges lie !
What streaks of meadows cross the eye !
A step, methinks, may cross the stream."

" You make your *lines ac*-cord," interrupted Tom Buoyant, " but let us *leave* the trees and flowers, and think of Mrs. Brindle and the Budds."

" Ah," exclaimed Mrs. Azure, " where can they be ? it is very strange."

" Very," echoed Mrs. Bodger ; " its two hours arter the time we was to a' had dinner ;" and she looked at her gold watch, which was about the elegant size of a small cheeseplate. " Why, I'm blessed," she continued, " its three o'clock. I feels precious peckish, and it strikes me that it won't be huncommon hodd if we have to toddle to the Star and Garter for our feed, for I have a ' *presongtimong*,' as Miss Hazzher says, that Jim won't bring the pannum."

" Ha ! ha ! ha !" shouted Smerke.

" Well, Mr. Grinner, wot do you mean by that horse-laugh ?" she asked indignantly of smiling Smerke, who could only put his hand to his heart, bow, and shake his head, while his whole frame was convulsed with a suppressed roar.

" Oh, don't mind him, mother," cried Miss Bodger, " nature will out—it is merely his natural stupidity displaying itself."

" Oh, well, if that's all," said Mrs. B , appeased.

Mrs. Bodger was interrupted at this moment, by an audible groan, accompanied by the exclamation—" Its of no use—none whatever—it won't do—won't—d—n it." Turning to the spot, Mr. Brindle was observed, in a state of perturbation, holding his hand half closed to his right eye, telescope fashion, walking forwards, and then receding, and then stamping, and scratching his head with great vigour, bewailing the loss of his glass in terms of ' bitterest woe."

" La !" cried the eldest Miss Brindle, " look at pa,—he ! he ! he ! what a way he's in—he said——"

" Shocking !" giggled her sister, " wasn't it ?"

" Partic'lar so—he ! he ! he !" was the response.

" Gals," said Mrs. Bodger, " wats keeping your——Oh, here they hare—here they hare," she shouted, as Mrs. Brindle appeared in sight, followed by three men, carrying as many hampers ; and her dear son devouring a ' maid of honour,' accompanied by the two Budds, who were exciting the anger of the men, by occasionally inserting pins in their understandings.

"Hurrah, here's the dinner," shouted Buoyant.

"That's plummy!" vociferated Mrs. Bodger."

"Glorious—puff—devilish—puff—good," intermittingly ejaculated Walter, who had not ceased smoking, and who had replenished his case in Richmond.

"*Now*, I hope, we shall enjoy ourselves," said Miss Bodger.

"What detained you so long, Mrs. B. dear," enquired Miss Azure.

"Why, my love," answered Mrs. Brindle, wiping her forehead, for she was still ' dripping dew,' " when I was drying my boy's and my own clothes, I remembered there was nobody to meet the villain Jim with the dinner, so I directly started off, and the Budds would go with me down to the bridge ; and there I waited—waited, till I was tired ; but I had enough to do to keep the boys from mischief ; the little sprightly dogs kept throwing stones, until they broke a window and cut a child's eye open, both of which I had to pay for ; just after, up c mes a large boat, a regular party barge, and four men got out, and brought out our parcels with them, which, as soon as I saw, I went up to them, and asked them how they came by them ; and, would you believe it, the rude fellows called me the ' fat cook,' but I soon undeceived them ; I enquired for Jim, and learned that he had opened the wine hamper, had got beastly intoxicated, and was lying fast asleep in the cabin, or whatever you call it, of the pleasure boat. I got one of the men to wake him ; and all I could get out of the wretch was, that he was thirsty, and water did not agree with him, and then he filthily hiccup'd in my face. I sent him to the cabin to sleep off his liquor, and the watermen offering to carry the dinner, I—I——Why, here we are," she concluded.

"By the bye," said Makemoney, " it would be no bad thing to return by the boat, if it is large enough ?"

"Oh, quite," answered Mrs. Brindle.

"A good thought, uncle," cried Sprightly ; " I imagine it will be a clear moonlight night, and that will make it delicious."

"Besides," broke in Flourish, " we shall not have to endure the heat of the steamer, nor return so soon,"

"Delightful," ejaculated Miss Azure. " *Le vent du bureau est bon.*"

"Out of evil cometh good," eagerly uttered Miss Young ; " there is no evil, says Du Moulin, but some good enters into the composition ; and as my illustrious ancestor observes——"

"Mrs. Brindle—my wife—ma'am," interrupted Mr. Brindle ; " did you put up, as I directed, my pocket-glass in the hamper ?"

"Yes, my dear," answered his wife.

"The loss, Sacharisse, of my telescope, induces a necessity for the pocket-glass,—give it me."

"Lor, my dear, we shan't have dinner to day,—do wait ?"

"D—n it, Mrs. Brindle—ma'am," muttered Mr. B.

"Boatman," cried Makemoney, "is your boat large enough to take us all back to London?"

"Plenty, sir," replied a man advancing from his companions.

"Then we engage you to do so," said Makemoney.

"And he engages to do so, I hope," urged Buoyant.

"The Neoteric Charon is monoculous,' observed Pundit.

"What's that?" interrogated Mrs. Bodger.

"That he has a *singular* vision," replied Buoyant.

"Why, he's only got one hi," answered Mrs. B.

"Exactly," exclaimed Buoyant.

"Saves trouble, mum," said the waterman, who overheard the remark; "because, you see——" He would have grown loquacious, but the general cry of "Where shall we dine? Dinner! dinner!" drowned the intended explanation.

A council was now called to arrange where to dine: the Park, Star and Garter, were to their left; an hotel, a row of houses, at their back; a quantity of ditto to their right, and *the* view in front of them. It was evident that this was not a place for Pic-nic-iana. To be within the gaze of the world had nothing very rural in it. So, after a slight deliberation, they filed off to the right, and, with a little winding about, found a nice place,—a spot encompassed by a few trees, and commanding an extensive view. Here they stopped, and, with as much speed as might be, the cloth was laid upon the grass; the eatables brought forth; and, in an inconceivable short period, were being discussed by the party.

"Well, I likes this," cried Mrs. Bodger, with her mouth full; "it certain'y is nice to heat your wittles in the hopen hair."

"Very," responded Mrs. Azure; "it makes me think on our last trip here: there was no houses then—all fields and tresses —eh?"

"Oh, its pleasant to think on hold times, han't it, Hazzher?"

"Very," growled Azure.

"Well, how do you like the dinner?" asked Mrs. Brindle, who had been serving every body, and stood a very good chance of getting none herself. "How do you like it?" she asked, with a flattering consciousness of receiving the highest commendation.

"Oh, delicious—very nice—does great credit—never enjoyed any thing more—lamb so young—so sweet—fowls so nice," &c. &c. uttered the party.

"Well, I am very glad of that—I tried to——bless me, Mr. Pundit, what is the matter?" asked Mrs. B. of Mr. P., on seeing him cram his handkerchief to his mouth, turn as pale as death, and rise hastily from his seat. He could not reply, but waved his hand, rushed from the spot, and was very ill behind a tree. This incident gave rise to various conjectures: he had been eating a small pigeon-pie.

PIC-NIC-ING on RICHMOND HILL.

" Its very singular," remarked Mrs. B.; " there is nothing in a pigeon-pie to make any one unwell."

" Ain't there though," said the elder Budd.

" What d'ye mean, my child?" asked Mrs. B., with an inward conviction of some unpleasant disclosure of youthful villainy.

" Why, I saw Bob empty a little bottle of physic in that pie. He! he! he!" he giggled.

" Ha! ha! ha!" roared Smerke.

" Bottle of physic!" faintly reiterated Mrs. B.; " then that's where my emetic went." She turned to Bob—" Oh, you naughty boy."

" Well," snivelled Bob, " Mr. Joe put some black beetles in that meat-pie Mr. Smerke has been eating."

On this disclosure every one laughed but Smerke; and the fear of similar discoveries taking place induced nearly every one to believe that they had eaten sufficiently; particularly on Pundit's return,—for his ghastly, pallid look, alarmed all of them; and Smerke, with the thoughts of the beetles, was waxing marvellously white. Various antidotes were prescribed for them.

" Gin!" cried Azure.

" Brandy!" said Mrs. Bodger.

" Cigar!" exclaimed Walter,—puff—" nothing—puff—like a —puff—cigar"—puff.

However, Mrs. Bodger's prescription was followed, and seemed to have a very good effect; for Pundit began to look redder, and Smerke to laugh. A general dispersing now took place. The two Budds were most industriously exerting themselves; they had already affixed a long paper-tail to the collar of Walter, and a dirty knife-cloth to the tye wig of Mr. Brindle, who still followed the old fashion, and who now was busy with his telescope, muttering, " Beautiful! charming!" and various other words expressive of delight. They (the Budds) then diverted themselves by several other mischievous tricks; and Joe, having gathered some wild flowers, decorated, with much perseverance and ingenuity, the cap with which Miss Young adorned her head; while Bob was busy emptying a bottle of port wine into the pocket of Mr. Pundit's plum-coloured coat, as he was conversing very earnestly with Miss Young, and endeavouring to persuade her to take a glass of wine, which she, with affected juvenile bashfulness, was declining.

" Look at—puff—Brindle's—puff—tail—puff," said Walter to Miss Bodger; " he's got a—puff—tail—puff. Ha! ha! ha! Those young dogs—puff—have pinned a—puff—cloth to his— puff—tail—puff—puff."

" Oh vastly entertaining, no doubt," replied Miss Bodger; " I wonder you don't get rid of that filthy habit of ejecting smoke; it is a propensity so disgustingly offensive to any but the

2 F

little-minded follower of it, that I am surprised decent people should tolerate it."

" Well, now—puff," answered Walter, not at all affected by the remark, " I have—puff—heard—"

A scream from Mrs. Bodger, and a smashing of plates, announced that Mr. Brindle had stepped back unconsciously into a quantity, which the last-mentioned lady had been gathering together, and drew from her a flood of invective upon his unfortunate propensity.

Sprightly, who was lying, ' *a la Hamlet*,' at the feet of Miss Azure, laughed heartily at this mishap, and drew a retrospective review of the events of the day, with so much humour, that Miss Azure felt highly amused.

" Poor Pundit," he smilingly continued, " looked horribly rueful after the emetic, and our grinning friend grew grave. Here's Brindle, in using his glass too freely, is breaking his plates, and——"

" You are spilling your wine," interrupted Miss Azure ;— " gracious me, look there," she exclaimed suddenly. Sprightly turned his head, and beheld his uncle, quite overcome by the intense heat, fast asleep under a tree ; while the elder Miss Brindle was dressing him in a shawl and bonnet, the property of Mrs. Bodger ; and Flourish, with some flowers and grass at the end of a cane, was tickling the old gentleman's nose, who every now and then rubbed the part affected, exciting the jocularity of Smerke ; which Miss B. the younger, giggling mightily herself, endeavoured ineffectually to repress.

Mr. Azure, who would attempt nothing sprightly after his failure in his leap from the boat to the shore, kept " drinking gin with great spirit," as Tom Buoyant observed ; and Mrs. Azure, who had a leaning to that pellucid liquid, waited with some patience to receive a portion , which, after seeing the departure of four or five glassfuls down his thirsty throat, she doubted the attainment of, and therefore made a snatch at the bottle, which came readily into her possession from the unsuspecting, unresisting hand of Azure ; but, as she unfortunately expected the reverse, and did not intend to carry on the attack, meaning the snatch merely as a hint, the consequence was, the bottle fell with some force, broke, and distributed the liquor upon the parched and thirsty turf. This accident was to Azure one of frightful importance ; for the only pleasure he had tasted on his trip came from that bottle. Here, in an instant, he saw the cup of bliss dashed from his lips ; he had been but little pleased during the day—he expected much less gratification for the remainder : all this flashed like lightning through his brain, and, turning to his wife, he gave vent to a tremendous exclamation, too horrid for " polite ears ;" and, contrary to his usual custom, added to it a quantity of words—" You've done it, you greedy old hag, you have ; I wish I hadn't come ; I didn't want to come, you know I didn't ; and if I don't go may I be —— ;" and off he started.

"My dear, I couldn't help it," replied his wife ; "you know I couldn't ; it was all——" and she followed.

"Mr. Buoyant, you haven't seen my Swallow, have you ? " asked Mrs. Brindle of the punster.

"No, ma'am," answered Buoyant ; "I was too much engaged with my own dinner to notice how much you eat."

"How much I ——? Ah, you mistake my meaning ;—I spoke of my son."

"Your *son* is in the *shade* of that tree ; I fancy I saw him *leave* the *Budds* for the *trees*," cried Buoyant, delighted at having an opportunity to pun.

Mrs. Brindle walked to the tree, and for an instant peeped over, but saw sufficient to make her dart forward, with a shout, and seize her son, who was in the act of devouring, with all possible swiftness, a jam tart, and dispensing frugally portions of his plenty to Flourish's dog ; who sat eagerly watching for the proffered bits, which, like angels' visits, were "few and far between ; " and, as Buoyant described it (for he followed Mrs. Brindle, and, looking over the tree, saw the whole affair), every piece from Swallow to Snap was *snapped* up and *swallowed* by the dog, who *sat* there *bolting* with all his speed.

"Ha! you naughty boy," screamed Mrs. Brindle ; "give me the tart ; "you'll kill yourself, you greedy little glutton, you will—you good for nothing," &c. &c. She was about to inflict coercion, when Buoyant restrained her.

"Nay," he observed, "do not look so *sour* about a little *tart ;* the young colt is only a trifle Brindle-*pied*. Nay, don't strike him—you know a *blow* is sure to bring on a *breeze*."

Mrs. Brindle refrained.

"There," said Buoyant, leading the weeping Swallow from his mother, "young gentleman, you were on the *eve* of being *caned ;* and, even if you were *able* to *bear* it, your mother is not *brute* enough to do it."

Miss Bodger overheard the last speech of Buoyant, and she did not fail to give him her opinion of it.

"How happy you must be, Buoyant," she exclaimed.

"Why ? " he asked.

"Oh," she laughed, "there is no need to ask why. However, as you really are the victim of such ineffable stupidity, I will enlighten your dull brain. You must find a great pleasure in giving birth to those immeasurably abortive attempts at wit, or you would not put the kindness of your acquaintances to so painful a test ; and if such extremely slight trifles, lighter than air, can 'give you joy great as your content,' why you can have nothing to create sorrow ; therefore, you must be happy. You verify the old proverb, 'Trifles please little minds.' "

"Oh, you are too flattering," bowed Buoyant.

"You don't say so; indeed," sneeringly, smilingly, uttered the pungent petticoat, as she curtseyed.

The smashing of the plates, the screaming of Mrs. Bodger, the breaking of the bottle, the outcry of Mrs. Brindle, the tricks of the Miss Brindles and Flourish, and the " Ha! ha! ha!" of smiling Smerke, had the effect of rousing Makemoney from, as Miss Young observed,

> ' Tir'd Nature's sweet restorer, balmy *Sleep!* '

quoting her eminently great ancestor; Complaint, Night 1.

The rousing and rising of Makemoney caused a simultaneous movement in the whole party; they gathered together, in hopes that something would be proposed to make the " visit pleasant." Makemoney, upon discovering that he had been decked in the garments of a lady, testified for an instant some surprise, but finding that it was " only their fun," entered into the feeling with great good humour; and, after a little ' *badinage,*' a stroll was proposed and agreed to. Off they started to Richmond Park; leaving Mrs. Azure and Mrs. Bodger to take up the fragments and replace them in the baskets, which they lost no time in doing. The watermen, who had waited at a short distance, had been presented with a good " blow out," and were now called by the two ladies to remove the hampers to the boat.

"Here, you one hied gunner," elegantly exclaimed Mrs. Bodger, "just drop that bottle, will you; its like your imperence to take other people's lush without asking; you're cheap at nothing, and no gammon."

" Vy, you see, marm," replied the monocular Charon, " I was werry thusty, and I knew your good natur wouldn't let you say no if I axed you: and so you see I thought I wouldn't trouble you to say yes; you see——"

" Humbug—precious humbug," replied Mrs. Bodger; " come, shoulder the hamper and trudge."

The man obeyed grinningly; for he had taken a long pull at the bottle before he heard, or rather would hear, the lady's command to " drop it."

Mrs. Brindle succeeded in stowing away the things very nicely and compactly. She took much trouble in so packing them that they would not run much hazard of breaking; yet she feared that they would not go safe, for the cord which had bound them so firmly on their passage here had been taken by the boys; therefore, she cautioned the men several times to be careful in carrying them. They shouldered the baskets, and Mrs. Brindle, with some trepidation, watched their departure: she feared some mishap—a presentiment of evil oppressed her, and in a few seconds it was verified. The one-eyed gentleman, in the height of his jocularity, regardless of any impediments lying in his **path**, trudged forward, chuckling to himself with pleasure at the success of his impudence—

> "They canst not say but I had the crown—
> I was not fool, as well as villain—"

when—dire misfortune—his toe caught an unseen stone, and he, and hamper, plates, dishes, glasses, knives, and forks, were scattered in grievous disorder upon the grass. Mrs. Brindle and Mrs. Bodger screamed in concert, and spontaneously rushed forward; but, alas! they reached the spot only in time to pick up the pieces. Upon seeing the extent of the destruction, Mrs. Brindle stood motionless with horror; scarcely a thing was whole; fragments were strewed in all parts. The man was least damaged: he arose, and for a moment shook himself, as if to ascertain whether any bones had followed the example of the plates; but finding that not to be the case, he set the hamper up, and then sat down upon it, crossed his arms upon his knees, and, rolling his one eye over the devastation, coolly contemplated the effects of his disaster; at length, he exclaimed,

"This is a rummy go."

Mrs. Bodger was of an irascible temperament: had the property been her own she could not have felt greater anger than she did now; for a moment her rage had taken away her speech; during which space of time she watched with astonishment the movement of our unfortunate water wight; when "This is a rummy go!" burst on her ear. Her passion now got the better of her prudence; had the consequences been ever so frightful, it would have been of no consequence; bursting with rage unutterable, she darted forward to the man. "Rummy go, is it?" she shouted, "there, take that;" and she bestowed upon him a tremendous smack on the side of the head, which, with terrific velocity, placed him again among the broken crockery; and with considerable satisfaction did she survey the effects of her gift. "There, there!" she muttered, with great enjoyment. Up bounded he of the one eye, with deeply crimsoned cheek, and a horrible singing in the ears, which lasted him a week: upon gaining his feet, he advanced speedily, with clenched hands, to Mrs. Bodger.

"Hallo, old gal!" he vociferated; "what's that for?"

But we will spare our readers the colloquy that ensued. Mrs. Brindle, growing terribly alarmed that a battle would take place, separated the belligerent parties; and, telling the man she would be at the loss of the crockery, sent him with the few things that were saved to the boat, rubbing his tingling cheek, and giving utterance to many and various names.

We must now turn and follow the strollers. Miss Young and Pundit had found so much pleasure in each other's company, that they paired off; Miss Azure and Miss Bodger did the same; Flourish, Sprightly, and Smerke, kept together, and Makemoney, who had strolled with them, was suddenly found wanting ; they, therefore, commenced a search for him ; Buoyant followed the perambulations of the Budds and Swallow, according to a wish expressed to that effect by Mrs. Brindle, but on seeing that lady approach, he advanced to her, resigned his charge, and underwent the infliction of a minute's history of the affray from Mrs. Bodger, who accompanied Mrs. Brindle; he laughed much at hearing of the *blow ;* asking if she gave it him in the *wind ;* and, saying she did right " to *pitch* into the *tar*," left them.

The whole of the party were now rambling, in different parties, in different parts of the park ; the motives inducing this separation were various ; on the ladies parts the desire of meeting with gipseys was the principal one, therefore, the two Miss Brindles sidled off. Miss Young tried all in her power to quit Mr. Pundit, but he was not to be shaken off, and she was compelled to give up all hopes of having her fortune told ; she, however, turned farther from the rest of the party, indulging a faint expectation that he would join them and leave her to the opportunity of learning whether, and when, she should have a husband, &c. But Mr. Pundit had found a person who professed great reverence for the ancients, and he indulged himself by giving excerpts from authors whose existence Miss Young had never heard of until now. The names of Phocylides, Isocrates, Epicurus, Antoninus, Theophrastus, Theognis, Archytas Empedocles, &c. &c., were ' *all Greek* ' to her; but the hope of being able to quote her illustrious ancestor, and the supposition that they might have been almost equally great, induced her to listen with some patience, and thus employed, they wandered through the park, the enjoyment of which oberration, Pundit declared was excessive.

Mrs. Bodger quitted Mrs. Brindle, and sought her daughter, whom she took from the company of Miss Azure, ' to have a go at the lines in her hand by the gipsez,' and Miss Azure finding herself thus deserted, joined Sprightly, Flourish, and Smerke, and accompanied them in their search for Makemoney ; they had not strolled far, when the voice of a gipsey dealing out fortune and happiness struck on their ear, and the voice was accompanied by a laugh, which Sprightly, in an instant, knew to be Makemoney's. " By all the Gods in the Mythology," cried he, "there is my uncle having his fortune told.—Hush ! hush !— softly—gently—we'll unkennel the old fox—this is what he gave us the slip for, is it ?"

A slight opening in the trees presenting itself, Sprightly and Flourish struggled to gain first peep, while Smerke stifled the ' Ha ! ha ! ha !' that rose to his lips ; the opening being of sufficient size to enable the two to see without being seen, they gazed with unfeigned delight upon the scene ; there they saw Makemoney leaning his back against a tree, while a young black-eyed gipsey with his right hand in her possession, was telling him

PORTLAND RANG BEUORT PARK.

all that nearly and dearly concerned him—the past, present, and to come.

"Here," she exclaimed, looking him steadfastly and roguishly in the face, with as bright and black a pair of eyes as ever laughed from underneath the long silken lashes of a Castilian beauty; "Here, I see," said she, "in these lines, much that tells of good fortune; you had prosperity in your business; you were born under Jupiter, which is a lucky planet; the stars decreed thy fortune, and their prophecy is fulfilled, am I right?"

Makemoney nodded.

"Jupiter did not enter the house of Venus till long after your birth; you have gained wealth; you have obtained fortune; you sought for it; have it; but you have not searched for a heart; not men's hearts, for those your money will acquire for you; but a woman's heart you have not looked for, and you yet remain alone—am I right?"

Makemoney looked peculiar, as he nodded.

"Ha! ha' ha!" swallowed Smerke.

"I know it," she continued; "but there is a heart in store for you; one which will cleave to you through weal and woe; she is a dark beauty, and it rests with yourself to be happy with her for life."

"Nonsense, you rogue," chuckled Makemoney.

"By heavens! she means herself," whispered Sprightly to Flourish.

"Very like it," was the answer; "it is to be hoped she will not prevail on your uncle's soft susceptibility, and lead him astray!"

"Deluding idea," uttered Sprightly.

"Ha! ha! ha!" smothered Smerke.

"Have I seen her?" asked Makemoney, and looked full into the flashing eyes of the gipsey; now it is no joke to look into such eyes, particularly when the owner is returning the gaze kindly, brightly, and meaningly; Makemoney felt 'all overish,' and—

> "You might hear the beatings of his heart,
>   Quick, but not strong."

"You have," softly and hesitatingly replied the girl.

"Um! I have, you little rascal, eh? and will you not tell me where, you bright eyed Egyptian pearl, eh?" asked Makemoney tenderly, and we think—mind, we only *think*, he squeezed her hand.

"Ye gods! my uncle grows affectionate," said Sprightly, "this will never do. Hallo! there's another," he cried, as a second gipsey, accompanied by a boy and girl, stole up to the tree against which Makemoney leaned, without attracting the old gentleman's attention.

"Your worthy nunkey," said Flourish, "will never be able to withstand the united attacks of those dark eyed damsels. I think we had better interpose, and save him from their gentle fascinations."

"Ha! ha! ha!" choked Smerke.

"I must appeal to you, as a lady, to advise us what course ——why, where's Miss Azure ?" enquired Sprightly, interrupting himself on missing the lady.

Neither Flourish, or Smerke, could tell ; but an object moving through the trees at a short distance, caught their eye, and just stepping a few paces, discovered Miss Azure being led by the little gipsey girl, to learn her fate, they supposed of some older branch of the fraternity.

"Oh, hang it," cried Sprightly, " let her go ; we must interrupt this insinuating demoiselle, or there is no telling what my uncle may be induced to do."

They again sought their hiding place, and saw Makemoney chucking the girl under the chin, and evidently growing very delighted and very excited.

"The case is growing desperate," said Sprightly ; " we must disturb them—we have no other course—our philanthropy will not suffer us to remain neuter."

" Decidedly not," answered Flourish ; " however it may grieve us to act so peremptorily; besides," he concluded, with mock gravity, " it is all for his good !"

" Undoubtedly," laughed Sprightly.

" Ha! ha! ha!" gurgled Smerke.

But they were spared the cruel necessity, by a sudden crash and a piercing shriek. They rushed from their place of concealment, and discovered, close to the spot, Mrs. Brindle, with out-stretched arms, preparing to catch Master Joe Budd, who, followed by his brother, had climbed a tree in search of a bird's nest for Master Swallow ; he mounted a branch which age had withered, although the spring had kindly decked it with a few green sprigs, and, not being of sufficient strength to retain him, crashed—broke—and deposited him, with tremendous violence, in the arms of Mrs. B., who also had not sufficient strength to bear the weight ; consequently, she and Joe were scattered on the ground in an instant with " lightning's speed." There she lay. Master Bob, who had not reached the branch, gazed with affright on his brother's *leaving* the *bough* (as Tom Buoyant observed, who, not being far distant, was attracted to the spot by the scream)—and wisely and quickly descended the way he arose ; while Master Swallow, with a pot of jam which he had purloined from a basket, gazed on his prostrate parent with the same cool indifference that he had seen "the Budd leave the tree." He had his pot of jam safe, which was all he loved or cared for.

As we have just now observed, there lay Mrs. Brindle and Joe, until they were assisted to their feet by Sprightly and Flourish, who forgot, for a moment, Makemoney's situation in the accident which just occurred; but, on ascertaining that neither Mrs. B. nor Joe were hurt, only "uncommonly frightened," they turned to seek the old gentleman, and just caught him giving money to the gypsies, and sending them away.

"Aha! ho! ho! my good uncle," shouted Sprightly; "is this why you departed from our presence so stealthily, eh?—Fairly caught. Ha! ha! ha!"

Makemoney turned hastily round, and discovered that the whole party were assembled; for the scream of Mrs. B., which was long and piercing, had brought the whole pack around him: for a moment he was quite disconcerted, and saw no way of escaping the jeers of the party.

"What!" exclaimed Pundit, "Mr. Makemoney in opertaneous, colloquial consultation with an oneirocritie!—I am almost obmutescent. 'Soothsayers, interpreters of dreams, and all who pretend to a knowledge of the dispensations of fate, are low, base, cunning impostors,' said Chrysippus, and Ennius tells us, that 'Augurs and soothsayers, astrologers and interpreters of dreams, with vain pretence to more than human skill, I ne'er consult and heartily despise.' This, and much more, do the ancients say, and I fully agree with them."

"Ah," cried Miss Young, "but my revered predecessor says that 'Old Rome consulted birds.' Now, the citizens of old Rome were ancients, and wasn't that worse than consulting gypsies."

Pundit hummed and ha'a'd for a reply.

In the mean time, Sprightly and Flourish kept bantering Makemoney most unmercifully.

"My dear uncle," cried Sprightly, "what did she promise you? what say the stars? are you to live all the days of your life, and die when you cease to breathe?"

"Who is the lady?" interrupted Flourish; "is she dark or fair—brown or white—blue eyes or black—short or tall—thin or stout—sweet-tempered or Xantippeious?"

"What's the first letters of her name?" asked Mrs. Azure.

"—— Her eyes,
Her hair, her features, all, to the very tone
Even of her voice—"

quoted Miss Azure.

"Did she say—puff—that you should—puff—have a—puff—partner for—puff—li-e-fe?" drawled and whiffed Walter.

"Nay," said Miss Bodger, "a person in the vale of years like Mr. Makemoney, needs a partner to soothe his descent to that 'bourne from whence no traveller returns;' and it shews a nice discrimination in him, who has not the impetuosity or the frailness of youth to precipitate him into the commission of an act which requires such foresight and forethought; and therefore, with a wisdom peculiar to himself, and a coolness which great age bestows, he sought for the decrees of fate from one

2 G

who knew—ha! ha! ha!—much less about them than he did himself. Poor Mr. Makemoney! It is a frightfully weak-mindedness in females, but in an elderly gentleman—oh, dear—dear."

"Oh, but they tells huncommon. true," ejaculated Mrs. Bodger.

"Humbug!" said Azure.

"Ha! ha! ha!" warbled Smerke.

"Oh, but they does," continued Mrs. B.; "I'm sure wot they told you, Sally," she observed, turning to her daughter, "was very strange—all about that dark young man, with the large whiskers and round hies; there was no gammon in that, was there?—All true—I should think so!"

There was an universal laugh at Miss Bodger's expence.

If looks were daggers, Mrs. Bodger would have fallen to the ground, mortally wounded; such a malignant, piercing glance flashed from the bright black eyes of Miss Sally Bodger.

Makemoney now endeavoured to change the subject, but Sprightly would not suffer him.

"No, no, my good uncle," he jovially cried, "you must tell us all she said. Were you not to have a *dark beauty*, who would cleave to you through weal and woe? Was she right? eh?"

"Ha! ha! ha!" laughed Smerke. The party joined in the mirth.

"A little rascal that gypsey, eh?" cried Flourish; "a bright-eyed Egyptian pearl."

"Ha! ha! ha!" roared Smerke: "Ha! ha! ha!" echoed the party; and Makemoney heartily joined.

"So, then," he cried, "you heard——"

"A trifle, so I believe," replied Sprightly.

"Indeed," exclaimed Miss Bodger; "a noble employment for *gentlemen*"—and she laid a particular stress upon the last word—"that same eaves-dropping, truly."

Both gentlemen made her a low bow, and Sprightly observed, with much irony,—"I shall certainly come to you, my dear girl, for absolution; for your keen perception of what is proper, your strong mindedness, your unprejudiced view of circumstances, induce me to believe I could not find a being more worthy of being my absolver of sins."

"There," cried Buoyant, "how can you *steel* yourself against his *irony*."

Miss Bodger felt her colour come and go; she bit her lips, and tried to laugh it off, but unfortunately made a dead failure; which Sprightly observing, felt almost sorry for what he had said, and endeavoured to remove the attention of the party from her; observing, "But, my dear Miss Bodger, you forget all this while we are suffering my uncle to slip through our fingers; come, sir," he said, turning to his uncle, "your mystery—your mystery."

"Well, if I must tell you," replied Makemoney, "why, of course——"

"Oh, certainly, oh, yes, do, do," cried the party.

"Well then, she told me, would you believe it?—that—but it will not interest you."

"Oh, yes, yes, it will, it must," exclaimed the party, whose curiosity was much excited.

"Well then, she said,—'There's ne'er a rogue in all Denmark, but he's an arrant knave.'—Ha! ha! ha!—would you have believed it?"

"Oh, shame—shame—nonsense," the party exclaimed.

At this moment, Makemoney suddenly began searching his garments; he thrust, first his right, and then his left hand into his coat pockets, and rummaged unsuccessfully; the curiosity of the party was again excited; he patted his pockets again, and again, then took off his hat and looked into it, but fruitlessly, and he ultimately exclaimed—"It is gone?"

"What was gone?" was the general question. "His handkerchief!" This loss created much merriment.

"My ighs!" suddenly shouted Mrs. Bodger, who was contemplating her pocket clock; "why, I'm blessed, if it arnt seven o'clock; so, if we're agoin to have any tea, we'ed better git it at wonce."

This was generally agreed to, and in about a quarter of an hour succeeding, they found themselves ensconced comfortably in the large room of the Star and Garter, and a tea equipage, with all its apparatus and appendages, arranged in prime taste before them; everything was good, and every thing was nice, and as those little disclosures at dinner had prevented most of the members eating as heartily as they would otherwise have done, they made up now for the deficiency by doing perfect justice to all before them; this meal seemed to be enjoyed by every one, more than any thing else which had occurred during the day; they laughed, joked, drank, smoked, chattered, and, indeed, seemed quite happy, when a powerful stopper was clapped upon their mirth and enjoyments.

As might be expected, the offsprings were the springs of the accident we are about to relate: it will be remembered that Mrs. Brindle complained that one of the boys had purloined the cord which had fastened the hampers; a portion of this line still remained in the possession of Master Joe Budd, who suddenly conceived a great affection for Flourish's dog, but as the dog was not singular in his attachment, he roved from person to person in pursuit of whatever eatables they might bestow upon him; this roving disposition created a desire in the youth to restrain him by some more powerful means than any hold on his affections, which might have been obtained by him at the expence of sundry large pieces of provision; he, therefore, doubting the strength of the animal's attachment, attached the said cord to the dog's neck and to the handle of the tea-tray, he then threw a piece of cold meat to the animal, which fell without the distance which the cord allowed him to reach, and the consequences were, that in making a violent bound, he drew the tea-tray, cups and saucers, basons, plates, tea-pot, &c., &c., from the table to the ground. The crash, the din, the screams, the horrid clatter, was frightfully stunning; in an instant, the landlord, followed by a tribe of waiters, maids, strangers, &c., filled the room, to ascertain the cause of the uproar; and what a scene presented itself! the floor was strewn with the demolished tea things—chairs and tables here and there, and the whole room presented one mass of disorder; the various members of the Pic-nic, mixed in glorious confusion, were loud in their calls for vengeance upon the delinquent; very few had escaped some grievous effects of this disaster; poor Mrs. Brindle, as usual, suffered most; that horrid disease of the nerves, ever rendered her suspicious of some evil; she saw the tea things on the wane, without knowing the cause; she had not a second look, she stretched out her arms to stay their fall, and received cups full of tea, plates of bread and butter, &c., &c., in her bosom, without the satisfaction of saving one from destruction. Mrs. Bodger had a quantity of cream poured into her lap; her lavender silk dress was, therefore, spoiled, and her outcry upon the discovery was outrageous. Pundit was just sipping a cup of tea, which was too hot to drink, when the bound of Buoyant, to escape the falling mass, caused a collision, which jerked the whole of the burning liquid into his face and neck; while Azure had the tea-urn popped suddenly into his possession. He instantly discovered that it was ' too hot to hold,' and immediately placed it upon the ground, with what might be termed a good throw; directly he had disposed of it thus, he commenced *quivering* both hands with great rapidity in the air, then squeezed them against his body with his arms, and then bowed himself to the ground, or rather, we would say, curtseyed, only the speed with which he committed the act, might render it doubtful as to the truth of the term: he accompanied his ' bobs ' with the hurried and angry exclamation of—" I wish I hadn't come—I didn't want to come—dolt, dolt, dog, fool, to come—won't come any more—never !"

The two Miss Brindles had the contents of a coffee biggen thrown over their white dresses, which were not improved in whiteness by the occurrence; in truth, the whole party, more or less, suffered by the catastrophe; and their reflections did not tend to increase the happiness or welfare of the offending Budd; the children were universally voted a bore, and in the last case of juvenile flagrancy, flogging was deemed highly necessary; however, as no one offered to put the general wish into execution, Master Budd escaped the castigation he so well deserved, and would, otherwise, have received. The broken tea things were removed, and fresh ones substituted; peace was restored, and the meal finished; it was now getting near nine o'clock, and it was, therefore, thought high time to leave the Inn and proceed to the boat: this was done, and every one, without the slightest accident, got safely into the vessel, and found themselves comfortably situated in a commodious pleasure barge. Universal satisfaction was expressed, and, when the bustle was over, the beauty of the night attracted particular attention: the moon was shedding the silver glory of its cloudless splendour over the blue landscape,—it was at the full; charming as moonlight nights had appeared many times preceding this evening, yet they had never seemed to all in the party so beautiful: the air was still and quiet, and the existence of a faint breeze was only discovered as it slightly cooled the cheek it kissed: every thing seemed imbued with a loveliness surpassing description; and those who gazed upon its charms felt powerfully

" Nature, how beautiful art thou ! "

" Well, I'm blessed if it aint the beautifullest night I was hever hout hin," observed Mrs. Bodger, who was the first to break the silence.

" Yes," replied Sprightly—

" Night is bare
From one lonely cloud,
The moon rains out her beams, and heaven is overflowed.'

" Beautiful ! exquisite ! " fervently exclaimed Miss Azure, who, in the present instance, really felt what she said; but she must quote; the propensity was too strong to be resisted; and, after expatiating on the glory of the moonbeams on blue waters, she spoke of the moon, " broad, and round, and bright," and its

' Light, through summer foliage stealing;
Shedding a glow of such mild hue,
So warm, and yet so shadowy too,
As makes the very darkness there
More beautiful than light elsewhere."

This drew from Miss Young a quotation from her relation. Here was the misfortune of Miss Azure's love for quoting; she never gave lines from an author; but Miss Young found means to give something from her illustrious, &c. ; or, if the latter was the first to quote, Miss Azure followed with something from somebody.

" Oh," cried Miss Young, " this lovely moonlight gives us all delight. Ah, how divinely my great ancestor wrote on night, and he says in his Seventh Night what we may see now:

" A crystalline transparency prevails,
And strikes full lustre through the human sphere."

" How beautiful Kew Bridge looks by moonlight," chimed in Makemoney.

" Beautiful! beautiful!" echoed the party, who were growing rather tired and rather sleepy: in fact, be it known, to the happiness of the adults, the youths were already soundly locked in the arms of Morpheus.

" I wonder," cried Sprightly, "if we shall see the 'white lady of Kew!'"

" Who is she?" inquired the ladies.

" A ghost!" replied Sprightly, and laughed.

" Mercy on us!" muttered the ladies, and shuddered; "we hope not."

" I don't like ghosts," said Mrs. Brindle, softly and timidly, as if she was afraid one would hear her.

" Ha! ha! ha!" grinned Smerke.

" Oh, but I can assure you," urged Sprightly, "that this is a most sweet, gentle ghost."

" What is it all about, Jem?" asked his uncle.

" I'll tell you," answered his nephew. "One evening, such an one as this, I was induced to hire a boat, and enjoy an hour or two upon the water. I came up here—it was rather later than this—and, in gazing around me, I fancied I saw, at no inconsiderable distance, something white gliding, like a small cloud, upon the surface of the water: I communicated what I saw to the waterman, and uttered a supposition that it was a white vapour or exhalation from the water.''

" 'Lord bless you, sir,' said the man, and almost seemed to shudder, 'that's no mist—no, no. That's the white lady of Kew,—the Lord of Heaven rest her soul.'

" 'And who is the white lady of Kew?' I asked. At that very moment a low plaintive melody was wafted along the bosom the of waters by the breeze, and struck with a peculiarly mournful beauty on my ear. I listened intensely, but it soon faded and died away.

" 'There, sir,' said the man, 'that's the song her lover used to sing to her; and now she sings it for him.'

" He then told me the whole story, which is not long; and, if you wish to hear it, I will tell it in my own words."

" Oh do, do," was the general cry.

" In the time of——

" Hark! hark!" interrupted Mrs. Brindle, whose nerves were horribly strained; " don't you hear music?—There—there—hush!"

A low sound came floating on their ears, very like music certainly. Mrs. B. was convinced that this was the "white lady."

" Look there—see—" cried Miss Azure; "there is something white moving, I declare. Oh, heaven, defend us!"

" Oh! o—oh!" almost shrieked Mrs. Brindle.

Every eye was stretched upon the spot, except Mrs. B.'s; and hers were buried in her handkerchief upon her lap. It was very extraordinary—there *was* something white moving upon the water—it neared them—Oh, it was only a sailing-boat, with some persons in it singing " Jack Robinson."

"How particularly unromantic," cried Sprightly.

" But how relieving," ejaculated Mrs. Brindle, as a deep sigh of relief escaped her.

" Proceed with the story—now with the story," was the outcry of the ladies, faintly echoed by Mrs. Brindle.

Sprightly bowed and proceeded.—" At the beginning of the fifteenth century, there dwelt on the banks of the river, at Kew, a man, who gained a scanty pittance by ferrying persons across the river in his boat ; occasionally he took some persons, who felt a pleasure in the scenery, up and down the river for an hour's enjoyment ; but this seldom occurred, as, if he felt no desire to go, no persuasion could induce him ; neither fair words, or glittering gold, had any effect upon him ; when he did go, he would take no more than one or two persons with him, and then accepted no remuneration ; he was a lone man. At that period, there was no houses nearer to his hut, on his side of the river, if I may so express myself, than the convent at Isleworth, then just built ; and down the river the little village of Puttelei, or Puttenheth, now called Putney ; nearly opposite to his hovel, on the other side of the river, was the house of a sea captain ; thus he lived remote from society, and had no further intercourse with it than what his ferry produced ; from whence, how, or when he came, many conjectured, but none knew. Here he was, and that was the only positive knowledge to be obtained. He was known by the name of Friedel, the ferryman, and that was all.

" One beautiful night he seated himself in his boat, and rowed down the river a short distance, and then suffered his boat to be borne by the tide, while he ceased rowing, and gazed upon the scenery around him.

" ' This paradise,' he exclaimed, ' oh man ! is thine ; all this beauty is given thee for thy happiness, and how dost thou abuse it ; oh, God, must this loveliness be changed by the unsparing love of——'

" His attention was caught by something floating on the water—he rowed towards it, and found a large basket covered with a dark cloth ; he pulled it into his boat, opened it, and discovered a beautiful child in a sweet calm sleep ; he started in horror. ' Oh, Cain, Cain, how terribly thy curse has fallen upon us,' he bitterly exclaimed ; ' poor child, hath thy mother so changed her nature from what it should be, that she should doom thee to a death so cruel ? but why should I doubt it ?' and he laughed in scorn: ' has not my heart been withered by one ?— but, no matter, it is past. Woman, beautiful as thou art, thy universal mother's frailty is a clinging, blighting curse to thee !

thou cans't not eradicate the evil implanted in thee, by her fall from purity, and man must still gaze on thee—and perish !'

" A low, faint cry from the child, awakened him from his reverie, and throwing the cloth carefully over it, he pondered an instant what to do with it.

"' It had been happier for thee had'st thou have died, poor helpless innocent,' he cried ; ' but thou shalt not perish, for thy mother's heartlessness—No ! I'll foster thee, cherish thee, and teach thee the speciousness of all things beautiful, but the lovely world man labours so much to destroy.'

" An old woman, who dwelt in Puttelei, and who was in the habit of crossing the river, now came to his memory, and he determined to place the child with her till he was old enough to live with him ; with this intention, he rowed down the river till he nearly reached the village, and fastening his boat to some trees, he proceeded to the woman's house ; he knocked and gained admittance ; he produced the child, to the astonishment of the old dame, and begged of her to take charge of it ; the child, which was now exposed to the bright light, Friedel saw was of great beauty, and he felt a something creeping over his heart which seemed to breathe to him—' this pure thing shalt thou foster and cherish, and he will twine round thy heart and love thee, and be to thee a sunbeam in the gloom of thy loneliness.'

" Friedel, in early years, had dwelt in wealth and happiness : his family were noble, and the possessors of extensive estates on the Rhine ; he sprang from youth to manhood rich in the possession of a noble open nature, and a love for all mankind ; he was kind and affable to all, and won the attachment of all around him, but none seemed to idolize him, as did a foster brother, who was the son of a vassal on his father's estate, and ' kindness begetteth kindness,' so Friedel returned his affection warmly and sincerely. They were ever together—united by the strongest ties of fraternal affection.

" On a neighbouring estate, dwelt a baron, a widower, with one fair daughter, who was—

' A creature to adore
No less than love, breathing out beams,
As flowers do fragrance at every pore.'

" Is it to be wondered that Friedel, who had so large a portion of affection for his fellow beings, should, upon seeing one 'more exquisite still,' feel for her that love which makes a paradise of a desert ? ' Love,' Plato beautifully tells us, ' showers benignity upon the world : in its presence all harsh passions are hushed and still, it is the author of all soft affections, and the expeller of all ungentle thoughts ; it is the parent of grace and delicacy, of gentleness and delight, of persuasion and desire ; the ornament and impulse of all things—the best—the loveliest !' "

"True," interrupted Pundit, "Epicurus says—'Love is esteemed for the happiness it can bestow,' and 'without love,' says Lucretius, 'there would be nothing charming, nothing amiable!'"

"Gammon!" cried Azure, half-tipsey, "nothing like gin!"

"Ha! ha! ha!" shouted Smerke.

"Oh its sweet to be loved," quoted Miss Azure, with the flushed cheek of one who felt what she uttered; "love is the highest and dearest gift of the Deity, it is sweet from all—and to all."

"The *sense* is ravish'd, and the *soul* is blest!"

"As my illustrious antecedent says," screamed Miss Young.

"Proceed, Sprightly, with your story," said Flourish, "or ——" he checked himself, he was about to utter a rudeness.

"Well," continued Sprightly, "one evening, Friedel communicated his passion for this maiden, to his foster brother, and commissioned him to bear his letters, and woo for him, but alas! he too soon discovered, that—

"Friendship is constant in all other things,
Save in the office, and affairs of love,
Therefore all hearts in love use your own tongues."

his foster brother, who was possessed of great personal beauty, was, also, of a susceptible nature, and the blaze of this creature's rare charms blinded him, as his, did her; Friedel found, with an anguish 'too deep for tears,' that she, who had plighted her faith to him, and swore to love him beyond all earthly things, had forgotten her vows, and wedded, notwithstanding his mean birth, the foster brother, who had not remembered—that he was destroying every hope of happiness in him, who had raised him from a rank earth to bloom on a fair soil.

"Friedel stood a blighted, broken-hearted man, his dreams of future bliss were crushed in this frightful reality, and he who had cherished a love for all his race, now turned on them his withering hate: every thing seemed imbued with a horrid ingratitude, but the bright and beautiful nature, which ever laughed, beneath the sun's warm smile.

"'Man! man! for whom this lovely world was created, who should have attuned nature's beauty to his own happiness, hath cast it from his heart and placed the canker 'self' there as the idol he would worship,' were the last words of Friedel, as he quitted his father-land for ever.—' Farewell, we meet not again, the ties which bound us are severed—the shaft hath sped from the hand of one, for whose truth, I would have pledged body and soul; and she—she was false—the lesson is a bitter one, and is graven on my heart, with a depth, that no time can eradicate; I leave ye for ever—Ye! who shonld have made this home my Elysium; ye shall not look upon the wreck ye have made here;' and he struck his breast with violence. 'Farewell, thou beauti-

2 H

ful land of my birth; thou sunny scene of my unclouded early
days; thy brightness *now* scorches my sight; I turn on thee my
last look—I quit thee for ever,' and the hot tears rolled down
his sunken cheek, as he gazed long and earnestly o'er the bloom-
ing, glittering land, he should never more behold.

"He sought the shores of England, and fixed upon his present
home, as one best suited to his misanthropical feeling; as one
which could be, when he desired it, a solitude; and, yet, one
in which he could see enough of society to feed his scorn.

"Seventeen years elapsed since his discovery of the child, and
he still dwelt on the same spot, and with him that child, who
had sprung up into a handsome, manly youth, rather dark com-
plexioned, with dark hair, a forehead open, as the thoughts it
was the home of; full, expressive eyes, straight nose, well made
lips, which, ever and anon, parted, displaying a set of even white
teeth, a face slightly inclined to roundness, and an expression
of noble ingenuousness playing over the features, which blended
them, and completed the head, his form was slight, but well
made, and there was an air of gentleness, hovering over him,
which was calculated to excite an interest in 'gentle eyes.'

"Friedel had watched and tended him from infancy, and cultivated and directed his mind to the possession of every virtue;
but, at the same time, he endeavoured to instil into him, a doubt
of the truth of all human creatures; which, his adopted child
could not feel, for there is a freshness in youthful feelings, that
tones things and actions to its own perceptions; and Alfreyd,
(so Friedel had named him,) would not, or rather could not
credit the existence of a deceit and heartlessness, which he did
not feel, and which he had never seen practised.

"I have before mentioned that nearly opposite to his hovel
was the house of a sea captain, who was a widower, his wife,
whom he had loved dearer than aught else in the world, who
had from his playmate in infant years, sprung up into the loving
girl, and thence to his devoted wife; had died in giving birth to
a daughter, during a voyage he made to Holland; he returned in
time to see all that he thought worth living for, placed in the
grave: his grief may be conceived, not described, language was
ever too feeble to express pangs which must be felt to be known;
had the child not have lived, the same grave would have contained the wife and husband; but he could not leave that child
to bloom, or fade, as fate might direct, without a friend to rear
and tend it, and so he lived on, and his daughter grew from the
infant into the smiling affectionate girl; every day she became
more like her mother, and her father, who had believed he would
never feel a joy again, saw with increasing pleasure, his tender
bud ripening into a beautiful blossom.

"Being accustomed to cross the river frequently, Friedel was
well known to him, in truth, their dispositions assimilating, a
sympathy was excited, and eventually a friendship subsisted

between them; thus Alfreyd became the companion of Mary Asphodel, the daughter of the captain, and when two young hearts are ever together, to seek their joys and pleasures, have the same hopes and fears, in common, share the same good and evils, both beautiful, and as innocent as they are beautiful; who should wonder that they were to each other, what they could never be to aught else?

" Years fleeted by as happy years will fleet, to make us wonder that we are so old. Alfreyd was more than a boy, and Mary was ripening into woman, and yet, there was something so young, so fresh, in her looks, you would wonder that she could ever look less youthful.

" Mary Asphodel was one of those rare productions of nature, more often existing in imagination, than in reality; all that was loving and loveable, seemed centred in her : she was a sun burst on the clouded world; the one bright flower on a herbless waste. The brightest star in heaven's glittering diadem never emitted sweeter rays than did the gentle blue eye of Mary Asphodel; never was the sweet name of sunny smile, more fully exemplified, than when her small delicate lips curved tenderly expressive of some joy she received, the tone of her ever kind voice trembled o'er the heart, like the memory of some rare melody, known and loved in early and happy days; her long fair hair fell caressingly down her shining neck, and her slight, wavy, graceful form confessed her one of nature's faultless models.

> " A maid,
> That paragons description, and wild fame ;
> One that excels the quirks of blazoning pens,
> And in the essential vesture of creation,
> Does bear all excellency."

quoted Miss Azure, interrupting Sprightly.

" You'll do, Jem, you'll do," cried Makemoney; " you should write a novel; I've published many, that used to have a great deal of that sort of nonsense."

" Nonsense !" scornfully echoed Miss Bodger, who felt some interest in the story, and had cast an eye of kindness on Sprightly.

" She must have—puff—been a—puff—de-vil-ish nice—puff —girl,"—puffed Walter.

" I should liked to have known her," said Flourish, pulling up his collar.

" Oh, but she only liked 'ansome chaps," observed Mrs. Bodger.

" Ha! ha! ha !" roared Smerke.

Buoyant bit his nails, he couldn't think of a pun.

" Oh, go on, go on, Mr. Sprightly ;" cried Mrs. Brindle, who longed to hear all about it.

A pause succeeding Mrs. Brindle's entreaty; Sprightly proceeded with his story .—

"As Mary Asphodel possessed as much kindness as she was beautiful, it may be expected, that she looked with a favouring eye upon one, who was devotedly attached to her, who had been brought up with her, whom she had been taught to love, and it is possible she might have required no teaching on that point; however, be that as it may, they were deeply in love with each other; that sweet, pure love, which knows no worldly distinction, which makes each—the other's world, wherein is contained all their joy, their brightness, their happiness; wherein no outward circumstance has any influence to brighten, or depress, without affecting each equally; a sympathy, which, like a pure stream, is coloured by the object, reflected in its glittering bosom: the sweetest, the most innocent—but no matter, they loved each other deeply and tenderly; they were never happy apart, and never apart when happy; though ever together, they were never tired of each other's sweet society; the few hours which nightly parted them, found them restless, till the morrow should bring the light of each other's countenance to them: they ever found a new joy in meeting, and a thousand little ways to beguile the time happily, besides gazing in each other's eyes, which, ever and anon, they did, till all things visible faded, and melted, away, and they would tremble, and almost faint, with too deep happiness, and when the sweet moon smiled tenderly, and serenely over the dreaming earth, in the warm and beautiful summer time, then, would Alfreyd steal from his home, and crossing the river in the boat, hasten to the dwelling of Mary, and in words, deep and earnest, would implore her to float on the river's silvery bosom with him; and a few faint refusals and blushes were all prostrated before the kindness, which could never deny a pleasure to any, much less to one, for whom her gentle heart beat so strongly; and then, as they glided calmly and quietly over the bright waters, would be heard the rich voice of Alfreyd, singing the following words:—

> Mary, the moon doth tint this stream,
>   With her own sweet, silver hue;
> Each glitt'ring star pour's forth its beam,
>   From the canopy of blue;
> The wind hath rocked the flowers, love,
>   To a sleep most light and free;
> Yet, I look not on their beauty, love,
>   I but gaze alone on thee,
>
>   Mary!

> Mary, 'tis said that other lands,
>   Have sunnier streams than this;
> Which boasts bright gems, and golden sands,
>   And flowers too fair to kiss.
> There is a charm, they fondly tell,
>   In every flower, and tree;
> Which in no other clime may dwell;
>   Ah! they have no flower like thee,
>
>   Mary!

"Thus happily glided by their hours; but, alas! its brightness was doomed to change, the sunniest day is succeeded by a clouded morrow; and these two guileless creatures were fated to endure the painful reverse of the happiness they were now enjoying; Mary's father had observed the attachment between her and Alfreyd, with much pleasure; he had watched the progress of the latter almost from infancy, and had never seen any tendency to vice in his disposition, on the contrary, he had ever found him gentle, kind, and possessing a nice sense of honour, which Friedel had inculcated, and had discovered no necessity to enforce his precepts; Alfreyd, in all his acts, ever developing an extreme fineness of feeling. Thus Asphodel knowing Friedel's story, and his intention of providing well for Alfreyd, conceived that his daughter in marrying Alfreyd, would unite herself to one every way worthy of her, and who would protect her when he had sunk into the grave; he, therefore, promoted their affection, and looked forward, with a pleasurable anticipation, for the day which should unite them; but all hopes and wishes are vain, and our best intentions are unhinged, and frustrated by the most unlooked for occurrences.

"It was the custom of Mary, three times in each week, to visit Puttelei, for the purpose of procuring for the house every thing necessary in the domestic way, Alfreyd usually attended her; but on the evening we refer to, she was alone; she was skipping along joyous and lightly, anticipating Alfreyd to pop from behind each tree she passed, when she overtook two men, who, by their garb, appeared to hold some rank in society; she turned her head to see that Alfreyd was really not one of these persons, and an exclamation of surprise, but more of admiration, burst from the stranger's lips.

"'By our lady,' cried one, 'that is the fairest damsel my eyes ever looked on; a gem almost too bright for a monarch's crown.'

"'Aye,' returned his companion, scornfully; 'a diamond truly, but one in the rough, a rustic damsel, whom a well filled purse, would make as kind as she is pretty.'

"'Bah!' returned the first speaker, 'do not measure the virtue of our village maids by the purity of your German fair ones: believe me, the sun, which ripens your vines, and warms your women into *such* kindness, is not so potent here; our women trust more to their eyes and hearts, than to the influence of his solar majesty, but by the mass, I'll have some words with yonder beauty, spite of who shall say me nay;' and he quickened his speed, shouting at the same time—'Ho, damsel —Ho, pretty one—so ho—Ho!'

"His companion looked with more interest than he cared to own, upon the beauty of Mary, and he therefore kept pace with his friend, determining to have some share in the conversation; but Mary who had been taught to shun all such strangers as

these when alone in her journies to market; on finding the strangers rapidly approaching her, and calling her, felt terrified, and
hurried forward as fast as she was able, until a turning in the
road hid them from her view; the pathway leading to the ferry
was encircled by trees, almost forming a wood ; and she seized
the opportunity, darted swiftly among the trees, and by a route,
known only to herself, and Alfreyd, gained the ferry ; the strangers on losing sight of her as she turned the road, redoubled
their speed, and quickly gained the spot where she had disappeared; but found no trace of her ; they however still kept
along the pathway, which was winding and intricate, and ultimately they reached the banks of the river without meeting
with her ; the first stranger looked along the banks of the river,
and searched round the trees which bordered it, in vain ; the
lady was not to be met with, while the German, casting his
eyes on the river, perceived her in a boat with a youth, nearly
on the opposite side ; noting the house which stood on the bank,
he concluded instantly that she dwelt there ; and he resolved
to pay a visit, to confirm his conjectures ; he turned to his companion and said, " Your fair country-woman has outwitted us,
we shall not discover her now, so it's useless to waste time
here, let us begone.

"' By my mother's kindness ; and that's a good oath,' returned
his friend, ' I would give the best purse-full of golden marks
in Christendom to have a loving glance from those exquisite
eyes,' and he sighed and gazed, in vacancy, most pathetically.

"' Ha! ha! ha!' laughed the German, ' your rank, fair sir,
without your purse, will buy you scores of most loving glances
from fairer eyes, and richer dames than the damsel we have
lost.'

"' Bah !' returned the stranger, and quitted the spot, followed
by the German.

"Some few days elapsed, when Mary, on a most beautiful
evening, quitted her home to meet her lover ; it was in May,
nearly the end of the month, when the air was scented by the
hawthorn and wild flowers, which grew in profusion, and decked
and spangled the ground with their wondrous beauty ; and the
birds whistled as they flew from branch to branch of the trees,
with which, at that period, the banks of the thames were clus-
tered with ; every thing teemed with a glory-surpassing description ; Mary felt her heart light and happy as she gathered some
wild flowers the rarest and most delicate she could cull to form
a nosegay for him, who to her, was the one world—the all—the
everything ; and her cheek glowed as she thought of the deep look
of joy, his sparkling eyes would beam upon her when she
presented him with her little gift; and foolish as it may seem to
those who cannot understand, and therefore cannot appreciate the
feeling ; she trembled, and panted, and sat herself down amid
the sweet flowers to tranquillize her beating heart: she placed

her hat beside her, and leaning her head against the tree she was sitting under, closed her eyes to gaze upon beautiful idealities ; a footstep near her made her unclose her eyes, and she almost shrieked as she saw the dark eye of one of the strangers, the German who had followed her few days since; she sprung from her seat, and would have fled, but the German caught her in his arms, and held her forcibly.

" ' Nay,' he exclaimed, ' whither so swiftly fairest, I will not harm thee—by Heaven, I love beauty far too well to breath a sting upon it, nay, tremble not so violently, foolish one,—I cannot harm thee.'

" ' Unhand me, I entreat you,' cried Mary, ' I know you not—suffer me to depart, I implore you,' and she struggled to free herself from his arms.

" ' Not so easily, my gentle one,' returned the German, ' promise to meet me again, and thou shalt depart ; swear to me that thou wilt. I'll seal the pledge on thy vermeil lips.' He attempted to kiss her : she uttered a most piercing shriek ; and some branches were torn aside, and Alfreyd rushed to the spot, he sprung upon the German, and Mary, uttering a cry of joy, threw herself into his arms. while the German, enraged at being thus thwarted, drew his dagger, and was about to plunge it into the breast of Alfreyd, when the voice of Friedel, who had witnessed the whole affray, cried fiercely ; ' hold !' at the sound, the German turned his head like lightning, and in an instant, uttering a bitter cry of recognition, darted from the spot ; while Friedel gave a faint cry, and staggering back a few paces, fell senseless to the ground.

" Alfreyd and Mary flew to his assistance, and in a few minutes he recovered, and cast his eyes wildly round, as if in horrid anticipation of meeting some blighting thing, but seeing nothing, he became more composed, and observing the questioning look of Alfreyd and Mary, he stayed them, and begged them to ask nothing, think nothing,—forget it all ; he motioned them to leave him,—they obeyed ; and when at some distance, they turned and saw him on the spot with his arms folded and his eyes fixed upon the ground.

" Friedel was aroused from his abstractions by Asphodel, who evincing great agitation, questioned him earnestly.—' Friedel,' he cried, ' you have told me you discovered Alfreyd in a basket floating up the river ?'

" ' Well,' uttered Friedel.

" ' Was there any token—any trinket, in the basket ?' asked Asphodel.

" ' Why, yes,' replied Friedel, ' a bauble to encircle a lady's arm, such as this—I have ever worn it on my person, for it resembled minutely one—oh, God !' and a recollection, which brought a pang with it, seemed to convulse his frame.

" ' Ha ! ha ! that is the one, great heaven, I thank thee,' cried

Asphodel, energetically; 'I may now atone for my crime! Know, Friedel, that some twenty years since, I brought a German and his lady from the Rhine to England; on the passage some trivial neglect incenced this German, and he struck me a vile blow, I would have laid him dead on the instant at my feet, but the thoughts of my sweet wife, who then waited my return, flashed like lightning through my brain, and on the instant, I determined to be revenged in a surer way, and one that would be fraught with less danger to myself; his young and beautiful wife had an infant—

Friedel recoiled a few paces.

" ' Nay, hear me to the end,' continued Asphodel; 'this child, I stole from its mother, while sleeping, and placing it in a basket, made water tight, with the bracelet, also taken from its mother that it might form a clue to the discovery of its family, if found, which I firmly trusted it would be, though not by its parents, I committed it to the tide; the mother, on missing her child, became distracted; all her servants, all the crew, and myself, were interrogated with a closeness, which, had my revenge been less powerful, or my actions less secret, must have discovered the whole truth; but judge of my feelings when I learned that the lady, who was good and gentle, whom my heart smote me to hurt in any way, had never smiled again—that the loss of her child, added to her husband's unkindness, had, in two short days, killed her; oh, how bitterly, dreadfully was she avenged; on my return to my home, I found my wife, whom I loved better than all the world, my beautiful—she—she was dead! from that moment the world has been a blank—a chaos, from which nothing joyous, or more horrible can spring into being!' He was silent, overpowered by his feelings, Friedel sympathized with him, but the excitement this tale had produced, gave his curiosity the spur, and induced him to break the silence.

" ' Then Alfreyd,' he observed; ' is the child you——

" ' Yes, yes,' answered Asphodel, ' he is that same child, and but now his *father* passed, in seeming excitement and agitation.'

·" ' Oh, heavens,' burst forth and interrupted Friedel; ' how was he attired ?—what his appearance ?—answer quick.'

" Asphodel described him.

" ' Ha! ha! ha!' wildly laughed Friedel; why this is well—very well; I have fostered the child of one false as water; and of my bitterest foe! Oh, brave world, that makes the dog lick the hand that strikes him.'

" ' What mean you ?' asked Asphodel, in astonishment.

" ' That I never knew pain, but by name,' bitterly returned Friedel; ' until that shameless, treacherous villain, Alfreyd's father, forsooth! blighted me—beggared my hopes—made me, from one of God's happiest creatures, the thing I am; but I am revenged!—poor Aldine, thou mightest have shared a happier——

THE WHITE LADY of KEW.

A scream—long, loud, and heart-rending, so piercing, so wild, that one's hair might have turned grey at the sound : burst upon their ears, and sent their blood rushing back to their hearts. A moment's pause, and it was repeated ; simultaneously they rushed to the spot from whence the sound proceeded, and beheld Mary struggling violently in the arms of the German, who was exerting his whole strength to drag her from the place. The instant they appeared Mary shrieked and burst from his arms. 'Oh, father!—Friedel!' she franticly cried, 'they have murdered him—Alfreyd, look, see, help him, oh, Almighty God! let him not perish. Hear me, hear me.' Like lightning their eyes followed the direction in which she pointed, and they saw two men masked at no great distance from the shore, cast the body of Alfreyd, covered with blood, into the river; in an instant, Friedel sprung upon the German.—'Bloody, remorseless tiger,' shouted he, ' thine hour is come : see, 'tis I, thy foster brother, slays thee ; this, this, for thy goodness ;' and he plunged a dagger, up to its hilt, in the bosom of the German ; who struggled fiercely with him, and who, upon receiving the steel in his heart, uttered a deep groan, and fell upon the ground ; while Friedel still kept firmly hold of his throat. ' See, see,' he shouted, ' how sure is retribution ; thou, whose life has been one long career of villainy ; thou, who hast destroyed my peace ; broken thy wife's heart ; and murdered—aye, foully, cruelly murdered —thine own child !'—The German started fearfully, and convulsively, as Friedel thundered the last sentence in his ear ; and with one strong effort, he disengaged his throat from Friedel's grasp, and feebly uttered, ' Nay, loose thine hold ; a few minutes and I shall be dust ; but say that was not my son ; I came but for the maiden, he would thwart me, cross me—oh, hell, this pang,—it is not my son !—I have no son—he died years since. Ha ! 'tis false,' he screamed, ' avaunt see, there he beckons—I —I—curse——' the blood gurgled in his throat ; his eyes rolled horribly ; then became fixed, and he fell back dead !

" Friedel gazed upon him long and silently : he then exclaimed ' All is over, my misery has found its end ; fate has done its worst ;' he turned to Asphodel, who sat with his face buried in his hands, in a state of deathlike stupor ; while at his feet lay Mary insensible ; he lifted her head from the ground, parted her fair hair, and looked sorrowfully on her face ; ' Poor frail flower,' he said, ' what hast thou done, that thy young heart should be crushed by this load of agony : I had hoped that thou and, and—what, tears ! I have not wept for long, long years, 'tis fit I should weep ; and now they are gone again, and my eyes are dry as fire ; oh, how cold—how dreary—joyless, will this world be to thee ; Mary, thou, who wert all trembling gentleness ; who hast ever had all the brightness—summer of life glowing round thee ; shall suffer now its most terrible reverse ; it will destroy thee—thou must perish, the sweet, slight flower, the sun smiled upon, the dew watered; and the faint wind kissed; that dwelt in a world of light, when the fierce storm has smote the earth, it has broken, destroyed, swept it from home, and it perishes; canst *thou* survive this storm? No! thou must die, this completes my sum of misery. Farewell, hapless maiden, I may never more behold thee; I did not dream we should sever thus; thou hast twined round my heart with him, like the young, green ivy round the withered oak; thou, and he, the only things that ever loved me—to——but it must be so, I stand alone, a withered, and a withering thing; blighted, and where I come, blighting; why did not this sear my brain ere now? Ha! ha! ha!' there was an icy hollowness of tone in his laugh, that was horrible; he bounded from the ground on which he was kneeling; and letting Mary fall heavily, rushed from the spot, never to be seen, or heard of more.

"Mary was restored to life; but not to her senses, her mind was quite gone; she would wander for hours, days, through the woods and fields in search of Alfreyd: and would enter the boat, and trust herself on the river, in vain search of him; while she sang the song she loved to hear him sing, in so low a voice, a tone so full of woe, of utter anguish, that the tears would force their way into the eyes of stern men, when the sound fell on their hearts; a few months passed away, and one evening, she was seen on the river in the boat, and her song was heard, but the boat was discovered, next morning, some distance up the river, empty—she was drowned!

"When the painful news reached her father, he pressed his hands to his brain, and staggered to a chair, in which he fell stone dead!—his heart had broken.

"Their fate had caused much sorrow to those who lived near them, and known and loved them, and many were the tears, which were shed for Mary, who, it was said, was to be seen in the calm and clear moonlight, floating in a fairy boat, and heard to sing, in a plaintive voice, the melody which sounded sweet, and yet sorrowful, as it was wafted o'er the water, and many a peasant has crossed himself, and offered up a prayer, as in passing the river's edge, he has heard the gentle tones of the ' WHITE LADY OF KEW."

Sprightly was silent, and the party, therefore, supposed the story had concluded; at least, Buoyant said as much; the story teller received thanks of those who were not asleep.

They now reached Blackfriars Bridge, and the gentlemen, nearly all of whom were asleep, were roused up, the whole of the party then landed, shook hands, parted, and in an hour or so, were locked in the arms of Morpheus, being well contented, taking all things into consideration, with their excursion *a la* PIC-NIC!

CHAPTER XI.

Makemoney's invitation to Charles Turf, Esq., to dine with him in London—accepted by the latter. Continuation of the interesting adventures of the Match-girl; strange, but true. Love letters; or, rather bargains of a Smithfield character—Vice reduced to a trade, and beauty a marketable commodity; but face painting not amongst the faults of the Match-girl. The dangers of fascination—Flourish's opinion and dislike of very beautiful women—some truth connected with his remarks. A female without a heart—yet not devoid of susceptibility—a touch of the pathetic—the afflicted father, fond mother, and inconsiderate son—grey hairs still respected. Greatness of the Match-girl! Introduction of young Rentroll, a country gentleman—a neck-or-nothing sort of personage—all to-day, and let to-morrow provide for itself.—A masquerade visit; or, how to pay off old debts. Dangerous to be safe. Prowess of the Match-girl—the sprig of quality reduced beneath the rank of a commoner—revenge sweet. No security in disguise, or, I am not what I seem to be? The bailiffs in the dark—a scene in a lock-up house —the amorous man-woman—One might be hanged as well for a sheep as a lamb. Holdfast in error—astonished —the secret unravelled—therefore, " go it," and finish the spree; it will amount to the same thing one hundred years hence;—but " all's well that ends well."

" The ghost story, or rather, the ' White Lady of Kew,'" observed Makemoney,—" I am ready to admit is, of a very interesting nature; but yet, I should like to hear another chapter respecting the match-girl—there is so much life attached to all her movements."

" I am equally anxious to hear it," replied Sprightly, " and if you send an invitation to Charles Turf, Esq., to dine with you, the affair is accomplished at once; nay, more, we shall have him all to ourselves, and under your own roof. Besides, we are indebted to him for his hospitality in more than one or two instances."

" Say no more, my dear nephew" answered Makemoney, " I regret it has never occurred to us before; but better late than never; I will send to Turf without delay, as my messenger shall not return from him without an answer."

" I second the proposition," urged Flourish, " time flies in the company of Charles Turf—his method of relating anecdotes is the most delightful I ever heard."

Charles Turf immediately acquiesced with the request of Makemoney, and a more splendid dinner could not have been provided for any gentleman. Makemoney, respecting his dinners, was one of the most liberal creatures alive. The cloth being removed—the wine going round briskly, and the Pilgrims in high spirits, Flourish addressed Turf,—"My dear sir, my friend Makemoney has been talking about scarcely anything else, since he heard you relate the singular adventures of the match-girl: therefore, if it is quite convenient to you to proceed with another chapter of her memoirs—I am sure delight will be the result, and no one will feel it more than your humble servant. I am sure you will not hesitate."

" I have not the slightest objection," replied Turf; " but I wish to premise, that in order to prevent any idea arising in your minds, of *exaggeration* on my part, I will deliver nothing else but 'a round, unvarnished tale', respecting the beautiful, but *depraved* Charlotte Partridge. Yet I have to regret, that her adventures are not in better hands; for, according to the biographers of the late *Dr. Johnson*, he was extremely fond of taking women of the town to taverns, (in company with his friend *Savage*, the poet), whom he casually met with in his nightly strolls, and listen to their histories with great patience and interest! but the 'Colussus of Literature', when he moved in better society, or rather company of a more moral description, became proverbial for his gravity and good conduct, and related nothing else but propriety at the 'table of the Thrales,' burying his former midnight sprees in oblivion; or else, the world, might have been benefitted by some penetrating sketches of female frailty—their origin—and cause—tending, as awful lessons towards the improvement of mankind in general.

"The *self*-importance which Charlotte possessed, astonished me," said Turf; " and it was quite ludicrous to witness some of the highest born men in the kingdom—and some of the proudest also, who valued themselves on their rank and station in society, succumb to her sneers and ridicule, when she reproved them for addressing her in a way that she did not approve of. She had no individual respect for persons ;* and maintained her ground with

---

* A celebrated French Duke, distinguished for his gallantries in all the countries he visited before the revolution in France, and quite promiscuous in his amours ; also immensely rich, but in meanness, equal to the veriest miser; and sooner than open his purse strings, he would shuffle off without paying, if he found a convenient opportunity. During his first visit to the house of a well known courtezan in Italy, he wished to quit her establishment without complying with the usual terms, and when pressed closely on the subject, he attempted to get off by boasting of his *rank* in life. " I am " said he, " the Duke of * * * *" " Very likely you are such a person," answered the courtezan, " I shall not dispute it; but under the circumstances you entered my house, it is immaterial to

the most consummate assurance I ever beheld : presuming, I apprehend, upon her great personal beauty."

" It has often occurred to me, though I do not mean to boast of much experience," said Flourish, "that beautiful women are so much in love with themselves, that they have scarcely any left—nay, none at all for any other persons. I dislike your *very* beautiful women—*flattery* being so much their idol, that they positively *doat*, and live upon it, and are *selfish* to the extent of the phrase; but when calculation, gain, and coldness are annexed to it, and the face and form are reduced to a sort of *merchandize*, and the best bidder can purchase it. Such a female *must* be devoid of a *heart*, and can only be denominated, the mere outline of a woman. But these are the sort of women who generally have it all their own way—can threaten and command—delude —ensnare—and ruin men with the most perfect finesse and indifference—therefore, my dear Makemoney, old as you are, I speak it without offence, and you, Sprightly, invulnerable as you boast to be,—have a care of all match-girls, say I, ha ! ha ! ha !

> Beauty is a witch;
> Against whose claims, faith melteth into blood.

" I have" said Turf, " some curious copies of letters which were addressed to the match-girl, and will serve to show the *bartered* feelings of some men, respecting women of a peculiar class in society, which I will read to you :—

My dear girl,
　　　　Your lovely figure, fine form, and admirable beauty of person,—in short, the *tout ensemble* delights me ; but I hate writing—talking,—or making what is called, *love*. Therefore, if you choose to *jump* into a carriage, without hesitation ; enjoy a capital house, furnished fit for a princess, without any trouole ; a carriage that will make all the women in the Metropolis sigh to have its parallel--and a purse well filled, at your command, only say, *Yes!* and the *bargain* is concluded. I would not write so much to an Empress. Now or never ?
　　　　　　　　　　　　　　　From your admirer,
To Miss Partridge.　　　　　　　　* * * * * * *

To which epistle, she wrote the following answer to the noble Lord ——, a person whom she detested.

My Lord !
　　　　What a mistake I have made, a most egregious blunder ? In my eyes, the term of beast would be far more appropriate. I am not to be bought and sold in a land of liberty ; I am no *slave*. More words are unnecessary, except to state that I despise your ugly person—and your gold, (although I am fond, very fond of the glittering ore) has not the weight of a single feather with
　　　　　　　　　　　　　　　CHARLOTTE PARTRIDGE.

---

me whether it is the Duke or his coachman, my demand must be discharged. However, I will just give your Grace a gentle *hint* upon the subject, and then you will decide as you think proper." She immediately rang a bell, when three or four bravoes appeared, with stilettoes in their hands, with countenances of the most murderous aspect. " Yes," replied the Duke, " I am perfectly convinced you are *now* in the right, my good lady ;" instantly paid the charge, and felt glad to depart in a whole skin.

P.S.—If you send any more messengers to annoy me with your proposals, they shall be horse-whipped; and if you dare, in person, to approach me, beware of the consequences, for I have a rod in pickle, even for a Lord.   So let this hint suffice—*beast!*

The following letter is from an old general, who was terribly *smitten* with the match-girl :—

" My dear girl,

I am an old soldier, and to command has been hitherto my forte, however in this instance, I leave the *command* in your hands. But fighting has been my trade, instead of making *love*. Therefore, anything like fine words, or complimentary phrases, you must not expect from me. The FORTRESS, I am quite aware, is of the most magnificent description ; but a long siege will not do —offer liberal terms of capitulation—*surrender* without delay—and you shall have no occasion to find fault with your admirer,

To Miss Partridge   GENERAL ————"

To which, the match-girl sent the following laconic reply ;—

" My worthy and respected old general,

I honour your laurels, and I love the brave, but this time, victory is out of the question ; therefore, my answer in the military phrase is—to the right about; quick ; march :

From your humble servant,

General ————.   CHARLOTTE PARTRIDGE.

" I rather think, Charles Turf," said Makemoney " that you must have been a great favourite with Miss Partridge; for you appear to be acquainted with all her secrets in life: ha ! ha! ha!"

" Nothing more than a friend, I assure you," replied Turf ; " I am in her confidence it is true, owing to a circumstance which occurred in the early part of her career, I was her adviser upon that occasion ; and she has never forgotten it—and owing to that kindness, as she termed it, she has been very communicative to me ever since.

" Quite *platonic !*" urged Flourish, with a smile, " and you, Mr. Turf, of all other men, know the extent and meaning of the word, *friend*, with a lady of her description.

" I will take the word of Mr. Turf, that it was truly *platonic*," said Sprightly, " and were it otherwise—kiss and tell of it, would never suit his book of life ; gallantry forbids it.   But he has previously told you, that he would ' nothing extenuate,' and I return him my thanks for the simple, straight-forward manner in which he has related the adventures of the match-girl, without *identifying* himself at all with them, the great fault of too many story-tellers—but I hope he will now proceed without any interruption.

" Charlotte was quite the *rage* with those sort of men who are continually on the look out for a *new* face in the public walks of the Metropolis ; in consequence of her character having run before her that she was a *Gay* woman.   Persons who prefer the company and conversation of *such* females, to the retired and modest community ; yet nevertheless it might be difficult to class them under the head of admirers—lovers—keepers—or gallants; true, perhaps, that one or two of them felt something like love for the *ci-devant* match-girl; others inclined to purchase her favours—yet most of them ready to deceive and outwit this splendid piece of frailty!"

" But never was the adage more the fact, in this case, ' that which went in at one ear, went out at the other,' she laughed in her sleeve at all of them; although she listened to the tales of every one of the gallants, with the utmost politeness, yet *artful* complacency; and, however, strange but true, Charlotte might be deemed a *chaste* woman, as to her feelings—the mere statue of a female —the exterior and fine form of a woman, that could not be excelled. But for warmth of disposition, or a soul inclined to love, were entirely out of the question. Charlotte had not the slightest touch of it in her composition. She could listen, listen, and listen again, to the most animated declaration of attachment made to her by her admirers, with as much indifference as a bill of the play offered to her for purchase. It was this sort of *coldness* of character that enabled the match girl to triumph over all her suitors. Her secret, an *invaluable* secret to a woman of this description, she kept inviolably to herself: this was the great danger to men who were fond of her company —they could not pluck out her mystery!

" Charlotte was all affability and condescension, she never refused a present, great or small, offered for her acceptance—and became quite an adept in pointing out in any of her visits to different jewellers; or other shops, where expensive articles of curiosity were to be met with, which exactly suited her taste and fancy, in so strong a manner to those gentlemen who were with her at the time, that her *hints* could not be mistaken. From this insinuating mode of conduct, her house was filled with some of the richest rarities in London. Her magnificent collection of shawls might have extorted a sigh from the heart of a Duchess—she had also a happy *knack* of pointing out to any new visitor, to render the gift more important, that the Duke of—— presented her with that inimitable *vase*; my Lord—— furnished me also with those elegant mirrors in the apartments, not to be excelled; and Sir Henry—— one of the most wealthy and ancient baronets on the list of men of rank, had been kind enough to send her those elegant chairs and sofas, not to be equalled in the great Metropolis; but that delightful creature—her most particular friend, Peregrine Crayon, Esq. had made her a present of a whole-length likeness of herself, said, at the least, to be worth £500, but she had refused £1000 for it, and will not sell it for any sum !

Her library, she urged with a smile on her beautiful face, she was well aware could not compete with the British Museum; but nevertheless, it had been collected for her by nothing else but scholars; and the *bindings* of all her books were of the most costly description. Her display of annuals, keepsakes, forget-me-not's were splendid in the extreme: she also took pride to herself that she had not the work of any author which had been tinctured in the slightest manner with any passages offensive to decency or morality in her book-case.

" ' I am not a prude neither,' said Charlotte, with a face as immoveable as clay, one day in conversation with a very rigid *out-of-door* man, a director of one of the societies for sanctity and reformation, who visited the match-girl privately; ' but I have always been most anxious to obtain a *character* for acting correctly in most points of view, knowing as I do, that the world is very censorius; therefore, it is highly necessary that an unprotected female like myself, should be armed at all points; and then you may bid defiance to newspaper writers, tatlers, and all the gossipers in the kingdom. True, people may be suspected; females calumniated; but when facts are wanting, and where evidence cannot be brought into court, then safety is the result.'

" Charlotte had at one period of her career, a distinguished literary man in her train, fond of her to excess, and who had taken great pains to improve her mind, and also instruct her in the ways of the world. When taxed with visiting such a female of this description, he exclaimed with the utmost indifference, ' O yes! I do know Charlotte Partridge, and my visits, are merely to become acquainted with *character* : writers should view every thing in life, either good or bad, otherwise it would be totally impossible for them to communicate to the public, the dangerous persons they are likely to meet with in society, under the garb of propriety.' " Therefore, excuses must be made for being seen in improper company,' observed Turf, " and according to the old proverb, ' any excuse is better than none.'

" I have often, and often gazed upon her face, with more hant ordinary delight, beautiful it is in a most eminent degree. NATURE has been liberal, more than liberal to Charlotte, in this respect, and the sensitive STERNE, who speaks of the monk's head and face that crossed his path, observing, that no one could have passed it without reverence, nay, almost worshipped it ! and although yet the *face* of the once poor dirty, distressed match-girl might have excited a different feeling towards it, yet it was so truly attractive, that it brought those persons to a complete *stand-still* the first time they beheld her countenance. They looked again—stopped—another glance—walked on a few steps—another peep—loitered—turned round again, and again —lingering look after lingering look—and could scarcely take leave of it, in the shape of a FAREWELL! Such were the sensations felt by those persons who encountered the face of Charlotte Partridge.

" But LAVATER, with all the knowledge that he possessed of the countenances of mankind, would have been puzzled to have pronounced a decisive opinion on her face; and Drs. Gall and Spurzheim equally at a loss to have described it accurately, as to the indication of her *mind*. In fact, OTWAY might have better supplied the text.

> Who was it occasioned a ten years siege?
> Woman! curst deceitful! damnable woman.

" Yet it is only common justice to her character to assert, that I have often heard Charlotte complain of her *heart*, or rather to observe, that she had none, 'I am affected to tears,' said she, 'at a tragedy; a tale of deep distress moved me more than I can express; and I cannot challenge myself with a want of feeling towards mankind.'

" 'I laugh heartily at a farce, enjoy a pantomime—fond of a bit of fun, and I am attached, that is to say, *friendly* attached to several persons of my acquaintances; and, perhaps, not a bad friend, where the necessity of the case requires it; but I have no *heart* for LOVE. I do not know what it means. Surely that is not the fault of my mind; and it must be a defect in the anatomy of my composition. Therefore, I am aware of the character I bear amongst men of the world; and which will account, in a great measure, for the various changes I have made in my life, and the singular connections I have hastily formed, and as hastily dissolved. However singular it may appear, I admit I have my *likes* and *dislikes*; but to speak honestly, I never was in LOVE in the whole course of my career; in consequence of which, I have not acted *foolishly*, neither have I suffered vain men to play tricks with me, or display tyranny in any shape, which, what are called fond women are too often exposed to in life; nay, more, I do not think that any individuals, gifted as they might be with the animating, exciting oratory of a Demosthenes; or, the powerful persuasive eloquence of a Cicero could have moved me, hitherto to have felt the force of love. Yet I am quite satisfied, from what I have seen of its terrible effects upon the minds of some persons, ultimately producing beggary and ruin. Therefore, I have *steeled* myself against it; and you, Charles Turf, have had my *secret*, which, to no other person did I ever impart it.

> Women you know but seldom fail
> To make the stoutest men turn tail;
> And bravely scorn to turn their backs
> Upon the desperatest attacks.

According to a celebrated French Author, La Bruyere, who gives it as his opinion, 'that man is more faithful to the secrets of others than to his own; whereas woman on the contrary, is more faithful to her *own*, than those of others.'

" For singularity of conduct, I never knew any female half-like Charlotte Partridge, in my knowledge of society; she is particularly fond of out-door company—sometimes proud to the echo—at others, she will unbend and mix with any sort, almost the *refuse* of mankind; but nevertheless, she will not let any persons behave rude, or take liberties with her, without resenting it in a manner that they do not expect, and which ensures afterwards respect and attention. Charlotte frequently goes out without a companion, but never without a servant either male or female, who have their cue to keep their distance, but to be within call, when he, or she, may be wanted to attend her home. And this accounts for meeting with her at races and fairs by herself; besides, it answers her purpose when she is without a *protector!* Charlotte considers herself quite at liberty to enter into conversation with any stranger who presents himself to her notice ; by so doing, she gives any person an opportunity of becoming acquainted with her without an introduction. She also dismisses them without the least ceremony, if they are not calculated to answer her purpose.

" Charlotte has, in several instances, adopted the language of Richard to his Queen, when she has got tired of her *keepers,* or when their funds were not able to support her high style of living, without any feeling or delicacy—by telling them that they had ' out-lived her liking,' and she should quit their company for ever ! The high *tone* she assumed, upon all occasions, with presuming, fashionable, young rakes—nay, she set *rank* at defiance; never failed to awe them with her superiority and independence of feeling, and it also had the desired effect of binding them faster in her charms : and singular as it may appear, it is nevertheless true, that a number of men admired her more strongly for this sort of pride which she possessed, by keeping inferior men, at all events, at a respectful distance ; and if she had not have been a woman of lax morals, her conduct, in many instances, might have proved a model, and worthy of imitation.

" The match-girl would often insist upon it that her *peculiar* conduct rested entirely upon herself—she had no *father* living to reproach her—no *mother* to cry over her errors—no *brothers* to threaten and abuse her for her behaviour—no *sisters* to shun her as a loose woman and an improper character—and no acquaintance, who could, or *dare* to take the liberty with her to call her to account for the mode of life she had adopted ! Therefore, I have *chalked* out a line for myself—I mean to play my cards well, and turn up trumps as often as I can, until I ultimately win the *game.* I love money, and I am also ambitious to rise in the world, which is to be achieved by perseverance of mind and coolness of disposition, and I feel assured that I possess them in no common degree. I do not care who knows it, I love money, vastly—to me, it possesses every charm—nay, I worship it. Does it not produce comforts, pleasures, aye, and *happiness* too : there are some few persons who may dispute the assertion, but I am not of that class of beings, therefore, I cherish to the echo that applauds again—' a *fat* sorrow, is better than a lean one !'

" To become a rich woman is my determined resolution, and I will never lose sight of any opportunity that can further my views to fill my coffers, and elevate my situation in society. And when I shew the quantity of gold I possess in the bank— when I display my massive service of plate—sport a splendid equipage—open my house, next to a palace, (by comparison), for the reception of company, I shall not want for visitors, and the question asked will not be—' *How* did she get it?' And if my riches do no absolutely wash out what is termed the *blot** at-

---

* It has been argued that there are as many sorts of feelings in the breasts of different men and women, as variety in fashions; and it is likewise totally impossible to describe them with any thing like accuracy on the subject. The inimitable POPE, has told us, ' that the proper study of mankind is man:' and that woman is a riddle altogether ; who—

> Shines in exposing knaves, and painting fools,
> Yet *is* what e'er she hates and ridicules !

But of all the studies which may cross the path of the student, none are half so difficult as the study of human nature. Therefore, what might be considered a *blot* in the character of some conscientious females, by many others might be looked upon as a mere *speck*; nay, almost *spot*-less ! a matter of course, a routine sort of feature, an every day occurrence, according to the old and dangerous axiom—to ' Get money *honestly* if you can. But *get* money !' "That is my creed," said Charlotte, "a fig for your recording angels, who might be disposed to drop a tear and *blot* out my errors for ever ! I value them not ! I pay no court to them !" The horrors likewise displayed by Lady Macbeth made no impression upon her feelings---' Out damned spot !' as to reformation in her character. Her ideas were more in unison with Richard on the subject of a great name---' They cannot say I was fool as well as rogue !' It is thus, that so many vicious characters lay the flattering unction to their souls in London ; who, if they cannot live by honest means, prefer an *infamous* notoriety.

It is urged---' That train up a child in the way it should go ; and when it is old, it will not depart therefrom !' Here the above excellent considered precept, in the present instance, improperly applied ; may lead to the most ruinous consequences in life, by instilling an avaricious feeling. The match-girl, it should seem, never forgot, but cherished the bad advice of Mrs. Feelnot, to view mankind only upon a decided interest---' to make *money* by them !' This principle had been so strongly engrafted upon *her* mind, that all the sermons ever preached, advice given to her, remonstrances made on the subject, could not remove, or overturn it a jot with Charlotte Partridge. The value of *chastity* was set at nought, a good name not of the slightest consequence, in comparison, that property must and would command respect.

True, she might have felt some annoyance that there was a *bar* to her introduction to some parts of society, who valued themselves on those delightful principles which do so much honour to the head and heart, that consoles virtue under all its difficulties and temptations, with conscious rectitude and unbroken feelings, though poor but honest, in spite of the rebuffs of the busy world. But the match-girl's mind was composed of different materials ; and Cocker was not more cold, or calculating upon all subjects, whenever her *interest* was concerned, than Charlotte Partridge. She could smother her feeling, with as much ease as a banker's clerk puts his bill book into his side-pocket.

Therefore, in describing some characters, their manners, and conduct, are so widely different from the general routine of society, that the writer runs the great danger of being challenged with *exaggeration* in his portraits of human nature, and colouring them too highly, when his descriptions can be vouched for as the plain and simple truth. The learned, and correctly considered Dr. Johnson, had quite forgotten that he had eaten his dinner once, thrashed his servant for reminding him of the circumstance, and was only induced to pardon the man on being shown the plates and dishes which he had removed from his table, occasioned by the mania of study, to a corner of the apartment.

tached to my origin in life, they will nearly obliterate the remembrance of it with the stupid, ignorant world—for after all, *what* is called 'the world,' are led away and imposed upon by shew, and I cannot quote any better authority than Shakspeare :—

'The world is still deceived by ornament!'

"One of the crowned heads of Russia, I have read, was only a trooper's daughter : but I need not quote history, nor go out of my own country to shew what wonders a pretty face can effect, and what *elevation* it may lead to, names can be mentioned if necessary—that a kitchen-maid became the mistress of a prime minister and a duke into the bargain, the reversion of her charms also claimed the attention of two others, and with one she made the grand tour of Europe, and afterwards, became one of the peerage, as the Countess of ———

"Yet with all these freezing, *icy* notions of money, I must mention one instance of her generosity, feeling, or good conduct ! Call it what you please, but you may rely upon the fact :—

"A fine young man—all impetuosity and passion, and thoughtless beyond description, an only son of rather aged parents, who had been her keeper for a short period ; but who, nevertheless, had made such a destruction of property, as to alarm his father and mother for their safety to escape from beggary and ruin. He was so fascinated with the ci-devant match-girl, that he positively refused to listen to any remonstrances on the subject from his parents, who had ascertained the cause of his extravagance and expenditure, that in the paroxysm of the moment, declared that he could not live without her, and that he would make her his wife. His parents dreading the result of his fascination—his father, at length, got an opportunity of introducing himself to Charlotte, by another name, on pretence of business, and quite unknown to his son.

"Upon entering the apartment, and beholding the match-girl, he was struck with her beautiful appearance and manners, and felt pity for his son, and almost could have found some excuse for the infatuation of his poor boy ; but rousing himself from his surprise and astonishment, with tears in his eyes, he mentioned to her the nature of his visit, related his fears that his wife and himself would be reduced to beggary, if not total ruin, if such a

---

We are rather afraid for the moral part of mankind, that there are too many females in existence, the exact counter part of the match-girl, without assuming any thing like *cant* upon the subject, and until they become, from a change in their circumstances, hacknied, despised, worn-out, diseased, wretched, heart-broken, and too late in the day to alter and amend their past lives, feel the severity, but just remark of the poet :—

Guilt is the source of sorrow ; 'tis the fiend,
Th' avenging fiend, that follows us behind
With whips and stings !

connection continued any longer. The appearance of a fine, old, gentlemanly man, his venerable face, and grey hairs, his eyes filled with drops of sorrow, his pathos, and the forcible manner in which he represented the feelings of the mother of his son, had the desired effect.

" The match-girl, although money was her idol, was subdued in an instant, the tears rolled down her cheeks, and as soon as she could give utterance to her faultering speech, she thus addressed him:—' My good old gentleman, you have *touched* my feelings more acutely than I thought you could have accomplished ; but say no more, the connection was not of my seeking ; nevertheless, it ends this moment, and your son shall never be admitted again into this house ! Yes, once more, to hear my determination, which is irrevocably fixed—that I have more real respect for his aged parents, than to be the cause of their ruin— perhaps, their deaths ; therefore, worthy sir, depart in comfort to your home, solace your wife, and do not act *harshly* towards your son, reason with him properly on the subject, point out his errors in the most lenient manner possible ! He is a sensible fellow, and I do flatter myself, you will yet find him an obedient, affectionate son.'

" The old man was lost in astonishment with the extreme beauty of the female before him, and her delightful form ; but the good feeling, sense, and mind she displayed, positively electrified him beyond the power of recital, and he left the house overwhelmed with joy, yet he could not help mentally exclaiming— ' Such a woman might *seduce* a bird from a tree ! What an escape for my poor boy !'

" The match-girl, in one or two instances, was rather unfortunate with her protectors. In a fit of desperation one of them committed a forgery to a large amount, so distractedly fond was he of Charlotte ; but the relatives of the young man, to save his life, though nearly the ruin of the family, raised the sum and paid it ; but banished her admirer from the country for ever. ' This unfortunate circumstance,' said she, to one of her friends, who taxed her with it, as being the cause and ruin of the young man in question: ' was not my fault ! I did not solicit his acquaintance, nor friendship, and I refused, positively refused to listen to his offers ! But he pressed his suit arduously, and said, that he would not be denied—nor no denial would he take. He was quite aware of my situation in society ; but he replied, that his fortune was ample enough—nay, twice enough to support me. It was not for me to enquire into his resources, I cannot find brains for other people ; I have difficulty enough to furnish common sense for myself. But I have always made a point never to swerve from—I never did—nor never will be, the cause of men doing wrong to themselves, or families ; however, if they will sin with their eyes open, the blame rests on their heads, and not upon mine. I never directly asked a favour of any man in my life, and if the men—the lords of the creation, who are *wiser*, and *know* every thing better than us poor weak-minded females, will run after us with their praises and admiration respecting my person—pester me with their fulsome, *insincere* compliments, who swear that I am as beautiful as Venus, a divinity, my eyes are more billiant that the stars in the sky, and that they will not *exist* without me, united with a variety of every day sort of hackneyed phrases, and strings of lies to gain their ends ! I would ask, how am I to blame ? Yes ; the scene ultimately sooner or later changes, when all their money is gone, and desire fled, then I become a demon, a fiend in petticoats, and every thing that is bad ! Be it so, I am answerable for my own conduct—ALONE. I think, and act for myself !'

" One of her most violent admirers was a young fellow, called RENTROLL ; and to whom Charlotte seemed more attached than to any other of her protectors, she had, what she termed—rather a sort of *liking* for him ; but nevertheless, Rentroll, like the rest of her gallants, had only his day. His outline does not require much difficulty to describe,—he was high-spirited, a fine and atheletic figure, a manly face, and his countenance full of animation and cheerfulness. If tuition, and excellent instructors, could have made him a scholar, he had been long enough at school to have obtained that title ; but reading and writing were not his forte ; yet, he could not be set down as an ignorant man. His taste lay in a different style altogether : he prefered the field to the closet, enamoured with all sorts of society, and company was his delight. Solitude, or any thing like it, he deemed a complete bore.

" Rentroll had spent the great portion of his time in the country, a distance of two hundred miles and upwards from the Metropolis—the immense, improving town of Liverpool, was his native place. His mother was taken from him when quite a child, and his father died before he had attained his thirteenth year. Rentroll was an only son, and the sole heir to his father's great property, one of the richest merchants in that celebrated place of commerce. He was under the control of guardians, according to a *strict* will made for that purpose ; but long before he had attained his majority, they found, to their sorrow, that they had a very troublesome young man to deal with: he was continually ' out-running the constable,' according to the proverb, in respect to extravagance and unnecessary expenses. He had a very liberal allowance to live as a young gentleman ; but his spirit and feelings had elevated him to assume the character of a man before the term of youth had left him.

" Liverpool, if not absolutely a second Metropolis, as to what is called *life*, in all its varieties ; nevertheless, is full of dissipated scenes nightly, with the sailors and their girls ; the fiddle, harp, glee-singers, dances, &c., are to be seen and heard at numerous taverns and saloons in the neighbourhood of Williamson Square, independently of saloons and several theatres. In the above respect, London does not equal it, and Wapping is a mere shadow also, for splendid rooms and lively amusements.

"Rentroll was a hero at all of these places, and distinguished for his *sprees* and fun at most of them ; and whenever he ' was at fault !' or detected in an error—' *How much to pay ?*' soon put it all to rights, and his character was a good fellow ! He was the life of all his acquaintances, and scarcely ever said, 'No !' to any proposition made to him. He made several trips to Dublin, and enjoyed all the amusements which that splendid city affords to the visitor, who possesses a gay turn of mind. In fact, *his* life might be said to be one continual round of pleasure. His days passed away briskly ; his nights merrily ; and *time* never loitered upon his hands. Sailing up and down the Mersey, hunting, coursing, shooting, with the races at their annual periods, Chester, Liverpool, &c., he never missed attending ; and, from one thing to another, kept Rentroll always upon the alert.

" The long-looked for, nay, much wished for day, at length arrived, when, according to law ; obtained the title of MAN for him, and guardianship and control were removed from his person. He had had, according to his own version of the matter, quite enough of Liverpool ; Dublin and Manchester had also lost their attractions, but London, dear London, where the resident can carry on ' the game,' without being subject, quite so much, to the *prying* qualities of his neighbours in the country, he determined, without any hesitation, to take up his abode in it.

" In quick succession he visited every place of amusement, either genteel or otherwise ; and kept it up with such animated spirits, as if he had only a few days to view every thing : he went on at a race-horse pace. He had a large sum of ready money at his command, which soon procured him introductions in every quarter ; and if he could not boast of having secured any *friends,* he could not find fault for the want of numerous acquaintances, always surrounding his person, and making him the hero of their company. Indeed, his estates were so extensive, that he obtained the nick-name of young RENTROLL, from their immense value.

" In one of his rambles, soon after his arrival in the Metropolis, it was at Ascot Races, I believe, that he first saw the match-girl in all her bloom and beauty ; he became instantly entranced, as it were, with her person and look altogether ; it is true, that Charlotte never omitted anything that could give interest, or loveliness to her countenance, but *face*-painting she detested ; and I have often heard her assert, with a smile of confidence— 'With all my errors, I will never be challenged as a painted sepulchre !'

" It is totally impossible to describe his *libertine* feelings upon this occasion, he could not take his eyes off her person, and in the ectasy of the moment, he exclaimed—' I never saw a woman half so fine, or beautiful; and if *money* and tempting offers, can make any impression on her feelings, I will not stand upon trifles until I get her consent to place herself under my *protection!* But is she comeatable? is the question, he asked himself. Yes; there is something after all about her appearance that one can hardly mistake, which tells me she is one of the *Gay* freaks of nature! Should that be the fact, I need not display much diffidence upon the subject.' Backed by riches, he assumed a confidence, rather call it an *assurance*, which, otherwise, he might not have possessed. After Rentroll had introduced himself to Charlotte by some common place observations about the weather, fineness of the days. &c., he begged that he might be permitted to call and enquire after her health, presenting her with his card at the same time. His request was granted almost as soon as he asked it. Charlotte never attempted *coyness*, she was no hypocrite as to assume a virtue which she did not possess.

" The match-girl who *would* not call it LOVE, yet she was ' struck with the appearance of the fellow !' as she observed to her maid, and that she had not seen so good-looking a young man for some time. There was also taste displayed about his horses and carriage ; and his person well attired, although the tailor might have rendered him great assistance towards obtaining the term—elegance.

" Rentroll, without further delay, became one of her professed admirers, She was his idol, and he teased her morning, noon, and night, to place herself under his immediate protection. He; therefore, unblushingly made her an offer of his purse to a certain extent, a carriage, a house, but not his *hand !* Yet he swore that he loved her better than any woman he had ever seen since he was born, she was his choice, his taste, and he felt assured that happiness would be the result to both of them being under one roof. However, as he did not like *restraint* himself, he would not ask her to pronounce the disagreeable word to the ears of many females—' *obey !*'

" In truth, he had made up his mind not to be *bound* by any exactment, tied like a stake to a hedge, and the terms for better worse, respecting women, he never could, nor would recognize in his vocubulary ! But nevertheless, *constancy*, was his motto, and if he really loved a female, it would be impossible to leave her, so much was he acquainted with his own feelings ; therefore, his heart was *whole* in the present instance.

" ' But,' said Rentroll, ' perhaps, that I am a young man, may not be the least recommendation to Charlotte; and as I have been candid in my own mode of dealing, I trust, I shall be treated with equal sincerity of disposition ?'

" ' You shall,' replied the match-girl, ' a fig for you professions of love, constancy, and all that sort of thing, which you do not, nor perhaps, never will possess ! They may be on the tip of your tongue, but not at all near your heart. No matter, your *purse* will be highly acceptable to me to prevent duns, and assist me in the hour of need; your carriage truly convenient for an airing; and your, or *the* house, a desirable residence; but on one condition, it must be with me—a FIXTURE! Your personal qualifications in my eyes are better than most of your sex, I candidly admit—*that*, you may be made an agreeable companion from what little I have seen of you, no doubt; but respecting your *youth*, give me leave to say, it is the worst recommendation you could have offered to *me*—without it is secured by a good *settlement*, to prevent your acting like a boy.

"'YOUTH is fickle, changeable, and at times, egotistical; I understand the *sneer*, and therefore, the *settlement* only with Charlotte Partridge, can change a young fellow into an old man! But bear in mind, that *my* house, and all that is in it, still remains my property, as a *reserve ;* according to some good old maxims laid down for my future conduct, by my late departed, highly esteemed friend, the banker. 'To day,' said he, ' the sun may shine brilliantly, the next, it may rain, the third day a tempest may arise, desolation overwhelm, and I become not only shipwrecked, but left alone almost on an uninhabited island !'

"'The above maxims, I am well aware, will not only be viewed as *cold*, calculating points; but tell against me, as not eminating from any thing like the warmth of affection; but they are my creed, and from which I shall never swerve. But to the point, your final answer, when the settlement is formally executed, and strictly legal, according to the forms of law, and revised by my solicitor, then Charlotte Partridge becomes the *chere amie* of Samuel Rentroll, Esq. Yet I am free to say, that I shall not be the worse acquaintance for the above *precautions !*

"'Women, too often, are foolish, fond, weak, and cannot see their way; but I am not one of the sex in that respect, therefore, I boast of nothing more than *friendship*, and you must deserve it, before Charlotte Partridge allows the term to have existence. One word more, and that must be observed most rigidly—I *brook* no command; authority over me, I will not recognize, but liberality and kindness no one can better appreciate. Now I hope we understand each other, so that no mistakes arise hereafter. I am to be depended upon when I give my word. I should advise you also to avoid all *jealousy*, should any compliments be paid to me, which I cannot avoid, and do not acknowledge. Under these circumstances, should any separation occur, the *fault* shall not be mine.'

"'I will agree to any, to every thing you propose !' Such was the ardour of young Rentroll.

"The independence of character, displayed by the match-girl, and delivered in a most emphatic, yet, pleasing tone, made an intense impression on the feelings of Rentroll, not exactly to be developed; her beauty and fine form had spoken for themselves. No man was deceived upon these points; but the knowledge she displayed respecting mankind, added to the conquest she had made over Rentroll, he sat her down far above an every day sort of woman: nay, more, had she have been placed in a more elevated rank in society, she would have obtained the character of a female of very superior abilities.

" We are not aware that her protector had ever perused the memoirs of the *Chevalier Faublas*, which so universally attracted not only all the lovers of gallantry in France, but throughout the City of Paris, and which also found its way into *boudoirs* of numbers of the English women of quality, after its translation in this country. However, the match-girl, under the auspices of her keeper, although not placed under the necessity of changing her dress to carry on her intrigues like the lovely Marchioness of B., in that gay and voluptuous work ; yet, a suit of male attire was made for Charlotte, under a pledge of honour and secrecy, by one of the most fashionable tailors at that period.

" The order was attended to with the greatest nicety of art, to transform her appearance and exterior to the exact resemblance of a *man !* The tailor had done his duty to the very letter, and highly rewarded for the talents he had displayed in procuring a good *fit*, allowing anatomically for the different proportions of frame between the sexes. Rentroll was delighted on viewing the dress, and Charlotte in rapture with the fun this change of apparel was likely to afford her, when the proper time arrived for her to assume, in public, the character of a dashing, young MAN !

" A wig was also produced, for elegance, and such a close resemblance to nature, quite different in colour to her own hair, that was pronounced matchless ; with whiskers, eye-brows, and mustachios, that would deceive the most rigid inspector of human nature—so much, and so cleverly had *art* performed her task. The advice given to Charlotte, how to act in her new character was—'To hear much, and speak little !'

" After a few lessons from her protector, added to strutting and fretting her hour in her own house, and when the private rehearsals were considered complete, and the *debut* might be made with safety, a card was engraved, with the name of Mr. John Summersett ! as a *finish* to the character altogether.

" But in case of accidents, or sudden rencounters might occur, Rentroll decided that it was absolutely necessary he should give her a few lessons of the art of self-defence : Charlotte thought so too, and cheerfully entered into the spirit of the thing, with all the fondness of an amateur. She was an apt pupil—did not want for courage or strength, and she soon acquired the knowledge to *stop* and *hit*, so as to give a semblance in reality to the character of a high-spirited young fellow. The pupil often drove her master over the room when in combat, and completely convinced him that Charlotte, at all events, for a short period, should her courage be put to the test, that she would not betray any thing like a *Coward!*

"But before any of the *sprees* commenced, the argument between Rentroll and Charlotte was—the designation of *Jack Summersett, Esq.*, 'I have it,' said the former; 'he is to be known as a young sprig of fashion, related to a noble family, and ultimately will succeed to a title. To which might be added— an only son, very rich, great expectations, and lately come of age; but perfectly *incog.* as to his movements in life!

"'Excellent,' replied Charlotte; 'only keep my secret to yourself, and Jack Summersett will never betray himself. Ha! ha! ha! I hope I shall be able to keep my gravity—I am sure, it will be often put to the test. However, I am not afraid! Only one favour, I request,—never quit my elbow?'

"'Most rigidly,' answered Rentroll, 'shall I attend to your request, for upon that circumstance, depends our safety!'

"In truth, the latter kept the secret of his most intimate friend, as he termed Summersett—boys together from their childhood; inviolably in his own breast; by which means he imposed on the whole of his acquaintances. But it was decided between them, that Jack Summersett was not to make his *(her) debut* upon the grand theatre of metropolitan life—the West-end of the town; but in the more quiet part of it, when from a little practice in her new character, and her male attire did not sit uneasy upon her frame, she might acquire a degree of confidence, not to be shaken by any trivial interruption which might accidentally cross the path of Summersett!

"The latter in the early part of his male career, only showed himself on particular occasions; but he very soon became a favourite amongst the dashing associates of Rentroll; however, the latter, never left him alone with any of his *rakes*, as he termed them, for fear of the consequence. Summersett was continually upon his guard, and always waited for the *cue* from his tutor, before he launched out into any thing like a display of eloquence.

"The conversation of men, at times, over their glass at mid-night, and at other periods, when the 'Juice of the grape,' may have elevated their spirits rather above the *par*, are not very scrupulous or nice in their remarks; and who relate circumstances, anecdotes, and amours, not at all calculated for the ears of females; but the match-girl was prepared for such events intuitively, she was not at all fastidious, nor squeamish, and Jack Summersett was not likely to betray his condition on that account.

"During one evening, while our female hero was absent— Rentroll only now and then indulged his friends with her company in male-attire; he was asked where he first became acquainted with Jack Summersett.

" ' He seems to be a nice young fellow—unassuming—well-bred—quiet—and full of the etiquette of good manners. He is quite the gentleman!'

" ' So, I would have him :' replied Rentroll, scarcely able to suppress the laugh upon his countenance : ' indeed, it would be very unpleasant to my feelings to have Jack Summersett taken for any thing else but a *perfect* man and a gentleman. True, he is young and inexperienced ; but I assure you, my friends, he is much better when you are acquainted with him more intimately. He is in leading strings at present, totally under my care, and I have promised, his friends, that I will take care of him. Hitherto he has been very tractable, and, if I realize my expectations, it is my wish that he should return to his relatives in Northamptonshire, evidently improved in his mind ; a more enlarged knowledge of society ; yet, without the slightest touch of *bronze*, rudeness, or vulgarity.'

" The above frank display concerning his friend Summersett, was quite satisfactory to all of his acquaintances, and the *taciturnity* of the latter, was rather viewed as a want of confidence, than an embargo laid upon his tongue by Rentroll. Thus the secret was secured, and if any opinions about Summersett, that he appeared rather *feminine,* were expressed, still not the slightest suspicion arose in their minds that *he* was a female in reality, and only *looked* like a man !

" Summersett could, with some difficulty, manage one cigar, or rather, play with it, so as not to appear singular in company ; but he refused to sing on all occasions ; therefore, detection was not likely to occur from the quality of his voice. The match-girl was quick in apprehension, lessons were not thrown away upon her, and either in the capacity of a female, or the exterior of a man, she proved herself a match for the most knowing of her opponents. She was abstemious almost to a fault, although she had no objection to a glass of generous wine, on the score that it strengthened the frame of either man or woman ; but anything beyond that, she never indulged in ; she was scrupulously rigid ; therefore, Rentroll was perfectly satisfied that either in the character of Jack Summersett, or the *ci-devant* match-girl—drinking to excess was not amongst her faults. Drinking parties, of course, were avoided ; and it was only by sheer accident that Charlotte ever appeared amongst them.

" Rentroll appeared always to pay so much attention to Jack Summersett, that he was often challenged by his friends—He was careful over much ! Also, that he used the curb too strongly —he held the reins too tight—and he would, ultimately, find out his mistake. If the door of the cage should be found open some day, most likely the bird might fly away!

" ' Leave that to me,' observed Rentroll, with a smile ; ' I know *my* game, and I shall play my cards accordingly. I am the best judge in this case ; then as a matter of favour, reserve your remarks, and bear in mind the old saying—' That opinions given unasked, often create offence !'' This hint had the desired effect ; and ever afterwards, Summersett became a free agent amongst them, whenever he appeared in their company.

" Rentroll would not have gone so far by suffering Jack Summersett to appear amongst his friends at home ; but it was done to prevent idle curiosity when they were met together at any place of amusement out of doors ! This was well done as a *russe de guerre ;* and answered, to prevent such questions as— ' Who have you got with you, Rentroll ?'—' What is the name of your friend ?'—' Where does he come from ?' &c. &c.

" The match-girl possessed amazing strength for a woman, and the exercise she took, privately, with Rentroll, in using the dumb bells, walking miles at a time, learning to fence, as an amusement, and acquiring, in some degree, nay, an expert pupil, in the art of self-defence, with the gloves, was quite capable, as the term goes, of ' Taking her own part,' in a more defensive, nay, offensive style, if necessity compelled her to show herself off in the Amazonian character.

" Charlotte was very fond of a *spree,* when out with her protector—talked loud, when she thought it necessary to show her importance—called some men *puppies,* for their insignificance of conduct—that she would pull their noses—cane them—and horsewhip others, for their impertinence and cowardice : keeping up the sport of the character which she had assumed, in first-rate style, appertaining to a buck, or blood of the highest grade ; and whenever a *row* assumed something like a tangible shape, a duel likely to be the consequence, she would pull out her card-case with the utmost indifference, and present her card in exchange :—

MR. JOHN SUMMERSETT,

Regent's Park.

Smiling to herself, that the above hero in disguise, was at other times—' *non est inventus !*' Rentroll enjoyed this sort of fun exceedingly, and kept up the delusion in the cleverest manner, observing, when recognized by some persons as being in the company of the *runaway* Jack Summersett—' That he had not seen him since the row occurred ; but when he did meet with him, if Summersett did not come forward and act *like* a man, he should *cut* his acquaintance for ever. He would never keep company with poltroons !'

" This sort of *fun,* to Rentroll and Charlotte, was carried on for some time, without the slightest suspicion, or detection ; but according to an old proverb—' The pitcher which goes so often to the well, gets broken at last!' and so it occurred to the match-girl. In the course of a short period, she had not only obtained perfect confidence in her male attire ; but in some respects, became over daring ; however, on the evening, I am about to describe, it was urged against her that she had taken more wine than usual, and exhiliirated beyond her usual spirits, which were of the highest description at all times, without any other impetus : but Charlotte, at an after period, not only repelled the assertion with great indignation, as a foul calumny ; but it ultimately was the cause of their separation !

" At one of those uproarious scenes at the Italian Opera House, in the Haymarket, denominated a masquerade, Charlotte and Rentroll had made up their minds, unknown to their most intimate friends, according to Rentroll's phraseology to—' Go it !' or, in other words, to have some fun at the expense of their acquaintances ; and also to teaze and put other persons on the *fret*, who had previously offended them, and by annoying their opponents in the most ludicrous manner possible, what is called ' *owing* them One !'

" Charlotte went in her male-attire, with merely a black silk mask over her face ; but fastened on so tightly, that nothing but a most outrageous attack could have removed it from its place. Rentroll by her side, arm-in-arm, determined not to separate from her, without some row occurred, and then afterwards to meet at a given box near the orchestra. This being understood, Rentroll, well primed with champagne, had scarcely joined the motley group, before he began to ' push along—keep moving,' as if he had been out of his senses, and Charlotte was equally on the *qui vive*.

" To enumerate the jostlings which occurred for the purpose —the attack which took place—*designedly*—insolent replies— and now and then, blows, which passed on the occasion, would be a waste of time ; for both Charlotte and Rentroll, were bent upon *mischief* !

" The former, on seeing a *puppy*, as she termed him, yet a sprig of nobility ; who had affronted her grossly at one period of her life, and whom, Charlotte used to observe, had no more *brains* than a flower pot ; but nevertheless, who prided himself on his rank, and looked down with scorn and contempt upon every individual in society, without they could lay claim to high birth.

" ' Here's a *spooney*,' said she to Rentroll, ' that I have long wished to ' serve out ' upon an old score, the time has arrived, so look out, and be ready for a row ! I will give it him !'

" ' Go your hardest,' replied Rentroll, ' your *second* is at hand ! We'll die game ! Ha ! ha ! ha ! A skirmish—a caper or a turn-up, is meat, drink, washing and lodging for me for a month—so Go it, my pippin !'

" ' Then I am ready,' said Charlotte, and swaggering up to the sprig, nearly pushing him down—' You are a disagreeable chap, an't you, never to bring home to my house, the cheese and butter that I ordered of your master? You are a careless, negligent wretch, and I'll get you discharged! No reply, chap —no impertinence—no prate!'

" ' I am no cheesemonger, rude fellow!' answered the sprig, quite indignant, at such an insult; 'I am a gentleman, fellow! Therefore, be off, fellow—or, else——'

" ' Or else, what!' replied Charlotte, shaking her fist at him; ' Ha! ha! ha! an apology of a man like you!—a mere thing! —a non-entity!—a mushroom in society! Dare to call me fellow again, and I'll make a tinder box of your eyes, and extract the only spark of fire you have about you! I'll also turn your nose into a pair of snuffers by pinching it! And if you dare to open your lips any more to me, good, bad, or indifferent, I will put you into my side pocket, and smother you for the benefit of society in general! Ha! ha! ha!'

" ' So do,' said Rentroll, laughing immoderately at the *patter* made use of by Charlotte; ' take the *rind* off the cheesemonger, and *wop* him into butter! Make *scrapings* of the wretch!' A crowd of masqueraders had by this time formed quite a mob round them, listening to the above harangue, and who joined in the loud laugh.

" ' You are a liar, and a blackguard,' answered the sprig, ready to burst with passion; ' for thus abusing me, I am no cheesemonger; and I'll chastise you for your insolence— you——'

" Charlotte did not wait for the sprig to finish the sentence; but said—' Come on, Mr. Know-nothing, and I'll give you a receipt in full of all demands.' Charlotte was not long in showing her knowledge of the art of self-defence upon the face of the sprig, who had not the slightest chance to ward off her blows, the *claret* following every *hit*, till the sprig ultimately measured his length upon the floor. The row became general, blows were dealt out like a shower of hail, and the strongest only came best off, when the parties were dispersed by a violent rush from the clowns, tumblers, watchmen, brigands, firemen, &c. in consequence of which interruption, Charlotte and Rentroll made a lucky escape, without any detection as to '*who* they were!'

" After keeping the ' game alive' until they were completely tired; indeed, no two persons present had endeavoured to create more mirth, than *Jack Summersett* (in disguise) and Rentroll, had done at the masquerade. Daylight now appeared as the signal for their departure, when the latter went out of doors to seek for his chariot, but not returning to Charlotte quite so soon as she expected, she advanced to the extremity of the door, to be in readiness for the carriage, which led to the following ludicrous adventure:—

" The match-girl, in her male attire, although she was not

aware of the circumstance, it appeared, looked like the *double* of a dashing, extravagant, young man, who was frequently in the hands of John Doe and Richard Roe! The bailiffs had been on the look out for him for some time; but, unknown to them, he had gone to Paris, when they suddenly popped on Charlotte, exclaiming—'Here he is!'

"Upon the bailiffs making their caption good, Summersett, with a spirit of indignation, enquired the meaning of their rude, unmannerly attack; and with all *(his)* her strength resisted them.

"' You are wanted, sir,' replied the bailiffs.

"' What does the fellow mean?'

"' You are our prisoner! And you must go along with us!'

"' Prisoner! What crime have I commited?'

"' Not any crime; perhaps, a *fault!* But no doubt, if you go to Bill Holdfast's you will soon be able to settle it!'

"' Crime!—fault!—settle it! I do not understand a word you say. What is the cause I am thus annoyed? Tell me without delay.'

"' You know well enough! On suspicion of debt to the amount of seven hundred pounds; nevertheless, we do not wish to be troublesome, nor rude to you, sir, if you will only conduct yourself like a gentleman.'

"' I am no ——— I am a ———' but recollecting herself—the *secret* of her sex was still in her keeping.—'I tell you, gentlemen,' in rather a subdued tone, 'you have made a mistake. I am not the person you take me for. And if you will go with me to my house, I will not only satisfy you of the error you have committed, but reward you well for your trouble.'

"' No, sir, we don't do business in that 'ere manner! We've *cotched* you, and we means to keep you, as the man says to his wife—for better or for vorse! Besides, as how, you need not affect so much ignorance upon the subject! We have *nabbed* you several times before this 'ere, upon the same suit. So we can't lose our time, as we have several other gents to wait upon, who are like yourself—*shy* cocks! Therefore, we cannot argufy the pint; but you must come along———'

"' Had me before? you are a couple of insolent, lying rascals, and I have a great mind to break every bone in your bodies. I will not stir an inch! I do not owe a shilling to any person in the world!'

"' Then, Jem, you see how it is, this here person means to be obstropolis, and we must go to vork! Ve must use force! You see as how, sir, if you strike Jem and I in our duty, you will, and no mistake, be tried for an assault, and the *caper* will be, we shall get heavy damages; therefore, submit like a gentleman.'

"' I tell you again—I am no ——— and upon my honour, you are mistaken, and you will find that out too late!'

" ' We know better than that ere—that *gammon* won't do for Jem and I—old birds are not to be caught with chaff. So Jem, be polite—and lend the gentleman your arm, and here is mine also at his service.'

" Summersett offered his purse, but all in vain. ' Well then,' said he, " as you are determined, right or wrong, to take me, I will go with you quietly ; so take away your arms, or you will repent of it.'

" ' Repent !' you said last. ' Ha ! ha ! ha! you must excuse us laughing, sir ; but there is no *repentance* about us chaps. No, no—we are always *hindemnified.* Catch us repenting ; what stuff.'

" Very soon after the above dialogue had occurred, Summersett found himself, at his ease, in person, at Holdfast's lock-up house, but not so in *mind* ; and requested that some one might be sent immediately to S. Rentroll Esq., to inform him of the circumstance, and also to procure bail.

" ' Lord bless you sir, bail could not be taken at this improper hour of the night. The security must be undeniable, £700 is no trifle ! Besides, we might be taken up as disorderly persons, knocking at doors, and enquiring after persons who are asleep. I would very readily do anything to serve you, but bail now, sir, is out of the hunt ! Make yourself happy and comfortable— you have nothing to fret about—there is in this ere house as fine a *down* bed as you ever slept upon in the whole course of your life. There is the bell, sir, call for what you please—but my advice is, only to be civil, and draw it *mild*, and then you will be as happy and comfortable as if you were at home. It is our duty to make the *wisit* pleasant. Shall we send the servant-maid, Nancy, to you, she is a *wery* nice young woman, and will do anything for you—good night, sir.'

" The match-girl now rather *cooled* upon the subject. She was inclosed within iron bars—and complaint was useless. To get out, till the next morning, was out of the question ; she, therefore, consoled herself with the cheerful idea, that in the course of a few fleeting hours, which might be slept away, would restore her to liberty. Charlotte could not help laughing at the singularity of her situation ; but nevertheless, she thought it was carrying the joke rather too far. However, as I am to be a gentleman, in spite of myself—I will keep up the character a little longer, and also have a *spree* here, as I am sure discovery must come at last. Charlotte rang the bell rather loudly.

" The door opened, when a handsome young servant-girl appeared with a night-light, and said, ' I am ready, sir, to shew you to your room. The bed is well aired.'

" ' That is right, my girl, proceed, and I will follow you.'

" ' You will find excellent accomodation here sir, I assure you ; my master, Mr. Holdfast, has got a character for doing every thing in the most handsome manner to gentlemen in your situation.'

"'Gentlemen!' I'll have a bit of fun, thought the match-girl, "I cannot do any harm.'

"'What time do you wish to be called in the morning, sir? I wish you a good night.'

"'Stop a minute, my pretty little maid, I have got something to say to you;' and immediately ran up to the girl, and began to kiss her violently—behaving also in rather an unbecoming manner, and dragging her forcibly towards the bed. The girl resisting with all her strength—calling out at the same time, 'Master! mistress! Help! help. I shall be ruined! murder, fire! help! help!' This bustle and loud noise soon brought to her assistance her master, in his shirt—Mrs. Holdfast in her night-clothes—and two or three other inmates from their beds, who were under the influence of lock and key. The consternation and fright are not to be described; and the host and hostess were alarmed, under the apprehension that the house was on fire.

"Upon their entrance into the room occupied by Summersett, they perceived the servant-maid sitting upon a chair, crying—and the former laughing heartily at the row he had created in the lock-up house. Holdfast observed in a rage to the match-girl, 'You are no gentleman, sir, to conduct yourself in such an infamous manner.'

"'No,' replied Summersett, "I know that, I told your harpies so before, but they would not believe me.'

"'I mean, sir, that you are a blackguard to behave in such an unwarrantable manner to my servant-girl, and I wish it was in my power to kick you out of the house.'

"'*Kick* me out of the house indeed! Use better words, Mr. Bailiff, or I'll make you repent of your insolence on the spot instantly. I have got a potent arm to keep such fellows as you at a distance. Kick me! what have I done? you are mighty squeamish, Mr. Holdfast, all in a minute; I suppose you want to make a *property* of me, by swearing that I have committed——'

"'We'll ascertain that, without delay," cried Holdfast. 'What has the worthless wretch done to you my girl?'

"'Done!' I don't know scarcely what he has done to me," answered the girl, blubbering loudly, with her hands up to her eyes, 'but I don't know what might have been the consequences if you had not have come to my assistance. He is as strong as a lion—I was nothing in his arms—he kissed me violently!—and he—he—he—'

"'Well, I am glad it is no worse; however, we will indict him for an *assault*. He shall pay handsomely for his rudeness —so get you to bed, my girl, and we'll leave the gentleman to his private reflections. I am sorry, sir, you should so far have forgot yourself.'

"The room was instantly cleared—and the house as silent as could be wished—the match-girl laughing heartily at the adventure: ' this is *masquerading*—it is real 'life,' said she, ' and I will keep it up now to the end of the chapter.'

" For a few minutes she rather hesitated whether she should *undress* herself, or lie down in her clothes: but she soon decided on the subject—the clothes of the representative of Mr. Summersett were thrown upon the chairs—when she popped into bed, tired with the night's amusement, the diversity of the scene, and was fast asleep in quick time.

" We must now return to Rentroll, whom we left on the lookout for his chariot: his surprise and astonishment were beyond expression, when he returned to the spot where he had left Summersett waiting for his return. He asked in the most anxious manner of all the servants and persons at the door, describing his person, if such a gentleman had been seen. To all his enquiries the direct NO was returned. This is some trick Charlotte has put upon me—a little bit of her fun—or, rather to teaze me for leaving her so long, but I could not avoid it. She must have got into a coach, and gone home, where I shall find her taking some refreshment on my arrival I have no doubt. Such were Rentroll's thoughts upon the subject. He enquired of his coachman, but no traces could he learn respecting the absence of Summersett. He drove rapidly home—but to his surprise, nay, violent jealousy in an instant—Charlotte had not arrived. Horrors accumulated upon his mind—he was desperately in love with the match-girl: ' Ah,' he exclaimed in a tone of misery, —" it was what I always was afraid would happen, sooner or later; she has made some assignation, an intrigue with some man of fashion. Charlotte had always so many fine rich fellows buzzing about her person, like flies at a sugar cask, that I never could wholly beat them off.'

> Oh, what damned minutes counts he o'er
> To him who doubts! yet fondly loves.

" Rentroll was lost in conjecture ; and after harrassing his feelings to madness, he went to bed in despair—blaming himself for leaving Summersett alone. But he had made up his mind, that Charlotte was lost to him for ever—in consequence of some *new ;* or, more flattering connection.

" The match-girl, on opening her eyes after a few hours sleep, could not for the moment contemplate where she was—in a strange apartment, and *alone.* The windows, too, secured by strong iron bars—exclaimed, ' where the deuce am I ?' but reflection immediately flashed across her memory—and she recollected the *row*—the *arrest* of last night—and her singular situation in the lock-up house. ' Ha! ha! ha! no matter.' She rang the bell violently, and after waiting some little time, she overheard a parley, between the master, the mistress, and the servant-girl, who should attend to it. ' Let him ring and be d—— for an insolent fellow,' said Holdfast.

" The match-girl again rang the bell, with force enough to break the wire attached to it—when a man-servant—with a gruff hoarse voice, popped his nose in at the door, and asked what was wanted.

" ' Send the servant-girl up to me, immediately, fellow.'

" ' She is afraid to come, sir,'

" ' Ha! ha! ha! What is she afraid of? Then let your mistress come directly, I must see her.'

" ' Not by no manner of means, master says his wife an't a' going to be pulled about, and slobbered over by any fellow— besides, she will not trust herself in such bad company—she is the mother of children—a modest woman—and she says that you did not behave like a gentleman. You know what you did best—it's nothing to me, you know.'

" ' Ha! ha! ha! Such a fuss about modesty—squeamishness—I should have thought I had have been in the Penitentiary, fellow, sooner than in a blackguard lock-up house—but no matter. Do you, sir, bring me up pens, ink, and paper immediately; and in about a quarter of an hour afterwards, come up to me again, and you will find a note on the table, directed to a friend of mine. Do you take it immediately, or cause it to be taken—and the sooner you bring the answer—the sooner you will be a *sovereign* the richer; perhaps *two*, if you do it quickly. So be off.'

" ' You shall be obeyed, sir,' said the fellow, grinning—' I shall be punctual; I don't know what mistress may think, but I am sure he is a gentleman, every inch of him. A stuck up little wretch like her to give herself airs, she thought, I suppose to make a *flat* of him, but he would'nt stand it. I shouldn't have thought on it—howsomdever I shall try it on for the two *sovs*. One I consider safe in my fob. The *blunt* makes the gemman, in my *idears*.'

" The match-girl, on obtaining the paper, immediately wrote this facetious note to her gallant:

" Dear Rentroll,

" Here is a precious *scrape* you have got me into— but your pal, Jack Summersett is off for ever. You will never see him again. No more masquerading for me: but nevertheless, your own dear Charlotte, as you have so often called her—is now in fresh *keeping* ; and my *new* keeper is so strongly attached to my person, that he will not suffer me to go out of doors. But don't be alarmed for my constancy at present—for the truth is—the bailiffs have mistaken me for a sprig of quality, and I have been arrested for £700. This is above a *joke* at all events : however, a truce to complaint.

Come my dear fellow to me immediately, and bring with you a complete dress of female attire; my maid, Fanny, will give it to you. I am determined not to *act* the gentleman any more : one pill is a dose. I am to be found, or, rather say the lost sheep is to be heard of at Mr. Holdfast's, Cursitor Street, Chancery Lane. I cannot say, in the sporting cant, that I am *up* and dressed ; but yet, I am *down* —in bed. I cannot run away, but as the song says,

Locks, bolts, and bars, soon fly asunder.

Then don't delay a minute, every second appears to me an hour.

From your's, in durance vile,
CHARLOTTE PARTRIDGE."

P.S. This will prove a rare *exposure;* and I shall have some difficulty, I am afraid, for a short time, to convince the bailiff that I am *not* Jack Summersett. I shall become the laughing stock of all your friends.

" Upon reading this note, Rentroll resumed his natural spirits—bursting out in a fit of loud laughter—capering and dancing all over the room—uttering, with ecstacy—' My dear Charlotte, it is a precious *lark,* I must admit—and has given me some pain and uneasines of mind, but it is all over now. I will soon be with you—and convince those *living* body-snatchers that you are a woman, a delightful woman ; and demand satisfaction for the capture, and also the insult they have put upon my Charlotte.' He procured, not only a complete, but one of the most elegant dresses in Charlotte's possession, from the maid-servant ; and lost no time to relieve the representative of Jack Summersett from his unpleasant situation. On his arrival at Holdfast's, in his chariot,—' I want' said he, ' a lady in your custody, I apprehend by mistake.'

" ' You have come to the wrong house, sir, we have no lady debtor here. We are not such flats as to mistake a lady for a gentleman. We have been too long in business to commit such a palpable error. But you are not serious, I am sure. Rest assured, sir, we have no female in this house confined for debt.'

" ' Say, you don't know, Mr. Bailiff. Much cleverer men than you have been deceived by women. I again tell you, I must see the lady you have got in your custody.'

" ' We have no such person here, I once more assure you. A wrong direction has been given to you.'

" ' If I must speak by the card then, I want to see the gentle man you arrested last night at the masquerade. Take me to his apartment immediately.'

" ' Ha ! ha ! ha ! a pretty lady, indeed ; a fellow that would have *ravished* my maid-servant last night—if his diabolical attempts had not been frustrated. A lady, indeed, ha ! ha ! ha !'

" ' You grow insolent, sir. Keep your discourse to yourself ; I am not in a humour to argue with bailiffs.'

" ' I do not wish to be insolent, and far from rude ; but you will find that I have only spoken the truth, convince yourself.'

On Rentroll and Charlotte meeting together, loud laughter occurred between them, at the singularity of the scene. He found the match-girl in bed. ' Have you brought a dress for me ?' asked Charlotte, ' for I am determined, whatever ridicule I may undergo, I will not quit this house as Jack Summersett ; I have been punished for assuming the character of *lordly* man ?'

" ' Be it so,' replied Rentroll ' and while you are changing your *sex* ; Ha ! ha ! ha ! I mean your dress, I will go down stairs, and make the discovery known to the lock-up hero.'

" ' Do, my dear Rentroll ; and I'll *astonish* the bailiff, strong as his nerves may be ; he shall find I am a woman, to his cost.

At all events, I will try to frighten him. It is my turn *now* to talk loud of the injury I have sustained—false imprisonment—large damages, &c. &c.   Ha! ha! ha!'

"Upon Rentroll meeting with the master of the house, he observed to him—'Your men made rather a bit of a mistake last night, but, of course, you will abide the consequences, and in the course of a few hours you will hear from my solicitor on the subject. A lady, most certainly, you have made prisoner, instead of a gentleman, with all your penetration in these matters!'

"'That will not do, sir, I am am not so easily imposed upon as you may imagine. A lady, instead of a gentleman, it is impossible! However, I will soon remove all doubts upon that head. Here, Nance!'   The servant maid instantly made her appearance. 'Did not that gentleman in No. 5, treat you in a rough, rude manner, last night, and would have——'

"'He *did* indeed, sir, and had not you and my mistress have ran to my help, I should have been *ruined* in spite of my exertions to have prevented it.'

"'Psha!' exclaimed Rentroll, '*ruined*, indeed, you have all taken leave of your senses. I now ask you seriously, my girl, are you sure the person who attacked you so *rudely*, as you term it, was not a lady?'

"'A lady! I'll take my oath of it, sir. I never met with a stronger man in my life—I had no chance to defend myself—I was a child in his hands.'

"'Amazement!' uttered Rentroll, 'however, the mistake shall be cleared up instantly. Let your wife go up stairs, Mr. Holdfast, to the person alluded to, and she will find her a woman!'

"'No, I thank you, sir, I will not. I do not choose to suffer the mother of my children to be insulted with impunity, after what occurred last night. I must be a fool, to act so unwisely.'

"'Well then, I ask it of you, as a favor, let us go up stairs in a body, there can be no danger of *insult*, when we are altogether?'

"After considerable persuasion on the subject in dispute, they all repaired to the supposed gentleman's apartment, when, to the surprise of Holdfast, his wife and the servant girl, they found Charlotte in a splendid dress, and her fine form and beautiful appearance, positively electrified them for the instant.

"'Ha! ha! ha!' taking up the mustachioes and false whiskers, said Rentroll, 'they are not to be sent to the British Museum as curiosities, but they will be kept as a *memento* to laugh at when the anecdote is related to some future companies, as a proof that the most experienced 'knowing ones!' are to be taken in.'

"'True, true, my dear Rentroll,' remarked Charlotte, 'and if the gentlemen will only retire for a few minutes, I will soon satisfy Mrs. Holdfast, and the servant girl that I have behaved so rudely to, as she says ; but I only kissed her lips, upon my veracity, that I have a right to wear a petticoat !'

" Holdfast and Rentroll immediately retired, when, in the course of a minute or two, the landlady and Nancy came laughing out of the room, asserting, ' Sure enough, it is a lady, and a finer woman,' said Mrs. Holdfast, ' I never saw in my life. I am quite in love with her.'

> How many pictures of one nymph we view,
> All how *unlike* each other, all how true !
> What then ? let blood and body bear the fault ;
> Her head's untouch'd, that noble seat of thought :
> That, nature gives ; and where the lesson taught,
> Is but to please, can *pleasure* seem a fault.

" ' I hope you are now satisfied, Mr. Holdfast, you have no more doubts on the subject ?'

" ' Perfectly satisfied, sir, and I can only express my astonishment—but hope——'

" ' Not another word,' replied Rentroll, ' instead of bringing an action against you for false imprisonment, only *keep* the secret, and Charlotte and I, (not Jack Summersett,) will stay and dine with you; therefore, order the best dinner that can be procured from the nearest tavern, with plenty of champagne, also, every thing in season : spare no expense, and I will pay for it. Over our glass of wine I will relate the whole of the *spree*, for it was nothing else but a *spree* from beginning to the end of it. I will likewise make you a present for your trouble and uneasiness, occasioned by the lady on her entrance into your house. The girl also shall not be overlooked in the settlement,' at the same time calling the servant maid to him : ' remember, my dear, there is a *punishment* for those who kiss and tell, so let your lips be sealed for ever on this subject.'

" ' I will be as *silent* as death, sir,' replied the girl, ' respecting the *kisses ;* but in case of any future attacks, it seems I must be doubly on my guard, in case, a right arnest man might assume the garb of a female, and *mischief* might be done to me, before I could help it !'

" Holdfast, from his long experience in the capacity of a *lock-up* house keeper, was determined to *make* the most of his guests during the time they remained under his roof, and also to prolong their stay, if possible ; and a better judge of human nature, according to the opinions of his own fraternity, did not exist among the whole mob of bailiffs and their followers. He, therefore, lost no time in giving orders for a most expensive dinner, all the delicacies of the season, a fine dessert, with wines of the richest quality ; besides, a good understanding existed between Holdfast and the tavern-keeper, the former being allowed what is termed a *feeling* out of every article brought into his house.

" Rentroll was in high spirits on the occasion that he had once more the possession of his dear Charlotte, and the latter, was not a jot behind him in rendering the scene pleasant, that liberty and pleasure were again at her command. Holdfast, full of mirth and spirits, acted the *amiable* to the life ; eating and drinking at the expense of other people, and also putting money into his pocket at the same time. Towards the rich, rogues, or any other persons, who could spend money in his house, he was a complete fawning sycophant, and the most *accommodating* creature alive. But to the poor and needy, whom cruel distress brought to his residence for a short period, he had the character of being the most hard-hearted man of *his* calling.

" Upon the removal of the cloth, Rentroll pushed the bottle about rather briskly, and called upon Holdfast for a toast !

" 'You shall not wait long for one—I could mention names, but no matter, here's good luck to those persons who will not pay their debts until they are *compelled !*'

" ' Ha ! ha ! ha ! what a strange toast,' observed Charlotte, ' then I shall never have any luck, if that is the case ; for I have a great aversion to being in debt ; and I always pay on demand, sometimes before hand.'

" ' Yes, m'am, that's all very right, if you like to do so,' replied Holdfast ; ' but I am anxious to take care of the *main chance*, or in other words—*business.*'

" ' I should very much like to hear an explanation of your toast, Holdfast,' said Rentroll, ' for I have always heard it laid down, as sound argument, that those persons who would not pay their debts without compulsion, were allied to dishonesty !'

" ' Honour, honesty, and integrity, are principles which I very much admire, as principles,' observed Holdfast, ' and they ought to be taught as precepts at every school in the kingdom ; but WE cannot live by them. Honest men are of no *use* to us. If all the men in the world were honest, we must *starve*, and the disciples of John Doe and Richard Roe, would not be able to boil their pots. But, observe me, sir, I argue this matter as a bailiff anxious to obtain business, for a most *useful*, if not respectable, class of men. Therefore, sir, I hope you will not write me down as a dishonest man. Besides, sir, there are a number of characters in this great Metropolis, who would sooner pay *sixty* shillings in the pound, than discharge a just debt when demanded ! Therefore, I repeat, but without offence, that honest men are of no *use* to Bill Holdfast !'

" ' At all events,' replied Charlotte, ' there is a great deal of candour about your remarks.'

" A few more glasses of wine made Holdfast quite eloquent, and he related several anecdotes respecting many persons who had been residents in his house ; ' And if you have the time to spare,' said he, ' a day or two would not be thrown away, and your hours pass rapidly, the scenes in a lock-up house are often worthy of observation ; besides you, my lady and gentleman, although the key would be turned upon you, confinement would not be the result. I will give you an instance: an artist of some celebrity, exceedingly thoughtless and extravagant, who was arrested, and brought to my house, was in my custody for a fortnight, before his business was settled ; and during that time he felt himself so much at his ease, and quite at home, that he did not like to quit my roof. In the course of a short time afterwards, to prevent any duns becoming troublesome to him, for he was one of those persons who could not keep out of debt ; he would only pursue his studies when dire necessity stared him in the face, and then, he would not allow himself sufficient time to *finish* any of his pictures. He proposed to board and lodge with me; and he paid me liberally for the accommodation. I accepted the artist as an inmate, and found him a most interesting and pleasing companion at all times, and he used to laugh heartily to his associates whom he could trust with his secret, observing at the same time, ' You see I am always now in *trouble*, but never in GRIEF !''

"' Every man to his *taste*,' observed Rentroll, ' but the *look only* of iron bars is too much for me; however, as time is on the wing, and we are anxious to be at home, let ushear the song you promised us !'

"' You shall have it directly, sir,' replied Holdfast——

> My name's *Sam Snatch*, a *grab*, d'ye see,
>   Never *vas* a bolder ;
> *Vith* high and low I can make free,
>   And tap 'em on the shoulder.
> *Vene'er* I call, *they're not at home*,
>   Such *shy* cocks, only mind 'em ;
> But *ven* to lodge *vith* me they come,
>   Then I knows *vere* to find 'em,
>   Fol de dol, de diddle dol, de, da.
>
> To *quod*, I never make 'em trip,
>   *Vile* they can come it freely ;
> And if they stand a handsome *tip*,
>   I uses 'em genteelly :
> 'Mong bucks of fashion I have plied,
>   They found me sly and cunning ;
> And often, *ven* my *nibbs* they spied,
>   Lord, how I set 'em running.
>   Fol de dol, de diddle dol, de, da.

" The time, at length arrived, when Rentroll and Charlotte left the residence of Holdfast without the office being searched for *Detainers*. The latter, by this time, was quite tipsey, and full of hic-coughs, and when bidding good night to his liberal guests, he observed to Charlotte, that he should be happy to see her again, as often as she thought proper, either in the character of a lady or a gentleman. Rentroll and Charlotte soon afterwards arrived at their own domus, not at all angry at what had occurred, when the latter observed—' ALL'S WELL THAT ENDS WELL !' '

CHAPTER XII.

Strolls on the water—a tour—anything ; or rather, days of observation by the PILGRIMS; a boat excursion—Stop where it suits you! Go where you like! Stay as long as you please! after the manner of the sailors idea upon the subject: any port in a storm? The "NATIONAL!" every thing in the mind of MAKEMONEY: an argument in favour of the BANKS OF THE THAMES, respecting their connection with history, politics, fine arts, literature, the drama, &c, including a host of "Great Creatures of by-gone days!" A spree—a bit of fun—an anecdote. How to astonish a landlord; a-row-a-way party to escape the reckoning. "It must be them! No, it ain't! Yes it is! No, I am wrong! Very much like 'em! At all events, they look more like thieves than horses!" FLOURISH's tale; nay more, a fact; in which are exhibited the feelings of gratitude, the value of friendship, and the purity of uncon-querable love ; realizing the adage, better to be born for-tunate than rich. Names not necessary, yet a reference to the London Directory, might, if the cue was obtained, put the matter beyond all doubt. But MYSTERY is effective ; or the characters of MARPLOT and PAUL PRY, would become dead letters, and be put upon the shelf. "Oh, the joys of angling"—a fishing party—a bite: the DOG fish! Over-board he went! A splashing match with the Eton boys; MAKEMONEY in the water ; not drowned ; a cooler and a complete ducking ! Those who play at bowls must expect rubs. The pleasing sound of Bow bells to the ear of a cockney !

"THE more I visit old Father Thames, the more I am delight-ed with my native country," observed Makemoney, "the in-roads of war can never interrupt its peace and happiness ; and the simple peasant sits down contented by his fire-side with the blessings of liberty attendant upon every meal ; other countries cannot make such a boast. Whether the object of your pleasure may be directed, either above or below bridge, you must be im-pressed with its attractive situation; therefore, my brother Pilgrims, I have no doubt, will acquiesce with me in favour of my NATIONAL feelings on the subject."

"True to the echo," replied Flourish, " and I have heard it observed, that the history of a river, is the history of whatever *appears* on its BANKS ; from Metropolitan magnificence to village simplicity; from the habitations of king's to the hut of the fisherman, from the woody brow, which is the pride of landscape, to the rare plant that is only known to the eye of the botanist. In addition to which, the recollection of *past* and *present* times are equally animating to the mind of the tourist!"

"Unanimous—carried unanimously!" cried Sprightly, "the Thames, as a river, must appear of the very first importance in the eyes of every Englishman; but to foreigners, a complete *astonishment*—to behold, borne on the tide, below bridge, the active fishing boat, the gentleman's yatcht, and the noble man-of-war, the pride of old England, and the envy of the world; together with the busy hum of trade and merchandize. I do not possess talents enough to describe the animating scene! And if not so striking a feature *above* bridge, yet the noisy wharfs, well filled warehouses, splendid mansions, venerable seats, the scattered hamlet, the lonely farm, and the high elm trees, are pleasing pictures of the rustic soil."

"Excellently described, my brother Pilgrims," said Make-money, in raptures; "every word you have uttered has been like a cordial to my heart; besides, the names associated with the BANKS of the THAMES, are enough to claim a reverence from all the lovers of history, politics, literature, the fine-arts, the drama, and every thing calculated to raise the character of human nature, and give importance to the country that gave us birth. Is not the spot dear to us, where THOMPSON wrote his seasons; also the the residence of the poet of a thousand years—POPE, where he translated Homer; composed his delightful poem of Windsor Forest—

> Thy forests, Windsor! and thy green retreats,
> At once the monarch's and the muse's seats,
> Invite my lays!

and may be added the birth-place of EDMUND GIBBON, the author of that splendid work, the 'Decline and Fall of the Roman Empire.' Besides, the lovers of liberty will always reverence a spot where the glorious revolution of 1688, was planned, in a vault, in Hurley House, the seat of Lord Lovelace."

"I do not profess to be much of an historian," replied Flourish, "but let me add the name of Lord Bolingbroke, that great master of men and books, of whom, it is said, he possessed the wisdom of Socrates, the dignity and ease of Pliny, and the wit of Horace! The residence of another great character, who not only made the world '*look* about them abroad;' but also the people at home—OLIVER CROMWELL, was once on the Banks of the Thames."

"Neither shall my praise be wanting to do justice to the favourite spot of my school-boy days and delight," said Sprightly, "I have been informed that the celebrated Dr. DEE, in the reign of Elizabeth, selected Mortlake as his residence, and so great.

was his thirst to obtain information and to be of service to mankind in general, that he only allowed himself *four* hours out of the twenty-four from his studies—two to sleep, and two for recreation. COWLEY, the poet, likewise selected a retired spot close to the Thames, for his retreat. It was also where the haughty, proud, overbearing Cardinal Wolsey dwelt, who carried his notions of grandeur to such an extent, before he presented Hampton Court to Henry the Eighth, that he had two hundred and eighty silken beds, besides suitable hangings, in order to impress on his visitors, and the people, the pomp and magnificence of his palace, and extent of his riches : but he was a memorable instance, in his own person, that—' *Pride* should have a fall !' "

" If *taste*," urged Makemoney, " has any weight in the spots chosen for the residences of the members of the fine arts, the late SIR JOSHUA REYNOLDS was so much delighted with the view of the river, and the prospect from his window, that he produced a most exquisite painting of Richmond Hill. In 1300, it was called Sheen, and had a palace. Edward the Third died there, in 1377. Also, Richard the Second's queen ; which he took so much to heart, that he left the palace, which then went into great decay. Henry the Fifth restored it ; but in 1498, it was burnt down. It was rebuilt, in the finest style of architecture, by Henry the Seventh, who bestowed his family name of *Richmond,* upon it. Henry the Eighth frequently visited it ; and it was a favourite residence of Queen Elizabeth, who died there. It, however, fell into decay, and in the last century was entirely removed. The Countess of Northampton, the Duke of Queensbury, and the late Wiltshed Keene, Esq., had houses built on a portion of the site which occupied ten acres of ground. The remains of GAINSBOROUGH, one of the brightest ornaments of the Royal Academy, are buried in the church yard at Richmond. SIR PETER LILY, one of the greatest portrait painters of his day, dwelt the latter part of his time, and died at Kew. HUDSON, the painter, if he did not acquire so distinguished a name as his competitors, it was, nevertheless, in his school that Sir Joshua Reynolds learned his art. And HOGARTH, one of the greatest creatures in his peculiar line, whose scenes of men and manners upon paper, are perfect dramatic representations in their way, and have acquired, for Hogarth, an immortality in the temple of fame : his ashes lie buried in Chiswick church-yard. The Banks of the Thames have also been distinguished for private theatricals at Brandenburg House, under the direction of the Margravine Anspach, and the actors and actresses were lords and ladies. The late Dowager Lady Craven, was a female of great eccentricity, talent, and notoriety. She was authoress of several works, besides plays ; the Margravine altered the comedy of ' She would, and she would not !' and performed the part of Hypolita. She was also a great traveller, and made the tour of the continent; and at Constantinople the Grand Sultan paid her great attention.   Her last work was under the following singular title—' Anecdotes, Modern and Ancient, of the Family of the Kinkervandotsdarsprakengotchderns !'"

" I think, sir," said Flourish, " that I am correct in stating that RICHANDSON, the novelist, wrote the life of Sir Charles Grandison, on the Banks of the Thames; and that celebrated, but unfortunate statesman, Sir Thomas More, and Bishop Lowth, of classic erudition, selected their dwellings upon the above spot !"

" In point of architectural beauty," said Sprightly, " I have been told that the Duke of Devonshire's villa at Chiswick, would not disgrace the banks of the Arno or Tyber. No matter, but the elegance of stone and brick work, melts, like snow before the sun, when CHELSEA COLLEGE appears to the view and feelings of an Englishman ; it does honour to its founder— James the First. Four hundred men are amply provided for in it, exhibiting the soldier's tear of gratitude, when he is enabled to make a *halt* in the downhill of life. To shoulder his crutch and talk over seiges manly endured, dreadful breaches made, the forlorn hope, and imperishable conquests obtained. Where also many an *Uncle Toby*, and lots of *Corporal Trims*, have heaved a sigh for the loss of some gallant comrade, or dropped a tear at *his* departure, who might, otherwise, have proved another General Wolfe.—

> Come fire a volley o'er his grave,
>   Dead marches let us beat ;
> War's honors well become the brave,
>   Who sound their last retreat.
> ALL must obey Fate's awful nod,
>   Whom life this moment warms :
> Death soon, or late beneath the sod,
>   Will ground the soldier's arms.

Such a place as Chelsea College, is only to be met with on the Banks of the Thames."

" Not in the whole world beside," cried Makemoney, knocking his stick with great animation, against the ground, in proof of his love towards that truly NATIONAL feature : " but it ought not to escape our memory, as lovers of dramatic talents, that the celebrated Mrs. CATHERINE CLIVE, of whom it is said, ' If ever there were a truly comic genius, she was one ;' perhaps, never equalled, but never excelled, and sketches in her hands became highly finished pictures ; retired, and died on the above spot. COLLEY CIBBER, equally distinguished in the annals of the stage ; Lord Dorset, the Lord Chamberlain at that period, said of him—' That for a young fellow to show himself such an actor, and such a writer in one day, was something extraordinary ;' he dwelt, at one period of his life, at Strawberry Hill. This distinguished residence afterwards became the property of HORACE WALPOLE, the author of the ' Castle of Otranto,' and from whose private press several other important works were issued. Also, the English Roscius, the immortal DAVID GARRICK, Esq., who united the poet, the actor, and the gentleman in the same person.* The Right Hon. CHARLES JAMES FOX, one of the most illustrious statesmen of his own, or any other period, and parallel with Demosthenes, as an orator; all of them dwelt upon the Banks of the Thames!"

"Oxford, sir, the first University in the world, and of an immense antiquity," said Flourish, " seems to have escaped your notice; it is connected with the river, and a seat of learning for at least a thousand years. Now, my old friend, if you can furnish us with any of the *sprees* of those gents, termed Oxford scholars, they might not only enliven your remarks, but set the table in a roar. It should seem they have often distinguished themselves in several rowing matches on the Thames, with more zeal to become the winners of the contest, than exerting themselves to obtain *a degree*. Although they have not been wanting to prove themselves tolerably good *Wranglers* upon the water."

" The Oxford scholars are rather dangerous subjects to meddle with at any time," answered Sprightly, " therefore we had better leave them to pore over their black-lettered folios to enlighten the community, and turn our thoughts to matters of another description. The Banks of the Thames, it appears, have been dedicated in the olden times to the meeting of lovers. The celebrated DEAN SWIFT, an author of immense power, as a satirist, a politician, and a high churchman, stole a few hours now and then, from severer studies, to enjoy the company of his STELLA, and talk of love. She was daughter of the steward of Sir William Temple. Such conversations, if they could have been handed down to the present period, might have been of the most essential service to the love-sick *Romeos'* and the all confiding *Juliets'!* Nay, invaluable! A reverend Dean in love!

---

* The following anecdote never before appeared in print: Garrick and Sir Joshua Reynolds, were in a large party, at the house of a gentleman in Westminster; and being all assembled in the drawing room, previous to dinner, the daughter of the host, quite a child, came bounding into the room, unconscious of any person being present, but immediately stopped short, finding herself amongst several gentlemen entirely strangers to her; several of the company endeavoured to coax her forward, but she hesitated for some time, looking about her, and surveying the whole of the group. After a minute or two had elapsed, she ran up to Garrick, who had a waistcoat on of a shot silk of bright colours. Sir Joshua, in a playful mood, observed—" Ah ! Miss, I see what made you prefer that gentleman, his pretty silk waistcoat attracted your attention." The child immediately answered—"No, indeed, it was not *that*." Sir Joshua still persisted that it was the silk waistcoat, and said, " If it was not that, what made you run to him first ?" " It was his EYES," answered the child with seeming rapture. The company were highly amused to see Garrick immediately afterwards seize the child in his arms, and almost smother her with caresses. The child in question, is now the mother of a family, and resident in the Metropolis. The Gentleman's name was ASTLE; and the family well-known for its respectability both in India and London.

—and that person of no less importance than Dean Swift! I should think, uncle, that the copyright of such a book, a 'manuel for sweethearts,' would soon have paid the amount of its purchase money from its immense sale. Ha! ha! ha!"

"You might have added another, and a greater personage to your list," said Makemoney, "the fair ROSAMOND; and not lost the *clue* neither. Woodstock is connected with the Thames. "Great doubts are entertained respecting the exact mode of her death; yet there are none about her beauty. It is said that the Queen of Henry the Second, who went, full of jealousy and rage, to kill her detested rival, yet, was so struck with her great beauty, that she paused, and gazed upon fair Rosamond for several minutes before she administered the cup of poison.

"I have little more to say on the subject," replied Flourish, "but I should not like to pass over in silence, MR. PHILLIPS, the author of the 'Splendid Shilling,' a poem that used to delight me very much for its regularity and spirit when I was at school :—

'Happy the man, who void of care and strife,
In silken, or in leathern purse retains
A splendid shilling.'

Likewise JACOB TONSON, the book-seller, (originally a footman-in-livery I believe) but afterwards, the proprietor of Down Place, a name connected with that constellation of genius, which, at one period, illuminated the literary world, in connection with the celebrated Kit-Cat Club, of whom Dr. Johnson, Garrick, Oliver Goldsmith, Sir Joshua Reynolds, &c. were members."

"And my last words on the pleasing subject are, persons who have been born and dwelt on the banks of the Thames," said Sprightly, "that Cromwell, the son of a blacksmith, who afterwards became Earl of Essex, from his splendid talents, through the patronage of Cardinal Wolsey; yet, from his integrity and love of truth, was beheaded by the order of Henry VIII; and West, the son of a baker, an unruly, naughty boy at school, changed in so extraordinary a degree as to have been created Bishop of Ely, and considered, for the remainder of his life, one of the most wise and pious prelates that adorned the bench. A convincing proof that at any period of English history, a man, with the possession of talents, may rise to the highest offices in the state, without any disparagement to his birth."

"In fact, my worthy brother Pilgrims, we might go on *ad infinitum*, the Banks of the Thames afford such a prolific source for great names and amusements connected with the River," urged Makemoney, "Chelsea alone would fill volumes. *Ranelagh* at one period, fifty years ago, it is said, was the climax of elegance and fashion, a superior place altogether—far, very far above *Vauxhall*, and all the places of resort in or near the Metropolis. People of the first rank and consequence in the state were its principle visitors; and few persons felt *courage* enough to show themselves at Ranelagh—their dress, manners, and behaviour were so soon detected as belonging to an inferior class of society. To shew the estimation the above place was held in by the lower orders,—the cook, in 'High Life below Stairs,' when she is asked which place of entertainment she will go to; her reply is, '*Run-ne-law* for my money!'

"But the times are very materially altered since that period," said Flourish, "I heard Mr. Matthews, a few years ago, in the lively farce of 'Hit or Miss!' sing a song, in which I recollect the two following lines :—

> ' The Peer and the Prentice, they dress so much the same,
> That you cannot tell the difference, excepting by the name.'

"You must not forget, sir, the *Red House*," urged Sprightly to his uncle—"which has been such a favourite place of resort for the last few years—as I do not think we ought exactly to lose sight of the *Moderns!*—Ha! ha! ha! I have seen some extraordinary shooting matches between Lord Kennedy, Mr. Osbaldeston, Capt. Ross, Lord Ranelagh, &c. I well remember to have seen a Mr. Arrowsmith, on a penny piece being thrown up in the air, to have put in it, above one *hundred* shots."

"You are quite in order," replied Flourish, "and you now remind me of another rather prominent feature connected with the Banks of the Thames—a celebrated tavern, both in the olden, and times of a more modern date, where the celebrated Colossus of Literature, and the author of the Vicar of Wakefield used frequently to *unbend* in company with other great wits, and men of first-rate talents—the COAL-HOLE. It still keeps up its name for the resort of men of abilities; although somewhat of a different class in society; but nevertheless, entitled to the character of CHOICE SPIRITS! I must say that I have spent many pleasant evenings at the Coal-Hole, with gentlemen of the press, authors, actors of note, composers, men of the world, merchants, and some first-rate vocalists, affording that variety of company, in which, *Time* might be said to fly. Most certainly, it has not a board outside of the door, as I have seen at some inns, 'good entertainment for man and horse:' yet the '*feeds*' are excellent, served up well: and the entertainment good; the glee-singers also of the first reputation; and the comic songs, several of which are from MSS. quite a treat; and to echo the words of mine host, (Mr. Rhodes) that ' dull care' is not to be met with at the Coal-Hole, except in the shape of a *chant*. The proprietor of the tavern is a musician, sings a good song, and well calculated, from his knowledge of society in general to amuse his patrons: and is likewise a punster of the highest grade. Puns escape from his lips, nearly as fast as he fills the glasses with liquor, ' I don't know the origin of my sign,' said he, when asked by a precise old gentleman, who said the allusion was a very odd one, ' but this I know sir, that the fire of intellect attached to it, is not kept up without plenty of *Cole!*' Soon after KEAN made his appearance in London, a society was established at the above tavern, under the title of '*the* WOLVES!' the members of which, carried their zeal to such an extent in favour of the great tragedian, that it was dangerous for any new performer to make his appearance in the Metropolis, in the character of Richard the Third."

Turf, who had remained silent during the whole of the above remarks, with a smile on his countenance observed, "deep research does not belong to *my* book; or, chronological events; but perhaps, it is worthy of your notice, that the late Lord Barrymore of extravagant, theatrical, and sporting notoriety, treated the bargemen upon the Thames with flagons of Rhenish wine, according to his notions of things, ' to make them men of *Taste.*'"

"The watermen are waiting for you at the bridge sir," announced the servant, "and they say you are all right for the tide, but the sooner you and the gentlemen are afloat, the better."

"Tell them we shall be on board immediately;" replied Makemoney, "so let us be off, brother Pilgrims to enjoy our *stroll* upon the water. The phrase has an odd sound, I admit—but what I mean is, that not having any direct object in view—we can either dine at Chelsea; sup at Richmond, Twickenham, or elsewhere."

"Nothing can be more welcome to all of us, I think," said Flourish—"therefore, let us make ourselves at home at every place where we sojourn."

The Pilgrims were soon under the care of the watermen, and Makemoney again, on his delightful Thames, quite enraptured with the picturesque scenery and objects by which it was surrounded, "I have heard the banks of the Clyde admired; the river Lee, with a beautiful country on each side of it, flowing towards the cove of Cork; and the lakes of Killarney, highly praised as incomparable; but nevertheless, I say there is nothing like the THAMES, take it for ' all in all.' And I agree with Pope to the extent of his description:"

No seas so rich, so gay no BANKS appear,
No lake so gentle, and no spring so clear:
Where tow'ring oaks, their growing honors rear,
And future NAVIES on thy shores appear.
Happy the man, whom this bright court approves,
His sov'reign favours, and his country loves:
Happy next him, who to these shades retires,
Whom NATURE charms, and whom the muse inspires.

"Bravo! bravo!" said Sprightly.

In the course of the day, Makemoney pointed to a house which caught his eye, observing, "it remind me of a circumstance, when I was a youth, under twenty years of age, during

2 o

an excursion with a boat party on the river. Most of the company were audacious dogs indeed for frolic and fun.

"The boat was an eight-oared cutter; and the sitters and rowers consisted of about fourteen persons. We landed at the above house, partook of refreshment, drank a variety of liquors, smoked our pipes, and no persons could have felt more happy than ourselves. One of the party, Jack Robinson, the foremost in all sorts of mischief, proposed that during the absence of the waiter, we should all get off in the best manner we could, without *paying* the reckoning, and come back on some future day and discharge the amount of the bill."

"The idea was adopted instantly; the whole of us being inclined for the joke."

"There was little difficulty in getting off unperceived—the room was situated at the end of the garden, fronting the river, with an ascent of steps—but at some distance from the tavern. The company *walked* off by degrees: and during the absence of the waiter, who had received an order to replenish the whole of the glasses with liquor; the remainder of the boat's crew were off like lightning; and never did any cutter leave the shore in quicker style. Before the waiter returned to the room, the boat was out of sight: but the crew could scarcely follow the strokesman for laughing, at the surprise the waiter would feel on his entering the room to find the whole of the company had *bolted*."

"We were quite strangers to the landlord; and the circumstance was a standing joke with us in London for several weeks; therefore, he had not the slightest clue to our directions. It served likewise, a tale for the landlord and his servants to all the different boat-parties that visited the tavern afterwards and a variety of comments were passed upon the subject, coming under the terms of dishonesty, trick, fraud, and shabby in the extreme."

"When the circumstance had subsided for a little time, and the landlord and his waiter had rather *cooled* about the run-away, or rather the *row*-away boat's party, Jack Robinson collected the whole of the same company together, and again started for the room alluded to; but previously begged of his companions, in the strongest manner, to put on the most demure faces possible; and not to betray the slightest hint of the former circumstance. After landing, and taking their seats exactly, as well as they could recollect, on the previous occasion, Robinson rang the bell, and upon the waiter entering the room for orders, he started back with astonishment:—

Like Garrick's Hamlet's, frighted ghost he stood!

and appeared quite confused: he would have taken to his heels immediately, to have acquainted his master, if Robinson had not have spoken sharply to him, saying, 'Waiter, you do not seem to pay attention to my orders?'

" ' Yes—sir—but—I—I—I—'

" ' But what,' replied Robinson.

" The waiter, on quitting the room, muttered to himself—' it must be the chaps that *bolted* from here some time ago, without paying their reckoning. I am sure it is them. However, I will tell my master what I think about it.' He immediately communicated his suspicions to the landlord, who returned with the waiter to take a synopsis of the party: when considerable whisperings took place between them, as to the best manner of conducting themselves towards the suspicious persons, in case they might be mistaken; and wavering in their minds, to charge the party with their bad conduct. However, they let it pass over for a short time, but when the next order was given to replenish the glasses, and something to eat, ' no, by Heavens,' said he to his waiter, ' I will not stand it a second time : therefore, tell them I shall not send any more liquor without paying for it on delivery,' and quitted the room in an angry mood.

" Upon the waiter asking for the money, ' it is our intention, most certainly, to pay what we call for ; but send your master to us,' said Robinson, ' we do not like to have this affront upon our honesty.'

" On the arrival of the landlord amongst them—he again scrutinized the whole of the party, with a most penetrating eye. But their general appearance of respectability, seemed to defy anything like dishonesty. Robinson, in a pompous style, asked, ' what doubts have you, sir, respecting our characters ?'

" ' None !' replied the landlord,—' yes—no,—yes I—have ; no, no—yes, it must be ! Both of us can't be mistaken. I am suspicious—.'

" ' Suspicious !' the whole of the boat's crew rising up indignantly. ' Do you wish for a good *ducking* in the Thames, Mr. Host, and afterwards well *kicked* to dry you ? we are not to be traduced with impunity. So have a care—.'

" The landlord being thus surrounded, and being assailed with so many loud voices, felt some little intimidation on the subject —and a sort of confusion in his ideas, whether he had not better make an apology for what he had said, and drop the matter, than to make a direct charge against them for having quitted his house without paying their reckoning. However, screwing his courage to the sticking place, he said, ' I am rather in a dilemma ; and I do not wish to give any offence ; but there was a company of gentlemen—no, not gentlemen—but——.''

" ' Be on your guard ! Mind what you say, sir,' from all the party. ' No unwarrantable allusions.'

" ' Well then,' continued mine Host, ' a party of thoughtless young men—whether for a lark—or, a bit of fun—I know not. But they forgot—or, I supposed it escaped their memories, to pay the reckoning.'

" ' Aye! that is nearer the mark,' said Bill Blunt, ' hear him out, give the *sinner* fair play.'

" ' Do you mean to assert then,' asked Jack Robinson, that *we* are the party that went off without paying our reckoning ?'

" ' I will not take my oath of it,' replied the landlord, ' but you cannot hurt me for *thinking* that I am right.'

" A loud burst of laughter followed the last sentence, and Jack Robinson, holding out his hand to the landlord, in token of friendship, said, ' you are right, my friend, we are the party that *bolted* ; but it originated in a bit of fun, the *lark* has been answered ; and if you will pardon us for the pain we have put you to—send in your bill, and it shall instantly be discharged. Neither shall the waiter be neglected ; nay, more, we are determined to have a dinner here, merely to establish the anecdote ; and also to convince you, that we are better than we look to be.'

" I shall never forget that dinner," observed Makemoney, " if I were to live for a thousand years ; none of the party were capable of returning home that night by *water*, they had made themseves so very jolly with the large portions of wine they swallowed, to make amends to the landlord, and drinking success to ' the *bolters !*'"

The Pilgrims were perfectly free, and easy in their movements—dining at one place, drinking tea at another ; and enjoying all the picturesque variety of the scene, until the shades of evening compelled them to retire from the watery element :—

> Let India boast her plants, nor envy we
> The weeping amber, or the balmy tree ;
> While by our OAKS, the precious loads are borne,
> And realms COMMANDED which those trees adorn.

The supper over, and the grog upon the table, " we cannot have a better opportunity, Flourish," said Sprightly, " than the present, for the anecdote you promised us ; and as we are well aware that you are a man of gallantry, and met with many adventures in your time, it is not too much, to expect something *spicy* from you, connected with society, in its gayest moments."

" I must acknowledge, our friend Makemoney, has never lost sight of the NATIONAL during our pilgrimage," replied Flourish, " Sprightly has also entertained us with the ' White Lady of Kew ;' and Mr. Turf, most interestingly occupied our time with the extraordinary adventures of the ' Match-girl,' therefore, I have no objection, with your leave and attention, to introduce to your notice, a slight sketch of ' PULL-AWAY JACK OF THE FERRY !' connected with old Father Thames ; but there is no touch of the *Frankenstien* about it, no ghost, or apparition to excite horror and fear, and nothing else but a down-right matter of fact substantial story, connected with flesh and blood: but with this difference, the match-girl was without a *heart* ; a mere machine ; a vile piece of clay ; and only the outline of a woman. However, the young lady, that I have to describe, was all tenderness, all SOUL, with love of the purest description, appreciat ing kindness offered to her, tremblingly alive to honour, and knew the value of constancy, but then she was a *modest* female :—

A women's seen in private life alone !

" By all means," replied Turf, " variety is, at all times, sure to please us, so no more preface, but proceed without delay."

" Respecting the birth, parentage, and family connections of ' Pull-away Jack,' " said Flourish, " I candidly confess, I am totally in the dark ; and so was every other person, I believe, that ever knew him. He was too young to give any account of himself. He dropped from the clouds as it were. But the fact is, Jack was *picked up,* soon after daylight, one morning, close alongside the ferry, at Twickenham. He could *cry* lustily, *smile* now and then, and call out dad, *dad*, and *mam*, but nothing more ; the clothes he had on him were tolerably decent, but not the slightest clue remained as to his unnatural parents.

" In after days, whenever his origin was enquired into by inquisitive persons, lots of whom are to be found in every parish, who delight to pick a hole in a man's coat if it answers their purpose, that Jack was a *love* begotten child, a natural son—a by blow—or, in the vulgar, course phrase of the illiterate and unfeeling—a *bastard !*

The child, who many fathers share,
Hath seldom known a father's care !

" Little Jack, it appears, was first discovered by an old bargeman of the name of honest Joe Morris, who had overslept himself, and was hurrying towards his craft, to make up for lost time, when his career was suddenly stopped by the crying of a little child. Joe lost sight of business in an instant, and immediately went up to him. The bargeman was the father of a large family ; and proverbially known in the neighbourhood as a good parent, a kind husband, a steady friend, and an honest man. ' How came you here,' said he, ' so early, my little one, this morning ?' But the boy was too young to answer the question, and cried incessantly.

Come on, poor babe !
Some powerful spirits instruct the kites and ravens
To be thy nurses ! Wolves and bears, they say,
(Casting their savageness aside), have done
Like offices of pity !

" ' Hard lines !' exclaimed Joe, ' what unfeeling brutes there must be in the world, to desert their offspring at such a tender age to starve, perhaps, to die, for what they care.' Then clenching his fist violently. ' D—n me, if I had but the father and mother of this poor child here, I would pay no respect to the law, but I'd give them such a sound drubbing for their brutal conduct, that they should not be able to leave their beds for a month, and remember it the longest day they had to live.

" ' What's to be done, I am behind hand with my work, and

time is precious. D—n the work! I could not find it in my heart to leave this poor baby to starve and die unheeded ! No, nor 1 will not,' taking the baby up in his arms and kissing it; ' you are a pretty fellow, and business must give way for a short time, when our humanity is put to the test. I am a father. Thank God, I know what are the feelings of a parent, and I will not disgrace them. I will return home to my wife. Old Bess is not one of the best tempered women in the world; but nevertheless, she has got a tender heart. I expect to be well *blowed* up by her at first, but she will soon afterwards *melt* into the mother. Well, never mind, I will run all risques ; I always have, and always shall cherish the notions that ' good deeds are never ill-bestowed.' '

"Old Joe hurried back to his cottage with the child in his arms, and upon entering the doors of it, he said to his wife,— ' Here, Bess, I've brought a present for you. I found this poor little fellow in the fields crying ready to break his heart, and no one near him. His forlorn situation touched my feelings, and I could not pass him by. I am sure his unfeeling, brutes of parents, have left him, either to perish, or to be picked up by some person and sent to the parish.'

" ' You need not have been so officious, Joe, what is every body's business, is nobody's business,' answered his wife, rather angrily ; ' therefore, you had better have minded your work, as you know you are behind hand with it ; and have left it to somebody else, who has more time on their hands, to have taken care of the child. Besides, you know we are too poor to do any thing for the neglected baby; we have already, too many children of our own. We can scarcely get bread for them.'

" ' What, Bess, do you refuse this poor child house room,' replied Joe, almost getting into a passion ; ' you do not mean it, I am sure. Suppose now, you had lost one of your children, *only* lost one of your boys or girls, what would you say to any person who took care of them for a short time, until they found out their parents ?'

" ' Say not another word, Joe,' said his wife, taking the boy in her arms ; ' he is a pretty fellow. Give him house room, aye, bread and butter too, and a bed, if he should want it. But I have no patience—my curses attend on all such wretches ! who could leave such a sweet boy unprotected in the wide world; but the punishment of God will overtake them in their wickedness !'

" ' Give me a kiss, Bess,' replied Joe, joy sparkling in his eyes ; ' take care of the boy till I have finished the job, and then we will see what can be done for him.'

" ' He shall want for nothing during your absence, Joe,' said his wife in a tone of voice that indicated true feeling—' I am a *mother* !'

" ' That's enough,' urged Joe, and took to his heels as fast as

he could to make up for the time he had lost; his mind was now
at rest, he felt that he had done his duty, yet, that he had only
performed the dictates of humanity, and while he was tugging
at the oar up the river, he appeared so pleased with what he had
done, that he sung a few lines of one of the late Charles
Dibdin's songs, with a zest that he had never felt before :—

> I'm called honest Ben, but for what I don't know,
>   I only, d'ye see, do my duty;
> 'Tis every one's place to lighten the woe
>   That presses down virtue and beauty!
> Why gold was first made, I can't tell to be sure,
>   To learning not being addicted;
> Unless it was made to cherish the poor,
>   To comfort and aid the afflicted!

" 'Perhaps,' said he, ' this little fellow, should I live to see him
grow up to manhood, may, one day or another, thank old Joe
for giving him a little succour in the hour of need ! But if he
does not, no matter, I have the consolation to think that I
acted like what every father would have done in the same
situation.'

" Old Joe worked double tides, as the watermen say, to get
his job finished, that he might return home to ascertain the fate
of little Jack. In the course of two or three days he found
himself at his own fireside, and was delighted to see the little
foundling, playing with his children near his hearth. ' This is,
as it should be,' said Joe, ' I knew, Bess, you was right at the
core, right as a trivet. Your heart was always in the right place,
and I shall love you for your *motherly* conduct to the little
stranger, better, much better, than ever I did in the whole course
of my life.'

" ' Did I not tell you, Joe, that I was a mother !' answered
Bess, ' and I have taken such a liking for the poor boy, that I
shall not like to part with him, and I am only sorry that we are
so very poor, and our family so large, that we cannot make room
for him.'

" ' We are poor indeed,' said Joe, ' I feel it keenly at this
moment; but I will go immediately to the overseers of the
parish, and take the child with me. I will relate the particulars
of my finding him to Mr. Halfloaf, who is not a hard-hearted
fellow upon the whole; and beg of the latter to see the foundling well done by.' The boy, as a matter of course, was received
into the workhouse, bills and advertisements were put forth,
offering a reward for his unnatural parents, in order to bring
them to justice. But all in vain, no clue could be obtained, or
explanation given on the subject; the overseer and churchwardens, therefore, put down in their books Jack-of-the-Ferry,
as one of their bad bargains; but determined to turn him to
some account when the opportunity offered.

" ' Old Joe and his wife, never lost sight of little Jack during his abode in the workhouse, and called, with a parental care, frequently to enquire after his improvement and welfare ; giving him halfpence, apples, and other little presents to please his mind and make him comfortable. This conduct towards little Jack produced a kindred feeling between them, he called old Joe his father, and Bess his mother ; and he expressed more attachment to them, than any other persons in the world. He grew apace a nice child, and in spite of his mean apparel— workhouse clothing, there seemed something about his person, that betokened better things.

"Personal appearance is, generally, considered one of the greatest recommendations in life ; respecting its existence there is no denial, however difficult it may be accurately to define! Dress *that* man in the best manner you can, is frequently the re- mark, and he will never *look* like a gentleman. You will like- wise hear it said, *that* lady has the appearance of a duchess ; her attitude is commanding, her appearance prepossessing, and her genteel air and carriage, speaks for her, without the aid of a trumpeter to announce her qualifications, that she is a female of superior pretentions. Also, such and such a child belongs to a gen- tleman, I am sure, his looks are so very different from other boys ; so it occurred with Jack, although in his very humble, nay, low occupation and condition in life ; yet, there was a certain some- thing about him altogether, which attracted the attention of a number of persons *en passant*, that they could not account for. But it is an every day feeling in society.

"In the course of a few years, when quite an urchin, he got tired of the confined limits and rules of the workhouse, and with- out taking any thing like a formal leave of the officers of the institution, he left them to seek his fortune in the wide world. The banks of the Thames was the first spot of ground that pro- duced him a *halfpenny*, amongst the boatmen in the character of ' *Jack-in-the-water* !'

"" At the period alluded to, he might have been compared to a *duck*, as he nearly lived in the river ; the expense of shoes he avoided, and a hat was of little account with Jack, his feet were scarcely ever dry, and his head frequently endured the ' pitiless, pelting storm.' But the rude elements did not appear to annoy him ; use, it is said, becomes second nature. In process of time his frame was like iron, he possessed prodigious strength, but he never used it improperly to irritate or ill use any person ; in dis- position, he was tractable, and inoffensive as a lamb. The world was almost a *blank* to him : and he, therefore, from this chasm in his mind, endeavoured to make every man his friend. In truth, Jack was a true child of nature: he was poor and content, and the luxury, which riches affords to the opulent man, were unknown to his feelings. He always appeared satisfied when he got a belly-full by his industry, and it is not unlikely but he ate his crust with more happiness than did his monarch!

"The designation of 'PULL-AWAY,' was given to him by the watermen, from the readiness he displayed when a passenger wanted a boat in a hurry, and which might have been at some distance from the shore ; his exertions were so great, that he would scarcely allow himself time to breathe, he rowed with such rapidity to earn a penny. The watermen calling out to him 'Pull-away Jack, here's a gentleman to be off! pull-away! pull-away !' But the overseers of the parish had him christened, being a foundling, JACK TWICKENHAM!

" His knowledge of men and manners was all acquired in the streets, or upon the banks of the river, as they crossed his path, therefore, observation, it might be read, rather than tuition. He listened to the stories of the watermen, when unemployed, for this class of society have their jokes and quaint sayings, like people of different grades in society ; and who also 'argufy the topic ' about the things going on in the great world, since the march of intellect has made such rapid progress in the minds of most men, with an earnestness of feeling commensurate with their betters.

" Time and tide wait for no man, according to an old proverb, and year after year rolled over Jack's head, with little improvement in his finances, or situation ; however, *poverty* did not stint his growth, and he obtained the appellation of a good looking, athletic lad. Fortune had never given him the *shadow* of a purse ; but Nature had been bountiful to him in the extreme, as a finely proportioned young man ; and had Jack have had the chance of having a suit of clothes made for him by those splendid apparel furnishers—a Stultz, or a Nugæ, who dress up so many *nothings* into something like the shape of men by the ingenuity of art and *padding*, the odds might have been in his favour, that he would have been taken for a man of more importance in the eyes of the population than the meagre, apologies, phantom-like, appearance of beings, who are classed as people of fortune and fashion.

" But, although he might have been called a sturdy John Bull sort of fellow, yet, he was never taunted with being a *grumbler*. ' All I want,' said he, when consulting old father Joe, on the subject, ' is plenty of customers to the boats, and that Jack-in-the-water should come in for the pence ! I have hitherto contrived to make a tidy living by putting THIS and THAT together, and never refusing any sort of job, heavy or light, so that it produced the cash.'

" ' That's the right mode, my boy,' answered old Joe, ' be a good lad, something will turn out for you, by and by, when you least expect it. You work very hard it is true, but it is a long lane that has no turning.'

"Old Joe Morris was looked up to as a bit of an oracle, amongst the bargemen and watermen on the Thames, and at the public-house door on a fine summer's day, along side of the river, when no work claimed his attention, or during a long winter's night, when stories beguile the time over their pots of porter and glasses of grog, if old Joe couldn't spin a yarn as long, or with as much talent as T. P. Cooke, in Black-eyed Susan, he, nevertheless, could tell some tough stories.

"Old Joe was also an arbitrator upon many knotty points respecting rowing-matches, and other events connected with the River Thames; and his decisions generally gave satisfaction. He was a kind of stud-book, in his own person—a racing, or rather a rowing calendar, upon the water. The pedigrees of all the crack-watermen were at his fingers ends—he knew all their bearings—their different styles—strength—and aquatic sporting tricks—equal to a Crockford or a Bland upon a Racecourse. He was a lively companion,—Joe could sing a good song—in short, his character went before him, that he was a fine, jolly, kind-hearted fellow, and ready to do a good turn, whenever it lay in his power; and in his peculiar situation in life—JOE MORRIS was looked upon as a hero. He was quite the idol of "pull-away Jack," the latter did not think there was half such a clever fellow as his old father, in the world :—

> All these to hear:
> Would Twickenham Jack seriously incline;
> But still the boat affairs would draw him hence,
> Which ever as he could, with haste dispatch,
> He'd come again, and with a greedy ear,
> Devour up old Joe's discourse.

"But an unexpected, accidental circumstance took place, in favour of Jack—which not only took him *out* of the water, but ultimately made a man of him. His high courage and humanity, were his recommendation to fame and fortune. Well may it be said, that from ' little causes, great events arise.'

"It should seem, that some dashing young sparks, who had been dining at Richmond—and who had also taken too much wine after it, nay, were completely inebriated; and quite incapable of conducting themselves with propriety, on the land; much more with correctness on the water, and to render it worse, altogether amateur rowers. In their violence and stupidity, and quarrelling amongst themselves, they struck against a boat, in which were seated, an elderly gentleman and his daughter, with such force, as nearly to upset it.

"This rude, ungentlemanly conduct, produced a strong remonstrance from the old man, to the youngsters in the eight-oared cutter: high words immediately ensued between them; the young lady became frightened—hastily left her seat in the scuffle—fell overboard, and was nearly drowned.

"The agony and exclamations uttered by the old gentleman, on seeing his only child in the water, and in danger of losing her life, cannot be portrayed: they were of the most heart-rending description.

"Jack, on witnessing the accident, plunged into the river, with the rapidity of lightning: he could swim like a fish—he soon came near the spot—and caught hold of the young lady, just as she was sinking, and nearly exhausted. He held her with one hand—and with the other, made his way safe to the shore, ran with his charge to the nearest tavern—called the land-lady and maid-servants—then darted off again, with the celerity of a greyhound for a medical man; he returned to the tavern, with the doctor, and soon had the satisfaction to learn, that the young lady had recovered, in some degree, from her exhausted state, and was likely to do well.

"The father also, upon ascertaining the report to be true, could not contain his joy, 'Brave, young fellow,' said he, 'you have recalled me from the grave! I should have died broken-hearted: I am sure I never could have survived her loss. It is impossible that I can ever repay you as you deserve in my estimation—to risk your own life, to preserve my dear child. Here, take my purse.'

"'Lord bless you, sir,' replied Jack, 'there was no risk about my life; I have only done my duty towards a fellow-creature. I can swim twice, three-times as far as I went, with ease; and you are quite welcome: but if you can spare a trifle for poor Jack-in-the-water, that will satisfy me, kind sir, and I will thank you kindly.'

"'A *trifle* for poor Jack,' said the old gentleman, 'I will make you a *rich* Jack. I am indebted to you for the future pleasure and happiness of my life. I will make it the best day's work you have ever done, since you was born. Here is my purse, and accept whatever sum is in it—you merit every reward that I can bestow upon you. Tell me who you are; what is your calling? that I may better your prospects in life. My daughter, when she is able to see you, shall make an acknowledgment for your humane exertions, in her behalf.'

"'I am a very poor young man, sir, with no other recom-mendation, that I knew of, sir, but my honesty; and am anxious to get a living in the best manner I am able. I never had a father, and mother.'

"'Not that you remember, perhaps,' replied the old gentle-man,—'left an orphan, I suppose.'

"'Yes, sir,' said Jack, ' you are right, I never knew them, nor any body else that I could call a relation: I am quite *alone* in the world. I get my bread out of doors, by the side of the river; but may God bless you, for your generosity to a poor lad.'

"'Well, never mind what you are—I will be a friend to you; and if your conduct hereafter merits my esteem, I will be as good as a father to you. In the first place, leave your *call-ing;* and with the trifling sum you may find in the purse, buy yourself some decent apparel; and, in the course of two or three days, call at my house in town. Here is my direction, handing his card over to Jack. 'MR. RUTHERFORD, *Dowgate Hill:*' where I shall be glad to see you,' at the same time, grasping the hand of Jack, with great warmth of friendship. The latter made a scrape with his foot, a nod with his head, something like a bow, and took leave of his benefactor.

"Upon the return of Jack to his wretched hovel of a lodging, he emptied the contents of the purse—and to his astonishment, his sparkling eyes beheld ten pounds. He could scarcely believe what he saw; and he counted them over and over again, before he could satisfy himself with the amount. Jack lost no time in buying himself a suit of clothes—two shirts, of a better texture than had ever covered his back—a hat—and every thing requisite to give him a *tidy,* if not a respectable appearance.

"In his new 'rig out,' he went for the opinion of his old father, Joe, before he would venture to show himself at the house of Mr. Rutherford—'How do I look in my new clothes?' said he, 'I should not like to disgrace the house of the gentleman, who has behaved so kind to me.'

"'*Look*, my boy, at all events, like a man,' answered Joe, delighted in the change of circumstances of the poor foundling child, that he had picked up at the ferry. 'But never mind your *looks*—don't get proud—and whatever good fortune awaits you—never let change of circumstances make you forget yourself. I think, saving the young lady's life, may do for you, more than you expect. Her father is a rich man, and may get you a good place in the Docks, or the Custom-House. So keep your weather-eye up, my boy.'

"At the appointed time, he presented himself at the merchant's door, and enquired with the greatest submission, not to say, accompanied with fright and apprehension, as to the reception he might meet with from Mr. Rutherford and his daughter. Jack gave a single knock at the door: or rather, no knock at all, but of the description which the late George Colman states,— 'as if the knocker, by chance, had slipped through his fingers!'

"Upon the servant opening the door to him, he scraped his foot, and bowed with the greatest modesty and diffidence. The servant seeing Jack was a novice, and a poor man, with an air of authority, asked his business, and what *name* he should tell his master.

"'Pull-away-Jack,' he replied, with a bow almost to the ground.

"'Pull-away-Jack!' echoed the man-servant—'Ha! ha! ha! What an odd name! I never heard of such a one before. You must be mistaken in the house. My master is too much of a gentleman to know such a person. So Mr. Pull-away-Jack, you had better try it on somewhere else. I should be afraid to take up such a name to my master. Ha! ha! ha! pull-away-Jack, indeed.'

" Such a reception confused the poor fellow beyond description : after some hesitation, scarcely knowing how to act, Jack said,—'be kind enough, sir, to inform your master, it is one, Jack Twickenham—from—who—.'

" 'I tell you again, my good man, you must be mistaken. What business can you have with my master? He is a very particular gentleman; and my orders are very strict, not to admit any person to him, without he has some knowledge of them.'

" ' Yes, sir,' replied Jack, ' he does know there is such a person : but I am quite a stranger to him. I only saw him two or three days ago; but he gave me his card, told me to call upon him, and here it is.'

" ' Aye, aye, that alters the case! you are right, my friend, and I will take it to my master. So come in, and remain in the hall, while I go to Mr. Rutherford.' Upon the livery-servant approaching his master, he observed, with a supercilious grin on his face, ' Here is a man, below stairs, sir, who calls himself Pull-away-Jack, wishes to see you; but I did not like to admit him.'

" ' And why not, sir?' I wish you was only half as good a man, or, lived so much in my memory, as Pull-away-Jack. Let me have no more impertinence, but shew the person up to me, immediately.'

" ' I beg your pardon, sir, what I did was for the best.'

" ' Well, then,' said Mr. Rutherford, ' behave better in future ; as it is my desire, that every person, who comes to enquire after me, may be treated with proper respect.'

" ' Who would have thought this pull-away-Jack was a man of so much consequence,' observed the servant, muttering to himself, in a whisper, as he quitted the apartment of his master.

" Jack's knees positively knocked together, he felt so much embarrassed, upon entering the elegant drawing-room of Mr. Rutherford, which the latter perceiving, said, ' compose yourself, my noble fellow.' Shaking him heartily by the hand. ' I am very glad to see you, sit yourself down, and make yourself as comfortable, and as easy in your mind, as if you was at home. I feel myself very much indebted to your courage and humanity ; and I am anxious to promote your interest. What can I do for you ?'

" ' I am thankful, sir, for your kindness already : I am well paid. Had the person have been a beggar, and in the same danger, I should have felt it my duty to have exerted myself to save the life of a fellow creature. It was neither trouble, risk, nor danger to me.'

"' Well said, my brave young man; I applaud your notions,' said Mr. Rutherford, ' you can read and write, I suppose ?'

"' Yes sir, a little,' answered Jack, ' I can write my own name, and another word or two, which Old Joe, the bargeman taught me, with a piece of chalk upon a board, when I had nothing else to do by the side of the river.   In return for Old Joe's kindness, I used to run of errands for him and his family. He has been very good to me—and many times he has filled my belly, when I must have gone without.   Several times, sir, in my life, I have been without the means to buy a bit of bread.'

"' Poor fellow! poor fellow!' escaped from the lips of Mr. Rutherford, with a sigh, ' that shall never happen again, while I live.   You must improve yourself, both in reading, and writing, as fast as you can ; and you shall not want for instruction. I have got a place for you, in my establishment.'

"' God bless you, sir,' replied Jack, ' I will pray for you the longest day I have to live : and you shall find me a grateful, and trusty servant.'

" At this juncture, entered Miss Rutherford, a very fine, prepossessing young lady ; who, if she could not be called a beauty, her amiability of character was beyond all praise: ' Here, Maria, my dear,' said her father, ' is the young man who saved your life! I told him to call and see me; and that you should thank him—I mean, reward him—.'

"' Thanks, my dear father ! *Thanks !*' replied Maria, ' would be a very inadequate reward, to the man who saved my life. But I do thank you, sir,' addressing Jack, ' in the warmest manner that my feelings are capable of conveying to you; so sincerely do I value your intrepidity.   I know it is my father's intention to better your condition in life; and he will provide you with a situation, that will enable you to live like a respectable man in society.'   Then taking a very handsome silk purse out of her reticule, with numerous pieces of money in it, presented it to Jack—' I beg your acceptance of this trifle, to purchase any little things that you may stand in need of—but the *purse*, I hope you will keep, as a remembrance for saving the life of a fellow creature.'

" Jack had not the slightest idea of the fine-looking female, which Miss Rutherford now appeared to him, when he had her in his arms, in the water, rescuing her from a watery grave— her countenance then, was as pale as death—her wet clothes clinging to her person—rendering her an object of pity—that he could scarcely believe it was the same person, added to the penetrating tones of the voice of Maria, and the warmth with which she addressed him; to assert he looked bashful—shy— confused—foolish, would not be half strong enough, to convey his real situation, and feelings, to the reader.

" Jack had never been in such company before in his life. He could not articulate a word, in return for the kindness and condescension which he had received, both from the father, and daughter—his tongue positively forsook its office; but after some little time, he faintly articulated, ' I—I—I—am but a poor ignorant young fellow, Miss! I do not know what to say. I am rewarded by your kind-hearted father, and yourself, much more than I required. I am satisfied, and I thank you, over and over again. But for the *purse*,' looking at it, and putting it to his lips, with a sigh that spoke volumes—' I never will part with it, but with my life.' This act of gallantry, —the effects of nature—let it be either one or the other, made his fortune.

" Jack's mode of distinguishing the value of the purse, *touched* the feelings of Maria, in a way that she could not have contemplated, ignorant as he might have been in the ways of the world, still there was *eloquence* about the transaction.

" 'I have a little advice to give you, young man, nay, a request,' observed Maria, with one of the most pleasing and persuasive tones ever uttered by any female—' that is, to be very circumspect in your conduct. Be particularly attentive to my dear father's instructions. The world you are now about to mix with is a very dazzling one, a different sphere altogether to what, hitherto, you have been acquainted with, and you must take care not to be deceived by the *shadows* instead of the substance. My father will have you instructed by clever and *patient* tutors; and so much interest do I feel in your future prosperity, that I will hear you repeat your lessons, whenever you think proper to ask me, in order that not a minute may be lost towards your capability to fill the situation which my father is about to confide in you; also, your improvement as a young man, and a recommendation to the good circles of society.'

" To have answered this delightful, most grateful creature, and the excellent advice given him by Miss Rutherford, might have shaken to the centre a much more experienced man than Jack. He blushed, stammered, bowed, looking up to the ceiling of the room, then down upon the floor, squeezed the rim of his hat almost to pieces unknowingly, his eyes full of tears; in short, description, however accurately penned, must fall short of the confused portrait of Pull-away Jack in the presence of Miss Rutherford. At last, almost blubbering, he said, 'I will do my best to please you and your father, miss, it is my duty to do so.' Then turning aside to wipe away the drops which were fast stealing down his iron cheeks ; such are the effects of kindness and generosity, where NATURE reigns paramount.

" ' I will provide a comfortable lodging for you, near to my house,' said Mr. Rutherford to Jack, ' and will also allow you a sufficient salary to render you respectable. You shall not want for my assistance, neither towards acquiring a good knowledge of accounts. For the first part of your servitude you will only have to attend upon me; until I find you capable of fulfilling a better situation in my establishment. However, I will point out to you in the clearest manner the things, or business, that you will have to transact, and I am not afraid but you will answer all my wishes.'

" Jack expressed his gratitude to Mr. Rutherford, and felt as light as a cork. The happiness which now seemed to surround him, gave him new life, a second creation; he became, as it were, regenerated, and to all intents and purposes, quite another sort of being.

" Jack entered upon the lodgings provided for him by his master, without delay, and the tailor of the latter, had orders to furnish him with a good suit of clothes, he, therefore, commenced his new career with no traces about him of his previous low condition in life. He was immediately placed under the requisite tutors to bring him forward as fast as possible, in order that he might be of service to himself and to his patrons. They were also requested to be *patient* with him upon all occasions, in consequence of his education having been totally neglected, and to explain every thing in the most clear and forcible mode in their power, that he might comprehend their meaning with ease and facility.

" Jack, who had been so long obscured in the walks of ignorance, and most likely, if the above *fortunate* accident for him, had not occurred, he might have remained in the *dark*, as to acquirements, all his life. His eyes were rapidly opened with surprise, unto the delightful subjects which were presented to his view; and he was determined to improve the *chance* which now displayed itself so favourably to himself. He had always been of an active mind, although he had not had the opportunity of improving it. He, therefore, listened with raptures to the instructions which were given to him daily, his improvement was great, his tutors were pleased with Jack's exertions and attention to their precepts, and his master was equally satisfied with his conduct. But Miss Rutherford was more than delighted with his quickness and perception, her views respecting Jack, were of another description, that will be clearly seen at a future part of the story, which might be out of place to develope here.

" Time rolled on pleasantly, and every minute was most sedulously employed by Jack to render himself of importance to his patron; he entered into all the spirit of the thing, and the incalculable advantage it might be to him at some future day, were the uppermost thoughts in his mind.

" In a short time his *readings* were considered tolerably good, his writing plain and distinct, united with quickness; but his knowledge of *accounts*, of which he seemed to be remarkably fond, rather astonished the whole of them, which endeared him to his master in so great a degree, as to make him a sort of confidential servant in money transactions. He was also, eminently indebted to Mr. Rutherford for an *insight* into those intricate matters for a novice to comprehend.

" But no one took so much pains with *Mr. Twickenham*, for that was the appellation he had acquired at the house of his benefactor, as did Miss Maria Rutherford. The improvement in his person, dress, manners, conversation, &c., were equally rapid; nay, in so great a degree, that it would have been a libel to have made a comparison between Mr. Twickenham, of Dowgate Hill, and ' *Jack-of-the-Ferry*,' so immense was the change altogether. But the *secret* of the ferry remained as close as possible within the hearts of the father and daughter.

" Maria had heard him repeat his lessons, looked over, and corrected, his writing for him, opened his eyes to a clear and distinct view of well-bred society in all its bearings; and to her great satisfaction, found, that not a single word she had ever bestowed upon him, in the form of instruction, but had indelibly been treasured up in his mind. But Miss Maria Rutherford before she could dismiss it form her bosom, found out that her pupil, her *preserver*, as she called him, was essential to her happiness by another *title;* she never told her love, it is true; neither did she ' conceal it in the bud,' yet any person conversant with the family might have perceived with half-an-eye, *who* was the object of her choice! The poor, but distant Jack-of-the-Ferry!

" There is little doubt but the latter saw it, and felt the passion with as much warmth as the love-sick Romeo; but then, he also felt, by comparison, his low origin and dependant state, when put in competition with Miss Rutherford, that it might be said of Jack, ' He pined in thought' with hopes that never could be realized.

" With a sightly person, a handsome fortune, and the only daughter of a rich merchant, it cannot excite any surprise that Miss Maria Rutherford in the bloom of youth, had a host of suitors aspiring to obtain her hand. Her father was continually assailed with offers to become the 'happy man!' Several of the proposals to wed his daughter were of the most undeniable nature in every point of view, but his answers to all of them—' The happiness of my daughter is nearest my heart; I will give her my advice on that most important event of her life, respecting her choice of a husband; but I will not use any thing like *command*, she shall be entirely free, and I am not afraid of her discretion, or judgment. Then I cannot be blamed; nor ill-nature, or selfish motives be levelled at my conduct!'

" All her suitors were rejected, and when pressed very closely on the subject by her admirers, her answer to one and all, was —' That she had made up her mind not to change her situation for several years:' in consequence of which declaration, they were all dismissed with politeness and respect.

" The frequent intercourse which Twickenham had with Maria, and with the permission of her father, was likely, in the end, to produce a much stronger attachment than applies to the term of friendship! A young lady reading to a gentleman, also pointing out to him a mode of life for his happiness; or *vice versa*, a gentleman acting upon the same principles to a female, often leads to the hymeneal altar. We read in Richardson's celebrated novel of Sir Charles Grandison, that the highly accomplished Baronet taught Clementina to read English, and admire the beauties of Shakspeare; at the same time, she lost her heart imperceptibly, and which had nearly led to tragical consequences. Therefore, it will not cause anything like astonishment to assert, that Miss Maria Rutherford was less invulnerable to the charms of love than her sex in general; or, that Twickenham was incapable of bowing to the powerful influence of NATURE!

" *Doomsday*, perhaps, might have arrived before the latter could have urged his suit, his own inferiority stared him too strongly in the face, he might have been spurned for his presumption, and he could not have *broken* silence in the character of a lover, admitting Maria to have been the sole object of his wishes. Twickenham had often and often expressed his *gratitude*, in the strongest manner possible, for her attention and kindness to promote his interests: and gratitude, it is said, is one of the stepping stones to love. His courage in every other point of view, might have been classed with a NELSON!

"He weighed all these things in his mind, one *rash* step— an offer of his hand to the daughter of his patron, might have blasted all his future prospects in life, driven him from her presence, and deprived him of the confidence and good-will of her father. He paused. This must account for his apparent *coldness;* yet this forbearance, on his part, added to the humility of his behaviour, when contrasted with the warmth which Miss Rutherford evinced for him, at length, secured his happiness, made him, not only a happy fellow, but a man of some weight in the eyes of his country, and the founder of a family!

" It has been laid down, as an argument, by the enlightened part of society, that if an individual possesses a ' strong mind,' and he feels determined to push his fortune if a chance is offered to him, that 'impediments vanish; and difficulties are overcome.' Cobbett, may be quoted as an instance, he acquired the French tongue while doing duty as a common soldier, in a sentry box; and ultimately published grammars both in the English and French languages; and numerous other instances might be produced to shew the advantages of *perseverance.* No sooner did the glorious opportunity present itself to Twickenham to extricate himself from misery and poverty, than he embraced it with the most enthusiastic ardour. A few days only, made a visible alteration in his person and knowledge; a month, did wonders; but at the expiration of a year, he had so far advanced in his studies, that, without offending propriety, he might have been viewed as a ' rising young man!' True, he, Jack, had, what is termed, the *stuff* about him, to become a prominent feature in life; but at one period of his career, the mere *anticipation* of such an event, would have been laughed at, and put down, as ' building castles in the air !'

" The *inherent* good qualities of Twickenham, soon began to display themselves, when he began to feel his way in society; and the remembrance of the kind offices which he had received at various times from old Joe and his wife, when he could not help himself, had fastened so strong upon his memory, that he lost no time in acting upon the old adage, that ' one good turn deserves another.'

"To the extent of their circumstances, they had behaved to Jack like parents; and if he did not intuitively feel, towards them, like a child does to his father and mother, according to the ties of nature, his real attachment towards the bargeman and his wife, was not a jot behind. He had been too well acquainted with *extreme* poverty, for nearly the whole of his life, and was well aware that they had a large family to provide for with very scanty means : they were also advancing in years, and that a trifling present, now and then, would not only prove acceptable, but, in a great measure, keep ' the wolf from the door !'

"To the credit of Jack, be it stated, the first few pounds that he had *saved* from his allowance, he did not forget his old friends at Twickenham. He called to see them, when he could spare the time conveniently; and although change of circumstances had given him the appellation of *Mister*, also dressed like a gentleman, yet in his respect and behaviour to Old Joe, and his wife, he was still as humble, when he appeared before them, as Jack-of-the-Ferry.

" He could not do much for them, yet it was a sort of hand-basket fortune to the old folks, for scarcely a week passed but they received a good joint of meat from him, half-a-pound of tea, sugar, cheese, a side of bacon, &c., that made their old hearts leap with joy, frequently accompanied with exclamations, ' God bless him, he was always a grateful boy ! He deserves good luck, he makes such good use of it !' ' And I hope, Joe,' said Bess, ' we shall live to see him ride in his carriage ! Ha! ha! ha ! what a thing that would be.'

" But to return to Miss Maria Rutherford, it is true, she might have had some severe struggles with herself respecting origin, family pride, degradation, and the sneers of the world to contend against ; but affection—true love, had taken such possession of her feelings as to triumph over all obstacles in favour of Twickenham. But then she wanted the resolution to make her passion known to the object of her choice. Delicacy, and all the refined notions of the sex forbade it. For years she never divulged her situation to her nearest female friend, her pride would not let her make a *confidante :* but the *secret* which had been so long confined within her bosom, at length burst forth like a raging fire ; her tender frame could not sustain the violent attack. An alarming fit of illness was the consequence ; she was confined to her bed, and her life in danger. The art of the physicians was of no avail ; and her complaint was pronounced out of the power of physic to cure !

> So holy and perfect is my love,
> And I in such poverty of grace,
> That I shall think it a most plentious crop,
> To glean the broken ears after the man,
> That the main harvest reaps : loose now and then
> A scatter'd smile, and that I'll live upon.

" ' My dear Maria,' said her father, ' the medical men, who have attended you, observe that you are not in want of medicines, but something weighs heavily on your mind, which is the real cause of your illness. I have always found you an ingenuous girl, therefore, in me, not only as your father, but friend, confide the source of your affliction. Treat me with candour !'

" Sighs, tears, and convulsive sobs, for several moments, prevented Maria from answering her indulgent parent, ' You have been to me from the moment I was born up to the present period of my life, dear father,' replied Maria, ' generous and liberal in the extreme ; but much as your love for me exists, and the liberality of mind which you have displayed upon the most trying occasions, I am afraid—I tremble for the consequence, when you become acquainted with the extent of my secret ; and that you will tear yourself away from me in anger.' Here she paused for some time. ' I am ashamed to tell you of my weakness, degradation, and want of respect to myself and family. For such, I anticipate, you will call my conduct. My choice is made, and the only man that I can ever give my hand to as a wife. But if you decide against me, if it breaks my heart, no one shall know it, and I will keep my sufferings within my own bosom. You shall never hear a sigh escape from my lips ; I will also endeavour to assume a cheerfulness in society although I possess it not. But I will not marry any man, however much I love him, without the free consent of my father : this resolution I would rather die than swerve from. His name—is—is—is—I cannot speak it, my courage fails me.'

" ' I must hear his name, my child,' replied her father, in the mildest tone ; ' Come, compose yourself—tell me !'

" ' His name is—is—is—Mr.—John—Twickenham,' answered Maria, hiding her face ; ' my mind, at all events, is relieved from a burthen, if I am not made happy by the declaration of my passion ; but Twickenham is entirely ignorant of it, I have never given him the slightest hint.'

" This declaration appeared to deprive her father of his faculties, and for the instant he stood motionless, when he observed, in a sorrowful accent, ' My poor girl, my beloved Maria, I must own this circumstance seriously affects me, the disparagement is great indeed. It is true, it was my intention to have forwarded his views in society on account of saving your life; but I could not have anticipated that I should have been called upon to have given him my daughter! However, I will not decide hastily, nor harshly on the matter; such a subject requires great consideration on both our parts, and some little time must elapse before I can give a decisive answer. I am very glad that Twickenham is in the dark upon the matter at issue; and that you have not made the first advances. I must confess, you have opened your mind to me like a good, prudent girl: and that will have great weight in my decision.'

" Her father was not one of those flinty-hearted old gentlemen that we see depicted in a novel, or who struts his hour upon the stage, like a raving lunatic, but on the contrary, Mr. Rutherford was a sensible considerate man.

" In point of argument, there was nothing so very objectionable against the match, if we pass over the obscurity, origin, and want of property on the part of Twickenham, and to a sensible mind, where the happiness of a beloved daughter was at stake, it might be said, he had been some years upon trial, and not found wanting in the scales of quality, either as to manners, sense, or good conduct. Twickenham also had been moulded to their wishes; he had likewise been taught under their eye all the acquirements requisite for a man to pass muster in the good circles of society.

" Respecting the *weakness*, infatuation, gratitude, or love, displayed by Miss Rutherford in making such a *choice*, and descending from her sphere in life, the celebrated Duke of Buckingham observed, 'That LOVE, Almighty LOVE, has made *Solomon* commit idolatry; David contrive a murder; and all the world, at some time or other, *play* the fool!' It is likewise well-known, nay, publicly declared in a court of justice, that the mind of a distinguished military marquis was, at one period of his life, so much overwhelmed with the *passion* of love, that he rushed at the head of his division, into the hottest fire of the enemy, more like the violence of a madman than the coolness of a general; and the lady, (the mother of a family,) the object of his wishes, resorted to prayers, day and night, to overcome the power of an unruly attachment towards the marquis, which agitated her bosom: therefore, some little allowance may be made for the amiable Miss Rutherford:—

Things base and vile, holding no quantity,
LOVE can transpose to form and dignity:
LOVE looks not with the eyes, but with the mind,
And therefore is wing'd Cupid painted *blind*.
Nor hath love's mind of any judgment taste,
Wings, and no eyes, figure unheedy haste:
And therefore is Love said to be a child,
Because in CHOICE he often is beguil'd!

"*Twickenham*, it should seem, was a young man, of all others, most likely to make the daughter of Mr. Rutherford, happy—if *love* did not reign paramount in his heart—*gratitude* must indelibly have been placed there—elevated from beggary to affluence—removed from ignorance to a state of sensibility and knowledge, in fact: he was indebted to his patron and his daughter for every thing in life.'

"However, Mr. Rutherford was determined to arrive at the truth of the matter in doubt; and in the course of conversation, one day, observed to Twickenham, as a touchstone of his feelings,—'I think, I could recommend to you an excellent match, whereby you would increase your importance in the eyes of society; add riches to your coffers; and ultimately, set down in life, happily, and contented; and the lady I am about to propose to you is of such inestimable value in her own person, as to be worth all the other considerations put together.'

"Twickenham appeared greatly agitated; and some time occurred before he could make a reply. 'Your offer, sir, I must admit, is a splendid one; but let me beg to observe, you always instilled upon my mind the advantages of truth; therefore, with the most respectful deference, permit me to say that circumstances, feelings—nay, a prior attachment, is a prohibition to such a material change in my life, that I should become a miserable being, instead of a happy man.'

"'Indeed!' said Mr. Rutherford. 'I certainly did not expect such an answer; but is the lady you allude to, aware of your passion? Is there reciprocity in your love?'

"'The lady is quite ignorant of my attachment; I never dared to presume to mention it to her. Therefore, I cannot say a word about reciprocity.'

"'This is candid, fair, and honorable, I must admit,' replied Mr. R. 'Do I know the female in question? Have I ever seen her; because I might be inclined to say a word or two in your behalf—as I am always anxious to promote your welfare?'

"'You have known the lady for a long time, sir; but I cannot flatter myself that you will give me a *recommendation* in that quarter? I do not expect it, however great your kindness towards me! There is an insurmountable bar between us. Because———

"'What! State your reasons,' said Mr. Rutherford.

"'My origin—obscurity of birth—and very low situation in life, during my earlier years, love always checked my presumption, and paralyzed my tongue whenever I was tempted to propose such a match; and, therefore, the *secret* of my attachment must, for ever, remain enveloped in my bosom; and most likely descend with me into the grave.'

"'Then you will not name the lady?' asked Mr. R.

"'To refuse you anything, sir, would be next to an impossbility to me—being under so many obligations to your kindness; but in the present instance, I cannot—dare not—I have not the courage ! Your displeasure might overwhelm—if not deprive me of your patronage, and order me for ever out of your sight.'

" ' Say no more !' answered Mr. Rutherford, ' I perceive your agitation ! I know it all, and I must applaud your circumspection and good conduct. But it is quite clear to me, that Miss Rutherford is the object of your choice. Be it so ! I will not check, nor disappoint your ambition ; and regardless of the sneers of society, my mind is made up—I will give you the hand of my daughter in marriage. A *richer* match might have been procured for her, there is no doubt ; but a *better* man, I am free to say, according to the best consideration I have given to the subject cannot be found to make her a good husband. Twickenham, you saved her life ; that circumstance will never be obliterated from my memory—then my only request is, that you will, for the remainder of her existence, make it happy and contented: as she may never have the slightest occasion to regret that she had wrongly estimated the man whom she had selected as her companion and protector. Here Maria !'

" Upon the entrance of his daughter, he caught hold of her hand, and presented it to Twickenham. ' I give my daughter freely to you—my heart applauds the deed ; and may every blessing await upon your union.' To describe the joy upon the countenances of Maria and her lover—the happiness of their minds ; and their anxiety to thank the liberality of feeling displayed by the father of Maria, is impossible ; but on their going to reply :—

" ' Not another word upon the subject ; ' said Mr. R. ' but from this hour, I look upon you as my SON-IN-LAW ! and also a *Partner* in the establishment.'

> How all the other passions, fleet to air,
> As doubtful thoughts, and rash embraced despair,
> And shuddering fear, and green-eyed jealously.
> O love, be moderate, allay thy ecstasy,
> In measure rein thy joy, scant this excess ;
> I feel too much thy blessing, make it less,
> For fear I surfeit !

" For years afterwards, the names of RUTHERFORD and TWICKENHAM were well known as the " Great House," near the Royal Exchange ; and when the senior partner was called to the tomb of his fathers—*Twickenham* ALONE, stood equally important in the eyes of the commercial world, on the change, embellished with civic honors, and in the House of Commons as an M. P. Several children blessed their union ; and the once *"poor Jack of the ferry"* became the FOUNDER of a family of repute, in the greatest city of the world. Such are the chances attached to life."

After breakfast, the next morning, *Turf*, who was a decided angler, proposed to the Pilgrims to have a day's fishing in the

the neighbourhood of Hampton; it being considered one of the best places on the river for good sport. The proposition met with approbation from the whole of the party.

"I am not very fond of the sport," said Makemoney, "and as to the character of a fisherman, I have not the slightest pretensions; there is nothing of the Izaak Walton about my composition; but nevertheless, I will not be singular upon the occasion; and I have no doubt but the variety of it, will afford me plenty of amusement."

"It is a most healthful pastime," observed Flourish, "and tends to longevity in a great degree; a proof of which is not wanting: according to Walton, Dr. Nowell lived to the great age of ninety-five years, forty-four of which he had been dean of St. Paul's Church; and that his age had neither impaired his *hearing*, nor *dimmed* his eyes, nor weakened his memory, nor made any of the faculties of the mind weak or useless. 'Tis said, that *angling* and *temperance* were great causes of these blessings' Besides, according to Plutarch, angling was a favorite amusement in the days of Marc Antony and Cleopatra, and that in the midst of their wonderful glory, they used angling as a principal recreation."

"True, every syllable of what you have uttered is the perfect truth," answered Sprightly; "and to add to your assertion, Izaak Walton also lived to the age of *ninety-three*!"

"I am pleased to find that my friends are such advocates for angling; and I must acknowlege," urged Turf, "that I never feel anything like so much gratified as when I am by the side of a river, engaged in the delightful sport." Singing to Makemoney:—

In the morning, up we rise, soon as daylight peeping,
Take a cup to cheer the heart, leave the sluggard sleeping,
Forth we walk, and merry talk, to some pleasant river,
Near the THAMES silver streams, there we stand, rod in hand,
Fixing right, for a bite, all the time the fish allure,
Come leaping, skipping, bobbing, biting,
Dangling at our hooks secure;
With this pastime, sweet and pure, we could fish for ever.

Turf, from his knowledge and experience as an angler, caught lots of fish; and Flourish and Sprightly were likewise tolerably successful; but Makemoney could not get a single *nibble*—a *bite*, was out of the question. Indeed, the mind of the latter was more occupied with the scenery and the different parties, passing up and down the river, than paying attention to his rod and line. "How is it?" said the old citizen, "that you are all so fortunate; and I am so very unlucky?"

"You do not *woo* the fish. You do not offer them any attraction," answered Turf—"the fish at times, require as much *coaxing* as the ladies before they are caught! Ha! ha! ha!

"If that is the case," replied Makemoney, "I am rather

PILGRIMS in DIFFICULTIES at WINDSOR.

afraid the chance is against me; but I will endeavour to follow your advice." Shortly afterwards Makemoney began to cry out, " Halloo! halloo! get your landing-net, Flourish; by the tugging, or weight at the end of my line, I must have caught a *whale*! Look out! look out! or else I shall lose the monster."

They were all directed to the calls of the old citizen, to witness what sort of a fish he was about to get into the landing-net.

"Gently! gently!" said Turf, "take care he does not break your line; be ready with the net, Mr. Flourish?"

Curiosity was now at the utmost stretch, to behold the prize; when the head of an old dog was perceived just above the water. " What the deuce have we got here? I never saw anything like it at Billingsgate," observed Makemoney.

The whole of them set up a loud laugh at the dog's head. " Not at Billingsgate?" said Turf. " No, no, more likely at Sharp's Alley, Cow Cross; but it has been rather too long in the water to make————"

" Confound the beast," replied Makemoney, a little out of temper for the moment, finding the laugh against him, and instantly pulling out his pen-knife, cut the line, " let the hook and dog go to the bottom, I will not use it any more."

In a short time afterwards, they returned to the Red Lion, at Hampton, to sup off their dish of fish; to spend the evening comfortably together; to laugh over the adventures of the line and rod; and on finishing the evening, Turf caught hold of the old citizen's hand in the most friendly manner, singing,

> " Then praise the jolly fisherman,
>   Who takes what he can get;
> Still going on his better's plan,
>   *All's* fish that comes to net.

Ha! ha! ha!"

" Have your joke." replied Makemoney; " I will not be angry with you, but after all, I have acted according to the hint on the board—FISH *may not be caught here.* Ha! ha! ha!"

The next day, Windsor Castle was the great object of attraction with the Pilgrims; the morning was inviting, the *row* up the river truly pleasant, and every thing went on as agreeably as they could wish; but during the time they were resting upon their oars, Makemoney was describing to the ladies some anecdotes, connected with the above ancient palace of royalty. " Windsor Castle," said he, " is thus described by Hogarth, in his Analysis of Beauty; it is a noble instance of *quantity.* The hugeness of its few distinct parts, strikes the eye with uncommon grandeur at a distance as well as nigh. It is quantity with simplicity which makes it one of the finest objects in the kingdom; though void of any regular order of architecture."

A boat full of Eton boys, whom it should seem, were determined for a *spree*, rowed right against them, as if by accident: and instead of apologizing for their rude behaviour, although they saw females in the boat; one of the scholars, a young sprig of nobility: one of those juvenile creatures, born with a silver spoon in his mouth, only to know misery and poverty by name; to threaten and command; to throw people out of window, if it pleased their fancy, and afterwards tell the waiter to charge them in the bill; to wrest off knockers from doors, at the very witching time of night; to ring bells, and alarm the nervous of both sexes in their beds; and other little harmless pranks, the mere effects of boyhood—and matters of no consequence to persons of rank in society. The *Etonians* looked upon Make-money as one of the right sort of plainly dressed folks that a *lark* might be practised upon with impunity, thus addressed him, —" I say, old tradesman, mind where you are driving with your flat-bottomed barge, do you want to upset us *children*? Attack your match, and don't meddle with us boys!"

" Better language, if you please, young gentlemen," said Makemoney, " such phrases do not become you, I'm sure; after endeavouring to insult us! Eton, I am aware, is distinguished for its scholastic acquirements; but if such rude conduct is a specimen of its good breeding: I shall pronounce it the worst seminary in the kingdom."

" Good breeding, indeed? Ha! ha! ha! A coalheaver like you, talking of what you do not understand. Why you don't know the right end of an oar. What do you call that *lump* upon your shoulders? But if you are not civil, we'll sprinkle your dusty jackets." Then in a low tone of voice to his companions, said, " let us give it to them." This was the signal for a row—when they began to splash the Pilgrims with water, without any further ceremony—and also putting themselves in fighting attitudes.

This outrageous conduct of the Eton boys so enraged Make-money, that in his exertions to catch hold of the ringleader, he missed his aim, and fell into the water.

This accident produced loud shouts and peals of laughter, during the time Flourish and Turf were rescuing Makemoney from his perilous situation; if not from a watery grave! The Eton scholars singing—" Overboard he vent; Chip, chow, cherry chow, fol-de-dol-de-da! How drunk the old chap is; well, he is only mixing his grog; perhaps adding a little water to his heavy whet! It will *cool* his courage, at all events. Ha! ha! ha!" Then dashing their oars into the water—splashing the Pilgrims all over. But to prevent any mischief to themselves, they began to row off with all their strength, and by way of a finish to the spree, said—" Good night, old butter-fir-kin; we wish you better luck another time. Talk of good breeding—' *Odi profanum vulgus!* ' " They were out of sight

before any redress could be obtained ; indeed, the Pilgrims were glad to make for the shore, to quiet the fears of the females, and also to get dry clothes for Makemoney.

When the effects of passion had subsided in the old citizen's breast, and he had procured a dry suit of clothes, he laughed heartily at the adventure over his grog ; "it might have been worse," said he, " I have been more frightened than hurt, it is true ; and I recollect I was once a boy myself, I'll forget it."

" Yes, sir," replied Flourish, " it is the enthusiasm and excitement of youth ; the *dry* studies of Horace, Juvenal ; and the Elements of Euclid, Ovid, &c., require some relaxation now and then, and these lads must *unbend,* and have a whiff or two, and a whet,—as they consider themselves great cigars, either on or off the water ! which makes them regardless of danger, or the consequences ; so that fun and mischief are the result. It is not fifty to one but some of those boys, at a future period, may be gravely sitting, as the judges of the land in the Courts of Law ; or gracing the woolsack, as sapient legislators ! Boys will be boys—and it would be loss of time to think any more about it."

" Fond as I am of the Thames," said Makemoney, " I have had rather too much of *water* this time ; but those who play at bowls, must expect rubs. Ha ! ha ! ha !"

" To prevent your being liable to cold," said Sprightly, " from your sudden immersion in the River, I propose that we return to town by the first stage-coach, and the sooner you arrive at home the better, where you can make yourself so much more comfortable." This proposition was acceded to—and in the course of a few hours—the ears of the Pilgrims were delighted once more with the sound of Bow bells.

CHAPTER XIII.

The PILGRIMS interested at a Rowing-match, between " Bill Prizeman's boy, and Coat and Badge Dick."   The spirit of the thing!   Times and manners.   Civility costs nothing.   A dialogue between a coalheaver and an old maid ; or, torturing the English language.   The dog and the hat ; a tiny bit of the marvellous!   A night scene on the banks of the Thames. —VAUXHALL to wit.   MAKEMONEY out of humour with the altered appearance of things ; or, nothing like by-gone days at the gardens.   SPRIGHTLY, vice versa, full of enjoyment with the present period ; and FLOURISH exulting, that " a bird in the hand is worth two in the bush?"   TURF, all happiness, contented with the idea of taking things as you find them.   Unexpected meeting with old friends and acquaintances.   The hoax ; Flourish and Makemoney the victims!   Women and wine—a row—the Pilgrims in trouble! an every day sort of thing at places of amusement.   " We won't go home till morning!   We won't go home till morning, &c."

Mirth admit me of thy crew?

THE attention of the PILGRIMS had been occupied for a short time, about a rowing-match, Flourish having backed a young waterman well known on the Thames as ' Bill Prizeman's boy !' against ' coat and badge Dick.'   They were both *crack* watermen ; and both equally successful as to a variety of matches they had won.   The amateurs of rowing were now anxious to ascertain which was the best man?   The Thames displayed a great deal of gaiety upon the occasion ; several of the different yacht clubs in their sailing boats : the cutter lads, wherries, &c., and both sides of the river lined with barges full of well-dressed persons to witness the contest.

The " boy," was rather the favorite, from the possession of strength, length, and wind ; but coat and badge Dick, it was contended knew the River much better than his opponent—he was up to all the windings of it—current, &c., to a T.   Sprightly felt a great interest in the match, and supported the opinion of his friend Flourish ; and Makemoney was induced on the same account to become one of the party.   But the old citizen preferred being safe, rather than trusting himself amongst the harem-scarem sort of fellows which are generally to be met with in boats on the river, on those sort of days, more especially after his late

The PILGRIMS at a FO[.]RAE

ducking at Windsor; therefore, he took his station on a heavily-laden coal-barge, that nothing but a violent tempest could shift from its moorings. Besides, Makemoney was fond of the mixture of society at such times; and the dialogue which passed between them afforded him considerable amusement.

An old maid who was equally anxious for the safety of her person, and being anxious to witness the match, Prizeman's boy being a near relation, wished to be perfectly assured by the coalheavers, before she parted with her money, whether there was any danger?

"Lord bless you, marm," answered one of the coalheavers, "you are as safe as if you *wos* in your coffin."

"I don't like that allusion," said the old maid, "I do not wish any remembrances connected with death."

"You may depend, marm, the greatest conwulsion on the earth would not stir a single bit of coal! My pal, Jem, and I have made this ere barge as fast as a rock. Here you can see every thing *wot* takes place without the help of a telescope; and also hear *wot* directions are given to them precious bits of stuff, who are about to enter upon this prime contest, without the help of an ear-trumpet."

"I hope I shall find what you say to be the truth; because I have been deceived before now, by men promising what they never perform."

"There is no deception about Jem and I, marm—no *bonneting*—only ask the company, (which is the genteelest on the river) we are patronized by nothing else but the *swells* upon these ere occasions. Jim and I would not take any person on board but wot are the right sort—we have nothing belonging to us of the *blackguard* but snuff; perhaps marm, you would like to take a pinch, it is the real *blackguard*, only so by name— being taken by the king upon his throne, as a most delicious treat for his nose—it wos given to us by the best gentleman *scull* on the river, my lord Goldring! O here he comes—this way, my lord—make way for his lordship! This here is the only barge for the out-and-outers.

An interruption was put to this dialogue, between the old maid and the coalheaver, for a little time, in consequence of a man's hat being blown off his head into the river, from the next barge, and a dog jumping off to get it—"I say governor," said one of the black diamonds, "you wouldn't be so foolish as to let that ere dog get hold of your castor!"

"Why, where's the harm: the hanimal won't hurt it?"

"If you are spooney enough to let him get hold of your tile, he will make a meal of it, and no mistake. He has not had a bit of grub for the last three days; and he is the most *ferociousest* dog in London; he is vorse than a wolf. I knows him well: he is quite the terror of Cow's Cross! and the *knacker* people have offered a reward to any hindividual who will kill him, and bring his head to them. It was only a few days ago that he bolted with the biggest part of a horse, and got clear off with it! He can kill *one hundred rats* in eight minutes, like winking; and kill anything else if it comes in his way.'

" That ere is not the dog I tell you as how once more; and if you insists upon taking away his character, I will shove your *nose* into the river; and then I knows your body must follow it, but I will charge you nothing for *bathing.* So don't kick up any more row about my dog; he is a Newfoundland, and the animal wot you takes him for is a *terrier!*"

" I have no doubt but he is a new found dog; that is a genteel word for *prigging* a tyke. You never saw him before to-day, I knows—so shut your mouth and be quiet, if you wishes to be safe: and not get into trouble. So be off while your shoes are good. We knows how you get your living."

" O dear," said the old maid, "I am quite alarmed; I hope there will be no quarrelling—we may all be drowned! I dread coroner's inquests, I do indeed!"

" No Marm; its only wot we calls a bit of civil jaw—it is wot we calls whopping a man with your *chaffer!*"

" Chaffer! chaff—what do you mean by that phrase—I cannot understand it?"

" Why marm, in genteel company, it is wot the female vomen call—*red rag!*"

" Dear me! how very odd; you would puzzle a dictionary maker."

" To cut the matter short—it means, marm, the *tongue!*"

" Bless my soul! what a strange world we live in. I don't know my own language!"

" Here's a start for you; wot chaps to pull! my eyes, how sweetly they cut along: six to four on the boy."

" Who do you want to *swindle;* are you upon the look out to pick up green horns? He's no boy; he's the father of a family. Call him a boy? where will you get your men I wonder?"

" Hold your jaw, Mr. Wiseacre; he is Bill Prizeman's boy, that's wot I mean; and he has won every thing upon the river, from Limehouse hole to Richmond Bridge. He is the out-and-out crack waterman on the Thames—either for sculls or oars, and I say, six to four he wins."

" Huzza! huzza! Bill Prizeman's boy has made a man of himself to-day. See! see, he is winning the match like fun; and giving Coat-and-Badge the go-by. It is quite play to Prizeman's boy; but Coat-and-Badge is nothing else but a good un! They can't both win—I wishes they could."

The contest, which was a very sharp one, was decided in favor of Prizeman's boy, amidst the shouts of the spectators; and to the complete satisfaction of Flourish, who had won a tolerable sum of money.

Just as Makemoney was about to quit the barge, he was

hailed by Sprightly and Flourish in a boat, to accompany them to Vauxhall Gardens, to meet Turf by appointment.

"I am now ready, sir, to fulfil my promise," said Flourish, "a handsome supper, at my expense; and a glass or two of champagne shall not be wanting to give a zest to the evening's entertainment, I have no doubt but we shall meet with some of the right sort of folks to spend a merry, happy, and gay evening together."

"I am quite ready," answered the old Citizen—"it was in my early days, a favorite place of amusement of mine, after business, and the fatigues of the day were over."

The merits of Prizeman's boy, and Coat-and-Badge Dick occupied their attention until they arrived at Vauxhall stairs.

The Pilgrims, after promenading the gardens for a short period—viewing the company—and different groups who had assembled together for the evening; "I may well assert," observed Makemoney, 'O the days when I were young!' VAUXHALL then, appeared to every visitor a decided place of fascination—a sort of Elysium—and all the cares of the world left outside of the gardens. Gaiety was the leading feature—heart'sease in abundance—pleasure in all its variety of taste—and happiness seemed to reign triumphant upon every brow. Hours flew away like minutes; and day-light intruded itself upon the minds of the spectators with astonishment. Yet, I must confess, the entertainments were not half so grand, nor half so good—but the visitors appear to me completely changed altogether! They walk about, appear indifferent; seem *stiff*, formal: and not inclined to recognize each other upon equal terms; but at the period I allude to, the company appeared like one family! Hail fellow, well met. Unbending with sociality of disposition and good nature; joining in the lively dance: and mirth and humour the presiding deities over the festive scene. Such a change is not at all the fault of the proprietors; on the contrary, they have out-heroded herod in their exertions to produce novelties: and to furnish every sort of intellectual amusement to attract the public to visit Vauxhall Gardens."

"I am not at all inclined," replied Flourish, "to dispute your assertions: and also to give you the benefit of your experience to its utmost extent; at the same time, my worthy friend, I am anxious not to convey the slightest affront whatever: but sir, you do not see with the same eyes—all your *boyish* friends have become old men—*repetition* palls upon the mind—and you have become tired as it were of your once delight and pleasure. But we, sir, are full of raptures with the gardens, and give it the preference to any other place of amusement of the kind, connected with the metropolis."

"A truce to argument!" cried Sprightly, "let us enjoy the illuminated scene as it presents itself—I never felt more delighted in my life—but let us all be free in our promenades. Yet we must make it a point to meet altogether at supper."

" Agreed," replied Turf.

" With all my heart," answered Makemoney.

" The Duchess for a rump and a dozen," said Sprightly, " and her stylish daughters."

" Then I'll be after them," replied Flourish, "I *owe* them something. But you are mistaken, I think. However, I'll put up the game; and bring down the birds, if I can. So excuse me, gents., I am off."

" Egad," observed Sprightly, " how very odd, I perceive a young lady a most intimate acquaintance of mine, walking without a companion. That must not be—the laws of gallantry will not permit it. I will just ask after her health, when I will return to you immediately, uncle, I don't like to leave you, but—"

" I'll be hanged if there an't an old acquaintance of mine— vulgarly called *slippery* Dick. I would not be seen with him but he owes me a handsome bet; and if I don't get it now, months may occur before I meet with him again. He *twigs* me; and is trying to bolt! I know you will pardon me, Makemoney; but necessity has no law. I would not have left you under any other circumstances," said Turf.

Makemoney found himself *alone*, in the midst of a vast throng of visitors. " 'Pon my word," he exclaimed, " this is very pleasant, but I suppose I must, like my brother Pilgrims, recognize *somebody ;* or else I must remain standing here like a finger-post. But no matter—I like to see the young ones enjoy themselves; therefore I will amuse myself in the best way I can."

Flourish, with almost the speed of a greyhound, ran over the gardens in search of the Duchess and her daughters, who had occupied his attention so much at Greenwich, anticipating some agreeable conversation with those sprightly females; and also with the hopes of obtaining a little more insight into their characters; and if the Duchess might in any way allude to the loan of the five pound note. But nothing like the gay Duchess met his eyes : although, in several instances, he *stared* some of the ladies out of countenance. At length he gave up the pursuit as hopeless; and began to entertain an idea that it was a pleasant *hoax* played off on him, by his friend Sprightly. Nevertheless, he did not like to give up the ' look out' altogether, and while he was holding a sort of parley with himself on the subject, Turf touched him on the shoulder—" what, at *fault*, my worthy Pilgrim?" said he, " Have you lost the scent ? Are the birds flown away? Ha! ha! ha!"

" I am at fault," replied Flourish, and " I cannot be put right to night; but never mind, I perceive Makemoney in rather a solitary mood, as if he was looking out for us. Can't we have a bit of fun with the old citizen? Nothing more than a harmless joke! How can we manage it? And Sprightly will not be implicated in it!"

"I have it! Ha! ha! ha!" answered Turf, "it will serve to amuse us after supper, over our wine!" Turf, who never stood upon niceties, and quite careless as to the remarks of any by-standers upon his behaviour, recognizing an old acquaintance of his, one of the *sisterhood,* but no *Nun,* went immediately up to her—"You see that old gentleman, with a good-natured face, *loitering* about the gardens, he belongs to our party, and we want to have a bit of fun with him, therefore, go and claim an acquaintance with him, but treat him as a gentleman, and try to persuade him, in a lady-like manner, that you know him very well; that once he was a *particular* friend of your's, and seriously enquire, of him, the reason of his *cruel* desertion? He is rather hasty in his temper at times, and this sort of unexpected attack will have the desired effect! But when we return to him, and pretend to detect him in making an *assignation* with you, then make your escape as soon as possible.

"Penelope ———, is a clever woman, and possesses superior talents for an actress, and had she have taken the right course in life, might have been an ornament to the stage; but owing to, what she terms an 'amiable weakness' in the first instance, proved her overthrow. Her situation, at the present moment, speaks for itself. But her manners are good, and she will play what 'is set down for her' to the very life. She is also fond of a joke, and will enter into the spirit of it."

"Excellent!" cried Flourish, "it would not be a bad incident for a comedy!"

Makemoney, who had been musing for some little time, not exactly in what is termed a *trance,* but scarcely knowing how to pass his time, during the absence of his brother Pilgrims, was then listening to a song in the Orchestra, viewing the transparencies, and other attractive features, and strolling up and down the different walks, when the young female alluded to, dressed in the very first style of fashion, thus accosted him—"I beg pardon, Sir, but you do not seem to recollect the face that you have so often praised, flattered, and caressed with feelings of delight. But I regret to say, that in my eyes your character seems changed altogether, and you now appear more like the 'Knight of the woeful countenance,' than the hitherto laughing, jolly fellow at the festive board. Yet, perhaps, I can account for it, you have lost an intimate acquaintance, a dear *friend!* which has produced that settled melancholy on your brow. I am sorry to see it!"

Makemoney could scarcely believe his own ears; and after recovering himself from such a sudden unexpected attack, he briefly answered—"True, madam, I am looking after a *friend!*"

2 s

" And so am I, my dear sir," replied Penelope, in a most plaintive tone of voice, " therefore, if we put our *losses* together, we can afford, to each other, consolation, and enjoy the luxury of woe undivided. There is a delightful little box which I see yonder, in which we can have a *tete-a-tete* : dissipate our grief over sparkling champagne, or arrack punch, if you give it the preference, as I always leave the choice of liquors, or wine, to the good taste of gentlemen ! A little refreshment will be necessary, and as I do not wish to be extravagant, a cold chicken, some ham, a cucumber, &c., will, I feel assured, render the evening truly pleasant to us both !"

" Amazement !" cried Makemoney, " you are taking liberties with an entire stranger ; and also making more free than welcome ! And, I desire, madam, you will quit my presence immediately. You are an improper character to be seen with ! Retire immediately, or else———"

" A stranger !" answered Penelope, putting up her handkerchief to her eyes, as if in tears ; " is it come to this ! after your expressions of love to your dear *Pen.* as you used to call me. Such base ingratitude and desertion, will, positively, be the death of me ! (Laying hold of Makemoney's arm,) I am getting faint, my head turns round, I shall expire before my wrongs are revenged ! Has the poor, forlorn, deserted Penelope, no friend to stand by her at this unprotected moment ? Oh ! oh ! oh ! I shall die !"

A small crowd began to gather round them, when at the juncture, like good actors waiting for their *cue*, Turf and Flourish appeared in sight to render assistance to Penelope.

" My dear friend, said Turf to Makemoney, " what is the matter ? What have you done to this young damsel in distress ?" Penelope throwing herself into the arms of Turf.

" Nothing !" replied Makemoney, quite out of breath with rage ; "it is all a mystery to me. The woman is out of her senses ! Positively insane ! I never saw her before in my life. It is a mistake altogether."

" Is it nothing to desert the dearest female friend you ever had in your life ;" answered Penelope, sobbing loudly. " Do you call it nothing ? You base, ungrateful man ! But you shall rue it ! I will have justice done me. Fine old London gentleman as you are. I will not stay in the horrid monster's company any longer. Pray, sir, let me have a little air, or else, I shall be suffocated with grief."

Turf immediately led her a little distance from Makemoney ; but she immediately returned, full of spirit, and said to the latter, " As you have promised to meet to-morrow night 'by moonlight *alone*,' to make amends for your tragedy conduct, which has lacerated my tender feelings beyond description, I will not expose you any more before such a number of persons."

Penelope was out of sight in an instant.

"Such assurance is not to be borne," observed Makemoney "I never promised to meet the wretch—the wicked im postor."

"Some of the crowd began to laugh heartily, and enjoy the row ; others interfering to support Penelope ; " I say, old chap, with one foot in the grave," cried a gay spark, "what have you been caught out in your wickedness ?" A second person, observed—"An old fellow like you to seduce a beautiful young woman as she appears to be, and young enough to be your grand daughter ! You ought to be pumped upon !" With a variety of other remarks, that rather alarmed the citizen for his safety.

"Take me away," said Makemoney, instantly, "from the sight of this base woman, or else I shall choke with passion. An infamous liar, and strumpet ! It is lucky for her that in my passion I had not done her some mischief."

" You see," observed Turf, "however *sly* we may be in our amours, there are times when we are unexpectedly caught. Ha ! ha ! ha ! But it is only a nine days wonder, and it will soon blow over. We have almost carried the *joke* too far," Turf whispered into the ear of Flourish ; "but *mum !* Not a sentence about the affair to Sprightly, when we meet. The talents displayed by Penelope made her assumed injuries, appear like reality !"

"Worse and worse," replied Makemoney, "do you Turf, believe a single word the wretch has uttered ? I shall go, stark, staring mad, if such a villainous falsehood should get abroad !"

" I did not believe her in the first instance, I must confess," answered Turf, with a smile on his countenance, and Flourish was compelled to retire to some little distance for fear he should burst out into a loud fit of laughter : "but when she said you had promised to meet her *alone :* I was rather staggered, and did not know what to think about it."

" Let us retire from this scene of confusion, and order supper," said Flourish, " it is a mistake—I am sure it is a mistake ; and the young lady in question has taken you, Makemoney, for one of the 'gallant gay Lotharios,' once in her train. Compose yourself, sir, and only laugh at the circumstance. It is one of those *funny* sort of adventures that sometimes crosses our paths at public places of amusement."

"It may be a laughing matter to you, I have little doubt," replied the old citizen, " but this is *coming out* in life, in rather a hazardous sort of manner. Such effrontery in a female, I never met with before in all my travels."

"If I might offer my advice upon the subject," urged Turf, with a face made up as seriously as a judge about to pronounce sentence upon a criminal ; "you would treat the affair altogether as the *impulse* of the moment ; the female has mistaken her

man, and you have an *alibi* to prove you never *kept* a woman
in your life. Ha! ha! ha! I am a witness to that effect, whenever you are in want of one. But if you promise to forgive the
poor deluded wench, and keep your temper, I will bring her before you, and convince her, beyond all doubt, that she has committed an error, and must make you a suitable apology. For I
overheard her observe, on her leaving me, ' Surely, I am not
mistaken in the person of my old gallant. If so, I am sorry, very
sorry for it. Perhaps, I have been rather too violent in my conduct, but he is very like my old Charles. Now, my friend
Makemoney, as your name is *Peter*, I have no doubt, but it may
be made all right over a glass of wine."

"If I could be satisfied that by agreeing to an interview with
her, the *fact* might be established that she was mistaken as to
my person," replied Makemoney, "I should have no objection.
I am anxious that that point should be cleared up, because I feel
uneasy under the accusation. I am not disposed to be ill-na-
tured, and always ready to make an allowance for mistakes,
when I am assured the error committed was *unintentional*."

"You have acted sensibly," said Turf, "the girl is not an
absolute stranger to me, and I am sure, when I point out the
mistake to her, and the unnecessary violence she used upon the
occasion, she will make any apology you may require; Penelope
————, is one of the ' *unfortunates!*' it is true; but, nevertheless, she has had a decent education; and is not deficient in good
manners. At all events, I will seek her out before she quits the
gardens; and an acknowledgement of her error, upon the spot
where it has been committed, will be worth twenty times more,
than after the circumstance has made its way into the City, or
obtained an extensive circulation in all the newspapers. Scandal and satire, my dear friend, are rich subjects for most of the
journals, the public *doat* upon rows; devour *police* intelligence;
but for an *intrigue* or amour, it is positively food for all the
breakfast, dinner, and tea-tables in the metropolis for a week!
Besides, sir, the mistake in question might be distorted into a
thousand horrid shapes; and the *desertion* of a lovely, interesting, beautiful female, promulgated as an act of the blackest die.
I am determined to see the *mistery* cleared up, and Penelope
shall make a curtsey before the Pilgrims!"

"Do so, my dear Turf," replied Makemoney, "let us have
the truth, and nothing else but the truth, at all events, and
then, perhaps, I may be inclined to laugh at the mistake."

Turf giving the wink to Flourish, went immediately in search
of Penelope————

"I think, my friend Turf," said Flourish, "is quite correct
in his view of the subject at issue, an explanation is decidedly
necessary: and he is acting towards you with sincerity. Here
he is, I see, returning with the young female. (Putting his

PILGRIMS at VAUXHALL GARDENS.

glass up to his eyes.) Egad, she is a very fine woman. A beautiful creature! and, I should say, there are few men but what would consider it a feather in their caps to be her *Protector*, rather than otherwise. Therefore, sir, you must show your gallantry upon this occasion. Remember the advice of the poet:—

> If to her share some common errors fall,
> Look on her face and you'll forget them all.

Penelope on approaching Makemoney, dropped him a most elegant curtsey, affected bashfulness, and rather hesitated before she attempted to address him.

"Be not afraid," observed Turf, "if you are now convinced that you have committed an error, acknowledge it with a good grace, and forgiveness is at hand. (*Turf aside.*) Compliment the forbearance of the old gentleman, and you may become a favourite with him, after all the fire and smoke. Your face and person will effect wonders." Penelope gave a nod.

"You will excuse me, sir, I hope," said Penelope, "taking a synopsis of your person, and rudely scanning your features, that I may decide with certainty; but notwithstanding those roguish, amorous-looking eyes in your head which are so very prominent, and so dangerous to females in general, I must confess that I have been *deceived;* and the error I have committed is now so palpable to myself, that I blush for my violent behaviour, and upon looking at you again, sir, *you* are Hyperion to a Satyr when compared with my old Charles. How could I have been so much mistaken—you are quite a boy in appearance to him. But I suppose it must have been owing to the *glare* of the vast number of lights in the gardens, which change the countenances of every person."

"I think it is likely," replied Flourish. "People do not look the same as at other places of amusement. But proceed."

"It was a mere *glance* at your person, sir, that has done all the mischief: besides, when you take into the scales of justice the pangs of disappointed love—neglect—abandonment—and all the other circumstances connected with wronged women, which accounts for my conduct, you will be inclined to grant me a pardon: therefore, sir, I hope you will accept of an apology; but I know you well as an admirer of the sex—"

"Madam! have a care!" replied Makemoney. "I am not to be *flattered* in turn out of my reason."

"To love the sex, sir, is not a crime, nor a fault; but in my humble opinion, an honor: and kindness from man to woman is one of his greatest attributes. I am sorry, very sorry for what has occurred this evening. Can I offer any thing more in extenuation. Only mention it—and you will find me, Penelope, perfectly willing and obedient."

"No! no! no!" exclaimed Flourish and Turf at the same

instant—"our friend has too much of the milk of human kindness in his composition to require any thing more from a female. You have acknowledged your error in a handsome way, and I am sure, the sooner it is buried in oblivion the better for all parties."

"Not exactly so abrupt," replied Penelope, "a *duel* now, between us, is out of the question. Yet a challenge may be given and accepted, without violating the bounds of decorum. Therefore, I am about to challenge my—"

"How?" asked Makemoney, almost relapsing into a passion, "a challenge from a lady? I do not understand it! What do you mean? explain!"

Turf, *(Aside.)* "This is carrying on the *joke* better than I could have anticipated. Penelope will now have the best of the argument," giving a significant nod to Flourish: "Is she not a very clever creature?"

"Do not be alarmed, sir knight. I am no female duellist! Powder, ball, and swords will not suit me. But my challenge is to your friends—I wish to drink your health over a glass of champagne, to convince you, if necessary, that my apology is sincere; therefore, you are quite safe for me. Here, waiter, bring a bottle of the best sparkling champagne that you have got in your cases—*Nectar* I would have called for, if it could have been purchased upon earth—(Feeling for her purse.) I will pay for it. Then sir, after the toast has been drank—I will not annoy you with my company any longer; but most respectfully take my leave."

"Not so fast! not so fast, young lady," replied Makemoney, who not only began to relax from his severity: but appeared rather smitten with the charms of Penelope, "Ladies do not pay for any thing in my company: besides, a pleasant hour's conversation or two is within our grasp; and we cannot part so readily with beauty and talent as you imagine. Therefore, you will sup with us.

"I acquiesce, sir, to your request," replied Penelope, "and I hope now that you will, *war* being at an end, not deny me the claim, at least, of an acquaintance; and perhaps, at some future period, should we ever cross each other's path, that of an old friend. Ha! ha! ha!

"Bravo! bravo," cried Flourish, "if we feel inclined at any time to quarrel about other circumstances, I hope we shall never quarrel with wit."

The health of Makemoney was drank with great spirit; and the waiter having filled another glass for Penelope, she thus addressed Makemoney:—"Kindness to the faults of others, and liberality to discern our own." The supper over, and a few glasses of generous wine had banished from the mind of the old Citizen all about the recent row; Flourish was in high spirits on the occasion: and Turf quite on the *qui vive*.

Taking wine with each other was the order of the night; and bottle after bottle was emptied of its contents with rapidity. The party soon became elevated; and at times, a little noisy, and Makemoney almost as young as a boy in his actions. The fine old adage of Shakspeare began to show itself amongst them—"O that a man will put an enemy into his mouth to steal away his brains." The handsome face of Penelope, added to her talent for repartee, attracted the attention of Makemoney: and in whispers, he began to say a thousand civil things to her; such are the effects of the bottle.

"To-morrow," replied Penelope, who had not yet *indulged* so much as to deprive her of self-possession, and who was of a sensitive nature, looking Makemoney full in the face, "when you are soberly seated at home, suffering from the effects of drink and fever, and blaming yourself for acts of intemperance, and also being seen in the company of a doubtful, nay, what is termed an improper character. What weight am I to attach to such expressions of admiration; only picture to yourself how galling it must be to my feelings, for I have not entirely lost sight of them—however situated I may be in life, to be treated as a *play-thing*, and made mere pastime of for the sport of men. The cruelty and deliberate injuries I have received from mankind; and the pains taken by men to seduce every pretty woman from the paths of virtue, and blast their characters in the estimation of virtuous society—makes me almost hate the name of man. Can you blame females for seeking revenge on their *betrayers*; and afterwards deserting them, to become the derision and insult of the world?"

This unexpected appeal to the feelings of Makemoney almost *sobered* him in an instant, and he hesitated for a reply—"No allusions, Miss Penelope—the present company I hope are excepted."

"No, no," said Flourish, "we won't have any thing in the way of *moralizing* here. Vauxhall Gardens is not the place for it. Come, cheer up, Penelope; give us one of your little songs—an anecdote—a pun: *preaching* will not do for us. Another glass of wine or two will make us as merry as players."

"Aye, wine is the thing to soothe our sorrows and banish grief," replied Turf, "and whenever I feel low-spirited, and unpleasant thoughts intrude themselves—this is the mode I adopt to dispel them." Filling himself a bumper and singing:

> Drink of this cup—you'll find there's a spell in
> Its every drop 'gainst the ills of mortality—
> Talk of the cordial that sparkled for *Helen*,
> Her cup was a fiction, but this is reality:

> Would you forget the dark world we are in,
>   Only taste of the bubble that gleams on the top of it,
> But would you rise above earth, till akin,
>   To immortal yourselves, you must drain every drop of it.
>   Send round the cup, &c.

"If such charms exist in wine," said Makemoney, "the sooner we have another glass all round the better. We came out to be cheerful and happy; and therefore, let us embrace the opportunity."

Penelope, like the rest of her companions, gave a truce to sensibility; and after the manner of most females of her description who are affected to tears by some unpleasant reflections, and laugh heartily at any occurrence the next—she once more became all gaiety. Her interesting conversation, and the little anecdotes which she now and then illustrated her stories with, made the wine go down like water; added to which a few *snatches* of songs from her favorite author, Tommy Moore, elevated Flourish, Makemoney, and Turf equal in spirit, to the finest jolly fellows in the world: they had courage enough now, or rather, *impetuosity* to have *scaled* fortresses ; mounted the deadly *breach ;* and entered the *forlorn* hope like heroes of the first description.

"The song ; Penelope's song ! the song," became the universal request of the Pilgrims.

She immediately complied with their request, and looking rather *smirkingly* in the face of the old Citizen—sang :—

> Can *love* be controled by advice ?

"Ah, this love;" said Penelope, "attachment—fondness—admiration, and all those phrases so often poured into the ears of females, are all deceit, I am afraid ; and almost begin to think that what is called *Love*, is nothing more than a farce : calculated to annoy and upset society in general. But no matter."— singing again to Makemoney :—

> Come rest in this bosom, my own stricken deer,
> Though the herd have fled from thee, thy home is still here ;
> Here still is the smile, that no cloud can o'ercast,
> And the heart and the hand, all thy own to the last.
>
> Oh, what was love made for, if 'tis not the same,
> Through joy, and through torments, through glory and shame ;
> I know not, I ask not, if guilt's in that heart,
> I but know that I love thee, whatever thou art !
>
> Thou hast called me *thy* angel, in moments of bliss—
> Still *thy* angel I'll be, 'mid the horrors of this,
> Through the furnace, unshrinking, thy steps to pursue,
> And shield thee, and save thee, or perish there too.

"Excellent !" observed Turf, "what a happy fellow you

must think yourself, Makemoney, to have so much love and constancy expressed for you, by such a handsome creature! You must forgive me, but I cannot help envying you."

"Bliss! perfect bliss to the echo!" replied Flourish, "I never heard any song better applied in my life. And a good bit of truth into the bargain."

"Too much! too much! you comical rogues," said Makemoney with a hic-cough, and appearing any thing but sober; "you are also a *satirist*, Miss Penelope, thus to quiz an old fellow! but I must f-o-r-g-i-v-e you! but I never felt more happy and pleased during my existence. Where's Sprightly all this time? I have not seen my nephew for the last two or three hours, and, you know, he promised to meet us again at supper. Let us go and look after him: he may have forgot himself, and what is due to propriety, lost his time with *naughty* company! I must point out to him the danger of such people."

"By all means," answered Flourish, "we will all start together. Naughty folks won't do at all for us Pilgrims."

Turf, by this time, was rather *freshish*, he had stuck to the bottle like glue; in fact, he was no flincher upon such occasions. Flourish also, a thing quite unusual for him, was like a sailor, 'three-sheets in the wind;' and Makemoney, a rare occurrence, 'how come you so?' Turf and Flourish sallied forth, and Makemoney, with Miss Penelope hanging upon his arm: it is true, they attempted to walk, but *reeling*, perhaps would be the better description of it. They had not moved forwards but a few steps, when some person rather rudely pushed by Miss Penelope, this excited the anger of Makemoney, and he exclaimed, "Who are you pushing against fellow? Don't you see I have a lady under my care? Have you left your manners at home?"

"Pushing against!" echoed a nicely apparelled dandy, "why, an old Pope, to be sure. A *ci-devant* member of Noah's flood. Ha! ha! Such old fogeys as you, ought, positively, to have been at *roost* long before this period: and not be seen strutting up and down the walks with a *questionable* female. Fie! fie! I am ashamed of you old man."

"Do not be insolent again to my friend, and the lady," said Turf, turning round to him with a sovereign look of contempt; "if you render yourself troublesome any more, beware of the consequences. A puppy like you to insult your elders! I have a great mind to chastise you for your impertinence. So, once more, beware!"

"Ha! ha! ha! A lady and a gentleman, forsooth! a precious pair of non-descripts! Where can they come from, I wonder? but I suppose from the mohawk country. Chastise indeed, take care, my Jonny Raw, gentleman farmer, clod-pole, that I do not annihilate you, if I display my science on your unmeaning *nob*! Ha! ha! A good joke, upon my word. Fellows from the wilds of Sussex, or the obscure parts of Yorkshire, to talk of chastising us Metropolitans. Here, Tom, take my kid gloves, I should not like to soil them upon this Ourang-outang! But, yet, I must punish the beast out of civilized society, and send him running back to his proper sphere—the woods and forests. Ha! ha! So come on my *Raw*, and receive the reward due to your merits; for I mean to give you a receipt in full of all demands: I do nothing by halves." Putting himself in a boxing attitude.

This challenge was most acceptable to the feelings of Turf, although a very peaceable fellow in the main; yet, nevertheless, he had not the slightest objection, at any time, to a trial of skill; nay, to speak the truth, he was fond of it: and in the early part of his career, had received lessons from the most expert professors on the list.

" I am ready," he replied, " and take care of yourself; you shall not wait long before you *hear* from me. All I require for both of us, is—fair play !"

It was quite evident to the by-standers that Turf and the dandy had paid too much attention to the bottle, to prove, in a serious point of view, mischievous, and *staggered* up to each other on setting-to. But after a few blows had been exchanged, Turf, put in a slight hit upon the jugular vein of his opponent, that instantly sent him sprawling on the ground. The friends of the dandy, (who it appeared, afterwards, was a sprig of quality,) on finding he was likely to be well thrashed for his boasting and impudence, joined in the row, and a general skirmish took place.

The screams of the females and the noise and bustle which took place altogether, excited the attention of Sprightly, who had also been drinking rather freely, and supping with some young fellows of his acquaintances, ripe and ready for any thing, he immediately ran to the spot, when, Sprightly, perceiving Flourish and Turf engaged in the contest, and his uncle in jeopardy, pushed about with a female on his arms, he did not stop to ask any questions on the subject, but hit away, right and left, until he had the satisfaction of seeing the Pilgrims masters of the field.

The dandy had been carried off by some of his friends during the row, for fear of the consequences, to get bled; for a long time he remained in a state of stupor, and it was generally expected that a Coroner's Inquest would have been the result of the affray. However, he recovered his *senses*, to the great joy of the whole of the party concerned in the quarrel.

The constables interfered when the danger was all over, and understanding that it was nothing more than a trifling quarrel between gentlemen; and cards having been exchanged to settle their differences in another way, the constables, on their own account, did not wish to give the *gentlemen* any trouble the next morning to *expose* themselves at a police office for their indiscreet conduct. Palm-oil, (i. e. *money*,) being given to them to let the row be buried in oblivion ; therefore, like sensible men in office, they preferred the old adage, that a still tongue, shews a wise head. And *silence* was the order of the day.

Penelope was so alarmed during the contest, that Make-money had his work to do to prevent her from fainting ; but on Sprightly learning her address, he relieved his uncle from his *dear* charge, by putting the elegant little ' piece of frailty,' into a hackney coach, settling the fare, and thus got rid of her company altogether.

On the Pilgrims looking and laughing at each other, after peace was restored, the face of Turf was a litttle bruised in the skirmish ; Flourish had received a *black* eye ; Sprightly a cut on his nose ; and Makemoney a sprained ancle, besides sundry blows in divers places.

It might have been imagined, after quietness had been obtained, that the PILGRIMS would have made the best of their way *home !* But not so, when the wine is in the head, the wit is out of it ; (which, in this instance, appeared to be the fact,) and the very last place thought of was HOME !

Turf, the leader upon this occasion, proposed to *finish* the night at a well-known coffee house, " Strictly in good taste," said he, " contiguous to the Banks of the Thames. Over our tea, or coffee, we shall get a little to rights ; besides, we shall have something to occupy our mind ; and we are told, that the ' proper study of mankind, *is* man :' we cannot have a finer illustration of the adage than in this place of refreshment. You will have, my worthy Pilgrims, a fine opportunity of viewing society in all its bearings, from high to low, rich and poor, honest men, depraved characters of all sorts, splendid cyprians, and ragged unfortunates—in short, a complete mirror of human nature.

The proprietor opens the door of this establishment, which commenced many years since, at four-o'clock in the morning, and originally it was intended for the accomodation of the market people only, but like every other thing in society, abuses will creep in ; therefore, it accounts for fellows like ourselves becoming visitors to obtain information, who can spend a pound without feeling the loss of it ; while there are others who can scarcely muster the price of a cup of coffee, to keep life and soul together, who have been prowling the streets all night. Splendour and misery, at times, are both very prominent in this receptacle, it being a sort of republic, distinction of persons is not attended to, and Jack is as good as his master."

Makemoney had scarcely seated himself amongst the motley crew, before he was astounded, although rather disordered in his intellects, from the effects of liquor. Flourish looked unutterable things, as much as to say, " Can such things be ?" Sprightly, who had never mixed with such a heterogenous mass of society, looked lost in wonder, and contemplated in silence, but Turf, felt himself quite at home as an old customer, and acquainted with every movement in life, enjoyed the surprise manifested by the Pilgrims, witnessing things they had never seen before between heaven and earth.

The Pilgrims strictly followed the advice of Turf, not to suffer themselves to be '*drawn out*,' upon any occasion whatever, "I will not suffer you," said he, "to be picked up as *flats*, while you are in my company." In consequence of this admonition, they resisted all attempts at conversation with either male or female, who had addressed them.

After a cup of coffee, Makemoney felt the effects of late hours, and 'keeping it up,' began to yawn, and ultimately fell asleep. Flourish and Sprightly were equally drowsy and stupid, and thought a few *winks* might refresh them; and the experienced Turf, with all his care and watchfulness, was compelled to succumb to the fatigues of nature, and, like the rest of his companions, lost in the arms of *Somnus*.

It is urged there is a time for all things, so it occurred with the worn-out Pilgrims; and HOME, ultimately became the object in view.

On Makemoney opening his eyes, he stared with astonishment, and looked round the room full of doubts and fears, "Where am I?" was the exclamation. The place was entirely cleared of all the visitors, except his three companions with their heads upon the table fast asleep. He aroused them from their lethargy, observing, "Don't you *think* it is almost time to go home?"

"Yes, yes," replied Turf, "ha! ha! ha! but we have had one advantage in not going to bed, we are up and dressed, and ready for any other adventure that may offer itself."

"Enough is as good as a feast," answered Flourish, "I am quite satisfied with the *experience* of this day and night's pilgrimage."

Makemoney, after looking about the room for some time, could not perceive his hat, when he immediately rang for the waiter, "Have you seen my hat?" said he, "I had it safe enough before I went to sleep!"

"I do not doubt your assertion, sir," replied the napkin hero, with a grin upon his countenance, "but gentlemen should never go to sleep *here*, without they keep *one* eye open! But you are lucky, sir, I see your shoes are safe."

"What do you mean by that?" asked the old Citizen, "I don't understand you—My shoes *safe*?"

"It is true, sir, that *shoes* have been known to walk off from this room without having any feet in them. Ha! ha! ha! There are a number of extraordinary clever artists who visit this establishment, who are not particular what they *take* besides tea and coffee! *Wigs* too have been missing here at times: and so, would the *heads* that belonged to them, if they had been loose?"

" My gloves are gone after the hat, I suppose ?" said Flourish, " they are not to be found where I left them."

"They have *kid*-did them, as the artist calls it," answered the waiter; " that is *boned* them ; or, in other words converted them to their own use, under the idea they were their own. Mistakes will happen you know, gentlemen."

" You are a wag," observed Sprightly, " and a punster into the bargain ! but the sooner we are off the better, *now* we are *wide*-awake! Ha! ha! ha!"

" True, my boy, true," answered Makemoney—" it won't do to be caught *napping* again. What is the hour, waiter ?"

" We take no note of *time* here, sir," replied the waiter, " our visitors, in general, have a very little to do with time, except the *loss* of it."

" Severe ; but just !" remarked Flourish, " Sprightly, you can tell us the hour?"

On Sprightly putting his hand to his pocket—his jollity forsook him in an instant, and his countenance was changed altogether—" My watch is gone !" said he.

" Gone !" exclaimed the old Citizen, " Impossible !"

" Gone !" observed Flourish, " you mistake ; feel for it again!"

" But you had a *guard* to it," said Turf, with a smile on his face; " and I thought from the look of it, a very strong one."

" The guard, watch, and seals are all gone !" answered Sprightly, " 1 must have slept sound, indeed, not to have felt any tug at it."

" If *your* guard has deserted you," replied Flourish, " it is hopeless. Are your teeth all safe ? Ha! ha! ha!"

" The *snoozing* system is always a dangerous one, where property is concerned," observed the waiter, with a sneer, " but we lost our dial one night, when our eyes were open, and *wide awake*. There is no *guard*-ing against such events."

" If that was the case," said Makemoney—" it is high time to be missing ; or, we may be lost ourselves ; and a reward offered for us; ha! ha! ha! Let us keep our own secrets, that we may not have the laugh of the public against us."

" Be it so," said Turf, " therefore, as soon as we can, let us *hide* ourselves in a drag, it will not do to show ourselves in the street at this time of day. A hackney coach was immediately at the door, the Pilgrims jumped into it, without delay, and in a very short time they found themselves comfortably seated in Makemoney's drawing-room, when Flourish exclaimed, " After all that I have seen, ' *L'experience est la maitresse des fous !*"

CHAPTER XIV.

The Pilgrims in training—a horse cannot always be running at the top of his speed; and the strongest men require rest when they put NATURE to the test. FLOURISH, SPRIGHTLY, and MAKEMONEY restored to their pristine state of health, and anxious to start upon another cruize. The Pilgrims once more on the Thames, enjoying all its nautical grandeur, united with the picturesque and pleasing variety of its scenery, developed on its banks. A character on board of the steamer—an ENGLISH DON JUAN—a man of sentiment—an appalling picture of the destruction occasioned, by dissipation and libertinism on the human frame: a portrait for inconsiderate young men to analyze, before it is too late, in all its bearings—depicted by TURF in an artist-like manner. Modern Antiquity; or, the mansion built with stones from old London Bridge—its various comical designations and allusions by the passengers, who pass and repass it, up and down the River. A sketch of the Proprietor, by the old Citizen. MAKEMONEY determined to participate in the amusements of GRAVESEND, without any restraint; according to the maxim, ' that when you are at Rome, do as Rome does.' Remarks, by the old Citizen, on the rapid rise of Gravesend in the estimation of the public, as a convenient and fashionable watering-place—contrasted with his boyhood days, to the downhill of life. With a variety of other circumstances which presented themselves to the PILGRIMS, during their trip to Grsvesend :—

> There's a *magnet* OLD THAMES firmly holds in his mouth,
>   To which all sorts of merchandize tend;
> And the trade of all nations—WEST, NORTH, EAST, and SOUTH—
>   Like the *needle*, points right to—GRAVESEND!

AFTER a storm comes a calm, it is said, and some little time occurred before the Pilgrims were again ready to start: they were compelled to undergo a kind of *training*, to recover from the effects of the Vauxhall row.

The *black* eye of Flourish induced him to keep within side of his house for a short period—he had too much good sense to show himself to the public; and, under any circumstances, nothing has so much the appearance of ' low life !' about a man's face, as that of a *damaged* eye.

Sprightly's *nose*, in point of look, was equally unpleasant to

THE ENGLISH DON JUAN.

his feelings; and he likewise preferred retirement, rather than brave the laugh and jeers of his acquaintance and friends; until time and repeated applications should have restored it to its original character.

Makemoney had nothing outwardly against his appearance; therefore, he could *hobble* about under an excuse of an attack of the gout; and Turf, retreated to his cottage, to enjoy the country air, and laugh at the plight in which he had left the Pilgrims. Thus matters stood for a short period.

However, possessing all the enjoyments of life at home, time did not hang heavily upon their hands, although they did not stir outside their doors. But at length, all impediments vanished, and a trip to GRAVESEND was carried *mem. con.* Timely intimation of their wishes were communicated to Turf; and he, without delay, sent the following letter:—

"Turf Cottage——

To one and all of you.

My dear Pilgrims!

I hope that none of your friends, Flourish, can *now* say that *black* is the white of your eye. Also, that Sprightly's *bowsprit* will soon be ready for actual service; and I rejoice to hear, the tough old Commodore, Peter Makemoney, Esq., will again hoist his flag for another cruize. Success to all sound hearts, and true bottoms. The loss of the Commodore's hat in his last voyage, is of no moment to me, when I am assured that his *head* is all right.

I met, yesterday, poor Penelope, on Richmond Hill, brim-full of grief, for the loss of her heart—which, she says, she has never *heard* of since she was in company with ——'O dear, what can the matter be?' But every man to his own business, therefore, I say, Gravesend, ahoy! I will be with you, my jolly boys, in good time.

Your's to the end of life,

To the Pilgrims.   CHARLES TURF."

"I am heartily glad that he has accepted of our invitation," said Makemoney, "either at home or abroad—over the bottle, or in any other shape, he is an invaluable companion. Turf, in my mind, is exactly the character which Shakspeare describes:—

A merrier man, I never met withal.

The night before starting, Turf arrived in London: and a jolly evening was the result: but sobriety the leading feature. The next morning they were all on board of the steamer before the bell gave notice—"off she goes!"

On the Pilgrims entering the saloon, accompanied by Turf, the latter almost stood aghast with horror and surprise, on beholding a person once well known at the West end of the town in all the gay circles of society, propped up in one corner and wrapped in a heavy cloak to keep himself warm; his face was deadly pale; in fact, he was an illustration of those emphatic words, sans teeth, sans eyes, sans taste, sans every thing; yet it did not appear from the effects of age. His voice was completely gone; and it appeared like a hollow whisper when he addressed Turf—"Don't you know me Mr. Turf? I think I am a *little* altered since you first knew me ? I am going to see what the fresh air will do for me in the neighbourhood of Gravesend ;" This exertion seemed too much for him, and he reclined his head against the side of the vessel

Turf, who did not like to play the hypocrite, nor to ill-treat an apparently dying man, replied—"Certainly you do not look well," and abruptly left the saloon, and went upon deck. He was followed by 'Sprightly, Makemoney, and Flourish, to know the cause of his hasty departure.

" I cannot, will not, sit down in the company of a wretch that I despise ; he is a disgrace to society." replied Turf, " His appearance is odious to my feelings."

" A more emaciated being I never saw in my life," said Make-money, " Who is he ? At all events, he is not long for this world !"

" He is well known amongst the people of fashion—under the title of the ' *English* DON JUAN ; or, *lady-killing Fred !*' He appears to have had a summons from death ; but while he can put one leg before the other, he will mix with society ; in-deed, I shall not be surprised to hear that he is found dead at one of the theatres: he is restless, and cannot stay at home ; but he never will be able to return to town."

" No," replied Flourish, " I think *Gravesend* will finish him !"

" Yes," urged Sprightly—" he is bound for *Grave's*-end !"

" Will you be kind enough to give us an outline of his cha-racter," said Makemoney—" an *English* Don Juan will be worth hearing about, I rather anticipate."

" He was," said Turf, " when I first knew him, considered a perfect Adonis in form : he valued himself highly on the beauty of his person ; and he likewise flattered himself that no female whatever could resist his advances. He commenced life when quite a youth, long before his majority, with a splendid fortune —fine estates, &c., but all his thoughts were bent upon the ruin of the sex ; and I regret to say, that too many of his schemes were successful ; yet, strange to say, he was a sordid miser in every thing else, but spending his money in profusion to over-throw the mind of the females he had set his roving eyes upon.

"His cruelty and desertion of some of his victims, were of so diabolical a nature ; that my indignation will not let me repeat them. He was a bully and a coward in the same breath. He was a *single* man, to all intents and purposes—and his love for women, was out of the question ; it was the most unbridled lust.

" He had studiously and indefatigably made himself master of every accomplishment that could tend to render him an ob-ject of attraction with the fair sex. He spoke French fluently, and with as good an accent as the most gentlemanly Parisian his dancing was elegance, personified ; and in manners, and politeness he was a perfect Chesterfield. In truth, he was a most dangerous, insinuating fellow in the company of females ; and had he taken a right course, must have been a hero amongst men. He had occasioned, by his vile arts and duplicity, more misery and destruction to several families of the most reputable description, than a life of a thousand years could ever make atonement for. His character became so notorious and despicable, that the door of every family, who valued their reputation, was closed against him ; but whenever his vile stratagems failed him, to complete the degradation of a female, he, demon-like, lost no time to blast her reputation, if possible, in the dark. He is an assassin of the blackest dye, a complete sensualist, and as to *feeling*, he only knows it by name.

" He boasts amongst his companions, that he has lived all the days of his life, if not a few days more, as if his opinion of men and manners could have any weight, except in circles where such wretches as himself, only meet.

" He has outraged NATURE to its fullest extent ! He appears to be now in the last stage of consumption, full of misery, excruciating pains, and agony. His premature imbecility is frightful ! for he has not reached any thing like the age of what is termed an old man ! Nothing can console his mind, according to report, horrors overwhelm him when he reflects on his wanton crimes. He is dying by inches, and nothing can conceal from him that he is fast approaching to death !

> A motley train—Fever with cheek of fire, diseases thick,
> Consumption wan ; Palsy half warm with life ;
> And a half clay clod lump ; joint-tottering gout,
> And even-gnawing rheumatism, convulsion wild ;
> Swollen dropsy, panting asthma, apoplex,
> Full gorg'd. These too the pestilence that walks
> In darkness, and the sickness that destroys
> At broad noon-day !

" I am sorry to say, however uncharitable it may appear, that I have not the slightest pity for him ; because, his errors were committed—wilfully ! He was cold and deliberate in all his attacks on females ; and the most calculating *seducer* that I ever knew, or heard of. There was not a single redeeming point point about his character.

" He was the complete destruction of a family, that came under my own immediate observation, who were most intimate acquaintances of mine. An only daughter, living with her father, a widower, beautiful as Hebe, with a host of suitors in her train, and the pride and envy of her sex. He proposed marriage to her father, and was accepted ; that circumstance gave him a familiarity of visiting in the house, which otherwise could not have taken place ; unhappily, she became fond of the wretch, and viewed him as her future husband. In an unfortunate hour, she became a victim to his machinations, and by his arts induced to elope from her father's residence. Villain like, he soon became tired of his victim, and deserted her for another, and fled to the Continent. Her venerable parent, one of the highest spirited men that ever existed, became so overwhelmed with grief, he died broken-hearted. The girl, without a friend or relative to call her seducer to account, and meeting with bad advisers, ultimately, became a miserable prostitute, and died in the hospital. Justice though slow, is sure ; he has been overtaken in his villainy, and he will die despised and hated by all mankind.

"I am not a vindictive man, neither do I wish to pursue vengeance beyond the grave ; but when we see the peace and happiness of whole families totally destroyed by such cold, deliberate wretches, patience, in my humble opinion, becomes a crime, and it is the duty of every man to express his detestation of such infamous conduct!

"He must be a bad man indeed, who cannot find some person that will offer a word, or two in mitigation of his conduct ; but of this I am assured, that none will pity, but many will rejoice at his death : the curses of wretched girls, and the maledictions of broken-hearted fathers and mothers, will hover over his grave, and serve as a monument to his infamous remembrance. I again repeat, I am not a vindictive man, but if I could erect a stone to convey the above information to the rising generation of females, as a beacon to avoid such monsters in human shape, no expense should deter me from such an act. His last moments must be dreadful to him if reason holds her seat :—

> Let no dark crimes,
> In all their hideous forms, then starting up,
> Plant themselves round my couch in grim array,
> And stab my bleeding heart with two edg'd torture,
> Sense of past guilt, and dread of future woe.

" Let us leave him to his fate," observed Flourish, " and attend to subjects of a more cheerful nature."

The Pilgrims after promenading up and down the deck of the steamer, and letting no object escape their notice, worthy of observation, on both sides of the Thames, when they came opposite *Greenhithe,* Flourish put up his telescope to take an accurate view of a new mansion which presented itself to his view.

A smartly dressed man, rather of a sporting aspect, with a certain sort of dash about his character, and one, who seemed to have lived all the days of his life, and, according to the vulgar phrase ' *up* to a thing or two !' thus addressed him, " That building, sir, is a great object of attraction to the passengers who daily pass, and repass it, on their trips to and from Gravesend."

" The situation is delightful," replied Flourish, and a splendid retreat from the fatigues and cares of office, that a monarch might be delighted with."

" It *must* always prove an interesting feature to the spectator from two circumstances connected with its erection. The stones which compose the building, formerly belonged to the Old London Bridge, therefore, as a matter of antiquity, united with modern taste, it becomes rather important as an object of curiosity."

" It has, I understand," replied Makemoney, " cost already a pretty round sum ; thousands of pounds have been expended upon it, and thousands of pounds are still required before the mansion is complete."

" It reminds me of an old song," said Sprightly, " which my nurse has often sung me to sleep with.

London Bridge is broken down,
Dance over my Lady Lea ;
London Bridge is broken down,
With a gay lady !
Build it up with silver and gold, &c.

" I do not care a fig for its architecture," observed the sporting man, " and the grounds beautifully as they are laid out, sink into insignificance by comparison, with the proprietor of the mansion, when his name is mentioned—Alderman HARMER. It has been jocularly called ' *Thieves Hall !*' and a variety of other designations, in allusion to the great success which attended the *practice** of Mr. Harmer, in the character of solicitor, and the frequent acquittals of certain parts of the population deemed cracksmen, *soft* robbers, high toby gloques, fogle hunters, &c. &c."

" I know him well, Horatio," said Turf, " the briefs of Solicitor Harmer, were short, pithy, and common sense : the counsel had only to cast their eyes over them, and the case presented itself to their notice at the first blush. There is no doubt but he has by his ingenuity, exertion, and knowledge of the criminal

---

* It is a sound maxim, that every man is presumed innocent until he is found guilty ; and every individual under *doubtful* circumstances, has a right to procure the best assistance within his grasp. When a man's liberty, or his life is in danger, *gentility* of feelings, or *practise*, is entirely out of the question, and reminds us of a dialogue which took place in a court of justice, between the late Judge Garrow, when a brow-beating barrister, and the well-known Bow-street officer, the late Jack Townshend, as ' to the mode *af getting a living !*'

Question.—How do you get your living, sir?
Answer.—You know me very well, Mr. Garrow.
Question.—I insist upon knowing how you get your livelihood. Recollect, sir, you are upon your oath.
Answer.—Yes, sir, I have taken a great many oaths in my time, but I ought to have said, *professionally.*
Question.—To the question, sir ; and no equivocation.
Answer.—Why then, sir, I get my living in the same way as you do.
Question.—How is that, fellow ?
Answer.—I am paid for *taking* up thieves ; and you are paid for ' *getting them off* !' that is much about the same sort of thing.
Question.—You consider yourself a *sharp* shot, don't you, fellow ?
Answer.—No, sir, but I like to *hit* the mark !
Question.—You may stand *down*, fellow !
Answer.—I am glad, sir, you found me UP !

law, saved the lives of several guilty men, almost with ropes round their necks. Although not considered an eloquent man, yet, he was viewed, in difficult cases, one of the most able defenders ; gentlemanly and persuasive in his manners and address ; and much better than all the rest, his orations before the magistrates, were short, but emphatic and decisive."

" True," answered Makemoney, " he had deservedly the character of a clever man, a first-rate lawyer in the criminal courts, and Mr. Harmer was listened to with the greatest attention. There was also a *firmness* about his mode of speaking which had great weight with the justices of peace in town and country ; he never appeared in doubt, *hesitation,* on his part, was entirely out of the question, his mind was always made up, that seemed to infer that he had the law at his fingers ends.

" His PERSONAL practise was immense at one period of his career," said the sporting man," and he might have been termed the *flying* solicitor, for he was daily to be seen at three or four of the police offices. The magistrates liked Mr. H., because he gave them little trouble ; he always saw his way clearly, and whenever danger appeared to any extent, to individuals, his assistance was sought after with avidity ; and if his clients only told the truth to *him*, it was two to one in their favour.

" The first case that brought him into *notoriety* with the public, as a lawyer, that I recollect," was the book he published respecting Holloway and Haggety, to prove their innocence. At the execution of the above men in the Old Bailey, upwards of thirty person were trod upon, and died from suffocation, and the immense crowd."

" But one of the most triumphant things of the sort," answer-Makemoney, " was his rescuing a young man of the name of *George Mathews,* from the jaws of death, removing him from the condemned cell, ultimately obtaining for him a free pardon, and also clearing him of the crime alleged against him, likewise exposing the cruelty and vengeance of his prosecutor, against the most overwhelming influence!"

" In most of the great criminal prosecutions, which agitated the mind of the public," said Flourish, " the name of Harmer, always stood conspicuous ; either *for* or against, his services were to valuable to remain idle."

" But in the immense law suit and trial of the House of Kinnear and Co.," urged Turf, " which excited the attention of the merchants both in London and Liverpool, placed the talents of Mr. Harmer, as a lawyer in the most eminent point of view. Kinnear was a host in himself, a perfect *Crichton* for a knowledge of the world, the study of mankind, and a giant at *finesse.* He might have have been compared to Cerberus ; for he possessed the talents of three heads on one pair of shoulders. Kinnear, by his arts, had completely duped several solicitors, who had been employed against him, they could not fathom his depth. But when Mr. Harmer removed the masqued battery, he was completely foiled, exposed, found guilty, and suffered some years imprisonment. However, strange to say, Kinnear was so delighted with the undaunted *perseverance*, and never-tiring talents of Mr. H., who was not to be diverted from his most difficult task, that he strongly solicited, on obtaining his liberty, the latter would become his solicitor. This alone speaks volumes, and the merchants of London presented Mr. Harmer, with a splendid piece of plate for his valuable services!"

" In obtaining the title of Alderman," observed Makemoney, " his numerous clients lost a valuable defender, as he could not exercise his talents as a solicitor before the magistrates by pleading for any person ; but, nevertheless, he serves his country in his character of Alderman, and his mode of disposing cases, always tempering justice with mercy has met with the highest approbation from the public !"

" He has always been a steady friend to the liberty of the subject," said Turf, " and I understand his vote upon all public questions, has been given on the liberal side."

" True, sir, true, he has been consistent in that respect," observed the sporting man, " and his name appears at the bottom of a widely circulated newspaper, as the principal proprietor— one of the boldest and most fearless on the list of journals. It once obtained a distinguished feature in the sporting world for its reports connected with the turf, &c., and which feature might have been said one of its stepping stones to fame and wealth for a rising circulation with the public ; but since which period, it has changed its character altogether, whether from a better notion of things, or an improved taste, I am not aware, but the pugilists, once its heroes, have been knocked about in all directions, nay, most of them *floored* without a hit on the sconce, it is urged that honesty is the best policy. The ' Blue-bottles,' according to the cant phrase of the day, have also been thrashed within an inch of their reputation, for tyranny of conduct, and unjust detection. Likewise, the ' *Swell-mob*,' (gentlemen thieves, who have a character to lose amongst their brother *artists*,) have been shown up with a kind of *knout*-castigation, which has not only made them wince again, but to hide their diminished heads.

> Since laws were made for every degree,
> To curb vice in others as well as me, &c.

yet, I have no doubt, that the DISPATCH, which has, and still continues to prove a mine of wealth to Mr. Harmer, is conducted under the motto of—' *Fiat justitia ruat cœlum.*'"

"Every hour of his life has been employed actively for the benefit of society," said Makemoney, " and the civic coach will never be better filled with a practical man, and one well versed in the duties of the office, than when on his road to Guildhall, and the chain of the Lord Mayor is placed round the neck of Alderman Harmer."

The Pilgrims, very soon afterwards, arrived safe at Gravesend ; and without loss of time, began to participate in all its amusements.

" It is of no use visiting a popular watering-place," said Makemoney, "without *unbending* and making yourself quite at home. It is a delightful trip from the metropolis, a sort of jump, only two hours, nay, you are wafted from one place to the other during the time you are occupied in reading a newspaper. What alterations and improvements occur in the course of a few years, united with enterprise and capital. When I was a boy, Gravesend was a mere dog-hole by comparison to its present appearance. It is now like a flourishing city ; fine houses, capital libraries, theatre, numerous steam boats, &c., in short it is like a new world."

" True, uncle," replied Sprightly, " there are delightful walks, unbounded prospects, and such facilities, not only to procure comforts, but amusements, until you are tired of them. Besides excellent company, and meeting with old acquaintances. A place like Gravesend, with such advantages near the Metropolis, must meet with immense patronage !"

" What do you say, sir," Turf asked Makemoney, " to a ride upon a Jerusalem pony ? You seem rather fatigued with your walk up hill, and a lift will refresh you."

" I most certainly would not trust myself upon the back of a race horse, or contest a match for gentleman's stakes at Doncaster, Epsom, &c., but I see no cause for fear on the outside of a donkey ; therefore, as our trip is entirely dedicated to pleasure, ease, and comfort, a man has a right to *unbend* in any way he my think proper ; provided it be of a harmless description, regardless of the remarks a joke of his friends, however ridiculous it may appear in the eyes of fastidious persons !"

" I have a nice donkey for you, sir," observed a fellow to the old Citizen. " She is as safe as a go-cart. An old lady of ninety, who is blind, has rode her without fear : and felt no reluctance to let the donkey go where she pleased—she is a sensible creature, and if there is a bit of fresh air to be had in Gravesend, she knows where to get it for my customers ; besides an infant might hold her with the most perfect ease. She can do everything but speak ; but howsomdever, she understands wot I says to her, and by sundry signs, best known to myself, she answers accordingly. Let me give you a leg up, sir ; you will find yourself as easy as if you vos on a bed of down."

Makemoney was induced to mount the Jerusalem poney— " she is quite safe, I hope," said he.

" Safe as the Bank of England, sir, you shall hear the naked truth, only listen. This ere donkey ought not to be called an

PILGRIMS at GRAVESEND.

hanimal; she possesses more abilities than many of the human race: without any reflections on the ladies and gents, who are by-standers. It is a she-donkey, sir, and a lady christened it *Tacita*, which she explained to me, meant the Goddess of Silence. But I doesn't understand any larning. Now Tacita, mind as how wot I tell you—be careful, and go slow; because you have got a gemman on your back. I knows him werry vell. In the vinter time I am a costermonger, and I sarves your house near the docks with wegetables; therefore, as how, I wouldn't let you have a shyer; or, a kicking poney for the vorld. Therefore, Tacita, you keep the line, and do not *bolt.*"

The donkey would not move a step; and the spectators were convulsed with laughter at the awkward situation of Makemoney.

"*Bolt!*" said Flourish, "why, she will not move a step. Ha! ha! ha!"

"If you don't go," observed the coster-monger, "I must use my *persuader*; therefore, don't you get *sulky*, or else I must *tip* it you, and no mistake. So *percede* at once."

Seeing the dilemma in which Makemoney was placed, a low-life fellow began to shout and sing—

> If I had a donkey what wouldn't go,
> Do you think I'd wollop him? oh, no, no.
> I'd give him some hay and cry ge woo!
> > And come up Neddy.
> If all had been like me, in fact
> There'd been no occasion for Martin's *hact!*
> Dumb hanimals to prevent getting crack't
> > Over the head.
> > Oh, if I had, &c.

"I say, ould chap, how long will you be getting to town? Three months, or half a year. The *steam* an't up, is it? Ha! ha! ha!"

"Come now, Mr. Spooney," said the coster-monger, don't you laugh at, and behave rude to the gemman; if you do as how, I will give you summut for yourself; so now you make your *lucky*, for fear of an accident. The gemman is going on werry vell, I'm sure—he only vants a little fresh air, and he'll get time, as much by sitting upon the donkey, as standing upon the turf. I am werry sorry, sir," said he to Makemoney, "but Tacita is not in spirits to-day, and harn't got the *pluck* to move; but to-morrow, sir, if you come to me on this ere werry spot of ground, I will not charge you a copper for a ride, when you will find *Tacita* as fresh as a four year old; and as lively as a race-horse." The old Citizen finding he had been imposed upon, got off the donkey, and retired amidst the laugh of the surrounding spectators: observing to Flourish, "I'll have nothing more to do with Jerusalem ponies."

The Pilgrims had scarcely descended the hill, when they observed a splendid mansion, and a female elegantly dressed, sitting at the window on the first floor. She immediately recognized Turf, and with a graceful nod, gave him to understand that she wished to speak to him. "It is the match-girl," said he to Makemoney, "go my friends to the inn, when I will join you as soon as possible; and relate the result of this interview." The Pilgrims left him, when a servant in a rich livery was waiting at the door to usher in Turf to his mistress.

"My dear Turf," she exclaimed, "I am delighted to see you: in brief—I am an altered creature since I last saw you—not the same woman! don't smile, but believe me, it is the truth. I am married to a gentleman who is connected with a noble family; and of some importance in the state; who really loves me! whose attention and liberal conduct towards me, since I have become his wife; makes me sincerely regret, that I ever was a *loose* female."

"You please me, beyond expression." replied Turf, "Better late than never."

"His proposals to me were so extremely generous, that I could not mistake his attachment for me; and when I found that he would take no denial, I was determined not to *deceive* him. I will be equally honorable and generous too I exclaimed—I have money enough with a little economy to keep me like a lady; during my life; but I will own to you, what I never felt before in my life—*Love* for a man; perhaps, when you hear my story, which you shall, and not a particle of it *disguised* from the first to the last—you may be inclined to assert, I ought not to have introduced the word—*Love!* I then told him the whole of my unfortunate, disgraceful career, and finished my tale in the following words.

"You astonish me," replied Turf.

"I have been looked upon as a bad, designing, artful sort of creature, without a soul, nothing like a *heart;* and to render men subservient to my purposes. Perhaps I had better plead guilty to the charges, or throw myself on the mercy of the Court. But, nevertheless, it is my intention to become a good woman, and by my future conduct, to make every reparation in my power to ensure my own happiness, and to obtain, if possible, respect from society.

I have *looked* into myself with a most scrutinizing eye—accompanied with an upbraiding conscience; and I now see myself in its true light. But have a care of *promises,* said I to my husband, the experiment on your part is truly a dangerous one; there have been many *backsliders* in the world; and it is not too much to assert, but I may *add* one to the number."

"I again repeat, be on your guard—recollect the taunts and sneers you are likely to meet from your friends respecting *such* a marriage. Look before you leap; but if after what I have related to you, you are determined to make me your WIFE—do not reproach me with past circumstances, should any foolish, trifling quarrel ensue between us—*all*; ALL, must be henceforward buried in oblivion. Six months will I allow you for serious consideration of the matter, that you may not be taken by surprise; and if after the end of that period, you renew the proposals, feeling convinced that I shall act up to my assertion, I will then say, there is my hand—my heart—my property; and will endeavour to fulfil all the honorable and sacred duties imposed upon a WIFE; and make your home a paradise.

"At the end of six months, he did renew his proposals of marriage; but I insisted he should take *three* months more: and after that period had elapsed, I still hesitated—and at the end of twelve months, I became his partner for life.

"His noble conduct has so endeared him to me, that I love him with an excess of admiration. He has raised me from *infamy* to happiness; and I will never lose sight of the chance I have obtained. Therefore, I am an altered woman, to all intents and purposes; do not believe me, but come and witness it. Not when my husband is out, but when he is at home. I will then introduce you to him: for in my opinion, to the open hearted—straight-forward Charles Turf—a king might consider such an introduction an honor. Farewell; but I shall expect a visit from you, without fail."

Turf made his bow, and returned to the Pilgrims, who were extremely anxious to know the result of his visit. "Wonders will never cease," said he, "the match-girl is married; yet it is nothing more than I expected. She is an extraordinary creature after all; possessing talents to achieve anything, however diffitult the task; Charlotte Partridge is united to a man of fortune; and of political importance in the country."

"How did she get rid of her gay spark, Rentroll? I should like to hear the way in which she managed that circumstance. I think your story only went as far as her exit from the lock-up house—perhaps you would have the kindness to give us the wind-up of it—as it may be considered now she is a married woman—the climax of her career?" asked Makemoney.

"I have no objection," answered Turf, "only listen."

"The match-girl, it should seem, never exactly overlooked the charge of her being rather flushed with liquor at the masquerade, by Rentroll; and also she rather thought there was neglect about him—he paid less attention to her—and she perceived a *cold*ness that did not suit her feelings. He therefore, was dismissed according to a vulgar proverb, with a flea in his ear. Such a change in the conduct of the match-girl was quite unexpected—he could scarcely believe it true; and treated it as a joke, merely to try the effects of his attachment. But he had slighted beauty—the worst crime he could have committed to a female—more especially with an *adept* in matters of *intrigue*. With pride, as the ci-devant match-girl now valued herself on her property; and in consequence of her mixture with men of the upper classes of society—her wretched origin, was nearly banished from her memory.

"Rentroll was caught before he was aware of it, paying his addresses to another shrine; and the decree of Charlotte was final. No appeal was suffered to be heard against her mandate.

"The sighs of Rentroll—the sorrow he expressed—his applications to be heard in extenuation, all, all, were useless: offers of atonement, accompanied with a rich present—she would not listen to. He was proved a traitor to the cause, and he must suffer judgment—'I cautioned you,' said Charlotte, 'on our first agreement, that it should not be *my fault* if a separation took place between us. I have kept my word; therefore, there is nothing harsh in my decision, and yourself only to blame. What I have decided upon is entirely out of respect to myself. I am once more free. And the name of Rentroll I shall not only erase from the tablet of my memory'; but cease to think that such a person ever had existence.'

"'You cannot do so! you will not, I am sure,' replied Rentroll, visibly touched—'no, no, you do not mean it.'

"'My mind is resolutely made up,' answered Charlotte, in a very lofty tone—'therefore, do not annoy me any more on this subject. If you persist—you will compel me to call for assistance, and expel you from the house.'

"'Expel me from this house,' replied Rentroll, rising in choler, and agitated.

"'Yes, *this* house; it is mine! I am aware that you presented it to me—but it is now mine by a legal claim; therefore, behave decorously, or else I shall put my threat into execution.'

"'Is it come to this?' observed Rentroll—'am I awake—are my eyes open—do not my ears deceive me?'

"'No, there is no deception,' replied Charlotte, 'Ha! ha! ha! It is true you have transferred your affections! Poor fellow! You could not help it. I am not at all angry for your so doing; perhaps, you have shown your taste, and I wish you every pleasure with your new idol, the lovely Maria ——— But such changes are mere matters of *routine* with men of gallantry; and women are equally as fickle-minded, I am well aware! But Charlotte Partridge is not one of that class. Ha! ha! ha! I am a *non*-descript; they do sneer at me, and say, I shall yet be *punished* severely for my coldness, calculation, system, indifference, and several other disagreeable phrases might be added—it may be so! I cannot peep into futurity! The wind changes, and so do women; some, I know, are moved by every blast, and there is no *fixing* them in any quarter.'

"'Do not enrage me beyond the limits of bearing, or perhaps, I may forget myself, and do that, which I should be sorry for afterwards," replied Rentroll, getting into a passion.

" ' Keep your temper, young man, and listen—Your threats are useless, I am too well prepared for you ; a good general will not suffer himself to be surprised. But to recur to the subject, I will put it out of my power to act foolishly, I will settle every shilling that I have got upon myself, while I possess *sanity* of mind, then I cannot be overtaken, or upset in my resolution.'

" ' How have I been mistaken in the character you now appear to me—I am thunder-struck !' said Rentroll.

" ' Yes, perhaps, the knowing one has been *duped ;* but you must pay for your learning !' replied Charlotte, ' Ha! ha! ha! and the knowledge you have received in my company, will prove of far more service to you, than all the dry routine lessons of education.'

" After the rage of Rentroll had subsided a little, and he could give utterance to speech, he observed, in a most indignant tone, ' My once violent attachment towards you, Charlotte, is now changed to the most violent hatred, and I despise myself for having spent one hour ; nay, a single minute, in the company of such a woman, or rather the exterior of one ! Your presence in future, would prove to me, disgusting beyond expression.'

" ' Moderate your resentment, Rentroll,' Charlotte replied, with a sneer, ' be gentlemanly ; and to show you how lady-like I can behave, here is my hand, which I offer to you in friendship. I sincerely wish you well, but the sooner you quit *my* house, will restore me to a state of convalescence: yet, remember, never to *annoy* me any more, for fear of the consequences. Here Betty, open the door, Mr. Rentroll is anxious to depart.'

" ' I must depart, or perhaps, I might commit murder: at all events, endanger your existence,' said Rentroll, ' but I do hope you will yet be punished for your ingratitude and treachery, and that form of clay, for it cannot be human, yet be taught to feel the most bitter sufferings, that can be inflicted on any person, for the remainder of your life !' He then rushed out of the house.

" ' Poor Rentroll, ha! ha! ha! He took it better, after all, than I expected,' observed Charlotte, ' so much for Buckingham.' "

" My indignation would have so far got the better of me," observed Flourish, " that I would have shot her without the slightest remorse ; surely, there could be no sin in ridding the world of such a demon in petticoats ?"

" Hold hard !" said Turf, "till I have finished her portrait, and then make what remarks you think proper ! The match-girl had since her elevation above rags and poverty, perused many books with great attention, during her leisure moments ; and also united her reading with a practical knowledge of society. She shuddered frequently with horror on viewing those outcasts of society— unfortunate women, who seek a *livelihood* in the public streets ; and who might have been, at one period of their lives, living equally in grandeur, if not superior, to herself. The match-girl despised the foolish motto, of a ' short life and a merry one; she preferred being called a creature of art, rather than the mere plaything of the hour, fondled, and carressed for a few fleeting weeks, or months, and then deserted like a pestilence.

" ' I have seen,' said she, ' some of the finest women in the world, in a shorter space of time than could be believed, reduced from thoughtlessness, dissipation, and beggary, worn out from disease, passed home, in a cart, to their parish, and end their wretched existence in a workhouse. Buried without a friend to follow them to their graves, or, a sigh for their loss, or memory. Such an end, I hope, will never be my fate.'

" ' But to prevent such a termination to my career, I have learnt the *value* of riches; if my health is in danger, I can procure the best advice, and the choice of physicians. And if *riches* will not procure respectabi::ty in society, for doubtful females, such a one as I am they will save me from the *cut* direct. Riches will also keep me honest, when perhaps, *poverty* might overbalance all my better feelings, and cause me to commit crimes under wretched circumstances. Besides, rich persons according to the average term of life, enjoy a greater *longevity*, than those who are in want of the necessaries of life. A poor man, or woman, is too often without a friend; and most people shun poverty almost as a crime, even old, intimate acquaintances, are lost sight of and forgotten in the world. The possession of riches make a distinction in every movement in life; there is a *distinction* felt between the rich thief and the petty larceny robber; the judges appear to pity the respectable looking man at the bar; and the officers of justice allow him favour, while the poor wretch may faint from exhaustion.'

" ' Besides, the *opinion* of the rich man has great weight in all companies without shewing traits of Oxford or Cambridge talents; therefore, the acquirement of riches has been my study, and I have found it superior to all the other accomplishments put together. RICHES have procured me comforts, pleasure, and attention, and few persons are to be met with, who will not bow, succumb, and flatter the rich person. Then my determination has long been fixed, never to lose sight of the value of property.

" 'I was a poor, miserable, wretched, poverty-stricken girl, at one period of my life, and almost as ignorant as a dumb animal, but, thanks to my instructor, the poor dead and gone banker, when the daylight opened upon me as to a better view of society, I then saw the world in a new light. I became a little better acquainted with men and manners, and with *practical* experience I improved, at every step I advanced, and I devoured all my lessons with avidity. It has been clearly pointed out to me that if I became a rich woman, my *origin* would never be questioned; my character, if it had been a little *loose*, might be bolstered up, and no questions asked whether I derived my income from the *funds*, landed property, or inherited it from my ancestors, so that I possessed the money to dazzle the eyes of mankind. I have found it to be the truth, the whole truth, and nothing else but the truth !'

" ' Charlotte Partridge, the dirty, beggarly-looking, half-starved match-girl, by a *single change of dress*, a slice of luck, and the golden, glorious opportunity having been seized upon, has transformed me into a rich woman, but nevertheless, it has taught me to look down with fright and horror from the height I have attained. I feel the *lift*, the great lift I have met with in the world ; and it will be my constant study and aim to act upon the system which has done so much for me, and keep me above the frowns of mankind, in despite of the detraction and envy of the world.'

" ' However, the old adage, assures us, the ' Devil is never half so black as he is painted !' This may be rather a saving clause to me, when I am seen at the Bank of England every half year, with a handsome dividend from a round sum of money, placed in the stocks at my disposal : it may tend, in a small degree to wash the ' *blackamoor white.*' It is my intention to retire to some part of England, where I am not known, live in good style, as a woman of fortune ; and if riches can procure a title, buy a place, obtain a character, a funeral sermon, an epitaph, I may yet have the chance before I quit this wicked world, to derive the appellation of an *honest* woman by— MARRIAGE !' "

" A fig for the promises of the match-girl," remarked Sprightly, " if she had the Bank of England for her fortune, and the waters of *oblivion* could cleanse her from her impurities, I would not have her for a companion. To me the thought is disgusting, a wife, indeed, after such a life !—No ! no !"

" Such systematic infamy," said Flourish, " I never heard of before, it is terrific to any thing like sensibility of disposition, the adage is fulfilled to the extent, ' a wolf in sheep's clothing.' "

" Can the match-girl," asked Makemoney, " be a woman ? There is nothing like flesh and blood about her, I am sure. If I remained in her company long, I should be afraid of being carried off in a flash of fire. A woman !—She is a devil ! A dealers by wholesale in intrigue ! Her web is as dangerous to men, as the spider, who entangles and destroys the fly !"

" Ha ! ha ! ha ! what a difference a word makes in the sense of a thing," said Turf, " come, come, my worthy Pilgrims, be more charitable, and do not set your faces against *reformation.* Accept it always at the eleventh hour.

" I am inclined to think it is *real ;* and that it springs from self-conviction ! Previous to her alteration of mind, Charlotte used to call it making a *provision* for herself. Putting a little something by for a rainy day. Keeping the wolf from the door. That a stitch in time saves nine. Ha ! ha ! ha ! Proverbs may be quoted, I am fully aware, to answer every purpose, and the devil, it is urged, can cite scripture to illustrate his argument; but, as a farewell to the match-girl, I will merely observe :—

> Yet believe me, good as well as ill,
> WOMAN's at best, a *contradiction* still!

The above discourse was relieved by the appearance of rather an elderly looking man, one of the tribe of Israel, bowing to Makemoney, and who thus addressed the old Citizen. "You are taking your pleasure, Mr. Makemoney, I perceive, I am very glad to see you, Also retired from the fatigues of business, like myself, I understand; and if you are fond of curiosisies, I have a treat in store for you. I shall be happy to give you, and your friends a seat in my carriage to Rochester, to view them.

" I call it a *Musuem*, and I do not think you will be inclined to quarrel with the term, when you visit it. The proprietor is a jew, like myself, but a most fortunate man. We have been told that the thrice Lord Mayor of London, made all his vast riches by a *cat;* and my friend, Mr. Levi, has realized all his great wealth from an *orange;* more properly speaking, and consistent with truth—A BASKET OF ORANGES! He is a complete pattern of industry and perseverance; and although, as the term goes, 'As rich as a jew!' Ha! ha! ha! up to the present time, there is no pleasure to him, like being in business."

" You have most certainly excited my curiosity," answered Makemoney, " Mr. Lovegold; and if my friends here have no objection to accompany me, I shall be delighted with such an opportunity."

" For my part," said Flourish, " novelty and character are the order of the day with us Pilgrims; we are out upon a tour of discovery : besides, it is not out of place ; neither do we travel out of our road, it being connected with the Banks of the Thames."

" True, my dear friend," observed Turf, " and it is also in unison with the ' search of the NATIONAL !' The tars of old England know how to keep the ' game alive !' at Rochester, while they have a leg to stand upon. In war time, it was a glorious place for the inhabitants. Fortunes were made in no time. The publicans and tradesmen could not take money fast enough. The theatre overflowed every evening ; and the tap-rooms and parlours were all converted into ball rooms, to accommodate the brave fellows belonging to the wooden walls of old England ; who were never happy but when the fiddles were heard, dancing with their girls, and getting rid of every shot in the locker before the anchor was weighed :—

> 'Tis said that with grog and our lasses,
> Because jolly sailors are free ;
> That money we squander like asses,
> Which, like horses, we earned when at sea.

But let them say this, that, or t'other,
In one thing they're forced to agree,
Honest hearts find a friend and a brother,
In each worthy that ploughs the salt sea!

"It is impossible I should assert," replied Sprightly, "to resist the opportunity of visiting the Museum, where the mind will not only be gratified; but surely some remnants of life and spirit remain in Rochester and Chatham, although we are at peace. At all events, let us try the experiment, and during our ride, perhaps, Mr. Lovegold will have the kindness by way of preface, to give a short outline of the proprietor of the Museum. I anticipate considerable touches of eccentricity about his character."

"Nothing, rest assured," replied Mr. Lovegold, "can give me greater pleasure, because Mr. Levi has been the architect of his own fortune, unaided by a single friend in the world; and who has brought up a large and rather expensive family. It might not be too much to observe, perhaps, that a great portion of the houses in Rochester, including two very large wharfs, call the above person—*master*. Be that as it may, to the credit of Mr. Levi, be it spoken, when quite a little urchin, *necessity* compelled him to procure a livelihood, or, go without sustenance. With a few halfpence for his *capital*, he first embarked on the precarious ocean of life.

"He obtained a small basket, and with a very *few* oranges, he made his way to the theatre, and with the old phrase of the people, 'Very cheap,' he invited his customers to taste the articles he offered for sale.

"This occurred during the time the inimitable DOWTON was the hero of the tale, and where the splendid talents of the latter were first discovered as a sound, legitimate actor, and intituled to the phrase of *genuine*. He was elevated to the boards of Old Drury, from this town. His *Sheva, Hassan, &c.* have never been surpassed for eliciting the emphatic effects of nature; if equalled! and who has stood his ground without a competitor.

"In addition to which, Master BETTY that *precocious* star in theatricals, whose fame and popularity reached from one end of, the kingdom to the other, visited Rochester, where his performances crammed the theatre every night. These circumstances had the desired effect for the poor boy—the excessive heat of the theatre produced excessive *thirst* amongst the spectators, and young Levi sold his oranges like wildfire—full basket after basket were disposed of—and the few halfpence from a quick profit were soon turned into shillings; and his trifling capital ultimately assumed a more important aspect in the scale of money matters, and derived the term of PROPERTY.

"Gradually rising from one step to another, the rapid accumulation of articles of all sorts, was the astonishment of every person acquainted with the once narrow means of Mr. Levi. He became a general merchant—and nothing came amiss to him, if he could turn an honest penny, either by his purchase or sale; he bought houses, lands, wharfs, old vessels, iron, musical instruments, books, paper, chairs, tables, jewellery, &c., and give me leave to assure you, gentlemen," observed Mr. Lovegold, "that you cannot ask for any article in general use; or others of a more rare and scarce character, but you can be instantly supplied with them from the museum of Mr. Levi."

Upon the arrival of the Pilgrims at the above place, on entering a very extensive yard, filled almost with cart-loads of old iron; various pieces of ship timber, broken up from worn-out vessels; large stones, wheels, carriages, &c., some of which appeared in the last state of destruction; and fragments of all descriptions, which appeared in the eyes of the Pilgrims absolutely useless: were surprised, when told they were worth, at least, several thousand pounds.

The building, or museum, consists of three stories of great length; but to describe the immense variety of articles in them, would require a thick volume; in fact, communication is out of the question: but strange to say, Mr. Levi could go in the dark and put his hand upon anything he might want, without any difficulty whatever; his memory has been so trained to it, that he has never been found at fault upon any occasion. He attends to his business, assisted by his wife; without any pride or ostentation—shewing every thing with the greatest civility, whether purchases are made or not, at the same time, gratifying the visitors with the most ready answers in his power.

The first story of the building contains the greatest diversity of articles that can be imagined—good and bad—toys for children; saddles, bird-cages, piano-fortes, &c., &c.

But the second gallery excited the astonishment of the Pilgrims, to behold every article that could be named; crowded with household furniture, plate, glass, china, oil-paintings, &c., worthy of situations in a palace.

The third gallery was equally well stored with beds, bedsteads, looking-glasses, decanters; papers of every description, printed books, colours for artists; wearing apparel, &c., &c., and with the utmost readiness, Mr. Levi put a price upon each article.

"It is worthy of remark," observed Mr. Lovegold, "to shew the extent and variety of articles to be met with in this museum of curiosities, that a gentleman made a heavy bet, that any article, however rare or scarce, upon being asked for, could be instantly purchased upon the spot."

The authority was doubtful; the thing was thought totally impossible; when the wager was accepted with the utmost confidence of success.

A SECOND HAND COFFIN was the article enquired for,

the person laughing in his sleeve, exclaimed with the greatest exultation, " now I have puzzled you, Mr. Levi: Ha! ha! ha! you can no more shew me such an article, than you can the man in the moon."

" I will soon put you right," answered Mr. Levi, with the greatest composure, "but do not hollow before you are out of the wood. Step a few yards along with me, when you shall decide the wager yourself, sir." Then pointing to the article in question—"I believe you call it a coffin; and that you may be prepared for such an event, and cause no expence to your survivors, you shall have it a *pargain*." The gentleman retired from the museum, astonished; congratulating himself that the wager had not been for a larger sum.

The above circumstance having been made public; and which also had created a great deal of conversation upon the subject, another person who still doubted the resources of Mr. Levi, offered a wager that he would name an article that the proprietor of the museum could not produce.

This bet likewise was accepted, without the slightest hesitation whatever; and, for a tolerable sum of money, when he was asked what he wanted.

" A SECOND-HAND PULPIT!" said he, " and no *juggling* : but produce it instantly."

" If you had named a church, or a synagogue," answered Mr. Levi, " ha! ha! ha! I must have been defeated ; but within three feet where you now stand, you will perceive a **PULPIT** ready made to your hands ; and if you wish to proclaim aloud that you have lost your bet, you have the opportunity of becoming an orator, to express your defeat."

" Had I been inclined to have made a bet" observed Turf, " most certainly I should have betted against the production of a **PULPIT**—but opposition to a *Second-hand COFFIN*, I should have offered without the slightest hesitation *ten to one!*"

" Strange incidents, I must admit," replied Flourish "but a *Second-hand Coffin*, was shewn to us, if it has not slipped your memory, containing a wax figure of the late George IV. lying in state belonging to the Show-Folks, and which might be exhibited again on a similar occasion."

" No assertion could be more in point or true " answered Makemoney, " that travellers see strange things. I have been highly amused with what I have seen, and the next time I visit Rochester, I shall give Mr. Levi a call, for his museum will bear inspection more than a second time."

" I really do not believe there is such another collection of good, bad, and indifferent articles in the kingdom," urged Mr. Lovegold, " but nevertheless, it is a repository of great utility to the neighbourhood of Stroud, Rochester, and Chatham. The convenience of such a place is beyond calculation, where all ranks in society may be accommodated by a visit to Mr. Levi, and lay out their money

3 E

to the best advantage. His *dealings* are on an immense scale. He will purchase large wharfs; old ships; cargoes, &c., with all the ease and indifference of selling a few sheets of paper. Those persons whose necessities compel them to raise money by an immediate sale of their property, either to a large or small extent, find a ready medium by an application to the proprietor of the above museum. Such are the advantages arising from industry, economy, and wealth—supported by integrity."

The Pilgrims retraced their steps to Gravesend; bade adieu to Mr. Lovegold for the kindness he had displayed in shewing them the museum; when the Steamer with all its celerity conveyed them safe to London Bridge; and a hackney coach brought them safe to their residence, in the first City in the world!

Over their glass of grog, before Somnus had the Pilgrims under his care, Sprightly asked his uncle how long he had known Mr. Lovegold. "He appears to me, a similar personage to the keeper of the museum; and I would wager a trifle, that he also sprang from nothing."

"You are right," replied the Old Citizen; "I knew Lovegold, as the Jews term it, when he was upon the 'top of the street:' but he was always a clever, shrewd *calculating* civil *fellow*. He had the art of turning *rags* into gold! The main chance was always before his eyes. In truth the sons of Abraham, understand the *tact* of getting money better than any other set of persons in the world: but it is easily explained—they act upon *system*—quick returns is their immediate object, and no article whatever will they suffer to remain in their hands for a single half hour, if they can get any profit by it. For instance, a Jew boy will start early in the morning with only sixpence in his pocket; and with this sum he purchases some article or other from servants; he then returns immediately to some of his fraternity, or others, and perhaps sells it for nine pence, and thus by buying and selling the whole of the day, his single sixpence, sometimes has realized for his exertions before night, five or six shillings."

"Mr. Lovegold commenced his career in the above manner, in early life, he was out in the streets soon after daylight appeared, with his bag upon his shoulder, he was extremely active on all occasions, and never let ' *a pargain*,' slip through his fingers. His pence were quickly turned into shillings, the latter became pounds, and step by step, he rose amongst the monied interest, into importance. He opened accounts with bankers—appeared on the change—bought and sold to a large amount—had an eye to politics—looked to passing events; and neglected no opportunity to fill his coffers. He was a careful and a lucky man in the same person: and he never spent a shilling that he could not avoid. He ultimately turned money-lender to the young sprigs of nobility who must have money at any price: and I have heard that forty, fifty, and even sixty per cent. have been paid to him for immediate cash: not thinking that 'Gold *may* be bought too dear.' He has retired with an immense fortune ; and it is but justice to say of him, that however 'hard bargains' he made in the way of trade ; he is now charitable in the extreme to his own people ; and not at all wanting in acts of generosity and feeling towards persons of other persuasions."

" Great an admirer as I am of Shakspeare, I think he has been rather too severe in his remarks repecting the *Jews*," said Turf. " SHYLOCK would have his bond, it is true, but in my intercourse with ' *the people* !' I have found many noble hearted and generous men, alive to all the distresses incident to human nature, and who were never backward in charitable acts. In trade, or merchandize, I am ready to admit—they will have the *advantage* if possible, but in other respects, I have found them excellent neighbours and sincere friends. The passage I allude to is :—

> You may as well go stand upon the beach,
> And bid the main flood bate his usual height ;
> You may as well use questions with the wolf,
> Why he hath made the ewe beat for the lamb ;
> You may as well forbid the mountain pines
> To wag their high tops, and to make no noise,
> When they are fretted with the gusts of heaven ;
> You may as well do any thing most hard,
> As seek to soften (than which what's harder,)
> His *Jewish* HEART !

" It is severe indeed ;" answered Flourish, " but I do not take it in a general sense : individually, it appears to me, directed against the unfeeling conduct of *Shylock !*"

" Our next trip will be to Richmond—that is, if it meets with the approbation of my brother Pilgrims," said Makemoney, " as I have a little affair to settle in the town ; and I feel assured you will agree with me, that if there is one spot more than another, where prospects and fine scenery be the object in view, on the Banks of the Thames—it is the Hill at Richmond."

" Any where? Every where !" replied Sprightly, " Only my dear Uncle, you lead the way ; and the Pilgrims will follow ! Therefore, good night to all !"

CHAPTER XV.

The Pilgrims always on the alert ; another trip to Richmond —the church yard—a visit to the grave of the late Edmund Kean, Esq., as an obligation to his splendid histrionic talents. De mortuis nil nisi bonum. Conversation between Makemoney, Turf, Sprightly, and Flourish, respecting no monument having been erected over the remains of so great an actor. Introduction of Launcelot Quarto, the tourist ; the author's MS. respecting his visit to Woodland Cottage, in the Isle of Bute, the selected retreat of Shakspeare's hero, including a variety of original anecdotes, never before published—description of the splendid picturesque scenery—beauties of the Clyde ; the interior of the cottage, paintings, books, presents made to Mr. Kean ; with a variety of interesting circumstances worthy the attention of the lovers of the drama.

RICHMOND HILL, and its picturesque beauty again proved a great source of delight to the Pilgrims, but on retiring from it, they immediately repaired to the church yard, to take a view of the monument of the late EDMUND KEAN, ESQ. But after traversing the church yard from one end of it to the other, and scrutinizing every thing in the shape of a tombstone, or monument, they felt greatly surprised to find nothing of the sort.

> " Can such things be,
> And overcome us like a summer's cloud,
> Without our special wonder !'

exclaimed Makemoney, "no monument erected to Kean ? Impossible ! We must have mistaken the church yard. Let us enquire of that old man yonder. Can you, my friend, point out to us the precise spot where we shall find Kean's monument ?"

" Nothing of the kind," replied the old man, " has been erected yet. There has been some *talk* about placing a tablet at the head of his grave, or upon the wall of the church ; but nothing more has been done ; however, a great many enquiries are almost daily taking place on the subject, and much *astonishment* has been expressed by every person visiting the church yard. After the grand funeral he had, and the number of persons that followed him, it is rather strange to be sure. But he's gone, and it is —' Out of sight, out of mind !' The remains of the great actor

KEAN'S GRAVE.

lay there, (pointing to the spot,) where you see those letters—
E. KEAN, said to have been written by a boy!"

"It has been urged, by a celebrated writer,''said Makemoney,
"that praises on tombs are trifles, vainly spent! Be it so!
But surely some token, or some land mark is necessary to point
out the *exact* spot where so much intellectual talents are deposited, more especially when it is recollected that the late Mr.
Kean, when in America, erected a monument to the late George
Frederick Cooke, Esq., at his own expense, in remembrance of
his great abilities in illustrating the text of our immortal bard."

"There is an *omission* somewhere," replied Flourish, "why,
a PENNY subscription would have effected so desirable and
grateful object to the feelings. GARRICK had his monument,
and why not KEAN?"

"It is, I think, a libel on the lovers of Shakspeare," observed
Sprightly, "to have let such a subject come under criticism. It
is not too late now to accomplish the erection of a monument
to so ' great a creature !' "

"Very true ;" replied Flourish, "I enter into all the spirit of
your wishes ; and better late then never ! Fulsome adulation is
not required ; but yet, common justice should be done! I am
for a plain monument, after the manner of the one erected in St.
Pancras Church-yard, to an authoress of first rate abilities ; the
late *Mary Woolstoncraft Godwin* ; the more simple the better:—

HERE LIES
EDMUND KEAN, Esq.

The above conversation was interrupted by a very spare, thin
looking man, a thread-paper sort of character, an author by profession bowing to the Old Citizen.

"My old friend, *Mr. Launcelot Quarto*! I hope you are well,"
said Makemoney, "but what brought *you* here?"

"The loss of talent," replied Quarto, "and to mourn with sincerity and silence over the grave of one of the most distinguished men that ever appeared on the English Stage ; but I have
been wandering about for some time, and cannot find any traces
of it! That should not be ! It is true, a whole length statue has
been erected to the memory of the late Mr. Kean, in the rotunda of
Drury Lane Theatre ; and reflects much credit on those persons,
who were the authors of it ; yet, nevertheless, I must insist, that
some *token*, a sort of finger post, should have been placed over
his ashes, that every passer by might heave a sigh to his
memory."

"That is my opinion," replied Makemoney, "but a monument
will yet be erected over his grave I have no doubt. I will lend
a helping hand towards it !"

"It was Mr. Kean's wish during his residence in the Isle of
Bute," said Quarto, "to have been interred under his favourite
oak tree."

"How, sir," asked Flourish, "are you aware of that circumstance?"

"In making a tour through Scotland, I visited the Banks of the Clyde; and as a lover of genius under any circumstances, I felt very anxious to see Woodland Cottage, the retreat of Shakspeare's hero, where I obtained the above information. I made several notes, upon every thing that came under my observation, which I intend to publish, and am enabled to vouch for their authenticity."

"I should very much like to peruse them," said Flourish, "Have you them with you?"

"I have," replied Quarto, "but perhaps the actor having been dead for some time, you may not *think* the MS. attractive?"

"You are wrong there," observed Makemoney, "Every thing, in my humble opinion, must be highly interesting respecting the late Edmund Kean; therefore, if you have no objection, Quarto, let us have the Manuscript to peruse without delay?"

"I have not the slightest objection," answered Launcelot Quarto, "and I also feel assured, that notwithstanding your great veneration for the Banks of the Thames,—the Clyde, with its romantic scenery, will highly excite your attention." The M.S. was immediately handed over to the Old Citizen.

The Pilgrims soon afterwards quitted Richmond Church-yard, for a splendid repast at the Star and Garter Tavern, and over their wine, Flourish entertained them with a perusal of the following sketch of Woodland Cottage:——

MR. KEAN'S COTTAGE AT BUTE—A sail down the Clyde—its picturesque scenery, romantic Situation—splendid Castles, Mountains, Antiquities——Port-Glasgow—Greenock—Rothsay—Argyleshire, and also a visit to Kean's Cottage in the Isle of Bute—with a description of the Grounds, House, Pictures, Library, Books, &c., with several original anecdotes, never before published, of the late Edmund Kean, Esq., Charles Incledon, and Oxberry, connected with the above subject.

> Praising what is lost
> Makes the remembrance more dear.
>
> SHAKSPEARE.

To those persons who are fond of the picturesque, sublime, and romantic scenery, united with a trip by water, let them take a sail down the River and Frith of Clyde, from Glasgow; and all their wishes will be gratified in the highest degree. On both sides of the River, its banks possess an interest of the most imposing character, either on account of its delightful, pleasing, fertility: or, for the appearance of wildness, terrific grandeur, and alpine sublimity.

We started from the Broomielaw, where steam vessels go to Liverpool, Belfast, England, Ireland, Wales, and the Highlands; Dumbarton, Port-Glasgow, Greenock, &c., to give anything like a description of the numerous Gentlemen's seats, Fortifications, Towns, Mountains, Watering-places, &c. which continually attract the eye of the traveller, on his passage to the Isle of Bute, in which the late Edmund Kean, Esq. selected his retreat, would require a volume, and that of no small dimensions—but it would be impossible not to notice one of the most magnificent views in Scotland, on the right of Donaldson's Quay, comprehending a group of the beautiful scenery on the Clyde. Equally fine on passing the ruinous fort of Dunglas. Of its remains, only a small round tower is seen, with part of the wall, situated on a rock, on the water's edge, which has a venerable appearance, and heightens very much this part of the river; the eastern aspect of the Rock of Dumbarton; on the left, the coast of Renfrew, and the towns of Port-Glasgow, and Greenock, their shipping, with the Peninsula of Rosneath, and the lofty mountains of Argyleshire, form altogether one of the most imposing prospects in North Britain.

Proceeding onwards, the view opens in the valley on the left, in which Loch-Lomond lies. This view is also enriched by the mountain Ben Lomond in the distance, and the neighbouring hills. Dumbarton Castle next appears—this famous rock was supposed, anciently, to have been a volcano—and considered to have been by some writers as the *Balclutha of* OSSIAN : it is a huge bicapitated rock, with nearly equal summits; and was once a fortress of great strength, and deemed almost impregnable. On the side next the river is seen the governor's house, and barracks, with the lower and upper castles, anciently under different governors. It is still the residence of a garrison, and very much frequented by travellers. Near the village of Renton, by its banks, is the old mansion-house of *Dulquhurn*, in which was born Dr. TOBIAS SMOLLETT, the celebrated historian novelist, and poet, who, in his delightful " *Ode to Leven Water*," beautifully describes the characteristic charms of his native stream. A lofty column has been erected to his memory.

Ardmore, distinguished by the name of the " *Great Promontory*," which is a beautiful wooded peninsula, and very attractive by its running out a considerable projection into the Frith. Newark Castle, a fine piece of antiquity, built in 1599, with a round tower near it. The castle appears much older; and it is viewed as one of the most perfect buildings of its kind, in Scotland. It was once fortified. From its situation and appearances it affords an admirable subject for an artist.

Not far distant from Newark Castle is Port-Glasgow, a compact, well built town, and a place of some importance; it has an excellent dry dock, capable of containing ships of 500 tons to be repaired. It has three excellent piers or quays; —and the harbour is safe and commodious, having about fifteen feet water at ordinary tides. Ship-building is carried on here, and an extensive rope-work, sugar-houses, &c.

About a mile from the above castle is seen, the town and harbour of *Greenock*, which, in the 18th. century, only consisted of a row of thatched houses—but it has increased so much in trade and population, that the inhabitants are calculated between twenty and thirty thousand. It contains many elegant houses. In its two harbours, the east, and west, are several excellent commodious quays, and a graving dock.

In 1812, a society was instituted for the encouragement of arts, and literature and taste is said to be much cultivated and cherished in Greenock—the Clyde here, expands into a beautiful and extensive basin, formed by the different promontories on the opposite coast of Dunbartonshire; and the scenery on the opposite coast, particularly the lofty rugged mountains, called Argyle's Bowling Green, (part of the western extremity of the Grampians,) exceedingly grand and romantic.

The village of Gourock is situated on one of the most beautiful bays in Scotland—hilly and mountainous, but extremely healthy; and few places of equal population, can boast equal instances of health and longevity; the air of Gourock is very beneficial in weaknesses of pulmonary complaints, and general debility. The view of the shipping on the Clyde, continually passing it—with its wherries and fishing-boats, renders it attractive.

Numerous other delightful situations might be pointed out before you arrive at Rothsay, the capital of Bute : which is a place of great antiquity, and enfranchised in the year 1400, and was at that period a royal residence; Rothsay, the present day, is a well-frequented watering-place in the summer months. It has an extensive bay, and several well-built houses; but the princfpal object of attraction and curiosity is, its very ancient Castle, and is frequently visited by travellers of the highest rank in society. It originally consisted of a circular court, one hundred and thirty eight feet in diameter, surrounded by a wall of eight feet in thickness, and seventeen feet high, with battlements. The Court was flanked by four towers, at nearly equal distances—the gateway was on the north side, betwixt two of the towers, and the lower part of it is still to be shewn in the vaults of the additional buildings; the whole was cased with hewn stone, and surrounded with a wet ditch of considerable breadth, and about fifteen feet deep; It was, however, considerably enlarged by King Robert II, who built a palace, projecting from the ancient gateway into the ditch. About fifteen years since, the Marquis of Bute directed the rubbish to be removed from its ruins; in consequence of which, the foundations of several buildings which were not known before, and several curiosities were also discovered. The " Ivy-mantled " wall, added to its great age, strongly interests the attention of the stranger. The island of Bute also contains many other vestiges of antiquity, amongst which is a " hill fort." The island extends from south-east to north-west, about eighteen miles, and about five in breadth. The air, in general, is considered temperate, having neither the violent heat of summer, nor the extreme cold of winter, as on the main land. Fogs seldom affect Rothsay. The island belongs mostly to the Marquis of Bute, who has an excellent seat at Mountstuart, situated on a delightful eminence, in the middle of a wood. The climate from its equableness and purity, is said to be rather favourable for persons afflicted with asthmas, and shortness of breath. There are six lochs on the island; but only three of considerable size; and which are full of perch, pike, and trout. The herring fishery has been a source of great improvement to the town within the last few years: also a large cotton manufactory contiguous to it; indeed, Rothsay is viewed as a rising place.

On Friday the 17th of May, 1833, at one o'clock, the *Inverary Castle, Steamer* put us on shore, near the Bute Arms, Rothsay, kept by Mr. D. M'Corkindale; a very splendid hotel, at which place we hired a noddy, and instantly set out for *Woodland Cottage*, the late Mr. Kean's retreat, nearly three miles from Rothsay. Perhaps it may be necessary to premise, that no person was admitted to visit the cottage, without obtaining a card of admission from M'Corkindale, or the appearance of one of his vehicles at the gate; the road to the cottage was of the most rugged and jolting description, in fact, it could not be called a road: we passed Rothsay Castle in our journey, and at length we arrived at the desired object of our pursuit the Lodge, distant from the cottage about a quarter of a mile. Over the gate, on the right side were placed the busts of *Massinger*, and *Garrick*; and upon the left were those of *Kean* and *Shakspeare*, all of them well executed; here we got out of the noddy, and accompanied by JOHN READ, the gardener, porter, &c., walked towards the cottage, delighted with the situation and prospects all around us; but the female who had the care of it, had gone to Rothsay for some provisions. In order to occupy our time till her return, we then took a synopsis of the exterior of the building, which is only one story in height and has nothing to recommend it to the notice of the visitor, in point of architecture, except its extreme simplicity; Mr. Kean, it appears, was his own architect; therefore style, or according to the rules of art, were entirely out of the question, and, it should seem, all that he required was a comfortable dwelling.

The situation of WOODLAND COTTAGE, is of the most romantic description; in the front of it, a large green plat is seen gradually sloping to the margin of *Loch-Fadd*—exhibiting a fine lake of water; but it had no boat upon it—the scenery all around the lake is enchanting and picturesque beyond communication; at the back of the cottage, stands a high hill covered with heather, and in beautiful bloom. We ascended by a circuitous route to the top of it, or nearly so, on which is situated the FOGG HOUSE; this building is circular, and capable of dining about a dozen persons; it is, however, of the rudest description, but nevertheless it may be said to be perfectly in keeping with the rest of the picture. Here the spectator might almost say with Dr. Goldsmith.—

I sit me down a pensive hour to spend,
And placed on high, above the storm's career,
Look downward, where a hundred things appear;
Lakes, forests, cities, plains, extending wide,
The pomp of Kings, the shepherd's humbler pride.

On the outside of the *Fogg House* the following words are to be seen;

'TIS GLORIOUS THROUGH THE LOOP-HOLES
OF RETREAT—TO PEEP AT SUCH
A WORLD !

In the interior of which, was a seat made of branches from trees, and also a small table, in the Fogg, (or *Moss*, as we term it in England,) in the roof, the coat of arms looked conspicuous, *adopted* by Mr. Kean, (the crest of which, the tragedian was at a loss to furnish, when Douglas Kinnard, Esq., suggested to him the boar's head, from his immense success in Richard. The latter gentleman, is the godfather to Charles Kean.) Indeed, it was a glorious sight to VIEW SUCH A WORLD from the glorious loop-holes of retreat at every point, the prospect from the elevated situation of the Fogg House, was truly fascinating. Description of it, however faithful it might be given, would not, in the slightest degree, convey the magnificence of the surrounding scenery to the reader, indeed, it must be seen to realize the great beauties of the situation altogether, something after the manner of Kean's beloved Shakspeare:—

The poet's eye in a fine frenzy rolling,
Doth glance from heav'n to earth, from earth to heav'n,
And as imagination bodies forth
The form of things unknown, the poet's pen,
Turns them to shape, and gives to airy nothing
A local habitation and a name !

We descended with reluctance, nay, with regret, to quit such a truly luxuriant, picturesque view, and therefore, cast many a longing, lingering look behind. The idea of the Fogg House, first originated with Charles Kean, but his father furnished the words which appear outside of it. The female had now returned from Bute, and was in waiting to show us over the cottage. Upon entering the hall, rather a small one, a bust of *Kean in Brutus*, on a pedestal, presented itself to our notice; but, from its youthful appearance, it must have been taken several years since; however, it was a fine likeness of the great actor.

The cottage consists of *nine rooms*, two or three of which, on the ground-floor, were nearly empty, and in a state of confusion. We then entered the library, a mere parlour, and nothing to recommend it, as what might have been anticipated from so great a reader as the late Mr. Kean. Here persons who were on intimate terms with the actor, have frequently found him, when he wished for something like quietness, and to be at his ease, in bed, surrounded by piles of books, not altogether unlike *Dominie Sampson's* predilection to obtain the works of the learned pundits; however, it did not portray the *character* of a LIBRARY as to good taste. Indeed, the books were by no means numerous, the principal part of which were secured by wires, and locked up in the bookcases, except a few scattered on some shelves, of minor importance: yet, there were several very valuable ones, folio editions of Shakspeare, presented by the Duke of Devonshire to Mr. Kean. Two very large globes upon handsome mahogany stands, with compasses underneath them, they were most certainly an embellishment to this apartment.

Over the fire-place in the middle of it, was an engraved portrait of *Lord Essex;* his lordship, we believe, was at one period, a great admirer and patron of Mr. K., also a whole length likeness of *Kean* in Brutus, and a portrait of *David Fisher* as the son of Brutus, a very fine, well-know theatrical print, and engraved at the great actor's expense, and merely made its way before the public as gifts to his friends and acquaintances, Likewise portraits of his two sons *Howard* and *Charles*. Howard died very young.

A whole length portrait, beautifully executed by the late Sir Thomas Lawrence, of the late *John Kemble*, in *Hamlet*, near to hichu was *Garrick*, in *Richard*, also a very small likeness of Kean, in Shylock, *Miss O'Neil* in the character of *Juliet*, and the late *Mrs. Siddons*, a well-known, remarkably fine engraving, as *Melpomne*. A whole length engraved portrait of *Curran*, the barrister, of great Irish popularity. A finely ornamented piece of writing of the speech made to Mr. Kean, on the presentation of the gold cup by his brother and sister performers of the Theatre Royal Drury Lane, with their signatures attached to it.

A very fine copy, an engraving of the face of Garrick; but not one oil painting was there to be seen in the library. A few mahogany chairs, a table of the same description, ink-stand, pens, &c., formed the whole of this apartment, and very unlike what might naturally have been expected on entering the library of so great an actor, and man of taste, as the late Mr. Kean.

We then ascended one flight of stairs to view the DRAWING ROOM, which, most certainly, partook of the character of a magnificent apartment; but its appearance suffered a considerable drawback by the splendid carpet belonging to it, not being down; and also the windows were destitute of the elegant, rich, and beautiful curtains, which were laid aside in one corner of the room. But the animating prospects of NATURE, clothed in all the richest beauties of vegetation, both in the front and rear of the cottage, left the other articles of ART, intended as objects of attraction, completely in the back ground. The room is rather lofty, the walls of which are covered with very handsome French paper, representing the Greek festivals, &c. A splendid looking-glass, over the fire-place, the chairs very good, made of the finest mahogany, with tables to correspond. Two very large mahogany boxes, handsomely shaped, one as a wine cooler, and the other for tea and sugar; also, an elegantly finished upright piano-forte. A large mahogany stool upon castors; several handsome bound volumes of music on the shelves, and a few other miscellaneous books scattered about; on the pianoforte there were three or four sheets of MS. music, composed for Mr. Kean, when he attempted the admirable and versatile character of the highly famed CRICHTON. A few curious and scarce stones in a glass case; and also a most beautiful model of the Alps. The drawing-room did not contain a single picture of any description. A small *boudoir* attached to the above room, was quite empty, the walls of which were covered with French paper, representing the Bay of Naples, Mount Vesuvius, &c. The above *boudoir*, divided the drawing-room from the sleeping apartment of the great actor. A very plain, but handsome, mahogany four-post bedstead, the hangings of which were rich and splendid, were lying on the bed, a plain chest of drawers, with mahogany chairs, composed this place of repose belonging to the inimitable representative of *Othello*.

The front parlour, on the right hand as you enter the hall, is also very plain, but very handsomely furnished. Over the fire-place is a finely painted likeness; said, by the servant, to have been an uncle of Mr. Kean; but from the striking likeness it bore to him, it might be presumed to have been the portrait of his father, the late *Moses Kean*, of highly talented abilities as a mimic and lecturer, after the manner of the celebrated *George Alexander Stevens*, indeed, the same opinion, according to the servant, had been expressed by several theatrical visitors to the cottage.

On the left hand side of the hall, in another parlour, stood a bedstead with a bed upon it, the *coverlid* of which was a very large buffalo's skin, brought by Mr. Kean from America. Also some swords and daggers: one of the swords was said to contain *poison* at the end of it; likewise, a terribly looking double pointed dagger, capable of dealing out death at every thrust, but the hand of the assailant was secured quite safe in the handle of it, and to have attempted to wrest it from the grasp of any person who held it, must have been attended with the most dangerous consequences. Here also, we discovered, upon the shelves of an open cupboard, the remains of a once perfect theatre, belonging to his son, Charles Kean, composed of elephants, Turks, horses, &c., for his amusement as a child,

since which period he has made such rapid strides towards attaining the highest situation of an actor, as to astonish the theatrical world. His animated representations of some of Shakspeare's characters ; are, in several instances, if not
equal to his great and unrivalled parent, very little inferior to him. At one period
of his life, the late Edmund Kean, Esq., publicly expressed his opinion that his
son had no talents for the stage to arrive above mediocrity ; but he lived long
enough, not only to alter that opinion, but also acknowledged that it had been
founded in error.

We then bid farewell to the HOUSE OF DEATH, (although the news had not
arrived of the mournful exit of Mr. Kean,) to take a last view of the fine OAK,
which the great actor often viewed with the highest feelings of delight :—

> Absurd to think to over-reach the GRAVE,
> And from the wreck of names to rescue ours;
> The best concerted schemes men lay for fame,
> Die fast away ; only *themselves* DIE faster.
> The far-famed sculptor, and the laurel'd bard,
> Those bold insurers of eternal fame,
> Supply their little feeble aids in vain.

The above OAK, was said to be the finest in the island, twelve feet in circum-
ference, situated at the declivity of a hill, under which runs a quiet murmuring
stream of water. "*Here*," said the late Mr. Kean, pointing to the spot, to his
gardener, JOHN READ, with great firmness, "*John Read, whenever I die, I should
like to be buried under this matchless Oak-tree; and I ask it of you as a promise,
that you will most sacredly keep, which is to watch the ground day and night for six
weeks after I am deposited under the Oak.*" The gardener, who appeared to us
to be rather an intelligent sort of man, thus replied to his master. "*If I should
outlive you, sir. But pray do not talk of dying. However, if that painful
moment should arrive, you may depend on my word to watch with assistance, night
and day for six weeks, in fact I will never quit the oak, until* NATURE *is quite exhausted.*"

On our making enquiries of John Read, *how* Mr. Kean spent his time at Bute.
He replied, " Principally, during the day time, he was out of doors, and very
fond of fishing : he would also, frequently dine at the very top of the hill, in the
Fogg House, contemplating the prospects and beauties of nature, which so delightfully presented themselves from this elevated spot, to his view: at other times, he
would take refreshment under the oak tree. Mr. Kean," he also observed, " appeared to him, to be quite delighted with his retirement at Woodland Cottage ; that
he was, in every point of view, a most excellent, and kind-hearted master, scarcely giving any thing like *trouble*, to those persons around him." John Read
told us, in Loch-Fadd, the stream of water before the house, contained great
quantities of fish, but principally perch and jack. He mentioned the names of Mr.
Beverly and his son, having visited Bute Cottage and the grounds, also SHERIDAN
KNOWLES, ESQ., likewise Mr. Francis Seymour, the well-known provincial
manager in Ireland, and also once the lessee of the celebrated theatre in Glasgow,
who was on terms of the greatest intimacy with Mr. Kean.

The gardener stated to us, that the summer of 1832, was quite a blank as
to visitors, which he thought was owing to the cholera in Bute, and that up to the
period we were engaged in conversation with him, (May 17, 1833,) scarcely any
person had solicited to see the retreat of Mr. Kean. John Read had lived in the
service of Mr. Kean, nearly eight years, he gathered some flowers for us out of
the grounds, and he likewise cut three small pieces off the OAK, (one of which I
gave to Mr. Duncan Shaw, of Greenock, who visited Woodland Cottage with me,)
to keep as a *remembrance* not only respecting our visit to Rothsay and the Oak
tree, under which Mr. Kean had often seated himself to view the distant prospect
of the fine country, and the luxuriant treat of his own grounds, but to the memory
of SHAKSPEARE'S HERO !

It appeared, that Mr. Kean had not visited Bute for the last sixteen months.
In January, 1832, he passed ten days at Woodland Cottage, with great satisfac-

tion and apparent delight; and he observed to those persons around him, that he thought his health was materially improved by his remaining *quiet;* his mind not disturbed, he retired to rest early; and that he also had the pleasure of asserting in his retreat, that he had *distanced* disgraceful sycophants, and fulsome flatterers, which men, like himself, were too often nauseated with in public life. The female servant, an intelligent Scotch girl, likewise good-natured and civil in the extreme, and who had lived in the service of Mr. Kean, for the last four years and a half, spoke of her master with raptures—"That he was kind, very kind, to every person about him, and upon his quitting Bute, he begged of her to have the fastenings of the house and windows always strongly secured before she went to rest: " I say so, (said this great master of the passions,) not merely on account of the little property I may leave behind me, under your immediate care, but to guard yourself against any ruffian, who might be tempted to ill-use a lonely woman, and that a thief might also commit his depredations with a better chance of success." ·

The gardener's lodge being at some distance from the house, and in consequence of the feeling advice given her by her master, a fine large house dog was immediately procured for her, as a protector. The servant maid told us, that she never felt the slightest fear, neither did she apprehend any thing like danger, when the above faithful creature of all other animals, slept at her door every night, "But I am sorry to say," said she, "he died about ten days ago." She described all the things in the house with clearness and perspicuity, very different in manner and tone from the dull, stupid, monotonous way of those persons whose *business* it is to describe the monuments in Westminster Abbey, or to give an account of the pictures in Windsor Castle. Upon her being asked in what manner Mr. Kean spent his time after having finished with his walks and other pursuits out of doors, she said, " Reading, at times; but principally at the pianoforte, and singing; and that she could have listened to his delightful manner of expressing the words of the various songs from morning until night, and never have been tired. He was a most extraordinary man altogether; and his manners and mode of address were mildness to the very echo."

" Mrs. Kean," she said, " and her son Charles, lived in retirement for upwards of twelve-months, at Bute."

The Jewess, so designated by the friends of the late Mr. Kean, and to whom the great actor unfortunately, not to say unhappily for himself and family, resided with him at *Woodland Cottage* for six weeks. The servant urged that the Jewess was very attentive, and kind to him in every respect, and administered all those little comforts, which Mr. Kean stood so much in need of, during the last few years of his existence; but ultimately, he paid very dearly for this sort of pretended feeling towards him, and according to report, she had *wheedled* (if not insisted) from Mr. Kean whilst at Bute, to satisfy some pressing demand she had to discharge; had obtained from him the sum of four hundred pounds; and at another period, very soon afterwards, the unsuspecting disposition of this " Great Creature," the man of all others, who might have been expected from his fine display and illustrations of the various passions of human nature, incapable of being deceived by the mysteries and duplicities of mankind, advanced, without the least hesitation, another five hundred pounds. He was so much *infatuated* with this woman, it is said, and so perfectly under her control, that he could not refuse her any demand from first to last—the sum of three thousand pounds would not pay for all the money he had lavished upon an ungrateful woman;—

> Women are ever masters when they please,
> And *cozen* with their kindness: they have *spells*
> Superior to the wand of the magician.

We now took our departure, often turning round to take a last look at the cottage and grounds, with the melancholy reflection pressing on our minds, that the arrival of the next post would bring an account of the decease of one of the greatest actors in the history of the Stage, until we arrived at the porter's lodge, to exclude us altogether from Mr. Kean's retreat at Bute. We immediately retraced our jolting journey to the Bute Arms, and had a different, but another very fine view of Rothsay Castle, and sat down to a most excellent dinner, and a capital glass of wine. Previous to our dinner, our worthy host, Mr. M'Corkindale behaved to us in the most polite manner, and shewed us the splendid gold cup, rather a large one, and given to Mr. Kean in the year 1816, by the performers of Drury Lane Theatre, with all the names of the subscribers engraved upon it.

Also the *Mosaic*, richly-worked gold box, representing a boar fight, which had been presented to Mr. Kean by the late Lord Byron, on account of the great actor's unrivalled illustrations of the characters of Shakspeare. This box, it was well known, Kean valued as the highest gift in the whole of his truly splendid presents. "When I received it from his lordship," said he, "I considered the circumstance, not only as one of the proudest moments of my chequer'd life, but the most gratifying to my feelings during my theatrical career. My highest hopes of ambition never amounted to this—such a compliment from so illustrious a character in the wide field of literature, and one of the greatest poets of the age—an immense judge of human nature in all its bearings—rewards me more, much *more*, for all the ills and 'proud contumely' I have met with in the early part of my life. To the last moment of my existence, this invaluable present, not for the splendid display of workmanship and talents on the box, or its weight in gold—but I shall cherish it with delight, as a grateful remembrance of its most enlightened author."

We likewise saw a very richly worked gold box with numerous figures upon the outside of it. In the inside was engraved,—"The gift of D. Bingham, Esq., of Montreal, a most sincere friend, and ardent admirer of Mr. Kean; for his unrivalled performances in the characters of Shakspeare." The workmanship and taste of the above gold box, are of the most exquisite description.

Also a gold medal, characteristically ornamented, representing the *Western Philanthropic Institution*, given to Mr. Kean for his noble and disinterested exertions, to promote the views of the above noble and humane institution.

A *Silver Bible*, to which was suspended a silver key, on a blue ribbon; engraved on the back of the bible appears—"*Lodge*, 240, *Waterford*." The above lodge made it a present to Mr. Kean. This present was the only article which came ashore from the wreck of a very large vessel.

The *gold box* we likewise saw, which had been presented to him by the members of the Theatre Royal Covent Garden, during their short stay at the English Opera House, when the former Theatre had a very narrow escape from being destroyed, by an escape of the gas. Mr. Kean, with the utmost liberality of disposition, performed a few nights, GRATIS—in aid of the salaries of his distressed brother actors.

All the above presents were deposited under the immediate care of Mr. M'Corkindale; for whom, it appears, Mr. Kean had a very sincere regard, and long established in his confidence. Mr. M'Corkindale, during the absence of Mr. Kean, managed the whole of the affairs connected with Woodland Cottage. Our worthy host shewed us Pierce Egan's Panorama of the Sporting World, in which appeared the following autograph—"*The gift of Edmund Kean, to his friend, D. Corkindale, July*, 1829—*Greenock.*

At five o'clock we left Rothsay, in the Rob Roy steamer, on our return to Greenock, and which proved a trip of the most delightful description—the prospects on both sides of the Clyde were really enchanting—the lofty Ben Lomond Dumbarton—Argyleshire—and a view of the mountains in which ROB ROY once dwelt. We landed at Greenock at seven o'clock; but had scarcely entered Mr. Shaw's house, when we were made acquainted with the death of Mr. Kean by the arrival of the Post. Therefore, we may assert, we were the last persons who paid a visit to the cottage of Mr. Kean at Bute.—"*Sic transit gloria Mundi!*"

This Cottage, it appears, was put up for sale in Glasgow, on May 1, 1834, by auction, at the Buck's Head, Argyle Street, by George Robins, but the "King's name was not a tower of strength" in this instance—and the recollection, or the mention of the splendid talents of the departed hero, Mr. Kean, who had nightly filled the Theatre Royal in this ancient city, and where his son (CHARLES, the successful representative of his father's characters) first met together, (as actors) and performed in the tragedy of Brutus to overwhelming applause, had not the slightest effect upon the minds of the bidders—who seemed like men without spirit, and cold as *ice*, as to any *offerings* for this most delightful retreat of a performer, whose like we shall not, for many a day, perhaps see again ; and fulfilling the melancholy truth, observed by the late brilliant, witty, and inimitable Richard Brinsley Sheridan, Esq.

> " The ACTOR *only* shrinks from Time's award:
> *Feeble* tradition is his memory's guard ;
> By whose faint breath his merits must subside,
> Unvouch'd by proof—to SUBSTANCE unallied !"

In spite of all the oratorical abilities of the auctioneer, to excite some liberal feelings in honor of the "*mighty dead*," a long tine elapsed before five hundred pounds was offered for *Woodland Cottage*, which, at the least farthing, cost six thousand pounds, independent of the value attached to it, as the residence of the late Mr. Kean. After great exertion had been made to procure something like a bidding, it was *knocked down* for one thousand and fifty pounds to a Mr. Railton, a writer of the Signet; or rather, it is said, "*bought in*" by that gentleman :—

> " Out, out brief candle !
> Life's but a walking shadow, a poor player
> That struts and frets his hour on the stage—
> And then is heard no more; It is a tale
> Told by an idiot, full of *sound* and *fury*,
> Signifying NOTHING ! ! !"

This satire is not only extremely *biting* to the utmost extent, but the truth of it does not admit of the the slightest doubt—and all actors must feel the severity *acutely* indeed, as to their peculiar traits being handed down, or impressed on the minds of posterity. The late JOHN KEMBLE, the greatest Roman of them all : MRS. SIDDONS, who positively stood *alone* on the stage ; and GEORGE FREDERICK COOKE, nature personified in the most animated style of excellence. LEWIS, the *gossamer* of his time, and rich as gold in the representations of Goldfinch, Tom Shuffleton, Squire Tally-ho, &c. Irish JOHNSTONE, without compare, in Sir Lucius o'Trigger, Dennis Brulgruddery, Looney M'Twolter, &c: QUICK's Little Isaac, and Old Cockletop. The blank which MUNDEN has left is, Old Dornton, Crack, Dosey, &c. EDWIN's Jemmy Jumps, Lingo, &c. Mrs. JORDAN's Nell, Country-Girl, Little Pickle, &c. ELLISTON's Rover, Duke Aranza, Three Singles, Mercutio, and a lover, that every actress seemed positively to feel in reality that her lover was at her feet—have ALL, within a few fleeting years, made their *exits*, and " gone to that bourne, from whence no traveller returns." Therefore, except those persons who can remember their *greatness*—relate the manner—speak of their unrivalled excellence, and tell their sons or relatives about their *peculiar* styles of acting—they are almost forgotten by the public in general ; and it is that sort of *taste* so difficult, if it can be at all communicated, so as to convey a lasting and accurate portrait of an actor for the amusement of the rising generation. JACK BANNISTER, once so truly celebrated, and deservedly so, as an actor ; and FAWCETT, equally brilliant as a performer of the very first class, both since dead, but whose names are scarcely ever mentioned—and KEAN, who saved Drury Lane Theatre from ruin, and SHAKSPEARE's hero, to all intents and purposes, has scarcely been interred four years—(" Die, two months ago, and not forgotten yet ! Then there's hope ; a great man's memory may outlive his life, half a year ; but by'r lady, he must build churches then.") and his memory, and great talents, it should seem, generally speaking, are almost consigned to OBLIVION.

To the lovers of retirement—*Woodland Cottage*, is the very reality of the thing, and might be viewed almost as a sort of Paradise on earth ; the poet might have dwelt upon its beauties again and again ; and still have found fresh subjects for the exercise of his pen :—

> The statesman, lawyer, merchant, man of trade,
> Pants for the refuge of some rural shade,
> Where all his long anxieties forgot—
> Amid the charms of a sequester'd spot;
> Or, recollected only to gild o'er,
> And add a smile, to what was sweet before.

We understand, and that from excellent authority, that the idea of having a cottage on the banks of the Clyde, or contiguous to it, first originated with Mr. Kean, whilst he was performing a round of his characters at the rising and improving town of Greenock, then under the management of Mr. Francis Seymour. During one of his aquatic trips on the Clyde, to enjoy its romantic scenery, he landed at Rothsay, and fixed on a spot of ground in the Isle of Bute, which took his fancy, with great delight ; an application was immediately made to the Marquis of Bute, to erect a cottage, and inclose the grounds as a park, about thirteen acres in extent, as a retreat and personal residence for Mr. Kean. The request was granted without delay, and on the most liberal terms, by the noble Peer, out of respect for the unrivalled talents of the great actor. Be that as it may. But it appears that Woodland Cottage was erected for other purposes besides being a splendid retreat for Mr Kean, in an *economical* point of view, also renovated his health, and kept him out of the temptations and dissipation which he was continually exposed to in the Metropolis. From its contiguity to *Glasgow*, not more than *six* hours sail from Bute ; also, in *ten* hours Mr. Kean could have arrived in *Edinburgh*, in a day and a half he might have acted at *Aberdeen*, from thence, in TWO days, he could have appeared either at Liverpool, or Manchester, and from the former town, in *twelve hours*, he conld have reached Dublin. From the capital of Ireland, *a day's ride* would have brought him to Limerick, Waterford, Cork, Belfast, &c., and from the sums he nightly received from managers, his income would have realized *three thousand pounds* per annum, the whole of which theatres would not have occupied his time above three months in the year, leaving the other nine for his most perfect enjoyment in his cottage at Bute.

We are assured that the above plan was first proposed to Mr. Kean by his friend, Seymour, at a moment, when the great actor, full of disgust, had expressed himself full of anger and regret, that after all his great exertions—lucrative provincial engagements—he was not able to meet his expenditure in London ; indeed, so readily did Mr. Kean enter into this plan, that he signed an agreement, for three years, with Mr. Seymour, for the sum of Ten thousand pounds. Mr. Seymour to procure the engagements—pay coach hire, &c., and to risk the loss, or obtain the profit of such a speculation; but owing to the illness of Mrs. Seymour, the agreement was cancelled.

The temptations of London, most certainly are, and must have been, very great and seducing—nay, expensive, if not injurious, to the health of a man of splendid talents like the late Mr. Kean. Where is the individual, a lover of the drama, who might not have been proud to have spent an evening in the company of so delightful an actor? But it should seem, Mr. Kean was not fond of the company of great folks, that is to say—"Titled personages !" there was an etiquette due to them, from their rank in society, which might have operated as a kind of reserve upon his general character and habits—the freedom of expression—something like a man being "ill at his ease;" or, rather in accordance with the notions expressed by the late Charles Incledon, respecting the company of "GREAT FOLKS." "My dear boy," said he, to one of his old and favourite cronies, to whom he could unbosom himself without the slighest hesitation—"you know, great folks are great folks—and they will be great folks ! They eat like great folks, they talk like great folks—they dress like great folks, and they *sing*—no, no by G— there Charles Incledon has the *pull*; he is one of the *great* folks—you are aware, as being the first English singer in the world. Yes, Charles is *great* in that instance, you will admit ; but I have always found the P.Q.'s, to me, the two most difficult letters in the alphabet to acquire, to render myself quite at home with the great folks. You know, my dear boy, that an early rehearsal in life is necesary, to become perfect to a letter—and I would not play a part, for the best manager in the kingdom, without a rehearsal. Therefore, as I never had a rehearsal on the P.Q. system, I must require the assistance of a Prompter at some time for "the *word*," and I should not like to appear imperfect, even in the character of a walking gentleman ; I only find myself at ease, in the company of great folks, when I am singing at the Theatre, and they are seated in the boxes. You know, my dear boy, I love the great folks in their proper places—and I do not think my friend, *Mr.* Devonshire—no, no—I am out—I want the word—I mean his Grace the Duke of Devonshire, an honor to the cloth, could have given a better definition of the great folks than Charles Incledon, the first English singer has done ; no, nor half so well explained by any of the black-lettered fraternity, either in, or out of Paternoster Row, or the British Museum into the bargain, I admire the word *great*, my dear boy ; there is substance attached to the thing—I like to be *the* great singer ; to have a *great* house—a *great* cash account ; a *great* number of friends ; *great* Provincial engagements—and a *great* creature in my way of expression. Also, to experience *great* ease—*great* luck—to be *great* in little things, and *great* before the public ; that's the greatness, my dear boy, next to Charles Incledon's heart, the first English singer on the stage ; therefore, being of a little consequence any where else, to me, does not signify a brass farthing. And last of all, my dear boy, you know that I never had a foul mouth in the course of my life ; and it has been said, that some of the sweetest notes have escaped from my lips, the first English singer of the day, that has beaten all the foreign trumpery of squallers and Jews to a stand still—and that's what I call being GREAT. Now, my dear boy, if you wish to know any more about the "GREAT FOLKS," you must look for them in Debrett's Peerage." How far this view of visiting " Great Folks" coincided with the opinions of the late Mr. Kean, we are not exactly aware ; but in the company of his brother actors, we have found him one of the most liberal men alive, and very loud in the praise of some of the Performers he had met with in the course of his different engagements in the country.

Dining one day with him at Billy Oxberry's, mine host of the Craven's Head, in Drury Lane, after the cloth had been removed, and ' *Non nobis domine*,' had been given with a spirit and harmonious effect, that would have made the members of the Philharmonics to have opened their ears with raptures, and the fine bass voice of George Smith had completely filled the room, with his song of the ' *Wolf*,' never excelled, and we have some doubts if it was ever rivalled, Mr. Kean gave the health of Mr. Bengough, (a respectable, pléasing, but who had never obtained the appellation of a great actor ; yet, nevertheless, he had strutted and fretted his hour on the boards of Drury Lane Theatre, for some seasons, but, ultimately, finished his career at the Coburg Theatre,) and in doing it, he prefaced the toast with the following observations, " I rise," said he, " to propose the health of my friend, Mr. Bengough, not only as a most worthy private character, but an excellent actor, and if I have derived any public fame for the personification of Othello, I thus publicly declare, that the knowledge of *acting* it, I derived from the brilliant efforts, I witnessed in the representation of Shakspeare's Moor of Venice, by Mr. Bengough.' The above toast was drank with enthusiasm during the absence of Mr. Bengough, but on his return to the table it was mentioned to him, the high panegynic which Mr. Kean had pronounced on his acting the part of Othello, when the immortal actor again rose, and repeated eyery word with the greatest animation, and also to the delight of the company present.

I have, on several other occasions, heard him speak in the highest terms of other performers ; the late Mr. Elliston was decidedly a great favourite of Mr. Kean, and to use his own words, he styled Mr. E. " a most brilliant actor !" The late Mr. William Oxberry, as a comedian, also stood very high in the opinion of Mr. Kean, and that his praises should not be considered emptyones, he presented

Oxberry with a very valuable gold ring, as a testimony of his preference and regard. Whenever the impulse offered itself, Oxberry's parlour, (so designated, although a room on the first floor,) Mr. Kean popped in, as it were on the sly, when the table was completely covered with punch, three bowls being his first order. He was extremely liberal to all the actors round him, and numerous instances might be related of his generosity and feeling to country actors, could time, or space, permit their insertion. Yet, notwithstanding the above little sort of ' break-outs!' we believe, on only one instance, did he absent himself from his duty, and then it was owing to a mistake about a stage coach leaving the town he was dining at for London.

Every person was eager to obtain the patronage of Mr. Kean ; indeed, at that time, his name *was* a tower of strength, and his residence, and the theatre were assailed with notes, letters, messages, and petitions, from morning till night, from persons of the first consequence in society, down to the veriest intruders and pretenders, and *duped* without end under the *garb* of charity. It is true, he was rather fond of what is termed ' a bit of life !' and to be met with frequently at the sporting dinners of Tom Cribb, and Belcher's, the first three or four seasons after he became the ' great creature ' in London : he had a *penchant* for the *Fancy ;* and those who were loud in their applause to see the abilities he displayed, nay, superior excellence, in FENCING, will have no doubt, that he could make a good and scientific hit with the *gloves*. He was a frequenter of the old rooms in Bond Street, when kept by Mr. Jackson, for the tuition of self-defence, on one day, and on the other, by Henry Angelo, Esq., for fencing.

I well remember at Belcher's one night, to have heard Mr. Kean call upon the late Joey Munden for a flash song. The latter unrivalled actor, made up one of his comical faces, and rolled about his expressive eyes with such an irresistable effect, that the whole company were immediately on the *titter*, when he began the well-known chaunt of ' NIBB'S POUND !' one of the old school of *slang*, belonging to the times of Johnathan Wild. I also heard Mr. Kean sing two or three charming duets with the late Jem Barnard, a great companion, at that period, of Mr. K's., but who, from dissipation and extravagance, lost his mind, his situation at the theatres, became the object of contempt and derision, and was utterly reduced to beggary before his death.

OXBERRY'S room, on some evenings, was a great treat to the visitor. Reporters were to be met with, literary men, actors, both town and country, and authors, singers, &c., were to be found, rubbing against each other over their cigars and grog ; theatrical subjects were generally the order of the day ; but politics have been debated here with almost as much vigour and talent, possessing something like the reality of the House of Commons. Mine host was truly a host in himself, and take him for ' all in all,' he was a brilliant of the first water, his tales and anecdotes claimed profound attention ; in fact he made them a sort of DRAMA, and suited the action to the word ; he possessed the art of magnifying a *mole* into a mountain ; nothing fell dead from his lips, there was no still life about his composition. His face seconded his efforts, he was likewise well-read, possessed also good tact as a compiler, could write off a short paragraph with good point, and he had the *nous* to hit off two or three successful melo-dramas. His edition of plays were much admired, and his likeness of actors the best published. His coffee room deserved the appellation of a portrait gallery, he was a great lover of the arts, and fond of paintings. He was a printer by profession, and a great hero, at one time amongst the private theatricals, from which the renowned showman, Richardson, extracted him, to become a more public character ; he then, to use his own words, experienced all the vicissitudes attached to the life of a strolling player, up one day, and *down* the next, a smoking joint, sometimes to be seen at the commencement of the week, and then only *smelling* a dinner as he might chance to pass a cook-shop ; but he never lost his spirits, or pined at his fate, on the contrary, if hunger teazed him at times, his wit sharpened on it, and he was always on the *qui vive* to improve his circumstances. The ' good time ' came at last, when he bade adieu to strolling, vagabondizing, gaffing, &c., he also took his leave of an empty cupboard, and farewell to swallowing, daily, pages of the drama, called ' fresh study,' and candle ends avaunt ! The *trea-*

sury was now regularly open to give him fresh supplies, full salaries always paid and Billy Oxberry himself again !   In addition to which, he was a master printer, and sent out his own works to the world, a member of the Theatre Royal Drury Lane, and mine host at the Craven's Head, all happiness !   But, just as he had established himself in all the above points, and beginning to make his way, the 'Grim King of Terrors' entered his domus on the sly, as if he had had a pique against the laughing comedian, and *floored* him at a single hit, to the great loss and lamentations of his numerous friends, at his unexpected and premature exit ! It is thus the late *Tom Greenwood*, the celebrated scene painter, described him :—

> Quite pleased so snug a shop to know,
> Where he could *stop* and take a Go !
> But ere he from the house retired,
> The landlord's *name*, below, inquired ;
> "'Tis OXBERRY," said the man, and bow'd ;
> The Frenchman stared, then roar'd aloud,
> " He's of de *dairy*, de large pan,
> PRINTER, *Poet*, Player, and Publican !"

As a convincing proof that the late Mr. Kean, possessed a great deal of liberality of mind, as well as setting no value upon money, during his visit to the lakes of Killarney, in company with Mr. Seymour, the manager, and two other persons, the whole of the party, not exceeding four individuals ; his tavern expences, boats, and boatmen, band of music, &c., the time of his stay altogether not exceeding a week, amounted to nearly, if not quite, seventy pounds !   The Irish manager advised Mr. Kean to look over the *items* of the bill, as he thought some mistake might have occurred, the sum being very large ; and not to be completely satisfied, as a matter of course, with the sum total of the bill.   " No, no," said Mr. Kean, " I will not examine the contents of it, the landlord, according to re-report, is a good, honest fellow, one of the right sort of men.   I have been delighted with the attention I have received, and the comforts I have had at the Inn ; indeed, so much so, that I am perfectly satisfied with the account.   I am well aware such trips are expensive, but they are not every day sort of things, and we must pay for superior accommodation every where.   Remember, Frank Seymour, we are a long way from London, also, a great distance from Dublin, and when I have been near the Metropolis of England—Epsom Races, I have been made to pay for accommodation *there* ; therefore, I will not grumble at the sum I have paid for visiting the Lakes of Killarney ; to witness scenes unrivalled, and to hear an ECHO, that is worth double the sum it has cost me.   I would not have missed the glorious sight—*seeing* what I have seen, for treble the money, for it is my opinion, there is no *comparison* between the enjoyment of intellectual pleasure, and amassing a large pile of cash.   I am obliged to you, Seymour, for your attention towards me ; but depend upon it, the expenses at the Lakes of Killarney, is not one of the worst *errors* I have committed in my life respecting the cash account, and I again repeat I have no regret about it, and we will leave the landlord to enjoy the fruits of his labour."

During the short stay of Mr. Kean at Greenock, one night, after the performances at the theatre were over, and rather late in the evening, spending an hour or two at a tavern, in a very jovial manner, and feats of agility being the argument amongst the party, all of them boasting in turn of the *leaps* they had made, when Kean, seeing the window open, and by way of silencing the ' great doings,' observed, " When I used to act the part of *Harlequin*, I have taken a far greater jump than that which now presents itself," (without looking at the height, and regardless of the danger, a row of iron rails being beneath the window,) " Impossible !" was the general cry, when to their utter astonishment, *out* Kean leaped, and it was supposed that he had fallen on the ground, and must have hurt himself.   The company immediately left the room, and it being a corner house, and the part alluded to, at the back part of it ; but to their great surprise, Kean was not to be found.   They returned to the room conversing on the strangeness of the affair, and a variety of conjectures were formed as to the result. However, Mr. Kean did not make his appearance, and the company left the tavern for their homes. It appeared afterwards that Mr. Kean had received a violent fall in his flight from the window, which had shook him to the very centre, and in the moment, he scrambled himself together, as well as he could, and strolled about he knew not whither. A poor old fisherman, who lived on one of the flats, in a house at no great distance, was awoke out of his sleep by a person groaning and full of pain, at the door of his apartment, where Mr. Kean had crawled to ; the poor old fisherman got out of bed, struck a light, and found the great actor perfectly insensible : although he did not know the value and consequence of his guest, yet, like the good Samaritan, if he did not pour oil into his wounds, he dressed himself, and placed the object of his commiseration in his stead, something like a bed, watching over him with all the care and kindness of the most attentive friend. After Mr. Kean had been asleep for about three or four hours, he started up, as if from a *trance*, and seeing the poor old fisherman's head decorated with a cap, then looking at the miserable state of the room, also at the rags and old pieces of sail made up for a bed, something after the manner of the affrighted *Hamlet* at the appearance of the ghost, addressing the old veteran with his eyes darting fire :—

Angels and ministers of grace
Be thou a spirit of health,
Or goblin——

"Puir body," answered the fisherman, in a tremulous tone ; "compose yourself—compose yourself! you dinna ken where you are. I am no *speerit*, but poor old Sandy Pike, the fisherman, at your bidding!" "Do not mock me, sir," (answered Kean, in a state of confusion, and theatrical sort of rage,) "but tell me where I am, and how I came here, undressed in this beggarly, wretched apartment?" "Puir body," said old Sandy Pike, "I dinna ken that circumstance. All I know is, that I found you insensible at my door-step, quite *foued*, when I put you into my bed, and I hope you are now much better, for you were, puir body, in a pitiable plight when I took you in." Kean looking at him, with a sort of expression, which, perhaps, no other man living could have done so much with his eyes, exclaimed, in a tone of gratitude, that penetrated the very soul of the old fisherman—"Kind creature! disinterested old man! worthy soul! and you did not know me?" "I dinna ken," replied the old fisherman, "that I ever saw you before, puir body, wfth my e'en!" "Know then, good old man, that my name is Kean, the actor," said the leaper. "Kean, the great mon," exclaimed the fisherman, surprised beyond description, "you! that I saw in King Richard, last night. I had heard of your great abilities and fame, and I could not resist the opportunity of going to the play-house. But do not deceive me!" Kean a little more composed, felt for his pocket book, and gave the old fisherman a five-pound Bank of England note, at the same time telling him to go to the Inn, and bring back with him a post-chaise with the blinds up, and not to mention to any person who had ordered the carriage. "I will never part with this bank bill," replied the old fisherman, overjoyed with the honour of having such a guest, "come what may, but treasure it up on account of the abilities of its once great owner." Sandy soon returned with the post-chaise, but during the short interval, Kean roused himself as well as he could, then grasping the hand of the old fisherman, and thanking him, a thousand times, for his humanity, darted like lightning into the post-chaise, and very soon afterwards was in bed at his own lodgings. He received no other hurt but a few bruises, which, after a day or two's care, he resumed his professional duties, laughing heartily at the circumstance, observing I forgot the old adage—'to look before you leap!' also gratefully praising the Samaritan like feeling and conduct of old Sandy Pike, the Greenock fisherman!

During his stay at Woodland Cottage, his secretary, Mr. Phillips, left him, thinking it incompatible with his idea of respectability, and also at variance with the rules of propriety, to remain any longer under the same roof with the JEWESS.

he, therefore, wrote the great, little man a letter, excellent in point of composition, on the subject, a sort of *moral* sermon, and recommending Mr. Kean to give up the lady in question, and to turn aside from his ERRORS.   He received the letter in good part, and read it over two or three times, smilingly, said to Seymour, who was then with him on a visit, " This is well done, and kind of the old boy, there is something like real friendship about it, and I cannot quarrel with his intentions ; but, I believe, it is generally understood that we are *born* in ERROR, *live* in ERROR, and, I am sadly afraid, there are too many of us who *die* in ERROR !   But no more of that—we have other fish to fry at present, and let us proceed with the business at issue."

The following sort of remembrance, by way of EPITAPH, is inserted here, that the proprietor may insert it under the leaves of the Oak Tree, at Woodland Cottage, if he thinks proper :—

IN ONE OF THE MOST SEQUESTERED,

YET TRULY DELIGHTFUL, ROMANTIC SPOTS IN THE

ISLE OF BUTE ;

AND FAR REMOVED FROM THE BUSY HUM OF THE GREAT WORLD,

HERE LIES—(OR, MIGHT HAVE LAIN,)

EDMUND KEAN, ESQ.,

WHO DIED AT THE PREMATURE AGE OF FORTY-FIVE YEARS,

ON WEDNESDAY, MAY 16, 1833, AT

RICHMOND, IN SURRY.

NO WORDS CAN BE MORE APPLICABLE TO THE MEMORY OF THIS

MOST DISTINGUISHED

ACTOR ON THE ENGLISH STAGE, THAN THOSE FROM OUR IMMORTAL BARD !

WHOSE VERY SOUL HE SEEMED TO INHERIT BY CONCEPTION;

BUT WHOSE IDENTITY OF CHARACTER AND ILLUSTRATIONS OF

SHAKSPEARE,

RENDERED HIM UNEQUALLED, UNRIVALLED, AND WITHOUT A COMPETITOR :

THEREFORE, TAKE HIM FOR " ALL IN ALL," WE SHALL NOT

LOOK UPON HIS LIKE AGAIN!

IT IS A TRUE RECORD OF THE MOVEMENTS OF THIS GREAT ACTOR IN HIS

BUSY CAREER THROUGH SOCIETY : AND THOUGH WITH SINCERE REGRET

FORM MANY ERRORS, WE ARE LED TO

EXCLAIM

ALAS ! POOR HUMAN NATURE !

YET, NEVERTHELESS,

HE WAS A MAN FOR A' AND A' THAT !

CHAPTER XVI.

*he PILGRIMS anxious to visit the SOURCE of the THAMES ;
one of the most important features in their Pilgrimage :
also to follow the STREAM to the finish of it. The NORE
—explanation and authorities upon the subject. A trip to
Gloucestershire ; friendly reception at Fox-hunter's Hall.
SIR HENRY TALLY-HO, Bart., a choice spirit, one of the
Olden Times : TURF, FLOURISH, and SPRIGHTLY, quite
at home ;—*

A southerly wind, and a cloudy sky,
  Proclaims a hunting morning :
Before the sun peeps we'll briskly fly,
  Sleep and a downy bed scorning.
Away, my boys, to horse away,
  The chase admits of no delay,
Now on horseback we've got—

*MAKEMONEY, in a new character, a second JOHNNY
GILPIN, who went faster and further than he intended—
(but a miss is as good as a mile,)—and, the Old Citizen,
none the worse for his unexpected gallop ! Outline of an
Oxford Scholar. Unlooked for incidents. The old Citizen
sporting a toe. Sketch of an accomplished thief, &c.*

" WE ought to see the *Source* of the THAMES, or else our Pilgrimage will not be complete," said Makemoney, " the trip, both by land and water, will afford us great variety of scenes ; and I am quite sure that *distance* is of no consequence to my brother Pilgrims, so that the trip is attended with pleasure and profit."

" *Distance,* my dear friend," replied Turf, " is quite out of consideration with me at any time ; and if Jerusalem, or Jericho, were named, I should not demur ! So let us be off !"

" Nor I," said Flourish, " under a good leader, I would march to the end of the world; and never acknowledge that I felt *tired.* But surely Gloucestershire cannot be termed a great distance from the Metropolis ?"

" A fig for distance," said Sprightly, " either rowing, sailing, turf, or turnpike, I am ready, only mention the place, my dear uncle, and you will find us jolly Pilgrims on the alert."

" Gloucestershire, I think, is the spot," said Makemoney,

" but I know that Wiltshire claimes the honour of it also.
However, I am not historian enough, or scholar, to decide the
question ; but I have read, that from an infant spring, near
Cricklade, not far from Malmesbury, denominated THAMES
HEAD ! is the source from whence the mighty river springs :—

> First the fam'd authors of his ancient name,
> The winding *Isis*, and the fruitful THAME ;
> The *Kennet* swift, for silver eels renown'd,
> The *Loddon* slow, with verdant alders crown'd ;
> *Cole*, whose dark streams his flow'ry island lave,
> And chalky *Wey*, that rolls a milky wave ;
> The blue, transparent *Vandalis* appears,
> The gulphy *Lee*, his sedgy tresses rears ;
> And sullen *Mole*, that hides his diving flood,
> And silent *Darent*, stained with Danish blood !

" I understand," replied Turf, " in a place called Trewsbury
Meadow, in the confines of Gloucestershire, called THAMES, or
Isis Head, the spring tumbles forth in a confined vale, from a
layer of loose, or flat stones, through Oxford, Henley, Maiden-
head, Windsor, Eton, Richmond, down to the Nore. The definition of the word Thames is not necessary for us Pilgrims to
enquire into ?"

" Not at all," answered Flourish, " it has occupied the time
and pens of some of our greatest writers, both in ancient and
modern times. Holinshed, Stowe, Speed, Pope, &c. It is
quite sufficient to our purpose to understand that however
Gloucester may claim the honour of the SOURCE of the Thames,
it first becomes navigable in Wiltshire. It is, I am told, 240
miles in length ; 188 of which are navigable, when it joins the
Medway. The latter river, it is said, embraces the sea. Therefore, I think, let us begin at the *Source*, and follow it until we
come to the NORE. Let us finish all well !"

" Nothing could be more apropos," replied Turf, " I have a
worthy friend of mine in Gloucestershire, not far from the spot,
Sir Henry Tally-ho, Bart., who will not only receive us with
all the warmth of a brother, but he will tell us all about the
matter, and furnish us with some fine cattle to visit the SOURCE
of the Thames. He is one of the old school, an accomplished
sportsman, of ancient pedigree and good, but a gentleman in
every point of view. He is a high-spirited fellow, and I know
we shall all be at home to a peg. His mansion is the seat of
hospitality ; and my brother Pilgrims will experience, at Fox-
hunter's Hall, all that they can wish for, where they will be
surrounded with pleasure ; comfort, at their elbows ; and
happiness wait upon *their* nightcap,"

" That's your sort," said Sprightly, " the character you have
given of this fine old fox hunter, is inviting in the extreme : but
my friend, Turf, is at home every where. In fact, he is a sort
of polar star to us wandering Pilgrims !"

"True, my nephew," echoed Makemoney, "Turf, is not only one of the most accommodating fellows that I ever met with in the course of my life, but the readiest man to point out the most agreeable, method of spending our time either by land or water. Let us make the best of our way to Gloucestershire, and on our return to London, afterwards, not a spot, or a creek, connected with the source of the Thames, to the finish of it, at the Nore, shall escape our notice."

No time was lost, the quickest conveyance was adopted, and in a short time, the Pilgrims found themselves comfortably seated at Foxhunter's Hall. It was the true scene of hospitality altogether, and so much sport and diversion were afforded to them, that the days and nights positively flew away.

But Makemoney, Sprightly, and Flourish, were rather out of their element respecting the conversation which took place between Turf and the baronet. Sir Henry Tally-ho, was a thorough-bred sportsman, and he took delight in scarcely any other subject. The pedigree, blood, and bone belonging to the crack horses, the winners of the St. Leger, the Derby, and the Oaks, he had at his fingers ends, without consulting any book of reference. The qualities of the jockies were also strongly impressed upon his memory, and there were few, if any race course in the kingdom, that he had not shown himself at one period or another, during his life.

At his own table, he was a choice spirit of the highest quality, and over his glass a most entertaining companion, in his *peculiar* way; he was fond of a song, cheerful upon all occasions to the echo, and his greatest delight appeared to be—to see and make every body happy around him.

The library, left to him by his predecessor, was seldom disturbed, and the works in it, he jocularly used to call—"Horses of another colour, and did not belong to *his* book." Yet, every thing *new*, respecting the field, he purchased with avidity, for his perusal when laid up with the gout, or compelled to remain within doors. The Racing Calender, he pointed out to his friends with delight: the Stud Book, was also a treat to him, the Sporting Magazine, from its commencement, was his 'History of England,' as he termed it; and Boxiana, reminded him of 'divers blows in sundry places! All the above books he had read so often, that he used to boast, he was as perfect about sporting events, as a clergyman, belonging to a cathedral, with his bible.

Sir Henry Tally-ho, had no ambition to become an M. P., nay, he had refused that honour several times, observing, with a smile, that he would be *distanced*, double-distanced, amongst the 'Great Creatures' in the nation, and the House that claimed his attention, when in London, was the *Red* house, and also the most attractive room, was the subscription parlour at Tattersalls.

The baronet likewise, at one period of his career, was a great patron of the art of self-defence: he was fond of a cudgelling-match, and could play a good bout at single-stick himself. The prize-ring in its zenith, had not a greater supporter, and the different styles and manners of the various boxers, he would often descant upon rather eloquently. He used to call himself an Englishman to the back-bone, and only exulted over Molineaux, the man of colour, when he was defeated by the champion, Tom Cribb, but apologized for this *partiality*, by observing, the *national* honour was at stake in the contest.

Sir Henry Tally-ho was a first-rate shot, and he could bring down his bird with the best marksman in Gloucestershire; but out of the sporting world he pronounced himself little more than a *dummy*, and had sense enough to keep his ' tongue within his teeth,' when subjects were broached that he was ignorant of, or could not comprehend. Such was the hero of Foxhunter' sHall.

Upon Makemoney's stating to the baronet that the principle object of their journey was to view the SOURCE OF THE THAMES.

"It is only a few miles from the hall," replied Tally-ho, "and a very pleasant ride through a delightful country. I have plenty of horses, gentlemen, at your service, therefore, I beg you will not stand upon any ceremony."

"We shall avail ourselves of your kind offer," answered Turf, "but to praise the cattle of Sir Henry Tally-ho, would be quite out of place."

"Stop a bit! stop a bit! said the old Citizen, "you forget that I am no horseman, Mr. Turf, therefore, I must go to see the *source* in a carriage of some description; I shall then run no risque of being thrown off my guard."

"My friend," replied the baronet, " you need not be under any alarm as to being thrown, I have an old hunter, who has seen the best of his days, and a baby might ride on him: besides, he is as quiet as a lamb. Old Spankaway was once a tip-top creature at a hunt, I admit, but his day has gone by, and, like the old ones in general, both men and horses, his speed has left him; therefore, sir, I recommend the animal to your notice. Any thing like danger, is not to be apprehended; but if you doubt my opinion of old Spankaway, my grooms will satisfy you in every respect!"

" I do not doubt your word, sir," answered Makemoney, "but I repeat I am no horseman, and I may say, that almost since I was a boy, I have not been across a horse; and I am afraid I might be rather *timid*."

" Never fear," said Turf, "we shall be all together and travel at a moderate pace; so that you may make up your mind no harm will come of it. The road is a quiet one, and not like the dangers to be apprehended on a race course."

PILGRIMS at the SOURCE of the THAMES.

Flourish and Sprightly also backed the argument of Turf ; and Makemoney was ultimately persuaded to mount old spankaway as a worn out hunter ; who would want the whip to make him go if required ; and that no spirit was left in him to become a *starter !* The old hunter in his day had never refused a leap, and could clear a five barred gate with the utmost ease and safety.

The old Citizen, like most persons who were unaccustomed to riding ; or who had acquired from practice how to manage a horse ; had not travelled above a mile or two before he found himself rather awkward in his seat, and went much faster, bobbing up and down upon the saddle, than the animal on which he rode. And to add to his discomfiture, unfortunately for Makemoney, the hounds were out, and the full cry of a musical pack came across the ears of old Spankaway, and off he went like lightening, to join the chase, before the old Citizen was aware of it, and giving the ' go-by ' to his brother Pilgrims. The situation of Makemoney was truly ludicrous in an instant, something after the manner of *Johnny Gilpin :—*

His horse, who never in that sort,
  Had handled been before,   ·
What thing upon his back had got,
  Did wonder more and more.

Away went Money, neck or nought,
  Away went hat and wig ;
He little dreamt, when he sat out,
  Of *running* such a rig !

His brother Pilgrims could not help laughing heartily at the sudden start made by old Spankaway, and the *instinct* he displayed to be in at the death, and compelling, as it were, the old Citizen to join the hunters, whether he would or not ; but they soon checked themselves, and became alarmed for his safety. Makemoney tried all his strength to stop him, but he had no more power over the mouth of the horse than a fly, and the first ditch that came in his way, over he went, with the utmost speed, and strange to say, Makemoney kept his seat, to the astonishment of his friends, who expected every minute to behold him prostrate on the ground. Turf clapped spurs to his horse, and rode after the old Citizen with all the speed he could make, to render him all the service in his power ; but on old Spankaway joining the huntsmen, and the hounds being at fault, he was stopped by Makemoney, without much difficulty.

Makemoney was not long before he dismounted, and never felt the ground under his feet half so pleasantly in his life, and upon recovering his wind, for all the breath was nearly out of his body ; what with the fright and the speed he had gone, he congratulated himself that it was no worse. And with a smile upon his face, " Miracles will never cease," said he, " to think that an

3 G

old fellow like me, should leap over a wide ditch, and not fall into it. I shall place it amongst the *extraordinary* incidents of my life !"

" My dear uncle," observed Sprightly, " to behold you once more safe and sound, has made me more happy than I can express : I dreaded the worst consequences to occur when I saw old Spankaway take the leap ! It is truly astonishing to me *how* you kept your seat. But your life is saved, and I am grateful for it !"

" To me also," said Flourish, " it is a high gratification that you have been restored to us without injury ; and it will be a memorable circumstance, connected with the *source* of old Father Thames, that you *hunted* it out ! Ha ! ha ! ha !"

" You may depend upon it, my dear Turf," said Makemoney, " I will never be seen as a rider any more ; and in the character of a fox-hunter, or follower of the hounds, one pill is a dose. And old Spankaway may live in retirement for the remainder of his days for me ; nor, no more leaping of ditches, or pantaloon tricks. It is true I might have been *in* at the death !"

" I am glad to find you so jocular on the subject," replied Turf, " at all events you have verified the old system, that a man never knows what he can accomplish, until he tries the experiment. With all your *discretion*, you cannot aver you *looked* before you took the leap ! Ha ! ha ! ha !"

" No person can regret more than I do," remarked Sir Tally-ho, " that the old horse should have *bolted* with you ; I could have betted twenty to one such an occurrence could not have taken place. I thought all the fire and speed had long since been taken out of Spankaway ; but I suppose he is like an old coachman, that likes to hear the smack of the whip. But we must endeavour to forget it over a bowl of punch."

The Pilgrims had a jolly night of it with the old baronet, before he would suffer them to take leave of Foxhunter's Hall.

The *windings* of the Thames, the object of their pilgrimage, once more became the point of consideration, and like surveyors of an estate, they left not a spot, or a creek, that could illustrate the argument in any shape whatever.

" I have it," said Flourish, in ectasy, " Oxford, illustrious Oxford, will be in our path home ; and a day or two spent with my friend at that celebrated seat of learning, may give us a little more information respecting the *source* of the Thames, than otherwise, we might acquire. The Oxonians *ought* to know something about the matter from their opportunities of *research ;* but yet, I believe, the scholars, in general, could give a much better dissertation upon the qualities of different wines, than any thing like a grave description of water ; the latter article is not their forte, I am aware. Be that as it may, I propose that we Pilgrims call upon my intimate friend, Stephen Giltleaf, Esq., one of the jolliest fellows upon earth ; if the musty, fusty rules of the College, have not *sobered* him down to propriety itself! However, I have been told he is rather an altered man, and sees things in a different point of view, to what he did, before he entered, as an inmate, the College of —— No matter. The name of the institution, is not at all necessary to my purpose, and for the respect I bear, and shall always entertain for that veneral seat of eruidition and classical knowledge, prevents me from offering any thing, in the slightest degree, that might be construed into a *slur* upon any of its members!"

"Excellently well said," replied Makemoney, "boys will be boys, and some of them never obtain the character of men. I need not be told that *learning* is one thing, and conduct in life another. Oxford scholars, it is admitted, *read* well, and better, perhaps, than most persons; but whether they *think* and act with more propriety than persons in different stations in life, is a question I am not called upon to solve at this moment, but I shall be happy to visit Mr. Giltleaf. I remember his old father, he died very rich and left his son a large fortune. He was a general merchant, lived near the Tower of London, and dealt largely in rags, to supply the paper mills. Old Giltleaf, was considered a very ignorant man as to education; but was anxious to make a bright fellow of his son, therefore, nothing that could improve his mind, and send him forth into the world as a scholar and a gentleman, was neglected: the ambition of the old man was such, that he would have liked to have seen his son fill the office of prime minister, if such chance ever came within his grasp. I hope the son has entered into all the views of his father, who, notwithstanding, the deficiency of scholarship, was one of the best calculators in the kingdom, and one of the greatest adepts, in the commercial world, at turning *pence* into pounds!"

"Should he ever arrive at that honour," observed Sprightly, "he will not be the first tradesman's son who has filled that high and important situation."

"Giltleaf is no *pedant*, I am sure," answered Flourish, "and I should think nothing of the *Dominie Sampson* character, will be found attached to his character—enveloped in books of the black-lettered school; although, I have heard, he has obtained a *degree* or two. However, I am sure he will make all of us heartily welcome."

"That is the only *token* we want," remarked Turf, "and he is welcome to keep every word from the Alpha to the Omega, to himself. We do not seek learning, but friendship!"

A rich man, like at every other place, does not long remain in obscurity at Oxford: *learning*, it is true, has its admirers, and is in great repute on this classic ground; but money, that all powerful coin, carries every thing before it, and GILTLEAF was *pounced* upon, without any trouble.

The Pilgrims immediately upon their introduction discovered

that Giltleaf came up to the discription given by Flourish. They understood each other at their first meeting ; and the Oxonian expressed himself honoured by their acquaintance. With a frankness of behaviour which delighted them, he said, " Such as I have, my worthy Pilgrims, I will give unto thee, further ceremony, might be troublesome unto both parties ; therefore, I once more repeat you are heartily welcome, and think and act as if you were at home ; I shall say no more on the subject. But in your characters of Pilgrims, I have a duty to perform, if you are hungry, I will give you something to eat, if you are dry, drink shall be in readiness to allay your thirst. If you are in want of attire, I will clothe thee, and when your eye-lids close with o'erwatching, I will find a resting place for thee. Ha! ha! ha!"

" You have our thanks, beggars as we are," replied Make-money, " and we shall accept of your favours, like mendicants of the first class. Ha! ha! ha!"

Every thing that was worthy of attention in Oxford, Giltleaf showed the Pilgrims with the greatest alacrity and attention. The venerable piles, magnificent libraries, stately halls, and the good old stingo, (fine ale,) for which some of the Colleges have so celebrated a character, also claimed their taste.

Over the farewell dinner, after the cloth had been removed, when the wine was going round with steam alacrity, reserve vanished, diffidence was out of sight, and Liberty Hall became the decided feature. Flourish asked his friend, Giltleaf, what work he had lately been employed upon. " I have heard that you have been exercising your pen very much lately. I expect to see your name enrolled with the first writers as you had rather a touch when at school, of the *cacoethes scribendi,* and now you have, as it were, withdrawn from the world, and can pursue your studies without interruption, there can be no excuse for you to give society a treat."

" Surely you are laughing at me, Flourish," replied Giltleaf, " talk of manuscripts, studies, no interruption, withdrawn from the world, &c. No, no, my boy, you are quite wrong in your con-jectures, the world, I consider too good to withdraw from it ; I cannot part with my old friends with so much indifference. I quarrel with no man for his *taste ;* but I assert that my habits will not do for the *cloister.* In the arts and sciences, Oxford is the finger-post ; but for life and character, I am still wedded to the metropolis. My father sent me to College to improve my education; and I flatter myself, as far as that goes, I have deriv-ed immense advantages from the able tuition I have received at Oxford ; but as to *my* writings, my friend, they only become valuable to the possessors, when they contain the words—' Pay to me, or my order, one hundred pounds,' and I honour them with a draft on my banker. The history of my talents will be much better appreciated in that way, than in any other *history* I might attempt to write. No! rest assured, I have always kept the two following lines before me, as a caution against sending any of my MSS. forth to the world, more especially, as I have not the slightest pretentions to authorship :—

> A little learning is a dangerous thing,
> Drink deep; or, taste not of the Pierian spring!"

"It gives me great pleasure, sir," said Makemoney, "to hear you express yourself with so much modesty. It encourages me to ask you a question, amongst your various readings, if you are acquainted with the *source* of the Thames."

"I know no touch of it," replied Giltleaf, "and to be candid with you, that is not a *source* from which I should derive any pleasure. I have nothing to do with *antiquity!*"

"Be it so," replied Flourish, "but let not your modesty prevent us from knowing what *degrees* you have obtained since you have been at Oxford."

"None!" answered Giltleaf, "as far as respects learning, if that is your question. But I will tell you what I have ever been anxious to obtain, according to my own idea of DEGREES. Listen, most worthy Pilgrims, the best horse according to the *degrees* of high-bred cattle. To have for a sincere friend, the best fellow according to the *degrees* of honour and gentleman-like conduct upon all occasions, and the finest creature of the female sex, not absolutely for her beautiful face, incomparable form, and lively wit! No, but answering according to the *degrees* of true love, without a particle of doubt on the subject; affection and sincerity, that cannot be questioned; and a *heart* in all its purity of sensibility, seated in the right place of the human frame, to feel and act properly in every situation of life. If they are not Oxford degrees, I trust I shall never lose sight of them until I cease to exist."

"Excellent," replied Turf, "to become acquainted with such degrees of comparison, are worth travelling, any time, a hundred miles, although out of one's road. Accept my best thanks, Mr. Giltleaf, for the knowledge you have displayed of society."

Oxford had had its day with the Pilgrims, and the hospitality and conversation of Giltleaf, they left with regret. They accordingly retraced their tour down the river until they arrived at the Custom House. Makemoney proposed they should sojourn for a day's rest at his house.

"It is rather fortunate," said the old Citizen, on looking over the letters which had arrived during his absence; "that invitation cards, from the commodore of the Yacht Club, have been sent to us, to witness the sailing match. A steam boat, it appears, has also been engaged for the purpose, to accommodate the numerous friends of the members of the club, from which, every tack made by the captains of the vessels who sail for the prize, can be seen with ease and comfort."

"That's lucky, uncle," replied Sprightly, "the invitation will answer a double purpose—a day's pleasure, and when we arrive at the Nore Light, our Pilgrimage may be then said to be complete. We have traced the *source* of the Thames in Gloucestershire, and also seen the finish of it, where it joins the Medway, and the Sea."

"True, my boy," said Turf, "it will be a prime day's pleasure, and with the right sort of folks too: a much better and more select description than the mere casual mixture of all sorts of persons which you meet with on board of a steamer going, or coming from Margate, &c. We, therefore, may anticipate a lively and pleasant excursion."

Makemoney, Flourish, Sprightly, and Turf, were on board of the steamer in good time, and all upon the *qui vive* when the match commenced. The company, as Turf had described, were of the most respectable and genteel character; the men well-dressed, and several of them fit for a ball room; indeed, it appeared like a *dress* party altogether. The females, it should seem, had put on their best bibs and tuckers, whether to *angle* for lovers, or to attract more attention than usual, was best known to themselves. However, Makemoney, in the ecstacy of the moment, declared, that the members of the Yacht Club, had displayed most excellent taste in their invitations to the ladies; "For a finer set of creatures," said he, "I never saw, their forms delightful, and their faces divine! I say, Sprightly, you must take care of your heart to-day. Old as I am, I must acknowledge, I am enchanted with the appearances of the fair sex around me; and well might Filch, in the Beggars Opera, sing :—

'Tis women that seduces all mankind !"

"I am delighted, my dear uncle, that you feel so happy; but more especially, although you have remained so long a bachelor, you are not unmindful of the attractions of the fair sex."

"He can soon alter his condition if he likes," answered Flourish, "a more glorious opportunity never presented itself to man : and let him pick and chuse amongst the lot, beauty will stare him in the face. Only listen to the amatory poet on the subject :—

To ladies' eyes a round boys,
    We can't refuse, we cant refuse ;
Though bright eyes so abound, boys,
    'Tis hard to chuse, 'tis hard to chuse."

How long this discourse respecting beauty, love, and matrimony, might have continued, we are not aware; but the loud, authorative voice of a well-known police officer, engaged upon all such days, whose knowledge of improper characters, had obtained for him a terrific name to the thieves, was overheard, threatening, to all appearances, a very elegantly dressed young man.

"If you do not call a boat, and instantly quit the vessel," said the officer, " I will take you into custody as a reputed thief, and you know the consequences of that charge. Therefore, no more impertinence, but depart while you are safe."

"You have ill-treated me," replied the *insinuating* artist, "you have exceeded your duty. I am not the person you take me for. What a shame it is to have one's character blasted in this vile manner!"

"Begone!—No more!—Silence!" replied the officer, with a frown, that might have almost frightened a lion. "Another word, and it will be too late——"

A boat was called, and the thief was soon out of sight, wisely preferring his liberty, to undergoing an examination at the police office, and should no other charge have been preferred against him, the magistrates might have sentenced him to three months.

Makemoney, who knew the officer, said, " I am glad you did his business so quietly. I was rather afraid he might have proved troublesome, and alarmed the ladies. I suppose you know him well? His person appears rather genteel; and his manners not at variance with his dress."

" Yes, sir," replied the officer, " according to the vulgar saying, he is better known to me than trusted! He has been a thief from his cradle: and he is a member of what is called the 'Swell Mob!' His father was hung, and his mother transported. The whole of his race are thieves! When quite a child he was received in the ' Refuge for the Destitute!' and every exertion made to reclaim him; for a short time some hopes were entertained that he had taken to the right course. According to the rules of the Institution, he was put out as an apprentice to a respectable tradesman; and his first crime was to plunder his master of some clothes, and he also took the whole contents of the till along with him.

"Nothing can *tame* him, he has been confined in the *Penitentiary*, also sentenced to the tread-mill for some months; in short, he has been at every thing he could lay his hands upon, from *clouting, pinching,* and *cracking!* I beg your pardon, sir, for using those slang phrases, but what I mean is, from picking pockets, robbing the shops of jewellers, and house-breaking, up to the highest rank in thieving!

Several bank robberies have been laid to his charge; at other times he appears to be a very devout character, and dresses like a clergyman, and attends charity sermons, for the benefit of himself. He is a capital actor; and can assume almost any shape that will answer his ' rogueries.' He has a very smooth, insinuating address; and no one can play ' the amiable,' as it is called, at watering-places, on board of steamers, &c., with such good effect and success. He is particularly attentive to the old ladies, and he tries it on with the young females, and if a watch is to be purloined, or a ring taken off the fingers by an apparent friendly shake of the hand, he is the thief that can do it with impunity.

" Amongst his fraternity, he has obtained the cognomination of the ' *insinuating* ARTIST !'

" He is a complete workman, and provided he is not taken in the fact, so expert, that he is seldom detected. The *insinuating* artist, to use his own words, had one unlucky day in his life—when he was transported for seven years ; but he served his time out, and returned to England with a considerable sum of money in his pockets. But his *propensity* for thieving could not keep him honest, or he had an excellent opportunity for leaving it off, and becoming a good member of society. But such a word as *honesty*, is not to be found in his book.

" During his career he has received sentence of death, but owing to some *flaw* in the indictment, his case being reserved for the twelve judges, the point of law was proved in his favour, and ultimately he was discharged. But no sooner did the *insinuating* artist obtain his liberty, than he returned t h: old practices with additional vigour.

" As a thief he has had an immense deal of luck . d at one period of his life he had accumulated together sever.. thousand pounds ; his vicissitudes have been equally great. But he is fond of gambling to excess; and will bet twenty, or thirty pounds at a time, on the single *toss* up of a half-penny. He has won and lost hundreds at one sitting, at the above game.

" He is not destitute of talents as a speaker, and studied the peculiar points of law, which apply to his own cases of imprisonment, with considerable ability. He has obtained his liberty several times, from his own ingenuity, and without any legal assistance whatever. He gives himself the airs of a gentleman when in custody, to the officers who do not know him ; but before the magistrates, he is very respectful, which conduct, at times, has been of great service to him.

" The *insinuating* artist has received several kind admonitions from the bench, begging of him to quit his evil ways ; but all to no purpose, I had lost sight of him for some time, but I understand, from my brother officers, that he figh *shy* of the public thoroughfares, being so well known ; and he makes his way with genteel company under false pretences, where his persuasive manners and address, have obtained *plunder* to a great amount, and almost defies suspicion, from his meekness of demeanour.

" The *insinuating* artist is a great admirer of the fair sex, and makes his boast that he has, by his own exertions, *kept* some of the finest women in the kingdo l. But, as *Macheath* observes, a highwayman may be as content with *one* guinea, as one women. He has been lavish in the extreme, in this respect, to some of the dashing women on the town.

"About twelve months since, he had nearly inveigled a widow in respectable life, with a large fortune, to become his wife, at a fashionable watering-place. The licence was procured, and his character was only discovered an hour or two before he was to appear in the church. The *insinuating* artist has contrived to elude the vigilance of the police for some time past, and his invention is continually on the alert to rob the public on a '*new suit!*'

"Take him for all in all, he is one of the most dangerous fellows that I ever met with in the course of my duty as an officer, and much as I am accustomed to hear *artful* tales told by thieves, who are the most ready people in the world to *invent* a story, he out-tops them all. In the first instance that I had any thing to do with him, his tale appeared so feasible, and he put on so innocent a look, appeared terribly agitated, that his person had been mistaken for another, and his character would be ruined if known that I thought I might have been mistaken, and did not detain him on suspicion. Improper company will intrude themselves on board these boats, although set apart for private company, a admitted by tickets. It was discovered upon one occasion, not till after the mischief had been done, a gentleman had had his pocket picked, and in his book were several admission tickets to a steam boat, to witness a sailing match."

The fineness of the day, the scene was all gaiety and cheerfulness, every body seemed anxious to render each other happy. An excellent band had been selected for the purpose, which performed several celebrated pieces of music, until it was proposed to have some quadrilles. The Pilgrims were full of fun and jollity, and had not been very particular it should seem as to the quantity of wine they had drank, it is not intended to infer that they were *tipsey*. Such a character would have been an untruth; but nevertheless, they were elevated, ripe, merry, and ready for any thing. Turf said, he had no objection to make one in a quadrille, if Makemoney would be another; Flourish and Sprightly, as a matter of course, were anxious to join the dance.

Makemoney made a thousand excuses—he was too old; did not know how to dance: he should appear ridiculous at his time of life, &c.; but, at length, all his denials were overcome by a beautiful young female, previously known to Turf, a citizen's daughter, soliciting him to be her partner. Turf had privately whispered in her ear the fun it might produce if they could get the old Citizen to stand up in a quadrille.

"You cannot refuse a lady, sir," said Flourish, "'tis beauty's queen who asks the favour You have too much gallantry about you for that! Come sir, the dance waits."

Makemoney was compelled, in a manner, to consent; but before the first figure had concluded, whether from the effects of the wine, or a piece of orange peel on the deck, he reeled about rather strangely for some time, as if quite *giddy*, and then fell down, almost dragging his lovely partner with him, to the no small amusement of the ladies and gentlemen promenading up and down the deck.

After the laugh had subsided a little, and Makemoney recovered from the fall, he said with a smile upon his face, " This is worse than hunting, or leaping over a ditch. Old Spankaway could not get me down. Ha! ha! ha! No matter, I found my head heavier than my heels. It was a punishment on me for attempting to *act* the boy; but if the young lady will pardon me, I shall make no other complaint, and solicit, in my turn, that she select a more suitable partner. *January and May* ought not to dance together."

The contest between the sailing boats as the match advanced; and several changes of situation had taken place among them, began to excite a gread deal of interest amongst the gentlemen on board of the steamer, in consequence of which, several glasses of grog, bottles of wine, rumps and dozens, and *new* hats, were betted upon the successful boat; the second best; the third, and so on. In truth, it was a jolly day altogether; and the Pilgrims made themselves quite *heroes* amongst the ladies, by their attention and politeness to them; but Makemoney could not be prevailed upon, a second time, to join the dance.

The match, upon the whole, afforded great satisfaction to all parties; and the seaman-like conduct of the captains belonging to the sailing boats, was loudly praised. This sort of amusement, may almost be said, within the last few years, to have become *professional,* and many of the captain's of gentlemens' yachts, have regular seamen forming the crews, on board of which, *duty*, and watch is kept, with all the regularity of a ship belonging to government.

The old Citizen appeared so enraptured with the lovely females which, at times, surrounded him, that he declared to Turf, if he had have been a young man, he must have lost his heart! " I do not know," said he, " that I ever felt so happy, and so much amused on any trip before, which, I think, is owing, in a great degree, to the company being intellectual, well-selected, and anxious to behave towards each other like ladies and gentlemen."

" So much for a glass of good wine," observed Turf, " it not only makes us more pleasant companions, but we view circumstances in a more favourable light. When a man is elevated and cheerful, then life is a bumper!" Turf singing to Makemoney with a glass of wine in his hand :—

Take wine like this,
Let looks of bliss,
Around it well be blended ;

PILGRIMS at the MOUTH of the THAMES.

Then bring wit's beam,
To warm the stream,
And there's your NECTAR—splendid!

The sailing match over, the steamer returned to London Bridge, to debark the passengers, just as they had become a little acquainted with each other, when the unpleasant moment arrived of saying 'Good night! or, bidding farewell!' Make-money made his bow to the company, and retired *heart*-whole. Flourish said some pleasant things to his partner, and like a man of the world, hoped they might meet again, when pleasure was the order of the day. Turf was quite at ease, but Sprightly was so enamoured with his dear partner, (the admiration of the whole company, as one of the handsomest creatures alive,) that he could not say 'Good night!' and 'Farewell!' would not leave his lips. He appeared to be in love, deeply in love, at first sight, and begged of her, that he might not only call the next day, to enquire after her health, but to name an important subject. The conversation was held in rather an under tone of voice, but whether the '*consent*' was granted, his brother Pilgrims could not ascertain! Yet the signs, looks, and nods, seemed to say—YES! and, in Turf's eye, was most likely to lead to a pilgrimage for life.

On their return home, the night was finished by a recital of the day's pleasure they had experienced, until the tell-tale told them that PILGRIMS, like other people, could not do without *rest!*

CHAPTER XVII.

The winding up of the Pilgrimage for the season ; MAKE-
MONEY, FLOURISH, and SPRIGHTLY, having a peep at the
Lord Mayor's Show, opposite Hungerford Market. Re-
marks of the crowd, and other incidents connected with
mobs in general. There is a time for every thing. The
Pilgrims' FAREWELL to CHARLES TURF, Esq., until the
long days and bright Sol, once more invite them to the
country :—

Parting is such sweet sorrow,
That I shall say, good night, till it be morrow !

THE cold weather and the *long* nights having made their
appearance, put an end to the travels of the Pilgrims, and they,
like ships in the navy, who had done some service, had made
up their minds to retire into port, until some new feature
might again call them into action, and to leave the Banks of the
Thames for a short period, to enjoy those amusements which
might cross their paths in the Metropolis.

The Pilgrims were in the neighbourhood of Westminster
Bridge, when being attracted by the bands of music, and the
procession of the Lord Mayor's Show by water, immediately repaired to the banks of the river, to enjoy the civic scene, opposite
Hungerford Market.

" This is a day of great triumph to a merchant, or tradesman,"
said Flourish, " and that individual who can elevate himself
above his neighbours, by his industry and talents, to obtain the
high and honourable situation of Lord Mayor of the City of London, has done himself and the state some service. This is one
of the sterling features and pride of old England ; that a man in
business—a shopkeeper, can hold so important a situation in the
eyes of his country ; by which circumstance he is introduced
to the notice of his sovereign, without being indebted to the
aid of sycophants and flatterers for his presence at court."

" It is well known," observed Sprightly, " that most of the
Lord Mayors of London, and the Mayors, in general, in provincial
towns, have been the architects of their own fame and fortune.
The Story of Whittington and his Cat, however questionable,
or divided in opinions on the subject, authors may be, it is nevertheless, an emulation and excitement to show what great fortunes may be made by industry and trade in England."

" Foreigners may laugh and sneer at us, if they please, and

PILGRIMS at the LORD MAYOR'S SHOW.

P. C. Egan Sun. delt

call us a nation of shopkeepers," said Turf, "but these shop-keepers not only form the bulk of the nation, when any great questions are at issue, connected with the prosperity of the country, or liberty of its subjects, but have their importance when numbers are counted. The wealth and property of Britain, in the aggregate, are inexhaustable! And I will have for the security of my money, the Bank of England against any other establishment of the sort in the wide world!"

The river was covered with boats, but the confusion on the water appeared so great, that Makemoney resisted all entreaties to put off in a wherry to join some of his old companions on board of the stationer's barge, where he was sure to have met with all the 'good things' of this life, the great delight of the aldermen and citizens of London. The recollection of the row with the Eton boys, at Windsor, remained too fresh in his memory, to run the risque of another aquatic row!

"No, no," said the old Citizen, "the crowd, bad as it may be, and to be pushed about from pillar to post, is very annoying and troublesome, I admit, but a *ducking* in November, won't do for an old fellow like I am! It might be the death of me!" However, Makemoney almost repented the decision he had made, being very soon afterwards engaged in a row, and hardly escaped being pushed in the river by a gang of thieves.

"You impudent rascal," said Sprightly, in a violent passion, turning round and catching a fellow's hand in his pocket, at the same time giving him a blow in the stomach, hard enough to knock all the breath out of his body; "How dare you be en-quiring into the worth of my pocket? If I could see an officer of justice, I would give you into custody!"

"You are too rash," replied the thief, "it was entirely a mis-take. Your pocket is so much like my own, that I can't tell one from the other. But I beg your pardon, sir, it shall not occur again during the show. The *stomacher* you gave me, might have deprived a horse of his *wind*, and may prove of more conse-quence to me, than the worth of a cart-load of *wipes*. But you have no right to take the law in your hands, and I have a great mind to employ my solicitor to enter an action against you for an assault!"

"Throw him into the river," urged Flourish, "a rascally thief like he is, talk of a solicitor and an action; make a duck of him, and if he is not web-footed to swim, it seems that every finger belonging to him is a fish-hook. I never met with such insolence!"

"Better not attempt that 'ere sort of rash conduct, my fine fellow," escaped the lips of three or four horrid looking fellows, as if belonging to a gang of pickpockets. Take care you don't get put in the river yourself. The man had no right to be hit in that cruel manner, enough to break every bone in his body! Hold your *gab*, if you wish to get home safe!"

At the same time, another robber, who was pretending to point out some interesting feature on the river amongst the city barges, with his left hand, employed his right in picking Makemoney's pocket. Turf observing this conduct, without any ceremony, laid the fellow sprawling on the ground, who roared out for help. This was the signal for a general rush of the thieves to commit depredations, and the old Citizen had a narrow escape from being forced into the river. "That's the fellow!" cried one of the thieves, "the big one, lets tip it to him; he's been annoying every body about him. He's no good!" In saving himself from the water, Makemoney got surrounded by a desperate set of villains ; and had it not been for the spirited exertions of Turf, who led the way, followed by Flourish and Sprightly, Makemoney would not only have lost every thing he had about him, but got a severe thrashing into the bargain. On the appearance of an officer, and before the old Citizen could recover his breath to point out any of the thieves, they were all off like lightening.

"Have you lost any thing?" asked Turf, "you are in luck if you have not! A more determined set of thieves, I never met with in my life."

"No !" replied Makemoney, "nothing else but my *wind*, and they have taken all that from me. I can scarcely breathe, I am so exhausted in trying to get out of their abominable clutches."

"Never mind, if it is only your wind!" said Turf, "that is recoverable, without any expense! It is an article that comes and goes when a man is employed in defending himself!"

"How soon a man may get into trouble," observed Makemoney, " and I have now made up my mind never again to enter a crowd ; nothing shall entice me. There is no protection from danger ; and the strongest man only has the best chance. Besides, I believe, I have had a *mark* set upon me, for if there is anything unpleasant occurs, I am sure to be the victim of it."

" It's the fortune of war, uncle !" said Sprightly, "and as the weather is disagreeable, the sooner we arrive at home the better. Upon the whole we have no right to complain. Storms overtake travellers, in spite of their precautions ; therefore, as we have disappointed the thieves, our adventures will serve us to laugh at over the gaily circling glass. We must now say, ' *Farewell !*' to our invaluable friend, Turf, whose presence is required in the country."

"Good-by, my jolly Pilgrims," said Turf, "it is impossible that I could part with you without feeling sincere regret. I have found you, upon all occasions, ready to do the thing that was right towards each other ; and such companions are not every day acquaintances. Therefore, I cannot repeat good-by, Makemoney, Flourish, and Sprightly, without the recollections of friendship, mirth, and harmony, being indelibly stamped upon the tablet of my memory."

" Let me return the compliment with interest," replied Flourish, " We feel much indebted to you upon all occasions ; your advice has been of the utmost importance to us Pilgrims, you have pointed out the dangers of mixed society, and your portraits of human nature have been delineated with the hand of a master ; therefore your absence is a heavy loss to us, where shall we look for that experience, and those explanations, which you have so liberally bestowed upon us *wandering* Pilgrims ?   Our gratitude teaches us to assert, we can never forget it !"

" *Farewell*, my dear friend Turf, for a short time," said Makemoney rather touched, it might be called pathetic ; at all events, there was a great deal of good feeling about his manner of expression ; " but necessity has no law.   Let me also add—*Farewell* to steam-boats, rowing, and sailing matches, for the season. Richmond Hill, and the unrivalled picturesque scenery, *adieu !* Windsor and thy delightful forest, farewell.   Greenwich Hospital, the pride and boast of the navy ; and Chelsea College, the retreat of the brave veterans ; until a more favourable opportunity presents itself, I say, again—*Farewell !*   But above all to the unrivalled

BANKS OF THE THAMES,

which have afforded us all so much real pleasure and interest ; I regret to state, that for a short period, I must bid those inviting scenes—ADIEU !   Nevertheless, I hope a time will arrive when we

JOLLY PILGRIMS;

SWORN FOES TO MELANCHOLY!

LIKE GIANTS REFRESHED;

WILL AGAIN BE ABLE TO SALLY FORTH

WITH

PEN AND PENCIL,

IN SEARCH OF THE

NATIONAL."